The Best
Sea
Stories

Upon this resolve I arose, and bought for myself goods and commodities and merchandise, with such other things as were required for travel; my mind had consented to my performing a sea voyage. So I embarked in a ship, and it descended to the city of El-Basrah, with a company of merchants, and we traversed the sea for many days and nights. We had passed by island after island, and from sea to sea, and from land to land and in every place by which we passed we sold and bought and exchanged merchandise. We continued our voyage until we arrived at an island like one of the gardens of Paradise, and there the master of the ship brought her to anchor. He put forth the landing-plank, and all who were in the ship landed upon that island. They had prepared for themselves fire-pots, and they lighted the fires in them; and their occupations were various. Some cooked, others washed and others amused themselves. I was among those who were amusing themselves upon the shores of the island, and the passengers were assembled to eat and drink and play and sport. But while we were thus engaged, lo, the master of the ship, standing upon its side, called out with his loudest voice,

'O ye passengers, whom may God preserve! Come up quickly into the ship, hasten to embark, and leave your merchandise, and flee with your lives, and save yourselves from destruction. For this apparent island, upon which ye are, is not really an island. It is a great fish that hath become stationary in the midst of the sea, and the sand hath accumulated upon it, so that it hath become like an island, and trees have grown upon it since times of old. And when ye lighted upon it the fire, it felt the heat, and put itself in motion, and now it will descend with you into the sea, and ye will all be drowned! Then seek for yourselves escape before destruction, and leave the merchandise!'

The passengers, therefore, hearing the words of the master of the ship, hastened to go up into the vessel, leaving the merchandise, and their other goods, and their copper cooking-pots, and their fire-pots; and some reached the ship, and others reached it not. The island had moved, and descended to the bottom of the sea, with all that were upon it, and the roaring sea, agitated with waves, closed over it.

I was among the number of those who remained behind upon the island; so I sank in the sea with the rest who sank. But God (whose name be exalted!) delivered me and saved me from drowning, and supplied me with a great wooden bowl, one of those in which the passengers had been washing, and I laid hold upon it and got into it, induced by the sweetness of life, and beat the water with my feet as with oars, while the waves sported with me, tossing me to the right and left. The master of the vessel had caused her sails to be spread, and pursued his voyage with those who had embarked, not regarding such as had been submerged, and I ceased not to look at that vessel until it was concealed

The First Voyage of
Es-Sindibad of the Sea

Adapted from Edward William Lane's translation of
The Thousand and One Nights
1839–1841

KNOW, O masters, O noble persons, that I had a father, a merchant, who was one of the first in rank among the people and the merchants, and who possessed abundant wealth and ample fortune. He died when I was a young child, leaving to me wealth and buildings and fields. When I grew up, I put my hand upon the whole of the property, ate well and drank well, associated with the young men, wore handsome apparel, and passed my life with my friends and companions, feeling confident that this course would continue and profit me, and I lived in this manner for a length of time. I then returned to my reason, and recovered from my heedlessness, and found that my wealth had passed away, and my condition had changed, and all the money that I had possessed had gone. I saw my situation in a state of fear and confusion of mind, and remembered the saying of our lord Suleiman the son of Daood (on both of whom be peace!): Three things are better than three: the day of death is better than the day of birth; and a living dog is better than a dead lion; and the grave is better than the palace.

Then I arose, and collected what I had of effects and apparel, and sold them; after which I sold my buildings and all that my hand possessed, and amassed three thousand pieces of silver. It occurred to my mind to travel to the countries of other people; and I remembered one of the sayings of the poets, which was this:

> In proportion to one's labour, eminences are gained; and he who seeketh eminence passeth sleepless nights.
> He diveth in the sea who seeketh for pearls, and succeedeth in acquiring lordship and good fortune.
> Whoso seeketh eminence without labouring for it, loseth his life in the search of vanity.

CONTENTS

The Best
Sea
Stories

Authors Include

JOSEPH CONRAD

JAMES GOULD COZZENS

C.S. FORESTER

JOHN MASEFIELD

HERMAN MELVILLE

NICHOLAS MONSARRAT

MALLARD PRESS

An Imprint of BDD Promotional Book Company, Inc.
666 Fifth Avenue
New York, NY 10103
Manufactured in Great Britain

from my eye. I was sure of destruction, and night came upon me while I was in this state. But I remained so a day and night, and the wind and the waves aided me until the bowl came to a stoppage with me under a high island, whereon were trees overhanging the sea. So I laid hold upon a branch of a lofty tree, and clung to it, and kept hold upon it until I landed on the island, when I found my legs benumbed, and saw marks of the nibbling of fish upon their hams, of which I had been insensible by reason of the violence of the anguish and fatigue that I was suffering.

I threw myself upon the island like one dead, and was unconscious of my existence, and drowned in my stupefaction, and I remained in this condition until the next day. The sun having then risen upon me, I awoke upon the island, and found that my feet were swollen, and that I had become reduced to the state in which I could not walk. Awhile I dragged myself along in a sitting posture, and then I crawled upon my knees. And there were in the island fruits in abundance, and springs of sweet water. I ate of those fruits, and continued in this state for many days and nights. My spirit had then revived, my soul had returned to me, and my power of motion was renewed.

I began to meditate, and to walk along the shore of the island, amusing myself among the trees with the sight of the things that God (whose name be exalted!) had created, and I had made for myself a staff from those trees, to lean upon it. Thus I remained until I walked, one day, upon the shore of the island, and there appeared unto me an indistinct object in the distance. I imagined that it was a wild beast, or one of the beasts of the sea, and I walked towards it, ceasing not to gaze at it; and, lo, it was a mare, of superb appearance, tethered in a part of the island by the sea-shore. I approached her; but she cried out against me with a great cry, and I trembled with fear of her, and was about to return, when, behold, a man came forth from beneath the earth, and he called to me and pursued me. 'Who art thou, and whence hast thou come, and what is the cause of thine arrival in this place?'

So I answered him, 'O my master, know that I am a stranger, and I was in a ship, and was submerged in the sea with certain others of the passengers. But God supplied me with a wooden bowl, and I got into it, and it bore me along until the waves cast me upon this island.'

When he heard my words, he laid hold of my hand and said to me, 'Come with me.'

I therefore went with him, and he descended with me into a grotto beneath the earth, and conducted me into a large subterranean chamber, and having seated me at the upper end of that chamber, brought me some food. I was hungry, so I ate until I was sated and contented, and my soul became at ease. Then he asked me respecting

my case, and what happened to me, wherefore I acquainted him with my whole affair from beginning to end, and he wondered at my story.

When I had finished my tale, I said, 'I conjure thee by Allah, O my master, that thou be not displeased with me. I have acquainted thee with the truth of my case and of what hath happened to me, and I desire of thee that thou inform me who thou art, and what is the cause of thy dwelling in this chamber that is beneath the earth, and what is the reason of thy tethering this mare by the sea-side?'

So he replied, 'Know that we are a party dispersed in this island, upon its shores, and we are the grooms of the King El-Mihraj, having under our care all his horses. Every month, when moonlight commences, we bring the swift mares, and tether them in this island, every mare that has not foaled, and conceal ourselves in this chamber beneath the earth, that they may attract the sea-horses. This is the time of the coming forth of the sea-horse; and afterwards, if it be the will of God (whose name be exalted!), I will take thee with me to the King El-Mihraj, and divert thee with the sight of our country. Know, moreover, that if thou hadst not met with us, thou hadst not seen anyone in this place, and wouldst have died in misery, none knowing of thee. But I will be the means of the preservation of thy life, and of thy return to thy country.'

I therefore prayed for him, and thanked him for his kindness and beneficence, and while we were thus talking the horse came forth from the sea, as he had said. Shortly after, his companions came, each leading a mare, and, seeing me with him, they inquired of me my story, and I told them what I had related to him. They then drew near to me, and spread the table, and ate, and invited me, so I ate with them. After which they arose and mounted the horses, taking me with them, having mounted me on a mare.

We commenced our journey, and proceeded without ceasing until we arrived at the city of King El-Mihraj, and they went in to him and acquainted him with my story. He therefore desired my presence, and they took me in to him. I saluted him, and he returned my salutation, and welcomed me, greeting me in an honourable manner, and inquired of me respecting my case. So I informed him of all that had happened to me, and of all that I had seen from beginning to end.

He wondered at that which had befallen me and happened to me, and said to me, 'O my son, by Allah thou hast experienced an extraordinary preservation, and had it not been for the predestined length of thy life, thou hadst not escaped from these difficulties. But praise be to God for thy safety!'

Then he treated me with beneficence and honour, caused me to draw near to him, and began to cheer me with conversation and courtesy, and he made me his superintendent of the sea-port, and registrar

THE FIRST VOYAGE OF ES-SINDIBAD OF THE SEA

of every vessel that came to the coast. I stood in his presence to transact his affairs, and he favoured me and benefited me in every respect. He invested me with a handsome and costly dress, and I became a person high in credit with him in intercessions, and in accomplishing the affairs of the people. I remained in his service for a long time, and whenever I went to the shore of the sea, I used to inquire of the merchants and travellers and sailors respecting the direction of the city of Baghdad, that perchance some one might inform me of it, and I might go with him thither and return to my country. But none knew it, nor knew anyone who went to it.

At this I was perplexed, and I was weary of the length of my absence from home. In this state I continued for a length of time, until I went in one day to the King El-Mihraj, and found with him a party of Indians. I saluted them, and they returned my salutations, and welcomed me, and asked me respecting my country. After which I questioned them as to their country, and they told me that they consisted of various races. Among them are the Shakireeyeh, who are the most noble of their races, who oppress no one, nor offer violence to any. And among them are a class called the Brahmans, a people who never drink wine; but they are persons of pleasure and joy and sport and merriment, and possessed of camels and horses and cattle. They informed me also that the Indians are divided into seventy-two classes; and I wondered at this extremely. And I saw, in the dominions of the King El-Mihraj, an island, among others, which is called Kasil, in which is heard the beating of tambourines and drums throughout the night, and the islanders and travellers informed us that Ed-Dejjal is in it. I saw too, in the sea in which that island is a fish two hundred cubits long, and the fishermen fear it. Wherefore they knock some pieces of wood, and it fleeth from them, and I saw a fish whose face was like that of the owl. I likewise saw during that voyage many wonderful and strange things, such that, if I related them to you, the description would be too long.

I continued to amuse myself with the sight of those islands and the things that they contained, until I stood one day upon the shore of the sea, with a staff in my hand, as was my custom, and, lo, a great vessel approached, wherein were many merchants. When it arrived at the harbour of the city, and its place of anchoring, the master furled its sails, brought it to an anchor by the shore, and put forth the landing-plank and the sailors brought out everything that was in that vessel to the shore.

They were slow in taking forth the goods, while I stood writing their account, and I said to the master of the ship, 'Doth ought remain in thy vessel?' He answered, 'Yes, O my master; I have some goods in the hold of the ship. But their owner was drowned in the sea at one of the islands during our voyage hither, and his goods are in our charge;

so we desire to sell them, and to take a note of their price, in order to convey it to his family in the city of Baghdad, the Abode of Peace.'

I therefore said to the master, 'What was the name of that man, the owner of the goods?' He answered, 'His name was Es-Sindibad of the Sea, and he was drowned on his voyage with us in the sea.'

When I heard his words I looked at him with a scrutinizing eye, and recognized him. I cried out at him with a great cry, and said, 'O master, know that I am the owner of the goods which thou hast mentioned, and I am Es-Sindibad of the Sea, who descended upon the island from the ship, with the other merchants who descended. When the fish that we were upon moved, and thou called out to us, some got up into the vessel, and the rest sank, and I was among those who sank. But God (whose name be exalted!) preserved me and saved me from drowning by means of a large wooden bowl, of those in which the passengers washed, and I got into it, and began to beat the water with my feet, and the wind and the waves aided me until I arrived at this island. When I landed on it, and God (whose name be exalted!) assisted me, I met the grooms of the King El-Mihraj, who took me with them and brought me to this city. They then led me in to the King El-Mihraj, and I acquainted him with my story; whereupon he bestowed benefits upon me, and appointed me clerk of the harbour of this city, and I obtained profit in his service, and favour with him. Therefore thou hast my goods and my portion.'

But the master said, 'There is no strength nor power but in God the High, the Great! There is no longer faith nor conscience in any one!' 'Wherefore, O master,' said I, 'when thou hast heard me tell thee my story?' He answered, 'Because thou heardest me say that I had goods whose owner was drowned, therefore thou desirest to take them without price, and this is unlawful to thee. For we saw him when he sank, and there were with him many of the passengers, not one of whom escaped. How then dost thou pretend that thou art the owner of the goods?'

So I said to him, 'O master, hear my story, and understand my words, and my veracity will become manifest to thee; for falsehood is a characteristic of the hypocrites.' Then I related to him all that I had done from the time that I went forth with him from the city of Baghdad until we arrived at that island upon which we were submerged in the sea, and I mentioned to him some circumstances that had occurred between me and him. Upon this, therefore, the master and the merchants were convinced of my veracity, and recognized me; and they congratulated me on my safety, all of them saying, 'By Allah, we believed not that thou hadst escaped drowning; but God hath granted thee a new life.'

They then gave me the goods, and I found my name written upon

The First Voyage of Es-Sindibad of the Sea

them, and nought of them was missing. So I opened them, and took forth from them something precious and costly. The sailors of the ship carried it with me, and I went up with it to the King to offer it as a present, and informed him that this ship was the one in which I was a passenger. I told him also that my goods had arrived all entire, and that this present was a part of them. And the King wondered at this affair extremely. My veracity in all that I had said became manifest to him, and he loved me greatly and treated me with exceeding honour, giving me a large present in return for mine.

Then I sold my bales, as well as the other goods that I had, and gained upon them abundantly, and I purchased other goods and merchandise and commodities of that city. And when the merchants of the ship desired to set forth on their voyage I stowed all that I had in the vessel and, going in to the King, thanked him for his beneficence and kindness; after which I begged him to grant me permission to depart on my voyage to my country and my family.

So he bade me farewell, and gave me an abundance of things at my departure, of the commodities of that city. And when I had taken leave of him, I embarked in the ship, and we set sail by the permission of God, whose name be exalted! Fortune served us, and destiny aided us until we arrived in safety at the city of El-Basrah. There we landed, and remained a short time, and I rejoiced at my safety, and my return to my country. After that I repaired to the city of Baghdad, the Abode of Peace, with abundance of bales and goods and merchandise of great value. Then I went to my quarter, and entered my house, and all my family and companions came to me. I procured for myself servants and other dependants, and mamelukes and concubines and male black slaves, so that I had a large establishment. I purchased houses and other immovable possessions, more than I had before. I enjoyed the society of my companions and friends, exceeding my former habits, and forgot all that I had suffered from fatigue, and absence from my native country, and difficulty, and the terrors of travel.

The Sailor and
the Pearl Merchant

Adapted from the translation by Reuben Levy, 1923.
(*MS. Ousely 231, Bodleian Library, Oxford*)

IT is related that in the city of Basrah there was a man, Abu'l Fawaris, who was the chief of the sailors of the town, for in the great ocean there was no port at which he had not landed.

One day, as he sat on the seashore, with his sailors round him, an old man arrived in a ship, landed where Abu'l Fawaris was sitting, and said: 'Friend, I desire you to give me your ship for six months, and I will pay you whatever you desire.'

'I demand a thousand gold dinars,' said the sailor, and at once received the gold from the old man, who, before departing, said that he would come again on the next day, and warned Abu'l Fawaris that there was to be no holding back.

The sailor took home his gold, made his ship ready, and then, taking leave of his wife and sons he went down to the shore, where he found the old man waiting for him with a slave and twenty ass-loads of empty sacks. Abu'l Fawaris greeted him, and together they loaded the ship and set sail. Taking a particular star for their mark, they sailed for three months, when an island appeared to one side of them. For this the old man steered, and they soon landed upon it. Having loaded his slave with some sacks, the old man with his companions set out towards a mountain which they could see in the distance. This they reached after some hours of travel, and climbed to the summit, upon which they found a broad plain where more than two hundred pits had been dug.

The old man then explained to the sailor that he was a merchant, and that he had, on that spot, found a mine of jewels. 'Now that I have given you my confidence,' he continued, 'I expect faithfulness from you too. I desire you to go down into this pit and send up sufficient pearls to fill these sacks. Half I will give to you, and we shall be able to spend the rest of our lives in luxury.'

The sailor thereupon asked how the pearls had found their way into these pits, to which the old man replied that there was a passage connecting the pits with the sea. Along this passage oysters swam, and settled in the pits, where by chance he had come upon them. He explained further that he had only brought the sailor because he needed help; but he desired not to disclose the matter to anyone else.

With great eagerness then the sailor descended into the pit, and there found oysters in great numbers. The old man let down a basket to him, which he filled again and again, until at last the merchant cried out that the oysters were useless, for they contained no pearls. Abu'l Fawaris therefore left that pit, and descended into another, where he found pearls in great number. By the time night fell he was utterly wearied, and called out to the old man to help him out of the pit. In reply the merchant shouted down that he intended to leave him in the pit, for he feared that Abu'l Fawaris might kill him for the sake of the jewels. With great vehemence the sailor protested that he was innocent of any such intention, but the old man was deaf to his entreaties, and, making his way back to the ship, sailed away.

For three days Abu'l Fawaris remained, hungry and thirsty. As he struggled to find a way out he came upon many human bones, and understood that the accursed old man had betrayed many others in the same fashion. In desperation he dug about, and at last he saw a small opening, which he enlarged with his hands. Soon it was big enough for him to crawl through, and he found himself in the darkness, standing upon mud. Along this he walked carefully, and then felt himself suddenly plunged to his neck in water, which was salt to the taste; and he knew that he was in the passage that led to the sea. He swam along in this for some way, till, in front of him, there appeared a faint light. Greatly heartened by the sight of it, he swam vigorously until he reached the mouth of the passage. On emerging, he found himself facing the sea, and threw himself on his face to give thanks for his delivery. Then he arose, and a little distance from him he found the cloak which he had left behind when he set out for the mountain; but of the old merchant there was no sign, and the ship had disappeared.

Full of trouble and despondency, he sat down at the water's brink, wondering what he was to do. As he gazed at the sea there came into view a ship, and he saw that it was filled with men. At sight of it the sailor leaped from his place; snatching his turban from his head, he waved it with all his might in the air, and shouted at the top of his voice. But as they approached he decided not to tell his rescuers the truth of his presence there; therefore when they landed and asked how he came to be on the island he told them that his ship had been wrecked at sea, that he had clung to a plank and been washed to the shore.

They praised his good fortune at his escape, and in reply to his questions with regard to the place of their origin, told him that they had sailed from Abyssinia, and were then on their way to Hindustan. At this, Abu'l Fawaris hesitated, saying that he had no business in Hindustan. They assured him, however, that they would meet ships going to Basrah, and would hand him over to one of them. He agreed then to go with them, and for forty days they sailed without seeing any inhabited spot. At last he asked them whether they had not mistaken their way, and they admitted that for five days they had been sailing without knowing whither they were going or what direction to follow. All together therefore set themselves to praying, and remained in prayer for some time.

Soon afterwards, as they sailed, something in appearance like a minaret emerged from the sea, and they seemed to behold the flash of a Chinese mirror. Also they perceived that their ship without their rowing, and without any greater force of wind, began to move at great speed over the water. In great amazement the sailors ran to Abu'l Fawaris and asked him what had come to the ship that it moved so fast. He raised his eyes, and groaned deeply as in the distance he saw a mountain that rose out of the sea. In terror he clapped his hand to his eyes and shouted out:

'We shall all perish! My father continually warned me that if ever I lost my way upon the sea I must steer to the East; for if I went to the West I would certainly fall into the Lion's Mouth. When I asked him what the Lion's Mouth was, he told me that the Almighty had created a great hole in the midst of the ocean, at the foot of a mountain. That is the Lion's Mouth. Over a hundred leagues of water it will attract a ship, and no vessel which encounters the mountain ever rises again. I believe that this is the place and that we are caught.'

In great terror the sailors saw their ship being carried like the wind against the mountain. Soon it was caught in the whirlpool, where the wrecks of ten thousand ancient ships were being carried around in the swirling current. The sailors and merchants in the ship crowded to Abu'l Fawaris, begging him to tell them what they could do. He cried out to them to prepare all the ropes which they had in the ship; he would then swim out of the whirlpool and on to the shore at the foot of the mountain, where he would make fast to some stout tree. Then they were to cast their ropes to him and so he would rescue them from their peril. By great good fortune the current cast him out upon the shore, and he made the rope of his ship fast to a stout tree.

Then, as soon as was possible, the sailor climbed to the top of the mountain in search of food, for neither he nor his shipmates had eaten for some days. When he reached the summit he found a pleasant plain stretching away in front of him, and in the midst of it he saw a lofty arch, made of green stone. As he approached it and entered, he observed a tall pillar made of steel, from which there hung by a chain a great drum of Damascus bronze covered with a lion's skin. From the arch also hung a great tablet of bronze, upon which was engraved the following inscription:

'O thou that dost reach this place, know that when Alexander voyaged round the world and reached the Lion's Mouth, he had been made aware of this place of calamity. He was therefore accompanied by four thousand wise men, whom he summoned and whom he commanded to provide a means of escape from this calamitous spot. For long the philosophers pondered on the matter, until at last Plato caused this drum to be made, whose quality is that if any one, being caught in the whirlpool, can come forth and strike the drum three times, he will bring out his ship to the surface.'

When the sailor had read the inscription, he quickly made his way to the shore and told his fellows of it. After much debate he agreed to risk his life by staying on the island and striking the drum, on condition that they would return to Basrah on their escape, and give to his wife and sons one-half of what treasure they had in the ship. He bound them with an oath to do this, and then returned to the arch. Taking up a club he struck the drum three times, and as the mighty roar of it echoed from the hills, the ship, like an arrow shot from a bow, was flung out of the whirlpool. Then, with a cry of farewell to Abu'l Fawaris from the crew, they sailed to Basrah, where they gave one-half the treasure which they had to the sailor's family.

With great mourning the wife and family of Abu'l Fawaris celebrated his loss; but he, after sleeping soundly in the archway and giving thanks to his Maker for preserving him alive, made his way again to the summit of the mountain. As he advanced across the plain he saw black smoke arising from it, and also in the plain were rivers, of which he passed nine. He was like to die of hunger and weariness, when suddenly he perceived on one side a meadow, in which flocks of sheep were grazing. In great joy he thought that he was at last reaching human habitation, and as he came towards the sheep, he saw with them a youth, tall in stature as a mountain, and covered with a tattered cloak of red felt, though his head and body were clad in mail.

The sailor greeted him, and received greeting in reply, and also the question 'Whence come you?' Abu'l Fawaris answered that he was a man upon whom catastrophe had fallen, and so related his adventures to the shepherd. He heard it with a laugh, and said: 'Count yourself fortunate to have escaped from that abyss. Do not fear now, I will bring you to a village.' Saying this he set bread and milk before him and bade him eat. When he had eaten he said: 'You cannot remain here all day, I will take you to my house, where you may rest for a time.'

Together they descended to the foot of the mountain, where stood a gateway. Against it leaned a mighty stone, which a hundred men could not have lifted, but the shepherd, putting his hand into a hole in the stone, lifted it away from the gateway and admitted Abu'l Fawaris. Then he restored the stone to its place, and continued on his way.

When the sailor had passed through the gateway he saw before him a beautiful garden in which were trees laden with fruit. In the midst of them was a kiosk, and this, the sailor thought, must be the shepherd's house. He entered and looked about from the roof, but though he saw many houses there was no person in sight. He descended therefore, and walked to the nearest house, which he entered.

Upon crossing the threshold he beheld ten men, all naked and all so fat that their eyes were almost closed. With their heads down upon their knees, all were weeping bitterly. But at the sound of his footsteps they raised their heads and called out 'Who are you?'

He told them that the shepherd had brought him and offered him hospitality. A great cry arose from them as they heard this.

'Here,' they said, 'is another unfortunate who has fallen, like ourselves, into the clutch of this monster. He is a vile creature, who in the guise of a shepherd goes about and seizes men and devours them. We are all merchants whom adverse winds have brought here. That devil has seized us and keeps us in this fashion.'

With a groan the sailor thought that now at last he was undone. At that moment he saw the shepherd coming, saw him let the sheep into the garden, and then close the gateway with the stone before entering the kiosk. He was carrying a bag full of almonds, dates, and pistachio nuts, with which he approached, and, giving it to the sailor, he told him to share it with the others. Abu'l Fawaris could say nothing, but sat down and ate the food with his companions. When they had finished their meal, the shepherd returned to them, took one of them by the hand, and then in sight of them all, slew, roasted, and devoured him. When he was sated, he brought out a skin of wine and drank until he fell into a drunken sleep.

Then the sailor turned to his companions and said: 'Since I am to die, let me first destroy him; if you will give me your help, I will do so.' They replied that they had no strength left; but he, seeing the two long spits on which the ogre had roasted his meat, put them into the fire until they were red hot, and then plunged them into the monster's eyes.

With a great cry the shepherd leaped up and tried to seize his tormentor, who sprang away and eluded him. Running to the stone, the shepherd moved it aside and began to let out the sheep one by one, in the hope that when the garden was emptier he could the more easily capture the sailor. Abu'l Fawaris understood his intention: without delay, he slew a sheep, put on the skin and tried to pass through. But the shepherd knew as soon as he felt him that this was not a sheep, and leaped after him in pursuit. Abu'l Fawaris flung off the pelt, and ran like the wind. Soon he came to the sea, and into this he plunged, while the shepherd after a few steps returned to the shore, for he could not swim.

Full of terror the sailor swam till he reached the other side of the mountain. There he met an old man who greeted him, and, after hearing his adventure, fed him and took him to his house. But soon, to his horror, Abu'l Fawaris found that this old man also was an ogre. With great cunning he told the ogre's wife that he could make many useful implements for her house, and she persuaded her husband to save him. After many days in the house, he was sent away to the care of a shepherd, and put to guard sheep. Day by day he planned to escape, but there was only one way across the mountain and that was guarded.

One day, as he wandered in a wood, he found in the hollow trunk of a tree a store of honey, of which he told the shepherd's wife when he went home. The next day, therefore, the woman sent her husband with Abu'l Fawaris, telling him to bring home some of the honey; but, on the way, the sailor leaped upon him and bound him to a tree. Then, taking the shepherd's ring, he returned and told the woman that her husband had given him leave to go, and that he sent his ring in token of this. But the woman was cunning and asked: 'Why did not my husband come himself to tell me this?'

Seizing him by the cloak, she told him that she would go with him and find out the truth. The sailor, however, tore himself free, and again fled to the sea, where he thought that he might escape death. In haste and terror he swam for many hours, until at last he espied a ship full of men, who steered towards him and took him on board. Full of wonder they asked how he came there, and he related to them all his adventures.

It happened by great good fortune that the ship's captain had business at one place only on the coast, and that from there he was sailing to Basrah. In the space of a month, therefore, Abu'l Fawaris was restored to his family, to the joy of them all.

The many dangers and sufferings of the sailor had turned his hair white. For many days he rested, and then, one day, as he walked by the seashore, that same old man who had before hired his ship again appeared. Without recognizing him, he asked if he would lend his ship on hire for six months. Abu'l Fawaris agreed to do so for a thousand dinars of gold, which the old man at once paid to him, saying that he would come in a boat on the morrow, ready to depart.

When the ancient departed, the sailor took home the money to his wife, who bade him beware not to cast himself again into danger. He replied that he must be avenged not only for himself, but also for the thousand Muslims whom the villainous old man had slain.

The next day, therefore, the sailor took on board the old man and a black slave, and for three months they sailed, until they once more reached the island of pearls. There they made fast the ship on the shore, and taking sacks, they ascended to the top of the mountains. Once arrived there, the old man made the same request to Abu'l Fawaris as before, namely, that he should go down into the pits and send up pearls. The sailor replied that he was unacquainted with the place, and preferred that the old man should go down first, in order to prove that there was no danger. He answered that there was surely no danger; he had never in his life harmed even an ant, and he would of a certainty never send Abu'l Fawaris down into the pits if he knew any peril lay there. But the sailor was obstinate, saying that until he knew how to carry it out, he could not undertake the task.

Very reluctantly, therefore, the old man allowed himself to be lowered into the first pit by a basket and a rope. He filled the basket with oysters and sent it up, crying out: 'You see, there is nothing to do harm in this pit. Draw me up now, for I am an old man and have no more strength left.'

The sailor replied, 'Now that you are there, it were better if you remained there to complete your task. To-morrow I myself will go into another pit and will send up so many pearls as to fill the ship.'

For a long time the old man worked, sending up pearls, and at last he cried out again, 'O my brother, I am utterly wearied, draw me out now.'

Then the sailor turned upon him with fury, and cried out: 'How is it that thou dost see ever thine own trouble and never that of others? Thou misbegotten dog, art thou blind that thou dost not know me? I am Abu'l Fawaris, the sailor, whom long ago you left in one of these pits. By the favour of Allah I was delivered, and now it is your turn. Open your eyes to the truth and remember what you have done to so many men.'

The old man cried aloud for mercy, but it availed him nothing, for Abu'l Fawaris brought a great stone and covered up the mouth of the pit. The slave too he overwhelmed with threats, and then together they carried down the pearls to the ship, in which they sat sail. In three months they arrived at Basrah. There Abu'l Fawaris related his adventures, to the amazement of all. Thenceforward he abandoned the sea and adopted a life of ease. Finally he died, and this story remains in memory of him. And Allah knoweth best.

Friedrich Martens of Hamburg

A Whaling Voyage into Spitzbergen

Adapted from an anonymous translation (1694) of *A Voyage into Spitzbergen and Greenland*

I

WE set sail the 15th of April, 1671, about noon, from the Elbe. The wind was north-east; at night, when we came by the Helgoland, it bore to north-north-east. The name of the ship was *Jonas in the Whale*, Peter Peterson, of Friesland, master.

The 27th, we had storms, hail and snow, with very cold weather, the wind north-east, and by east; we were in seventy-one degrees, and came to the ice, and turned back again. The island of Jan Mayen bore from us south-west and by west, as near as we could guess within ten miles. We might have seen the Island plain enough, but the air was hazy, and full of fogs and snow, so that we could not see far. About noon it blew a storm, whereupon we took down our topsails, and, furling our mainsail, drove with the mizzensail towards south-east.

The 29th, it was foggy all day, the wind north-east, and by north; we came to the ice, and sailed from it again.

The 30th, the first Sunday after Easter, was foggy, with rain and snow, the wind at north; at night we came to the ice, but sailed from it again; the sea was temptestuous, and tossed our ship very much.

The 3rd of May was cold, snowy, with hail, and misty sunshine; the wind north-west and by west; the sun set no more, we saw it as well by night as by day.

The 4th, we had snow, hail, and gloomy sunshine, with cold weather, but not excessive; the wind at north-west; the weather every day unconstant. Here we saw abundance of seals; they jumped out of the water before the ship, and, which was strange, they would stand half out of the water, and, as it were, dance together.

The 5th, in the forenoon, it was moderately cold, and sunshine, but toward noon darkish and cloudy, with snow and great frost; the wind north-west and by north. We saw daily many ships, sailing about the ice; I observed that as they passed by one another, they hailed one another, crying *Holla*, and asked each other how many fish they had caught; but they would not stick sometimes to tell more than they had. When it was windy, that they could not hear one another, they waved their hats to signify the number caught. But when they have their full freight of whales, they put up their great flag as a sign thereof: then if any hath a message to be sent, he delivers it to them.

The 7th we had moderate frosts, clouds, and snow, with rain. In the evening we sailed to the ice; the wind was quite contrary to us, and the ice too small, wherefore we sailed from it. In the afternoon we saw Spitzbergen, the south point of the North Foreland; we supposed it the true harbour. The land appeared like a dark cloud, full of white streaks; we turned to the west again, that is, according to the compass, which is also to be understood of the ice and harbour.

The 9th was the same weather, and cold as before, the wind south-west and by west. In the afternoon a fin-fish swam by our ship, which we took at first to be a whale, before we saw the high fins of his tail and came near to it. We had let down our sloop from the ship, but that labour was lost, for he was not worth taking.

On the 14th, the wind was north-west, fine weather with sunshine; we were within seventy-five degrees and twenty-two minutes. We told twenty ships about us. The sea was very even, and we hardly felt any wind, and yet it was very cold. In this place the sea becomes smooth presently again after a storm, chiefly when the wind blows from the ice; but when it blows off the sea, it always makes a great sea. The same day we saw a whale, not far off from our ship. We put out four boats from on board after him, but this labour was also in vain, for he run under the water and we saw him no more.

On the 20th, it was exceeding cold, so that the very sea was all frozen over. Yet it was so calm and still that we could hardly perceive the wind, which was north. There were nine ships in our company, which sailed about the ice. We found still, the longer we sailed the bigger the ice.

On the 21st (which was the fourth Sunday after Easter), we sailed into the ice in the forenoon, with another Hamburger-ship called the *Lepeler*, with eight Hollanders. We fixed our ship with ice-hooks to a large ice-field, when the sun was south-west and by south. We numbered thirty ships in the sea; they lay, as it were, in an harbour or haven. Thus, they venture their ships in the ice at great hazard.

On the 30th, it was fair weather in the morning, snowy about noon; the wind was south-west, and very calm. We rowed in the great sloop, before the ship, farther into the ice. In the morning we heard a whale blow when the sun was in the east, and brought the whale to the ship when the sun was at south-west and by east. The same day we cut the fat from it, and filled with it seventy barrels (which they call kardels).

A WHALING VOYAGE INTO SPITZBERGEN

By this fish we found abundance of birds, most of them were malle-mucks [fulmars, petrels], that is to say, foolish gnats, which were so greedy of their food, that we killed them with sticks. This fish was found out by the birds, for we saw everywhere by them in the sea where the whale had been, for he was wounded by an harpooning iron that stuck still in his flesh, and he had also spent himself by hard swimming; he blowed also very hollow.

In the morning, June 4th, we were a-hunting again after a whale, and we came so near unto one, that the harpoonier was just going to fling his harpoon into her, but she sank down behind and held her head out of the water, and so sunk down like a stone, and we saw her no more. It is very like that the great ice-field was full of holes in the middle, so that the whale could fetch breath underneath the ice. A great many more ships lay about this sheet of ice. One hunted the whales to the other, and so they were frighted and became very shy. So one gets as many fishes as the other, and sometimes they all get one. We were there several times a-hunting that very day, and yet we get never a one.

On the 12th, it was cold and stormy all day, at night sunshine. He that takes not exact notice, knows no difference whether it be day or night.

On the 13th, in the afternoon, it was windy and foggy. We were in seventy-seven degrees; we sailed along by the ice somewhat easterly towards Spitzbergen. That night we saw more than twenty whales, that run one after another towards the ice. Out of them we got our second fish, which was a male one, and this fish, when they wounded him with lances, bled very much, so that the sea was tinged by it where he swam. We brought him to the ship when the sun was in the north, for the sun is the clock to the seamen in Spitzbergen, or else they would live without order, and mistake in the usual seven weekly days.

We arrived at Spitzbergen June the 14th. First we came to the Fore-land thereof, then to the seven Ice-hills or mountains, then we passed the harbours (or bays) of the Hamburgers, Magdalens, of the English-men, the Danes, and sailed into the South Bay. We were followed by seven ships, three Hamburgers and four Hollanders.

That night we sailed with three boats into the English harbour or bay, and saw a whale, and flung into him three harpoons, and threw our lances into him. The whale ran underneath the small ice, and remained a great while under water before he came up again, and then ran but a very little way before he came up again, and this he repeated very often, so that we were forced to wait upon him above half an hour before he came from underneath the ice. The harpoons broke out at length, and we lost him.

On the 22nd, we had very fair weather, and pretty warm. We were by Rehenfelt, where the ice stood firm. We saw six whales, and got one of them that was a male and our third fish. He was killed at night when the sun stood westward. This fish was killed by one man who flung the harpoon into him, and killed him also, while the other boats were busy in pursuing or hunting after another whale. This fish ran to the ice, and before he died beat about with his tail. The ice settled about him, so that the other boats could not come to this boat to assist him, till the ice separated again that they might row, when they tied one boat behind the other, and so towed the whale to the great ship, where they cut him up into the vessels, and filled with him forty-five barrels. This night the sun shined very brightly.

On the 1st July, about noon, two whales came near to our ship. We saw that they had a mind to couple together; we set our boat for them, and the harpoonier hit the female, which when the other found, he did not stay at all, but made away. The female ran all along above the water, straight forward, beating about with her tail and fins, so that we durst not come near to lance her. Yet one of our harpooniers was so foolhardy to venture too near the fish, which saluted him with a stroke of her tail over his back so vehemently that he had much ado to recover his breath again. Those in the other boat, to show their valour also, hastened to the fish, which overturned their boat, so that the harpoonier was forced to dive for it, and hide his head underneath the water. The rest did the same; they thought it very long before they come out, for it was cold, so that they came quaking to the ship again. In the same morning a whale appeared near our ship, before the wide harbour. We put out four boats from our ship after him, but two Holland ships were about half a league from us. One of them sent a boat towards us; we used great diligence and care to take him, but the fish came up just before the Dutchman's boat, and was struck by him with the harpoon. Thus he took the bread out of our mouths.

On the 5th July, in the forenoon, it was bright sunshine and pretty warm. In the afternoon it was foggy; at night sunshine again, which lasted all the night. We hunted all that day long, and in the morning we struck a whale before the Weigatt. This fish run round about under the water, and so fastened the line whereon our harpoon was about a rock, so that the harpoon lost its hold, and that fish got away. This whale did blow the water so fiercely, that one might hear it at a league's distance.

On the 6th, we had the same weather, and warm sunshine all night. Hard by us rode a Hollander, and the ship's crew busy in cutting the fat of a whale, when the fish burst with so great a bounce as if a cannon had been discharged, and bespattered the workmen all over.

On the 8th, the wind turned north-west, with snow and rain. We were forced to leave one of our anchors, and thank'd God for getting off from land, for the ice came on fiercely upon us. At night the wind was laid, and it was colder, although the sun shined.

On the 12th, we had gloomy sunshine all day. We saw but very few whales more, and those we did see were quite wild, that we could not come near them. That night it was so dark and foggy, that we could hardly see the ship's length. We might have got sea-horses [walrus] enough, but we were afraid of losing our ships, for we had examples enough of them that had lost their ships, and could not come to them again, but have been forced to return home in other ships. When after this manner they have lost their ships, and cannot be seen, they discharge a cannon from the ship, or sound the trumpets, or hautboys, according as they are provided in their ships, that the men that are lost may find their ship again.

On the 13th, the ice came afloating down apace. We sailed from the south-east land to the west, and we could but just get through by the north side from the Bear Harbour or Bay. We sailed on to the Rehenfelt, where the ice was already fixed to the land, so that we could but just get through; we sailed further to the Vogelsang. Then we turned to the east with a north-east wind, in company with twelve ships more, to see whether there were many more whales left, with *George* and *Cornelius Manglesen*, and *Michael Appel*, who sailed in four fathoms water, and touched upon the wreck of a ship that was lost there.

On the 14th, in the morning, we sailed still among the ice, the wind being north-east and by east. We had a fog all that day with sunshine, with a rainbow of two colours, white and pale yellow, and it was very cold, and we saw the sun a great deal lower.

On the 15th, it was windy, cold and foggy the whole day. The wind turned north-west, and the ice come on in abundance, so that we could hardly sail, for it was everywhere full of small sheets of ice. At this time there were many ships beset with ice in the Deer or Muscle Bay. We sailed all along near the shore. At night we entered the south harbour, where twenty-eight ships lay at anchor, eight whereof were Hamburgers, the rest Dutchmen. From that time when we sailed out of the South Haven we kept always within sight of the land, and saw it always, except it was foggy. And so long the skippers stay by the ice to see if there are any more whales to be had.

On the 22nd day of July, in the morning, when the sun was north-east, we weighed our anchors, and sailed out of the South Haven.

On the 24th, it was so warm with sunshine, that the tar wherewith the ship was daubed over melted. We drove, it being calm, before the haven or Bay of Magdalen.

On the 25th, at night we came to the Forelands, the night was foggy, the wind south-west.

On the 28th, we turned from the side of the North Foreland towards the west, when the sun was south-east, and we did sail south-west and by west towards the sea . . .

II

THE fish properly called the whale, for whose sake our ships chiefly undertake the voyage to Spitzbergen, is differing from other whales in his fins and mouth, which is without teeth, but instead thereof long, black, somewhat broad and horny flakes, all jagged like hairs. He differs from the fin-fish in his fins, for the fin-fish hath a great fin on his back but the whale properly so called, hath none on his back. And there are two fins behind his eyes of a bigness proportionable to the whale, covered with a thick black skin, delicately marbled with white strokes; or as you see in marble, trees, houses or the like things represented. In the tail of one of the fishes was marbled very delicately this number, 1222, very even and exact, as if they had been painted on it on purpose. This marbling on the whale is like veins in a piece of wood, that run straight through, or else round about the centre or pith of a tree, and so go both white and yellow strokes, through the thick and the thin strokes, that is like parchment or vellum, and give to the whale an incomparable beauty and ornament. When these fins are cut up, you find underneath the thick skin bones that look like unto a man's hand, when it is opened and the fingers are expanded or spread. Between these joints there are stiff sinews, which fly up and rebound again if you fling them hard against the ground, as the sinews of great fish, as of a sturgeon, or of some four-footed beasts generally do.

Their tail doth not stand up as the tails of almost any other fish, but it doth lie horizontal, as that of the fin-fish, butskopf [grampus, or killer whale], dolphin, and the like, and it is three, three and a half, and four fathoms broad. The head is the third part of the fish, and some have bigger heads. On the upper and under lips are short hairs before. Their lips are quite plain, somewhat bended like an S, and they end underneath black streaks; some are darkish brown, and they are crooked as the lips are. Their lips are smooth and quite black, round like the quarter of a circle; when they draw them together they lock into one another. Within, on the uppermost lip, is the whalebone of a brown, black, and yellow colour, with streaks of several colours, as the bones of a fin-fish. The whalebones of some of the whales are blue, and light blue, which two are reckoned to come from young whales. Just before, on the under lip, is a cavity or hole, which the upper lip fits exactly into, as a knife into a sheath. I do really believe that he draws the water that he bloweth out through this hole, and so I have been informed also by seamen. Within his mouth is the whalebone, all hairy as horse's hair, as it is also in the fin-fish, and it hangs down from both sides all about his tongue. The whalebone of some whales is bended like unto a scimitar, and others like unto a half-moon. The lower part of the whale's mouth is commonly white. The tongue lieth amongst the whalebones; it is very close tied to the undermost chap or lip. It is very large and white, with black spots at the edges.

Upon his head is the hovel or bump before the eyes and fins. At the top of this lump on each side, is a spout-hole, two over-against one another, which are bended on each side like an S, or as the hole that is cut in a violin, whereout he doth blow the water very fiercely, that it roars like a hollow wind which we hear when the wind bloweth into a cave, or against the corner of a board, or like an organ-pipe. This may be heard at a league's distance, although you do not see him by reason of the thick and foggy air.

The whale bloweth or spouts the water fiercest of all when he is wounded, then it sounds as the roaring of the sea in a great storm, and as we hear the wind in a very hard storm. The head of the whale is not round at the top, but somewhat flat, and goeth down sloping, like unto the tiling of an house, to the under lip. The under lip is broader than the whale is in any part of his body, and broadest in the middle. Before and behind it is something narrower, according to the shape of the head. In one word, all the whole fish is shaped like unto a shoemaker's last, if you look upon it from beneath. Behind the knob or bump where the fins are, between that and the fins, are his eyes, which are not much bigger than those of a bullock, with eyelids and hair, like men's eyes. The crystal of the eye is not much bigger than a pea, clear, white, and transparent as crystal; the colour of some is yellowish, of others quite white. The seal's are three times as big as those of the whale. The eyes of the whale are placed very low, almost at the end of the upper lip.

Some bring along with them from Spitzbergen some bones, which they pretend to be the ears of the whale. But I can say nothing to this, because I never saw any; but thus much I do remember, that I have heard them say that they lie very deep. The whale doth not hear when he spouts the water, wherefore he is easiest to be struck at that time. His belly and back are quite red, and underneath the belly they are commonly white, yet some of them are coal black; most of them that I saw were white. They look very beautiful when the sun shines upon them, the small clear waves of the sea that are over him glisten like silver. Some of them are marbled on their back and tail; where he hath been wounded there remaineth always a white scar. I understood one of our harpooniers that he once caught a whale at Spitzbergen that was white all over. Half white I have seen some, but one above the rest, which was a female, was a beautiful one; she was all over marbled black and yellow. Those that are as black are not all of the same colour, for some of them are black as velvet, others of a coal black, others of the colour of a tench.

The yard [penis] of a whale is a strong sinew, and according as they are in bigness, six, seven, or eight feet long, as I have seen myself. Where this yard is fixed the skin is doubled, so that it lies just like a knife in a sheath, where you can see nothing of the knife, but only a little of the haft. Where the yard doth begin it is four-square, consisting of many strong sinews; if you dry them they are as transparent as fish glue; out of these sinews the seamen make twisted whips. Their bones are hard, like unto them of great four-footed beasts, but porous, like unto a sponge, and filled with marrow; when that is consumed out, they will hold a great deal of water, for the holes are big like unto the wax of a honey-comb.

The other strong sinews are chiefly about the tail, where it is thinnest, for with it he turns and winds himself as a ship is turn'd by the rudder. But his fins are his oars, and according to his bigness he rows himself along with them as swiftly as a bird flies, and doth make a long track in the sea, as a great ship doth when under sail.

George Mackay Brown

Perilous Seas

ON the afternoon of 5 November 1724 a merchant ship *Caroline* of Guernsey dipped gently northwards through the Mediterranean. She had weighed anchor at Santa Cruz that morning with a cargo of Turkish leather, woollen cloth, and beeswax, bound for Genoa. The *Caroline* mounted twelve guns. She carried a crew of twenty-three, including five officers; the crew was a mixture of Swedes, Scotsmen, Irishmen, Danes, Englishmen, Welshmen. She was under charter to a company of Dutch merchants. In that year the Netherlands were at war with the Dey of Algiers, and so the Dutch were glad to charter neutral ships to carry on their rich Mediterranean trade. The master and owner of the galley was a middle-aged Channel Islander, Oliver Ferneau.

To Captain Ferneau on the quarter-deck that afternoon came the first officer, Bonadventure Jelfs, who asked with all deference but some unease when he expected that the *Caroline* should reach Genoa.

Captain Ferneau, speaking English that had only a slight foreign spice to it, answered that they should see the coast of Italy before nightfall. He put his hand on the bright hair of the cabin-boy who was standing beside him. They should reach the harbour of Genoa, he said, sometime the next day; it depended on wind and weather, and also of course on God's will.

The skipper told his cabin-boy, a Swedish child ten years old called Peter Hanson, to fetch his snuff-horn from the cabin; he had forgotten it. The angelic-looking messenger went off at once.

As soon as they were alone, Mr Jelfs said, 'If I'm not mistaken, it depends even more on the intentions of Mister Williams.'

'What do you mean?' said Ferneau sharply, but he spoke as if Jelf's remark had reverberated from a private doubt of his own.

'There is a bad element in the crew,' said Jelfs. 'That Welshman, he is the worst of all. He is the ringleader.'

'What are you afraid of, Jelfs? Tell me, please,' said Ferneau.

'I am not easy in my mind, that is all, captain,' said Jelfs.

'Allow me to say what is in *my* mind,' said Ferneau. 'You are troubling yourself unnecessarily. You have bad imaginings. This happens when one has been at sea for too long a time.'

'I hope so, indeed,' said Jelfs.

'Sailors were never angels,' said Ferneau. 'I have sailed with worse than this crew. I can control them. I have been a shipmaster twenty years. I can handle men well enough. You spoke of Williams.'

'Yes,' said Jelfs.

'He *is* a bad one, that Williams,' said Ferneau. 'You are right about him. We have a rat with sharp teeth in our hold.'

'There are others,' said Jelfs gloomily. 'Winter, Macaulay, Melvin.'

'Silly loud-mouthed boys,' said Ferneau. 'Card-players with knives. They rant and rave in their rum cans. There is also on board this ship, fortunately for us, I am glad to say, John Gow.'

Mr Jelfs, with a coldness about his mouth, said nothing. He put a steady look on the cold grey heave of water in the west. The coast of Africa was a thin line on the horizon behind.

'So,' said Ferneau, 'you do not trust Mr Gow either, Jelfs?'

'It is my opinion,' said Jelfs, 'since you ask, that it was not a good thing you did, to advance Gow from the crew.'

'I did right,' said Ferneau. 'John Gow is a good sailor. He is an honest open lad, well-educated too. I will not have you say anything against him. I trust him very much.'

Peter Hanson stood between the two officers with the silver-mounted snuff-horn in his hand.

Again, Mr Jelfs made no reply. He took the snuff-horn from Peter Hanson, and sent the boy away with a curt sweep of his hand. He passed the horn wordlessly to Captain Ferneau.

'There is something more,' said Ferneau. 'Gow is well-liked by all the crew. He has a way with him. I am not well-liked, I am what you call a Frog, a Frenchman. You are not popular either, Jelfs – you have been too free with that ropes-end since we left the Texel. You are meagre with the rum also. But Gow is very much respected. Let there be any kind of trouble, I will send Gow to speak with them. He will stamp it out. That is a young sailor who will go far.'

'Winter threw his plate of beef at the cook,' said Jelfs. 'That is why I am here. I have come to report the incident.'

'Who did?' said Ferneau.

'Winter,' said Jelfs. 'The Swede.'

'I don't like that,' said Ferneau. 'This is the first food complaint since Santa Cruz. Did anyone else refuse?'

'No, sir,' said Jelfs. 'Only Winter.'

'The complaints at Santa Cruz, they were without cause,' said Ferneau. 'It was good food, plenty of fruit, wine, new bread. I did not like that then. I do not like this now. It was only Winter, you say?'

'Winter,' said Jelfs, 'the Swede. At Santa Cruz, as you say, sir, they complained of the food without reason. If there had been scurvy, or scab, or bowel flux. But there was nothing. They ate with both hands. Someone is putting them up to it. There is an evil intelligence at work on this ship.'

'That in Santa Cruz was indeed a shameful thing,' said Ferneau. 'The gentlemen merchants of Santa Cruz on board, drinking my brandy, so pleasant, black men and white men mingling, as in a courteous game of chess. Then three sailors from the hold with their caps on their heads – who, again? – yes, Winter, Petersen, Macaulay. Winter says, *The food we get to eat, Captain, it is bad, it is rotten, it is not fit for beasts*. Winter shouts this at me, in front of the merchants of Santa Cruz, my guests! My dear Jelfs, I am red in the face at this moment, only thinking of it.'

'That is why I will be thankful,' said Jelfs, 'when this voyage is over.'

They were aware that a third presence had been on the quarterdeck for some time. They turned. It was John Gow, the sailor from Hamnavoe in the Orkneys that Ferneau had promoted to second mate in the Bay of Biscay. He stood smiling at them with his hat under his arm. Captain Ferneau raised his hand in welcome; but the new officer lured no respondent smile from Bonadventure Jelfs.

'Never wish that, Mr Jelfs,' said Gow. 'We will have a good prosperous voyage. I know it.'

'All is quiet below, John, yes?' said Ferneau.

'Dice, cards, bible-reading,' said Gow. 'Winter is in his hammock. There is a request, sir. One of the sailors, James Williams, is wanting to see you. I made so bold as to bring him with me.'

'Again, Williams,' said Ferneau. 'What does Mister Williams want?'

'O, I couldn't say, sir,' said Gow. 'He's always on his high horse about something. I took the liberty of bidding him follow me. He's standing below. I knew you would wish to grant him a hearing.'

'Show him up, John,' said Ferneau.

Gow turned and called for the man to take off his cap and enter.

James Williams, a sailor with a dark vivid restless face, entered. He bowed and said, 'Your pardon, Captain Ferneau.' Under the pleasant sing-song of his speech there might have been, for those who are attuned to the music of fate, a whine and a snarl.

'You desire to see me, man?' said Captain Ferneau.

'Indeed yes, captain, if you will allow it,' said Williams.

'It is another complaint, like in Santa Cruz?' said Ferneau.

'No indeed, captain,' said Williams. 'I would not dream of complaining at all.'

'What is it, the food?' said Ferneau. 'No? You cannot stomach the food?'

'Goodness, captain,' said Williams, 'the food is excellent food. I have not tasted better on any voyage.'

'State your business then, as briefly as possible,' said Ferneau. 'I have work to do.'

'It is, look you, the matter of my wages,' said Williams.

'You are not paid enough?' said Ferneau. 'Is that what it is? You signed on for so much in Amsterdam.'

'More than enough I am paid,' said Williams.

'Well?' said Ferneau.

'I would like, as it were,' said Williams, 'to be paid in English money, captain, considering as it were that I am to spend the money in London in all likelihood at the end of the voyage.'

'That is impossible,' said Ferneau.

'I would like it paid so,' said Williams, 'in English money, however-er.'

'Look here, man,' said Ferneau. 'This ship, the *Caroline*, is under charter to a Dutch company. Do you understand that?'

'I understand nothing, captain,' said Williams, 'except that I serve you to the best of my ability.'

'I was given the currency of the Netherlands to pay the crew,' said Ferneau. 'Not the currency of France, England, Ethiopia, or the Eskimos, but the currency of the Netherlands. Do you understand that?'

'Indeed I am not caring,' said Williams.

'God damn you, man,' cried Ferneau, 'what do you take me for, a high-sea banker? When you reach London take your Netherlands money to any merchant and he will give you English equivalent money. Dutch currency is in good standing in the exchanges. I am telling you so. Is that plain?'

'It is not plain to me at all, captain,' said Williams. 'There is many grumbles among the sailors about this wrong money.'

'Let me speak to him, captain,' said Jelfs, stepping forward.

'Very well, Mr Jelfs,' said Ferneau. 'I lose my temper. Netherlands silver – what could be better!'

Mr Jelfs put his thin white face close to the flashing face of the Welshman.

'It is to the captain alone I wish to speak,' cried Williams, 'not to his subordinate.'

'You will do what you are told,' said Jelfs.

'Always I have done that,' said Williams. 'I know my station. I am a simple sailor. It is just, look you, that I am uneasy in my mind about my wages.'

'You are a bad influence in this ship,' said Jelfs.

'I would not have that said,' said Williams. 'You do not like me, Mr Jelfs. Mr Gow here, Jack Gow, he may have another opinion of my character.'

'Speak civilly to your officers,' said Gow in a low voice. 'Don't drag me into this.'

'It is my own private opinion,' said Jelfs, 'that you would be none the worse of a good flogging.'

'That is another matter,' cried Williams. 'You are too fond of the ropes-end, Mr Jelfs. All the sailors think this. The sailors will not endure it for ever, no indeed. They will stand only so much. We are not animals to be beaten and kicked.'

'That's enough, Williams,' said Gow. 'You'd better go now before you say anything else.'

'Between your floggings and your pig-swill and your bad money, look you, there will be funny things done on board this ship,' chanted Williams. 'We are on the open sea. We have thoughts and we have whisperings. Make of that what you will. We have teeth. We have knives.'

Gow came between Jelfs and Williams. He took Williams roughly by the shoulder. He whispered intensely to him, 'Be quiet, for God's sake! You'll ruin everything.'

The vivid possessed face of the seaman went from Jelfs to Gow to Ferneau. It shivered with rage and impotence.

'What did you say then, Mr Gow?' said Ferneau.

'The man's tongue ran away with him, sir,' said Gow. 'He is a Welshman. He gets drunk on words.'

'He has said too much,' said Ferneau. He turned on Williams. 'Get out of here,' he cried. 'Get back where you came from. I will consider what should be done with you.'

'Don't let him go, sir,' cried Jelfs. 'Teeth, knives – that was mutiny. Put the irons on him now. There are other bad characters down below. It is like a candle-flame among gunpowder, to let him go now.'

'No, no, let him go,' said Gow. 'He's one of those windbags, brave enough with his tongue, but a poor thing really. I know him. He's neither liked nor trusted by the other men. A sniveller, a bad loser. He has no influence over them.'

'But you have influence, Mr Gow,' said Jelfs.

'You're quite right, Mr Jelfs,' said Gow. 'And I don't use the ropes-end either.'

'Mr Jelfs, Mr Gow,' said Ferneau, 'that's enough.' He turned once more to Williams. 'Get out,' he said. 'I will consider your case. Perhaps it will be necessary to put you ashore in Genoa. You are a bad influence. Mr Jelfs is correct.'

Williams, five steps down, turned to say, 'It is a long way to Genoa.' Then his dark head disappeared.

'There again!' cried Jelfs. 'What did he mean by that? – *It's a long way to Genoa* . . .'

'He meant nothing,' said Gow. 'A fool with a hot loose tongue, that's what he is. I intend to say a thing or two to Williams before nightfall.'

'Nevertheless I did not like what he said,' said Ferneau. 'Mr Jelfs, you will tell the supercargo, the surgeon, and the boatswain to come here at once. Say it is important. Say it is a question of the safety of this ship.'

Jelfs left the quarter-deck at one.

'Sir, I assure you, nothing is amiss,' said Gow.

Ferneau held up his hand. 'You are too trustful, John,' he said. 'Mr Jelfs is right. I have set my mind against it for a long time, but now I know. There is a wicked element on board my ship. We must stamp on the smoulder before it takes hold. You are our gunner, John. I have appointed you to that position in Santa Cruz.'

'Yes, sir,' said Gow. 'Thank you.'

'See that the small-arms are cleaned and loaded immediately,' said Ferneau. 'They have not been used for a long time. I will give you the key of the arms chest presently. It is in my cabin. So long as we have the pistols they can do nothing. The pistols must be ready at a moment's notice. I know the stink of evil.'

'Mr Ferneau!' cried Jelfs from below.

'I will give you the key presently,' said Ferneau. He shouted over the rail, 'I am coming.' He said to Gow in a low voice, 'Yes, good. Our lives may depend upon it.' He tugged his hat over his troubled brow, and turned, and left Gow alone on the quarter-deck.

'The pistols will be cocked,' said Gow.

The prow smashed gently through the sea. The sails creaked. The voices of the officers below sounded like remote empty echoes . . . 'arms chest' . . . 'Genoa' . . . 'complaints' . . . Someone came running up from below, a rapid tattoo of feet on the ladder, random violent words; there appeared again on the quarter-deck the livid face of Williams.

'And here's something else I forgot to tell you, Captain Ferneau,' he yelled. He saw Gow standing there alone. 'You, is it, Jack,' he said. 'Tell me, where is the frogging scum of a Frenchman? Where is Jelfs? I'll –'

Gow gathered the filthy blouse-front into his fist. 'You've done

enough howling and singing for one day,' he said quietly. 'O, you poor
damned idiot, you nearly let everything out.'

'Me, Jack?' said Williams. 'I was very discreet, I thought. Only –'

'Shut your bloody gab, and do as I say,' said Gow. 'You've turned
them all into watch-dogs.' He let go of the excited man in front of him,
and dropped his voice to a whisper. 'Listen, James, do exactly what I
say. We are to go for them tonight. Tomorrow might be too late.
Melvin, Macaulay, Moore, Petersen, Winter, Rollson – tell them the
operation is to be advanced by twenty-four hours. They are to go to
their hammocks but they are not to sleep. The pistols will be ready. I
will give you the word.'

'Whatever you say, Jack,' said Williams.

'Only the men whose names I gave you. Tell them at once, in whispers, one after the other,' said Gow.

'Tell the men what?' said Jelfs' voice behind them.

'Tell the men to obey their orders,' said Gow sternly to Williams,
'or they'll find they've lost a good friend in Jack Gow. Now get out of
here.'

'I'm sorry, sir. Yes,' said Williams humbly and thankfully, like one
who has been given absolution, and left the quarter-deck.

'I'll help you with the firearms, Gow,' said Jelfs. 'Algier and I will
be only too glad to help you.'

'I'll manage very well by myself,' said Gow. 'It's a part of my duties
to see to the firearms. No one is to handle them but me.'

There entered the quarter-deck Captain Ferneau with his arm about
Peter Hanson's shoulder; Mr Algier the supercargo; Mr Guy the ship's
surgeon.

'So, gentlemen,' Ferneau was saying, 'that's the situation. It may
be the fartings of a windbag. It may be nothing at all. John here thinks
so. On the other hand, we may be on the brink of great danger. Do
be very careful. John here is to get the firearms ready immediately.
You will all be issued with a pistol. You will keep it by you always.
You are to sleep with the pistols under your pillows.'

Gow bowed and smiled to the group of officers.

'With our pistols we will quickly put a stop to any nonsense,' said
Ferneau. 'We will blow them to pieces.'

Peter Hanson pointed his hand at Mr Jelfs and cocked his forefinger
and made a violent noise with his mouth.

'If there should chance to be any trouble,' said Ferneau, 'the child
is to be put in my cabin out of harm's way.'

Gently the wind shook the shrouds, and the winter sun slid from
behind a cloud and made the water all blue and silver about them.

A three-quarter moon had risen over Sardinia, and dimmed a little
the light of the stars. The *Caroline* sailed slowly northwards through a

sea that was roughened only occasionally by a breath of wind. Captain Oliver Ferneau stood alone on the quarter-deck. He heard a step coming up from below, a laboured breath, a creak of leather. He laid a finger on the pistol on the table, then turned to face the intruder. It was James Belbin the boatswain.

'Nothing to report, sir,' said Belbin.

'All is quiet, yes?' said the skipper.

'They're mostly asleep in their hammocks, sir,' said Belbin. 'Mr Jelfs, Mr Algier, and the surgeon are in their hammocks too, but their eyes are open.'

'Where is Mr Gow?' said Ferneau.

'I haven't seen him, sir,' said Belbin.

The night was so still that their voices were keyed to whispering; as if a fuller articulation might sully the purity and silence.

'That's good, Belbin,' said Ferneau. 'I think all might be well, after all.'

'Nothing else you want, sir?' said Belbin.

'Nothing,' said Ferneau. 'We are all, I'm sure, in the hand of God.'

'Beg pardon, sir?' said Belbin.

'Do you believe in evil, Belbin?' said Ferneau earnestly. 'Do you believe in the power of evil?'

'Why, sir,' said Belbin. 'I've never rightly thought about that. I leave that kind of thing to the parsons.'

'But there is light and darkness, Belbin,' said Ferneau. 'There is a virtuous power, and also there is a wicked power that goes about in the night time.'

Belbin bent his head. He passed his hand lightly over his brow once or twice. 'I look at it this way, sir,' he said. 'Power is good in itself, whatever colour it comes in. Them that has power – kings and captains and bishops – they decide what's good and virtuous, and everybody else has got to toe the line whatever they feel about it. Excuse me, sir, I'm just an ignorant fellow.'

'No, go on,' said Ferneau.

'Well, sir,' said Belbin, 'the kings and captains are hard to put down. But sometimes the virtue goes out of them, and then somebody else has got to take over. My grandfather now, he was a trooper under Fairfax, when there was the civil wars in England.'

'Was he, Belbin?' said Ferneau: 'I am very interested in what you say. You must have thought deeply on these matters.'

'O no, sir,' said Belbin. 'I never went to school. My father shipped me on board a whaler in Hull when I was twelve.'

'All right, Belbin,' said Ferneau. 'Goodnight.'

'Goodnight to you, sir,' said Belbin.

The blunt moon rose higher between Sardinia and Corsica. There was no sound on the ship but the creaking of canvas and the rhythmic plangent wash of the sea from her bow.

Captain Ferneau, noting the sluggish heave of the *Caroline* through the water, considered that she must be careened and caulked as soon as they were back in Amsterdam; at any rate before the winter was over. The ship was old and must soon be broken up; he doubted if anyone would be interested in buying her. She had been a good fast vessel in his grandfather's time.

The worry of the past day, the contention of the officers, his conversation with the boatswain, led him to think of the solid secure stock he had sprung from – those merchants and sailors of Guernsey – and further back to the Breton countryside that had bred them. Ancient and magnificent and secure seemed the establishment in France, firmly built into history. Yet there were clever men, lawyers and philosophers, who saw mildew and decay everywhere. Belbin the Englishman was perhaps right: it was all a flux, a rooting and a ripening and a rotting. Nothing held. If one could look on those stars that shine in order nightly across the heavens like the implements laid up in some barn for the winter, symbols of the careful husbandry of heaven – men think of them as eternal – yet if one could look on the firmament with the eye of God, one would know that yesterday they were a chaos of fire, and tomorrow they will be cold rust and ashes; and then, perhaps, the great Harvester might turn his energies to another seedtime.

He felt very old and tired. This ship now – perhaps with some young cruel master in command, she would once more leap over the waves like a dolphin.

There was a single cold scream from below.

Ferneau went to the rail. He leaned over and called, 'What is wrong down there?'

There was running, scuffling, a confusion and babble and outcry, another terrible scream.

'Belbin,' cried Ferneau, 'please say what is wrong!'

'I think, sir,' came Belbin's drowsy voice from below, 'there's a man overboard.'

'Lower the boat, then,' cried Ferneau. 'What hinders you?'

Hands gripped him from behind, thrust his head out and forward. He was staring down into the water, all torn silk, and the moon's gently breaking and reforming image. His hat fell into the sea. Hands seized his thighs and tried to lever him off his feet.

Captain Ferneau turned his head round on his thick neck; he recognized the two Swedes Rollson and Winter and the Scotsman Melvin. He flung his hands at the shrouds and clutched and hung on there, swaying.

'Jelfs!' he cried. 'Algier!'

Winter crooked his arm round the skipper's neck and forced the head down into the chest. He levered down, grimacing, waiting for the neck-bone to break. 'Is very strong,' he said, gasping.

Melvin let go of the captain's thigh and took a knife out of his belt.

'Jelfs, captain?' he said. 'Is it Jelfs you're shouting for? His throat is cut. Your turn now, my bonny man.'

Melvin thrust the blade under Winter's lock-grip into the fat white neck; his hand was laved with warmth; he drew the dulled knife out.

Ferneau whispered, 'You will be shot like dogs when Mr Gow comes.'

Blood came out of his neck in quick short gushes. His knuckles shone white among the ropes.

Gow said behind them, 'I *am* here, monsieur.'

Winter took his arm from Ferneau's head. His arm was stiff. He shook the numbness out of it. 'Is sticking to his ship like limpets,' he said.

Rollson put his foot in the small of Ferneau's back and wound his hands through his hair and tried to drag him from the shrouds. The wound at the skipper's neck gaped. There was a dark growing stain down his jacket.

They heard a frantic familiar voice down below, saying the same thing over and over.

'I think Mr Jelfs is speaking,' said John Gow. 'That's strange. Someone told me his throat was cut.'

It was a terrified intense quavering whisper: 'For God's sake, please, time to pray, please, I will do anything, please God, no, not yet' . . . Then Williams' sing-song, 'Indeed to goodness, Mr Jelfs, this is all the prayers I'll let you pray,' followed immediately by a shot.

John Gow examined his pistol carefully. He cocked it. He held it straight out, pointed to the back of Ferneau's head.

The boy Peter Hanson came running in bare feet and grabbed Gow by the jacket. 'Jack, save me,' said the boy. 'Williams says he'll kill us all.'

'You'll be all right with me,' said Gow to the boy. 'Just stand over there till I finish what I'm doing' . . . To Rollston he said, 'You would oblige me by removing your hands from Monsieur Ferneau's hair.'

The boy recognized his master through the blood and dazzle of moonlight. 'What are they doing to you, sir?' he said.

Ferneau looked round at him. 'God bless you, boy,' he said. 'You have new masters now.'

'But I don't want any other master but you,' said Peter Hanson, and began to cry.

'Don't you, boy?' said Ferneau. 'Well then, Belbin was wrong after all.'

Peter Hanson stuck his fist into his mouth.

Ferneau said in a loud voice, 'Have you no strength, you evil men, to throw your old captain from his ship?'

Gow immediately shot him in the nape of the neck; and reloaded at once and put a second ball into his head higher up. There was a brief smell of burnt hair and flesh.

The dying hands relaxed in the shroud. The large body sagged slowly and slithered and fell face down on the deck. The head was a dark clot.

Gow blew a wisp of smoke from his pistol and reloaded it.

Peter Hanson said, 'Why are you angry with Mr Ferneau, Jack?'

There were random shouts and cries from below – a slither, a shot, paddings and flutterings of bare feet here and there. 'Wake up, you scum,' Williams shouted among the hammocks.

Winter took the dead skipper by the shoulders and Rollson took him by the ankles. He was hardly easier to manoeuvre dead than alive. They levered the body up with their knees and forearms, balanced it awkwardly, staggered, heaved it overboard, and staggered back splotched with red. The body went into the sea with a small splash.

'You'll go home to your mother with your pockets full of gold,' said Gow to the boy who was dredging sobs now deep out of his body.

Williams came rushing up from below. He seemed to be half insane from the night's work, dancing and laughing and leaping here and there like a clown. Across his hands lay Ferneau's sword, and Ferneau's silver watch dangled between his fingers. (He had been rifling the skipper's cabin.) After him, more quietly, came MacAulay and Moore and Petersen. They were like men who had drunk a lot and were tired.

Williams went up to Gow and kissed him. 'Give you joy, Captain Jack!' he cried. He handed over the sword and watch.

'God keep you, Captain Gow,' said MacAulay in his soft Hebridean voice.

The boy had stopped crying. He stood and looked the other way, at no-one. A spasm went through him from time to time: silent wondering gasps.

The boatswain, James Belbin, came up from below.

'Belbin,' said Gow quietly, 'and whose side are you on?'

Belbin said, 'I'm disappointed.'

'We had debates about you,' said Gow. 'We balanced your life anxiously. Disappointed, are you? Your throat's uncut – you should be pleased enough about that.'

'I'm very disappointed,' said Belbin. 'Why did you not tell me that this was brewing? I can cut a throat as well as the next man. Give me leave now to pledge my support to the mutiny.'

'Mr Belbin,' said Gow gravely, 'you will continue as boatswain.'

Williams took Belbin by the lapel. 'Realize, Belbin,' he said, 'that you are inferior to me. I am lieutenant.'

'Very good, lieutenant,' said Belbin, smiling. He turned once more to Gow. 'I have rounded up the crew,' he said. 'I have spoken to them. I have reassured one or two doubters. There will be no trouble.'

'I will speak to them now,' said Gow.

Belbin herded up from below a dozen bewildered sailors. They stood about the quarter-deck like sheep in the vicinity of a shambles, eyeing the knives and the pistols, eyeing with little starts and whisperings the dark clots and splashes and runnels everywhere.

'Be quiet there,' said Williams. 'The captain is speaking.'

'Men,' said Gow, 'this ship has a new name. She is no longer the *Caroline*. She is called the *Revenge*. We are no longer bound on errands from port to port. We are not any more the slaves of merchants or bankers. We are a free brotherhood of the sea. We are winged and strong as the albatross. Life on board this ship will be different from now on. There will be no ropes end. There will be no beef with maggots in it. If you don't want to join us, just say the word and we'll think of some place to put you ashore – Senegal, maybe, or Greenland. We'll think of something to do with you, never fear. But if you decide to be free men, there will be adventure and excitement aplenty, full flagons of it. Mr Williams here will sign you on in the morning; it's just a matter of taking a drop of blood from your wrists and making your mark in the book. You know me, Jack Gow. I'm not a hard man to work with, so long as you do what you're told. This is a democratic ship. We're all equal. We all work along with each other for the good of all. If in the days to come I let you down in any way – such as, stint you of women and rum, or navigate wrong, or turn out to be an unlucky man, a Jonah – you have the right and the power in such a case to put me down. The plunder we take we will divide equally among us. We on the *Revenge* are all comrades together. If one of you should in the course of duty meet with an injury – lose a leg or an eye for example – he will be compensated in the recognized sum of five hundred pieces-of-eight. If on the other hand you get poxed up you get nothing – that's your own private affair. That's all I have to say meantime.'

'Well spoken, captain,' said Williams.

An Irish sailor called Phinnes said gloomily, 'What if we're captured?'

'In that case, Paddy,' said Gow, 'we'll all jig for five minutes or so at Wapping Steps. That's where they hang pirates.' He laughed. 'But I assure you, a lot of silver and gold will run through our fingers before that.'

'Speak when you're spoken to,' said Williams to Phinnes.

'Now then,' said Gow, 'does anyone object to sailing on the *Revenge*?'

'We have no choice, do we?' said James Newport, another Irish sailor. 'We have to go along with you willy-nilly.'

'You're a clever salt, James,' said Gow, 'You've grasped the essence of the situation . . . You, Booth, what about you?'

'I'm with you,' said Booth.

'And you, Milne?' said Gow to a tall flame-headed freckle-faced sailor.

Milne said, in a Scottish lowland voice, 'I'm like the bosun, Jack, I'm just sorry you didn't break this to us before.'

'Well spoken,' said Gow. 'I'm sure we'll all get on together well. Thank you. Now then, if you don't mind, I want to be left alone for a while. There's a lot of things to be thought of before morning: such as, how are we going to break out of this bloody sea into the Atlantic. Westwards, that's where the gold and the wine-barrels are. Mr Williams, in order to celebrate this new brotherhood of the sea, I request you to let every sailor have a double tapping of rum. Then back to your hammocks, men. There'll be work for all of us in the morning.'

There were a few ragged cheers. Then the sailors dispersed in groups, whispering, until only Gow and Peter Hanson were left on the quarter-deck.

'You'd better go and get some shut-eye,' said Gow to the boy. 'It's all right. Nobody's going to hurt you.'

'Yes, Jack,' said Peter Hanson.

'That's a good boy,' said Gow. 'But you mustn't call me Jack any more. I'm your skipper now. This is a new ship. The *Revenge*, that's her name. I'm Captain Gow.'

'It must be cold for Mr Ferneau in the sea,' said Peter Hanson. 'Not a drop of rum to warm him at all.'

'He isn't feeling a thing, Peter,' said Gow.

'Mr Ferneau was a kind man to me,' said Peter Hanson. 'Could you not have kept him? He could have scrubbed the decks. He could have peeled potatoes with me in the galley.'

'No, boy. The laws of change are too quick and too cruel,' said Gow.

John Howison

Vanderdecken's Message Home

OUR ship, after touching at the Cape, went out again, and soon losing sight of the Table Mountain, began to be assailed by the impetuous attacks of the sea, which is well known to be more formidable there than in most parts of the known ocean. The day had grown dull and hazy, and the breeze, which had formerly blown fresh, now sometimes subsided almost entirely, and then recovering its strength, for a short time, and changing its direction, blew with temporary violence, and died away again, as if exercising a melancholy caprice. A heavy swell began to come from the south-east. Our sails flapped against the masts, and the ship rolled from side to side, as heavily as if she had been waterlogged. There was so little wind that she would not steer.

At two p.m. we had a squall, accompanied by thunder and rain. The seamen, growing restless, looked anxiously ahead. They said we would have a dirty night of it, and that it would not be worth while to turn into their hammocks. As the second mate was describing a gale he had encountered off Cape Race, Newfoundland, we were suddenly taken all aback, and the blast came upon us furiously. We continued to scud under a double reefed mainsail and foretopsail till dusk; but, as the sea ran high, the captain thought it safest to bring her to. The watch on deck consisted of four men, one of whom was appointed to keep a look-out ahead, for the weather was so hazy that we could not see two cables' length from the bows. This man, whose name was Tom Willis, went frequently to the bows, as if to observe something; and when the others called to him, inquiring what he was looking at, he would give no definite answer. They therefore went also to the bows, and appeared startled, and at first said nothing. But presently one of them cried, 'William, go call the watch.'

The seamen, having been asleep in their hamocks, murmured at this unseasonable summons, and called to know how it looked upon deck. To which Tom Willis replied, 'Come up and see. What we are minding is not on deck, but ahead.'

On hearing this, they ran up without putting on their jackets, and when they came to the bows there was a whispering.

One of them asked, 'Where is she? I do not see her.' To which another replied, 'The last flash of lightning showed there was not a reef in one of her sails; but we, who know her history, know that all her canvas will never carry her into port.'

By this time, the talking of the seamen had brought some of the passengers on deck. They could see nothing, however, for the ship was surrounded by thick darkness, and by the noise of the dashing waters, and the seamen evaded the questions that were put to them.

At this juncture the chaplain came on deck. He was a man of grave and modest demeanour, and was much liked among the seamen, who called him Gentle George. He overheard one of the men asking another if he had ever seen the Flying Dutchman before, and if he knew the story about her. To which the other replied, 'I have heard of her beating about in these seas. What is the reason she never reaches port?'

The first speaker replied, 'They give different reasons for it, but my story is this. She was an Amsterdam vessel, and sailed from that port seventy years ago. Her master's name was Vanderdecken. He was a staunch seaman, and would have his own way, in spite of the devil. For all that, never a sailor under him had reason to complain; though how it is on board with them now, nobody knows. The story is this, that in doubling the Cape, they were a long day trying to weather the Table Bay, which we saw this morning. However, the wind headed them, and went against them more and more, and Vanderdecken walked the deck, swearing at the wind. Just after sunset, a vessel spoke him, asking if he did not mean to go into the Bay that night. Vanderdecken replied, "May I be eternally d—d if I do, though I should beat about here till the day of judgment!" And to be sure, Vanderdecken never did go into that bay; for it is believed that he continues to beat about in these seas still, and will do so long enough. This vessel is never seen but with foul weather along with her.'

To this another replied, 'We must keep clear of her. They say that her captain mans his jolly boat when a vessel comes in sight and tries hard to get alongside, to put letters on board, but no good comes to them who have communication with him.'

Tom Willis said, 'There is such a sea between us at present, as should keep us safe from such visits.'

The other answered: 'We cannot trust to that, if Vanderdecken sends out his men.'

Some of this conversation having been overheard by the passengers, there was a commotion among them. In the meantime, the noise of the waves against the vessel could scarcely be distinguished from the sounds of the distant thunder. The wind had extinguished the light in the binnacle where the compass was, and no one could tell which way the ship's head lay. The passengers were afraid to ask questions, lest they should augment the secret sensation of fear which chilled every heart, or learn any more than they already knew. For while they attributed their agitation of mind to the state of the weather, it was sufficiently perceptible that their alarms also arose from a cause which they did not acknowledge.

The lamp at the binnacle being relighted, they perceived that the ship lay closer to the wind than she had hitherto done, and the spirits of the passengers were somewhat revived.

Nevertheless, neither the tempestuous state of the atmosphere, nor the thunder had ceased; and soon a vivid flash of lightning showed the waves tumbling around us, and, in the distance, the Flying Dutchman scudding furiously before the wind, under a press of canvas. The sight was but momentary, but it was sufficient to remove all doubt from the minds of the passengers. One of the men cried aloud, 'There she goes, top-gallants and all.'

The chaplain had brought up his prayer-book, in order that he might draw from thence something to fortify and tranquillize the minds of the rest. Therefore, taking his seat near the binnacle, so that the light shone upon the white leaves of the book, he, in a solemn tone, read out the service for those distressed at sea. The sailors stood round with folded arms, and looked as if they thought it would be of little use. But this served to occupy the attention of those on deck for a while.

In the meantime, the flashes of lightning becoming less vivid, showed nothing else, far or near, but the billows weltering round the vessel. The sailors seemed to think that they had not yet seen the worst, but confined their remarks and prognostications to their own circle.

At this time, the captain, who had hitherto remained in his berth, came on deck, and, with a gay and unconcerned air, inquired what was the cause of the general dread. He said he thought they had already seen the worst of the weather, and wondered that his men had raised such a hubbub about a capful of wind. Mention being made of the Flying Dutchman, the captain laughed. He said he would like very much to see any vessel carrying top-gallant-sails in such a night, for it would be a sight worth looking at. The chaplain, taking him by one of the buttons of his coat, drew him aside, and appeared to enter into serious conversation with him.

While they were talking together the captain was heard to say, 'Let us look to our own ship, and not mind such things.' And accordingly, he sent a man aloft to see if all was right about the foretop-sail yard, which was chafing the mast with a loud noise.

It was Tom Willis who went up; and when he came down, he said that all was tight, and that he hoped it would soon get clearer; and that they would see no more of what they were most afraid of.

The captain and first mate were heard laughing loudly together, while the chaplain observed that it would be better to repress such unseasonable gaiety. The second mate, a native of Scotland, whose name was Duncan Saunderson, having attended one of the University classes at Aberdeen, thought himself too wise to believe all that the sailors said, and took part with the captain. He jestingly told Tom Willis to borrow his grandma's spectacles the next time he was sent to keep a look-out ahead. Tom walked sulkily away, muttering that he would nevertheless trust to his own eyes till morning, and accordingly took his station at the bow, and appeared to watch as attentively as before.

The sound of talking soon ceased, for many returned to their berths, and we heard nothing but the clanking of the ropes upon the masts, and the bursting of the billows ahead, as the vessel successively took the seas.

But after a considerable interval of darkness, gleams of lightning began to reappear. Tom Willis suddenly called out, 'Vanderdecken, again! Vanderdecken, again! I see them letting down a boat.'

All who were on deck ran to the bows. The next flash of lightning shone far and wide over the raging sea, and showed us not only the Flying Dutchman at a distance, but also a boat coming from her with four men. The boat was within two cables' length of our ship's side.

The man who first saw her ran to the captain and asked whether they should hail her or not. The captain, walking about in great agitation, made no reply. The first mate cried, 'Who's going to heave a rope to that boat?' The men looked at each other without offering to do anything.

The boat had come very near the chains, when Tom Willis called out, 'What do you want? Or what devil has blown you here in such weather?'

A piercing voice from the boat replied in English, 'We want to speak with your captain.'

The captain took no notice of this, and Vanderdecken's boat having come close alongside, one of the men came up on the deck and appeared like a fatigued and weatherbeaten seaman, holding some letters in his hand.

Our sailors all drew back. The chaplain, however, looking steadfastly upon him, went forward a few steps, and asked, 'What is the purpose of this visit?'

The stranger replied, 'We have long been kept here by foul weather, and Vanderdecken wishes to send these letters to his friends in Europe.'

Our captain now came forward, and said as firmly as he could, 'I wish Vanderdecken would put his letters on board another vessel rather than mine.'

The stranger replied, 'We have tried many a ship, but most of them refuse our letters.'

Tom Willis muttered, 'It will be best for us if we do the same, for they say there is sometimes a sinking weight in your papers.'

The stranger took no notice of this, but asked where we were from. On being told that we were from Portsmouth, he said, as if with strong feeling, 'Would that you had rather been from Amsterdam. Oh that we saw it again! We must see our friends again.'

When he uttered these words, the men who were in the boat below wrung their hands and cried in a piercing tone, in Dutch, 'Oh that we saw it again! We have been long here here beating about; but we must see our friends again.'

The chaplain asked the stranger, 'How long have you been at sea?'

He replied, 'We have lost our count; for our almanac was blown overboard. Our ship, you see, is there still; so why should you ask how long we have been at sea? Vanderdecken only wishes to write home and comfort his friends.'

The chaplain replied, 'Your letters, I fear, would be of no use in Amsterdam, even if they were delivered, for the persons to whom they are addressed are probably no longer to be found there, except under very ancient green turf in the churchyard.'

The unwelcome stranger then wrung his hands, and appeared to weep. 'It is impossible,' he replied. 'We cannot believe you. We have been long driving about here, but country or relations cannot be so easily forgotten. There is not a raindrop in the air but feels itself kindred to all the rest, and they fall back into the sea to meet with each other again. How then can kindred blood be made to forget where it came from? Even our bodies are part of the ground of Holland; and Vanderdecken says if he once were to come to Amsterdam, he would rather be changed into a stone post, well fixed into the ground, than leave it again; if that were to die elsewhere. But in the meantime, we only ask you to take these letters.'

The chaplain, looking at him with astonishment, said, 'This is the insanity of natural affection, which rebels against all measures of time and distance.'

The stranger continued: 'Here is a letter from our second mate to his dear and only remaining friend, his uncle, the merchant who lives in the second house on Stuncken Yacht Quay.'

He helf forth the letter, but no one would approach to take it.

Tom Willis raised his voice, and said, 'One of our men here says that he was in Amsterdam last summer, and he knows for certain that the street called Stuncken Yacht Quay was pulled down sixty years ago, and now there is only a large church at that place.'

The man from the Flying Dutchman said, 'It is impossible; we cannot believe you. Here is another letter from myself, in which I have sent a bank-note to my dear sister, to buy some gallant lace, to make her a high headdress.'

Tom Willis hearing this, said, 'It is most likely that her head now lies under a tombstone, which will outlast all the changes of the fashion. But on what house is your banknote?'

The stranger replied, 'On the house of Vanderbrucker and Company.'

The man of whom Tom Willis had spoken, said, 'I guess there will now be some discount upon it, for that banking-house was gone to destruction forty years ago; and Vanderbrucker was afterwards amissing. But to remember these things is like raking up the bottom of an old canal.'

The stranger called our passionately: 'It is impossible. We cannot believe it! It is cruel to say such things to people in our condition. There is a letter from our captain himself, to his much-beloved and faithful wife, whom he left at a pleasant summer dwelling, on the border of the Haarlemer Mer. She promised to have the house beautifully painted the gilded before he came back, and to get a new set of looking-glasses for the principal chamber, that she might see as many images of Vanderdecken, as if she had six husbands at once.'

The man replied, 'There has been time enough for her to have had six husbands since then; but were she alive still, there is no fear that Vanderdecken would ever get home to disturb her.'

On hearing this the stranger again shed tears, and said that if they would not take the letters, he would leave them; and looking round he offered the parcel to the captain, chaplain, and to the rest of the crew successively, but each drew back as it was offered, and put his hands behind his back. He then laid the letters upon the deck, and placed upon them a piece of iron to prevent them from being blown away. Having done this, he swung himself over the gangway, and went into the boat.

He heard the others speak to him, but the rise of a sudden squall prevented us from distinguishing his reply. The boat was seen to quit the ship's side, and, in a few moments, there were no more traces of her than if she had never been there. The sailors rubbed their eyes, as if doubting what they had witnessed, but the parcel still lay upon deck, and proved the reality of all that had passed.

Duncan Saunderson, the Scotch mate, asked the captain if he should take them up, and put them in the letterbag. Receiving no reply, he would have lifted them if it had not been for Tom Willis, who pulled him back, saying that nobody should touch them.

The captain went down to the cabin, and the chaplain having followed him, found him at his bottle-case, pouring out a large dram of brandy. The captain, although somewhat disconcerted, immediately offered the glass to him, saying, 'Here, Charters, is what is good in a cold night.'

The chaplain declined drinking anything, and the captain having swallowed the bumper, they both returned to the deck, where they found the seamen giving their opinions concerning what should be done with the letters. Tom Willis proposed to pick them up on a harpoon, and throw them overboard.

Another speaker said, 'I have always heard it asserted that it is neither safe to accept them voluntarily, nor when they are left to throw them out of the ship.'

'Let no one touch them,' said the carpenter. 'The way to do with the letters from the Flying Dutchman is to case them upon deck, by nailing boards over them, so that if he sends back for them, they are still there to give him.'

The carpenter went to fetch his tools. During his absence, the ship gave so violent a pitch that the piece of iron slid off the letters, and they were whirled overboard by the wind, like birds of evil omen whirring through the air. There was a cry of joy among the sailors, and they ascribed the favourable change which soon took place in the weather to our having got quit of Vanderdecken. We soon got under way again. The night watch being set, the rest of the crew retired to their berths.

Herman Melville

Benito Cereno

IN the year 1799, Captain Amasa Delano, of Duxbury, in Massachusetts, commanding a large sealer and general trader, lay at anchor with a valuable cargo, in the harbour of St Maria – a small, desert, uninhabited island toward the southern extremity of the long coast of Chili. There he had touched for water.

On the second day, not long after dawn, while lying in his berth, his mate came below, informing him that a strange sail was coming into the bay. Ships were then not so plenty in those waters as now. He rose, dressed, and went on deck.

The morning was one peculiar to that coast. Everything was mute and calm; everything grey. The sea, though undulated into long roods of swells, seemed fixed, and was sleeked at the surface like waved lead that has cooled and set in the smelter's mould. The sky seemed a grey surtout. Flights of troubled grey fowl, kith and kin with flights of troubled grey vapours among which they were mixed, skimmed low and fitfully over the waters, as swallows over meadows before storms. Shadows present, foreshadowing deeper shadows to come.

To Captain Delano's surprise, the stranger, viewed through the glass, showed no colours; though to do so upon entering a haven, however uninhabited in its shores, where but a single other ship might be lying, was the custom among peaceful seamen of all nations. Considering the lawlessness and loneliness of the spot, and the sort of stories, at that day, associated with those seas, Captain Delano's surprise might have deepened into some uneasiness had he not been a person of a singularly undistrustful good-nature, not liable, except on extraordinary and repeated incentives, and hardly then, to indulge in personal alarms, any way involving the imputation of malign evil in man. Whether, in view of what humanity is capable, such a trait implies, along with a benevolent heart, more than ordinary quickness and accuracy of intellectual perception, may be left to the wise to determine.

But whatever misgivings might have obtruded on first seeing the stranger, would almost, in any seaman's mind, have been dissipated by observing that the ship, in navigating into the harbour, was drawing too near the land; a sunken reef making out off her bow. This seemed to prove her a stranger, indeed, not only to the sealer, but the island; consequently, she could be no wonted freebooter on that ocean. With no small interest, Captain Delano continued to watch her – a proceeding not much facilitated by the vapours partly mantling the hull, through which the far matin light from her cabin streamed equivocally enough; much like the sun – by this time hemisphered on the rim of the horizon, and, apparently, in company with the strange ship entering the harbour – which, wimpled by the same low, creeping clouds, showed not unlike a Lima intriguante's one sinister eye peering across the Plaza from the Indian loop-hole of her dusk *saya-y-manta*.

It might have been but a deception of the vapours, but the longer the stranger was watched the more singular appeared her manoeuvres. Ere long it seemed hard to decide whether she meant to come in or no – what she wanted, or what she was about. The wind, which had breezed up a little during the night, was now extremely light and baffling, which the more increased the apparent uncertainty of her movements.

Surmising, at last, that it might be a ship in distress, Captain Delano ordered his whale-boat to be dropped, and, much to the wary opposition of his mate, prepared to board her, and, at the least, pilot her in. On the night previous, a fishing-party of the seamen had gone a long distance to some detached rocks out of sight from the sealer, and, an hour or two before daybreak, had returned, having met with no small success. Presuming that the stranger might have been long off soundings, the good captain put several baskets of the fish, for presents, into his boat, and so pulled away. From her continuing too near the sunken reef, deeming her in danger, calling to his men, he made all haste to apprise those on board of their situation. But, some time ere the boat came up, the wind, light thought it was, having shifted, had headed the vessel off, as well as partly broken the vapours from about her.

Upon gaining a less remote view, the ship, when made signally visible on the verge of the leaden-hued swells, with the shreds of fog here and there raggedly furring her, appeared like a whitewashed monastery after a thunder-storm, seen perched upon some dun cliff among the Pyrenees. But it was no purely fanciful resemblance which now, for a moment, almost led Captain Delano to think that nothing less than a ship-load of monks was before him. Peering over the bulwarks were what really seemed, in the hazy distance, throngs of dark cowls; while, fitfully revealed through the open port-holes, other dark moving figures were dimly descried, as of Black Friars pacing the cloisters.

Upon a still nigher approach, this appearance was modified, and the true character of the vessel was plain – a Spanish merchantman of the first class, carrying negro slaves, amongst other valuable freight, from one colonial port to another. A very large, and, in its time, a very fine vessel, such as in those days were at intervals encountered along that main; sometimes superseded Acapulco treasure-ships, or retired frigates of the Spanish king's navy, which, like superannuated Italian palaces, still, under a decline of masters, preserved signs of former state.

As the whale-boat drew more and more nigh, the cause of the peculiar pipe-clayed aspect of the stranger was seen in the slovenly neglect pervading her. The spars, ropes, and great part of the bulwarks, looked woolly, from long unacquaintance with the scraper, tar, and the brush. Her keel seemed laid, her ribs put together, and she launched, from Ezekiel's Valley of Dry Bones.

In the present business in which she was engaged, the ship's general model and rig appeared to have undergone no material change from their original warlike and Froissart pattern. However, no guns were seen.

The tops were large, and were railed about with what had once been octagonal net-work, all now in sad disrepair. These tops hung overhead like three ruinous aviaries, in one of which was seen perched, on a rattlin, a white noddy, a strange fowl, so called from its lethargic, somnambulistic character, being frequently caught by hand at sea. Battered and mouldy, the castellated forecastle seemed some ancient turret, long ago taken by assault, and then left to decay. Toward the stern, two high-raised quarter-galleries – the balustrades here and there covered with dry, tindery sea-moss – opening out from the unoccupied state-cabin, whose dead-lights, for all the mild weather, were hermetically closed and caulked – these tenantless balconies hung over the sea as if it were the grand Venetian canal. But the principal relic of faded grandeur was the ample oval of the shield-like stern-piece, intricately carved with the arms of Castile and Leon, medallioned about by groups of mythological or symbolical devices; uppermost and central of which was a dark satyr in a mask, holding his foot on the prostrate neck of a writhing figure, likewise masked.

Whether the ship had a figure-head, or only a plain beak, was not quite certain, owing to canvas wrapped about that part, either to protect it while undergoing a refurbishing, or else decently to hide its decay. Rudely painted or chalked, as in a sailor freak, along the forward side of a sort of pedestal below the canvas, was the sentence, '*Seguid vuestro jefe*' (follow your leader); while upon the tarnished head-boards, near by, appeared in stately capitals, once gilt, the ship's name, *San Dominick*, each letter streakingly corroded with tricklings of copper-spike rust; while, like mourning weeds, dark festoons of sea-grass slimily swept to and fro over the name, with every hearse-like roll of the hull.

As, at last, the boat was hooked from the bow along toward the gangway amidship, its keel, while yet some inches separated from the hull, harshly grated as on a sunken coral reef. It proved a huge bunch of conglobated barnacles adhering below the water to the side like a wen – a token of baffling airs and long calms passed somewhere in those seas.

Climbing the side, the visitor was at once surrounded by a clamorous throng of whites and blacks, but the latter outnumbering the former more than could have been expected, negro transportation-ship as the stranger in port was. But, in one language, and as with one voice, all poured out a common tale of suffering; in which the negresses, of whom there were not a few, exceeded the others in their dolorous vehemence. The scurvy, together with the fever, had swept off a great part of their number, more especially the Spaniards. Off Cape Horn they had narrowly escaped shipwreck; then, for days together, they had lain tranced without wind; their provisions were low; their water next to none; their lips that moment were baked.

While Captain Delano was thus made the mark of all eager tongues, his one eager glance took in all faces, with every other object about him.

Always upon first boarding a large and populous ship at sea, especially a foreign one, with a nondescript crew such as Lascars or Manilla men, the impression varies in a peculiar way from that produced by first entering a strange house with strange inmates in a strange land. Both house and ship – the one by its walls and blinds, the other by its high bulwarks like ramparts – hoard from view their interiors till the last moment; but in the case of the ship there is this addition: that the living spectacle it contains, upon its sudden and complete disclosure, has, in contrast with the blank ocean which zones it, something of the effect of enchantment. The ship seems unreal; these strange costumes, gestures, and faces, but a shadowy tableau just emerged from the deep, which directly must receive back what it gave.

Perhaps it was some such influence, as above is attempted to be described, which, in Captain Delano's mind, heightened whatever, upon a staid scrutiny, might have seemed unusual; especially the conspicuous figures of four elderly grizzled negroes, their heads like black, doddered willow-tops, who, in venerable contrast to the tumult below them, were couched, sphinx-like, one on the starboard cat-head, another on the larboard, and the remaining pair face to face on the opposite bulwarks above the main-chains. They each had bits of unstranded old junk in their hands, and, with a sort of stoical self-content, were picking the junk into oakum, a small heap of which lay by their sides. They accompanied the task with a continuous, low, monotonous chant; droning and druling away like so many grey-headed bagpipers playing a funeral march.

The quarter-deck rose into an ample elevated poop, upon the forward verge of which, lifted, like the oakum-pickers, some eight feet above the general throng, sat along in a row, separated by regular spaces, the cross-legged figures of six other blacks; each with a rusty hatchet in his hand, which, with a bit of brick and a rag, he was engaged like a scullion in scouring; while between each two was a small stack of hatchets, their rusted edges turned forward awaiting a like operation. Though occasionally the four oakum-pickers would briefly address some person or persons in the crowd below, yet the six hatchet-polishers neither spoke to others, nor breathed a whisper among themselves, but sat intent upon their task, except at intervals, when, with the peculiar love in negroes of uniting industry with pastime, two and two they sideways clashed their hatchets together, like cymbals, with a barbarous din. All six, unlike the generality, had the raw aspect of unsophisticated Africans.

But that first comprehensive glance which took in those ten figures, with scores less conspicuous, rested but an instant upon them, as, impatient of the hubbub of voices, the visitor turned in quest of whomsoever it might be that commanded the ship.

But as if not unwilling to let nature make known her own case among his suffering charge, or else in despair of restraining it for the time, the Spanish captain, a gentlemanly, reserved-looking, and rather young man to a stranger's eye, dressed with singular richness, but bearing plain traces of recent sleepless cares and disquietudes, stood passively by, leaning against the mainmast, at one moment casting a dreary, spiritless look upon his excited people, at the next an unhappy glance toward his visitor. By his side stood a black of small stature, in whose rude face, as occasionally, like a shepherd's dog, he mutely turned it up into the Spaniard's, sorrow and affection were equally blended.

Struggling through the throng, the American advanced to the Spaniard, assuring him of his sympathies, and offering to render whatever assistance might be in his power. To which the Spaniard returned for the present but grave and ceremonious acknowledgements, his national formality dusked by the saturnine mood of ill-health.

But losing no time in mere compliments, Captain Delano, returning to the gangway, had his basket of fish brought up; and as the wind still continued light, so that some hours at least must elapse ere the ship could be brought to the anchorage, he bade his men return to the sealer, and fetch back as much water as the whale-boat could carry, with whatever soft bread the steward might have, all the remaining pumpkins on board, with a box of sugar, and a dozen of his private bottles of cider.

Not many minutes after the boat's pushing off, to the vexation of all, the wind entirely died away, and the tide turning, began drifting back the ship helplessly seaward. But trusting this would not last long, Captain Delano sought, with good hopes, to cheer up the strangers, feeling no small satisfaction that, with persons in their condition, he could – thanks to his frequent voyages along the Spanish main – converse with some freedom in their native tongue.

While left alone with them, he was not long in observing some things tending to heighten his first impressions. But surprise was lost in pity, both for the Spaniards and blacks, alike evidently reduced from scarcity of water and provisions; while long-continued suffering seemed to have brought out the less good-natured qualities of the negroes, besides, at the same time, impairing the Spaniard's authority over them. But, under the circumstances, precisely this condition of things was to have been anticipated. In armies, navies, cities, or families, in nature herself, nothing more relaxes good order than misery. Still, Captain Delano was not without the idea, that had Benito Cereno been a man of greater energy, misrule would hardly have come to the present pass. But the debility, constitutional or induced by hardships, bodily and mental, of the Spanish captain, was too obvious to be overlooked. A prey to settled dejection, as if long mocked with hope he would not now indulge it, even when it had ceased to be a mock, the prospect of that day, or evening at furthest, lying at anchor, with plenty of water for his people, and a brother captain to counsel and befriend, seemed in no perceptible degree to encourage him. His mind appeared unstrung, if not still more seriously affected. Shut up in these oaken walls, chained to one dull round of command, whose unconditionality cloyed him, like some hypochondriac abbot he moved slowly about, at times suddenly pausing, starting, or staring, biting his lip, biting his finger-nail, flushing, paling, twitching his beard, with other symptoms of an absent or moody mind. This distempered spirit was lodged, as before hinted, in as distempered a frame. He was rather tall, but seemed never to have been robust, and now with nervous suffering was almost worn to a skeleton. A tendency to some pulmonary complaint appeared to have been lately confirmed. His voice was like that of one with lungs half gone – hoarsely suppressed, a husky whisper. No wonder that, as in this state he tottered about, his private servant apprehensively followed him. Sometimes the negro gave his master his arm, or took his handkerchief out of his pocket for him; performing these and similar offices with that affectionate zeal which transmutes into something filial or fraternal acts in themselves but menial; and which has gained for the negro the repute of making the most pleasing body-servant in the world; one, too, whom a master need be on no stiffly superior terms with, but may treat with familiar trust; less a servant than a devoted companion.

Marking the noisy indocility of the blacks in general, as well as what seemed the sullen ineffiency of the whites, it was not without humane satisfaction that Captain Delano witnessed the steady good conduct of Babo.

But the good conduct of Babo, hardly more than the ill-behaviour of others, seemed to withdraw the half-lunatic Don Benito from his cloudy languor. Not that such precisely was the impression made by the Spaniard on the mind of his visitor. The Spaniard's individual unrest was, for the present, but noted as a conspicuous feature in the ship's general affliction. Still, Captain Delano was not a little concerned at what he could not help taking for the time to be Don Benito's unfriendly indifference toward himself. The Spaniard's manner, too, conveyed a sort of sour and gloomy disdain, which he seemed at no pains to disguise. But this the American in charity ascribed to the harassing effects of sickness, since, in former instances, he had noted that there are peculiar natures on whom prolonged physical suffering seems to cancel every social instinct of kindness; as if, forced to black bread themselves, they deemed it but equity that each person coming nigh them should, indirectly, by some slight or affront, be made to partake of their fare.

But ere long Captain Delano bethought him that, indulgent as he was at the first, in judging the Spaniard, he might not, after all, have exercised charity enough. At bottom it was Don Benito's reserve which displeased him; but the same reserve was shown toward all but his faithful personal attendant. Even the formal reports which, according to sea-usage, were, at stated times, made to him by some petty underling, either a white, mulatto, or black, he hardly had patience enough to listen to, without betraying contemptuous aversion. His manner upon such occasions was, in its degree, not unlike that which might be supposed to have been his imperial countryman's, Charles V, just previous to the anchoritish retirement of that monarch from the throne.

This splenetic disrelish of his place was evinced in almost every function pertaining to it. Proud as he was moody, he condescended to no personal mandate. Whatever special orders were necessary, their delivery was delegated to his body-servant, who in turn transferred them to the ultimate destination, through runners, alert Spanish boys or slave-boys, like pages or pilot-fish within easy call continually hovering round Don Benito. So that to have beheld this undemonstrative invalid gliding about, apathetic and mute, no landsman could have dreamed that in him was lodged a dictatorship beyond which, while at sea, there was no earthly appeal.

Thus, the Spaniard, regarded in his reserve, seemed the involuntary victim of mental disorder. But, in fact, his reserve might, in some degree, have proceeded from design. If so, then here was evinced the unhealthy climax of that icy though conscientious policy, more or less adopted by all commanders of large ships, which, except in signal emergencies, obliterates alike the manifestation of sway with every trace of sociality; transforming the man into a block, or rather into a loaded cannon, which, until there is call for thunder, has nothing to say.

Viewing him in this light, it seemed but a natural token of the perverse habit induced by a long course of such hard self-restraint, that, notwithstanding the present condition of his ship, the Spaniard should still persist in a demeanour, which, however harmless, or, it may be, appropriate, in a well-appointed vessel, such as the *San Dominick* might have been at the outset of the voyage, was anything but judicious now. But the Spaniard, perhaps, thought that it was with captains as with gods: reserve, under all events, must still be their cue. But probably this appearance of slumbering dominion might have been but an attempted disguise to conscious imbecility – not deep policy, but shallow device. But be all this as it might, whether Don Benito's manner was designed or not, the more Captain Delano noted its pervading reserve, the less he felt uneasiness at any particularly manifestation of that reserve toward himself.

Neither were his thoughts taken up by the captain alone. Wonted to the quiet orderliness of the sealer's comfortable family of a crew, the noisy confusion of the *San Dominick*'s suffering host repeatedly challenged his eye. Some prominent breaches, not only of discipline but of decency, were observed. These Captain Delano could not but ascribe, in the main, to the absence of those subordinate deck-officers to whom along with higher duties, is entrusted what may be styled the police department of a populous ship. True, the old oakum-pickers appeared at times to act the part of monitorial constables to their countrymen, the blacks; but though occasionally succeeding in allaying trifling outbreaks now and then between man and man, they could do little or nothing toward establishing general quiet. The *San Dominick* was in the condition of a transatlantic emigrant ship, along whose multitude of living freight are some individuals, doubtless, as little troublesome as crates and bales; but the friendly remonstrances of such with their ruder companions are not so much avail as the unfriendly arm of the mate. What the *San Dominick* wanted was, what the emigrant ship has, stern superior officers. But on these decks not so much as a fourth mate was to be seen.

The visitor's curiosity was roused to learn the particulars of those mishaps which had brought about such absenteeism, with its consequences; because, though deriving some inkling of the voyage from the wails which at the first moment had greeted him, yet of the details no clear understanding had been had. The best account would, doubtless, be given by the captain. Yet at first the visitor was loth to ask it, unwilling to provoke some distant rebuff. But plucking up courage, he at last accosted Don Benito, renewing the expression of his benevolent interest, adding, that did he (Captain Delano) but know the particulars of the ship's misfortunes, he would, perhaps, be better able in the end to relieve them. Would Don Benito favour him with the whole story.

Don Benito faltered; then, like some somnambulist suddenly interfered with, vacantly stared at his visitor, and ended by looking down on the deck. He maintained this posture so long, that Captain Delano, almost equally disconcerted, and involuntarily almost as rude, turned suddenly from him, walking forward to accost one of the Spanish seaman for the desired information, but he had hardly gone five paces, when, with a sort of eagerness, Don Benito invited him back, regretting his momentary absence of mind, and professing readiness to gratify him.

While most part of the story was being given, the two captains stood on the after part of the main-deck, a privileged spot, no one being near but the servant.

'It is now a hundred and ninety days,' began the Spaniard, in his husky whisper, 'that this ship, well officered and well manned, with several cabin passengers – some fifty Spaniards in all – sailed from Buenos Ayres bound to Lima, with a general cargo, hardware, Paraguay tea and the like – and,' pointing forward, 'that parcel of negroes, now not more than an hundred and fifty, as you see, but then numbering over three hundred souls. Off Cape Horn we had heavy gales. In one moment, by night, three of my best officers, with fifteen sailors, were lost, with the main-yard; the spare snapping under them in the slings, as they sought, with heavers, to beat down the icy sail. To lighten the hull, the heavier sacks of mata were thrown into the sea, with most of the water-pipes lashed on deck at the time. And this last necessity it was, combined with the prolonged detentions afterward experienced, which eventually brought about our chief causes of suffering. When –'

Here there was a sudden fainting attack of his cough, brought on, no doubt, by his mental distress. His servant sustained him, and drawing a cordial from his pocket placed it to his lips. He a little revived. But unwilling to leave him unsupported while yet imperfectly restored, the black with one arm still encircled his master, at the same time keeping his eye fixed on his face, as if to watch for the first sign of complete restoration, or relapse, as the event might prove.

The Spaniard proceeded, but brokenly and obscurely, as one in a dream.

Oh, my God! rather than pass through what I have, with joy I would have hailed the most terrible gales; but –'

His cough returned and with increased violence; this subsiding, with reddened lips and closed eyes he fell heavily against his supporter.

'His mind wanders. He was thinking of the plague that followed the gales,' plaintively sighed the servant; 'my poor, poor master!' wringing one hand, and with the other wiping the mouth. 'But be patient, señor,' again turning to Captain Delano, 'these fits do not last long; master will soon be himself.'

Don Benito reviving, went on; but as this portion of the story was very brokenly delivered, the substance only will here be set down.

It appeared that after the ship had been many days tossed in storms off the Cape, the scurvy broke out, carrying off numbers of the whites and blacks. When at last they had worked round into the Pacific, their spars and sails were so damaged, and so inadequately handled by the surviving mariners, most of whom were become invalids, that, unable to lay her northerly course by the wind, which was powerful, the unmanageable ship, for successive days and nights, was blown north-westward, where the breeze suddenly deserted her, in unknown waters, to sultry calms. The absence of the water-pipes now proved as fatal to life as before their presence had menaced it. Induced, or at least aggravated, by the more than scanty allowance of water, a malignant fever followed the scurvy; with the excessive heat of the lengthened calm, making such short work of it as to sweep away, as by billows, whole families of the Africans, and a yet larger number, proportionably, of the Spaniards, including, by a luckless fatality, every remaining officer on board. Consequently, in the smart west winds eventually following the calm, the already rent sails, having to be simply dropped, not furled, at need, had been gradually reduced to the beggars' rags they were now. To procure substitutes for his lost sailors, as well as supplies of water and sails, the captain, at the earliest opportunity, had made for Baldivia, the southernmost civilized port of Chili and South America; but upon nearing the coast the thick weather had prevented him from so much as sighting that harbour. Since which period, almost without a crew, and almost without canvas, and almost without water, and, at intervals, giving its added dead to the sea, the *San Dominick* had been battledored about by contrary winds, inveigled by currents, or grown weedy in calms. Like a man lost in woods, more than once she had doubled upon her own track.

'But throughout these calamities,' huskily continued Don Benito, painfully turning in the half-embrace of his servant, 'I have to thank those negroes you see, who, though to your inexperienced eyes appearing unruly, have, indeed, conducted themselves with less of restlessness than even their owner could have thought possible under such circumstances.'

Here he again fell faintly back. Again his mind wandered; but he rallied, and less obscurely proceeded.

'Yes, their owner was quite right in assuring me that no fetters would be needed with his blacks; so that while, as is wont in this transportation, these negroes have always remained upon deck – not thrust below, as in the Guinea-men – they have, also, from the beginning, been freely permitted to range within given bounds at their pleasure.'

Once more the faintness returned – his mind roved – but, recovering, he resumed.

'But it is Babo here to whom, under God, I owe not only my own preservation, but likewise to him, chiefly, the merit is due, of pacifying his more ignorant brethren, when at intervals tempted to murmurings.'

'Ah, master,' sighed the black, bowing his face, 'don't speak of me; Babo is nothing; what Babo has done was but duty.'

'Faithful fellow!' cried Captain Delano. 'Don Benito, I envy you such a friend; slave I cannot call him.'

As master and man stood before him, the black upholding the white, Captain Delano could not but bethink him of the beauty of that relationship which could present such a spectacle of fidelity on the one hand and confidence on the other. The scene was heightened by the contrast in dress, denoting their relative positions. The Spaniard wore a loose Chili jacket of dark velvet; white small-clothes and stockings, with silver buckles at the knee and instep; a high-crowned sombrero, of fine grass; a slender sword, silver mounted, hung from a knot in his sash – the last being an almost invariable adjunct, more for utility than ornament, of a South American gentleman's dress to this hour. Excepting when his occasional nervous contortions brought about disarray, there was a certain precision in his attire curiously at variance with the unsightly disorder around; especially in the belittered ghetto, forward of the mainmast, wholly occupied by the blacks.

The servant wore nothing but wide trousers, apparently, from their coarseness and patches, made out of some old topsails; they were clean and confined at the waist by a bit of unstranded rope, which, with his composed, deprecatory air at times, made him look something like a begging friar of St Francis.

However unsuitable for the time and place, at least in the blunt-thinking American's eyes, and however strangely surviving in the midst of all his afflictions, the toilet of Don Benito might not, in fashion at least, have gone beyond the style of the day among South Americans of his class. Though on the present voyage sailing from Buenos Ayres, he had avowed himself a native and resident of Chili, whose inhabitants had not so generally adopted the plain coat and once plebeian pantaloons; but, with a becoming modification, adhered to their provincial costume, picturesque as any in the world. Still, relatively to the pale history of the voyage, and his own pale face, there seemed something so incongruous in the Spaniard's apparel, as almost to suggest the image of an invalid courtier tottering about London streets in the time of the plague.

The portion of the narrative which, perhaps, most excited interest, as well as some surprise, considering the latitudes in question, was the long calms spoken of, and more particularly the ship's so long drifting about. Without communicating the opinion, of course, the American could not but impute at least part of the detentions both to clumsy seamanship and faulty navigation. Eyeing Don Benito's small, yellow hands, he easily inferred that the young captain had not got into command at the hawse-hole, but the cabin window; and if so, why wonder at incompetence, in youth, sickness, and gentility united?

But drowning criticism in compassion, after a fresh repetition of his sympathies, Captain Delano, having heard out his story, not only engaged, as in the first place, to see Don Benito and his people supplied in their immediate bodily needs, but, also, now further promised to assist him in procuring a large permanent supply of water, as well as some sails and rigging; and, though it would involve no small embarrassment to himself, yet he would spare three of his best seamen for temporary deck officers; so that without delay the ship might proceed to Conception, there fully to refit for Lima, her destined port.

Such generosity was not without its effect, even upon the invalid. His face lighted up; eager and hectic, he met the honest glance of his visitor. With gratitude he seemed overcome.

'This excitement is bad for master,' whispered the servant, taking his arm, and with soothing words gently drawing him aside.

When Don Benito returned, the American was pained to observe that his hopefulness, like the sudden kindling in his cheek, was but febrile and transient.

Ere long, with a joyless mien, looking up toward the poop, the host invited his guest to accompany him there, for the benefit of what little breath of wind might be stirring.

As, during the telling of the story, Captain Delano had once or twice started at the occasional cymballing of the hatchet-polishers, wondering why such an interruption should be allowed, especially in that part of the ship, and in the ears of an invalid; and moreover, as the hatchets had anything but an attractive look, and the handlers of them still less so, it was, therefore, to tell the truth not without some lurking reluctance, or even shrinking, it may be, that Captain Delano, with apparent complaisance, acquiesced in his host's invitation. The more, since, with an untimely caprice of punctilio, rendered distressing by his cadaverous aspect, Don Benito, with Castilian bows, solemnly insisted upon his guest's preceding him up the ladder leading to the elevation; where, one on each side of the last step, sat for armorial supporters and sentries two of the ominous file. Gingerly enough stepped good Captain Delano between them, and in the instant of leaving them behind, like one running the gauntlet, he felt an apprehensive twitch in the calves of his legs.

But when, facing about, he saw the whole file, like so many organ-grinders, still stupidly intent on their work, unmindful of everything besides, he could not but smile at his late fidgety panic.

Presently, while standing with his host, looking forward upon the decks below, he was struck by one of those instances of insubordination previously alluded to. Three black boys, with two Spanish boys, were sitting together on the hatches, scraping a rude wooden platter, in which some scanty mess had recently been cooked. Suddenly, one of the black boys, enraged at a word dropped by one of his white companions, seized a knife, and, though called to forbear by one of the oakum-pickers, struck the lad over the head, inflicting a gash from which blood flowed.

In amazement, Captain Delano inquired what this meant. To which the pale Don Benito dully muttered, that it was merely the sport of the lad.

'Pretty serious sport, truly,' rejoined Captain Delano. 'Had such a thing happened on board the *Bachelor's Delight*, instant punishment would have followed.'

At these words the Spaniard turned upon the American one of his sudden, staring, half-lunatic looks; then, relapsing into his torpor, answered. 'Doubtless, doubtless, señor.'

Is it, thought Captain Delano, that this hapless man is one of those paper captains I've known, who by policy wink at what by power they cannot put down! I know no sadder sight than a commander who has little of command but the name.

'I should think, Don Benito,' he now said, glancing toward the oakum-picker who had sought to interfere with the boys, 'that you would find it advantageous to keep all your blacks employed, especially the younger ones, no matter at what useless task, and no matter what happens to the ship. Why, even with my little band, I find such a course indispensable. I once kept a crew on my quarter-deck thrumming mats for my cabin, when, for three days, I have given up my ship – mats, men, and all – for a speedy loss, owing to the violence of a gale, in which we could do nothing but helplessly drive before it.'

'Doubtless, doubtless,' muttered Don Benito.

'But,' continued Captain Delano, again glancing upon the oakum-pickers and then at the hatchet-polishers, near by, 'I see you keep some, at least, of your host employed.'

'Yes,' was again the vacant response.

'Those old men there, shaking their pows from their pulpits,' continued Captain Delano, pointing to the oakum-pickers, 'seem to act the part of old dominies to the rest, little heeded as their admonitions are at times. Is this voluntary on their part, Don Benito, or have you appointed them shepherds to your flock of black sheep?'

'What posts they fill, I appointed them,' rejoined the Spaniard, in an acrid tone, as if resenting some supposed satiric reflection.

'And these others, these Ashantee conjurers here,' continued Captain Delano, rather uneasily eyeing the brandished steel of the hatchet-polishers, where, in spots, it had been brought to a shine, 'this seems a curious business they are at, Don Benito?'

'In the gales we met,' answered the Spaniard, 'what of our general cargo was not thrown overboard was much damaged by the brine. Since coming into calm weather, I have had several cases of knives and hatchets daily brought up for overhauling and cleaning.'

'A prudent idea, Don Benito. You are part owner of ship and cargo, I presume; but none of the slaves, perhaps?'

'I am owner of all you see,' impatiently returned Don Benito, 'except the main company of blacks, who belonged to my late friend, Alexandro Aranda.'

As he mentioned this name, his air was heart-broken; his knees shook; his servant supported him.

Thinking he divined the cause of such unusual emotion, to confirm his surmise, Captain Delano, after a pause, said: 'And may I ask, Don Benito, whether – since a while ago you spoke of some cabin passengers – the friend, whose loss so afflicts you, at the outset of the voyage accompanied his blacks?'

'Yes.'

'But died of the fever?'

'Died of the fever. Oh, could I but –'

Again quivering, the Spaniard paused.

'Pardon me,' said Captain Delano lowly, 'but I think that, by a sympathetic experience, I conjecture, Don Benito, what it is that gives the keener edge to your grief. It was once my hard fortune to lose, at sea, a dear friend, my own brother, then supercargo. Assured of the welfare of his spirit, its departure I could have borne like a man; but that honest eye, that honest hand – both of which had so often met mine – and that warm heart; all, all – like scraps to the dogs – to throw all to the sharks! It was then I vowed never to have for fellow-voyager a man I loved, unless, unbeknown to him, I have provided every

requisite, in case of a fatality, for embalming his mortal part for interment on shore. Were your friend's remains now on board this ship,
Don Benito, not thus strangely would the mention of his name affect
you.'

'On board this ship?' echoed the Spaniard. Then, with horrified
gestures, as directed against some spectre, he unconsciously fell into
the ready arms of his attendant, who, with a silent appeal toward Captain Delano, seemed beseeching him not again to broach a theme so
unspeakably distressing to his master.

This poor fellow now, thought the pained American, is the victim
of that sad superstition which associates goblins with the deserted body
of man, as ghosts with an abandoned house. How unlike are we made!
What to me, in like case, would have been a solemn satisfaction, the
bare suggestion, even, terrifies the Spaniard into this trance. Poor
Alexandro Aranda! What would you say could you here see your friend
– who, on former voyages, when you, for months, were left behind,
has, I dare say, often longed, and longed, for one peep at you – now
transported with terror at the least thought of having you any way nigh
him.

At this moment, with a dreary graveyard toll, betokening a flaw,
the ship's forecastle bell, smote by one of the grizzled oakum-pickers,
proclaimed ten o'clock through the leaden calm: when Captain Delano's
attention was caught by the moving figure of a gigantic black, emerging
from the general crowd below, and slowly advancing toward the elevated poop. An iron collar was about his neck, from which depended
a chain, thrice wound round his body; the terminating links padlocked
together at a broad band of iron, his girdle.

'How like a mute Atufal moves,' murmured the servant.

The black mounted the steps of the poop, and, like a brave prisoner,
brought up to receive sentence, stood in unquailing muteness before
Don Benito, now recovered from his attack.

At the first glimpse of his approach, Don Benito had started, a
resentful shadow swept over his face; and, as with the sudden memory
of bootless rage, his white lips glued together.

This is some mulish mutineer, thought Captain Delano, surveying,
not without a mixture of admiration, the colossal form of the negro.

'See, he waits your question, master,' said the servant.

Thus reminded, Don Benito, nervously averting his glance, as if
shunning, by anticipation, some rebellious response, in a disconcerted
voice, thus spoke:

'Atufal, will you ask my pardon now?'

The black was silent.

'Again, master,' murmured the servant, with bitter upbraiding eyeing his countryman, 'again, master; he will bend to master yet.'

'Answer,' said Don Benito, still averting his glance, 'say but the one word, *pardon*, and your chains shall be off.'

Upon this, the black, slowly raising both arms, let them lifelessly fall, his links clanking, his head bowed; as much as to say, 'No, I am content.'

'Go,' said Don Benito, with inkept and unknown emotion.

Deliberately as he had come, the black obeyed.

'Excuse me, Don Benito,' said Captain Delano, 'but this scene surprises me; what means it, pray?'

'It means that that negro alone, of all the band, has given me peculiar cause of offence. I have put him in chains; I –'

Here he paused; his hand to his head, as if there were a swimming there, or a sudden bewilderment of memory had come over him; but meeting his servant's kindly glance seemed reassured, and proceeded:

'I could not scourge such a form. But I told him he must ask my pardon. As yet he has not. At my command, every two hours he stands before me.'

'And how long has this been?'

'Some sixty days.'

'And obedient in all else? And respectful?'

'Yes.'

'Upon my conscience, then,' exclaimed Captain Delano impulsively, 'he has a royal spirit in him, this fellow.'

'He may have some right to it,' bitterly returned Don Benito, 'he says he was king in his own land.'

'Yes,' said the servant, entering a word, 'those slits in Atufal's ears once held wedges of gold; but poor Babo here, in his own land, was only a poor slave; a black man's slave was Babo, who now is the white's.'

Somewhat annoyed by these conversational familiarities, Captain Delano turned curiously upon the attendant, then glanced inquiringly at his master; but, as if long wonted to these little informalities, neither master nor man seemed to understand him.

'What, pray, was Atufal's offence, Don Benito?' asked Captain Delano; 'if it was not something very serious, take a fool's advice, and, in view of his general docility, as well as in some natural respect for his spirit, remit him his penalty.'

'No, no, master never will do that,' here murmured the servant to himself, 'proud Atufal must first ask master's pardon. The slave there carries the padlock, but master here carries the key.'

His attention thus directed, Captain Delano now noticed for the first, that, suspended by a slender silken cord from Don Benito's neck, hung a key. At once, from the servant's muttered syllables, divining the key's purpose, he smiled and said: – 'So, Don Benito – padlock and key – significant symbols, truly.'

Biting his lip, Don Benito faltered.

Though the remark of Captain Delano, a man of such native simplicity as to be incapable of satire or irony, had been dropped in playful allusion to the Spaniard's singularly evidenced lordship over the black; yet the hypochondriac seemed some way to have taken it as a malicious reflection upon his confessed inability thus far to break down, at least, on a verbal summons, the entrenched will of the slave. Deploring this supposed misconception, yet despairing of correcting it, Captain Delano shifted the subject; but finding his companion more than ever withdrawn, as if still sourly digesting the lees of the presumed affront above mentioned, by and by Captain Delano likewise became less talkative, oppressed, against his own will, by what seemed the secret vindictiveness of the morbidly sensitive Spaniard. But the good sailor, himself of a quite contrary disposition, refrained, on his part, alike from the appearance as from the feeling of resentment, and if silent, was only so from contagion.

Presently the Spaniard, assisted by his servant, somewhat discourteously crossed over from his guest; a procedure which, sensibly enough, might have been allowed to pass for idle caprice of ill-humour, had not master and man, lingering round the corner of the elevated skylight, began whispering together in low voices. This was unpleasing. And more; the moody air of the Spaniard, which at times had not been without a sort of valetudinarian stateliness, now seemed anything but dignified; while the menial familiarity of the servant lost its original charm of simple-hearted attachment.

In his embarrassment, the visitor turned his face to the other side of the ship. By so doing, his glance accidentally fell on a young Spanish sailor, a coil of rope in his hand, just stepped from the deck to the first round of the mizen-rigging. Perhaps the man would not have been particularly noticed, were it not that, during his ascent to one of the yards, he, with a sort of covert intentness, kept his eye fixed in Captain Delano, from whom, presently, it passed, as if by natural sequence, to the two whisperers.

His own attention thus redirected to that quarter, Captain Delano gave a slight start. From something in Don Benito's manner just then, it seemed as if the visitor had, at least partly, been the subject of the withdrawn consultation going on – a conjecture as little agreeable to the guest as it was little flattering to the host.

The singular alternations of courtesy and ill-breeding in the Spanish captain were unaccountable, except on one of two suppositions – innocent lunacy, or wicked imposture.

But the first idea, though it might naturally have occurred to an indifferent observer, and, in some respect, had not hitherto been wholly a stranger to Captain Delano's mind, yet, now that, in an incipient way, he began to regard the stranger's conduct something in the light of an intentional affront, of course the idea of lunacy was virtually vacated. But if not a lunatic, what then? Under the circumstances, would a gentleman, nay, any honest boor, act the part now acted by his host? The man was an impostor. Some low-born adventurer, masquerading as an oceanic grandee; yet so ignorant of the first requisites of mere gentlemanhood as to be betrayed into the present remarkable indecorum. That strange ceremoniousness, too, at other times evinced, seemed not uncharacteristic of one playing a part above his real level. Benito Cereno – Don Benito Cereno – a sounding name. One, too, at that period, not unknown, in the surname, to supercargoes and sea-captains trading along the Spanish Main, as belonging to one of the most enterprising and extensive mercantile familes in all those provinces; several members of it having titles; a sort of Castilian Rothschild, with a noble brother, or cousin, in every great trading town of South America. The alleged Don Benito was in an early manhood, about twenty-nine or thirty. To assume a sort of roving cadetship in the maritime affairs of such a house, what more likely scheme for a young knave of talent and spirit? But the Spaniard was a pale invalid. Never mind. For even to the degree of simulating mortal disease, the craft of some tricksters had been known to attain. To think that, under the aspect of infantile weakness, the most savage energies might be couched – those velvets of the Spaniard but the silky paw to his fangs.

From no train of thought did these fancies come; not from within, but from without; suddenly, too, and in one throng, like hoar frost; yet as soon to vanish as the mild sun of Captain Delano's good-nature regained its meridian.

Glancing over once more toward his host – whose side-face, revealed above the skylight, was now turned toward him – he was struck by the profile, whose clearness of cut was refined by the thinness, incident to ill-health, as well as ennobled about the chin by the beard. Away with suspicion. He was a true off-shoot of a true hidalgo Cereno.

Relieved by these and other better thoughts, the visitor, lightly humming a tune, now began indifferently pacing the poop, so as not to betray to Don Benito that he had at all mistrusted incivility, much less duplicity; for such mistrust would yet be proved illusory, and by the event; though, for the present, the circumstance which had provoked that distrust remained unexplained. But when that little mystery should have been cleared up, Captain Delano thought he might extremely regret it, did he allow Don Benito to become aware that he had indulged in ungenerous surmises. In short, to the Spaniard's black-letter text, it was best, for a while, to leave open margin.

Presently, his pale face twitching and overcast, the Spaniard, still supported by his attendant, moved over toward his guest, when, with even more than his usual embarrassment, and a strange sort of intriguing intonation in his husky whisper, the following conversation began:

'Señor, may I ask how long you have lain at this isle?'

'Oh, but a day or two, Don Benito.'

'And from what port are you last?'

'Canton.'

'And there, señor, you exchanged your seal-skins for teas and silks, I think you said?'

'Yes. Silks, mostly.'

'And the balance you took in specie, perhaps?'

Captain Delano, fidgeting a little, answered:

'Yes; some silver; not a very great deal, though.'

'Ah – well. May I ask how many men have you, señor?'

Captain Delano slightly started, but answered:

'About five-and-twenty, all told.'

'And at present, señor, all on board, I suppose?'

'All aboard, Don Benito,' replied the captain, now with satisfaction.

'And will be tonight, señor?'

At this last question, following so many pertinacious ones, for the soul of him Captain Delano could not but look very earnestly at the questioner, who, instead of meeting the glance, with every token of craven discomposure dropped his eyes to the deck; presenting an unworthy contrast to his servant, who, just then, was kneeling at his feet, adjusting a loose shoe-buckle; his disengaged face meantime, with humble curiosity, turned openly up into his master's downcast one.

The Spaniard, still with a guilty shuffle, repeated his question:

'And – and will be tonight, señor?'

'Yes, for aught I know,' returned Captain Delano – 'but nay,' rallying himself into fearless truth, 'some of them talked of going off on another fishing party about midnight.'

'Your ships generally go – go more or less armed, I believe, señor?'

'Oh, a six-pounder or two, in case of emergency,' was the intrepidly indifferent reply, 'with a small stock of muskets, sealing-spears, and cutlasses, you know.'

As he thus responded, Captain Delano again glanced at Don Benito, but the latter's eyes were averted; while abruptly and awkwardly shifting the subject, he made some peevish allusion to the calm, and then, without apology, once more, with his attendant, withdrew to the opposite bulwarks, where the whispering was resumed.

At this moment, and 'ere Captain Delano could cast a cool thought upon what had just passed, the young Spanish sailor, before mentioned, was seen descending from the rigging. In act of stooping over to spring inboard to the deck, his voluminous, unconfined frock, or shirt, of coarse woollen, much spotted with tar, opened out far down the chest, revealing a soiled under-garment of what seemed the finest linen, edged, about the neck, with a narrow blue ribbon, sadly faded and worn. At this moment the young sailor's eye was again fixed on the whisperers, and Captain Delano thought he observed a lurking significance in it, as if silent signs, of some Freemason sort, had that instant been interchanged.

This once more impelled his own glance in the direction of Don Benito, and, as before, he could not but infer that himself formed the subject of conference. He paused. The sound of the hatchet-polishing fell on his ears. He cast another swift side-look at the two. They had the air of conspirators. In connection with the late questionings, and the incident of the young sailor, these things now begat such return of involuntary suspicion, that the singular guilelessness of the American could not endure it. Plucking up a gay and humorous expression, he crossed over to the two rapidly, saying: 'Ha, Don Benito, your black here seems high in your trust; a sort of privy-counsellor, in fact.'

Upon this, the servant looked up with a good-natured grin, but the master started as from a venomous bite. It was a moment or two before the Spaniard sufficiently recovered himself to reply; which he did, at last, with cold constraint: 'Yes, señor, I have trust in Babo.'

Here Babo, changing his previous grin of mere animal humour into an intelligent smile, not ungratefully eyed his master.

Finding that the Spaniard now stood silent and reserved, as if involuntarily, or purposely giving hint that his guest's proximity was inconvenient just then, Captain Delano, unwilling to appear uncivil even to incivility itself, made some trivial remark and moved off; again and again turning over in his mind the mysterious demeanour of Don Benito Cereno.

He had descended from the poop, and, wrapped in thought, was passing near a dark hatchway, leading down into the steerage, when, perceiving motion there, he looked to see what moved. The same instant there was a sparkle in the shadowy hatchway, and he saw one of the Spanish sailors, prowling there, hurriedly placing his hand in the bosom of his frock, as if hiding something. Before the man could have been certain who it was that was passing, he slunk below out of sight. But enough was seen of him to make it sure that he was the same young sailor before noticed in the rigging.

What was that which so sparkled? thought Captain Delano. It was no lamp – no match – no live coal. Could it have been a jewel? But how come sailors with jewels? – or with silk-trimmed under-shirts either? Has he been robbing the trunks of the dead cabin passengers? But if so, he would hardly wear one of the stolen articles on board ship here. Ah, ah – if, now, that was, indeed, a secret sign I saw passing between this suspicious fellow and his captain a while since; if I could only be certain that, in my uneasiness, my senses did not deceive me, then –

Here, passing from one suspicious thing to another, his mind revolved the strange questions put to him concerning his ship.

By a curious coincidence, as each point was recalled, the black wizards of Ashantee would strike up with their hatchets, as in ominous comment on the white stranger's thoughts. Pressed by such enigmas and portents, it would have been almost against nature, had not, even into the least distrustful heart, some ugly misgivings obtruded.

Observing the ship, now helplessly fallen into a current, with enchanted sails, drifting with increased rapidity seaward; and noting that, from a lately intercepted projection of the land, the sealer was hidden, the stout mariner began to quake at thoughts which he barely durst confess to himself. Above all, he began to feel a ghostly dread of Don Benito. And yet, when he roused himself, dilated his chest, felt himself strong on his legs, and coolly considered it – what did all these phantoms amount to?

Had the Spaniard any sinister scheme, it must have reference not so much to him (Captain Delano) as to his ship (the *Bachelor's Delight*). Hence the present drifting away of the one ship from the other, instead of favouring any such possible scheme, was, for the time, at least, opposed to it. Clearly any suspicion, combining such contradiction, must needs be delusive. Besides, was it not absurd to think of a vessel in distress – a vessel by sickness almost dismanned of her crew – a vessel whose inmates were parched for water – was it not a thousand times absurd that such a craft should, at present, be of a piratical character; or her commander, either for himself or those under him, cherish any desire but for speedy relief and refreshment? But then, might not general distress, and thirst in particular, be affected? And might not that same undiminished Spanish crew, alleged to have perished off to a remnant, be at that very moment lurking in the hold? On heartbroken pretence of entreating a cup of cold water, fiends in human form had got into lonely dwellings, nor retired until a dark deed had been done. And among the Malay pirates, it was no unusual thing to lure ships after them into their treacherous harbours, or entice boarders from a declared enemy at sea, by the spectacle of thinly manned or vacant decks, beneath which prowled a hundred spears with yellow arms ready to upthrust them through the mats. Not that Captain Delano had entirely credited such things. He had heard of them – and now, as stories, they recurred. The present destination of the ship was the anchorage. There she would be near his own vessel. Upon gaining that vicinity, might not the *San Dominick*, like a slumbering volcano, suddenly let loose energies now hid?

He recalled the Spaniard's manner while telling his story. There was a gloomy hesitancy and subterfuge about it. It was just the manner of one making up his tale for evil purposes as he goes. But if that story was not true, what was the truth? That the ship had unlawfully come into the Spaniard's possession? But in many of its details, especially in reference to the more calamitous parts, such as the fatalities among the seamen, the consequent prolonged beating about, the past sufferings from obstinate calms, and still continued suffering from thirst; in all these points, as well as others, Don Benito's story had corroborated not only the wailing ejaculations of the indiscriminate multitude, white and black, but likewise – what seemed impossible to be counterfeit – by the very expression and play of every human feature, which Captain Delano saw. If Don Benito's story was, throughout, an invention, then every soul on board, down to the youngest negress, was his carefully drilled recruit in the plot: an incredible inference. And yet, if there was ground for mistrusting his veracity, that inference was a legitimate one.

But those questions of the Spaniard. There, indeed, one might pause. Did they not seem put with much the same object with which the burglar or assassin, by day-time, reconnoitres of the walls of a house? But, with ill purposes, to solicit such information openly of the chief person endangered, and so, in effect, setting him on his guard; how unlikely a procedure was that. Absurd, then, to suppose that those questions had been prompted by evil designs. Thus, the same conduct, which, in this instance, had raised the alarm, served to dispel it. In short, scarce any suspicion or uneasiness, however apparently reasonable at the time, which was not now, with equal apparent reason, dismissed.

At last he began to laugh at his former forebodings; and laugh at the strange ship for, in its aspect, some way siding with them, as it were; and laugh, too, at the odd-looking blacks, particularly those old scissors-grinders, the Ashantees; and those bedridden old knitting women, the oakum-pickers; and almost at the dark Spaniard himself, the central hobgoblin of all.

For the rest, whatever in a serious way seemed enigmatical, was now good-naturedly explained away by the thought that, for the most part, the poor invalid scarcely knew what he was about; either sulking in black vapours, or putting idle questions without sense or object. Evidently, for the present, the man was not fit to be entrusted with the ship. On some benevolent plea withdrawing the command from him, Captain Delano would yet have to send her to Conception, in charge of his second mate, a worthy person and good navigator – a plan not more convenient for the *San Dominick* than for Don Benito; for, relieved from all anxiety, keeping wholly to his cabin, the sick man, under the good nursing of his servant would, probably, by the end of the passage, be in a measure restored to health, and with that he should also be restored to authority.

Such were the American's thoughts. They were tranquillizing. There was a difference between the idea of Don Benito's darkly preordaining Captain Delano's fate, and Captain Delano's lightly arranging Don Benito's. Nevertheless, it was not without something of relief that the good seaman presently perceived his whale-boat in the distance. Its absence had been prolonged by unexpected detention at the sealer's side, as well as its returning trip lengthened by the continual recession of the goal.

The advancing speck was observed by the blacks. Their shouts attracted the attention of Don Benito, who with a return of courtesy, approaching Captain Delano, expressed satisfaction at the coming of some supplies, slight and temporary as they must necessarily prove.

Captain Delano responded; but while doing so, his attention was drawn to something passing on the deck below: among the crowd climbing the landward bulwarks, anxiously watching the coming boat, two blacks, to all appearances accidentally incommoded by one of the sailors, violently pushed him aside, which the sailor some way resenting, they dashed him to the deck, despite the earnest cries of the oakumpickers.

'Don Benito,' said Captain Delano quickly, 'do you see what is going on there? Look!'

But, seized by his cough, the Spaniard staggered, with both hands to his face, on the point of falling. Captain Delano would have supported him, but the servant was more alert, who, with one hand sustaining his master, with the other applied the cordial. Don Benito restored, the black withdrew his support, slipping aside a little, but dutifully remaining within call of a whisper. Such discretion was here evinced as quite wiped away, in the visitor's eyes, any blemish of impropriety which might have attached to the attendant from the indecorous conferences before mentioned; showing, too, that if the servant were to blame, it might be more the master's fault than his own, since, when left to himself, he could conduct thus well.

His glance called away from the spectacle of disorder to the more pleasing one before him, Captain Delano could not avoid again congratulating his host upon possessing such a servant, who, though perhaps a little too forward now and then, must upon the whole be invaluable to one in the invalid's situation.

'Tell me, Don Benito,' he added, with a smile – 'I should like to have your man here, myself – what will you take for him? Would fifty doubloons be any object?'

'Master wouldn't part with Babo for a thousand doubloons,' murmured the black, overhearing the offer, and taking it in earnest, and, with the strange vanity of a faithful slave, appreciated by his master, scorning to hear so paltry a valuation put upon him by a stranger. But Don Benito, apparently hardly yet completely restored, and again interrupted by his cough, made but some broken reply.

Soon his physical distress became so great, affecting his mind, too, apparently that, as if to screen the sad spectacle, the servant gently conducted his master below.

Left to himself, the American, to while away the time till his boat should arrive, would have pleasantly accosted some one of the few Spanish seamen he saw; but recalling something that Don Benito had said touching their ill conduct, he refrained; as a shipmaster indisposed to countenance cowardice or unfaithfulness in seamen.

While, with these thoughts, standing with eye directed forward toward that handful of sailors, suddenly he thought that one or two of them returned the glance and with a sort of meaning. He rubbed his eyes, and looked again; but again seemed to see the same thing. Under a new form, but more obscure than any previous one, the old suspicions recurred, but, in the absence of Don Benito, with less of panic than before. Despite the bad account given of the sailors, Captain Delano resolved forthwith to accost one of them. Descending the poop, he made his way through the blacks, his movement drawing a queer cry from the oakum-pickers, prompted by whom, the negroes, twitching each other aside, divided before him; but, as if curious to see what was the object of this deliberate visit to their ghetto, closing in behind, in tolerable order, followed the white stranger up. His progress thus proclaimed as by mounted kings-at-arms, and escorted as by a Caffre guard of honour, Captain Delano, assuming a good-humoured, off-handed air, continued to advance; now and then saying a blithe word to the negroes, and his eye curiously surveying the white faces, here and there sparsely mixed in with the blacks, like stray white pawns venturously involved in the ranks of the chessmen opposed.

While thinking which of them to select for his purpose, he chanced to observe a sailor seated on the deck engaged in tarring the strap of a large block, a circle of blacks squatted round him inquisitively eyeing the process.

The mean employment of the man was in contrast with something superior in his figure. His hand, black with continually thrusting it into the tar-pot held for him by a negro, seemed not naturally allied to his face, a face which would have been a very fine one but for its haggardness. Whether this haggardness had aught to do with criminality, could not be determined; since, as intense heat and cold, though unlike, produce like sensations, so innocence and guilt, when, through casual association with mental pain, stamping any visible impress, use one seal – a hacked one.

Not again that this reflection occurred to Captain Delano at the time, charitable man as he was. Rather another idea. Because observing so singular a haggardness combined with a dark eye, averted as in trouble and shame, and then again recalling Don Benito's confessed ill opinion of his crew, insensibly he was operated upon by certain general notions which, while disconnecting pain and abashment from virtue, invariably link them with vice.

If, indeed, there be any wickedness on board this ship, thought Captain Delano, be sure that man there has fouled his hand in it, even as now he fouls it in the pitch. I don't like to accost him. I will speak to this other, this old Jack here on the windlass.

He advanced to an old Barcelona tar, in ragged red breeches and dirty night-cap, cheeks trenched and bronzed, whiskers dense as thorn hedges. Seated between two sleepy-looking Africans, this mariner, like his younger shipmate, was employed upon some rigging – splicing a cable – the sleepy-looking blacks performing the inferior function of holding the outer parts of the ropes for him.

Upon Captain Delano's approach, the man at once hung his head below its previous level; the one necessary for business. It appeared as if he desired to be thought absorbed, with more than common fidelity, in his task. Being addressed, he glanced up, but with what seemed a furtive, diffident air, which sat strangely enough on his weather-beaten visage, much as if a grizzly bear, instead of growling and biting, should simper and cast sheep's eyes. He was asked several questions concerning the voyage – questions purposely referring to several particulars in Don Benito's narrative, not previously corroborated by those impulsive cries greeting the visitor on first coming on board. The questions were briefly answered, confirming all that remained to be confirmed of the story. The negroes about the windlass joined in with the old sailor; but, as they became talkative, he by degrees became mute, and at length quite glum, seemed morosely unwilling to answer more questions, and yet, all the while, this ursine air was somehow mixed with his sheepish one.

Despairing of getting into unembarrassed talk with such a centaur, Captain Delano, after glancing round for a more promising countenance, but seeing none, spoke pleasantly to the blacks to make way for him; and so, amid various grins and grimaces, returned to the poop, feeling a little strange at first, he could hardly tell why, but upon the whole with regained confidence in Benito Cereno.

How plainly, thought he, did that old whiskerando yonder betray a consciousness of ill desert. No doubt, when he saw me coming, he dreaded lest I, apprised by his captain of the crew's general misbehaviour, came with sharp words for him, and so down with his head. And yet – and yet, now that I think of it, that very old fellow, if I err not, was one of those who seemed so earnestly eyeing me here a while since. Ah, these currents spin one's head round almost as much as they do the ship. Ha, there now's a pleasant sort of sunny sight; quite sociable, too.

His attention had been drawn to a slumbering negress, partly disclosed through the lacework of some rigging, lying, with youthful limbs carelessly disposed, under the lee of the bulwarks, like a doe in the shade of a woodland rock. Sprawling at her lapped breasts was her wide-awake fawn, stark naked, its black little body half lifted from the deck, crosswise with its dam's; its hands, like two paws, clambering upon her; its mouth and nose ineffectually rooting to get at the mark; and meantime giving a vexatious half-grunt, blending with the composed snore of the negress.

The uncommon vigour of the child at length roused the mother. She started up, at a distance facing Captain Delano. But as if not at all concerned at the attitude in which she had been caught, delightedly she caught the child up, with maternal transports, covering it with kisses.

There's naked nature, now; pure tenderness and love, thought Captain Delano, well pleased.

This incident prompted him to remark the other negresses more particularly than before. He was gratified with their manners: like most uncivilized women, they seemed at once tender of heart and tough of constitution; equally ready to die for their infants or fight for them. Unsophisticated as leopardesses; loving as doves. Ah! thought Captain Delano, these, perhaps, are some of the very women whom Ledyard saw in Africa, and gave such a noble account of.

These natural sights somehow insensibly deepened his confidence and ease. At last he looked to see how his boat was getting on; but it was still pretty remote. He turned to see if Don Benito had returned; but he had not.

To change the scene, as well as to please himself with a leisurely observation of the coming boat, stepping over into the mizen-chains, he clambered his way into the starboard quarter-gallery – one of those abandoned Venetian-looking water-balconies previously mentioned – retreats cut off from the deck. As his foot pressed the half-damp, half-dry sea-mosses matting the place, and a chance phantom cat's-paw – an islet of breeze, unheralded, unfollowed – as this ghostly cat's paw came fanning his cheek; as his glance fell upon the row of small, round dead-lights – all closed like coppered eyes of the coffined – and the state-cabin door, once connecting with the gallery, even as the dead-lights had once looked out upon it, but now caulked fast like a sarcophagus lid; and to a purple-black, tarred-over panel, threshold, and post; and he bethought him of the time, when that state-cabin and this state-balcony had heard the voices of the Spanish king's officers, and the forms of the Lima viceroy's daughters had perhaps leaned where he stood – as these and other images flitted through his mind, as the cat's paw through the calm, gradually he felt rising a dreamy inquietude, like that of one who alone on the prairie feels unrest from the repose of the noon.

He leaned against the carved balustrade, again looking off toward his boat; but found his eye falling upon the ribbon grass, trailing along the ship's water-line, straight as a border of green box; and parterres of seaweed, broad ovals and crescents, floating nigh and far, with what seemed long formal alleys between, crossing the terraces of swells, and sweeping round as if leading to the grottoes below. And overhanging all was the balustrade by his arm, which, partly stained with pitch and partly embossed with moss, seemed the charred ruin of some summer-house in a grand garden long running to waste.

Trying to break one charm, he was but becharmed anew. Though upon the wide sea, he seemed in some far inland country; prisoner in some deserted château, left to stare at empty grounds, and peer out at vague roads, where never wagon or wayfarer passed.

But these enchantments were a little disenchanted as his eye fell on the corroded main-chains. Of an ancient style, massy and rusty in link, shackle, and bolt, they seemed even more fit for the ship's present business than the one for which she had been built.

Presently he thought something moved nigh the chains. He rubbed his eyes, and looked hard. Groves of rigging were about the chains; and there, peering from behind a great stay, like an Indian from behind a hemlock, a Spanish sailor, a marling-spike in his hand, was seen, who made what seemed an imperfect gesture toward the balcony, but immediately, as if alarmed by some advancing step along the deck within, vanished into the recesses of the hempen forest, like a poacher.

What meant this? Something the man had sought to communicate, unbeknown to anyone, even to his captain. Did the secret involve aught unfavourable to his captain? Were those previous misgivings of Captain Delano's about to be verified? Or, in his haunted mood at the moment, had some random, unintentional motion of the man, while busy with the stay, as if repairing it, been mistaken for a significant beckoning?

Not unbewildered, again he gazed off for his boat. But it was temporarily hidden by a rocky spur of the isle. As with some eagerness he bent forward, watching for the first shooting view of its beak, the balustrade gave way before him like charcoal. Had he not clutched an outreaching rope he would have fallen into the sea. The crash, though feeble, and the fall, though hollow, of the rotten fragments, must have been overheard. He glanced up. With sober curiosity peering down upon him was one of the old oakum-pickers, slipped from his perch to an outside boom; while below the old negro, and, invisible to him, reconnoitring from a port-hole like a fox from the mouth of its den, crouched the Spanish sailor again. From something suddenly suggested by the man's air, the mad idea now darted into Captain Delano's mind, that Don Benito's plea of indisposition, in withdrawing below, was but a pretence: that he was engaged there maturing his plot, of which the sailor, by some means gaining an inkling, had a mind to warn the stranger against; incited, it may be, by gratitude for a kind word on first boarding the ship. Was it from foreseeing some possible interference like this, that Don Benito had, before hand, given such a bad character of his sailors, while praising the negroes; though, indeed, the former seemed as docile as the latter the contrary? The whites, too, by nature, were the shrewder race. A man with some evil design, would he not be likely to speak well of that stupidity which was blind to his depravity, and malign that intelligence from which it might not be hidden? Not unlikely perhaps. But if the whites had dark secrets concerning Don Benito, could then Don Benito be any way in complicity with the blacks? But they were too stupid. Besides, who ever heard of a white so far a renegade as to apostatize from his very species almost, by leaguing in against it with negroes? These difficulties recalled former ones. Lost in their mazes, Captain Delano, who had now regained the deck, was uneasily advancing along it, when he observed a new face; an aged sailor seated cross-legged near the main hatchway. His skin was shrunk up with wrinkles like a pelican's empty pouch; his hair frosted; his countenance grave and composed. His hands were full of ropes, which he was working into a large knot. Some blacks were about him obligingly dipping the strands for him, here and there, as the exigencies of the operations demanded.

Captain Delano crossed over to him, and stood in silence surveying the knot; his mind, by a not uncongenial transition, passing from its own entanglements to those of the hemp. For intricacy, such a knot he had never seen in an American ship, nor indeed any other. The old man looked like an Egyptian priest, making Gordian knots for the temple of Ammon. The knot seemed a combination of double-bowline-knot, treble-crown-knot, back-handed-well-knot, knot-in-and-out-knot, and jamming-knot.

At last, puzzled to comprehend the meaning of such a knot, Captain Delano addressed the knotter:

'What are you knotting there, my man?'

'The knot,' was the brief reply, without looking up.

'So it seems; but what is it for?'

'For someone else to undo,' muttered back the old man, plying his fingers harder than ever, the knot being now nearly completed.

While Captain Delano stood watching him, suddenly the old man threw the knot toward him, saying in broken English – the first heard in the ship – something to this effect: 'Undo it, cut it, quick.' It was said lowly, but with such condensation of rapidity that the long, slow words in Spanish, which had preceded and followed, almost operated as covers to the brief English between.

For a moment, knot in hand, and knot in head, Captain Delano stood mute; while, without further heeding him, the old man was now intent upon ropes. Presently there was a slight stir behind Captain Delano. Turning, he saw the chained negro, Atufal, standing quietly there. The next moment the old sailor rose, muttering, and, followed by his subordinate negroes, removed to the forward part of the ship, where in the crowd he disappeared.

An elderly negro, in a clout like an infant's, and with a pepper-and-salt head, and a kind of attorney air, now approached Captain Delano. In tolerable Spanish and with a good-natured, knowing wink, he informed him that the old knotter was simple-witted, but harmless; often playing his odd tricks. The negro concluded by begging the knot, for of course the stranger would not care to be troubled with it. Unconsciously, it was handed to him. With a sort of *congé*, the negro received it, and, turning his back, ferreted into it like a detective custom-house officer after smuggled laces. Soon, with some African word, equivalent to pshaw, he tossed the knot overboard.

All this is very queer now, thought Captain Delano, with a qualmish sort of emotion; but, as one feeling incipient sea-sickness, he strove, by ignoring the symptoms, to get rid of the malady. Once more he looked off for his boat. To his delight, it was now again in view, leaving the rocky spur astern.

The sensation here experienced, after at first relieving his uneasiness, with unforeseen efficacy soon began to remove it. The less distant sight of that well-known boat – showing it, not as before, half blended with the haze, but with outline defined, so that its individuality, like a man's, was manifest; that boat, *Rover* by name, which, though now in strange seas, had often pressed the beach of Captain Delano's home, and, brought to its threshold for repairs, had familiarly lain there, as a Newfoundland dog; the sight of that household boat evoked a thousand trustful associations, which, contrasted with previous suspicions, filled him not only with lightsome confidence, but somehow with half-humorous self-reproaches at his former lack of it.

'What, I, Amasa Delano – Jack of the Beach, as they called me when a lad – I, Amasa; the same that, duck-satchel in hand, used to paddle along the water-side to the school-house made from the old hulk – I, little Jack of the Beach, that used to go berrying with cousin Nat and the rest; I to be murdered here at the ends of the earth on board a haunted pirate-ship by a horrible Spaniard? Too nonsensical to think of! Who would murder Amasa Delano? His conscience is clean.

There is someone above. Fie, fie, Jack of the Beach! you are a child indeed; a child of the second childhood, old boy; you are beginning to dote and drule, I'm afraid.'

Light of heart and foot, he stepped aft, and there was met by Don Benito's servant who, with a pleasing expression, responsive to his own present feelings, informed him that his master had recovered from the effects of his coughing fit, and had just ordered him to go present his compliments to his good guest, Don Amasa, and say that he (Don Benito) would soon have the happiness to rejoin him.

There now, do you mark that? again thought Captain Delano, walking the poop. What a donkey I was. This kind gentleman who here sends me his kind compliments, he, but ten minutes ago, dark-lantern in hand, was dodging round some old grindstone in the hold, sharpening a hatchet for me, I thought. Well, well; these long calms have a morbid effect on the mind, I've often heard, though I never believed it before. Ha! Glancing toward the boat; there's *Rover*; good dog; a white bone in her mouth. A pretty big bone though, seems to me. What? Yes, she has fallen afoul of the bubbling tide-rip there. It sets her the other way, too, for the time. Patience.

It was now about noon, though from the greyness of everything it seemed to be getting toward dusk.

The calm was confirmed. In the far distance, away from the influence of land, the leaden ocean seemed laid out and leaded up, its course finished, soul gone, defunct. But the current from landward, where the ship was, increased; silently sweeping her further and further toward the tranced waters beyond.

Still, from his knowledge of those latitudes, cherishing hopes of a breeze, and a fair and fresh one, at any moment, Captain Delano, despite present prospects, buoyantly counted upon bringing the *San Dominick* safely to anchor ere night. The distance swept over was nothing; since, with a good wind, ten minutes' sailing would retrace more than sixty minutes' drifting. Meantime, one moment turning to mark *Rover* fighting the tide-rip, and the next to see Don Benito approaching, he continued walking the poop.

Gradually he felt a vexation arising from the delay of his boat; this soon merged into uneasiness; and at last – his eye falling continually, as from a stage-box into the pit, upon the strange crowd before and below him, and, by and by, recognizing there the face – now composed to indifference – of the Spanish sailor who had seemed to beckon from the main-chains – something of his old trepidations returned.

Ah, thought he – gravely enough – this is like the ague: because it went off, if follows not that it won't come back.

Though ashamed of the relapse, he could not altogether subdue it;

and so, exerting his good-nature to the utmost, insensibly he came to a compromise.

Yes, this is a strange craft; a strange history, too, and strange folks on board. But – nothing more.

By way of keeping his mind out of mischief till the boat should arrive, he tried to occupy it with turning over and over, in a purely speculative sort of way, some lesser peculiarities of the captain and crew. Among others, four curious points recurred:

First, the affair of the Spanish lad assailed with a knife by the slave-boy; an act winked at by Don Benito. Second, the tyranny in Don Benito's treatment of Atufal, the black; as if a child should lead a bull of the Nile by the ring in his nose. Third, the trampling of the sailor by the two negroes; a piece of insolence passed over without so much as a reprimand. Fourth, the cringing submission to their master of all the ship's underlings, mostly blacks; as if by the least inadvertence they feared to draw down his despotic displeasure.

Coupling these points, they seemed somewhat contradictory. But what then, thought Captain Delano, glancing toward his now nearing boat – what then? Why, Don Benito is a very capricious commander. But he is not the first of the sort I have seen; though it's true he rather exceeds any other. But as a nation – continued he in his reveries – these Spaniards are all an odd set; the very word Spaniard has a curious, conspirator, Guy-Fawkish twang to it. And yet, I dare say, Spaniards in the main are as good folks as any in Duxbury, Massachusetts. Ah, good! At last *Rover* has come.

As, with its welcome freight, the boat touched the side, the oakum-pickers, with venerable gestures, sought to restrain the blacks, who, at the sight of three gurried water-casks in his bottom, and a pile of wilted pumpkins in its bow, hung over the bulwarks in disorderly raptures.

Don Benito, with his servant, now appeared; his coming, perhaps, hastened by hearing the noise. Of him Captain Delano sought permission to serve out the water, so that all might share alike, and none injure themselves by unfair excess. But sensible, and, on Don Benito's account, kind as this offer was, it was received with what seemed impatience; as if aware that he lacked energy as a commander, Don Benito, with the true jealousy of weakness, resented as an affront any interference. So, at least, Captain Delano inferred.

In another moment the casks were being hoisted in, when some of the eager negroes accidentally jostled Captain Delano, where he stood by the gangway; so that, unmindful of Don Benito, yielding to the impulse of the moment, with good-natured authority he bade the blacks stand back; to enforce his words making use of a half-mirthful, half-menacing gesture. Instantly the blacks paused, just where they were, each negro and negress suspended in his or her posture, exactly as the word had found them – for a few seconds continuing so – while, as between the responsive posts of a telegraph, an unknown syllable ran from man to man among the perched oakum-pickers. While the visitor's attention was fixed by this scene, suddenly the hatchet-polishers half rose, and a rapid cry came from Don Benito.

Thinking that at the signal of the Spaniard he was about to be massacred, Captain Delano would have sprung for his boat, but paused, as the oakum-pickers, dropping down into the crowd with earnest exclamations, forced every white and every negro back, at the same moment, with gestures friendly and familiar, almost jocose, bidding him, in substance, not be a fool. Simultaneously the hatchet-polishers resumed their seats, quietly as so many tailors, and at once, as if nothing had happened, the work of hoisting in the casks was resumed, whites and blacks singing at the tackle.

Captain Delano glanced toward Don Benito. As he saw his meagre form in the act of recovering itself from reclining in the servant's arms, into which the agitated invalid had fallen, he could not but marvel at the panic by which himself had been surprised, on the darting supposition that such a commander, who, upon a legitimate occasion, so trivial, too, as it now appeared, could lose all self-command, was, with energetic iniquity, going to bring about his murder.

The casks being on deck, Captain Delano was handed a number of jars and cups by one of the steward's aids, who, in the name of his captain, entreated him to do as he had proposed – dole out the water. He complied, with republican impartiality as to this republican element, which always seeks one level, serving the oldest white no better than the youngest black; excepting, indeed, poor Don Benito, whose condition, if not rank, demanded an extra allowance. To him, in the first place, Captain Delano presented a fair pitcher of the fluid; but, thirsting as he was for it, the Spaniard quaffed not a drop until after several grave bows and salutes. A reciprocation of courtesies which the sight-loving Africans hailed with clapping of hands.

Two of the less wilted pumpkins being reserved for the cabin table, the residue were minced up on the spot for the general regalement. But the soft bread, sugar, and bottled cider, Captain Delano would have given the whites alone, and in chief Don Benito; but the latter objected; which disinterestedness not a little pleased the American; and so mouthfuls all around were given alike to whites and blacks; excepting one bottle of cider, which Babo insisted upon setting aside for his master.

Here it may be observed that as on the first visit of the boat, the American had not permitted his men to board the ship, neither did he now; being unwilling to add to the confusion of the decks.

BENITO CERENO

Not uninfluenced by the peculiar good-humour at present prevailing, and for the time oblivious of any but benevolent thoughts, Captain Delano, who, from recent indications, counted upon a breeze within an hour or two at furthest, dispatched the boat back to the sealer, with orders for all the hands that could be spared immediately to set about rafting casks to the watering-place and filling them. Likewise he bade word be carried to his chief officer, that if, against present expectation, the ship was not brought to anchor by sunset, he need be under no concern; for as there was to be a full moon that night, he (Captain Delano) would remain on board ready to play the pilot, come the wind soon or late.

As the two captains stood together, observing the departing boat – the servant, as it happened, having just spied a spot on his master's velvet sleeve, and silently engaged rubbing it out – the American expressed his regrets that the *San Dominick* had no boats; none, at least, but the unseaworthy old hulk of the long-boat, which, warped as a camel's skeleton in the desert, and almost as bleached, lay pot-wise inverted amidships, one side a little tipped, furnishing a subterranean sort of den for family groups of the blacks, mostly women and small children; who, squatting on old mats below, or perched above in the dark dome, on the elevated seats, were descried, some distance within, like a social circle of bats, sheltering in some friendly cave; at intervals, ebon flights of naked boys and girls, three or four years old, darting in and out of the den's mouth.

'Had you three of four boats now, Don Benito,' said Captain Delano. 'I think that, by tugging at the oars, your negroes here might help along matters some. Did you sail from port without boats, Don Benito?'

'They were stove in the gales, señor.'

'That was bad. Many men, too, you lost then. Boats and men. Those must have been hard gales, Don Benito.'

'Past all speech,' cringed the Spaniard.

'Tell me, Don Benito,' continued his companion with increased interest, 'tell me, were these gales immediately off the pitch of Cape Horn?'

'Cape Horn? – who spoke of Cape Horn?'

'Y'urself did, when giving me an account of your voyage,' answered Captain Delano, with almost equal astonishment at this eating of his own words, even as he ever seemed eating his own heart, on the part of the Spaniard. 'You yourself, Don Benito, spoke of Cape Horn,' he emphatically repeated.

The Spaniard turned, in a sort of stooping posture, pausing an instant, as one about to make a plunging exchange of elements, as from air to water.

At this moment a messenger-boy, a white, hurried by, in the regular performance of his function carrying the last expired half-house forward to the forecastle, from the cabin time-piece, to have it struck at the ship's large bell.

'Master,' said the servant, discontinuing his work on the coat sleeve, and addressing the rapt Spaniard with a sort of timid apprehensiveness, as one charged with a duty, the discharge of which, it was foreseen, would prove irksome to the very person who had imposed it, and for whose benefit it was intended, 'master told me never mind where he was, or how engaged, always to remind him, to a minute, when shaving-time comes. Miguel has gone to strike the half-hour afternoon. it is *now*, master. Will master go into the cuddy?'

'Ah – yes,' answered the Spaniard, starting, as from dreams into realities; then turning upon Captain Delano, he said that 'ere long he would resume the conversation.

'Then if master means to talk more to Don Amasa,' said the servant, 'why not let Don Amasa sit by master in the cuddy, and master can talk, and Don Amasa can listen, while Babo here lathers and strops.'

'Yes,' said Captain Delano, not unpleased with this sociable plan, 'yes, Don Benito, unless you had rather not, I will go with you.'

'Be it so, señor.'

As the three passed aft, the American could not but think it another strange instance of his host's capriciousness, this being shaved with such uncommon punctuality in the middle of the day. But he deemed it more than likely that the servant's anxious fidelity had something to do with the matter; inasmuch as the timely interruption served to rally his master from the mood which had evidently been coming upon him.

The place called the cuddy was a light deck-cabin formed by the poop, a sort of attic to the large cabin below. Part of it had formerly been the quarters of officers; but since their death all the partitionings had been thrown down, and the whole interior converted into one spacious and airy marine hall; for absence of fine furniture and picturesque disarray of odd appurtenances, somewhat answering to the wide, cluttered hall of some eccentric bachelor-squire in the country, who hangs his shooting-jacket and tobacco-pouch on deer antlers, and keeps his fishing-rod, tongs, and walking-stick in the same corner.

The similitude was heightened, if not originally suggested, by glimpses of the surrounding sea; since, in one aspect, the country and the ocean seen cousins-german.

The floor of the cuddy was matted. Overhead, four or five old muskets were stuck into horizontal holes along the beams. On one side was a claw-footed old table lashed to the deck; a thumbed missal on it, and over it a small, meagre crucifix attached to the bulkhead. Under the table lay a dented cutlass or two, with a hacked harpoon, among some melancholy old rigging, like a heap of poor friars' girdles. There were also two long, sharp-ribbed settees of Malacca cane, black with age, and uncomfortable to look at as inquisitors' racks, with a large, misshapen arm-chair, which, furnished with a rude barber's crotch at the back, working with a screw, seemed some grotesque engine of torment. A flag locker was in one corner, open, exposing various coloured bunting, some rolled up, others half unrolled, still others tumbled. Opposite was a cumbrous washstand, of black mahogany, all of one block, with a pedestal, like a font, and over it a railed shelf, containing combs, brushes, and other implements of the toilet. A torn hammock of stained grass swung near; the sheets tossed, and the pillow wrinkled up like a brow, as if whoever slept here slept but ill, with alternate visitations of sad thoughts and bad dreams.

The further extremity of the cuddy, overhanging the ship's stern, was pierced with three openings, windows or port-holes, according as men or cannon might peer, socially or unsocially, out of them. At present neither men nor cannon were seen, though huge ring-bolts and other rusty iron fixtures of the woodwork hinted of twenty-four-pounders.

Glancing toward the hammock as he entered, Captain Delano said, 'You sleep here, Don Benito?'

'Yes, señor, since we got into mild weather.'

'This seems a sort of dormitory, sitting-room, sail-loft, chapel, armoury, and private closet all together, Don Benito,' added Captain Delano, looking round.

'Yes, señor; events have not been favourable to much order in my arrangements.'

Here the servant, napkin on arm, made a motion as if waiting his master's good pleasure. Don Benito signified his readiness, when, seating him in the Malacca arm-chair, and for the guest's convenience drawing opposite one of the settees, the servant commenced operations by throwing back his master's collar and loosening his cravat.

There is something in the negro which, in a peculiar way, fits him for avocations about one's person. Most negroes are natural valets and hair-dressers; taking to the comb and brush congenially as to the castanets, and flourishing them apparently with almost equal satisfaction. There is, too, a smooth tact about them in this employment, with a marvellous, noiseless, gliding briskness, not ungraceful in its way, singularly pleasing to behold, and still more so to be the manipulated subject of. And above all is the great gift of good-humour. Not the mere grin or laugh is here meant. Those were unsuitable. But a certain easy cheerfulness, harmonious in every glance and gesture; as though God had set the whole negro to some pleasant tune.

When to this is added the docility arising from the unaspiring contentment of a limited mind, and that susceptibility of blind attachment sometimes inhering in indisputable inferiors, one readily perceives why those hypochondriacs, Johnson and Byron – it may be, something like the hypochondriac Benito Cereno – took to their hearts, almost to the exclusion of the entire white race, their serving-men, the negroes, Barber and Fletcher. But if there be that in the negro which exempts him from the inflicted sourness of the morbid or cynical mind, how, in his most prepossessing aspects, must he appear to a benevolent one? When at ease with respect to exterior things, Captain Delano's nature was not only benign, but familiarly and humorously so. At home, he had often taken rare satisfaction in sitting in his door, watching some free man of colour at his work or play. If on a voyage he chanced to have a black sailor, invariably he was on chatty and half-gamesome terms with him. In fact, like most men of a good, blithe heart, Captain Delano took to negroes, not philanthropically, but genially, just as other men to Newfoundland dogs.

Hitherto, the circumstances in which he found the *San Dominick* had repressed the tendency. But in the cuddy, relieved from his former uneasiness, and, for various reasons, more sociably inclined than at any previous period of the day, and seeing the coloured servant, napkin on arm, so debonair about his master, in a business so familiar as that of shaving, too, all his old weakness for negroes returned.

Among other things, he was amused with an odd instance of the African love of bright colours and fine shows, in the black's informally taking from the flag-locker a great piece of bunting of all hues, and lavishly tucking it under his master's chin for an apron.

The mode of shaving among the Spaniards is a little different from what it is with other nations. They have a basin, specifically called a barber's basin, which on one side is scooped out, so as accurately to receive the chin, against which it is closely held in lathering; which is done, not with a brush, but with soap dipped in the water of the basin and rubbed on the face.

In the present instance salt water was used for lack of better; and the parts lathered were only the upper lip, and low down under the throat, all the rest being cultivated beard.

The preliminaries being somewhat novel to Captain Delano, he sat curiously eyeing them, so that no conversation took place, nor, for the present, did Don Benito appear disposed to renew any.

Setting down his basin, the negro searched among the razors, as for the sharpest, and having found it, gave it an additional edge by expertly stropping it on the firm, smooth, oily skin of his open palm; he then made a gesture as if to begin, but midway stood suspended for an instant, one hand elevating the razor, the other professionally dabbling among the bubbling suds on the Spaniard's lank neck. Not unaffected by the close sight of the gleaming steel, Don Benito nervously shuddered; his usual ghastliness was heightened by the lather, which lather, again, was intensified in its hue by the contrasting sootiness of the negro's body. Altogether the scene was somewhat peculiar, at least to Captain Delano, nor, as he saw the two thus postured, could he resist the vagary, that in the black he saw a headsman, and in the white a man at the block. But this was one of those antic conceits, appearing and vanishing in a breath, from which, perhaps, the best regulated mind is not always free.

Meantime the agitation of the Spaniard had a little loosened the bunting from around him, so that one broad fold swept curtain-like over the chair-arm to the floor, revealing, amid a profusion of armorial bars and ground-colours – black, blue and yellow – a closed castle in a blood-red field diagonal with a lion rampant in a white.

'The castle and the lion,' exclaimed Captain Delano – 'why, Don Benito, this is the flag of Spain you use here. It's well it's only I, and not the king, that sees this,' he added, with a smile, 'but' – turning toward the black – 'it's all one, I suppose, so the colours be gay'; which playful remark did not fail somewhat to tickle the negro.

'Now, master,' he said, readjusting the flag, and pressing the head gently further back into the crotch of the chair; 'now, master,' and the steel glanced nigh the throat.'

Again Don Benito faintly shuddered.

'You must not shake so, master. See, Don Amasa, master always shakes when I shave him. And yet master knows I never yet have drawn blood, though it's true, if master will shake so, I may some of these times. Now, master,' he continued. 'And now, Don Amasa, please, go on with your talk about the gale, and all that; master can hear, and, between times, master can answer.'

'Ah yes, these gales,' said Captain Delano; 'but the more I think of your voyage, Don Benito, the more I wonder, not at the gales, terrible as they must have been, but at the disastrous interval following them. For here, by your account, have you been these two months and more getting from Cape Horn to St Maria, a distance which I myself, with a good wind, have sailed in a few days. True, you had calms, and long ones, but to be becalmed for two months, that is, at least, unusual. Why, Don Benito, had almost any other gentleman told me such a story, I should have been half disposed to a little incredulity.'

Here an involuntary expression came over the Spaniard, similar to that just before on the deck, and whether it was the start he gave, or a sudden gawky roll of the hull in the calm, or a momentary unsteadiness of the servant's hand, however it was, just then the razor drew blood, spots of which stained the creamy lather under the throat: immediately the black barber drew back his steel, and, remaining in his professional attitude, back to Captain Delano, and face to Don Benito, held up the trickling razor, saying, with a sort of half-humorous sorrow, 'See, master – you shook so – here's Babo's first blood.'

No sword drawn before James the First of England, no assassination in that timid king's presence, could have produced a more terrified aspect than was now presented by Don Benito.

Poor fellow, thought Captain Delano, so nervous he can't even bear the sight of barber's blood; and this unstrung, sick man, is it credible that I should have imagined he meant to spill all my blood, who can't endure the sight of one little drop of his own? Surely, Amasa Delano, you have been beside yourself this day. Tell it not when you get home, sappy Amasa. Well, well, he looks like a murderer, doesn't he? More like as if himself were to be done for. Well, well, this day's experience shall be a good lesson.

Meantime, while these things were running through the honest seaman's mind, the servant had taken the napkin from his arm, and to Don Benito had said: 'But answer Don Amasa, please, master, while I wipe this ugly stuff off the razor, and strop it again.'

As he said the words, his face was turned half round, so as to be alike visible to the Spaniard and the American, and seemed, by its expression, to hint, that he was desirous, by getting his master to go on with the conversation, considerably to withdraw his attention from the recent annoying accident. As if glad to snatch the offered relief, Don Benito resumed, rehearsing to Captain Delano, that not only were the calms of unusual duration, but the ship had fallen in with obstinate currents; and other things he added, some of which were but repetitions of former statements, to explain how it came to pass that the passage from Cape Horn to St Maria had been so exceedingly long; now and then mingling with his words incidental praises, less qualified than before, to the blacks, for their general good conduct. These particulars were not given consecutively, the servant, at convenient times, using his razor, and so, between the intervals of shaving, the story and panegyric went on with more than usual huskiness.

To Captain Delano's imagination, now again not wholly at rest, there was something so hollow in the Spaniard's manner, with apparently some reciprocal hollowness in the servant's dusky comment of silence, that the idea flashed across him, that possibly master and man, for some unknown purpose, were acting out, both in word and deed, nay, to the very tremor of Don Benito's limbs, some juggling play before him. Neither did the suspicion of collusion lack apparent support, from the fact of those whispered conferences before mentioned. But then, what could be the object of enacting this play of the barber before him? At last, regarding the notion as a whimsy, insensibly suggested, perhaps, by the theatrical aspect of Don Benito in his harlequin ensign, Captain Delano speedily banished it.

The shaving over, the servant bestirred himself with a small bottle of scented waters, pouring a few drops on the head, and then diligently rubbing; the vehemence of the exercise causing the muscles of his face to twitch rather strangely.

His next operation was with comb, scissors, and brush; going round and round, smoothing a curl here, clipping an unruly whisker-hair there, giving a graceful sweep to the temple-lock, with other impromptu touches evincing the hand of a master; while, like any resigned gentleman in barber's hands, Don Benito bore all, much less uneasily, at least, than he had done the razoring; indeed, he sat so pale and rigid now, that the negro seemed a Nubian sculptor finishing off a white statue-head.

All being over at last, the standard of Spain removed, tumbled up, and tossed back into the flag-locker, the negro's warm breath blowing away any stray hair which might have lodged down his master's neck; collar and cravat readjusted; a speck of lint whisked off the velvet lapel; all this being done; backing off a little space, and pausing with an expression of subdued self-complacency, the servant for a moment surveyed his master, as, in toilet at least, the creature of his own tasteful hands.

Captain Delano playfully complimented him upon his achievement; at the same time congratulating Don Benito.

But neither sweet waters, nor shampooing, nor fidelity, nor sociality, delighted the Spaniard. Seeing him relapsing into forbidding gloom, and still remaining seated, Captain Delano, thinkiing that his presence was undesired just then, withdrew, on pretence of seeing whether, as he had prophesied, any signs of a breeze were visible.

Walking forward to the mainmast, he stood a while thinking over the scene, and not without some undefined misgivings, when he heard a noise near the cuddy, and turning, saw the negro, his hand to his cheek. Advancing, Captain Delano perceived that the cheek was bleeding. He was about to ask the cause, when the negro's wailing soliloquy enlightened him.

'Ah, when will master get better from his sickness; only the sour heart that sour sickness breeds made him serve Babo so; cutting Babo with the razor, because, only by accident, Babo had given master one little scratch; and for the first time in so many a day, too. Ah, ah, ah,' holding his hand to his face.

Is it possible, thought Captain Delano; was it to wreak in private his Spanish spite against this poor friend of his, that Don Benito, by his sullen manner, impelled me to withdraw? Ah, this slavery breeds ugly passions in man. Poor fellow!

He was about to speak in sympathy to the negro, but with a timid reluctance he now re-entered the cuddy.

Presently master and man came forth; Don Benito leaning on his servant as if nothing had happened.

But a sort of love-quarrel, after all, thought Captain Delano.

He accosted Don Benito, and they slowly walked together. They had gone but a few paces, when the steward – a tall, rajah-looking mulatto, orientally set off with a pagoda turban formed by three or four Madras handkerchiefs wound about his head, tier on tier – approaching with a salaam, announced lunch in the cabin.

On their way thither, the two captains were preceded by the mulatto, who, turning round as he advanced, with continual smiles and bows, ushered them on, a display of elegance which quite completed the insignificance of the small bare-headed Babo, who, as if not unconscious of inferiority, eyed askance the graceful steward. But in part, Captain Delano imputed his jealous watchfulness to that peculiar feeling which the full-blooded African entertains for the adulterated one. As for the steward, his manner, if not bespeaking much dignity of self-respect, yet evidenced his extreme desire to please; which is doubly meritorious, as at once Christian and Chesterfieldian.

Captain Delano observed with interest that while the complexion of the mulatto was hybrid, his physiognomy was European – classically so.

'Don Benito,' whispered he, 'I am glad to see this usher-of-the-golden-rod of yours; the sight refutes an ugly remark once made to me by a Barbados planter; that when a mulatto has a regular European face, look out for him; he is a devil. But see, your steward here has features more regular than King George's of England; and yet there he nods, and bows, and smiles; a king, indeed – the king of kind hearts and polite fellows. What a pleasant voice he has, too!'

'He has, señor.'

'But tell me, has he not, so far as you have known him, always proved a good, worthy fellow?' said Captain Delano, pausing, while with a final genuflection the steward disappeared into the cabin; 'come, for the reason just mentioned, I am curious to know.'

'Francesco is a good man,' a sort of sluggishly responded Don Benito, like a phlegmatic appreciator, who would neither find fault nor flatter.

'Ah, I thought so. For it were strange, indeed, and not very creditable to us white-skins, if a little of our blood mixed with the African's should, far from improving the latter's quality, have the sad effect of pouring vitriolic acid into black broth; improving the hue, perhaps, but not the wholesomeness.'

'Doubtless, doubtless, señor, but' – glancing at Babo – 'not to speak of negroes, your planter's remark I have heard applied to the Spanish and Indian intermixtures in our provinces. But I know nothing about the matter,' he listlessly added.

And here they entered the cabin.

The lunch was a frugal one. Some of Captain Delano's fresh fish and pumpkins, biscuit and salt beef, the reserved bottle of cider, and the *San Dominick*'s last bottle of Canary.

As they entered, Francesco, with two or three coloured aids, was hovering over the table giving the last adjustments. Upon perceiving their master they withdrew, Francesco making a smiling *congé*, and the Spaniard, without condescending to notice it, fastidiously remarking to his companion that he relished not superfluous attendance.

Without companions, host and guest sat down, like a childless married couple, at opposite ends of the table, Don Benito waving Captain Delano to his place, and, weak as he was, insisting upon that gentleman being seated before himself.

The negro placed a rug under Don Benito's feet, and a cushion behind his back, and then stood behind, not his master's chair, but Captain Delano's. At first, this a little surprised the latter. But it was soon evident that, in taking his position, the black was still true to his master; since by facing him he could the more readily anticipate his slightest want.

'This is an uncommonly intelligent fellow of yours, Don Benito,' whispered Captain Delano across the table.

'You say true, señor.'

During the repast, the guest again reverted to parts of Don Benito's story, begging further particulars here and there. He inquired how it was that the scurvy and fever should have committed such wholesale havoc upon the whites, while destroying less than half of the blacks. As if this question reproduced the whole scene of plague before the Spaniard's eyes, miserably reminding him of his solitude in a cabin where before he had had so many friends and officers round him, his hand shook, his face became hueless, broken words escaped; but directly the sane memory of the past seemed replaced by insane terrors of the present. With starting eyes he stared before him at vacancy. For nothing was to be seen but the hand of his servant pushing the Canary over toward him. At length a few sips served partially to restore him. He made random reference to the different constitution of races, enabling one to offer more resistance to certain maladies than another. The thought was new to his companion.

Presently Captain Delano, intending to say something to his host concerning the pecuniary part of the business he had undertaken for him, especially – since he was strictly accountable to his owners – with reference to the new suit of sails, and other things of that sort; and naturally preferring to conduct such affairs in private, was desirous that the servant should withdraw; imagining that Don Benito for a few minutes could dispense with his attendance. He, however, waited a while; thinking that, as the conversation proceeded, Don Benito, without being prompted, would perceive the propriety of the step.

But it was otherwise. At last catching his host's eye, Captain Delano, with a slight backward gesture of his thumb, whispered, 'Don Benito, pardon me, but there is an interference with the full expression of what I have to say to you.'

Upon this the Spaniard changed countenance; which was imputed to his resenting the hint, as in some way a reflection upon his servant. After a moment's pause, he assured his guest that the black's remaining with them could be of no disservice; because since losing his officers he had made Babo (whose original office, it now appeared, had been captain of the slaves) not only his constant attendant and companion, but in all things his confidant.

After this, nothing more could be said; though, indeed, Captain Delano could hardly avoid some little tinge of irritation upon being left ungratified in so inconsiderable a wish, by one, too, for whom he intended such solid services. But it is only his querulousness, thought he; and so filling his glass he proceeded to business.

The price of the sails and other matters was fixed upon. But while this was being done, the American observed that, though his original offer of assistance had been hailed with hectic animation, yet now when it was reduced to a business transaction, indifference and apathy were betrayed. Don Benito, in fact, appeared to submit to hearing the details more out of regard to common propriety than from any impression that weighty benefit to himself and his voyage was involved.

Soon, his manner became still more reserved. The effort was vain to seek to draw him into social talk. Gnawed by his splenetic mood, he sat twitching his beard, while to little purpose the hand of his servant, mute as that on the wall, slowly pushed over the Canary.

Lunch being over, they sat down on the cushioned transom; the servant placing a pillow behind his master. The long continuance of the calm had now affected the atmosphere. Don Benito sighed heavily, as if for breath.

'Why not adjourn to the cuddy,' said Captain Delano; 'there is more air there.' But the host sat silent and motionless.

Meantime his servant knelt before him, with a large fan of feathers. And Francesco, coming in on tiptoes, handed the negro a little cup of aromatic waters, with which at intervals he chafed his master's brow;

smoothing the hair along the temples as a nurse does a child's. He spoke no word. He only rested his eye on his master's, as if, amid all Don Benito's distress, a little to refresh his spirit by the silent sight of fidelity.

Presently the ship's bell sounded two o'clock; and through the cabin windows a slight rippling of the sea was discerned; and from the desired direction.

'There,' exclaimed Captain Delano, 'I told you so, Don Benito, look!'

He had risen to his feet, speaking in a very animated tone, with a view the more to rouse his companion. But though the crimson curtain of the stern window near him that moment fluttered against his pale cheek, Don Benito seemed to have even less welcome for the breeze than the calm.

Poor fellow, thought Captain Delano, bitter experience has taught him that one ripple does not make a wind, any more than one swallow a summer. But he is mistaken for once. I will get his ship in for him, and prove it.

Briefly alluding to his weak condition, he urged his host to remain quietly where he was, since he (Captain Delano) would with pleasure take upon himself the responsibility of making the best use of the wind.

Upon gaining the deck, Captain Delano started at the unexpected figure of Atufal, monumentally fixed at the threshold, like one of those sculptured porters of black marble guarding the porches of Egyptian tombs.

But this time the start was, perhaps, purely physical. Atufal's presence, singularly attesting docility even in sullenness, was contrasted with that of the hatchet-polishers, who in patience evinced their industry; while both spectacles showed, that lax as Don Benito's general authority might be, still, whenever he chose to exert it, no man so savage or colossal but must, more or less, bow.

Snatching a trumpet which hung from the bulwarks, with a free step Captain Delano advanced to the forward edge of the poop, issuing his orders in his best Spanish. The few sailors and many negroes, all equally pleased, obediently set about heading the ship toward the harbour.

While giving some directions about setting a lower stun'-sail, suddenly Captain Delano heard a voice faithfully repeating his orders. Turning, he saw Babo, now for the time acting, under the pilot, his original part of captain of the slaves. This assistance proved valuable. Tattered sails and warped yards were soon brought into some trim. And no brace or halyard was pulled but to the blithe songs of the inspirited negroes.

Good fellows, thought Captain Delano, a little training would make fine sailors of them. Why, see, the very women pull and sing too. These must be some of those Ashantee negresses that make such capital soldiers, I've heard. But who's at the helm? I must have a good hand there.

He went to see.

The *San Dominick* steered with a cumbrous tiller, with large horizontal pulleys attached. At each pulley-end stood a subordinate black, and between them, at the tiller-head, the responsible post, a Spanish seaman, whose countenance evinced his due share in the gereral hopefulness and confidence at the coming of the breeze.

He proved the same man who had behaved with so shamefaced an air on the windlass.

'Ah – it is you, my man,' exclaimed Captain Delano – 'well, no more sheep's-eyes now; – look straight forward and keep the ship so. Good hand, I trust? And want to get into the harbour, don't you?'

The man assented with an inward chuckle, grasping the tiller-head firmly. Upon this, unperceived by the American, the two blacks eyed the sailor intently.

Finding all right at the helm, the pilot went forward to the forecastle, to see how matters stood there.

The ship now had way enough to breast the current. With the approach of evening, the breeze would be sure to freshen.

Having done all that was needed for the present, Captain Delano, giving his last orders to the sailors, turned aft to report affairs to Don Benito in the cabin; perhaps additionally incited to rejoin him by the hope of snatching a moment's private chat while the servant was engaged upon deck.

From opposite sides, there were, beneath the poop, two approaches to the cabin; one farther forward than the other, and consequently communicating with a longer passage. Marking the servant still above, Captain Delano, taking the nighest entrance – the one last named, and at whose porch Atufal still stood – hurried on his way, till, arrived at the cabin threshold, he paused an instant, a little to recover from his eagerness. Then, with the words of his intended business upon his lips, he entered. As he advanced toward the seated Spaniard, he heard another footstep, keeping time with his. From the opposite door, a salver in hand, the servant was likewise advancing.

'Confound the faithful fellow,' thought Captain Delano; 'what a vexatious coincidence.'

Possibly the vexation might have been something different, were it not for brisk confidence inspired by the breeze. But even as it was, he felt a slight twinge, from a sudden indefinite association in his mind of Babo with Atufal.

'Don Benito,' said he 'I give you joy; the breeze will hold, and will increase. By the way, your tall man and time-piece, Atufal, stands without. By your order, of course?'

Don Benito recoiled, as if at some bland satirical touch, delivered with such adroit garnish of apparent good breeding as to present no handle for retort.

He is like one flayed alive, thought Captain Delano; where may one touch him without causing a shrink?

The servant moved before his master, adjusting a cushion; recalled to civility, the Spaniard stiffly replied: 'You are right. The slave appears where you saw him, according to my command; which is, that if at the given hour I am below, he must take his stand and abide my coming.'

'Ah now, pardon me, but that is treating the poor fellow like an ex-king indeed. Ah, Don Benito,' smiling, 'for all the licence you permit in some things, I fear lest, at bottom, you are a bitter hard master.'

Again Don Benito shrank; and this time, as the good sailor thought, from a genuine twinge of his conscience.

Again conversation became constrained. In vain Captain Delano called attention to the now perceptible motion of the keel gently cleaving the sea; with lacklustre eye, Don Benito returned words few and reserved.

By and by, the wind having steadily risen, and still blowing right into the harbour, bore the *San Dominick* swiftly on. Rounding a point of land, the sealer at distance came into open view.

Meantime Captain Delano had again repaired to the deck, remaining there some time. Having at last altered the ship's course, so as to give the reef a wide berth, he returned for a few moments below.

I will cheer up my poor friend this time, thought he.

'Better and better, Don Benito,' he cried as he blithely re-entered: 'there will soon be an end to your cares, at least for a while. For when, after a long, sad voyage, you know, the anchor drops into the haven, all its vast weight seems lifted from the captain's heart. We are getting on famously, Don Benito. My ship is in sight. Look through this side-light here; there she is; all a-taunt-o! The *Bachelor's Delight*, my good friend. Ah, how this wind braces one up. Come, you must take a cup of coffee with me this evening. My old steward will give you as fine a cup as ever any sultan tasted. What say you, Don Benito, will you?'

At first, the Spaniard glanced feverishly up, casting a longing look toward the sealer, while with mute concern his servant gazed into his face. Suddenly the old ague of coldness returned, and dropping back to his cushions he was silent.

'You do not answer. Come, all day you have been my host; would you have hospitality all on one side?'

'I cannot go,' was the response.

'What? It will not fatigue you. The ships will lie together as near as they can, without swinging foul. It will be little more than stepping from deck to deck; which is but as from room to room. Come, come, you must not refuse me.'

'I cannot go,' decisively and repulsively repeated Don Benito.

Renouncing all but the last appearance of courtesy, with a sort of cadaverous sullenness, and biting his thin nails to the quick, he glanced, almost glared, at his guest, as if impatient that a stranger's presence should interfere with the full indulgence of his morbid hour. Meantime the sound of the parted waters came more and more gurgingly and merrily in at the windows; as reproaching him for his dark spleen; as telling him that, sulk as he might, and go mad with it, nature cared not a jot; since, whose fault was it, pray?

But the foul mood was now at its depth, as the fair wind at its height.

There was something in the man so far beyond any mere unsociality or sourness previously evinced, that even the forbearing good-nature of his guest could no longer endure it. Wholly at a loss to account for such demeanour, and deeming sickness with eccentricity, however extreme, no adequate excuse, well satisfied, too, that nothing in his own conduct could justify it, Captain Delano's pride began to be roused. Himself became reserved. But all seemed one to the Spaniard. Quitting him, therefore, Captain Delano once more went to the deck.

The ship was now within less than two miles of the sealer. The whaleboat was seen darting over the interval.

To be brief, the two vessels, thanks to the pilot's skill, ere long in neighbourly style lay anchored together.

Before returning to his own vessel, Captain Delano had intended communicating to Don Benito the smaller details of the proposed services to be rendered. But, as it was, unwilling anew to subject himself to rebuffs, he resolved, now that he had seen the *San Dominick* safely moored, immediately to quit her, without further allusion to hospitality or business. Indefinitely postponing his ulterior plans, he would regulate his future actions according to future circumstances. His boat was ready to receive him; but his host still tarried below. Well, thought Captain Delano, if he has little breeding, the more need to show mine. He descended to the cabin to bid a ceremonious, and, it may be, tacitly rebukeful adieu. But to his great satisfaction, Don Benito, as if he began to feel the weight of that treatment with which his slighted guest had, not indecorously, retaliated upon him, now supported by his servant, rose to his feet, and grasping Captain Delano's hand, stood tremulous; too much agitated to speak. But the good augury hence drawn was suddenly dashed, by his resuming all his previous reserve, with augmented gloom as, with half-averted eyes, he silently reseated himself on his cushions. With a corresponding return of his own chilled feelings, Captain Delano bowed and withdrew.

He was hardly midway in the narrow corridor, dim as a tunnel, leading from the cabin to the stairs, when a sound, as of the tolling for execution in some jail-yard, fell on his ears. It was the echo of the ship's flawed bell, striking the hour, drearily reverberated in this subterranean vault. Instantly, by a fatality not to be withstood, his mind, responsive to the portent, swarmed with superstitious suspicions. He paused. In images far swifter than these sentences, the minutest details of all his former distrusts swept through him.

Hitherto, credulous good-nature had been too ready to furnish excuses for reasonable fears. Why was the Spaniard, so superfluously punctilious at times, now heedless of common propriety in not accompanying to the side his departing guest? Did indisposition forbid? Indisposition had not forbidden more irksome exertion that day. His last equivocal demeanour recurred. He had risen to his feet, grasped his guest's hand, motioned toward his hat; then, in an instant, all was eclipsed in sinister muteness and gloom. Did this imply one brief, repentant relenting at the final moment, from some iniquitous plot, followed by remorseless return to it? His last glance seemed to express a calamitous, yet acquiescent farewell to Captain Delano forever. Why decline the invitation to visit the sealer that evening? Or was the Spaniard less hardened than the Jew, who refrained not from supping at the board of him whom the same night he meant to betray? What imported all those day-long enigmas and contradictions, except they were intended to mystify, preliminary to some stealthy blow? Atufal, the pretended rebel, but punctual shadow, that moment lurked by the threshold without. He seemed a sentry, and more. Who, by his own confession, had stationed him there? Was the negro now lying in wait?

The Spaniard behind – his creature before: to rush from darkness to light was the involuntary choice.

The next moment, with clenched jaw and hand, he passed Atufal, and stood unharmed in the light. As he saw his trim ship lying peacefully at anchor, and almost within ordinary call; as he saw his household boat, with familiar faces in it, patiently rising and falling on the short waves by the *San Dominick*'s side; and then, glancing about the decks where he stood, saw the oakum-pickers still gravely plying their fingers; and heard the low, buzzing whistle and industrious hum of the hatchet-polishers, still bestirring themselves over their endless occupation; and more than all, as he saw the benign aspect of nature, taking her innocent repose in the evening; the screened sun in the quiet camp of the west shining out like the mild light from Abraham's tent; as charmed eyes and ear took in all these, with the chained figure of the black, clenched jaw and hand relaxed. Once again he smiled at the phantoms which had mocked him, and felt something like a tinge of remorse,

that, by harbouring them even for a moment, he should, by implication, have betrayed an atheist doubt of the ever-watchful Providence
above.

There was a few minutes' delay, while, in obedience to his orders,
the boat was being hooked along to the gangway. During this interval,
a sort of saddened satisfaction stole over Captain Delano, at thinking
of the kindly offices he had that day discharged for a stranger. Ah,
thought he, after good actions one's conscience is never ungrateful,
however much so the benefited party may be.

Presently, his foot, in the first act of descent into the boat, pressed
the first round of the side-ladder, his face presented inward upon the
deck. In the same moment, he heard his name courteously sounded;
and, to his pleased surprise, saw Don Benito advancing – an unwonted
energy in his air, as if, at the last moment, intent upon making amends
for his recent discourtesy. With instinctive good feeling, Captain
Delano, withdrawing his foot, turned and reciprocally advanced. As
he did so, the Spaniard's nervous eagerness increased, but his vital
energy failed; so that, the better to support him, the servant, placing
his master's hand on his naked shoulder, and gently holding it there,
formed himself into a sort of crutch.

When the two captains met, the Spaniard again fervently took the
hand of the American, at the same time casting an earnest glance into
his eyes, but, as before, too much overcome to speak.

I have done him wrong, self-reproachfully thought Captain Delano;
his apparent coldness has deceived me; in no instance has he meant to
offend.

Meantime, as if fearful that the continuance of the scene might too
much unstring his master, the servant seemed anxious to terminate it.
And so, still presenting himself as a crutch, and walking between the
two captains, he advanced with them toward the gangway; while still,
as if full of kindly contrition, Don Benito would not let go the hand of
Captain Delano, but retained it in his, across the black's body.

Soon they were standing by the side, looking over into the boat,
whose crew turned up their curious eyes. Waiting a moment for the
Spaniard to relinquish his hold, the now embarrassed Captain Delano
lifted his foot, to overstep the threshold of the open gangway; but still
Don Benito would not let go his hand. And yet, with an agitated tone,
he said, 'I can go no further; here I must bid you adieu. Adieu, my
dear, dear Don Amasa. Go – go!' suddenly tearing his hand loose,
'go, and God guard you better than me, my best friend.'

Not unaffected, Captain Delano would now have lingered; but catching the meekly admonitory eye of the servant, with a hasty farewell
he descended into his boat, followed by the continual adieus of Don
Benito, standing rooted in the gangway.

Seating himself in the stern, Captain Delano, making a last salute, ordered the boat shoved off. The crew had their oars on end. The bowsmen pushed the boat a sufficient distant for the oars to be length-wise dropped. The instant that was done, Don Benito sprang over the bulwarks, falling at the feet of Captain Delano; at the same time calling toward his ship, but in tones so frenzied, that none in the boat could understand him. But, as if not equally obtuse, three sailors, from three different and distant parts of the ship, splashed into the sea, swimming after their captain, as if intent upon his rescue.

The dismayed officer of the boat eagerly asked what this meant. To which, Captain Delano, turning a disdainful smile upon the unaccount-able Spaniard, answered that, for his part, he neither knew nor cared; but it seemed as if Don Benito had taken it into his head to produce the impression among his people that the boat wanted to kidnap him. 'Or else – give way for your lives,' he wildly added, starting at a clattering hubbub in the ship, above which rang the tocsin of the hatchet-polish-ers; and seizing Don Benito by the throat he added, 'This plotting pirate means murder!' Here, in apparent verification of the words, the serv-ant, a dagger in his hand, was seen on the rail overhead, poised, in the act of leaping, as if with desperate fidelity to befriend his master to the last; while, seemingly to aid the black, the three white sailors were trying to clamber into the hampered bow. Meantime, the whole host of negroes, as if inflamed at the sight of their jeopardized captain, impended in one sooty avalanche over the bulwarks.

All this, with what preceded, and what followed, occurred with such involutions of rapidity, that past, present, and future seemed one.

Seeing the negro coming, Captain Delano had flung the Spaniard aside, almost in the very act of clutching him, and, by the unconscious recoil, shifting his place, with arms thrown up, so promptly grappled the servant in his descent, that with dagger presented at Captain Delano's heart, the black seemed of purpose to have leaped there as to his mark. But the weapon was wrenched away, and the assailant dashed down into the bottom of the boat, which now, with disentangled oars, began to speed through the sea.

At this juncture, the left hand of Captain Delano, on one side, again clutched the half-reclined Don Benito, heedless that he was in a speechless faint, while his right foot, on the other side, ground the prostrate negro; and his right arm pressed for added speed on the after-oar, his eye bent forward, encouraging his men to their utmost.

But here, the officer of the boat, who had at last succeeded in beating off the towing sailors, and was now, with face turned aft, assisting the bowsman at his oar, suddenly called to Captain Delano, to see what the black was about; while a Portuguese oarsman shouted to him to give heed to what the Spaniard was saying.

Glancing down at his feet, Captain Delano saw the freed hand of the servant aiming with a second dagger – a small one, before concealed in his wool – with this he was snakishly writhing up from the boat's bottom, at the heart of his master, his countenance lividly vindictive, expressing the centred purpose of his soul; while the Spaniard, half choked, was vainly shrinking away, with husky words, incoherent to all but the Portuguese.

That moment, across the long-benighted mind of Captain Delano, a flash of revelation swept, illuminating, in unanticipated clearness, his host's whole mysterious demeanour, with every enigmatic event of the day, as well as the entire past voyage of the *San Dominick*. He smote Babo's hand down, but his own heart smote him harder. With infinite pity he withdrew his hold from Don Benito. Not Captain Delano, but Don Benito, the black, in leaping into the boat, had intended to stab.

Both the black's hands were held, as, glancing up toward the *San Dominick*, Captain Delano, now with scales dropped from his eyes, saw the negroes, not in misrule, not in tumult, not as if frantically concerned for Don Benito, but with mask torn away, flourishing hatchets and knives, in ferocious piratical revolt. Like delirious black dervishes, the six Ashantees danced on the poop. Prevented by their foes from springing into the water, the Spanish boys were hurrying up to the topmost spars, while such of the few Spanish sailors, not already in the sea, less alert, were descried, helplessly mixed in, on deck, with the blacks.

Meantime Captain Delano hailed his own vessel, ordering the ports up, and the guns run out. But by this time the cable of the *San Dominick* had been cut; and the fag-end, in lashing out, whipped away the canvas shroud about the beak, suddenly revealing, as the bleached hull swung round toward the open ocean, death for the figure-head, in a human skeleton; chalky comment on the chalked words below, '*Follow your leader.*'

At the sight, Don Benito, covering his face, wailed out: ' 'Tis he, Aranda! my murdered, unburied friend!'

Upon reaching the sealer, calling for ropes, Captain Delano bound the negro, who made no resistance, and had him hoisted to the deck. He would then have assisted the now almost helpless Don Benito up the side; but Don Benito, wan as he was, refused to move, or be moved, until the negro should have been first put below out of view. When, presently assured that it was done, he no more shrank from the ascent.

The boat was immediately dispatched back to pick up the three swimming sailors. Meantime, the guns were in readiness, though, owing to the *San Dominick* having glided somewhat astern of the sealer, only the aftermost one could be brought to bear. With this, they fired six times; thinking to cripple the fugitive ship by bringing down her spars. But only a few inconsiderable ropes were shot away. Soon the ship was beyond the gun's range, steering broad out of the bay; the blacks thickly clustering round the bowsprit, one moment with taunting cries toward the whites, the next with upthrown gestures hailing the now dusky moors of ocean – cawing crows escaped from the hand of the fowler.

The first impulse was to slip the cables and give chase. But, upon second thoughts, to pursue with whale-boat and yawl seemed more promising.

Upon inquiring of Don Benito what firearms they had on board the *San Dominick*, Captain Delano was answered that they had none that could be used; because, in the earlier stages of the mutiny, a cabin passenger, since dead, had secretly put out of order the locks of what few muskets there were. But with all his remaining strength, Don Benito entreated the American not to give chase, either with ship or boat; for the negroes had already proved themselves such desperadoes, that, in case of a present assault, nothing but a total massacre of the whites could be looked for. But, regarding this warning as coming from one whose spirit had been crushed by misery, the American did not give up his design.

The boats were got ready and armed. Captain Delano ordered his men into them. He was going himself when Don Benito grasped his arm.

'What! Have you saved my life, señor, and are you now going to throw away your own?'

The officers also, for reasons connected with their interests and those of the voyage, and a duty owing to the owners, strongly objected against their commander's going. Weighing their remonstrances a moment, Captain Delano felt bound to remain; appointing his chief mate – an athletic and resolute man, who had been a privateer's-man – to head the party. The more to encourage the sailors, they were told, that the Spanish captain considered his ship good as lost; that she and her cargo, including some gold and silver, were worth more than a thousand doubloons. Take her, and no small part should be theirs. The sailors replied with a shout.

The fugitives had now almost gained an offing. It was nearly night; but the moon was rising. After hard, prolonged pulling, the boats came up on the ship's quarters, at a suitable distance laying upon their oars to discharge their muskets. Having no bullets to return, the negroes sent their yells. But, upon the second volley, Indian-like, they hurtled their hatchets. One took off a sailor's fingers. Another struck the whaleboat's bow, cutting off the rope there, and remaining stuck in the gunwale like a woodman's axe. Snatching it, quivering from its lodgment, the mate hurled it back. The returned gauntlet now stuck in the ship's broken quarter-gallery, and so remained.

The negroes giving too hot a reception, the whites kept a more respectful distance. Hovering now just out of reach of the hurtling hatchets, they, with a view to the close encounter which must soon come, sought to decoy the blacks into entirely disarming themselves of their most murderous weapons in a hand-to-hand fight, by foolishly flinging them, as missiles, short of the mark, into the sea. But, ere long, perceiving the stratagem, the negroes desisted, though not before many of them had to replace their lost hatchets with handspikes; an exchange which, as counted upon, proved, in the end, favourable to the assailants.

Meantime, with a strong wind, the ship still clove the water; the boats alternately falling behind, and pulling up, to discharge fresh volleys.

The fire was mostly directed toward the stern, since there, chiefly, the negroes, at present, were clustering. But to kill or maim the negroes was not the object. To take them, with the ship, was the object. To do it, the ship must be boarded; which could not be done by boats while she was sailing so fast.

A thought now struck the mate. Observing the Spanish boys still aloft, high as they could get, he called to them to descend to the yards, and cut adrift the sails. It was done. About this time, owing to causes hereafter to be shown, two Spaniards, in the dress of sailors, and conspicuously showing themselves, were killed; not by volleys, but by deliberate marksman's shots; while, as it afterward appeared, by one of the general discharges, Atufal, the black, and Spaniard at the helm likewise were killed. What now with the loss of the sails, and loss of leaders, the ship became unmanagaeble to the negroes.

With creaking masts, she came heavily round to the wind; the prow slowly swinging into view of the boats, its skeleton gleaming in the horizontal moonlight, and casting a gigantic ribbed shadow upon the water. One extended arm of the ghost seemed beckoning the whites to avenge it.

'Follow your leader!' cried the mate; and, one on each bow, the boats boarded. Sealing-spears and cutlasses crossed hatchets and handspikes. Huddled upon the long-boat amidships, the negresses raised a wailing chant, whose chorus was the clash of the steel.

For a time, the attack wavered; the negroes wedging themselves to beat it back; the half-repelled sailors, as yet unable to gain a footing, fighting as troopers in the saddle, one leg sideways flung over the bulwarks, and one without, plying their cutlasses like carters' whips. But in vain. They were almost overborne, when, rallying themselves into a squad as one man, with a huzza, they sprang inboard, where, entangled, they involuntarily separated again. For a few breaths' space, there was a vague, muffled, inner sound, as of submerged sword-fish rushing hither and thither through shoals of black-fish. Soon, in a reunited band, and joined by the Spanish seamen, the whites came to the surface, irresistibly driving the negroes toward the stern. But a barricade of casks and sacks, from side to side, had been thrown up by the mainmast. Here the negroes faced about, and though scorning peace or truce, yet fain would have had respite. But, without pause, overleaping the barrier, the unflagging sailors again closed. Exhausted, the blacks now fought in despair. Their red tongues lolled, wolf-like, from their black mouths. But the pale sailors' teeth were set; not a word was spoken; and, in five minutes more, the ship was won.

Nearly a score of the negroes were killed. Exclusive of those by the balls, many were mangled; their wounds – mostly inflicted by the long-edged sealing-spears – resembling those shaven ones of the English at Prestonpans, made by the poled scythes of the Highlanders. On the other side, none were killed, though several were wounded; some severely, including the mate. The surviving negroes were temporarily secured, and the ship, towed back into the harbour at midnight, once more lay anchored.

Omitting the incidents and arrangements ensuing, suffice it that, after two days spent in refitting, the ships sailed in company for Conception, in Chili, and thence for Lima, in Peru; where, before the vice-regal courts, the whole affair, from the beginning, underwent investigation.

Though, midway on the passage, the ill-fated Spaniard, relaxed from constraint, showed some signs of regaining health with free-will; yet, agreeably to his own foreboding, shortly before arriving at Lima, he relapsed, finally becoming so reduced as to be carried ashore in arms. Hearing of his story and plight, one of the many religious institutions of the City of Kings opened an hospitable refuge for him, where both physician and priest were his nurses, and a member of the order volunteered to be his one special guardian and consoler, by night and by day.

The following extracts, translated from one of the official Spanish documents, will, it is hoped, shed light on the preceding narrative, as well as, in the first place, reveal the true port of departure and true history of the *San Dominick*'s voyage, down to the time of her touching at the island of St Maria.

But, ere the extracts come, it may be well to preface them with a remark.

The document selected, from among many others, for partial translation, contains the deposition of Benito Cereno; the first taken in the case. Some disclosures therein were, at the time, held dubious for both learned and natural reasons. The tribunal inclined to the opinion that the dependent, not undisturbed in his mind by recent events, raved of some things which could never have happened. But subsequent depositions of the surviving sailors, bearing out the revelations of their captain in several of the strangest particulars, gave credence to the rest. So that the tribunal, in its final decision, rested its capital sentences upon statements which, had they lacked confirmation, it would have deemed it but duty to reject.

I, Don José de Abos and Padilla, His Majesty's Notary for the Royal Revenue, and Register of this Province, and Notary Public of the Holy Crusade of this Bishopric, etc.

Do certify and declare, as much as is requisite in law, that, in the criminal cause commenced the twenty-fourth of the month of September, in the year seventeen hundred and ninety-nine, against the negroes of the ship *San Dominick*, the following declaration before me was made:

Declaration of the first witness, Don Benito Cereno.

The same day, and month, and year, His Honour, Doctor Juan Martinez de Rozas, Councillor of the Royal Audience of this Kingdom, and learned in the law of this Intendency, ordered the captain of the ship *San Dominick*, Don Benito Cereno, to appear; which he did in his litter, attended by the monk Infelez; of whom he received the oath, which he took by God, our Lord, and a sign of the Cross; under which he promised to tell the truth of whatever he should know and should be asked; – and being interrogated agreeably to the tenor of the act commencing the process, he said, that on the twentieth of May last, he set sail with his ship from the port of Valparaiso, bound to that of Callao; loaded with the produce of the country besides thirty cases of hardware and one hundred and sixty blacks, of both sexes, mostly belonging to Don Alexandro Aranda, gentleman, of the city of Mendoza; that the crew of the ship consisted of thirty-six men, besides the persons who went as passengers; that the negroes were in part as follows:

[Here, in the original, follows a list of some fifty names, descriptions, and ages, compiled from certain recovered documents of Aranda's, and

also from recollections of the deponent, from which portions only are extracted.]

One, from about eighteen to nineteen years, named José, and this was the man that waited upon his master, Don Alexandro, and who speaks well the Spanish, having served him four or five years; * * * a mulatto, named Francesco, the cabin steward, of a good person and voice, having sung in the Valparaiso churches, native of the province of Buenos Aires, aged about thirty-five years. * * * A smart negro, named Dago, who had been for many years a gravedigger among the Spaniards, aged forty-six years. * * * Four old negroes, born in Africa, from sixty to seventy, but sound, caulkers by trade, whose names are as follows: – the first was named Muri, and he was killed (as was also his son named Diamelo); the second, Nacta; the third, Yola, likewise killed; the fourth, Ghofan; and six full-grown negroes, aged from thirty to forty-five, all raw, and born among the Ashantees – Matiluqui, Yan, Lecbe, Mapenda, Yambaio, Akim; four of whom were killed; * * * a powerful negro named Atufal, who being supposed to have been a chief in Africa, his owner set great store by him. * * * And a small negro of Senegal, but some years among the Spaniards, aged about thirty, which negro's name was Babo; * * * that he does not remember the names of the others, but that still expecting the residue of Don Alexandro's papers will be found, will then take due account of them all, and remit to the court; * * * and thirty-nine women and children of all ages.

[*The catalogue over, the deposition goes on:*]

* * * That all the negroes slept upon deck, as is customary in this navigation, and none wore fetters, because the owner, his friend Aranda, told him that they were all tractable; * * * that on the seventh day after leaving port, at three o'clock in the morning, all the Spaniards being asleep except the two officers on the watch, who were the boatswain, Juan Robles, and the carpenter, Juan Bautista Gayete, and the helmsman and his boy, the negroes revolted suddenly, wounded dangerously the boatswain and the carpenter, and successively killed eighteen men of those who were sleeping upon deck, some with handspikes and hatchets, and others by throwing them alive overboard, after tying them; that of the Spaniards upon deck, they left about seven, as he thinks, alive and tied, to manoeuvre the ship, and three or four more, who hid themselves, remained also alive. Although in the act of revolt the negroes made themselves masters of the hatchway, six or seven wounded went through it to the cockpit, without any hindrance on their part; that during the act of revolt, the mate and another person, whose name he does not recollect, attempted to come up through the

hatchway, but being quickly wounded, were obliged to return to the cabin; that the deponent resolved at break of day to come up the companion-way, where the negro Babo was, being the ringleader, and Atufal, who assisted him, and having spoken to them, exhorted them to cease committing such atrocities, asking them, at the same time, what they wanted and intended to do, offering, himself, to obey their commands; that notwithstanding this, they threw, in his presence, three men, alive and tied, overboard; that they told the deponent to come up, and that they would not kill him; which having done, the negro Babo asked him whether there were in these seas any negro countries where they might be carried, and he answered them, No; that the negro Babo afterward told him to carry them to Senegal, or to the neighbouring islands of St Nicholas; and he answered, that this was impossible, on account of the great distance, the necessity involved of rounding Cape Horn, the bad condition of the vessel, the want of provisions, sails, and water; but that the negro Babo replied to him he must carry them in any way; that they would do and conform themselves to everything the deponent should require as to eating and drinking; that after a long conference, being absolutely compelled to please them, for they threatened to kill all the whites if they were not, at all events, carried to Senegal, he told them that what was most wanting for the voyage was water; that they would go near the coast to take it, and thence they would proceed on their course; that the negro Babo agreed to it; and the deponent steered toward the intermediate ports, hoping to meet some Spanish or foreign vessel that would save them; that within ten or eleven days they saw the land, and continued their course by it in the vicinity of Nasca; that the deponent observed that the negroes were now restless and mutinous, because he did not effect the taking in of water, the negro Babo having required, with threats, that it should be done, without fail, the following day; he told him he saw plainly that the coast was steep, and the rivers designated in the maps were not to be found, with other reasons suitable to the circumstances; that the best way would be to go to the island of Santa Maria, where they might water easily, it being a solitary island, as the foreigners did; that the deponent did not go to Pisco, that was near, nor make any other port of the coast, because the negro Babo had intimated to him several times, that he would kill all the whites the very moment he should perceive any city, town, or settlement of any kind on the shores to which they should be carried: that having determined to go to the island of Santa Maria, as the deponent had planned, for the purpose of trying whether, on the passage or near the island itself, they could find any vessel that should favour them, or whether he could escape from it in a boat to the neighbouring coast of Arruco, to adopt the necessary means he immediately changed his course, steering for the island; that the negroes Babo and Atufal held daily conferences, in which they discussed what was necessary for their design of returning to Senegal, whether they were to kill all the Spaniards, and particularly the deponent; that eight days after parting with the coast of Nasca, the deponent being on the watch a little after daybreak, and soon after the negroes had their meeting, the negro Babo came to the place where the deponent was, and told him that he had determined to kill his master, Don Alexandro Aranda, both because he and his companions could not otherwise be sure of their liberty, and that to keep the seamen in subjection, he wanted to prepare a warning of what road they should be made to take did they or any of them oppose him; and that, by means of the death of Don Alexandro, that warning would best be given; but, that what this last meant, the deponent did not at the time comprehend, nor could not, further than that the death of Don Alexandro was intended; and moreover the negro Babo proposed to the deponent to call the mate Raneds, who was sleeping in the cabin, before the thing was done, for fear, as the deponent understood it, that the mate, who was a good navigator, should be killed with Don Alexandro and the rest; that the deponent, who was the friend, from youth, of Don Alexandro, prayed and conjured, but all was useless; for the negro Babo answered him that the thing could not be prevented, and that all the Spaniards risked their death if they should attempt to frustrate his will in this matter, or any other; that, in this conflict, the deponent called the mate, Raneds, who was forced to go apart, and immediately the negro Babo commanded the Ashantee Matiluqui and the Ashantee Lecbe to go and commit the murder; that those two went down with hatchets to the berth of Don Alexandro; that, yet half alive and mangled, they dragged him on deck; that they were going to throw him overboard in that state, but the negro Babo stopped them, bidding the murder be completed on the deck before him, which was done, when, by his orders, the body was carried below, forward; that nothing more was seen of it by the deponent for three days; * * * that Don Alonzo Sidonia, an old man, long resident at Valparaiso, and lately appointed to a civil office in Peru, whither he had taken passage, was at the time sleeping in the berth opposite Don Alexandro's; that awakening at his cries, surprised by them, and at the sight of the negroes with their bloody hatchets in their hands, he threw himself into the sea through a window which was near him, and was drowned, without it being in the power of the deponent to assist or take him up; * * * that a short time after killing Aranda, they brought upon deck his german-cousin, of middle-age, Don Francisco Masa, of Mendoza, and the young Don Joaquin, Marques de Aramboalaza, then lately from Spain, with his Spanish servant Ponce, and the three young clerks of Aranda, José Mozairi, Lorenzo Bargas, and Hermenegildo Gandix, all of Cadiz;

that Don Joaquin and Hermenegildo Gandix, the negro Babo, for purposes hereafter to appear, preserved alive; but Don Francisco Masa José Mozairi, and Lorenzo Bargas, with Ponce the servant, besides the boatswain, Juan Robles, the boatswain's mates, Manuel Viscaya and Roderigo Hurta, and four of the sailors, the negro Babo ordered to be thrown alive into the sea, although they made no resistance, nor begged for anything else but mercy; that the boatswain, Juan Robles, who knew how to swim, kept the longest above water, making acts of contrition, and, in the last words he uttered, charged this deponent to cause mass to be said for his soul to our Lady of Succour: * * * that, during the three days which followed, the deponent, uncertain what fate had befallen the remains of Don Alexandro, frequently asked the negro Babo where they were, and, if still on board, whether they were to be preserved for interment ashore, entreating him so to order it; that the negro Babo answered nothing till the fourth day, when at sunrise, the deponent coming on deck, the negro Babo showed him a skeleton, which had been substituted for the ship's proper figure-head – the image of Christopher Colon, the discoverer of the New World; that the negro Babo asked him whose skeleton that was, and whether from its whiteness, he should not think it a white's; that, upon discovering his face, the negro Babo, coming close, said words to this effect: 'Keep faith with the blacks from here to Senegal, or you shall in spirit, as now in body, follow your leader,' pointing to the prow; * * * that the same morning the negro Babo took by succession each Spaniard forward, and asked him whose skeleton that was, and whether, from its whiteness, he should not think it a white's; that each Spaniard covered his face; that then to each the negro Babo repeated the words in the first place said to the deponent; * * * that they (the Spaniards), being then assembled aft, the negro Babo harangued them, saying that he had now done all; that the deponent (as navigator for the negroes) might pursue his course, warning him and all of them that they should, soul and body, go the way of Don Alexandro, if he saw them (the Spaniards) speak or plot anything against them (the negroes) – a threat which was repeated every day; that, before the events last mentioned, they had tied the cook to throw him overboard, for it is not known what thing they heard him speak, but finally the negro Babo spared his life, at the request of the deponent; that a few days after, the deponent, endeavouring not to omit any means to preserve the lives of the remaining whites, spoke to the negroes peace and tranquillity, and agreed to draw up a paper, signed by the deponent and the sailors who could write, as also by the negro Babo, for himself and all the blacks, in which the deponent obliged himself to carry them to Senegal, and they not to kill any more, and he formally to make over to them the ship, with the cargo, with which they were for that time satisfied and quieted. * * *

But the next day, the more surely to guard against the sailors' escape, the negro Babo commanded all the boats to be destroyed but the long-boat, which was unseaworthy, and another, a cutter in good condition, which knowing it would yet be wanted for towing the water-casks, he had it lowered down into the hold.

[*Various particulars of the prolonged and perplexed navigation ensuing here follow, with incidents of a calamitous calm, from which portion one passage is extracted, to wit:*]

That on the fifth day of the calm, all on board suffering much from the heat, and want of water, and five having died in fits, and mad, the negroes became irritable, and for a chance gesture, which they deemed suspicious – though it was harmless – made by the mate, Raneds, to the deponent in the act of handing a quadrant, they killed him; but that for this they afterward were sorry, the mate being the only remaining navigator on board, except the deponent.

That omitting other events, which daily happened, and which can only serve uselessly to recall past misfortunes and conflicts, after seventy-three days' navigation, reckoned from the time they sailed from Nasca, during which they navigated under a scanty allowance of water, and were afflicted with the calms before-mentioned, they at last arrived at the island of Santa Maria, on the seventeenth of the month of August, at about six o'clock in the afternoon, at which hour they cast anchor very near the American ship, *Bachelor's Delight*, which lay in the same bay, commanded by the generous Captain Amasa Delano; but at six o'clock in the morning, they had already descried the port, and the negroes became uneasy, as soon as at distance they saw the ship, not having expected to see one there; that the negro Babo pacified them, assuring them that no fear need be had; that straightway he ordered the figure on the bow to be covered with canvas, as for repairs, and had the decks a little set in order; that for a time the negro Babo and the negro Atufal conferred; that the negro Atufal was for sailing away, but the negro Babo would not, and, by himself, cast about what to do; that at last he came to the deponent, proposing to him to say and do all that the deponent declares to have said and done to the American captain; * * * that the negro Babo warned him that if he varied in the least, or uttered any word, or gave any look that should give the least intimation of the past events or present state, he would instantly kill him, with all his companions, showing a dagger, which he carried hid, saying something which, as he understood it, meant that that dagger would be alert as his eye; that the negro Babo then announced the plan to all his companions, which pleased them; that he then, the better to disguise the truth, devised many expedients, in some of them united deceit and defence; that of this sort was the device of the six Ashantees beforenamed, who were his bravos; that them he stationed on the break of the poop, as if to clean certain hatchets (in cases, which were part of the cargo), but in reality to use them, and distribute them at need, and at a given word he told them; that, among other devices, was the device of presenting Atufal, his right-hand man, as chained, though in a moment the chains could be dropped; that in every particular he informed the deponent what part he was expected to enact in every device, and what story he was to tell on every occasion, always threatening him with instant death if he varied in the least; that, conscious that many of the negroes would be turbulent, the negro Babo appointed the four aged negroes, who were caulkers, to keep what domestic order they could on the decks; that again and again he harangued the Spaniards and his companions, informing them of his intent, and of his devices, and of the invented story that this deponent was to tell; charging them lest any of them varied from that story; that these arrangements were made and matured during the interval of two or three hours, between their first sighting the ship and the arrival on board of Captain Amasa Delano; that this happened about half-past seven o'clock in the morning, Captain Amasa Delano coming in his boat, and all gladly receiving him; that the deponent, as well as he could force himself, acting then the part of principal owner, and a free captain of the ship, told Captain Amasa Delano, when called upon, that he came from Buenos Aires, bound to Lima, with three hundred negroes; that off Cape Horn, and in a subsequent fever, many negroes had died; that also, by similar casualties, all the sea-officers and the greatest part of the crew had died.

[*And so the deposition goes on, circumstantially recounting the fictitious story dictated to the deponent by Babo, and through the deponent imposed upon Captain Delano; and also recounting the friendly offers of Captain Delano, with other things, but all of which is here omitted. After the fictitious story, etc., the deposition proceeds:*]

That the generous Captain Amasa Delano remained on board all the day, till he left the ship anchored at six o'clock in the evening, deponent speaking to him always of his pretended misfortunes, under the forementioned principles, without having had it in his power to tell a single word, or give him the least hint, that he might know the truth and state of things; because the negro Babo, performing the office of an officious servant with all the appearance of submission of the humble slave, did not leave the deponent one moment; that this was in order to observe the deponent's actions and words, for the negro Babo understands well the Spanish; and besides, there were thereabout some others who were constantly on the watch, and likewise understood the Spanish; * * * that upon one occasion, while deponent was standing on the deck conversing with Amasa Delano, by a secret sign the negro Babo drew him (the deponent) aside, the act appearing as if originating with the deponent; that then, he being drawn aside, the negro Babo proposed to him to gain from Amasa Delano full particulars about his ship, and crew, and arms; that the deponent asked 'For what?' that the negro Babo answered he might conceive; that, grieved at the prospect of what might overtake the generous Captain Amasa Delano, the deponent at first refused to ask the desired questions, and used every argument to induce the negro Babo to give up this new design; that the negro Babo showed the point of his dagger; that, after the information had been obtained, the negro Babo again drew him aside, telling him that very night he (the deponent) would be captain of two ships, instead of one, for that, great part of the American's ship's crew being to be absent fishing, the six Ashantees, without anyone else, would easily take it; that at this time he said other things to the same purpose; that no entreaties availed; that, before Amasa Delano's coming on board, no hint had been given touching the capture of the American ship: that to prevent this project the deponent was powerless; * * * – that in some things his memory is confused, he cannot distinctly recall every event; * * * – that as soon as they had cast anchor at six of the clock in the evening, as has before been stated, the American captain took leave, to return to his vessel; that upon a sudden impulse, which the deponent believes to have come from God and his angels, he, after the farewell had been said, followed the generous Captain Amasa Delano as far as the gunwale, where he stayed, under pretence of taking leave, until Amasa Delano should have been seated in his boat; that on shoving off, the deponent sprang from the gunwale into the boat, and fell into it, he knows not how, God guarding him; that

[*Here, in the original, follows the account of what further happened at the escape, and how the* San Dominick *was retaken, and of the passage to the coast; including in the recital many expressions of 'eternal gratitude' to the 'generous Captain Amasa Delano.' The deposition then proceeds with recapitulatory remarks, and a partial renumeration of the negroes, making record of their individual part in the past events, with a view to furnishing, according to command of the court, the data whereon to found the criminal sentences to be pronounced. From this portion is the following:*]

That he believes that all the negroes, though not in the first place knowing to the design of revolt, when it was accomplished, approved it. * * * That the negro, José, eighteen years old, and in the personal service of Don Alexandro, was the one who communicated the information to the negro Babo, about the state of things in the cabin, before the revolt; that this is known, because, in the preceding midnight, he used to come from his berth, which was under his master's, in the cabin, to the deck where the ringleader and his associates were, and had secret conversations with the negro Babo, in which he was several times seen by the mate; that, one night, the mate drove him away twice; * * * that this same negro José was the one who, without being commanded to do so by the negro Babo, as Lecbe and Matiluqui were, stabbed his master, Don Alexandro, after he had been dragged half-lifeless to the deck; * * * that the mulatto steward, Francesco, was of the first band of revolters, that he was, in all things, the creature and tool of the negro Babo; that, to make his court, he, just before a repast in the cabin, proposed to the negro Babo, poisoning a dish for the generous Captain Amasa Delano; this is known and believed, because the negroes have said it; but that the negro Babo, having another design, forbade Francesco; * * * that the Ashantee Lecbe was one of the worst of them; for that, on the day the ship was retaken, he assisted in the defence of her, with a hatchet in each hand, with one of which he wounded, in the breast, the chief mate of Amasa Delano, in the first act of boarding; this all knew; that, in sight of the deponent, Lecbe struck, with a hatchet, Don Francisco Masa, when, by the negro Babo's orders, he was carrying him to throw him overboard, alive, besides participating in the murder, before mentioned, of Don Alexandro Aranda, and others of the cabin passengers; that, owing to the fury with which the Ashantees fought in the engagement with the boats, but this Lecbe and Yan survived; that Yan was bad as Lecbe; that Yan was the man who, by Babo's command, willingly prepared the skeleton of Don Alexandro, in a way the negroes afterward told the deponent, but which he, so long as reason is left him, can never divulge; that Yan and Lecbe were the two who, in a calm by night, riveted the skeleton to the bow; this also the negroes told him; that the negro Babo was he who traced the inscription below it; that the negro Babo was the plotter from first to last; he ordered every murder, and was the helm and keel of the revolt; that Atufal was his lieutenant in all; but Atufal, with his own hand, committed no murder; nor did the negro Babo; * * * that Atufal was shot, being killed in the fight with the boats, ere boarding; * * * that the negresses, of age, were knowing to the revolt, and testified themselves satisfied at the death of their master, Don Alexandro; that, had the negroes not restrained them, they would have tortured to death, instead of simply killing, the Spaniards slain by command of the negro Babo; that the negresses used their utmost influence to have the deponent made away with; that, in the various acts of murder, they sang songs and danced – not gaily, but solemnly; and before the engagement with the boats, as well as during the action, they sang melancholy songs to the negroes, and that this melancholy tone was more inflaming than a different one would have been, and was so intended; that all this is believed, because the negroes have said it.

That of the thirty-six men of the crew, exclusive of the passengers (all of whom are now dead), which the deponent had knowledge of, six only remained alive, with four cabin-boys and ship-boys, not included with the crew; * * * – that the negroes broke an arm of one of the cabin-boys and gave him strokes with hatchets.

[*Then follow various random disclosures referring to various periods of time. The following are extracted:*]

That during the presence of Captain Amasa Delano on board, some attempts were made by the sailors, and one by Hermenegildo Gandix, to convey hints to him of the true state of affairs; but that these attempts were ineffectual, owing to fear of incurring death, and, furthermore, owing to the devices which offered contradictions to the true state of affairs, as well as owing to the generosity and piety of Amasa Delano incapable of sounding such wickedness; * * * that Luys Galgo, a sailor about sixty years of age, and formerly of the king's navy, was one of those who sought to convey tokens to Captain Amasa Delano; but his intent, though undiscovered, being suspected, he was, on a pretence, made to retire out of sight, and at last into the hold, and there was made away with. This the negroes have since said; * * * that one of the ship-boys feeling, from Captain Amasa Delano's presence, some hopes of release, and not having enough prudence, dropped some chance word respecting his expectations, which being overheard and understood by a slave-boy with whom he was eating at the time, the latter struck him on the head with a knife, inflicting a bad wound, but of which the boy is now healing; that likewise, not long before the ship was brought to anchor, one of the seamen, steering at the time, endangered himself by letting the blacks remark some expression in his countenance, arising from a cause similar to the above; but this sailor, by his heedful after conduct, escaped; * * * that these statements are made to show the court that from the beginning to the end of the revolt, it was impossible for the deponent and his men to act otherwise than they did; * * * – that the third clerk, Hermenegildo Gandix, who before had been forced to live among the seamen, wearing a seaman's habit, and in all respects appearing to be one for the time, he, Gandix, was killed by a musket-ball fired through mistake from the boats before boarding; having in his fright run up the mizen-rigging, calling to the boats – 'don't board,' lest upon their boarding the negroes should kill him; that this inducing the Americans to believe he some way favoured the cause of the negroes, they fired two balls at him, so that he fell wounded from the rigging, and was drowned in the sea; * * * – that the young Don Joaquin, Marques de Aramboalaza, like Hermenegildo Gandix, the third clerk, was degraded to the office and appearance of a common seaman; that upon one occasion when Don Joaquin shrank, the negro Babo commanded the Ashantee Lecbe to take tar and heat it, and pour it upon Don Joaquin's hands; * * * – that Don Joaquin was killed owing to another mistake of the Americans, but one impossible to be avoided, as upon the approach of the boats, Don Joaquin, with a hatchet tied edge out and upright to his hand, was made by the negroes to appear on the bulwarks; whereupon, seen with arms in his hands and in a questionable attitude, he was shot for a renegade seaman; * * * – that on the person of Don Joaquin was found secreted a jewel, which, by papers that were discovered, proved to have been meant for the shrine of our Lady of Mercy in Lima; a votive offering, beforehand prepared and guarded, to attest his gratitude, when he should have landed in Peru, his last destination, for the safe conclusion of his entire voyage from Spain; * * * – that the jewel, with the other effects of the late Don Joaquin, is in the custody of the brethren of the Hospital de Sacerdotes, awaiting the disposition of the honourable court; * * * – that, owing to the condition of the deponent, as well as the haste in which the boats departed for the attack, the Americans were not forewarned that there were, among the apparent crew, a passenger and one of the clerks disguised by the negro Babo; * * * – that, besides the negroes killed in the action, some were killed after the capture and re-anchoring at night, when shackled to the ring-bolts on deck; that these deaths were committed by the sailors, ere they could be prevented. That so soon as informed of it, Captain Amasa Delano used all his authority, and, in particular with his own hand, struck down Martinez Gola, who, having found a razor in the pocket of an old jacket of his, which one of the shackled negroes had on, was aiming it at the negro's throat; that the noble Captain Amasa Delano also wrenched from the hand of Bartholomew Barlo a dagger, secreted at the time of the massacre of the whites, with which he was in the act of stabbing a shackled negro, who, the same day, with another negro, had thrown him down and jumped upon him; * * * – that, for all the events, befalling through so long a time, during which the ship was in the hands of the negro Babo, he cannot here give account; but that, what he has said is the most substantial of what occurs to him at present, and is the truth under the oath which he has taken; which declaration he affirmed and ratified, after hearing it read to him.

He said that he is twenty-nine years of age, and broken in body and mind; that when finally dismissed by the court, he shall not return home to Chile, but betake himself to the monastery on Mount Agonia without; and signed with his honour, and crossed himself, and, for the time, departed as he came, in his litter, with the monk Infelez, to the Hospital de Sacerdotes.

Benito Cereno.

Doctor Rozas.

If the Deposition have served as the key to fit into the lock of the complications which precede it, then, as a vault whose door has been flung back, the *San Dominick*'s hull lies open to-day.

Hitherto the nature of this narrative, besides rendering the intricacies in the beginning unavoidable, has more or less required that many things, instead of being set down in the order of occurrence, should be retrospectively, or irregularly given; this last is the case with the following passages, which will conclude the account:

During the long, mild voyage to Lima, there was, as before hinted, a period during which the sufferer a little recovered his health, or, at least in some degree, his tranquillity. Ere the decided relapse which came, the two captains had many cordial conversations – their fraternal unreserve in singular contrast with former withdrawments.

Again and again it was repeated, how hard it had been to enact the part forced on the Spaniard by Babo.

'Ah, my dear friend,' Don Benito once said, 'at those very times when you thought me so morose and ungrateful, nay, when, as you now admit, you half thought me plotting your murder, at those very times my heart was frozen; I could not look at you, thinking of what, both on board this ship and your own, hung, from other hands, over my kind benefactor. And as God lives, Don Amasa, I know not whether desire for my own safety alone could have nerved me to that leap into your boat, had it not been for the thought that, did you, unenlightened, return to your ship, you, my best friend, with all who might be with you, stolen upon, that night, in your hammocks, would never in this world have wakened again. Do but think how you walked this deck, how you sat in this cabin, every inch of ground mined into honeycombs under you. Had I dropped the least hint, made the least advance toward an understanding between us, death, explosive death – yours as mine – would have ended the scene.'

'True, true,' cried Captain Delano, starting, 'you have saved my life, Don Benito, more than I yours; saved it, too, against my knowledge and will.'

'Nay, my friend,' rejoined the Spaniard, courteous even to the point of religion, 'God charmed your life, but you saved mine. To think of some things you did – those smilings and chattings, rash pointings and gesturings. For less than these, they slew my mate, Raneds; but you had the Prince of Heaven's safe-conduct through all ambuscades.'

'Yes, all is owing to Providence, I know: but the temper of my mind that morning was more than commonly pleasant, while the sight of so much suffering, more apparent than real, added to my good-nature, compassion, and charity, happily interweaving the three. Had it been otherwise, doubtless, as you hint, some of my interferences might have ended unhappily enough. Besides, those feelings I spoke of enabled me to get the better of momentary distrust, at times when acuteness might have cost me my life, without saving another's. Only at the end did my suspicions get the better of me, and you know how wide of the mark they then proved.'

'Wide, indeed,' said Don Benito sadly; 'you were with me all day; stood with me, sat with me, talked with me, looked at me, ate with me, drank with me; and yet, your last act was to clutch for a monster, not only an innocent man, but the most pitiable of all men. To such degree may malign machinations and deceptions impose. So far may even the best man err, in judging the conduct of one with the recesses of whose condition he is not acquainted. But you were forced to it; and you were in time undeceived. Would that, in both respects, it was so ever, and with all men.'

'You generalize, Don Benito; and mournfully enough. But the past is past; why moralize upon it? Forget it. See, yon bright sun has forgotten it all, and the blue sea, and the blue sky; these have turned over new leaves.'

'Because they have no memory,' he dejectedly replied; 'because they are not human.'

'But these mild Trades that now fan your cheek, do they not come with a human-like healing to you? Warm friends, steadfast friends are the Trades.'

'With their steadfastness they but waft me to my tomb, señor,' was the foreboding response.

'You are saved,' cried Captain Delano, more and more astonished and pained; 'you are saved: what has cast such a shadow upon you?'

'The negro.'

There was silence, while the moody man sat, slowly and unconsciously gathering his mantle about him, as if it were a pall.

There was no more conversation that day.

But if the Spaniard's melancholy sometimes ended in muteness upon topics like the above, there were others upon which he never spoke at all; on which, indeed, all his old reserves were piled. Pass over the worst, and, only to elucidate, let an item or two of these be cited. The dress, so precise and costly, worn by him on the day whose events have been narrated, had not willingly been put on. And that silver-mounted sword, apparent symbol of despotic command, was not, indeed, a sword, but the ghost of one. The scabbard, artificially stiffened, was empty.

As for the black – whose brain, not body, had schemed and led the revolt, with the plot – his slight frame, inadequate to that which it held, had at once yielded to the superior muscular strength of his captor, in the boat. Seeing all was over, he uttered no sound, and could not be forced to. His aspect seemed to say, since I cannot do deeds, I will not speak words. Put in irons in the hold, with the rest, he was carried to Lima. During the passage, Don Benito did not visit him. Nor then, nor at any time after, would he look at him. Before the tribunal he refused. When pressed by the judges he fainted. On the testimony of the sailors alone rested the legal identity of Babo.

Some months after, dragged to the gibbet at the tail of a mule, the black met his voiceless end. The body was burned to ashes; but for many days the head, that hive of subtlety, fixed on a pole in the Plaza, met, unabashed, the gaze of the whites; and across the Plaza looked toward St Bartholomew's church, in whose vaults slept then, as now, the recovered bones of Aranda: and across the Rimac bridge looked toward the monastery, on Mount Agonia without; where, three months after being dismissed by the court, Benito Cereno, borne on the bier, did, indeed, follow his leader.

Stephen Crane

The Open Boat

A Tale intended to be after the Fact. Being the Experience of Four Men from the Sunk Steamer *Commodore*.

I

NONE OF them knew the colour of the sky. Their eyes glanced level, and were fastened upon the waves that swept toward them. These waves were of the hue of slate, save for the tops, which were of foaming white, and all of the men knew the colours of the sea. The horizon narrowed and widened, and dipped and rose, and at all times its edge was jagged with waves that seemed thrust up in points like rocks.

Many a man ought to have a bath-tub larger than the boat which here rode upon the sea. These waves were most wrongfully and barbarously abrupt and tall, and each froth-top was a problem in small boat navigation.

The cook squatted in the bottom and looked with both eyes at the six inches of gunwale which separated him from the ocean. His sleeves were rolled over his fat forearms and the two flaps of his unbuttoned vest dangled as he bent to bail out the boat. Often he said: 'Gawd! That was a narrow clip.' As he remarked it he invariably gazed eastward over the broken sea.

The oiler, steering with one of the two oars in the boat, sometimes raised himself suddenly to keep clear of water that swirled in over the stern. It was a thin little oar and it seemed often ready to snap.

The correspondent, pulling at the other oar, watched the waves and wondered why he was there.

The injured captain, lying in the bow, was at this time buried in that profound dejection and indifference which comes, temporarily at least, to even the bravest and most enduring when, willy nilly, the firm fails, the army loses, the ship goes down. The mind of the master of a vessel is rooted deep in the timbers of her, though he commanded for a day or a decade, and this captain had on him the stern impression of a scene in the greys of dawn of seven turned faces, and later a stump of a top-mast with a white ball on it that slashed to and fro at the waves, went low and lower, and down. Thereafter there was something strange in his voice. Although steady, it was deep with mourning, and of a quality beyond oration or tears.

'Keep 'er a little more south, Billie,' said he.

'A little more south, sir,' said the oiler in the stern.

A seat in this boat was not unlike a seat upon a bucking broncho, and, by the same token, a broncho is not much smaller. The craft pranced and reared, and plunged like an animal. As each wave came, and she rose for it, she seemed like a horse making at a fence outrageously high. The manner of her scramble over these walls of water is a mystic thing and, moreover, at the top of them were ordinarily these problems in white water, the foam racing down from the summit of each wave, requiring a new leap, and a leap from the air. Then, after scornfully bumping a crest, she would slide, and race, and splash down a long incline, and arrive bobbing and nodding in front of the next menace.

A singular disadvantage of the sea lies in the fact that after successfully surmounting one wave you discover that there is another behind it just as important and just as nervously anxious to do something effective in the way of swamping boats. In a ten-foot dinghy one can get an idea of the resources of the sea in the line of waves that is not probable to the average experience which is never at sea in a dinghy. As each slaty wall of water approached, it shut all else from the view of the men in the boat, and it was not difficult to imagine that this particular wave was the final outburst of the ocean, the last effort of the grim water. There was a terrible grace in the move of the waves, and they came in silence, save for the snarling of the crests.

In the wan light, the faces of the men must have been grey. Their eyes must have glinted in strange ways as they gazed steadily astern. Viewed from a balcony, the whole thing would doubtlessly have been weirdly picturesque. But the men in the boat had no time to see it, and if they had had leisure there were other things to occupy their minds. The sun swung steadily up the sky, and they knew it was broad day because the colour of the sea changed from slate to emerald-green, streaked with amber lights, and the foam was like tumbling snow. The process of the breaking day was unknown to them. They were aware only of this effect upon the colour of the waves that rolled toward them.

In disjointed sentences the cook and the correspondent argued as to the difference between a life-saving station and a house of refuge. The cook had said: 'There's a house of refuge just north of the Mosquito Inlet Light, and as soon as they see us, they'll come off in their boat and pick us up.'

'As soon as who see us?' said the correspondent.

'The crew,' said the cook.

'Houses of refuge don't have crews,' said the correspondent. 'As I understand them, they are only places where clothes and grub are stored for the benefit of shipwrecked people. They don't carry crews.'

'Oh, yes, they do,' said the cook.

'No, they don't,' said the correspondent.

'Well, we're not there yet, anyhow,' said the oiler, in the stern.

'Well,' said the cook, 'perhaps it's not a house of refuge that I'm thinking of as being near Mosquito Inlet Light. Perhaps it's a life-saving station.'

'We're not there yet,' said the oiler, in the stern.

II

As the boat bounced from the top of each wave, the wind tore through the hair of the hatless men, and as the craft plopped her stern down again the spray slashed past them. The crest of each of these waves was a hill, from the top of which the men surveyed, for a moment, a broad tumultuous expanse, shining and wind-riven. It was probably splendid. It was probably glorious, this play of the free sea, wild with lights of emerald and white and amber.

'Bully good thing it's an on-shore wind,' said the cook. 'If not, where would we be? Wouldn't have a show.'

'That's right,' said the correspondent.

The busy oiler nodded his assent.

Then the captain, in the bow, chuckled in a way that expressed humour, contempt, tragedy, all in one. 'Do you think we've got much of a show now, boys?' said he.

Whereupon the three were silent, save for a trifle of hemming and hawing. To express any particular optimism at this time they felt to be childish and stupid, but they all doubtless possessed this sense of the situation in their mind. A young man thinks doggedly at such times. On the other hand, the ethics of their condition was decidedly against any open suggestion of hopelessness. So they were silent.

'Oh, well,' said the captain, soothing his children, 'we'll get ashore all right.'

But there was that in his tone which made them think, so the oiler quoth: 'Yes! If this wind holds!'

The cook was bailing: 'Yes! If we don't catch hell in the surf.'

Canton flannel gulls flew near and far. Sometimes they sat down on the sea, near patches of brown seaweed that rolled over the waves with a movement like carpets on a line in a gale. The birds sat comfortably in groups, and they were envied by some in the dinghy, for the wrath of the sea was no more to them than it was to a covey of prairie chickens a thousand miles inland. Often they came very close and stared at the men with black bead-like eyes. At these times they were uncanny and sinister in their unblinking scrutiny, and the men hooted angrily at them, telling them to be gone. One came, and evidently decided to alight on the top of the captain's head. The bird flew parallel to the boat and did not circle, but made short sidelong jumps in the air in chicken-fashion. His black eyes were wistfully fixed upon the captain's head. 'Ugly brute,' said the oiler to the bird. 'You look as if you were made with a jack-knife.' The cook and the correspondent swore darkly at the creature. The captain naturally wished to knock it away with the end of the heavy painter; but he did not dare do it, because anything resembling an emphatic gesture would have capsized this freighted boat, and so with his open hand, the captain gently and carefully waved the gull away. After it had been discouraged from the pursuit the captain breathed easier on account of his hair, and others breathed easier because the bird struck their minds at this time as being somehow gruesome and ominous.

In the meantime the oiler and the correspondent rowed. And also they rowed.

They sat together in the same seat, and each rowed an oar. Then the oiler took both oars; then the correspondent took both oars; then the oiler; then the correspondent. They rowed and they rowed. The very ticklish part of the business was when the time came for the reclining one in the stern to take his turn at the oars. By the very last star of truth, it is easier to steal eggs from under a hen than it was to change seats in the dinghy. First the man in the stern slid his hand along the thwart and moved with care, as if he were of Sèvres. Then the man in the rowing seat slid his hand along the other thwart. It was all done with the most extraordinary care. As the two sidled past each other, the whole party kept watchful eyes on the coming wave, and the captain cried: 'Look out now! Steady there!'

The brown mats of sea-weed that appeared from time to time were like islands, bits of earth. They were travelling, apparently, neither one way nor the other. They were, to all intents, stationary. They informed the men in the boat that it was making progress slowly toward the land.

The captain, rearing cautiously in the bow, after the dinghy soared on a great swell, said that he had seen the lighthouse at Mosquito Inlet. Presently the cook remarked that he had seen it. The correspondent was at the oars then, and for some reason he too wished to look at the lighthouse, but his back was toward the far shore and the waves were important, and for some time he could not seize an opportunity to turn his head. But at last there came a wave more gentle than the others, and when at the crest of it he swiftly scoured the western horizon.

'See it?' said the captain.

'No,' said the correspondent slowly, 'I didn't see anything.'

'Look again,' said the captain. He pointed. 'It's exactly in that direction.'

At the top of another wave, the correspondent did as he was bid, and this time his eyes chanced on a small still thing on the edge of the swaying horizon. It was precisely like the point of a pin. It took an anxious eye to find a lighthouse so tiny.

'Think we'll make it, captain?'

'If this wind holds and the boat don't swamp, we can't do much else,' said the captain.

The little boat, lifted by each towering sea, and splashed viciously by the crests, made progress that in the absence of seaweed was not apparent to those in her. She seemed just a wee thing wallowing, miraculously top-up, at the mercy of five oceans. Occasionally, a great spread of water, like white flames, swarmed into her.

'Bail her, cook,' said the captain serenely.

'All right, captain,' said the cheerful cook.

III

It would be difficult to describe the subtle brotherhood of men that was here established on the seas. No one said that it was so. No one mentioned it. But it dwelt in the boat, and each man felt it warm him. They were a captain, an oiler, a cook, and a correspondent, and they were friends, friends in a more curiously iron-bound degree than may be common. The hurt captain, lying against the water-jar in the bow, spoke always in a low voice and calmly, but he could never command a more ready and swiftly obedient crew than the motley three of the dinghy. It was more than a mere recognition of what was best for the common safety. There was surely in it a quality that was personal and heartfelt. And after this devotion to the commander of the boat there was this comradeship that the correspondent, for instance, who had been taught to be cynical of men, knew even at the time was the best experience of his life. But no one said that it was so. No one mentioned it.

'I wish we had a sail,' remarked the captain. 'We might try my overcoat on the end of an oar and give you two boys a chance to rest.' So the cook and the correspondent held the mast and spread wide the overcoat. The oiler steered, and the little boat made good way with her new rig. Sometimes the oiler had to scull sharply to keep a sea from breaking into the boat, but otherwise sailing was a success.

Meanwhile the lighthouse had been growing slowly larger. It had now almost assumed colour, and appeared like a little grey shadow on the sky. The man at the oars could not be prevented from turning his head rather often to try for a glimpse of this little grey shadow.

At last, from the top of each wave the men in the tossing boat could see land. Even as the lighthouse was an upright shadow on the sky, this land seemed but a long black shadow on the sea. It certainly was thinner than paper. 'We must be about opposite New Smyrna,' said the cook, who had coasted this shore often in schooners. 'Captain, by the way, I believe they abandoned that life-saving station there about a year ago.'

'Did they?' said the captain.

The wind slowly died away. The cook and the correspondent were not now obliged to slave in order to hold high the oar. But the waves continued their old impetuous swooping at the dinghy, and the little craft, no longer under way, struggled woundily over them. The oiler or the correspondent took the oars again.

Shipwrecks are *à propos* of nothing. If men could only train for them and have them occur when the men had reached pink condition, there would be less drowning at sea. Of the four in the dinghy none had slept any time worth mentioning for two days and two nights previous to embarking in the dinghy, and in the excitement of clambering about the deck of a foundering ship they had also forgotten to eat heartily.

For these reasons, and for others, neither the oiler nor the correspondent was fond of rowing at this time. The correspondent wondered ingeniously how in the name of all that was sane could there be people who thought it amusing to row a boat. It was not an amusement; it was a diabolical punishment, and even a genius of mental aberrations could never conclude that it was anything but a horror to the muscles and a crime against the back. He mentioned to the boat in general how the amusement of rowing struck him, and the weary-faced oiler smiled in full sympathy. Previously to the foundering, by the way, the oiler had worked double-watch in the engine-room of the ship.

'Take her easy, now, boys,' said the captain. 'Don't spend yourselves. If we have to run a surf you'll need all your strength, because we'll sure have to swim for it. Take your time.'

Slowly the land rose from the sea. From a black line it became a line of black and a line of white, trees and sand. Finally, the captain said that he could make out a house on the shore. 'That's the house of refuge, sure,' said the cook. 'They'll see us before long, and come out after us.'

The distant lighthouse reared high. 'The keeper ought to be able to make us out now, if he's looking through a glass,' said the captain. 'He'll notify the life-saving people.'

'None of those other boats could have got ashore to give word of the wreck,' said the oiler, in a low voice. 'Else the lifeboat would be out hunting us.'

Slowly and beautifully the land loomed out of the sea. The wind came again. It had veered from the north-east to the south-east. Finally, a new sound struck the ears of the men in the boat. It was the low thunder of the surf on the shore. 'We'll never be able to make the lighthouse now,' said the captain. 'Swing her head a little more north, Billie,' said he.

' "A little more north," sir,' said the oiler.

Whereupon the little boat turned her nose once more down the wind, and all but the oarsman watched the shore grow. Under the influence of this expansion doubt and direful apprehension was leaving the minds of the men. The management of the boat was still most absorbing, but it could not prevent a quiet cheerfulness. In an hour, perhaps, they would be ashore.

Their backbones had become thoroughly used to balancing in the boat, and they now rode this wild colt of a dinghy like circus men. The correspondent thought that he had been drenched to the skin, but happening to feel in the top pocket of his coat, he found therein eight cigars. Four of them were soaked with sea-water; four were perfectly scatheless. After a search, somebody produced three dry matches, and thereupon the four waifs rode impudently in their little boat, and with an assurance of an impending rescue shining in their eyes, puffed at the big cigars and judged well and ill of all men. Everybody took a drink of water.

IV

'Cook,' remarked the captain, 'there don't seem to be any sign of life about your house of refuge.'

'No,' replied the cook. 'Funny they don't see us!'

A broad stretch of lowly coast lay before the eyes of the men. It was of dunes topped with dark vegetation. The roar of the surf was plain, and sometimes they could see the white lip of a wave as it spun up the beach. A tiny house was blocked out black upon the sky. Southward, the slim lighthouse lifted its little grey length.

Tide, wind, and waves were swinging the dinghy northward. 'Funny they don't see us,' said the men.

The surf's roar was here dulled, but its tone was, nevertheless, thunderous and mighty. As the boat swam over the great rollers, the men sat listening to this roar. 'We'll swamp sure,' said everybody.

It is fair to say here that there was not a life-saving station within twenty miles in either direction, but the men did not know this fact, and in consequence they made dark and opprobrious remarks concerning the eyesight of the nation's life-savers. Four scowling men sat in the dinghy and surpassed records in the invention of epithets.

'Funny they don't see us.'

The light-heartedness of a former time had completely faded. To their sharpened minds it was easy to conjure pictures of all kinds of incompetency and blindness, and, indeed, cowardice. There was the shore of the populous land, and it was bitter and bitter to them that from it came no sign.

'Well,' said the captain, ultimately, 'I suppose we'll have to make a try for ourselves. If we stay out here too long, we'll none of us have strength left to swim after the boat swamps.'

And so the oiler, who was at the oars, turned the boat straight for the shore. There was a sudden tightening of muscles. There was some thinking.

'If we don't all get ashore –' said the captain. 'If we don't all get ashore, I suppose you fellows know where to send news of my finish?'

They then briefly exchanged some addresses and admonitions. As for the reflections of the men, there was a great deal of rage in them. Perchance they might be formulated thus: 'If I am going to be drowned – if I am going to be drowned – if I am going to be drowned, why, in the name of the seven mad gods who rule the sea, was I allowed to come thus far and contemplate sand and trees? Was I brought here merely to have my nose dragged away as I was about to nibble the sacred cheese of life? It is preposterous. If this old ninny-woman, Fate, cannot do better than this, she should be deprived of the management of men's fortunes. She is an old hen who knows not her intention. If she has decided to drown me, why did she not do it in the beginning and save me all this trouble? The whole affair is absurd . . . But no, she cannot mean to drown me. She dare not drown me. She cannot drown me. Not after all this work.' Afterward the man might have had an impulse to shake his fist at the clouds: 'Just you drown me, now, and then hear what I call you!'

The billows that came at this time were more formidable. They seemed always just about to break and roll over the little boat in a turmoil of foam. There was a preparatory and long growl in the speech of them. No mind unused to the sea would have concluded that the dinghy could ascend these sheer heights in time. The shore was still afar. The oiler was a wily surfman. 'Boys,' he said swiftly, 'she won't live three minutes more, and we're too far out to swim. Shall I take her to sea again, captain?'

'Yes! Go ahead!' said the captain.

This oiler, by a series of quick miracles, and fast and steady oarsmanship, turned the boat in the middle of the surf and took her safely to sea again.

There was a considerable silence as the boat bumped over the furrowed sea to deeper water. Then somebody in gloom spoke. 'Well, anyhow, they must have seen us from the shore by now.'

The gulls went in slanting flight up the wind toward the grey desolate east. A squall, marked by dingy clouds, and clouds brick-red, like smoke from a burning building, appeared from the south-east.

'What do you think of those life-saving people? Ain't they peaches?'

'Funny they haven't seen us.'

'Maybe they think we're out here for sport! Maybe they think we're fishin'. Maybe they think we're damned fools.'

It was a long afternoon. A changed tide tried to force them southward, but wind and wave said northward. Far ahead, where coast-line, sea, and sky formed their mighty angle, there were little dots which seemed to indicate a city on the shore.

'St Augustine?'

The captain shook his head. 'Too near Mosquito Inlet.'

And the oiler rowed, and then the correspondent rowed. Then the oiler rowed. It was a weary business. The human back can become the seat of more aches and pains than are registered in books for the composite anatomy of a regiment. It is a limited area, but it can become the theatre of innumerable muscular conflicts, tangles, wrenches, knots, and other comforts.

'Did you ever like to row, Billie?' asked the correspondent.

'No,' said the oiler. 'Hang it.'

When one exchanged the rowing-seat for a place in the bottom of the boat, he suffered a bodily depression that caused him to be careless of everything save an obligation to wiggle one finger. There was cold sea-water swashing to and fro in the boat, and he lay in it. His head, pillowed on a thwart, was within an inch of the swirl of a wave crest, and sometimes a particularly obstreperous sea came in-board and drenched him once more. But these matters did not annoy him. It is almost certain that if the boat had capsized he would have tumbled comfortably out upon the ocean as if he felt sure that it was a great soft mattress.

'Look! There's a man on the shore!'

'Where?'

'There! See 'im? See 'im?'

'Yes, sure! He's walking along.'

'Now he's stopped. Look! He's facing us!'

'He's waving at us!'

'So he is! By thunder!'

'Ah, now we're all right! Now we're all right! There'll be a boat out here for us in half-an-hour.'

'He's going on. He's running. He's going up to that house there.'

The remote beach seemed lower than the sea, and it required a searching glance to discern the little black figure. The captain saw a floating stick and they rowed to it. A bath-towel was by some weird chance in the boat, and, tying this on the stick, the captain waved it. The oarsman did not dare turn his head, so he was obliged to ask questions.

'What's he doing now?'

'He's standing still again. He's looking, I think . . . There he goes again. Towards the house . . . Now he's stopped again.'

'Is he waving at us?'

'No, not now! he was, though.'

'Look! There comes another man!'

'He's running.'

'Look at him go, would you.'

'Why, he's on a bicycle. Now he's met the other man. They're both waving at us. Look!'

'There comes something up the beach.'

'What the devil is that thing?'

'Why, it looks like a boat.'

'Why, certainly it's a boat.'

'No, it's on wheels.'

'Yes, so it is. Well, that must be the life-boat. They drag them along shore on a wagon.'

'That's the life-boat, sure.'

'No, by —, it's – it's an omnibus.'

'I tell you it's a life-boat.'

'It is not! It's an omnibus. I can see it plain. See? One of these big hotel omnibuses.'

'By thunder, you're right. It's an omnibus, sure as fate. What do you suppose they are doing with an omnibus? Maybe they are going around collecting the life-crew, hey?'

'That's it, likely. Look! There's a fellow waving a little black flag. He's standing on the steps of the omnibus. There come those other two fellows. Now they're all talking together. Look at the fellow with the flag. Maybe he ain't waving it.'

'That ain't a flag, is it? That's his coat. Why certainly, that's his coat.'

'So it is. It's his coat. He's taken it off and is waving it around his head. But would you look at him swing it.'

'Oh, say, there isn't any life-saving station there. That's just a winter resort omnibus that has brought over some of the boarders to see us drown.'

'What's that idiot with the coat mean? What's he signalling, anyhow?'

'It looks as if he were trying to tell us to go north. There must be a life-saving station up there.'

'No! He thinks we're fishing. Just giving us a merry hand. See? Ah, there, Billie.'

'Well, I wish I could make something out of those signals. What do you suppose he means?'

'He don't mean anything. He's just playing.'

'Well, if he'd just signal us to try the surf again, or to go to sea, and wait, or go north, or go south, or go to hell – there would be some reason in it. But look at him. He just stands there and keeps his coat revolving like a wheel. The ass!'

'There come more people.'

'Now there's quite a mob. Look! Isn't that a boat?'

'Where? Oh, I see where you mean. No, that's no boat.'

'That fellow is still waving his coat.'

'He must think we like to see him do that. Why don't he quit it? It don't mean anything.'

'I don't know. I think he is trying to make us go north. It must be that there's a life-saving station there somewhere.'

'Say, he ain't tired yet. Look at 'im wave.'

'Wonder how long he can keep that up. He's been revolving his coat ever since he caught sight of us. He's an idiot. Why aren't they getting men to bring a boat out? A fishing boat – one of those big yawls – could come out here all right. Why don't he do something?'

'Oh, it's all right, now.'

'They'll have a boat out here for us in less than no time, now that they've seen us.'

A faint yellow tone came into the sky over the low land. The shadows on the sea slowly deepened. The wind bore coldness with it, and the men began to shiver.

'Holy smoke!' said one, allowing his voice to express his impious mood, 'if we keep on monkeying out here! If we've got to flounder out here all night!'

'Oh, we'll never have to stay here all night! Don't you worry. They've seen us now, and it won't be long before they'll come chasing out after us.'

The shore grew dusky. The man waving a coat blended gradually into this gloom, and it swallowed in the same manner the omnibus and the group of people. The spray, when it dashed uproariously over the side, made the voyagers shrink and swear like men who were being branded.

'I'd like to catch the chump who waved the coat. I feel like soaking him one, just for luck.'

'Why? What did he do?'

'Oh, nothing, but then he seemed so damned cheerful.'

In the meantime the oiler rowed, and then the correspondent rowed, and then the oiler rowed. Grey-faced and bowed forward, they mechanically, turn by turn, plied the leaden oars. The form of the lighthouse had vanished from the southern horizon, but finally a pale star appeared, just lifting from the sea. The streaked saffron in the west passed before the all-merging darkness, and the sea to the east was black. The land had vanished, and was expressed only by the low and drear thunder of the surf.

'If I am going to be drowned – if I am going to be drowned – if I am going to be drowned, why, in the name of the seven mad gods who rule the sea, was I allowed to come thus far and contemplate sand and trees? Was I brought here merely to have my nose dragged away as I was about to nibble the sacred cheese of life?'

The patient captain, drooped over the water-jar, was sometimes obliged to speak to the oarsman.

'Keep her head up! Keep her head up!'

' "Keep her head up," sir.' The voices were weary and low.

This was surely a quiet evening. All save the oarsman lay heavily and listlessly in the boat's bottom. As for him, his eyes were just capable of noting the tall black waves that swept forward in a most sinister silence, save for an occasional subdued growl of a crest.

The cook's head was on a thwart, and he looked without interest at the water under his nose. He was deep in other scenes. Finally he spoke. 'Billie,' he murmured, dreamfully, 'what kind of pie do you like best?'

V

'Pie,' said the oiler and the correspondent, agitatedly. 'Don't talk about those things, blast you!'

'Well,' said the cook, 'I was just thinking about ham sandwiches, and –'

A night on the sea in an open boat is a long night. As darkness settled finally, the shine of the light, lifting from the sea in the south, changed to full gold. On the northern horizon a new light appeared, a small bluish gleam on the edge of the waters. These two lights were the furniture of the world. Otherwise there was nothing but waves.

Two men huddled in the stern, and distances were so magnificent in the dinghy that the rower was enabled to keep his feet partly warmed by thrusting them under his companions. Their legs indeed extended far under the rowing-seat until they touched the feet of the captain forward. Sometimes, despite the efforts of the tired oarsman, a wave came piling into the boat, an icy wave of the night, and the chilling water soaked them anew. They would twist their bodies for a moment and groan, and sleep the dead sleep once more, while the water in the boat gurgled, about them as the craft rocked.

The plan of the oiler and the correspondent was for one to row until he lost the ability, and then arouse the other from his sea-water couch in the bottom of the boat.

The oiler plied the oars until his head drooped forward, and the overpowering sleep blinded him. And he rowed yet afterward. Then he touched a man in the bottom of the boat, and called his name. 'Will you spell me for a little while?' he said, meekly.

'Sure, Billie,' said the correspondent, awakening and dragging himself to a sitting position. They exchanged places carefully, and the oiler, cuddling down in the sea-water at the cook's side, seemed to go to sleep instantly.

The particular violence of the sea had ceased. The waves came without snarling. The obligation of the man at the oars was to keep the boat headed so that the tilt of the rollers would not capsize her, and to preserve her from filling when the crests rushed past. The black waves were silent and hard to be seen in the darkness. Often one was almost upon the boat before the oarsman was aware.

In a low voice the correspondent addressed the captain. He was not sure that the captain was awake, although this iron man seemed to be always awake. 'Captain, shall I keep her making for that light north, sir?'

The same steady voice answered him. 'Yes. Keep it about two points off the port bow.'

The cook had tied a life-belt around himself in order to get even the warmth which this clumsy cork contrivance could donate, and he seemed almost stove-like when a rower, whose teeth invariably chattered wildly as soon as he ceased his labour, dropped down to sleep.

The correspondent, as he rowed, looked down at the two men sleeping under-foot. The cook's arm was around the oiler's shoulders, and, with their fragmentary clothing and haggard faces, they were the babes of the sea, a grotesque rendering of the old babes in the wood.

Later he must have grown stupid at his work. for suddenly there was a growling of water, and a crest came with a roar and a swash into the boat, and it was a wonder that it did not set the cook afloat in his life-belt. The cook continued to sleep, but the oiler sat up, blinking his eyes and shaking with the new cold.

'Oh, I'm awful sorry, Billie,' said the correspondent contritely.

'That's all right, old boy,' said the oiler, and lay down again and was asleep.

Presently it seemed that even the captain dozed, and the correspondent thought that he was the one man afloat on all the oceans. The wind had a voice as it came over the waves, and it was sadder than the end.

There was a long, loud swishing astern of the boat, and a gleaming trail of phosphorescence, like blue flame, was furrowed on the black waters. It might have been made by a monstrous knife.

Then there came a stillness, while the correspondent breathed with the open mouth and looked at the sea.

Suddenly there was another swish and another long flash of bluish light, and this time it was alongside the boat, and might almost have been reached with an oar. The correspondent saw an enormous fin speed like a shadow through the water, hurling the crystalline spray and leaving the long glowing trail.

The correspondent looked over his shoulder at the captain. His face was hidden, and he seemed to be asleep. He looked at the babes of the sea. They certainly were asleep. So, being bereft of sympathy, he leaned a little way to one side and swore softly into the sea.

But the thing did not then leave the vicinity of the boat. Ahead or astern, on one side or the other, at intervals long or short, fled the long sparkling streak, and there was to be heard the whiroo of the dark fin. The speed and power of the thing was greatly to be admired. It cut the water like a gigantic and keen projectile.

The presence of this biding thing did not affect the man with the same horror that it would if he had been a picnicker. He simply looked at the sea dully and swore in an undertone.

Nevertheless, it is true that he did not wish to be alone. He wished one of his companions to awaken by chance and keep him company with it. But the captain hung motionless over the water-jar, and the oiler and the cook in the bottom of the boat were plunged in slumber.

VI

''If I am going to be drowned – if I am going to be drowned – if I am going to be drowned, why, in the name of the seven mad gods who rule the sea, was I allowed to come thus far and contemplate sand and trees?'

During this dismal night, it may be remarked that a man would conclude that it was really the intention of the seven mad gods to drown him, despite the abominable injustice of it. For it was certainly an abominable injustice to drown a man who had worked so hard, so hard. The man felt it would be a crime most unnatural. Other people had drowned at sea since galleys swarmed with painted sails, but still –

When it occurs to a man that nature does not regard him as important, and that she feels she would not maim the universe by disposing of him, he at first wishes to throw bricks at the temple, and he hates deeply the fact that there are no bricks and no temples. Any visible expression of nature would surely be pelleted with his jeers.

Then, if there be no tangible thing to hoot at he feels, perhaps, the desire to confront a personification and indulge in pleas, bowed to one knee, and with hands supplicant, saying: 'Yes, but I love myself.'

A high cold star on a winter's night is the word he feels that she says to him. Thereafter he knows the pathos of his situation.

The men in the dinghy had not discussed these matters, but each had, no doubt, reflected upon them in silence and according to his mind. There was seldom any expression upon their faces save the general one of complete weariness. Speech was devoted to the business of the boat.

To chime the notes of his emotion, a verse mysteriously entered the correspondent's head. He had even forgotten that he had forgotten this verse, but it was suddenly in his mind.

A soldier of the Legion lay dying in Algiers,
There was lack of woman's nursing, there was dearth of woman's
    tears;
But a comrade stood beside him, and he took that comrade's hand,
And he said: 'I shall never see my own, my native land.'

In his childhood, the correspondent had been made acquainted with the fact that a soldier of the Legion lay dying in Algiers, but he had never regarded the fact as important. Myriads of his school-fellows had informed him of the soldier's plight, but the dinning had naturally ended by making him perfectly indifferent. He had never considered it his affair that a soldier of the Legion lay dying in Algiers, nor had it appeared to him as a matter for sorrow. It was less to him than the breaking of a pencil's point.

Now, however, it quaintly came to him as a human, living thing. It was no longer merely a picture of a few throes in the breast of a poet, meanwhile drinking tea and warming his feet at the grate; it was an actuality – stern, mournful, and fine.

The correspondent plainly saw the soldier. He lay on the sand with his feet out straight and still. While his pale left hand was upon his chest in an attempt to thwart the going of his life, the blood came between his fingers. In the far Algerian distance, a city of low square forms was set against a sky that was faint with the last sunset hues. The correspondent, plying the oars and dreaming of the slow and slower movements of the lips of the soldier, was moved by a profound and perfectly impersonal comprehension. He was sorry for the soldier of the Legion who lay dying in Algiers.

The thing which had followed the boat and waited, had evidently grown bored at the delay. There was no longer to be heard the slash of the cut-water, and there was no longer the flame of the long trail. The light in the north still glimmered, but it was apparently no nearer to the boat. Sometimes the boom of the surf rang in the correspondent's ears, and he turned the craft seaward then and rowed harder. Southward, some one had evidently built a watch-fire on the beach. It was too low and too far to be seen, but it made a shimmering, roseate reflection upon the bluff back of it, and this could be discerned from the boat. The wind came stronger, and sometimes a wave suddenly raged out like a mountain-cat, and there was to be seen the sheen and sparkle of a broken crest.

The captain, in the bow, moved on his water-jar and sat erect. 'Pretty long night,' he observed to the correspondent. He looked at the shore. 'Those life-saving people take their time.'

'Did you see that shark playing around?'

'Yes, I saw him. He was a big fellow, all right.'

'Wish I had known you were awake.'

Later the correspondent spoke into the bottom of the boat.

'Billie!' There was a slow and gradual disentanglement. 'Billie, will you spell me?'

'Sure,' said the oiler.

As soon as the correspondent touched the cold comfortable sea-water in the bottom of the boat, and had huddled close to the cook's life-belt he was deep in sleep, despite the fact that his teeth played all the popular airs. This sleep was so good to him that it was but a moment before he heard a voice call his name in a tone that demonstrated the last stages of exhaustion. 'Will you spell me?'

'Sure, Billie.'

The light in the north had mysteriously vanished, but the correspondent took his course from the wide-awake captain.

Later in the night they took the boat farther out to sea, and the captain directed the cook to take one oar at the stern and keep the boat facing the seas. He was to call out if he should hear the thunder of the surf. This plan enabled the oiler and the correspondent to get respite together. 'We'll give those boys a chance to get into shape again,' said the captain. They curled down and, after a few preliminary chatterings and trembles, slept once more the dead sleep. Neither knew they had bequeathed to the cook the company of another shark, or perhaps the same shark.

As the boat caroused on the waves, spray occasionally bumped over the side and gave them a fresh soaking, but this had no power to break their repose. The ominous slash of the wind and the water affected them as it would have affected mummies.

'Boys,' said the cook, with the notes of every reluctance in his voice, 'she's drifted in pretty close. I guess one of you had better take her to sea again.' The correspondent, aroused, heard the crash of the toppled crests.

As he was rowing, the captain gave him some whisky-and-water, and this steadied the chills out of him. 'If I ever get ashore and anybody shows me even a photograph of an oar –'

At last there was a short conversation.

'Billie . . . Billie, will you spell me?'

'Sure,' said the oiler.

VII

WHEN the correspondent again opened his eyes, the sea and the sky were each of the grey hue of the dawning. Later, carmine and gold was painted upon the waters. The morning appeared finally, in its splendour, with a sky of pure blue, and the sunlight flamed on the tips of the waves.

On the distant dunes were set many little black cottages, and a tall white windmill reared above them. No man, nor dog, nor bicycle appeared on the beach. The cottages might have formed a deserted village.

The voyagers scanned the shore. A conference was held in the boat. 'Well,' said the captain, 'if no help is coming we might better try a run through the surf right away. If we stay out here much longer we will be too weak to do anything for ourselves at all.' The others silently acquiesced in this reasoning. The boat was headed for the beach. The correspondent wondered if none ever ascended the tall wind-tower, and if then they never looked seaward. This tower was a giant, standing with its back to the plight of the ants. It represented in a degree, to the correspondent, the serenity of nature amid the struggles of the individual – nature in the wind, and nature in the vision of men. She did not seem cruel to him then, nor beneficent, nor treacherous, nor wise. But she was indifferent, flatly indifferent. It is, perhaps, plausible that a man in this situation, impressed with the unconcern of the universe, should see the innumerable flaws of his life, and have them taste wickedly in his mind and wish for another chance. A distinction between right and wrong seems absurdly clear to him, then, in this new ignorance of the grave-edge, and he understands that if he were given another opportunity he would mend his conduct and his words, and be better and brighter during an introduction or at a tea.

'Now, boys,' said the captain, 'she is going to swamp, sure. All we can do is to work her in as far as possible, and then when she swamps, pile out and scramble for the beach. Keep cool now, and don't jump until she swamps sure.'

The oiler took the oars. Over his shoulders he scanned the surf. 'Captain,' he said, 'I think I'd better bring her about, and keep her head-on to the seas and back her in.'

'All right, Billie,' said the captain. 'Back her in.' The oiler swung the boat then and, seated in the stern, the cook and the correspondent were obliged to look over their shoulders to contemplate the lonely and indifferent shore.

The monstrous in-shore rollers heaved the boat high until the men were again enabled to see the white sheets of water scudding up the slanted beach. 'We won't get in very close,' said the captain. Each time a man could wrest his attention from the rollers, he turned his glance toward the shore, and in the expression of the eyes during this contemplation there was a singular quality. The correspondent, observing the others, knew that they were not afraid, but the full meaning of their glances was shrouded.

As for himself, he was too tired to grapple fundamentally with the fact. He tried to coerce his mind into thinking of it, but the mind was dominated at this time by the muscles, and the muscles said they did not care. It merely occurred to him that if he should drown it would be a shame.

There were no hurried words, no pallor, no plain agitation. The men simply looked at the shore. 'Now, remember to get well clear of the boat when you jump,' said the captain.

Seaward the crest of a roller suddenly fell with a thunderous crash, and the long white comber came roaring down upon the boat.

'Steady now,' said the captain. The men were silent. They turned their eyes from the shore to the comber and waited. The boat slid up the incline, leaped at the furious top, bounced over it, and swung down the long back of the wave. Some water had been shipped and the cook bailed it out.

But the next crest crashed also. The tumbling boiling flood of white water caught the boat and whirled it almost perpendicular. Water swarmed in from all sides. The correspondent had his hands on the gunwale at this time, and when the water entered at that place he swiftly withdrew his fingers, as if he objected to wetting them.

The little boat, drunken with this weight of water, reeled and snuggled deeper into the sea.

'Bail her out, cook! Bail her out,' said the captain.

'All right, captain,' said the cook.

'Now, boys, the next one will do for us, sure,' said the oiler. 'Mind to jump clear of the boat.'

The third wave moved forward, huge, furious, implacable. It fairly swallowed the dinghy, and almost simultaneously the men tumbled into the sea. A piece of lifebelt had lain in the bottom of the boat, and as the correspondent went overboard he held this to his chest with his left hand.

The January water was icy, and he reflected immediately that it was colder than he had expected to find it off the coast of Florida. This appeared to his dazed mind as a fact important enough to be noted at the time. The coldness of the water was sad; it was tragic. This fact was somehow so mixed and confused with his opinion of his own situation that it seemed almost a proper reason for tears. The water was cold.

When he came to the surface he was conscious of little but the noisy water. Afterward he saw his companions in the sea. The oiler was ahead in the race. He was swimming strongly and rapidly. Off to the correspondent's left, the cook's great white and corked back bulged out of the water, and in the rear the captain was hanging with his one good hand to the keel of the overturned dinghy.

There is a certain immovable quality to a shore, and the correspondent wondered at it amid the confusion of the sea.

It seemed also very attractive, but the correspondent knew that it was a long journey, and he paddled leisurely. The piece of life-preserver lay under him, and sometimes he whirled down the incline of a wave as if he were on a hand-sled.

But finally he arrived at a place in the sea where travel was beset with difficulty. He did not pause swimming to inquire what manner of current had caught him, but there his progress ceased. The shore was set before him like a bit of scenery on a stage, and he looked at it and understood with his eyes each detail of it.

As the cook passed, much farther to the left, the captain was calling to him, 'Turn over on your back, cook! Turn over on your back and use the oar.'

'All right, sir.' The cook turned on his back, and, paddling with an oar, went ahead as if he were a canoe.

Presently the boat also passed to the left of the correspondent with the captain clinging with one hand to the keel. He would have appeared like a man raising himself to look over a board fence, if it were not for the extraordinary gymnastics of the boat. The correspondent marvelled that the captain could still hold to it.

They passed on, nearer to shore – the oiler, the cook, the captain – and following them went the water-jar, bouncing gaily over the seas.

The correspondent remained in the grip of this strange new enemy – a current. The shore, with its white slope of sand and its green bluff, topped with little silent cottages, was spread like a picture before him. It was very near to him then, but he was impressed as one who in a gallery looks at a scene from Brittany or Holland.

He thought: 'I am going to drown? Can it be possible? Can it be possible? Can it be possible?' Perhaps an individual must consider his own death to be the final phenomenon of nature.

But later a wave perhaps whirled him out of this small deadly current, for he found suddenly that he could again make progress toward the shore. Later still, he was aware that the captain, clinging with one hand to the keel of the dinghy, had his face turned away from the shore and toward him, and was calling his name. 'Come to the boat! Come to the boat!'

In his struggle to reach the captain and the boat, he reflected that when one gets properly wearied, drowning must really be a comfortable arrangement, a cessation of hostilities accompanied by a large degree of relief, and he was glad of it, for the main thing in his mind for some moments had been horror of the temporary agony. He did not wish to be hurt.

Presently he saw a man running along the shore. He was undressing with most remarkable speed. Coat, trousers, shirt, everything flew magically off him.

'Come to the boat,' called the captain.

'All right, captain.' As the correspondent paddled, he saw the captain let himself down to bottom and leave the boat. Then the correspondent performed his one little marvel of the voyage. A large wave caught him and flung him with ease and supreme speed completely over the boat and far beyond it. It struck him even then as an event in gymnastics, and a true miracle of the sea. An overturned boat in the surf is not a plaything to a swimming man.

The correspondent arrived in water that reached only to his waist, but his condition did not enable him to stand for more than a moment. Each wave knocked him into a heap, and the under-tow pulled at him.

Then he saw the man who had been running and undressing, and undressing and running, come bounding into the water. He dragged ashore the cook, and then waded towards the captain, but the captain waved him away, and sent him to the correspondent. He was naked, naked as a tree in winter, but a halo was about his head, and he shone like a saint. He gave a strong pull, and a long drag, and a bully heave at the correspondent's hand. The correspondent, schooled in the minor formulae, said: 'Thanks, old man.' But suddenly the man cried: 'What's that?' He pointed a swift finger. The correspondent said: 'Go.'

In the shallows, face downward, lay the oiler. His forehead touched sand that was periodically, between each wave, clear of the sea.

The correspondent did not know all that transpired afterward. When he achieved safe ground he fell, striking the sand with each particular part of his body. It was as if he had dropped from a roof, but the thud was grateful to him.

It seems that instantly the beach was populated with men with blankets, clothes, and flasks, and women with coffee-pots and all the remedies sacred to their minds. The welcome of the land to the men from the sea was warm and generous, but a still and dripping shape was carried slowly up the beach, and the land's welcome for it could only be the different and sinister hospitality of the grave.

When it came night, the white waves paced to and fro in the moonlight, and the wind brought the sound of the great sea's voice to the men on shore, and they felt that they could then be interpreters.

A. E. Dingle

Bound for Rio Grande

I

THE old man's broken teeth gleamed through tight, thin lips whenever his rheumy eyes glimpsed the lofty spars of the clipper in the bay. She was the only deepwaterman in port.

'Blood boat!' he chattered. 'A blood boat. But you don't git no more o' my blood, not by a damn sight!'

Hastily turning away, the old man shambled along the wharf, at the end of which stood an office. Opposite the office, bright and cheery against the grey and dirt of the waterside, a tiny store kept its door open, revealing an interior to set the pulses of an ancient mariner leaping. Never a yellow oilskin, nor a bit of rope; nor one block or shackle offended the eye grown weary through half a century of salty servitude.

Glossy plugs of black tobacco; clay pipes of virgin whiteness and lissome shape; woolly comforters and stout shore-going winter socks; old, tasty cheese and soft, white bread; fat sausage and luscious, boneless ham; all these things mere fancies of the dreaming sailor-man at sea, were clear to the view of old Pegwell through the open door of the little store as he paced up and down before the office, waiting for the man to whom he was to make application for the job of watchman of the wharf.

There was a sharp hint of frost in the air; a sharper threat of wind. There was just enough of brine and breeze, just a trace. It smelt of salt water and of boats, with never an obstrusive reminder of hardcase deepwater ships.

Ah! There was a snug harbour indeed for a battered old seadog. If a chap could expect to come at last into such a fair haven as that little store now he wouldn't mind a few decades of bitter travail at sea.

'Hell's delight! Fat chance I got o' savin' money now!' he growled.

He sought for a match, found none. It was just his luck. But he had a few pennies. He would buy matches in that store. He waited until the stream of lunch customers thinned out, and entered.

'Box o' lucifers,' he demanded, slapping down the coin. His eyes wandered around the homey little place. There were things he had not noticed before from outside. Red candy; bright painted toys; rubber balls. Children came there evidently. What sort of children would come to that neighbourhood for toys?

'Your matches, sir,' said a rippling, laughing voice; and old Pegwell turned around sharply and discovered why children might well come to that store. Men, too. A twenty-year-old girl was offering him matches. Her big brown eyes danced mischievously. She was as trim as a brand-new China clipper.

'Thank e' ma'am,' said Pegwell, as he grabbed the matches and shuffled out, dazzled and confused by the vision. He was still dazzled, his box of matches unopened, when he stumbled against the man he had waited to see.

'Heard you wanted a watchman, sir,' said old Pegwell respectfully. He proffered a bundle of ship's discharges as evidence of character. The man glanced through them, glanced keenly at the old man, and nodded.

'Night work,' he said. 'Six to six. If you suit, in a month I'll give you a day shift, turn and turn about. Nothing much to do here, but you'll have to watch out for strangers. Lot of crooks on the water nowadays. Rum, dope, all sorts. Start tonight.'

Old Pegwell had landed his first shore job. For the first time since starting out to earn his own living he could afford to gaze curiously at a sailorman, going large, staggering along to the next blind pig.

'Sailors is a lot o' lummoxes,' he decided.

'Like kids.'

> If yuh save up yer money, an' don't git on th' rocks,
> Yuh'll have plenty o' tobacker in yer old tobacker box,

he sang quaveringly.

He pulled up sharply, ceasing his song, and drifted over toward the little store again. He would have to find some place to live, to sleep at least. That girl looked different from others he had known. Perhaps she would tell him where to seek. He walked in, more confidently than before. He had a shore job now.

'Plug o' tobacker, miss,' he asked for. The girl appeared from behind a provision case, putting on a smile as she emerged. A man thrust back deeper into the shadow. Pegwell saw nothing of the forced smile or the man. His eyes were roving, taking in the wealth of the stock. When he turned to take his tobacco the girl's smile was sunny enough. He felt encouraged.

'Beg y' pardon, miss, I just got a job on th' wharf, and thought likely you could direc' me where to git a bed, cheap. I ain't a pertickler chap. Just es long 's there ain't too many bugs, or –'

'You got a job on the wharf?' interrupted a man's voice. A youth, who might have been good-looking if he could have changed his eyes, came from behind the provision case and scowled surlily. 'What job?'

'Watchman,' said Pegwell importantly. 'Night watchman. Know any place I kin get a doss?'

'How did you get to hear about this job? I'm livin' here right along, lookin' for a job, and a stranger comes along and lands it over my head. You're a sailor, ain't you?'

'No; watchman,' retorted old Pegwell. 'Was a sailorman. Had good discharges. I'm a watchman now. D'you know of a place I kin sleep, miss?'

The youth dragged the girl aside, and they muttered together, ignoring Pegwell. Presently the girl spoke sharply angrily.

'It's best for you to go away, Larry. It's a good thing you never heard of the wharf job. Too many old friends hanging around there! You're signed on in the *Stella*. Now you go. You know what the judge said. Go to work, like a decent fellow, and you won't be watched like a –'

'Go to work? Hell! I'm willing to go to work, Mary, but what d'you want to shove me off into a damned old square rigger for? Ain't there work to be got –'

'It's best that you go away for a while,' insisted the girl. 'You were lucky to escape jail when that gang of smugglers got caught. I'm not sure now that the judge was satisfied about you. If you stay around here they're sure to watch you –'

'Beg pardon, miss, but if you know of a place –' interrupted Pegwell impatiently. Larry swung around and grinned crookedly.

'All right, sister,' he told her. 'I'll do it to please you.' He took Pegwell's arms. 'I'll find you a bed, old timer. What time d'you go to work?'

'Six. Want to get a sleepin' place afore that.'

'Meet me here at five-thirty. I'll have a bunk for you by then.'

Pegwell started off for a walk, but streets were a barren wilderness to him. He gravitated toward the harbour. He found himself somehow in front of the little store. It was a long time from five-thirty. Methodically he noted the contents of the window, grew amazed at the number and variety.

'Larry hasn't come back yet,' the girl called out from the store. 'Won't you wait inside?'

Pegwell looked sheepish. Sailors of the deep waters were always easily abashed in the presence of a decent woman. Pegwell scarcely dared to look up from the floor as he entered. But the girl began to chatter to him, and he felt at ease when she handed him a match for his cold pipe. In ten minutes he was spinning her fearsome yarns. In half an hour they were friends. She confided little scraps of her own affairs.

'Larry's a good fellow,' she said, a bit sadly. 'Too good. He's easy to lead. There has been a lot of smuggling along the front lately, and he ought to have kept away. But he always seems to have money, never goes to work, and when a big capture was made he was under suspicion. The judge told him he had better go to work, then folks would be apt to believe that he was innocent. Of course he is innocent! My brother Larry couldn't be a crook, Mr Pegwell. But he has been under suspicion, and I made him join that big sailing ship, the *Stella*, for a voyage. When he comes back everything will be forgotten, and he can – Oh, here's Jack! Excuse me, Mr Pegwell.'

A tall, brown-faced man of thirty limped in. Pegwell was no keen-eyed Solon concerning women of Mary Bland's sort; but when he saw her pretty face light up and her big brown eyes flash at the appearance of this good-looking fellow who limped on a shortened leg, he knew he was intruding. Puffing furiously at his pipe, he stumped out upon the front.

At five-thirty Larry found Pegwell sitting on the cap log of the wharf.

'Come on, old timer. I got a fine bunk for you,' said Larry. Pegwell followed him.

'I heared you be goin' in th' *Stella*,' remarked Pegwell.

'I ain't proud of it,' retorted Larry.

'I just come home in her. A hell ship, she is! Can sail, though. You ain't old an' stiff. Do yer work an' don't give th' mates no slack, an' you'll be all kiff, me son.'

Larry glanced curiously at the queer old man who thought fit to preach duty to him.

They turned down by a disused and evil-smelling fish dock, out of sight of a growing district.

'Have to cross the creek in a boat,' grinned Larry. 'Save time, see. You have to be on the job, now, but other times you can walk around. Here y' are.'

At the foot of a perpendicular ladder of boards nailed on a slimy pile a boat lay. Three husky boatmen grinned up knowingly at Larry. A blue canvas sea bag lay in the bottom of the boat, doubled up, like a dead man.

'Take good care of my old friend,' Larry ordered. He gently drew Pegwell to the ladder. 'Hurry up, old timer. Soon's they see you snug they have to come back for me.'

Pegwell stepped on the ladder.

'Ho!' he said. 'That's your sea bag, hey? Well, me son, do yer work an' give the mates no slack, an' –'

Something heavy fell upon his grey old head. He tumbled into the boat. As he pitched forward Pegwell heard the laugh of his friend Larry, and he realized the treatment awaiting him.

The tall clipper put to sea. On her forecastlehead men tramped drearily around the capstan. Hard-bitten officers cursed them; an exasperated tugboat skipper bawled; the anchor clung tenaciously to the mud.

> An' awa-ay, Rio! Awa-ay, Rio!
> Sing fare yew well, my bonny young gal,
> We are boun' fer Rio Grande!

A quavery, broken old pipe raised that chantey. The mate left the knighthead, plunging in among the desolate crew, thumping, thumping, cursing venomously.

'You sojers!' he yelped. 'You double-left-legged sojers! Here's old Noah come to life again, and you let him show you your work! Heave, blind you! Heave! Sing out, old Noah! Why, damn my eyes, if it ain't old Pegwell come with us again!'

The mate stood off a pace, staring at Pegwell. Sailormen rarely made two voyages in the *Stella*.

'I didn't join, sir,' protested Pegwell, ceasing his song. All the men stopped. Pegwell had tried to persuade the captain he was not one of his crew as soon as he recovered his wits. The result had been painful. 'I got to be on the job at six, sir. I'll lose my new job. I wuz shanghaied–'

A fist thumped him hard between the shoulders, driving him back to his capstan bar with coughing lungs.

'Sing out! Start something! Heave, damn you!' retorted the mate, and fell upon the miserable gang tooth and nail. The tug hooted owlishly.

> A jolly good ship, an' a jolly good crew:
> Awa-ay, Rio!
> A jolly good mate, an' a good skipper, too,
> An' we're boun' for Rio Grande!

Pegwell tramped around the capstan. A donkey yoked to the bar of a mill. A sailor bound by a lifetime of hard usage to a habit of obedience.

Pegwell's bunk had bugs. All the bunks had bugs. Pegwell's bunk was beneath a sweat leak where a bit of dry rot had crumbled a corner of a deck beam. But Larry's sea bag, a blue canvas bag made by a sailorman, revealed itself full of amazing comforts. The old fellow had never owned such a bag. There were blankets. Woollen, not woolly. Warm underwear, stockings, shirts. Good oilskins, leakproof boots. There was a real steel razor; a real steel sheath-knife. A great bundle of soap and matches; white enamelware dish and pannikin; and a dainty thing that puzzled Pegwell until he opened it. It was a folder of blue

141

BOUND FOR RIO GRANDE

cloth, tied about with a silken cord. On the flat side was worked in silk, beautifully, 'Larry; from Mary.'

Inside, cunning pockets were full of needles, thread, buttons, scissors. And tucked into the innermost fold was a note, in a slender hand bearing signs of stress, bidding Larry act the man, wishing him luck, praying for his safe return. The feel of it gave old Pegwell a warm thrill.

'Hey, me son, I want that bunk!' he announced grimly, shaking the shoulder of a sleeping ordinary seaman whose bunk was leakless. 'C'm on. Out of it! Able seamen comes fust, me lad.'

Pegwell carefully placed his needle case in a dry place, then hauled the youth out onto the filthy floor, cotton blanket and all. Even youth must yield to experience when youth is seasick, and experience runs along lines of deep water pully-haul.

Pegwell now had the cleanest, driest bunk in the forecastle. He stole lemons from the steward, which he hid cunningly. From time to time he cut one in slices, fastened it to ship's side or bunk board, thereby driving puzzled bugs to other, less exclusive quarters. He stole nails from Chips; made shelves for his little comforts, pegs for his fine new clothes. He stole a bit of white line from the bosun and made a pair of flat sennit bands by which his spare blanket swung from the bunk above.

By the time the clipper crossed the line Pegwell only dimly remembered Larry's treachery. He only mistily recalled the job he had got but had never worked at. It was easy for the old man to slip back into the habits of a lifetime; even though the ship was a hard place. The great outstanding point was that for the first time in his dreary life old Pegwell sailed deep water possessed of everything necessary for comfort, and some luxuries to boot. And this he owed to Mary Bland.

Old Pegwell usually fell asleep with a flash-back of memory to a snug little store on a dingy waterside, overladen with a stock of wonders, presided over by a laughing girl whose big, brown, friendly eyes sometimes held just a trace of trouble. Then he would think darkly of Larry, only to sink into sound slumber in the warmth of Larry's woollies under Larry's blankets.

II

PEGWELL'S bunk was no longer dry. No man's bunk was. The forecastle was a reeling, freezing, weeping dungeon peopled with miserable devils to whom hell would have been heaven. For thirty days the clipper had been battered by a northwesterly gale off Cape Horn.

When a man came from the wheel after a two hours' trick he was blue, and tottery, and grinning, and more than a little insane.

Pegwell stood his wheel warm and dry. He felt the bitterness of the weather and the ship's stress, but for once his old bones were not racked with extreme cold. The ship steered badly. They sent the young ordinary seamen to hold the lee spokes.

'You just put yer weight to it when I shoves the helm up or down, me son,' said Pegwell. The lad's teeth chattered; his lanky body, undernourished, 'twixt boy and man, shook like a royal mast under a thrashing sail.

'Y – yessir!' he chattered, fearfully.

Pegwell glanced sharply at the lad once or twice. Since their first encounter over the change of bunks, the lad had not been remarkable for politeness toward the old man. But there was no hint of impudence in that 'Yessir!' The boy looked blue.

Grumbling, taking a hand from the wheel when he could, gripping a spoke desperately to check it, the old man peeled off his heavy monkey jacket.

'Slip into this yer jacket, me son!' he roared, and put his shoulder to the spokes, bringing the ship to her course before the mate arrived. The lad thawed. When the watch was up, he was glowing. Old Pegwell was warm, but wet through with driving snow. He watched his chance to shuffle along the main deck between seas. The lad, less cautious, started first.

When they were in the deep waist, the new helmsman let the ship go off and a mile long hissing sea reared up and fell aboard the length of her. Pegwell grabbed a lifeline. When the decks cleared themselves through the ports, he clawed his way choking and blinded to the forecastle, soaked to the skin, his broken teeth chattering with the icy chill.

'Where's th' young feller?' he chattered.

'I see him bashed up against th' galley,' growled the man nearest. 'He'll git here. Can't lose them kind.'

He didn't 'git here'. The young ordinary seaman never rounded the Horn. He went overboard to death wearing old Pegwell's monkey jacket.

Making northing and westing with dry decks, though the wind was bitterly cold, men with all the sailorman's improvidence discarded tattered oilskins and soggy socks. And with all the fiendish frailty of Cape Horn weather, the fair wind blew itself out, a rolling calm followed, and then another, fiercer northwesterly gale shrieked down and drove the ship back into the murderous grey seas to the southward.

Pegwell clambered stiffly out of the rigging after re-tying the points of the reefed main topsail. The maindeck was a seething chaos of rope-snarled water. In the roaring torrent men were being hurled along the deck. Only a frantically waving arm or leg indicated that a man was not dead. Then a greater sea thundered aboard. It smashed the boat gallows. The boats hung over the side, precariously held by the ropes.

A spare topmast was torn loose from chain lashings and chocks: a massive stick of Oregon pine, roughly squared, it hurtled aft on the torrent, broke a sailor's half drowned body cruelly, and crashed end on against the poop bulkhead.

Pegwell and the watch fought with the spar. The seas enbued the timber with devilish spite. Twice all hands were torn from their hold, rolled about the flooded decks in the icy water, battered near to death by the murderous stick.

In a lull they secured the spar. The boats were gone. They picked up tangled gear, and took two mangled men from the meshes.

The wind struck afresh. It staggered the ship. And while she staggered and hung poised another chuckling sea climbed over the six foot bulwarks and filled her decks.

'Bill's hurted bad, now, sir,' screamed Pegwell, shivering in the grip of cold and numb agony. Bill was the bosun. He hung twisted and pallid between the two men who lifted him. They bore him forward. Chips stood across the sill of the smashed door of the tiny cabin they shared.

'This ain't no place for a hurted man!' Chips grumbled. 'Tell th' Old Man he ought t' be took care of aft.'

They told the skipper.

'No room aft,' the skipper howled at them. 'Put him in the forecastle if it's any drier.'

They bore the man below. Instinctively they laid him in old Pegwell's bunk, for it was driest. All were wet. Pegwell's at least boasted woollen coverings.

Pegwell himself covered the silent form with a blanket. He needed no hint to cover the pallid face too. He made no protest when a sailor gently pulled another blanket from under the bosun.

'Jack's cruel cold, mate,' said the sailor. He wrapped Jack, another storm victim, in the blanket with roughened hands that trembled.

Overhead the seas thundered on deck. The *Stella* fought her stubborn away against the gale under three lower topsails, reefed upper main topsail, and treble reefed foresail with a ribbon of fore topmast staysail.

The gale died out. A fair wind came. The ship sped north again, scarred but sound, clothed in new canvas, triumphant. They buried Bill and Jack in Pegwell's bedding.

By this time Pegwell had little left of his grand outfit. As the rags of his mates gave out, he grumblingly gave of his store. Grumbled and gave. That was Pegwell. But he never let go of that little blue cloth needle case inscribed, 'Larry; from Mary.' Slyly he had picked at the stitches until the word 'Larry' was becoming indistinguishable. When a few more threads fell out he could show his treasure to incredulous sailormen, and they would never know that the obliterated name was not his own.

The crew scuttled from the *Stella* like rats when she docked. Only Pegwell hung on. Alone of the outward bound crew before the mast, he stubbornly resisted all the efforts of the mates to get him out. They could ship a new crew homeward at half the wages paid outward. None of the deserters waited for their wages. Their forfeited pay was so much profit to the ship. But Pegwell refused to be driven out. Cheerless and bare his bunk might be. It was. There was always the little blue folded housewife to remind him that he had a shore job once over against a snug little store. And the ambition that had flamed then still burned.

As for quitting the ship, Pegwell had wages due. Not a lot, but wages still. If he completed the voyage, drawing no advance whatever, buying nothing from the slop chest, he would have coming to him a nice little nest egg which might hatch into a home at last. The nest egg loomed big to the captain.

'Set him to chipping cable,' said the skipper. 'Work him up!'

The mates worked him up, cruelly, but they could not work him out.

Homeward bound round the Horn, Pegwell showed his little blue housewife to the new hands. They were a hard lot. They made ribald fun about it. They stole his poor bedding, and dared him to identify it. He endured. They stole his sea boots. Pegwell endured that, too. But somebody stole his little blue housewife, worked in silk, '–; from Mary,' and there was a fight.

It was a young weasel of a wastrel who tried to prevent Pegwell from taking back his treasure. A weasel bred in the muck of the water front; cunning and full of devious fighting tricks. But the old seaman fought on sure feet on a reeling deck; fought with righteous fury swelling his breast; fought without feeling the brutal knee or the gouging thumb. And he beat his man, recovered his treasure, and earned much freedom from molestation.

In the bleak, soul-searching gales off Cape Stiff, Pegwell suffered intensely. He shivered and froze in silence.

The old sailor had always his little blue cloth treasure. He whispered his troubles to it as he shivered in his wet bed – it was the one comfort nobody could take from him. He might shake with cold and wet all through a watch below, but there was ever before him the vision of that snug little store, the pretty, laughing girl whose big brown eyes yet held a trace of trouble. Somehow he grew to fasten the responsibility for that trouble on Larry. And, once established, his own grievance against the man smouldered fiercer.

When the tall clipper furled her sails in her home port again, Pegwell's bitterness against Larry Bland had intensified to such a degree as to surprise the old chap himself. Bitterness formed no part of his real nature. But it was winter again; the snow fell; the streets, from the ship, looked dreary and inhospitable. And old Pegwell had nothing but rags to cover his aching bones.

The rest of the fo'mast hands had drawn something on account of wages and gone ashore to spend that and mortgage the balance due. But not old Pegwell. He would carry ashore every dollar coming to him from the voyage he ought never to have made. He would buy a suit of clothes and stout shoes that would last, put the rest of his money in safe hands, then look for Larry.

'It'll be him and me fer it!' he muttered.

III

THE ship paid off. Soulless wretches who had whined and cringed under the punishment of the sea rolled up bold and blusterous, full of hot courage at twenty-five cents a hot shot, cursing captain and mates and ship as they took their pitiful pay.

In an hour Pegwell entered the little store, and in ten seconds more a Cape Horn Voyage in a cardcase packet was a vanished horror. The big brown eyes of Mary Bland glistened with welcome, even though at first they had been cloudy with uncertainty.

'I am so glad to see you again, Pegwell,' she cried. 'It was so good of you to change places with Larry. I hope you had a good voyage. Won't you come inside?'

Pegwell grinned sourly as he followed her into the snug little room behind the shop. He had meant to say something about that change of jobs. Instead, with a warmth seeping through his bones clear to his heart, mellowing it again, he forgot Larry and smoked himself into rosy visions under the musical spell of her voice.

In an hour they were as intimate as before the *Stella* went out. Mary had told him, shyly, that Jack wanted a speedy wedding; she had barely hinted that brother Larry was a stumbling block, immediately suppressing the hint. She had offered to work Pegwell's name into the little blue housewife where the word 'Larry' had been picked out; and when she took it from him her eyes were suspiciously moist. Pegwell noticed it, though the girl tried hard to hide her feelings.

Then Jack came in and old Pegwell went out. The gladness in Mary's eyes, the pride in those of the stalwart cripple, gave the old mariner a thrill. It made him boil, too. There was a couple just aching for each other, hindered by a waster of a brother not worth a crocodile's tear.

'Hullo, old Pegwell,' smiled Jack as he passed. He stuck out a strong brown hand in a hearty grip. 'Mighty glad to see you again. Ought to stay this time. Going to buy Mary's shop, she tells me. Hurry up, old fellow. She's keeping me waiting all on your account.'

Jack laughed, and went to Mary's side, leaving Pegwell wondering.

He waited out in the cold street until Jack came out, then joined him in his walk and put the question bluntly:

'What's Larry up to?'

Jack was serious. His smile fled at the blunt demand. Anger was in his eyes, but he dismissed it. Pegwell, shrewder perhaps than he was given credit for being, noticed these little things. He put two and two together handily enough, and found the amount was four – no more or less.

'I wish Larry would either get bumped off or caught with the goods, Pegwell,' Jack said. 'He's breaking Mary's heart. She won't believe any wrong about him, yet she knows he's bound hellbent for ruin. If he was dead she would be better off. The rat has taken all her little savings and is about eating up her profits now. She won't marry, though God knows Larry's way of living don't influence me a bit where she's concerned. If Larry got sent up for a long stretch it would be better for Mary, though she would mourn him as if he was dead. I wish she would get rid of the store, quite this neighbourhood, and let me make her happy. But she won't, as long as that rat is loose.'

'Didn't 'e go to work on the dock?' asked Pegwell, raging. ' 'E bunged me off in th' *Stella* and took my job, didn't he?'

'He held the job for one week and quit,' Jack replied. 'He said he'd made a killing at the races. Two watchmen since have either fallen off the dock at night or been thrown off.' Jack was silent for a moment.

'Pegwell,' said Jack at length, 'I'm glad you're home. You can do a lot for Mary. I ought not to mention this to a soul; but I believe you are her friend.'

'Friend?' rasped Pegwell. 'Mister, you're bloody foolish! That little gal kin use me fer a door mat an' I'll show you what sort of a friend I am fust time I set eyes on that Larry!'

'Not so loud,' Jack whispered. They passed a policeman, who nodded to Jack. 'Pegwell, they're out to get Larry now! I have done all I can. I can't shield him any longer. He's out of town for a while, but when he comes back he's going to be jumped on, and he'll get ten years.'

'Wot d'you think I can do?' demanded Pegwell. 'Can I save him when you can't? Want me to go up for him, same as I made a Cape voyage in a hell ship for him?' The old man was furious.

'You can only be a friend and comfort to Mary,' said Jack quietly. Pegwell's wrinkled face was screwed up grotesquely with the intensity of his thought.

'Seems to me,' he said, 'if you was to sort of hurry her into a wed-din', maybe you could do a bit o' comfortin' yourself. If I had money enough to offer to buy her shop off her I c'd take care o' the Larry rat.'

'Oh, you have money enough,' retorted Jack quietly. 'Mary said long ago you could pay out of the profits. You only need about a hundred to pay down. I guess you have that much.'

Pegwell was apparently not listening; yet in fact he was. He seemed to be looking sheer through the cold, grey drizzle into the future, and if his worn, lined old face was any guide, what he saw in the dim perspective if imagination held more light than shadow.

'What's th' wust this yer Larry's done?' he suddenly asked. 'Killed anybody?'

'Oh, no,' replied Jack swiftly. 'Nothing like that.'

'Been wreckin' some young gal –'

'No more than he has wrecked Mary's youth,' Jack interrupted. 'He's just a plain crook. Dope smuggling; peddling, too. The worst he's done is to sell dope to school kids. Bad enough I'd say.'

'Not quite es bad es murder, I s'pose,' Pegwell growled, 'though be damned ef I know why it ain't. Anyhow, Jack, me lad, you take the advice of a old lummox, marry Mary whether she wants to or not, and I'll promise to take care o' Larry. I'll see he don't git sent up. You tell her. I be going round tonight again and see how fur you're right about that hunderd down and hunderd when you ketch me shop purchase proppisition. S'long, Jack. Set them weddin' bells to ringin'.'

Late that night Mary Bland bade Pegwell good night at the door of the little shop. She was rosy and smiling. Her brown eyes were wide and bright. Pegwell had never seen her so completely alive and gladsome. She shook his hand twice, and just for a tiny instant a speck of cloud flickered in her eyes.

'If you believe you can help Larry, I know you can,' she said. 'I know he will be safe in your care, old Pegwell.'

'He'll git a man's chance, you kin make sartin,' stated Pegwell. 'Good night, Missy, an' Gawd keep you smilin'. I'll be around to meet Jack in the mornin' and settle about the shop. Forgit yer troubles. Th' cops don't want Larry. If they did they couldn't git him.'

At the end of the week old Pegwell took undivided charge of the little shop, while Jack and Mary went about on some mysterious business connected with a license. Old Pegwell stood in the door watching them, and his old pipe emitted clouds of smoke in sympathy with the depth of his breathing. He felt queerly tight about the heart.

'Gawd bless 'em, goddammit!' he barked chokily.

A man came to buy tobacco. The two men stared at each other.

'Damn my eyes if't ain't old Pegwell!' roared the mate of the *Stella* 'Come to moorings at last, hey, you old fox?'

'Aye, mister, you won't bullydam old Pegwell no more. When d'ye sail?'

The mate laughed, picking up his change.

'Next Saturday. I'll put yer name on yer old bunk. Or p'raps you'd like to sail bosun, hey?'

Pegwell laughed comfortably. He spread his feet wide as he stood again in the doorway, gazing after the rolling figure of the mate. At last, at last he was man enough to tell a first mate to go scratch his ear. He turned to go inside, for the air was cold in spite of the sun, and the shop must be kept warm, when a scurrying figure doubled the corner, burst in after him, and slammed the door.

Larry Bland stood there before him, panting, wild-eyed.

'Where's Mary?' he rasped.

'Gone out, me son,' said Pegwell grimly. 'Just calm down. I own this here shop now. What kin I do for you?'

Larry glanced around the place furtively. He had a hunted look. Pegwell remembered Jack's words. A dark shape appeared against the glass of the door outside and Larry made for the inside room. Pegwell hastened him in as the door opened and a policeman entered.

'Larry Bland just came in here. Where is he?' he demanded.

'Orf'cer, Larry Bland shanghaied me a v'yage round Cape Stiff,' grinned Pegwell. 'D'you 'magine he'd come where I be?'

'I saw him open the door.'

'Aye, an' he dam' soon shut it again!'

The policeman stepped to the door of the inner room and peered inside. Old Pegwell heaved a tremendous sigh of relief when he quickly turned and bolted from the shop. Larry had taken care of his own concealment. He crawled in through a rear window when Pegwell called his name.

'Where's Mary gone?' he asked hoarsely. Larry looked scared. 'I got to get to her.'

'You can't get to her,' returned Pegwell. 'If it's the coppers you're scared of, lay low and keep your head. I won't let no cops git you, 'less you cuts up rought. You git upstairs to yer own room, while I thinks out what to do.'

'You ain't gettin' even are you?' snarled Larry suspiciously.

'In my own way, yes, me son. My way don't mean lettin' no cops git Mary Bland's brother. You duck into cover.'

When Mary and Jack returned she ran up to old Pegwell and kissed him warmly. She blushed at his gaze and shyly showed him a brand-new wedding ring. Jack laughed.

'I took your advice, Pegwell,' he said. 'No time like the present. So now you're sole proprietor here. We'll come back to-morrow to get Mary's few belongings Just now I want her to myself. So long. Come, Mary!'

They left quickly, leaving old Pegwell hot with unspoken felicitations. Larry crept down. He had heard Mary's voice.

'Get outa sight!' snapped Pegwell. 'Dammit! The street's full o' coppers!'

Larry ducked. He was frankly terrified.

When Mary appeared in the morning to pack her things Larry was securely out of sight. Old Pegwell had been busy all night. He had made a stout, roomy chest, iron cleated and hinged. He had made Larry help him, keeping him in mind of the police. Now Larry crouched in the big chest in the cellar, while Mary sang happily and packed her small trifles in the bright little rooms above.

'I do hope you will enjoy every hour here, Pegwell,' Mary said when ready to leave. 'Jack rather rushed me off my feet; but I'm glad, because he said you promised to see that Larry comes to no harm.'

'Missy,' replied Pegwell gravely, 'I won't let Larry get into no trouble with the police. I'm goin' to try to make a man outa him. So good luck to you, and God bless you. May all yer troubles be little 'uns, and if so be you wants a rattle, why –'

The old fellow glanced around the little shop, seeking for the bundle of rattles that hung somewhere; but he felt a warm, moist kiss on his cheek, the door opened, and she was gone.

On Thursday the police visited the shop again. Larry was known to be in the district.

'He wuz here, but I ain't seen him today,' said Pegwell. The old chap was in a sweating fret. Larry was getting impatient. He had demanded to see his sister and threatened to take his chance on the street. Pegwell had to lock the chest on him.

'He's likely to come back then,' decided the officer in charge. 'One o' you camp here,' he told one of his men.

'I don't think he'll bother me much,' Pegwell volunteered. 'He done me dirt and knows I'll git even.'

Pegwell was outwardly cool; inwardly, when that policeman took up his station in the inner room, he was all a-quiver. The noon stream of customers came in and kept him busy; but he dreaded the quiet of the afternoon. Another policeman came to take a turn of duty over night, and slept in a chair in the back room. Pegwell, upstairs, remained awake all night, listening lest the officer go exploring, dreading every moment to hear some betraying sound from the cramped Larry in the cellar.

All day Friday he had no chance to give Larry either food or water. All he could do was to pass hurriedly by and murmur through the lid of the chest a few harsh words of reassurance that relief was at hand. In the evening he closed the shop, left the policeman in sole charge, and went out for an hour. When he came back again he began to make up several small parcels of tobacco.

'Got a bit o' trade from the *Stella*,' he told the policeman. 'Nothin' like slops and tobacker for profits, mister. Ever think o' startin' a shop?'

'Shop, hell!' growled the policeman. 'I deal in men, old salt.'

'Men is queer, that's true,' said Pegwell.

At eleven o'clock a cart rattled up to the door, loaded up with sea chests and bags, with two husky toughs beside the driver and a heap of brutish bodies snoring in the back.

'Come for th' slops an' tobacker,' they said.

'Here's th' tobacker,' said Pegwell. 'Slop chest is in th' basement. Pretty heavy. I'll give y' a hand.'

'We can handle it,' returned the huskies, and one of them winked at Pegwell.

Pegwell chatted to the policeman as he handed out the tobacco parcels. He talked loudly, calling the policeman 'officer' as the chest was carried past. That was for Larry's benefit. Otherwise Larry might wonder what was being done to him and make some unfortunate noise.

'All right?' asked Pegwell.

'O.K.,' the leader said, and paid over the money he had been counting out to Pegwell. Pegwell carefully set it aside, to buy a wedding present for somebody he knew; then he joined the policeman for a goodnight smoke, chatting quite brilliantly, surprising himself.

Before daylight the next morning, old Pegwell was busy with broom and scraper on his sidewalk, for snow had fallen in the night. The water of the harbour was grey and cruel. Old Pegwell glanced out, shivered, and plied his broom. He was glad he had not to be out there, perhaps stamping around a capstan. It felt good to know that. It made him sing.

> And awa-ay, Rio! Awa-ay, Rio!
> Then fare you well, my bonny young gal,
> For we're bound for Rio Grande!

From down the bay came the hoot of a tug. And, clear and sharp, metallically shattering the morning heaviness, came also the clack, clack, clack of capstan pawls, the 'fare you well' of an outward bounder.

W. W. Jacobs

The Rival Beauties

IF you hadn't asked me, said the night watchman, I should never have told you; but, seeing as you've put the question point blank, I will tell you my experience of it. You're the first person I've ever opened my lips to upon the subject, for it was so eggstraordinary that all our chaps swore as they'd keep it to theirselves for fear of being disbelieved and jeered at.

It happened in '84, on board the steamer *George Washington*, bound from Liverpool to New York. The first eight days passed without anything unusual happening, but on the ninth I was standing aft with the first mate, hauling in the log, when we hears a yell from aloft an' a chap what we called Stuttering Sam come down as if he was possessed, and rushed up to the mate with his eyes nearly starting out of his 'ed.

'There's the s-s-s-s-s-s-sis-sis-sip!' ses he.

'The what?' ses the mate.

'The s-s-sea-sea-sssssip!'

'Look here, my lad,' ses the mate, taking out a pocket-handkerchief an' wiping his face, 'you just tarn your 'ed away till you get your breath. It's like opening a bottle o' soda water to stand talking to you. Now, what is it?'

'It's the sssssssis-sea-sea-sea-sarpint!' ses Sam, with a bust.

'Rather a long un by your account of it,' ses the mate, with a grin.

'What's the matter?' ses the skipper, who just came up.

'This man has seen the sea-sarpint, sir, that's all,' ses the mate.

'Y-y-yes,' said Sam, with a sort o' sob.

'Well, there ain't much doing just now,' ses the skipper, 'so you'd better get a slice o' bread and feed it.'

The mate bust out larfing, an' I could see by the way the skipper smiled he was rather tickled at it himself.

The skipper an' the mate was still larfing very hearty when we heard a dreadful 'owl from the bridge, an' one o' the chaps suddenly leaves the wheel, jumps on to the deck, and bolts below as though he was mad. T'other one follows 'im a'most d'reckly, and the second mate caught hold o' the wheel as he left it, and called out something we couldn't catch to the skipper.

'What the d—'s the matter?' yells the skipper.

The mate pointed to starboard, but as 'is 'and was shaking so that one minute it was pointing to the sky an' the next to the bottom o' the sea, it wasn't much of a guide to us. Even when he got it steady we couldn't see anything, till all of a sudden, about two miles off, something like a telegraph pole stuck up out of the water for a few seconds, and then ducked down again and made straight for the ship.

Sam was the fust to speak, and, without wasting time stuttering or stammering, he said he'd go down and see about that bit o' bread, an' he went afore the skipper or the mate could stop 'im.

In less than 'arf a minute there was only the three officers an' me on the deck. The second mate was holding the wheel, the skipper was holding his breath, and the first mate was holding me. It was one o' the most exciting times I ever had.

'Better fire the gun at it,' ses the skipper, in a trembling voice, looking at the little brass cannon we had for signalling.

'Better not give him any cause for offence,' ses the mate, shaking his head.

'I wonder whether it eats men,' ses the skipper. 'Perhaps it'll come for some of us.'

'There ain't many on deck for it to choose from,' ses the mate, looking at 'im significant like.

'That's true,' ses the skipper, very thoughtful; 'I'll go an' send all hands on deck. As captain, it's my duty not to leave the ship till the *last*, if I can anyways help it.'

How he got them on deck has always been a wonder to me, but he did it. He was a brutal sort o' a man at the best o' times, an' he carried on so much that I s'pose they thought even the sarpint couldn't be worse. Anyway, up they came, an' we all stood in a crowd watching the sarpint as it came closer and closer.

We reckoned it to be about a hundred yards long, an' it was about the most awful-looking creetur you could ever imagine. If you took all the ugliest things in the earth and mixed 'em up – gorillas an' the like – you'd only make a hangel compared to what that was. It just hung off our quarter, keeping up with us, and every now and then it would open its mouth and let us see about four yards down its throat.

'It seems peaceable,' whispers the fust mate, arter awhile.

'P'raps it ain't hungry,' ses the skipper. 'We'd better not let it get peckish. Try it with a loaf o' bread.'

The cook went below and fetched up half-a-dozen, an' one o' the chaps, plucking up courage, slung it over the side, an' afore you could say 'Jack Robinson' the sarpint had woffled it up an' was looking for more. It stuck its head up and came close to the side just like the swans in Victoria Park, an' it kept that game up until it had 'ad ten loaves an' a hunk o' pork.

'I'm afraid we're encouraging it,' ses the skipper, looking at it as it swam alongside with an eye as big as a saucer cocked on the ship.

'P'raps it'll go away soon if we don't take no more notice of it,' ses the mate. 'Just pretend it isn't here.'

Well, we did pretend as well as we could; but everybody hugged the port side o' the ship, and was ready to bolt down below at the shortest notice; and at last, when the beast got craning its neck up over the side as though it was looking for something, we gave it some more grub. We thought if we didn't give it he might take it, and take it off the wrong shelf, so to speak. But, as the mate said, it was encouraging it, and long arter it was dark we could hear it snorting and splashing behind us, until at last it 'ad such effect on us the mate sent one o' the chaps down to rouse the skipper.

'I don't think it'll do no 'arm,' ses the skipper, peering over the side, and speaking as though he knew all about sea-sarpints and their ways.

'S'pose it puts its 'ead over the side and takes one o' the men,' ses the mate.

'Let me know at once,' ses the skipper firmly; an' he went below agin and left us.

Well, I was jolly glad when eight bells struck, an' I went below; an' if ever I hoped anything I hoped that when I go up that ugly brute would have gone, but, instead o' that, when I went on deck it was playing alongside like a kitten a'most, an' one o' the chaps told me as the skipper had been feeding it agin.

'It's a wonderful animal,' ses the skipper, 'an' there's none of you now but has seen the sea-sarpint; but I forbid any man here to say a word about it when we get ashore.'

'Why not, sir?' ses the second mate.

'Becos you wouldn't be believed,' said the skipper sternly. 'You might all go ashore and kiss the Book an' make affidavits an' not a soul 'ud believe you. The comic papers 'ud make fun of it, and the respectable papers 'ud say it was seaweed or gulls.'

'Why not take it to New York with us?' ses the fust mate suddenly.

'What?' ses the skipper.

'Feed it every day,' ses the mate, getting excited, 'and bait a couple of shark hooks and keep 'em ready, together with some wire rope. Git 'im to foller us as far as he will, and then hook him. We might git him in alive and show him at a sovereign a head. Anyway, we can take in his carcase if we manage it properly.'

'By Jove! if we only could,' ses the skipper, getting excited too.

'We can try,' ses the mate. 'Why, we could have noosed it this mornin' if we had liked; and if it breaks the lines we must blow its head to pieces with the gun.'

It seemed a most eggstraordinary thing to try and catch it that way; but the beast was so tame, and stuck so close to us, that it wasn't quite so ridikilous as it seemed at fust.

Arter a couple o' days nobody minded the animal a bit, for it was about the most nervous thing of its size you ever saw. It hadn't got the soul of a mouse; and one day when the second mate, just for a lark, took the line of the foghorn in his hand and tooted it a bit, it flung up its 'ead in a scared sort o' way, and, after backing a bit, turned clean round and bolted.

I thought the skipper 'ud have gone mad. He chucked over loaves o'bread, bits o' beef and pork, an' scores o' biskits, and by-and-by, when the brute plucked up heart an' came arter us again, he fairly beamed with joy. Then he gave orders that nobody was to touch the horn for any reason whatever, not even if there was a fog, or chance of collision, or anything of the kind; an' he also gave orders that the bells wasn't to be struck, but that the bosen was just to shove 'is 'ead in the fo'c's'le and call 'em out instead.

Arter three days had passed, and the thing was still follering us, everybody made certain of taking it to New York, an' I b'leeve if it hadn't been for Joe Cooper the question about the sea-sarpint would ha' been settled long ago. He was a most eggstraordinary ugly chap was Joe. He had a perfic cartoon of a face, an' he was delikit-minded and sensitive about it that if a chap only stopped in the street and whistled as he passed him, or pointed him out to a friend, he didn't like it. He told me once when I was symperthizing with him, that the only time a woman ever spoke civilly to him was one night down Poplar way in a fog, an' he was so 'appy about it that they both walked into the canal afore he knew where they was.

On the fourth morning, when we was only about three days from Sandy Hook, the skipper got out o' bed wrong side, an' when he went on deck he was ready to snap at anybody, an' as luck would have it, as he walked a bit forrard, he sees Joe a-sticking his phiz over the side looking at the sarpint.

'What the d are you doing?' shouts the skipper. 'What do you mean by it?'

'Mean by what, sir?' asks Joe.

'Putting your black ugly face over the side o' the ship an' frightening my sea-sarpint!' bellows the skipper. 'You know how easy it's skeered.'

'Frightening the sea-sarpint?' ses Joe, trembling all over, an' turning very white.

'If I see that face o' yours over the side agin, my lad,' ses the skipper very fierce, 'I'll give it a black eye. Now cut!'

Joe cut, an' the skipper, having worked off some of his ill-temper, went aft again and began to chat with the mate quite pleasant like. I was down below at the time, an' didn't know anything about it for hours arter, and then I heard it from one o' the firemen. He comes up to me very mysterious like, an' ses, 'Bill,' he ses, 'you're a pal o' Joe's; come down here an' see what you can make of 'im.'

Not knowing what he meant, I follered 'im below to the engine-room, an' there was Joe sitting on a bucket staring wildly in front of 'im, and two or three of 'em standing round looking at 'im with their 'eads on one side.

'He's been like that for three hours,' ses the second engineer in a whisper, 'dazed like.'

As he spoke Joe gave a little shudder; 'Frighten the sea-sarpint!' ses he. 'O Lord!'

'It's turned his brain,' ses one o' the firemen, 'he keeps saying nothing but that.'

'If we could only make 'im cry,' ses the second engineer, who had a brother what was a medical student, 'it might save his reason. But how to do it, that's the question.'

'Speak kind to 'im, sir,' ses the fireman. 'I'll have a try if you don't mind.' He cleared his throat first, an' then he walks over to Joe and puts his hand on his shoulder an' ses very soft an' pitiful like,

'Don't take on, Joe, don't take on, there's many a ugly mug 'ides a good 'art.'

Afore he could think o' anything else to say, Joe ups with his fist an' gives 'im one in the ribs as nearly broke 'em. Then he turns away 'is 'ead an' shivers again, an' the old dazed look comes back.

'Joe,' I ses, shaking him, 'Joe!'

'Frightened the sea-sarpint!' whispers Joe, staring.

'Joe,' I ses, 'Joe. You know me, I'm your pal, Bill.'

'Ah, ay,' ses Joe, coming round a bit.

'Come away,' I ses, 'come an' git to bed, that's the best place for you.'

I took 'im by the sleeve, and he gets up quiet an' obedient and follers me like a little child. I got 'im straight into 'is bunk, an' arter a time he fell into a soft slumber, an' I thought the worst had passed, but I was mistaken. He got up in three hours' time an' seemed all right, 'cept that he walked about as though he was thinking very hard about something, an' before I could make out what it was he had a fit.

He was in that fit ten minutes, an' he was no sooner out o' that one than he was in another. In twenty-four hours he had six full-sized fits, and I'll allow I was fairly puzzled. What pleasure he could find in tumbling down hard and stiff an' kicking at everybody an' everything I couldn't see. He'd be standing quiet and peaceable like one minute, and the next he'd catch hold o' the nearest thing to him and have a bad fit, and lie on his back and kick us while we was trying to force open his hands to pat 'em.

The other chaps said the skipper's insult had turned his brain, but I wasn't quite so soft, an' one time when he was alone I put it to him.

'Joe, old man,' I ses, 'you an' me's been very good pals.'

'Ay, ay,' ses he, suspicious like.

'Joe,' I whispers, 'what's yer little game?'

'Wodyermean?' ses he, very short.

'I mean the fits,' ses I, looking at 'im very steady. 'It's no good looking hinnercent like that, 'cos I see yer chewing soap with my own eyes.'

'Soap,' ses Joe, in a nasty sneering way, 'you wouldn't reckernize a piece if you saw it.'

Arter that I could see there was nothing to be got out of 'im an' I just kept my eyes open and watched. The skipper didn't worry about his fits, 'cept that he said he wasn't to let the sarpint see his face when he was in 'em for fear of scaring it; an' when the mate wanted to leave him out o' the watch, he ses, 'No, he might as well have fits while at work as well as anywhere else.'

We were about twenty-four hours from port, an' the sarpint was still following us; and at six o'clock in the evening the officers puffected all their arrangements for ketching the creetur at eight o'clock next morning. To make quite sure of it an extra watch was kept on deck all night to chuck it food every half-hour; an' when I turned in at ten o'clock that night it was so close I could have reached it with a clothes-prop.

I think I'd been abed about 'arf-an-hour when I was awoke by the most infernal row I ever heard. The foghorn was going incessantly, an' there was a lot o' shouting and running about on deck. It struck us all as 'ow the sarpint was gitting tired o' bread, and was misbehaving himself, consequently we just shoved our 'eds out o' the fore-scuttle and listened. All the hullaballoo seemed to be on the bridge, an' as we didn't see the sarpint there we plucked up courage and went on deck.

Then we saw what had happened. Joe had 'ad another fit while at the wheel, and, *not knowing what he was doing*, had clutched the line of the foghorn, and was holding on to it like grim death, and kicking right and left. The skipper was in his bedclothes, raving worse than Joe; and just as we got there Joe came round a bit, and, letting go o' the line, asked in a faint voice what the foghorn was blowing for. I thought the skipper 'ud have killed him; but the second mate held him back, an', of course, when things quieted down a bit, an' we went to the side, we found the sea-sarpint had vanished.

We stayed there all that night, but it warn't no use. When day broke there wasn't the slightest trace of it, an' I think the men was as sorry to lose it as the officers. All 'cept Joe, that is, which shows how people should never be rude, even to the humblest; for I'm sartin that if the skipper hadn't hurt his feelings the way he did we should now know as much about the sea-sarpint as we do about our own brothers.

Jack London

Make Westing

'Whatever you do, make westing! make westing!'
– Sailing directions for Cape Horn.

For seven weeks the *Mary Rogers* had been between 50° south in the Atlantic and 50° south in the Pacific, which meant that for seven weeks she had been struggling to round Cape Horn. For seven weeks she had been either in dirt, or close to dirt, save once, and then, following upon six days of excessive dirt, which she had ridden out under the shelter of the redoubtable Tierra del Fuego coast, she had almost gone ashore during a heavy swell in the dead calm that had suddenly fallen. For seven weeks she had wrestled with the Cape Horn greybeards, and in return been buffeted and smashed by them. She was a wooden ship, and her ceaseless straining had opened her seams, so that twice a day the watch took its turn at the pumps.

The *Mary Rogers* was strained, the crew was strained, and big Dan Cullen, master, was likewise strained. Perhaps he was strained most of all, for upon him rested the responsibility of that titanic struggle. He slept most of the time in his clothes, though he rarely slept. He haunted the deck at night, a great, burly, robust ghost, black with the sunburn of thirty years of sea and hairy as an orang-outang. He, in turn, was haunted by one thought of action, a sailing direction for the Horn: *Whatever you do, make westing! make westing!* It was an obsession. He thought of nothing else, except, at times, to blaspheme God for sending such bitter weather.

Make westing! He hugged the Horn, and a dozen times lay hove to with the iron Cape bearing east-by-north, or north-north-east, a score of miles away. And each time the eternal west wind smote him back and he made easting. He fought gale after gale, south to 64°, inside the Antarctic drift-ice, and pledged his immortal soul to the powers of darkness, for a bit of westing, for a slant to take him around. And he made easting. In despair, he had tried to make the passage through the Straits of Le Maire. Halfway through, the wind hauled to the north'ard of north-west, the glass dropped to 28·88, and he turned and ran before a gale of cyclonic fury, missing, by a hair's breadth, piling up the *Mary Rogers* on the black-toothed rocks. Twice he had made west to the Diego Ramirez Rocks, one of the times saved between two snow-squalls by sighting the gravestones of ships a quarter of a mile dead ahead.

Blow! Captain Dan Cullen instanced all his thirty years at sea to prove that never had it blown so before. The *Mary Rogers* was hove to at the time he gave the evidence, and, to clinch it, inside half an hour the *Mary Rogers* was hove down to the hatches. Her new maintopsail and brand new spencer were blown away like tissue paper; and five sails, furled and fast under double gaskets, were blown loose and stripped from the yards. And before morning the *Mary Rogers* was hove down twice again, and holes were knocked in her bulwarks to ease her decks from the weight of ocean that pressed her down.

On an average of once a week Captain Dan Cullen caught glimpses of the sun. Once, for ten minutes, the sun shone at midday, and ten minutes afterwards a new gale was piping up, both watches were short-ening sail, and all was buried in the obscurity of a driving snow-squall. For a fortnight, once, Captain Dan Cullen was without a meridian or a chronometer sight. Rarely did he know his position within half of a degree, except when in sight of land; for sun and stars remained hidden behind the sky, and it was so gloomy that even at the best the horizons were poor for accurate observations. A grey gloom shrouded the world. The clouds were grey; the great driving seas were leaden grey; the smoking crests were a grey churning; even the occasional albatrosses were grey, while the snow-flurries were not white, but grey, under the sombre pall of the heavens.

Life board the *Mary Rogers* was grey – grey and gloomy. The faces of the sailors were blue grey; they were afflicted with sea-cuts and sea-boils, and suffered exquisitely. They were shadows of men. For seven weeks, in the forecastle or on deck, they had not known what it was to be dry. They had forgotten what it was to sleep out a watch, and all watches it was, 'All hands on deck!' They caught the snatches of agon-ized sleep, and they slept in their oil-skins ready for the everlasting call. So weak and worn were they that it took both watches to do the work of one. That was why both watches were on deck so much of the time. And no shadow of a man could shirk duty. Nothing less than a broken leg could enable a man to knock off work; and there were two such, who had been mauled and pulped by the seas that broke aboard.

One other man who was the shadow of a man was George Dorety. He was the only passenger on board, a friend of the firm, and he had elected to make the voyage for his health. But seven weeks off Cape Horn had not bettered his health. He gasped and panted in his bunk through the long, heaving nights; and when on deck he was so bundled up for warmth that he resembled a peripatetic old-clothes shop. At midday, eating at the cabin table in a gloom so deep that the swinging sea-lamps burned always, he looked as blue-grey as the sickest, saddest man for'ard. Nor did gazing across the table at Captain Dan Cullen have any cheering effect upon him. Captain Cullen chewed and scowled and kept silent. The scowls were for God, and with every chew he reiterated the sole thought of his existence, which was *make westing*. He was a big, hairy brute, and the sight of him was not stimulating to the other's appetite. He looked upon George Dorety as a Jonah, and told him so once each meal savagely transferring the scowl from God to the passenger and back again.

Nor did the mate prove a first aid to a languid appetite. Joshua Higgins by name, a seaman by profession and pull, but a pot-walloper by capacity, he was a loose-jointed, sniffling creature, heartless and selfish and cowardly, without a soul, in fear of his life of Dan Cullen, and a bully over the sailors, who knew that behind the mate was Captain Cullen, the law-giver and compeller, the driver and the destroyer, the incarnation of a dozen bucko mates. In that wild weather at the southern end of the earth, Joshua Higgins ceased washing. His grimy face usually robbed George Dorety of what little appetite he managed to accumulate. Ordinarily this lavatorial dereliction would have caught Captain Cullen's eye and vocabulary, but in the present his mind was filled with making westing, to the exclusion of all other things not contributory thereto. Whether the mate's face was clean or dirty had no bearing upon westing. Later on, when 50° south in the Pacific had been reached, Joshua Higgins would wash his face very abruptly. In the meantime, at the cabin table, where grey twilight alternated with lamp-light while the lamps were being filled, George Dorety sat between the two men, one a tiger and the other a hyena, and wondered why God had made them. The second mate, Matthew Turner, was a true sailor and a man, but George Dorety did not have the solace of his company, for he ate by himself, solitary, when they had finished.

On Saturday morning, July 24, George Dorety awoke to a feeling of life and headlong movement. On deck he found the *Mary Rogers* running off before a howling south-easter. Nothing was set but the lower topsails and the foresail. It was all she could stand, yet she was making fourteen knots, as Mr Turner shouted in Dorety's ear when he came on deck. And it was all westing. She was going round the Horn at last . . . if the wind held. Mr Turner looked happy. The end of the struggle was in sight. But Captain Cullen did not look happy. He scowled at Dorety in passing. Captain Cullen did not want God to know that he was pleased with that wind. He had a conception of a malicious God, and believed in his secret soul that if God knew it was a desirable wind, God would promptly efface it and send a snorter from the west.

So he walked softly before God, smothering his joy down under scowls and muttered curses, and, so, fooling God, for God was the only thing in the universe of which Dan Cullen was afraid.

All Saturday and Saturday night the *Mary Rogers* raced her westing. Persistently she logged her fourteen knots, so that by Sunday morning she had covered three hundred and fifty miles. If the wind held, she would make around. If it failed, and the snorter came from anywhere between south-west and north, back the *Mary Rogers* would he hurled and be no better off than she had been seven weeks before. And on Sunday morning the wind *was* failing. The big sea was going down and running smooth. Both watches were on deck setting sail after sail as fast as the ship could stand it. And now Captain Cullen went around brazenly before God, smoking a big cigar, smiling jubilantly, as if the failing wind delighted him, while down underneath he was raging against God for taking the life out of the blessed wind. *Make westing!* So he would, if God would only leave him alone. Secretly, he pledged himself anew to the Powers of Darkness, if they would let him make westing. He pledged himself so easily because he did not believe in the Powers of Darkness. He really believed only in God, though he did not know it. And in his inverted theology God was really the Prince of Darkness. Captain Cullen was a devil-worshipper, but he called the devil by another name, that was all.

At midday, after calling eight bells, Captain Cullen ordered the royals on. The men went aloft faster than they had gone in weeks. Not alone were they nimble because of the westing, but a benignant sun was shining down and limbering their stiff bodies. George Dorety stood aft, near Captain Cullen, less bundled in clothes than usual, soaking in the grateful warmth as he watched the scene. Swiftly and abruptly the incident occurred. There was a cry from the foreroyal-yard of 'Man overboard!' Somebody threw a lifebuoy over the side, and at the same instant the second mate's voice came aft, ringing and peremptory –

'Hard down your helm!'

The man at the wheel never moved a spoke. He knew better, for Captain Dan Cullen was standing alongside of him. He wanted to move a spoke, to move all the spokes, to grind the wheel down, hard down, for his comrade drowning in the sea. He glanced at Captain Dan Cullen, and Captain Dan Cullen gave no sign.

'Down! Hard down!' the second mate roared, as he sprang aft.

But he ceased springing and commanding, and stood still, when he saw Dan Cullen by the wheel. And big Dan Cullen puffed at his cigar and said nothing. Astern, and going astern fast, could be seen the sailor. He had caught the life-buoy and was clinging to it. Nobody spoke. Nobody moved. The men aloft clung to the royal yards and watched with terror-stricken faces. And the *Mary Rogers* raced on, making her westing. A long, silent minute passed.

'Who was it?' Captain Cullen demanded.

'Mops, sir,' eagerly answered the sailor at the wheel.

Mops topped a wave astern and disappeared temporarily in the trough. It was a large wave, but it was no greybeard. A small boat could live easily in such a sea, and in such a sea the *Mary Rogers* could easily come to. But she could not come to and make westing at the same time.

For the first time in all his years, George Dorety was seeing a real drama of life and death – a sordid little drama in which the scales balanced an unknown sailor named Mops against a few miles of longitude. At first he had watched the man astern, but now he watched big Dan Cullen, hairy and black, vested with power of life and death, smoking a cigar.

Captain Dan Cullen smoked another long, silent minute. Then he removed the cigar from his mouth. He glanced aloft at the spars of the *Mary Rogers*, and overside at the sea.

'Sheet home the royals!' he cried.

Fifteen minutes later they sat at table, in the cabin, with food served before them. On one side of George Dorety sat Dan Cullen, the tiger, on the other side, Joshua Higgins, the hyena. Nobody spoke. On deck the men were sheeting home the skysails. George Dorety could hear their cries, while a persistent vision haunted him of a man called Mops, alive and well, clinging to a life-buoy miles astern in that lonely ocean. He glanced at Captain Cullen, and experienced a feeling of nausea, for the man was eating his food with relish, almost bolting it.

'Captain Cullen,' Dorety said, 'you are in command of this ship, and it is not proper for me to comment now upon what you do. But I wish to say one thing. There is a hereafter, and yours will be a hot one.'

Captain Cullen did not even scowl. In his voice was regret as he said –

'It was blowing a living gale. It was impossible to save the man.'

'He fell from the royal-yard,' Dorety cried hotly. 'You were setting the royals at the time. Fifteen minutes afterwards you were setting the skysails.'

'It was a living gale, wasn't it, Mr Higgins?' Captain Cullen said, turning to the mate.

'If you'd brought her to, it'd have taken the sticks out of her' was the mate's answer. 'You did the proper thing, Captain Cullen. The man hadn't a ghost of a show.'

George Dorety made no answer, and to the meal's end no one spoke. After that, Dorety had his meals served in his state-room.

Captain Cullen scowled at him no longer, though no speech was exchanged between them, while the *Mary Rogers* sped north towards warmer latitudes. At the end of the week, Dan Cullen cornered Dorety on deck.

'What are you going to do when we get to 'Frisco?' he demanded bluntly.

'I am going to swear out a warrant for your arrest,' Dorety answered quietly. 'I am going to charge you with murder, and I am going to see you hanged for it.'

'You're almighty sure of yourself,' Captain Cullen sneered, turning on his heel.

A second week passed, and one morning found George Dorety standing in the coach-house companionway at the for'ard end of the long poop, taking his first gaze around the deck. The *Mary Rogers* was reaching full-and-by, in a stiff breeze. Every sail was set and drawing, including the staysails. Captain Cullen strolled for'ard along the poop. He strolled carelessly, glancing at the passenger out of the corner of his eye. Dorety was looking the other way, standing with head and shoulders outside the companionway, and only the back of his head was to be seen. Captain Cullen, with swift eye, embraced the mainstaysail-block and the head and estimated the distance. He glanced about him. Nobody was looking. Aft, Joshua Higgins, pacing up and down, had just turned his back and was going the other way. Captain Cullen bent over suddenly and cast the staysail-sheet off from its pin. The heavy block hurtled through the air, smashing Dorety's head like an egg-shell and hurtling on and back and forth as the staysail whipped and slatted in the wind. Joshua Higgins turned around to see what had carried away, and met the full blast of the vilest portion of Captain Cullen's profanity.

'I made the sheet fast myself,' whimpered the mate in the first lull, 'with an extra turn to make sure. I remember it distinctly.'

'Made fast?' the Captain snarled back, for the benefit of the watch as it struggled to capture the flying sail before it tore to ribbons. 'You couldn't make your grandmother fast, you useless hell's scullion. If you made that sheet fast with an extra turn, why in hell didn't it stay fast? That's what I want to know. Why in hell didn't it stay fast?'

The mate whined inarticulately.

'Oh, shut up!' was the final word of Captain Cullen.

Half an hour later he was as surprised as any when the body of George Dorety was found inside the companionway on the floor. In the afternoon, alone in his room, he doctored up the log.

'Ordinary seaman, Karl Brun,' he wrote, 'lost overboard from fore-royal-yard in a gale of wind. Was running at the time, and for the safety of *the ship did not dare to come up the wind. Nor could a boat have lived in the sea that was running.'*

On another page he wrote:

'Had often warned Mr Dorety about the danger he ran because of his carelessness on deck. I told him, once, that some day he would get his head knocked off by a block. A carelessly fastened mainstaysail sheet was the cause of the accident, which was deeply to be regretted because Mr Dorety was a favourite with all of us.'

Captain Dan Cullen read over his literary effort with admiration, blotted the page, and closed the log. He lighted a cigar and stared before him. He felt the *Mary Rogers* lift, and heel, and surge along, and knew that she was making nine knots. A smile of satisfaction slowly dawned on his black and hairy face. Well, anyway, he had made his westing and fooled God.

Joseph Conrad

Youth: A Narrative

THIS could have occurred nowhere but in England, where men and sea interpenetrate, so to speak – the sea entering into the life of most men, and the men knowing something or everything about the sea, in the way of amusement, of travel, or of breadwinning.

We were sitting around a mahogany table that reflected the bottle, the claret-glasses, and our faces as we leaned on our elbows. There was a director of companies, an accountant, a lawyer, Marlow, and myself. The director had been a *Conway* boy, the accountant had served four years at sea, the lawyer – a fine crusted Tory, High Churchman, the best of old fellows, the soul of honour – had been chief officer in the P & O service in the good old days when mail-boats were square-rigged at least on two masts, and used to come down the China Sea before a fair monsoon with stun'-sails set alow and aloft. We all began life in the merchant service. Between the five of us there was the strong bond of the sea, and also the fellowship of the craft, which no amount of enthusiasm for yachting, cruising, and so on can give, since one is only the amusement of life and the other is life itself.

Marlow (at least I think that is how he spelt his name) told the story, or rather the chronicle, of a voyager:–

'Yes, I have seen a little of the Eastern seas; but what I remember best is my first voyage there. You fellows know there are those voyages that seem ordered for the illustration of life, that might stand for a symbol of existence. You fight, work, sweat, nearly kill yourself, sometimes do kill yourself, trying to accomplish something – and you can't. Not from any fault of yours. You simply can do nothing, neither great nor little – not a thing in the world – not even marry an old maid, or get a wretched 600-ton cargo of coal to its port of destination.

'It was altogether a memorable affair. It was my first voyage to the East, and my first voyage as second mate; it was also my skipper's first command. You'll admit it was time. He was sixty if a day; a little man, with a broad, not very straight back, with bowed shoulders and one leg more bandy than the other, he had that queer twisted-about appearance you see so often in men who work in the fields. He had a nut-cracker face – chin and nose trying to come together over a sunken mouth – and it was framed in iron-grey fluffy hair, that looked like a chin-strap of cotton-wool sprinkled with coal-dust. And he had blue eyes in that old face of his, which were amazingly like a boy's, with that candid expression some quite common men preserve to the end of their days by a rare internal gift of simplicity of heart and rectitude of soul. What induced him to accept me was a wonder. I had come out of a crack Australian clipper, where I had been third officer, and he seemed to have a prejudice against crack clippers as aristocratic and high-toned. He said to me, "You know, in this ship you will have to work." I said I had to work in every ship I had ever been in. "Ah, but this is different, and you gentlemen out of them big ships; . . . but there! I dare say you will do. Join tomorrow."

'I joined tomorrow. It was twenty-two years ago; and I was just twenty. How time passes! It was one of the happiest days of my life. Fancy! Second mate for the first time – a really responsible officer! I wouldn't have thrown up my new billet for a fortune. The mate looked me over carefully. He was also an old chap, but of another stamp. He had a Roman nose, a snow-white, long beard, and his name was Mahon, but he insisted that it should be pronounced Mann. He was well connected; yet there was something wrong with his luck, and he had never got on.

'As to the captain, he had been for years in coasters, then in the Mediterranean, and last in the West Indian trade. He had never been round the Capes. He could just write a kind of sketchy hand, and didn't care for writing at all. Both were thorough good seamen of course, and between those two old chaps I felt like a small boy between two grandfathers.

'The ship was also old. Her name was the *Judea*. Queer name, isn't it? She belonged to a man Wilmer, Wilcox – some name like that; but he has been bankrupt and dead these twenty years or more, and his name don't matter. She had been laid up in Shadwell basin for ever so long. You may imagine her state. She was all rust, dust, grime – soot aloft, dirt on deck. To me it was like coming out of a palace into a ruined cottage. She was about 400 tons, had a primitive windlass, wooden latches to the doors, not a bit of brass about her, and a big square stern. There was on it, below her name in big letters, a lot of scrollwork, with the gilt off, and some sort of a coat of arms, with the motto "Do or Die" underneath. I remember it took my fancy immensely. There was a touch of romance in it, something that made me love the old thing – something that appealed to my youth!

'We left London in ballast – sand ballast – to load a cargo of coal in a northern port for Bangkok. Bangkok! I thrilled. I had been six years at sea, but had only seen Melbourne and Sydney, very good places, charming places in their way – but Bangkok!

'We worked out of the Thames under canvas, with a North Sea pilot on board. His name was Jermyn, and he dodged all day long about the galley drying his handkerchief before the stove. Apparently he never slept. He was a dismal man, with a perpetual tear sparkling at the end of his nose, who either had been in trouble, or was in trouble, or expected to be in trouble – couldn't be happy unless something went wrong. He mistrusted my youth, my common-sense, and my seamanship, and made a point of showing it in a hundred little ways. I dare say he was right. It seems to me I knew very little then, and I know not much more now; but I cherish a hate for that Jermyn to this day.

'We were a week working up as far as Yarmouth Roads, and then we got into a gale – the famous October gale of twenty-two years ago. It was wind, lightning, sleet, snow, and a terrific sea. We were flying light, and you may imagine how bad it was when I tell you we had smashed bulwarks and a flooded deck. On the second night she shifted her ballast into the lee bow, and by that time we had been blown off somewhere on the Dogger Bank. There was nothing for it but to go below with shovels and try to right her, and there we were in that vast hold, gloomy like a cavern, the tallow dips stuck and flickering on the beams, the gale howling above, the ship tossing about like mad on her side; there we all were, Jermyn, the captain, every one, hardly able to keep our feet, engaged on that gravedigger's work, and trying to toss shovelfuls of wet sand up to windward. At every tumble of the ship you could see vaguely in the dim light men falling down with a great flourish of shovels. One of the ship's boys (we had two), impressed by the weirdness of the scene, wept as if his heart would break. We could hear him blubbering somewhere in the shadows.

'On the third day the gale died out, and by-and-by a north-country tug picked us up. We took sixteen days in all to get from London to the Tyne! When we got into dock we had lost our turn for loading, and they hauled us off to a tier where we remained for a month. Mrs Beard (the captain's name was Beard) came from Colchester to see the old man. She lived on board. The crew of runners had left, and there remained only the officers, one boy and the steward, a mulatto who answered to the name of Abraham. Mrs Beard was an old woman, with a face all wrinkled and ruddy like a winter apple, and the figure of a young girl. She caught sight of me once, sewing on a button, and insisted on having my shirts to repair. This was something different from the captains' wives I had known on board crack clippers. When I brought her the shirts, she said: "And the socks? They want mending, I am sure, and John's – Captain Beard's – things are all in order now.

I would be glad of something to do." Bless the old woman. She overhauled my outfit for me, and meantime I read for the first time *Sartor Resartus* and Burnaby's *Ride to Khiva*. I didn't understand much of the first then; but I remember I preferred the soldier to the philosopher at the time; a preference which life has only confirmed. One was a man, and the other was either more – or less. However, they are both dead and Mrs Beard is dead, and youth, strength, genius, thoughts, achievements, simple hearts – all dies . . . No matter.

'They loaded us at last. We shipped a crew. Eight able seamen and two boys. We hauled off one evening to the buoys at the dock-gates, ready to go out, and with a fair prospect of beginning the voyage next day. Mrs Beard was to start for home by a late train. When the ship was fast we went to tea. We sat rather silent through the meal – Mahon, the old couple, and I. I finished first, and slipped away for a smoke, my cabin being in a deck-house just against the poop. It was high water, blowing fresh with a drizzle; the double dock-gates were opened, and the steam-colliers were going in and out in the darkness with their lights burning bright, a great plashing of propellers, rattling of winches, and a lot of hailing on the pier-heads. I watched the procession of head-lights gliding high and of green lights gliding low in the night, when suddenly a red gleam flashed at me, vanished, came into view again, and remained. The fore-end of a steamer loomed up close. I shouted down the cabin, "Come up, quick!" and then heard a startled voice saying afar in the dark, "Stop her, sir." A bell jingled. Another voice cried warningly, "We are going right into that barque, sir." The answer to this was a gruff "All right," and the next thing was a heavy crash as the steamer struck a glancing blow with the bluff of her bow about our fore-rigging. There was a moment of confusion, yelling and running about. Steam roared. Then somebody was heard saying, "All clear, sir" . . . "Are you all right?" asked the gruff voice. I had jumped forward to see the damage, and hailed back, "I think so." "Easy astern," said the gruff voice. A bell jingled. "What steamer is that?" screamed Mahon. By that time she was no more to us than a bulky shadow manoeuvring a little way off. They shouted at us some name – a woman's name, Miranda or Melissa – or some such thing. "This means another month in this beastly hole," said Mahon to me, as we peered with lamps about the splattered bulwarks and broken braces. "But where's the captain?"

'We had not heard or seen anything of him all that time. We went aft to look. A doleful voice arose hailing somewhere in the middle of the dock, "*Judea* ahoy!". . . How the devil did he get there? . . . "Hallo!" we shouted. "I am adrift in our boat without oars," he cried. A belated water-man offered his services, and Mahon struck a bargain with him for half-a-crown to tow our skipper alongside; but it was Mrs

Beard that came up the ladder first. They had been floating about the dock in that mizzly cold rain for nearly an hour. I was never so surprised in my life.

'It appears that when he heard my shout "Come up" he understood at once what was the matter, caught up his wife, ran on deck and across, and down into our boat, which was fast to the ladder. Not bad for a sixty-year-old. Just imagine that old fellow saving heroically in his arms that old woman – the woman of his life. He set her down on a thwart, and was ready to climb back on board when the painter came adrift somehow, and away they went together. Of course in the confusion we did not hear him shouting. He looked abashed. She said cheerfully, "I suppose it does not matter my losing the train now?" "No, Jenny – you go below and get warm," he growled. Then to us: "A sailor has no business with a wife – I say. There I was, out of the ship. Well, no harm done this time. Let's go and look at what that fool of a steamer smashed."

'It wasn't much, but it delayed us three weeks. At the end of that time, the captain being engaged with his agents, I carried Mrs Beard's bag to the railway station and put her all comfy into a third-class carriage. She lowered the window to say, "You are a good young man. If you see John – Captain Beard – without his muffler at night, just remind him from me to keep his throat well wrapped up." "Certainly, Mrs Beard," I said. "You are a good young man; I noticed how attentive you are to John – to Captain –" The train pulled out suddenly; I took my cap off to the old woman: I never saw her again . . . Pass the bottle.

'We went to sea next day. When we made that start for Bangkok we had been already three months out of London. We had expected to be a fortnight or so – at the outside.

'It was January, and the weather was beautiful – the beautiful sunny winter weather that has more charm than in the summertime, because it is unexpected, and crisp, and you know it won't, it can't, last long. It's like a windfall, like a godsend, like an unexpected piece of luck.

'It lasted all down the North Sea, all down Channel; and it lasted till we were three hundred miles or so the westward of the Lizards: then the wind went round to the sou'west and began to pipe up. In two days it blew a gale. The *Judea*, hove to, wallowed on the Atlantic like an old candle-box. It blew day after day: it blew with spite, without interval, without mercy, without rest. The world was nothing but an immensity of great foaming waves rushing at us, under a sky low enough to touch with the hand and dirty like a smoked ceiling. In the stormy space surrounding us there was as much flying spray as air. Day after day and night after night there was nothing round the ship but the howl of the wind, the tumult of the sea, the noise of water pouring over her deck.

There was no rest for her and no rest for us. She tossed, she pitched, she stood on her head, she sat on her tail, she rolled, she groaned, and we had to hold on while on deck and cling to our bunks when below, in a constant effort of body and worry of mind.

'One night Mahon spoke through the small window of my berth. It opened right into my very bed, and I was lying there sleepless, in my boots, feeling as though I had not slept for years, and could not if I tried. He said excitedly –

' "You got the sounding-rod in here, Marlow? I can't get the pumps to suck. By God! it's no child's play."

'I gave him the sounding-rod and lay down again, trying to think of various things – but I thought only of the pumps. When I came on deck they were still at it, and my watch relieved at the pumps. By the light of the lantern brought on deck to examine the sounding-rod I caught a glimpse of their weary, serious faces. We pumped all the four hours. We pumped all night, all day, all the week – watch and watch. She was working herself loose, and leaked badly – not enough to drown us at once, but enough to kill us with the work at the pumps. And while we pumped the ship was going from us piecemeal: the bulwarks went, the stanchions were torn out, the ventilators smashed, the cabin-door burst in. There was not a dry spot in the ship. She was being gutted bit by bit. The long-boat changed, as if by magic, into matchwood where she stood in her gripes. I had lashed her myself, and was rather proud of my handiwork, which had withstood so long the malice of the sea. And we pumped. And there was no break in the weather. The sea was white like a sheet of foam, like a cauldron of boiling milk; there was not a break in the clouds, no – not the size of a man's hand – no, not for so much as ten seconds. There was for us no sky, there were for us no stars, no sun, no universe – nothing but angry clouds and an infuriated sea. We pumped watch and watch, for dear life; and it seemed to last for months, for years, for all eternity, as though we had been dead and gone to a hell for sailors. We forgot the day of the week, the name of the month, what year it was, and whether we had ever been ashore. The sails blew away, she lay broadside on under a weather-cloth, the ocean poured over her, and we did not care. We turned those handles and had the eyes of idiots. As soon as we had crawled on deck I used to take a round turn with a rope about the men, the pumps, and the mainmast, and we turned, we turned incessantly, with the water to our waists, to our necks, over our heads. It was all one. We had forgotten how it felt to be dry.

'And there was somewhere in me the thought: By Jove! this is the deuce of an adventure – something you read about; and it is my first voyage as second mate – and I am only twenty – and here I am lasting it out as well as any of these men, and keeping my chaps up to the mark. I was pleased. I would not have given up the experience for worlds. I had moments of exultation. Whenever the old dismantled craft pitched heavily with her counter high in the air, she seemed to me to throw up, like an appeal, like a defiance, like a cry to the clouds without mercy, the words written on her stern: "*Judea*, London. Do or Die".

'O youth! The strength of it, the faith of it, the imagination of it! To me she was not an old rattle-trap carting about the world a lot of coal for a freight – to me she was the endeavour, the test, the trial of life. I think of her with pleasure, with affection, with regret – as you would think of someone dead you have loved. I shall never forget her . . . Pass the bottle.

'One night when tied to the mast, as I explained, we were pumping on, defeated with the wind, and without spirit enough in us to wish ourselves dead, a heavy sea crashed aboard and swept clean over us. As soon as I got my breath I shouted, as in duty bound, "Keep on, boys!" when suddenly I felt something hard floating on deck strike the calf of my leg. I made a grab at it and missed. It was so dark we could not see each other's faces within a foot – you understand.

'After that thump the ship kept quiet for a while, and the thing, whatever it was, struck my leg again. This time I caught it – and it was a saucepan. At first, being stupid with fatigue and thinking of nothing but the pumps, I did not understand what I had in my hand. Suddenly it dawned upon me, and I shouted, "Boys, the house deck is gone. Leave this, and let's look for the cook."

'There was a deck-house forward, which contained the galley, the cook's berth, and the quarters of the crew. As we had expected for days to see it swept away, the hands had been ordered to sleep in the cabin – the only safe place in the ship. The steward, Abraham, however, persisted in clinging to his berth, stupidly, like a mule – from sheer fright I believe, like an animal that won't leave a stable falling in an earthquake. So we went to look for him. It was chancing death, since once out of our lashings we were as exposed as if on a raft. But we went. The house was shattered as if a shell had exploded inside. Most of it had gone overboard – stove, men's quarters, and their property, all was gone; but two posts, holding a portion of the bulkhead to which Abraham's bunk was attached, remained as if by a miracle. We groped in the ruins and came upon this, and there he was, sitting in his bunk, surrounded by foam and wreckage, jabbering cheerfully to himself. He was out of his mind; completely and for ever mad, with this sudden shock coming down the fag-end of his endurance. We snatched him up, lugged him aft, and pitched him head-first down the cabin companion. You understand there was no time to carry him down with infinite precautions and wait to see how he got on. Those below would pick him up at the bottom of the stairs all right. We were in a hurry to go back to the pumps. That business could not wait. A bad leak is an inhuman thing.

'One would think that the sole purpose of that fiendish gale had been to make a lunatic of that poor devil of a mulatto. It eased before morning, and next day the sky cleared, and as the sea went down the leak took up. When it came to bending a fresh set of sails the crew demanded to put back – and really there was nothing else to do. Boats gone, decks swept clean, cabin gutted, men without a stitch but what they stood in, stores spoiled, ship strained. We put her head for home, and – would you believe it? The wind came east right in our teeth. It blew fresh, it blew continuously. We had to beat up every inch of the way, but she did not leak so badly, the water keeping comparatively smooth. Two hours' pumping in every four is no joke – but it kept her afloat as far as Falmouth.

'The good people there live on casualties of the sea, and no doubt were glad to see us. A hungry crowd of shipwrights sharpened their chisels at the sight of that carcass of a ship. And, by Jove! they had pretty pickings off us before they were done. I fancy the owner was already in a tight place. There were delays. Then it was decided to take part of the cargo out and caulk her topsides. This was done, the repairs finished, cargo reshipped; a new crew came on board, and we went out – for Bangkok. At the end of a week we were back again. The crew said they weren't going to Bangkok – a hundred and fifty days' passage – in a something hooker that wanted pumping eight hours out of the twenty-four; and the nautical papers inserted again the little paragraph: "*Judea*. Barque. Tyne to Bangkok; coals; put back to Falmouth leaky and with crew refusing duty."

'There were more delays – more tinkering. The owner came down for a day, and said she was as right as a little fiddle. Poor old Captain Beard looked like the ghost of a Geordie skipper – through the worry and humiliation of it. Remember he was sixty, and it was his first command. Mahon said it was a foolish business, and would end badly. I loved the ship more then ever, and wanted awfully to get to Bangkok. To Bangkok! Magic name, blessed name. Mesopotamia wasn't a patch on it. Remember I was twenty, and it was my first second-mate's billet, and the East was waiting for me.

'We went out and anchored in the outer roads with a fresh crew – the third. She leaked worse than ever. It was as if those confounded shipwrights had actually made a hole in her. This time we did not even go outside. The crew simply refused to man the windlass.

'They towed us back to the inner harbour, and we became a fixture, a feature, an institution of the place. People pointed us out to visitors as "That 'ere barque that's going to Bangkok – has been here six months – put back three times." On holidays the small boys pulling about in boats would hail, "*Judea*, ahoy!" and if a head showed above the rail shouted, "Where you bound to? – Bangkok?" and jeered. We were only three on board. The poor old skipper mooned in the cabin. Mahon undertook the cooking, and unexpectedly developed all a Frenchman's genius for preparing nice little messes. I looked languidly after the rigging. We became citizens of Falmouth. Every shopkeeper knew us. At the barber's or tobacconist's they asked familiarly, "Do you think you will ever get to Bangkok?" Meantime the owner, the underwriters, and the charterers squabbled amongst themselves in London, and our pay went on . . . Pass the bottle.

'It was horrid. Morally it was worse than pumping for life. It seemed as though we had been forgotten by the world, belonged to nobody, would get nowhere; it seemed that, as if bewitched, we would have to live for ever and ever in that inner harbour, a derision and a by-word to generations of long-shore loafers and dishonest boatmen. I obtained three months' pay and a five days' leave, and made a rush for London. It took me a day to get there and pretty well another to come back – but three months' pay went all the same. I don't know what I did with it. I went to a music hall, I believe, lunched, dined, and supped in a swell place in Regent Street, and was back to time, with nothing but a complete set of Byron's works and a new railway rug to show for three months' work. The boat-man who pulled me off to the ship said: "Hallo! I thought you had left the old thing. *She* will never get to Bangkok." "That's all *you* know about it," I said, scornfully – but I didn't like that prophecy at all.

'Suddenly a man, some kind of agent to somebody, appeared with full powers. He had grog-blossoms all over his face, an indomitable energy, and was a jolly soul. We leaped into life again. A hulk came alongside, took our cargo, and then we went into dry dock to get our copper stripped. No wonder she leaked. The poor thing, strained beyond endurance by the gale, had, as if in disgust, spat out all the oakum of her lower seams. She was recaulked, new coppered, and made as tight as a bottle. We went back to the hulk and reshipped our cargo.

'Then, on a fine moonlight night, all the rats left the ship.

'We had been infested with them. They had destroyed our sails, consumed more stores than the crew, affably shared our beds and our dangers, and now, when the ship was made seaworthy, concluded to clear out. I called Mahon to enjoy the spectacle. Rat after rat appeared on our rail, took a last look over his shoulder, and leaped with a hollow thud into the empty hulk. We tried to count them, but soon lost the tale. Mahon said: "Well, well! Don't talk to me about the intelligence of rats. They ought to have left before, when we had that narrow squeak from foundering. There you have the proof how silly is the superstition about them. They leave a good ship for an old rotten hulk, where there is nothing to eat, too, the fools! . . . I don't believe they know what is safe or what is good for them, any more than you or I."

'And after some more talk we agreed that the wisdom of rats had been grossly overrated, being in fact no greater than that of men.

'The story of the ship was known, by this, all up the Channel from Land's End to the Forelands, and we could get no crew on the south coast. They sent us one all complete from Liverpool, and we left once more – for Bangkok.

'We had fair breezes, smooth water right into the tropics and the old *Judea* lumbered along in the sunshine. When she went eight knots everything cracked aloft, and we tied our caps to our heads; but mostly she strolled on at a rate of three miles an hour. What could you expect? She was tired – that old ship. Her youth was where mine is – where yours is – you fellows who listen to this yarn; and what friend would throw your years and your weariness in your face? We didn't grumble at her. To us aft, at least, it seemed as though we had been born in her, reared in her, had lived in her for ages, had never known any other ship. I would just as soon have abused the old village church at home for not being a cathedral.

'And for me there was also my youth to make me patient. There was all the East before me, and all life, and the thought that I had been tried in that ship and had come out pretty well. And I thought of men of old who, centuries ago, went that road in ships that sailed no better, to the land of palms, and spices, and yellow sands, and of brown nations ruled by kings more cruel than Nero the Roman, and more splendid than Solomon the Jew. The old bark lumbered on, heavy with her age and the burden of her cargo, while I lived the life of youth in ignorance and hope. She lumbered on through an interminable procession of days; and the fresh gilding flashed back at the setting sun, seemed to cry out over the darkening sea the words painted on her stern, "*Judea*, London. Do or Die".

'Then we entered the Indian Ocean and steered northerly for Java Head. The winds were light. Weeks slipped by. She crawled on, do or die, and people at home began to think of posting us as overdue.

'One Saturday evening, I being off duty, the men asked me to give them an extra bucket of water or so – for washing clothes. As I did not wish to screw on the fresh-water pump so late, I went forward whistling, and with a key in my hand to unlock the forepeak scuttle, intending to serve the water out of a spare tank we kept there.

'The smell down below was as unexpected as it was frightful. One would have thought hundreds of paraffin-lamps had been flaring and smoking in that hole for days. I was glad to get out. The man with me coughed and said, "Funny smell, sir." I answered negligently, "It's good for the health they say," and walked aft.

'The first thing I did was to put my head down the square of the midship ventilator. As I lifted the lid a visible breath, something like a thin fog, a puff of faint haze, rose from the opening. The ascending air was hot, and had a heavy, sooty, paraffiny smell. I gave one sniff, and put down the lid gently. It was no use choking myself. The cargo was on fire.

'Next day she began to smoke in earnest. You see it was to be expected, for though the coal was of a safe kind, that cargo had been so handled, so broken up with handling, that it looked more like smithy coal than anything else. Then it had been wetted – more than once. It rained all the time we were taking it back from the hulk, and now with this long passage it got heated, and there was another case of spontaneous combustion.

'The captain called us into the cabin. He had a chart spread on the table, and looked unhappy. He said, "The coast of West Australia is near, but I mean to proceed to our destination. It is the hurricane month, too; but we will just keep her head for Bangkok, and fight the fire. No more putting back anywhere, if we all get roasted. We will try first to stifle this 'ere damned combustion by want of air."

'We tried. We battened down everything, and still she smoked. The smoke kept coming out through imperceptible crevices; it forced itself through bulkheads and covers; it oozed here and there and everywhere in slender threads, in an invisible film, in an incomprehensible manner. It made its way into the cabin, into the forecastle; it poisoned the sheltered places on the deck, it could be sniffed as high as the mainyard. It was clear that if the smoke came out the air came in. This was disheartening. This combustion refused to be stifled.

'We resolved to try water, and took the hatches off. Enormous volumes of smoke, whitish, yellowish, thick, greasy, misty, choking, ascended as high as the trucks. All hands cleared out aft. Then the poisonous cloud blew away, and we went back to work in a smoke that was no thicker now than that of an ordinary factory chimney.

'We rigged the force-pump, got the hose along, and by-and-by it burst. Well, it was as old as the ship – a prehistoric hose, and past repair. Then we pumped with the feeble head-pump, drew water with buckets, and in this way managed in time to pour lots of Indian Ocean into the main hatch. The bright stream flashed in sunshine, fell into a layer of white crawling smoke, and vanished on the black surface of coal. Steam ascended mingling with the smoke. We poured salt water as into a barrel without a bottom. It was our fate to pump in that ship, to pump out of her, to pump into her; and after keeping water out of her to save ourselves from being drowned, we frantically poured water into her to save ourselves from being burnt.

'And she crawled on, do or die, in the serene weather. The sky was a miracle of purity, a miracle of azure. The sea was polished, was blue, was pellucid, was sparkling like a precious stone, extending on all sides, all round to the horizon – as if the whole terrestrial globe had been one jewel, one colossal sapphire, a single gem fashioned into a planet. And on the lustre of the great calm waters the *Judea* glided imperceptibly, enveloped in languid and unclean vapours, in a lazy cloud that drifted to leeward, light and slow; a pestiferous cloud defiling the splendour of sea and sky.

'All this time of course we saw no fire. The cargo smouldered at the bottom somewhere. Once Mahon, as we were working side by side, said to me with a queer smile: "Now, if she only would spring a tidy leak – like that time when we first left the Channel – it would put a stopper on this fire. Wouldn't it?" I remarked irrelevantly, "Do you remember the rats?"

'We fought the fire and sailed the ship too as carefully as though nothing had been the matter. The steward cooked and attended on us. Of the other twelve men, eight worked while four rested. Everyone took his turn, captain included. There was equality, and if not exactly fraternity, then a deal of good feeling. Sometimes a man, as he dashed a bucketful of water down the hatchway, would yell out, "Hurrah for Bangkok!" and the rest laughed. But generally we were taciturn and serious – and thirsty. Oh! how thirsty! And we had to be careful with the water. Strict allowance. The ship smoked, the sun blazed . . . Pass the bottle.

'We tried everything. We even made an attempt to dig down to the fire. No good, of course. No man could remain more than a minute below. Mahon, who went first, fainted there, and the man who went to fetch him out did likewise. We lugged them out on deck. Then I leaped down to show how easily it could be done. They had learned wisdom by that time, and contented themselves by fishing for me with a chain-hook tied to a broomhandle, I believe. I did not offer to go and fetch up my shovel, which was left down below.

'Things began to look bad. We put the long boat into the water. The second boat was ready to swing out. We had also another, a 14-foot thing on davits aft, where it was quite safe.

'Then, behold, the smoke suddenly decreased. We redoubled our efforts to flood the bottom of the ship. In two days there was no smoke at all. Everybody was on the broad grin. This was on a Friday. On Saturday no work, but sailing the ship of course, was done. The men washed their clothes and their faces for the first time in a fortnight and had a special dinner given them. They spoke of spontaneous combustion with contempt, and implied *they* were the boys to put out combustions. Somehow we all felt as though we each had inherited a large fortune. But a beastly smell of burning hung about the ship. Captain Beard had hollow eyes and sunken cheeks. I had never noticed so much before how twisted and bowed he was. He and Mahon prowled soberly about hatches and ventilators, sniffing. It struck me suddenly poor Mahon was a very, very old chap. As to me, I was as pleased and proud as though I had helped to win a great naval battle. O! Youth!

'The night was fine. In the morning a homeward-bound ship passed us hull down – the first we had seen for months; but we were nearing the land at last, Java Head being about 190 miles off, and nearly due north.

'Next day it was my watch on deck from eight to twelve. At breakfast the captain observed, "It's wonderful how that smell hangs about the cabin." About ten, the mate being on the poop, I stepped down on the main-deck for a moment. The carpenter's bench stood abaft the mainmast: I leaned against it sucking at my pipe, and the carpenter, a young chap, came to talk to me. He remarked, "I think we have done very well, haven't we?" and then I perceived with annoyance the fool was trying to tilt the bench. I said curtly, "Don't, Chips," and immediately became aware of a queer sensation, of an absurd delusion – I seemed somehow to be in the air. I heard all round me like a pent-up breath released – as if a thousand giants simultaneously had said Phoo! – and felt a dull concussion which made by ribs ache suddenly. No doubt about it – I was in the air, and my body was describing a short parabola. But short as it was, I had the time to think several thoughts in, as far as I can remember, the following order: "This can't be the carpenter – What is it? – Some accident – Submarine volcano? – Coals, gas! – By Jove! we are being blown up – Everybody's dead – I am falling into the after-hatch – I see fire in it.'

'The coal-dust suspended in the air of the hold had glowed dull-red at the moment of the explosion. In the twinkling of an eye, in an infinitesimal fraction of a second since the first tilt of the bench, I was sprawling full length on the cargo. I picked myself up and scrambled out. It was quick like a rebound. The deck was a wilderness of smashed timber, lying crosswise like trees in a wood after a hurricane; an immense curtain of soiled rags waved gently before me – it was the main-sail blown to strips. I thought, The masts will be toppling over directly; and to get out of the way bolted on all-fours towards the poop-ladder. The first person I saw was Mahon, with eyes like saucers, his mouth open, and the long white hair standing straight on end round his head like a silver halo. He was just about to go down when the sight of the main-deck stirring, heaving up, and changing into splinters before his eyes, petrified him on the top step. I stared at him in unbelief, and he stared at me with a queer kind of shocked curiosity. I did not know that I had no hair, no eyebrows, no eyelashes, that my young mousta-che was burnt off, that my face was black, one cheek laid open, my nose cut, and my chin bleeding. I had lost my cap, one of my slippers, and my shirt was torn to rags. Of all this I was not aware. I was amazed to see the ship still afloat, the poop-deck whole – and, most of all, to see anybody alive. Also the peace of the sky and the serenity of the sea were distinctly surprising. I suppose I expected to see them convulsed with horror . . . Pass the bottle.

'There was a voice hailing the ship from somewhere – in the air, in the sky – I couldn't tell. Presently I saw the captain – and he was mad. He asked me eagerly, "Where's the cabin-table?" and to hear such a question was a frightful shock. I had just been blown up, you under-stand, and vibrated with that experience – I wasn't quite sure whether I was alive. Mahon began to stamp with both feet and yelled at him, "Good God! don't you see the deck's blown out of her?" I found my voice, and stammered out as if conscious of some gross neglect of duty, "I don't know where the cabin-table is." It was like an absurd dream.

'Do you know what he wanted next? Well, he wanted to trim the yards. Very placidly, and as if lost in thought, he insisted on having the foreyard squared. "I don't know if there's anybody alive," said Mahon, almost tearfully. "Surely," he said, gently, "there will be enough left to square the foreyard."

'The old chap, it seems, was in his own berth winding up the chronom-eters, when the shock sent him spinning. Immediately it occurred to him – as he said afterwards – that the ship had struck something, and ran out into the cabin. There, he saw, the cabin-table had vanished somewhere. The deck being blown up, it had fallen down into the lazarette of course. Where we had our breakfast that morning he saw only a great hole in the floor. This appeared to him so awfully mysteri-ous, and impressed him so immensely, that what he saw and heard after he got on deck were mere trifles in comparison. And mark, he noticed directly the wheel deserted and his barque off her course – and his only thought was to get that miserable, stripped, undecked, smouldering shell of a ship back again with her head pointing at her port of destination. Bangkok! That's what he was after. I tell you this quiet, bowed, bandy-legged, almost deformed little man was immense in singleness of his idea and in his placid ignorance of our agitation. He motioned us forward with a commanding gesture, and went to take the wheel himself.

'Yes; that was the first thing we did – trim the yards of that wreck! No one was killed, or even disabled, but everyone was more or less hurt. You should have seen them! Some were in rags, with black faces, like coalheavers, like sweeps, and had bullet heads that seemed close cropped, but were in fact singed to the skin. Others of the watch below, awakened by being shot out from their collapsing bunks, shivered incessantly, and kept on groaning even as we went about our work. But they all worked. That crew of Liverpool hard cases had in them the right stuff. It's my experience they always have. It is the sea that gives it – the vastness, the loneliness surrounding their dark stolid souls. Ah! Well! We stumbled, we crept, we fell, we barked our shins on the wreckage, we hauled. The masts stood, but we did not know how much they might be charred down below. It was nearly calm, but a long swell ran from the west and made her roll. They might go at any moment. We looked at them with apprehension. One could not foresee which way they would fall.

'Then we retreated aft and looked about us. The deck was a tangle of planks on edge, of planks on end, of splinters, of ruined woodwork. The masts rose from that chaos like big trees above a matted undergrowth. The interstices of that mass of wreckage were full of something whitish, sluggish, stirring – of something that was like a greasy fog. The smoke of the invisible fire was coming up again, was trailing, like poisonous thick mist in some valley choked with dead wood. Already lazy wisps were beginning to curl upwards amongst the mass of splinters. Here and there a piece of timber, stuck upright, resembled a post. Half of a fife-rail had been shot through the foresail, and the sky made a patch of glorious blue in the ignobly soiled canvas. A portion of several boards holding together had fallen across the rail, and one end protruded overboard, like a gangway leading upon nothing, like a gangway leading over the deep sea, leading to death – as if inviting us to walk the plank at once and be done with our ridiculous troubles. And still the air, the sky – a ghost, something invisible was hailing the ship.

'Someone had the sense to look over, and there was the helmsman, who had impulsively jumped overboard, anxious to come back. He yelled and swam lustily like a merman, keeping up with the ship. We threw him a rope, and presently he stood amongst us streaming with water and very crestfallen. The captain had surrendered the wheel, and apart, elbow on rail, and chin in hand, gazed at the sea wistfully. We asked ourselves, What next? I thought, now, this is something like. This is great. I wonder what will happen. O youth!

'Suddenly Mahon sighted a steamer far astern. Captain Beard said, "We may do something with her yet." We hoisted two flags, which said in the international language of the sea, "On fire. Want immediate assistance." The steamer grew bigger rapidly, and by-and-by spoke with two flags on her foremast, "I am coming to your assistance."

'In half an hour she was abreast, to windward, within hail, and rolling slightly, with her engines stopped. We lost our composure, and yelled all together with excitement, "We've been blown up." A man in a white helmet, on the bridge, cried "Yes! All right! all right!" and he nodded his head, and smiled, and made soothing motions with his hand as though at a lot of frightened children. One of the boats dropped in the water, and walked towards us upon the sea with her long oars. Four Calashes pulled a swinging stroke. This was my first sight of Malay seamen. I've known them since, but what struck me then was their unconcern: they came alongside, and even the bowman standing up and holding to our main-chains with the boathook did not deign to lift his head for a glance. I thought people who had been blown up deserved more attention.

'A little man, dry like a chip and agile like a monkey, clambered up. It was the mate of the steamer. He gave one look, and cried, "O boys – you had better quit."

'We were silent. He talked apart with the captain for a time – seemed to argue with him. Then they went away together to the steamer.

'When our skipper came back we learned that the steamer was the *Somerville*, Captain Nash, from West Australia to Singapore *via* Batavia with mails, and that the agreement was she should tow us to Anjer or Batavia, if possible, where we could extinguish the fire by scuttling, and then proceed on our voyage – to Bangkok! The old man seemed excited, "We will do it yet," he said to Mahon, fiercely. He shook his fist at the sky. Nobody else said a word.

'At noon the steamer began to tow. She went ahead slim and high, and what was left of the *Judea* followed at the end of seventy fathom of tow-rope – followed her swiftly like a cloud of smoke with mast-heads protruding above. We went aloft to furl the sails. We coughed on the yards, and were careful about the bunts. Do you see the lot of us there, putting a neat furl on the sails of that ship doomed to arrive nowhere? There was not a man who didn't think that at any moment the masts would topple over. From aloft we could not see the ship for smoke, and they worked carefully, passing the gaskets with even turns. "Harbour furl – aloft there!" cried Mahon from below.

'You understand this? I don't think one of those chaps expected to get down in the usual way. When we did I heard them saying to each other, "Well, I thought we could come down overboard, in a lump – sticks and all – blame me if I didn't." "That's what I was thinking to myself," would answer wearily another battered and bandaged scarecrow. And, mind, these were men without the drilled-in habit of obedience. To an onlooker they would be a lot of profane scallywags without a redeeming point. What made them do it – what made them obey me when I, thinking consciously how fine it was, made them drop the bunt of the foresail twice to try and do it better? What? They had no professional reputation – no examples, no praise. It wasn't a sense of duty; they all knew well enough how to shirk, and laze, and dodge – when they had a mind to do it – and mostly they had. Was it the two pounds ten a month that sent them there? They didn't think their pay half good enough. No; it was something in them, something inborn and subtle and everlasting. I don't say positively that the crew of a French or German merchantman wouldn't have done it, but I doubt whether it would have been done in the same way. There was a completeness in it, something solid like a principle, and masterful like an instinct – a disclosure of something secret – of that hidden something, that gift of good or evil that makes racial difference, that shapes the fate of nations.

'It was that night at ten that, for the first time since we had been fighting it, we saw the fire. The speed of the towing had fanned the smouldering destruction. A blue gleam appeared forward, shining below the wreck of the deck. It wavered in patches, it seemed to stir and creep like the light of a glow-worm. I saw it first, and told Mahon. "Then the game's up," he said. "We had better stop this towing, or she will burst out suddenly fore and aft before we can clear out." We set up a yell; rang bells to attract their attention; they towed on. At last Mahon and I had to crawl forward and cut the rope with an axe. There was no time to cast off the lashings. Red tongues could be seen licking the wilderness of splinters under our feet as we made our way back to the poop.

'Of course they very soon found out in the steamer that the rope was gone. She gave a loud blast of her whistle, her lights were seen sweeping in a wide circle, she came up ranging close alongside, and stopped. We were all in a tight group on the poop looking at her. Every man had saved a little bundle or a bag. Suddenly a conical flame with a twisted top shot up forward and threw upon the black sea a circle of light, with the two vessels side by side and heaving gently in its centre. Captain Beard had been sitting on the gratings still and mute for hours, but now he rose slowly and advanced in front of us, to the mizzen-shrouds. Captain Nash hailed: "Come along! Look sharp. I have mail-bags on board. I will take you and your boats to Singapore."

' "Thank you! No!" said our skipper. "We must see the last of the ship."

' "I can't stand by any longer," shouted the other. "Mails – you know."

' "Ay! ay! We are all right."

' "Very well! I'll report you in Singapore . . . Goodbye!"

'He waved his hand. Our men dropped their bundles quietly. The steamer moved ahead, and passing out of the circle of light, vanished at once from our sight, dazzled by the fire which burned fiercely. And then I knew that I would see the East first as commander of a small boat. I thought it fine; and the fidelity to the old ship was fine. We should see the last of her. Oh, the glamour of youth! Oh, the fire of it, more dazzling than the flames of the burning ship, throwing a magic light on the wide earth, leaping audaciously to the sky, presently to be quenched by time, more cruel, more pitiless, more bitter than the sea – and like the flames of the burning ship surrounded by an impenetrable night.

'The old man warned us in his gentle and inflexible way that it was part of our duty to save for the underwriters as much as we could of the ship's gear. Accordingly we went to work aft, while she blazed forward to give us plenty of light. We lugged out a lot of rubbish. What didn't we save? An old barometer fixed with an absurd quantity of screws nearly cost me my life: a sudden rush of smoke came upon me, and I just got away in time. There were various stores, bolts of canvas, coils of rope; the poop looked like a marine bazaar, and the boats were lumbered to the gunwales. One would have thought the old man wanted to take as much as he could of his first command with him. He was very, very quiet, but off his balance evidently. Would you believe it? He wanted to take a length of old stream-cable and a kedge-anchor with him in the long-boat. We said, "Ay, ay, sir," deferentially, and on the quiet let the thing slip overboard. The heavy medicine-chest went that way, two bags of green coffee, tins of paint – fancy, paint! – a whole lot of things. Then I was ordered with two hands into the boats to make a stowage and get them ready against the time it would be proper for us to leave the ship.
'We put everything straight, stepped the long-boat's mast for our skipper, who was to take charge of her, and I was not sorry to sit down for a moment. My face felt raw, every limb ached as if broken, I was aware of all my ribs, and would have sworn to a twist in the backbone. The boats, fast astern, lay in a deep shadow, and all around I could see the circle of the sea lighted by the fire. A gigantic flame arose forward straight and clear. It flared fierce, with noises like the whirr of wings, with rumbles as of thunder. There were cracks, detonations, and from the cone of flame the sparks flew upwards, as man is born to trouble to leaky ships, and to ships that burn.
'What bothered me was that the ship, lying broadside to the swell and to such wind as there was – a mere breath – the boats would not keep astern where they were safe, but persisted, in a pig-headed way boats have, in getting under the counter and then swinging alongside. They were knocking about dangerously and coming near the flame, while the ship rolled on them, and, of course, there was always the danger of the masts going over the side at any moment. I and my two boat-keepers kept them off as best we could, with oars and boat-hooks; but to be constantly at it became exasperating, since there was no

reason why we should not leave at once. We could not see those on board, nor could we imagine what caused the delay. The boat-keepers were swearing feebly, and I had not only my share of the work but also had to keep at it two men who showed a constant inclination to lay themselves down and let things slide.

'At last I hailed, "On deck there," and someone looked over. "We're ready here," I said. The head disappeared, and very soon popped up again. "The captain says, All right, sir, and to keep the boats well clear of the ship."

'Half an hour passed. Suddenly there was a frightful racket, rattle, clanking of chain, hiss of water, and millions of sparks flew up into the shivering column of smoke that stood leaning slightly above the ship. The cat-heads had burned away, and the two red-hot anchors had gone to the bottom, tearing out after them two hundred fathom of red-hot chains. The ship trembled, the mass of flame swayed as if ready to collapse, and the fore top-gallant-mast fell. It darted down like an arrow of fire, shot under, and instantly leaping up within an oar's length of the boats, floated quietly, very black on the luminous sea. I hailed the deck again. After some time a man in an unexpectedly cheerful but also muffled tone, as though he had been trying to speak with his mouth shut, informed me, "Coming directly, sir," and vanished. For a long time I heard nothing but the whirr and roar of the fire. There were also whistling sounds. The boats jumped, tugged at the painters, ran at each other playfully, knocked their sides together, or, do what we would, swung in a bunch against the ship's side. I couldn't stand it any longer, and swarming up a rope, clambered aboard over the stern.

'It was as bright as day. Coming up like this, the sheet of fire facing me was a terrifying sight, and the heat seemed hardly bearable at first. On a settee cushion dragged out of the cabin Captain Beard, his legs drawn up and one arm under his head, slept with the light playing on him. Do you know what the rest were busy about? They were sitting on deck right aft, round an open case, eating bread and cheese and drinking bottled stout.

'On the background of flames twisting in fierce tongues above their heads they seemed at home like salamanders, and looked like a band of desperate pirates. The fire sparkled in the whites of their eyes, gleamed on patches of white skin seen through the torn shirts. Each had the marks as of a battle about him – bandaged heads, tied-up arms, a strip of dirty rag round a knee – and each man had a bottle between his legs and a chunk of cheese in his hand. Mahon got up. With his handsome and disreputable head, his hooked profile, his long white beard, and with an uncorked bottle in his hand, he resembled one of those reckless sea-robbers of old making merry amidst violence and disaster. "The last meal on board," he explained solemnly. "We had nothing to eat all day, and it was no use leaving all this." He flourished the bottle and indicated the sleeping skipper. "He said he couldn't swallow anything, so I got him to lie down," he went on; and as I stared, "I don't know whether you are aware, young fellow, the man had no sleep to speak of for days – and there will be dam' little sleep in the boats." "There will be no boats by-and-by if you fool about much longer," I said, indignantly. I walked up to the skipper and shook him by the shoulder. At last he opened his eyes, but did not move. "Time to leave her, sir," I said quietly.

'He got up painfully, looked at the flames, at the sea sparkling round the ship, and black, black as ink farther away; he looked at the stars shining dim through a thin veil of smoke in a sky black, black as Erebus.

' "Youngest first," he said.

'And the ordinary seaman, wiping his mouth with the back of his hand, got up, clambered over the taffrail, and vanished. Others followed. One, on the point of going over, stopped short to drain his bottle, and with a great swing of his arm flung it at the fire. "Take this!" he cried.

'The skipper lingered disconsolately, and we left him to commune for a while with his first command. Then I went up again and brought him away at last. It was time. The ironwork on the poop was hot to the touch.

'Then the painter of the long-boat was cut, and the three boats, tied together, drifted clear of the ship. It was just sixteen hours after the explosion when we abandoned her. Mahon had charge of the second boat, and I had the smallest – the 14-foot thing. The long-boat would have taken the lot of us; but the skipper said we must save as much property as we could – for the underwriters – and so I got my first command. I had two men with me, a bag of biscuits, a few tins of meat, and a breaker of water. I was ordered to keep close to the long-boat, that in case of bad weather we might be taken into her.

'And do you know what I thought? I thought I would part company as soon as I could. I wanted to have my first command all to myself. I wasn't going to sail in a squadron if there were a chance of independent cruising. I would make land by myself. I would beat the other boats. Youth! All youth! The silly, charming, beautiful youth.

'But we did not make a start at once. We must see the last of the ship. And so the boats drifted about that night, heaving and setting on the swell. The men dozed, waked, sighed, groaned. I looked at the burning ship.

'Between the darkness of earth and heaven she was burning fiercely upon a disc of purple sea shot by the blood-red play of gleams; upon a disc of water glittering and sinister. A high, clear flame, an immense and lonely flame, ascended from the ocean, and from its summit the black smoke poured continuously at the sky. She burned furiously; mournful and imposing like a funeral pile kindled in the night, surrounded by the sea, watched over by the stars. A magnificent death had come like a grace, like a gift, like a reward to that old ship at the end of her laborious days. The surrender of her weary ghost to the keeping of stars and sea was stirring like the sight of a glorious triumph. The masts fell just before daybreak, and for a moment there was a burst and turmoil of sparks that seemed to fill with flying fire the night patient and watchful, the vast night lying silent upon the sea. At daylight she was only a charred shell, floating still under a cloud of smoke and bearing a glowing mass of coal within.

'Then the oars were got out, and the boats forming in a line moved round her remains as if in procession – the long-boat leading. As we pulled across her stern a slim dart of fire shot out viciously at us, and suddenly she went down, head first, in a great hiss of steam. The unconsumed stern was the last to sink; but the paint had gone, had cracked, had peeled off, and there were no letters, there was no word, no stubborn device that was like her soul, to flash at the rising sun her creed and her name.

'We made our way north. A breeze spang up, and about noon all the boats came together for the last time. I had no mast or sail in mine, but I made a mast out of a spare oar and hoisted a boat-awning for a sail, with a boat-hook for a yard. She was certainly over-masted, but I had the satisfaction of knowing that with the wind aft I could beat the other two. I had to wait for them. Then we all had a look at the captain's chart, and after a sociable meal of hard bread and water, got our last instructions. These were simple: steer north, and keep together as much as possible. "Be careful with that jury-rig, Marlow," said the captain; and Mahon, as I sailed proudly past his boat, wrinkled his curved nose, and hailed, "You will sail that ship of yours under water, if you don't look out, young fellow." He was a malicious old man – and may the deep sea where he sleeps now rock him gently, rock him tenderly to the end of time!

'Before sunset a thick rain-squall passed over the two boats, which were far astern, and that was the last I saw of them for a time. Next day I sat steering my cockle-shell – my first command – with nothing but water and sky around me. I did sight in the afternoon the upper sails of a ship far away, but said nothing, and my men did not notice her. You see I was afraid she might be homeward bound, and I had no mind to turn back from the portals of the East. I was steering for Java – another blessed name – like Bangkok, you know. I steered many days.

'I need not tell you what it is to be knocking about in an open boat. I remember nights and days of calm, when we pulled, we pulled, and the boat seemed to stand still, as if bewitched within the circle of the sea horizon. I remember the heat, the deluge of rain-squalls that kept us bailing for dear life (but filled our water-cask), and I remember sixteen hours on end with a mouth dry as a cinder and a steering-oar over the stern to keep my first command head on to a breaking sea. I did not know how good a man I was till then. I remember the drawn faces, the dejected figures of my two men, and I remember my youth and the feeling that will never come back any more – the feeling that I could last for ever, outlast the sea, the earth, and all men; the deceitful feeling that lures us on to joys, to perils, to love, to vain effort – to death; the triumphant conviction of strength, the heat of life in the handful of dust, the glow in the heart that with every year grows dim, grows cold, grows small, and expires – and expires, too soon, too soon – before life itself.

'And this is how I see the East. I have seen its secret places and have looked into its very soul; but now I see it always from a small boat, a high outline of mountains, blue and afar in the morning; like faint mist at noon; a jagged wall of purple at sunset. I have the feel of the oar in my hand, the vision of a scorching blue sea in my eyes. And I see a bay, a wide bay, smooth as glass and polished like ice, shimmering in the dark. A red light burns far off upon the gloom of the land, and the night is soft and warm. We drag at the oars with aching arms, and suddenly a puff of wind, a puff faint and tepid and laden with strange odours of blossoms, of aromatic wood, comes out of the still night – the first sigh of the East on my face. That I can never forget. It was impalpable and enslaving, like a charm, like a whispered promise of mysterious delight.

'We had been pulling this finishing spell for eleven hours. Two pulled, and he whose turn it was to rest sat at the tiller. We had made out the red light in that bay and steered for it, guessing it must mark some small coasting port. We passed two vessels, outlandish and high-sterned, sleeping at anchor, and, approaching the light, now very dim, ran the boat's nose against the end of a jutting wharf. We were blind with fatigue. My men dropped the oars and fell off the thwarts as if dead. I made fast to a pile. A current rippled softly. The scented obscurity of the shore was grouped into vast masses, a density of colossal clumps of vegetation, probably – mute and fantastic shapes. And at their foot the semicircle of a bench gleamed faintly, like an illusion. There was not a light, not a stir, not a sound. The mysterious East faced me, perfumed like a flower, silent like death, dark like a grave.

'And I sat weary beyond expression, exulting like a conqueror, sleepless and entranced as if before a profound, a fateful enigma.

'A splashing of oars, a measured dip reverberating on the level of water, intensified by the silence of the shore into loud claps, made me jump up. A boat, a European boat, was coming in. I invoked the name of the dead; I hailed: *Judea* ahoy! A thin shout answered.

'It was the captain. I had beaten the flagship by three hours, and I was glad to hear the old man's voice again, tremulous and tired. "Is it you, Marlow?" "Mind the end of that jetty, sir," I cried.

'He approached cautiously, and brought up with the deep-sea lead-line which he had saved – for the underwriters. I eased my painter and fell alongside. He sat, a broken figure at the stern, wet with dew, his hands clasped in his lap. His men were asleep already. "I had a terrible time of it," he murmured. "Mahon is behind – not very far." We conversed in whispers, in low whispers, as if afraid to wake up the land. Guns, thunder, earthquakes would not have awakened the men just then.

'Looking round as we talked, I saw away at sea a bright light travelling in the night. "There's a steamer passing the bay," I said. She was not passing, she was entering, and she even came close and anchored. "I wish," said the old man, "you would find out whether she is English. Perhaps they could give us a passage somewhere." He seemed nervously anxious. So by dint of punching and kicking I started one of my men into a state of somnambulism, and giving him an oar, took another and pulled towards the lights of the steamer.

'There was a murmur of voices in her, metallic hollow clangs of the engine-room, footsteps on the deck. Her ports shone, round like dilated eyes. Shapes moved about, and there was a shadowy man high up on the bridge. He heard my oars.

'And then, before I could open my lips, the East spoke to me, but it was in a Western voice. A torrent of words was poured into the enigmatical, the fateful silence; outlandish, angry words, mixed with words and even whole sentences of good English, less strange but even more surprising. The voice swore and cursed violently; it riddled the solemn peace of the bay by a volley of abuse. It began by calling me Pig, and from that went crescendo into unmentionable adjectives – in English. The man up there raged aloud in two languages, and with a sincerity in his fury that almost convinced me I had, in some way, sinned against the harmony of the universe. I could hardly see him, but began to think he would work himself into a fit.

'Suddenly he ceased, and I could hear him snorting and blowing like a porpoise. I said –

' "What steamer is this, pray?'

' "Eh? What's this? And who are you?"

' "Castaway crew of an English barque burnt at sea. We came here tonight. I am the second mate. The captain is in the long-boat, and wishes to know if you would give us a passage somewhere."

' "Oh, my goodness! I say . . . This is the *Celestial* from Singapore

on her return trip. I'll arrange with your captain in the morning, . . .
and, . . . I say, . . . did you hear me just now?'

' "I should think the whole bay heard you."

' "I thought you were a shore-boat. Now, look here – this infernal
lazy scoundrel of a caretaker has gone to sleep again – curse him. The
light is out, and I nearly ran foul of the end of this damned jetty. This
is the third time he plays me this trick. Now, I ask you, can anybody
stand this kind of thing? It's enough to drive a man out of his mind. I'll
report him . . . I'll get the Assistant Resident to give him the sack,
by . . .! See – there's no light. It's out, isn't it? I take you to witness
the light's out. There should be a light, you know. A red light on the –"

' "There was a light," I said, mildly.

' "But it's out, man! What's the use of talking like this? You can see
for yourself it's out – don't you? If you had to take a valuable steamer
along this Godforsaken coast you would want a light, too. I'll kick him
from end to end of this miserable wharf. You'll see if I don't. I will –"

' "So I may tell my captain you'll take us?" I broke in.

' "Yes, I'll take you. Good night," he said, brusquely.

'I pulled back, made fast again to the jetty, and then went to sleep
at last. I had faced the silence of the East. I had heard some of its
language. But when I opened my eyes again the silence was as complete
as though it had never been broken. I was lying in a flood of light, and
the sky had never looked so far, so high, before. I opened my eyes and
lay without moving.

'And then I saw the men of the East – they were looking at me. The
whole length of the jetty was full of people. I saw brown, bronze,
yellow faces, the black eyes, the glitter, the colour of an Eastern
crowd. And all these beings stared without a murmur, without a sigh,
without a movement. They stared down at the boats, at the sleeping
men who at night had come to them from the sea. Nothing moved. The
fronds of palms stood still against the sky. Not a branch stirred along
the shore, and the brown roofs of hidden houses peeped through the
green foliage, through the big leaves that hung shining and still like
leaves forged of heavy metal. This was the East of the ancient naviga-
tors, so old, so mysterious, resplendent and sombre, living and unch-
anged, full of danger and promise. And these were the men. I sat up
suddenly. A wave of movement passed through the crowd from end to
end, passed along the heads, swayed the bodies, ran along the jetty
like a ripple on the water, like a breath of wind on a field – and all was
still again. I see it now – the wide sweep of the bay, the glittering sands,
the wealth of green infinite and varied, the sea blue like the sea of a
dream, the crowd of attentive faces, the blaze of vivid colour – the
water reflecting it all, the curve of the shore, the jetty, the high-sterned
outlandish craft floating still, and the three boats with the tired men

from the West sleeping, unconscious of the land and the people and of the violence of sunshine. They slept thrown across the thwarts, curled on bottom-boards, in the careless attitudes of death. The head of the old skipper, leaning back in the stern of the long-boat, had fallen on his breast, and he looked as though he would never wake. Farther out old Mahon's face was upturned to the sky, with the long white beard spread out on his breast, as though he had been shot where he sat at the tiller; and a man, all in a heap in the bows of the boat, slept with both arms embracing the stem-head and with his cheek laid on the gunwale. The East looked at them without a sound.

'I have known its fascination since; I have seen the mysterious shores, the still water, the lands of brown nations, where a stealthy Nemesis lies in wait, pursues, overtakes so many of the conquering race, who are proud of their wisdom, of their knowledge, of their strength. But for me all the East is contained in that vision of my youth. It is all in that moment when I opened my young eyes on it. I came upon it from a tussle with the sea – and I was young – and I saw it looking at me. And this is all that is left of it! Only a moment; a moment of strength, of romance, of glamour – of youth! . . . A flick of sunshine upon a strange shore, the time to remember, the time for a sigh, and – good-bye! – Night – Good-bye . . .!'

He drank.

'Ah! The good old time – the good old time. Youth and the sea. Glamour and the sea! The good, strong sea, the salt, bitter sea, that could whisper to you and roar at you and knock your breath out of you.'

He drank again.

'By all that's wonderful it is the sea, I believe, the sea itself – or is it youth alone? Who can tell? But you here – you all had something out of life: money, love – whatever one gets on shore – and, tell me, wasn't that the best time, that time when we were young at sea; young and had nothing, on the sea that gives nothing, except hard knocks – and sometimes a chance to feel your strength – that only – what you all regret?'

And we all nodded at him: the man of finance, the man of accounts, the man of law, we all nodded at him over the polished table that like a still sheet of brown water reflected our faces, lined, wrinkled; our faces marked by toil, by deceptions, by success, by love; our weary eyes looking still, looking always, looking anxiously for something out of life, that while it is expected is already gone – has passed unseen, in a sigh, in a flash – together with the youth, with the strength, with the romance of illusions.

Joseph Conrad

Typhoon

CAPTAIN MACWHIRR, of the steamer *Nan-Shan*, had a physiognomy that, in order of material appearances, was the exact counterpart of his mind: it presented no marked characteristics of firmness or stupidity; it had no pronounced characteristics whatever; it was simply ordinary, irresponsive, and unruffled.

The only thing his aspect might have been said to suggest, at times, was bashfulness; because he would sit, in business offices ashore, sunburnt and smiling faintly, with downcast eyes. When he raised them, they were perceived to be direct in their glance and of blue colour. His hair was fair and extremely fine, clasping from temple to temple the bald dome of his skull in a clamp as of fluffy silk. The hair of his face, on the contrary, carrotty and flaming, resembled a growth of copper wire clipped short to the line of the lip; while, no matter how close he shaved, fiery metallic gleams passed, when he moved his head, over the surface of his cheeks. He was rather below the medium height, a bit round-shouldered, and so sturdy of limb that his clothes always looked a shade too tight for his arms and legs. As if unable to grasp what is due to the difference of latitudes, he wore a brown bowler hat, a complete suit of a brownish hue, and clumsy black boots. These harbour togs gave to his thick figure an air of stiff and uncouth smartness. A thin silver watch-chain looped his waistcoat, and he never left his ship for the shore without clutching in his powerful, hairy fist an elegant umbrella of the very best quality, but generally unrolled. Young Jukes, the chief mate, attending his commander to the gangway, would sometimes venture to say, with the greatest gentleness, 'Allow me, sir' – and possessing himself of the umbrella deferentially, would elevate the ferrule, shake the folds, twirl a neat furl in a jiffy, and hand it back; going through the performance with a face of such portentous gravity, that Mr Solomon Rout, the chief engineer, smoking his morning cigar over the skylight, would turn away his head in order to hide a smile. 'Oh! aye! The blessed gamp. . . . Thank 'ee,

TYPHOON

Jukes, thank 'ee,' would mutter Captain MacWhirr, heartily, without looking up.

Having just enough imagination to carry him through each successive day, and no more, he was tranquilly sure of himself; and from the very same cause he was not in the least conceited. It is your imaginative superior who is touchy, overbearing, and difficult to please; but every ship Captain MacWhirr commanded was the floating abode of harmony and peace. It was, in truth, as impossible for him to take a flight of fancy as it would be for a watchmaker to put together a chronometer with nothing except a two-pound hammer and a whip-saw in the way of tools. Yet the uninteresting lives of men so entirely given to the actuality of the bare existence have their mysterious side. It was impossible in Captain MacWhirr's case, for instance, to understand what under heaven could have induced that perfectly satisfactory son of a petty grocer in Belfast to run away to sea. And yet he had done that very thing at the age of fifteen. It was enough, when you thought it over, to give you the idea of an immense, potent, and invisible hand thrust into the ant-heap of the earth, laying hold of shoulders, knocking heads together, and setting the unconscious faces of the multitude towards inconceivable goals and in undreamt-of directions.

His father never really forgave him for this undutiful stupidity. 'We could have got on without him,' he used to say later on, 'but there's the business. And he an only son, too!' His mother wept very much after his disappearance. As it had never occurred to him to leave word behind, he was mourned over for dead till, after eight months, his first letter arrived from Talcahuano. It was short, and contained the statement: 'We had very fine weather on our passage out.' But evidently, in the writer's mind, the only important intelligence was to the effect that his captain had, on the very day of writing, entered him regularly on the ship's articles as Ordinary Seaman. 'Because I can do the work,' he explained. The mother again wept copiously, while the remark, 'Tom's an ass,' expressed the emotions of the father. He was a corpulent man, with a gift for sly chaffing, which to the end of his life he exercised in his intercourse with his son, a little pityingly, as if upon a half-witted person.

MacWhirr's visits to his home were necessarily rare, and in the course of years he dispatched other letters to his parents, informing them of his successive promotions and of his movements upon the vast earth. In these missives could be found sentences like this: 'The heat here is very great.' Or: 'On Christmas day at 4 p.m. we fell in with some icebergs.' The old people ultimately became acquainted with a good many names of ships, and with the names of the skippers who commanded them – with the names of Scots and English shipowners – with the names of seas, oceans, straits, promontories – with outlandish names of lumber-ports, of rice-ports, of cotton-ports – with the names of islands – with the name of their son's young woman. She was called Lucy. It did not suggest itself to him to mention whether he thought the name pretty. And then they died.

The great day of MacWhirr's marriage came in due course, following shortly upon the great day when he got his first command.

All these events had taken place many years before the morning when, in the chart-room of the steamer *Nan-Shan*, he stood confronted by the fall of a barometer he had no reason to distrust. The fall – taking into account the excellence of the instrument, the time of the year, and the ship's position on the terrestrial globe – was of a nature ominously prophetic; but the red face of the man betrayed no sort of inward disturbance. Omens were as nothing to him, and he was unable to discover the message of a prophecy till the fulfilment had brought it home to his very door. 'That's a fall, and no mistake,' he thought. 'There must be some uncommonly dirty weather knocking about.'

The *Nan-Shan* was on her way from the southward to the treaty port of Fu-chau, with some cargo in her lower holds, and two hundred Chinese coolies returning to their village homes in the province of Fo-kien, after a few years of work in various tropical colonies. The morning was fine, the oily sea heaved without a sparkle, and there was a queer white misty patch in the sky like a halo of the sun. The fore-deck, packed with Chinamen, was full of sombre clothing, yellow faces, and pigtails, sprinkled over with a good many naked shoulders, for there was no wind, and the heat was close. The coolies lounged, talked, smoked, or stared over the rail; some, drawing water over the side, sluiced each other; a few slept on hatches, while several small parties of six sat on their heels surrounding iron trays with plates of rice and tiny teacups; and every single Celestial of them was carrying with him all he had in the world – a wooden chest with a ringing lock and brass on the corners, containing the savings of his labours: some clothes of ceremony, sticks of incense, a little opium maybe, bits of nameless rubbish of conventional value, and a small hoard of silver dollars, toiled for in coal-lighters, won in gambling-houses or in petty trading, grubbed out of earth, sweated out in mines, on railway lines, in deadly jungle, under heavy burdens – amassed patiently, guarded with care, cherished fiercely.

A cross swell had set in from the direction of Formosa Channel about ten o'clock, without disturbing these passengers much, because the *Nan-Shan*, with her flat bottom, rolling chocks on bilges, and great breadth of beam, had the reputation of an exceptionally steady ship in a sea-way. Mr Jukes, in moments of expansion on shore, would proclaim loudly that the 'old girl was as good as she was pretty'. It would never have occurred to Captain MacWhirr to express his favourable opinion so loud or in terms so fanciful.

She was a good ship, undoubtedly, and not old either. She had been built in Dumbarton less than three years before, to the order of a firm of merchants in Siam – Messrs Sigg and Son. When she lay afloat, finished in every detail and ready to take up the work of her life, the builders contemplated her with pride.

'Sigg has asked us for a reliable skipper to take her out,' remarked one of the partners; and the other, after reflecting for a while, said: 'I think MacWhirr is ashore just at present.' 'Is he? Then wire him at once. He's the very man,' declared the senior, without a moment's hesitation.

Next morning MacWhirr stood before them unperturbed, having travelled from London by the midnight express after a sudden but undemonstrative parting with his wife. She was the daughter of a superior couple who had seen better days.

'We had better be going together over the ship, Captain,' said the senior partner; and the three men started to view the perfections of the *Nan-Shan* from stem to stern, and from her keelson to the trucks of her two stumpy pole-masts.

Captain MacWhirr had begun by taking off his coat, which he hung on the end of a steam windlass embodying all the latest improvements.

'My uncle wrote of you favourably by yesterday's mail to our good friends – Messrs Sigg, you know – and doubtless they'll continue you out there in command,' said the junior partner. 'You'll be able to boast of being in charge of the handiest boat of her size on the coast of China, Captain,' he added.

'Have you? Thank 'ee,' mumbled vaguely MacWhirr, to whom the view of a distant eventuality could appeal no more than the beauty of a wide landscape to a purblind tourist; and his eyes happening at the moment to be at rest upon the lock of the cabin door, he walked up to it, full of purpose, and began to rattle the handle vigorously, while he observed, in his low, earnest voice, 'You can't trust the workmen nowadays. A brand-new lock, and it won't act at all. Stuck fast. See? See?'

As soon as they found themselves alone in their office across the yard: 'You praised that fellow up to Sigg. What is it you see in him?' asked the nephew, with faint contempt.

'I admit he has nothing of your fancy skipper about him, if that's what you mean,' said the elder man, curtly. 'Is the foreman of the joiners on the *Nan-Shan* outside? . . . Come in, Bates. How is it that you let Tait's people put us off with a defective lock on the cabin door? The Captain could see directly he set eye on it. Have it replaced at once. The little straws, Bates . . . the little straws . . .'

The lock was replaced accordingly, and a few days afterwards the *Nan-Shan* steamed out to the East, without MacWhirr having offered any further remark as to her fittings, or having been heard to utter a single word hinting at pride in his ship, gratitude for his appointment, or satisfaction at his prospects.

With a temperament neither loquacious nor taciturn he found very little occasion to talk. There were matters of duty, of course – directions, orders, and so on; but the past being to his mind done with, and the future not there yet, the more general actualities of the day required no comment – because facts can speak for themselves with overwhelming precision.

Old Mr Sigg liked a man of few words, and one that 'you could be sure would not try to improve his instructions'. MacWhirr, satisfying these requirements, was continued in command of the *Nan-Shan*, and applied himself to the careful navigation of his ship in the China seas. She had come out on a British register, but after some time Messrs Sigg judged it expedient to transfer her to the Siamese flag.

At the news of the contemplated transfer Jukes grew restless, as if under a sense of personal affront. He went about grumbling to himself, and uttering short scornful laughs. 'Fancy having a ridiculous Noah's Ark elephant in the ensign of one's ship,' he said once at the engine-room door. 'Dash me if I can stand it: I'll throw up the billet. Don't it make *you* sick, Mr Rout?' The chief engineer only cleared his throat with the air of a man who knows the value of a good billet.

The first morning the new flag floated over the stern of the *Nan-Shan* Juke stood looking at it bitterly from the bridge. He struggled with his feelings for a while, and then remarked, 'Queer flag for a man to sail under, sir.'

'What's the matter with the flag?' inquired Captain MacWhirr. 'Seems all right to me.' And he walked across to the end of the bridge to have a good look.

'Well, it looks queer to me,' burst out Jukes, great exasperated, and flung off the bridge.

Captain MacWhirr was amazed at these manners. After a while he stepped quietly into the chart-room, and opened his International Signal Code-book at the plate where the flags of all the nations are correctly figured in gaudy rows. He ran his finger over them, and when he came to Siam he contemplated with great attention the red field and the white elephant. Nothing could be more simple; but to make sure he brought the book out on the bridge for the purpose of comparing the coloured drawing with the real thing at the flag-staff astern. When next Jukes, who was carrying on the duty that day with a sort of suppressed fierceness, happened on the bridge, his commander observed:

'There's nothing amiss with that flag.'

'Isn't there?' mumbled Jukes, falling on his knees before a deck-locker and jerking therefrom viciously a spare lead-line.

'No. I looked up the book. Length twice the breadth and the elephant exactly in the middle. I thought the people ashore would know how to make the local flag. Stands to reason. You were wrong, Jukes . . .'

'Well, sir,' began Jukes, getting up excitedly, 'all I can say –' He fumbled for the end of the coil of line with trembling hands.

'That's all right.' Captain MacWhirr soothed him, sitting heavily on a little canvas folding-stool he greatly affected. 'All you have to do is to take care they don't hoist the elephant upside-down before they get quite used to it.'

Jukes flung the new lead-line over on the fore-deck with a loud 'Here you are, bos'n – don't forget to wet it thoroughly,' and turned with immense resolution towards his commander; but Captain MacWhirr spread his elbows on the bridge-rail comfortably.

'Because it would be, I suppose, understood as a signal of distress,' he went on. 'What do you think? That elephant there, I take it, stands for something in the nature of the Union Jack in the flag . . .'

'Does it!' yelled Jukes, so that every head on the *Nan-Shan*'s deck looked towards the bridge. Then he sighed, and with sudden resignation: 'It would certainly be a damn distressful sight,' he said, meekly.

Later in the day he accosted the chief engineer with a confidential, 'Here, let me tell you the old man's latest.'

Mr Solomon Rout (frequently alluded to as Long Sol, Old Sol, or Father Rout), from finding himself almost invariably the tallest man on board every ship he joined, had acquired the habit of a stooping, leisurely condescension. His hair was scant and sandy, his flat cheeks were pale, his bony wrists and long scholarly hands were pale, too, as though he had lived all his life in the shade.

He smiled from on high at Jukes, and went on smoking and glancing about quietly, in the manner of a kind uncle lending an ear to the tale of an excited schoolboy. Then, greatly amused but impassive, he asked:

'And did you throw up the billet?'

'No,' cried Jukes, raising a weary, discouraged voice above the harsh buzz of the *Nan-Shan*'s friction winches. All of them were hard at work, snatching slings of cargo, high up, to the end of long derricks, only, as it seemed, to let them rip down recklessly by the run. The cargo chains groaned in the gins, clinked on coamings, rattled over the side; and the whole ship quivered, with her long grey flanks smoking in wreaths of steam. 'No,' cried Jukes, 'I didn't. What's the good? I might just as well fling my resignation at this bulk head. I don't believe you can make a man like that understand anything. He simply knocks me over.'

At that moment Captain MacWhirr, back from the shore, crossed the deck, umbrella in hand, escorted by a mournful, self-possessed Chinaman, walking behind in paper-soled silk shoes, and who also carried an umbrella.

The master of the *Nan-Shan*, speaking just audibly and gazing at his boots as his manner was, remarked that it would be necessary to call at Fu-chau this trip, and desired Mr Rout to have steam up tomorrow afternoon at one o'clock sharp. He pushed back his hat to wipe his forehead, observing at the same time that he hated going ashore anyhow; while overtopping him Mr Rout, without deigning a word, smoked austerely, nursing his right elbow in the palm of his left hand. Then Jukes was directed in the same subdued voice to keep the forward 'tween-deck clear of cargo. Two hundred coolies were going to be put down there. The Bun Hin Company were sending that lot home. Twenty-five bags of rice would be coming off in a sampan directly, for stores. All seven-years' men they were, said Captain MacWhirr, with a camphor-wood chest to every man. The carpenter should be set to work nailing three-inch battens along the deck below, fore and aft, to keep these boxes from shifting in a sea-way. Jukes had better look to it at once. 'D'ye hear, Jukes?' This Chinaman here was coming with the ship as far as Fu-chau – a sort of interpreter he would be. Bun Hin's clerk he was, and wanted to have a look at the space. Jukes had better take him forward. 'D'ye hear, Jukes?'

Jukes took care to punctuate these instructions in proper places with the obligatory 'Yes, sir', ejaculated without enthusiasm. His brusque 'Come along, John; make look see' set the Chinaman in motion at his heels.

'Wanchee look see, all same look see can do,' said Jukes, who having no talent for foreign languages mangled the very pidgin-English cruelly. He pointed at the open hatch. 'Catchee number one piecie place to sleep in. Eh?'

He was gruff, as became his racial superiority, but not unfriendly. The Chinaman, gazing sad and speechless into the darkness of the hatchway, seemed to stand at the head of a yawning grave.

'No catchee rain down there – savee?' pointed out Jukes. 'Suppose all'ee same fine weather, one piecie coolie-man come topside,' he pursued, warming up imaginatively. 'Make so – Phooooo!' He expanded his chest and blew out his cheeks. 'Savee, John? Breathe – fresh air. Good. Eh? Washee him piecie pants, chow-chow top-side – see, John?'

With his mouth and hands he made exuberant motions of eating rice and washing clothes; and the Chinaman, who concealed his distrust of this pantomime under a collected demeanour tinged by a gentle and refined melancholy, glanced out of his almond eyes from Jukes to the hatch and back again. 'Velly good,' he murmured, in a disconsolate undertone, and hastened smoothly along the decks, dodging obstacles in his course. He disappeared, ducking low under a sling of ten dirty gunny-bags full of some costly merchandise and exhaling a repulsive smell.

Captain MacWhirr meantime had gone on the bridge, and into the chart-room, where a letter, commenced two days before, awaited termination. These long letters began with the words, 'My darling wife,' and the steward, between the scrubbing of the floors and the dusting of chronometer-boxes, snatched at every opportunity to read them. They interested him much more than they possibly could the woman for whose eye they were intended; and this for the reason that they related in minute detail each successive trip of the *Nan-Shan*.

Her master, faithful to facts, which alone his consciousness reflected, would set them down with painstaking care upon many pages. The house in a northern suburb to which these pages were addressed had a bit of garden before the bow-windows, a deep porch of good appearance, coloured glass with imitation lead frame in the front door. He paid five-and-forty pounds a year for it, and did not think the rent too high, because Mrs MacWhirr (a pretentious person with a scraggy neck and a disdainful manner) was admittedly ladylike, and in the neighbourhood considered as 'quite superior'. The only secret of her life was her abject terror of the time when her husband would come home to stay for good. Under the same roof there dwelt also a daughter called Lydia and a son, Tom. These two were but slightly acquainted with their father. Mainly, they knew him as a rare but privileged visitor, who of an evening smoked his pipe in the dining-room and slept in the house. The lanky girl, upon the whole, was rather ashamed of him; the boy was frankly and utterly indifferent in a straightforward, delightful, unaffected way manly boys have.

And Captain MacWhirr wrote home from the coast of China twelve times every year, desiring quaintly to be 'remembered to the children', and subscribing himself 'your loving husband', as calmly as if the words so long used by so many men were, apart from their shape, worn-out things, and of a faded meaning.

The China seas north and south are narrow seas. They are seas full of everyday, eloquent facts, such as islands, sand-banks, reefs, swift and changeable currents – tangled facts that nevertheless speak to a seaman in clear and definite language. Their speech appealed to Captain MacWhirr's sense of realities so forcibly that he had given up his state-room below and practically lived all his days on the bridge of his ship, often having his meals sent up, and sleeping at night in the chart-room. And he indited there his home letters. Each of them, without exception, contained the phrase, 'The weather has been very fine this trip,' or some other form of a statement to that effect. And this statement, too, in its wonderful persistence, was of the same perfect accuracy as all the others they contained.

Mr Rout likewise wrote letters; only no one on board knew how chatty he could be pen in hand, because the chief engineer had enough imagination to keep his desk locked. His wife relished his style greatly. They were a childless couple, and Mrs Rout, a big, high-bosomed jolly woman of forty, shared with Mr Rout's toothless and venerable mother a little cottage near Teddington. She would run over her correspondence, at breakfast, with lively eyes, and scream out interesting passages in a joyous voice at the deaf old lady, prefacing each extract by the warning shout, 'Solomon says!' She had the trick of firing off Solomon's utterances also upon strangers, astonishing them easily by the unfamiliar text and the unexpectedly jocular vein of these quotations. On the day the new curate called for the first time at the cottage, she found occasion to remark, 'As Solomon says: "the engineers that go down to the sea in ships behold the wonders of sailor nature" '; when a change in the visitor's countenance made her stop and stare.

'Solomon . . . Oh! . . . Mrs Rout,' stuttered the young man, very red in the face, 'I must say . . . I don't . . .'

'He's my husband,' she announced in a great shout, throwing herself back in the chair. Perceiving the joke, she laughed immoderately with a handkerchief to her eyes, while he sat wearing a forced smile, and, from his inexperience of jolly women, fully persuaded that she must be deplorably insane. They were excellent friends afterwards; for, absolving her from irreverent intention, he came to think she was a very worthy person indeed; and he learned in time to receive without flinching other scraps of Solomon's wisdom.

'For my part,' Solomon was reported by his wife to have said once, 'give me the dullest ass for a skipper before a rogue. There is a way to take a fool; but a rogue is smart and slippery.' This was an airy generalization drawn from the particular case of Captain MacWhirr's honesty, which, in itself, had the heavy obviousness of a lump of clay. On the other hand, Mr Jukes, unable to generalize, unmarried, and unengaged, was in the habit of opening his heart after another fashion to an old chum and former shipmate, actually serving as second officer on board an Atlantic liner.

First of all he would insist upon the advantages of the Eastern trade, hinting at its superiority to the Western ocean service. He extolled the sky, the seas, the ships, and the easy life of the Far East. The *Nan-Shan*, he affirmed, was second to none as a sea-boat.

'We have no brass-bound uniforms, but then we are like brothers here,' he wrote. 'We all mess together and live like fighting-cocks . . . All the chaps of the black-squad are as decent as they make that kind, and old Sol, the Chief, is a dry stick. We are good friends. As to our old man, you could not find a quieter skipper. Sometimes you would think he hadn't sense enough to see anything wrong. And yet it isn't that. Can't be. He has been in command for a good few years now. He doesn't do anything actually foolish, and gets his ship along all right without worrying anybody. I believe he hasn't brains enough to enjoy kicking up a row. I don't take advantage of him. I would scorn it. Outside the routine of duty he doesn't seem to understand more than half of what you tell him. We get a laugh out of this at times; but it is dull, too, to be with a man like this – in the long run. Old Sol says he hasn't much conversation. Conversation! O Lord! He never talks. The other day I had been yarning under the bridge with one of the engineers, and he must have heard us. When I came up to take my watch, he steps out of the chart-room and has a good look all round, peeps over at the sidelights, glances at the compass, squints upwards at the stars. That's his regular performance. By-and-by he says: "Was that you talking just now in the port-alleyway?" "Yes, sir." "With the third engineer?" "Yes, sir." He walks off to starboard, and sits under the dodger on a little camp-stool of his, and for half an hour perhaps he makes no sound, except that I heard him sneeze once. Then after a while I hear him getting up over there, and he strolls across to port, where I was. "I can't understand what you can find to talk about," says he. "Two solid hours. I am not blaming you. I see people ashore at it all day long, and then in the evening they sit down and keep at it over the drinks. Must be saying the same things over and over again. I can't understand." '

'Did you ever hear anything like that? And he was so patient about it. It made me quite sorry for him. But he is exasperating, too, sometimes. Of course one would not do anything to vex him even if it were worth while. But it isn't. He's so jolly innocent that if you were to put your thumb to your nose and wave your fingers at him he would only wonder gravely to himself what got into you. He told me once quite simply that he found it very difficult to make out what made people always act so queerly. He's too dense to trouble about, and that's the truth.'

Thus wrote Mr Jukes to his chum in the Western ocean trade, out of the fulness of his heart and the liveliness of his fancy.

He had expressed his honest opinion. It was not worth while trying to impress a man of that sort. If the world had been full of such men, life would have probably appeared to Jukes an unentertaining and unprofitable business. He was not alone in his opinion. The sea itself, as if sharing Mr Jukes's good-natured forbearance, had never put itself out to startle the silent man, who seldom looked up, and wandered innocently over the waters with the only visible purpose of getting food, raiment, and house-room for three people ashore. Dirty weather he had known, of course. He had been made wet, uncomfortable, tired in the usual way, felt at the time and presently forgotten. So that upon the whole he had been justified in reporting fine weather at home. But he had never been given a glimpse of immeasurable strength and of immoderate wrath, the wrath that passes exhausted but never appeased – the wrath and fury of the passionate sea. He knew it existed, as we know that crime and abominations exist; he had heard of it as a peaceable citizen in a town hears of battles, famines, and floods, and yet knows nothing of what these things mean – though, indeed, he may have been mixed up in a street row, have gone without his dinner once, or been soaked to the skin in a shower. Captain MacWhirr had sailed over the surface of the oceans as some men go skimming over the years of existence to sink gently into a placid grave, ignorant of life to the last, without ever having been made to see all it may contain of perfidy, of violence, and of terror. There are on sea and land such men thus fortunate – or thus disdained by destiny or by the sea.

II

OBSERVING the steady fall of the barometer, Captain MacWhirr thought, 'There's some dirty weather knocking about.' This is precisely what he thought. He had had an experience of moderately dirty weather – the term dirty as applied to the weather implying only moderate discomfort to the seaman. Had he been informed by an indisputable authority that the end of the world was to be finally accomplished by a catastrophic disturbance of the atmosphere, he would have assimilated the information under the simple idea of dirty weather, and no other, because he had no experience of cataclysms, and belief does not necessarily imply comprehension. The wisdom of his country had pronounced by means of an Act of Parliament that before he could be considered as fit to take charge of a ship he should be able to answer certain simple questions on the subject of circular storms such as hurricanes, cyclones, typhoons; and apparently he had answered them, since he was now in command of the *Nan-Shan* in the China seas during the season of typhoons. But if he had answered he remembered nothing of it. He was, however, conscious of being made uncomfortable by the clammy heat. He came out on the bridge, and found no relief to this oppression. The air seemed thick. He gasped like a fish, and began to believe himself greatly out of sorts.

The *Nan-Shan* was ploughing a vanishing furrow upon the circle of the sea that had the surface and the shimmer of an undulating piece of grey silk. The sun, pale and without rays, poured down leaden heat in a strangely indecisive light, and the Chinamen were lying prostrate about the decks. Their bloodless, pinched, yellow faces were like the faces of bilious invalids. Captain MacWhirr noticed two of them especially, stretched out on their backs below the bridge. As soon as they had closed their eyes they seemed dead. Three others, however, were quarrelling barbarously away forward; and one big fellow, half naked, with herculean shoulders, was hanging limping over a winch; another, sitting on the deck, his knees up and his head drooping sideways in a girlish attitude, was plaiting his pigtail with infinite languor depicted in his whole person and in the very movement of his fingers. The smoke struggled with difficulty out of the funnel, and instead of streaming away spread itself out like an infernal sort of cloud, smelling of sulphur and raining soot all over the decks.

'What the devil are you doing there, Mr Jukes?' asked Captain MacWhirr.

This unusual form of address, though mumbled rather than spoken, caused the body of Mr Jukes to start as though it had been prodded under the fifth rib. He had had a low bench brought on the bridge, and sitting on it, with a length of rope curled about his feet and a piece of canvas stretched over his knees, was pushing a sail-needle vigorously. He looked up, and his surprise gave to his eyes an expression of innocence and candour.

'I am only roping some of that new set of bags we made last trip for whipping up coals,' he remonstrated, gently. 'We shall want them for the next coaling, sir.'

'What became of the others?'

'Why, worn out of course, sir.'

Captain MacWhirr, after glaring down irresolutely at his chief mate, disclosed the gloomy and cynical conviction that more than half of them had been lost overboard, 'if only the truth was known', and retired to the other end of the bridge. Jukes, exasperated by this unprovoked attack, broke the needle at the second stitch, and dropping his work got up and cursed the heat in a violent undertone.

The propeller thumped, the three Chinamen forward had given up squabbling very suddenly, and the one who had been plaiting his tail clasped his legs and stared dejectedly over his knees. The lurid sunshine cast faint and sickly shadows. The swell ran higher and swifter every moment, and the ship lurched heavily in the smooth, deep hollows of the sea.

'I wonder where that beastly swell comes from,' said Jukes aloud, recovering himself after a stagger.

'North-east,' grunted the literal MacWhirr, from his side of the bridge. 'There's some dirty weather knocking about. Go and look at the glass.'

When Jukes came out of the chart-room, the cast of his countenance had changed to thoughtfulness and concern. He caught hold of the bridge-rail and stared ahead.

The temperature in the engine-room had gone up to a hundred and seventeen degrees. Irritated voices were ascending through the skylight and through the fiddle of the stokehold in a harsh and resonant uproar, mingled with angry clangs and scrapes of metal, as if men with limbs of iron and throats of bronze had been quarrelling down there. The second engineer was falling foul of the stokers for letting the steam go down. He was a man with arms like a blacksmith, and generally feared; but that afternoon the stokers were answering him back recklessly, and slammed the furnace doors with the fury of despair. Then the noise ceased suddenly, and the second engineer appeared, emerging out of the stokehold streaked with grime and soaking wet like a chimney-sweep coming out of a well. As soon as his head was clear of the fiddle he began to scold Jukes for not trimming properly the stokehold ventilators; and in answer Jukes made with his hands deprecatory soothing signs meaning: No wind – can't be helped – you can see for yourself. But the other wouldn't hear reason. His teeth flashed angrily in his dirty face. He didn't mind, he said, the trouble of punching their blanked heads down there, blank his soul, but did the condemned sailors think you could keep steam up in the Godforsaken boilers simply by knocking the blanked stokers about? No, by George! You had to get some draught, too – may he be everlastingly blanked for a swab-headed deck-hand if you didn't! And the chief, too, rampaging before the steam-gauge and carrying on like a lunatic up and down the engine-room ever since noon. What did Jukes think he was stuck up there for, if he couldn't get one of his decayed, good-for-nothing deck-cripples to turn the ventilators to the wind?

The relations of the 'engine-room' and the 'deck' of the *Nan-Shan* were, as is known, of a brotherly nature; therefore Jukes leaned over and begged the other in a restrained tone not to make a disgusting ass of himself; the skipper was on the other side of the bridge. But the second declared mutinously that he didn't care a rap who was on the other side of the bridge, and Jukes, passing in a flash from lofty disapproval into a state of exaltation, invited him in unflattering terms to come up and twist the beastly things to please himself, and catch such wind as a donkey of his sort could find. The second rushed up to the fray. He flung himself at the port ventilator as though he meant to tear it out bodily and toss it overboard. All he did was to move the cowl round a few inches, with an enormous expenditure of force, and seemed spent in the effort. He leaned against the back of the wheel-house, and Jukes walked up to him.

'Oh, Heavens!' ejaculated the engineer in a feeble voice. He lifted his eyes to the sky, and then let his glassy stare descend to meet the horizon that, tilting up to an angle of forty degrees, seemed to hang on a slant for a while and settled down slowly. 'Heavens! Phew! What's up, anyhow?'

Jukes, straddling his long legs like a pair of compasses, put on an air of superiority. 'We're going to catch it this time,' he said. 'The barometer is tumbling down like anything, Harry. And you trying to kick up that silly row . . .'

The word 'barometer' seemed to revive the second engineer's mad animosity. Collecting afresh all his energies, he directed Jukes in a low and brutal tone to shove the unmentionable instrument down his gory throat. Who cared for his crimson barometer? It was the steam – the steam – that was going down; and what between the firemen going faint and the chief going silly, it was worse than a dog's life for him; he didn't care a tinker's curse how soon the whole show was blown out of the water. He seemed on the point of having a cry, but after regaining his breath he muttered darkly, 'I'll faint them,' and dashed off. He stopped upon the fiddle long enough to shake his fist at the unnatural daylight, and dropped into the dark hole with a whoop.

When Jukes turned, his eyes fell upon the rounded back and the big red ears of Captain MacWhirr, who had come across. He did not look at his chief officer, but said at once, 'That's a very violent man, that second engineer.'

'Jolly good second, anyhow,' grunted Jukes. 'They can't keep up steam,' he added, rapidly, and made a grab at the rail against the coming lurch.

Captain MacWhirr, unprepared, took a run and brought himself up with a jerk by an awning stanchion.

'A profane man,' he said, obstinately. 'If this goes on, I'll have to get rid of him the first chance.'

'It's the heat,' said Jukes. 'The weather's awful. It would make a saint swear. Even up here I feel exactly as if I had my head tied up in a woollen blanket.'

Captain MacWhirr looked up. 'D'ye mean to say, Mr Jukes, you ever had your head tied up in a blanket? What was that for?'

'It's a manner of speaking, sir,' said Jukes, stolidly.

'Some of you fellows do go on! What's that about saints swearing? I wish you wouldn't talk so wild. What sort of saint would that be that would swear? No more saint than yourself, I expect. And what's a blanket got to do with it – or the weather either . . . The heat does not make me swear – does it? It's filthy bad temper. That's what it is. And what's the good of your talking like this?'

Thus Captain MacWhirr expostulated against the use of images in speech, and at the end electrified Jukes by a contemptuous snort, followed by words of passion and resentment: 'Damme! I'll fire him out of the ship if he don't look out.'

And Jukes, incorrigible, thought: 'Goodness me! Somebody's put a new inside to my old man. Here's temper, if you like. Of course it's the weather; what else? It would make an angel quarrelsome – let alone a saint.'

All the Chinamen on deck appeared at their last gasp.

At its setting the sun had a diminished diameter and an expiring brown, rayless glow, as if millions of centuries elapsing since the morning had brought it near its end. A dense bank of cloud became visible to the northward; it had a sinister dark olive tint, and lay low and motionless upon the sea, resembling a solid obstacle in the path of the ship. She went floundering towards it like an exhausted creature driven to its death. The coppery twilight retired slowly, and the darkness brought out overhead a swarm of unsteady, big stars, that, as if blown upon, flickered exceedingly and seemed to hang very near the earth. At eight o'clock Jukes went into the chart-room to write up the ship's log.

He copied neatly out of the rough-book the number of miles, the course of the ship, and in the column for 'wind' scrawled the word 'calm' from top to bottom of the eight hours since noon. He was exasperated by the continuous, monotonous rolling of the ship. The heavy inkstand would slide away in a manner that suggested perverse intelligence in dodging the pen. Having written in the large space under the head of 'Remarks' 'Heat very oppressive', he stuck the end of the penholder in his teeth, pip fashion, and mopped his face carefully.

'Ship rolling heavily in a high cross-swell,' he began again, and commented to himself, 'Heavily is no word for it.' Then he wrote: 'Sunset threatening with a low bank of clouds to N. and E. Sky clear overhead.'

Sprawling over the table with arrested pen, he glanced out of the door, and in that frame of his vision he saw all the stars flying upwards between the teak-wood jambs on a black sky. The whole lot took flight together and disappeared, leaving only a blackness flecked with white flashes, for the sea was as black as the sky and speckled with foam afar. The stars that had flown to the roll came back on the return swing of the ship, rushing downwards in their glittering multitude, not of fiery points, but enlarged to tiny discs brilliant with a clear wet sheen.

Jukes watched the flying big stars for a moment, and then wrote: '8 p.m. Swell increasing. Ship labouring and taking water on her decks. Battened down the coolies for the night. Barometer still falling.' He paused, and thought to himself, 'Perhaps nothing whatever'll come of it.' And then he closed resolutely his entries: 'Every appearance of a typhoon coming on.'

On going out he had to stand aside, and Captain MacWhirr strode over the doorstep without saying a word or making a sign.

'Shut the door, Mr Jukes, will you?' he cried from within.

Jukes turned back to do so, muttering ironically: 'Afraid to catch cold, I suppose.' It was his watch below, but he yearned for communion with his kind; and he remarked cheerily to the second mate: 'Doesn't look so bad, after all – does it?'

The second mate was marching to and fro on the bridge, tripping down with small steps one moment, and the next climbing with difficulty the shifting slope of the deck. At the sound of Jukes's voice he stood still, facing forward, but made no reply.

'Hallo! That's a heavy one,' said Jukes, swaying to meet the long roll till his lowered hand touched the planks. This time the second mate made in his throat a noise of an unfriendly nature.

He was an oldish, shabby little fellow, with bad teeth and no hair on his face. He had been shipped in a hurry in Shanghai, that trip when the second officer brought from home had delayed the ship three hours in port by contriving (in some manner Captain MacWhirr could never understand) to fall overboard into an empty coal-lighter lying along-side, and had to be sent ashore to the hospital with concussion of the brain and a broken limb or two.

Jukes was not discouraged by the unsympathetic sound. 'The China-men must be having a lovely time of it down there,' he said. 'It's lucky for them the old girl has the easiest roll of any ship I've ever been in. There now! This one wasn's so bad.'

'You wait,' snarled the second mate.

With his sharp nose, red at the tip, and his thin pinched lips, he always looked as though he were raging inwardly; and he was concise in his speech to the point of rudeness. All his time off duty he spent in his cabin with the door shut, keeping so still in there that he was supposed to fall asleep as soon as he had disappeared; but the man who came in to wake him for his watch on deck would invariably find him with his eyes wide open, flat on his back in the bunk, and glaring irritably from a soiled pillow. He never wrote any letters, did not seem to hope for news from anywhere; and though he had been heard once to mention West Hartlepool, it was with extreme bitterness, and only in connection with the extortionate charges of a boarding-house. He was one of those men who are picked up at need in the ports of the world. They are competent enough, appear hopelessly hard up, show no evidence of any sort of vice, and carry about them all the signs of manifest failure. They come aboard on an emergency, care for no ship afloat, live in their own atmosphere of casual connection amongst their shipmates who know nothing of them, and make up their minds to leave at inconvenient times. They clear out with no words of leave-taking in some God-forsaken port other men would fear to be stranded in, and go ashore in company of a shabby sea-chest, corded like a treasure-box, and with an air of shaking the ship's dust off their feet.

'You wait,' he repeated, balanced in great swings with his back to Jukes, motionless and implacable.

'Do you mean to say we are going to catch it hot?' asked Jukes with boyish interest.

'Say? . . . I say nothing. You don't catch me,' snapped the little second mate, with a mixture of pride, scorn, and cunning, as if Jukes's question had been a trap cleverly detected. 'Oh, no! None of you here shall make a fool of me if I know it,' he mumbled to himself.

Jukes reflected rapidly that his second mate was a mean little beast, and in his heart he wished poor Jack Allen had never smashed himself up in the coal-lighter. The far-off blackness ahead of the ship was like another night seen through the starry night of the earth – the starless night of the immensities beyond the creative universe, revealed in its appalling stillness through a low fissure in the glittering sphere of which the earth is the kernel.

'Whatever there might be about,' said Jukes, 'we are steaming straight into it.'

'*You've* said it,' caught up the second mate, always with his back to Jukes. 'You've said it, mind – not I.'

'Oh, go to Jericho!' asked Jukes, frankly; and the other emitted a triumphant little chuckle.

'You've said it,' he repeated.

'And what of that?'

'I've known some real good men get into trouble with their skippers for saying a damn sight less,' answered the second mate feverishly. 'Oh, no! You don't catch me.'

'You seem deucedly anxious not to give yourself away,' said Jukes, completely soured by such absurdity. 'I wouldn't be afraid to say what I think.'

'Aye, to me. That's no great trick. I am nobody, and well I know it.'

The ship, after a pause of comparative steadiness, started upon a series of rolls, one worse than the other, and for a time Jukes, preserving his equilibrium, was too busy to open his mouth. As soon as the violent swinging had quieted down somewhat, he said: 'This is a bit too much of a good thing. Whether anything is coming or not I think she ought to be put head on to that swell. The old man is just gone in to lie down. Hang me if I don't speak to him.'

But when he opened the door of the chart-room he saw his captain reading a book. Captain MacWhirr was not lying down; he was standing up with one hand grasping the edge of the bookshelf and the other holding open before his face a thick volume. The lamp wriggled in the gimbals, the loosened books toppled from side to side on the shelf, the long barometer swung in jerky circles, the table altered its slant every moment. In the midst of all this stir and movement Captain MacWhirr, holding on, showed his eyes above the upper edge, and asked, 'What's the matter?'

'Swell getting worse, sir.'

'Noticed that in here,' muttered Captain MacWhirr. 'Anything wrong?'

Jukes, inwardly disconcerted by the seriousness of the eyes looking at him over the top of the book, produced an embarrassed grin.

'Rolling like old boots,' he said, sheepishly.

'Aye! Very heavy – very heavy. What do you want?'

At this Jukes lost his footing and began to flounder.

'I was thinking of our passengers,' he said, in the manner of a man clutching at a straw.

'Passengers?' wondered the Captain, gravely. 'What passengers?'

'Why, the Chinamen, sir,' explained Jukes, very sick of this conversation.

'The Chinamen! Why don't you speak plainly? Couldn't tell what you meant. Never heard a lot of coolies spoken of as passengers before. Passengers, indeed! What's come to you?'

Captain MacWhirr, closing the book on his forefinger, lowered his arm and looked completely mystified. 'Why are you thinking of the Chinamen, Mr Jukes?' he inquired.

Jukes took a plunge, like a man driven to it. 'She's rolling her decks full of water, sir. Thought you might put her head on perhaps – for a while. Till this goes down a bit – very soon, I dare say. Head to the eastward. I never knew a ship roll like this.'

He held on in the doorway, and Captain MacWhirr, feeling his grip on the shelf inadequate, made up his mind to let go in a hurry, and fell heavily on the couch.

'Head to the eastward?' he said, struggling to sit up. 'That's more than four points off her course.'

'Yes, sir. Fifty degrees . . . Would just bring her head far enough round to meet this . . .'

Captain MacWhirr was now sitting up. he had not dropped the book, and he had not lost his place.

'To the eastward?' he repeated, with dawning astonishment. 'To the . . . Where do you think we are bound to? You want me to haul a full-powered steamship four points off her course to make the Chinamen comfortable! Now, I've heard more than enough of mad things done in the world – but this . . . If I didn't know you Jukes, I would think you were in liquor. Steer four points off . . . And what after-wards? Steer four points over the other way, I suppose, to make the course good. What put it into your head that I would start to tack a steamer as if she were a sailing-ship?'

'Jolly good thing she isn't,' threw in Jukes, with bitter readiness. 'She would have rolled every blessed stick out of her this afternoon.'

'Aye! And you just would have had to stand and see them go,' said Captain MacWhirr, showing a certain animation. 'It's a dead calm, isn't it?'

'It is, sir. But there's something out of the common coming, for sure.'

'Maybe. I suppose you have a notion I should be getting out of the way of that dirt,' said Captain MacWhirr, speaking with the utmost simplicity of manner and tone, and fixing the oilcloth on the floor with a heavy stare. Thus he noticed neither Jukes's discomfiture nor the mixture of vexation and astonished respect on his face.

'Now, here's this book,' he continued with deliberation, slapping his thigh with the closed volume. 'I've been reading the chapter on the storms there.'

This was true. He had been reading the chapter on the storms. When he had entered the chart-room, it was with no intention of taking the book down. Some influence in the air – the same influence, pro-bably, that caused the steward to bring without orders the Captain's sea-boots and oilskin coat up to the chart-room – had as it were guided his hand to the shelf; and without taking the time to sit down he had waded with a conscious effort into the terminology of the subject. He lost himself amongst advancing semicircles, left- and right-hand qua-drants, the curves of the tracks, the probable bearing of the centre, the shifts of wind, and the readings of barometer. He tried to bring all these things into a definite relation to himself, and ended by becoming contemptuously angry with such a lot of words and with so much advice, all head-work and supposition, without a glimmer of certitude.

'It's the damnedest thing, Jukes,' he said. 'If a fellow was to believe all that's in there, he would be running most of his time all over the sea trying to get behind the weather.'

Again he slapped his leg with the book; and Jukes opened his mouth, but said nothing.

'Running to get behind the weather! Do you understand that, Mr Jukes? It's the maddest thing!' ejaculated Captain MacWhirr, with pauses, gazing at the floor profoundly. 'You would think an old woman had been writing this. It passes me. If that thing means anything useful, then it means that I should at once alter the course away, away to the devil somewhere, and come booming down on Fu-chau from the northward at the tail of this dirty weather thats supposed to be knocking about in our way. From the north! Do you understand, Mr Jukes? Three hundred extra miles to the distance, and a pretty coal bill to show. I couldn't bring myself to do that if every word in there was gospel truth, Mr Jukes. Don't you expect me . . .'

And Jukes, silent, marvelled at this display of feeling and loquacity.

'But the truth is that you don't know if the fellow is right, anyhow. How can you tell what a gale is made of till you get it? He isn't aboard here, is he? Very well. Here he says that the centre of them things bears eight points off the wind; but we haven't got any wind, for all the barometer falling. Where's his centre now?'

'We will get the wind presently,' mumbled Jukes.

'Let it come then,' said Captain MacWhirr, with dignified indignation. 'It's only to let you see, Mr Jukes, that you don't find everything in books. All these rules for dodging breezes and circumventing the winds of heaven, Mr Jukes, seem to me the maddest thing, when you come to look at it sensibly.'

He raised his eyes, saw Jukes gazing at him dubiously, and tried to illustrate his meaning.

'About as queer as your extraordinary notion of dodging the ship head to sea, for I don't know how long, to make the Chinamen comfortable; whereas all we've got to do is to take them to Fu-chau, being timed to get there before noon on Friday. If the weather delays me – very well. There's your logbook to talk straight about the weather. But suppose I went swinging off my course and came in two days late and they asked me: "Where have you been all that time, Captain?" What could I say to that? "Went around to dodge the bad weather," I would say. "It must've been damn bad," they would say. 'Don't know," I would have to say; "I've dodged clear of it." See that, Jukes? I have been thinking it all out this afternoon.'

He looked up again in his unseeing, unimaginative way. No one had ever heard him say so much at one time. Jukes, with his arms open in the doorway, was like a man invited to behold a miracle. Unbounded wonder was the intellectual meaning of his eye, while incredulity was seated in his whole countenance.

'A gale is a gale, Mr Jukes,' resumed the Captain, 'and a full-powered steamship has got to face it. There's just so much dirty weather knocking about the world and the proper thing is to go through it with none of what old Captain Wilson of the *Melita* calls "storm strategy". The other day ashore I heard him hold forth about it to a lot of shipmasters who came in and sat at a table next to mine. It seemed to me the greatest nonsense. He was telling them how he out-manoeuvred, I think he said, a terrific gale so that it never came nearer than fifty miles to him. A neat piece of head-work he called it. How he knew there was a terrific gale fifty miles off beats me altogether. It was like listening to a crazy man. I would have thought Captain Wilson was old enough to know better.'

Captain MacWhirr ceased for a moment, then said, 'It's your watch below, Mr Jukes?'

Jukes came to himself with a start. 'Yes, sir.'

'Leave orders to call me at the slightest change,' said the Captain. He reached up to put the book away, and tucked his legs upon the couch. 'Shut the door so that it don't fly open, will you? I can't stand a door banging. They've put a lot of rubbishy locks into this ship, I must say.'

Captain MacWhirr closed his eyes.

He did so to rest himself. He was tired, and he experienced that state of mental vacuity which comes at the end of an exhaustive discussion that had liberated some belief matured in the course of meditative years. He had indeed been making his confession of faith, had he only known it; and its effect was to make Jukes, on the other side of the door, stand scratching his head for a good while.

Captain MacWhirr opened his eyes.

He thought he must have been asleep. What was that loud noise? Wind? Why had he not been called? The lamp wriggled in its gimbals, the barometer swung in circles, the table altered its slant every moment; a pair of limp sea-boots with collapsed tops went sliding past the couch. He put out his hand instantly, and captured one.

Jukes's face appeared in a crack of the door: only his face, very red, with staring eyes. The flame of the lamp leaped, a piece of paper flew up, a rush of air enveloped Captain MacWhirr. Beginning to draw on the boot, he directed an expectant gaze at Jukes's swollen, excited features.

'Came on like this,' shouted Jukes, 'five minutes ago . . . all of a sudden.'

The head disappeared with a bang, and a heavy splash and patter of drops swept past the closed door as if a pailful of melted lead had been flung against the house. A whistling could be heard now upon the deep vibrating noise outside. The stuffy chart-room seemed as full of draughts as a shed. Captain MacWhirr collared the other sea-boot on its violent passage along the floor. He was not flustered, but he could not find at once the opening for inserting his foot. The shoes he had flung off were scurrying from end to end of the cabin, gambolling playfully over each other like puppies. As soon as he stood up he kicked at them viciously, but without effect.

He threw himself into the attitude of a lunging fencer, to reach after his oilskin coat; and afterwards he staggered all over the confined space while he jerked himself into it. Very grave, straddling his legs far apart, and stretching his neck, he started to tie deliberately the strings of his sou'wester under his chin, with thick fingers that trembled slightly. He went through all the movements of a woman putting on her bonnet before a glass, with a strained, listening attention, as though he had expected every moment to hear the shout of his name in the confused clamour that had suddenly beset his ship. Its increase filled his ears while he was getting ready to go out and confront whatever it might mean. It was tumultuous and very loud – made up of the rush of the wind, the crashes of the sea, with that prolonged deep vibration of the air, like the roll of an immense and remote drum beating the charge of the gale.

He stood for a moment in the light of the lamp, thick, clumsy, shapeless in his panoply of combat, vigilant and red-faced.

'There's a lot of weight in this,' he muttered.

As soon as he attempted to open the door the wind caught it. Clinging to the handle, he was dragged out over the doorstep, and at once found himself engaged with the wind in a sort of personal scuffle whose object was the shutting of that door. At the last moment a tongue of air scurried in and licked out the flame of the lamp.

Ahead of the ship he perceived a great darkness lying upon a multitude of white flashes; on the starboard beam a few amazing stars drooped, dim and fitful, above an immense waste of broken seas, as if seen through a mad drift of smoke.

On the bridge a knot of men, indistinct and toiling, were making great efforts in the light of the wheelhouse windows that shone mistily on their heads and backs. Suddenly darkness closed upon one pane, then on another. The voices of the lost group reached him after the manner of men's voices in a gale, in shreds and fragments of forlorn shouting snatched past the ear. All at once Jukes appeared at his side, yelling, with his head down.

'Watch – put in – wheelhouse shutters – glass – afraid – blow in.'

Jukes heard his commander upbraiding.

'This – coming – anything – warning – call me.'

He tried to explain, with the uproar pressing on his lips.

'Light air – remained – bridge – sudden – north-east – could turn – thought – you – sure – hear.'

They had gained the shelter of the weather-cloth, and could converse with raised voices, as people quarrel.

'I got the hands along to cover up all the ventilators. Good job I had remained on deck. I didn't think you would be asleep, and so . . . What did you say, sir? What?'

'Nothing,' cried Captain MacWhirr. 'I said – all right.'

'By all the powers! We've got it this time,' observed Jukes in a howl.

'No, sir. Certainly not. Wind came out right ahead. And here comes the head sea.'

A plunge of the ship ended in a shock as if she had landed her forefoot upon something solid. After a moment of stillness a lofty flight of sprays drove hard with the wind upon their faces.

'Keep her at it as long as we can,' shouted Captain MacWhirr.

Before Jukes had squeezed the salt water out of his eyes all the stars had disappeared.

III

JUKES was as ready a man as any half-dozen young mates that may be caught by casting a net upon the waters; and though he had been somewhat taken aback by the startling viciousness of the first squall, he had pulled himself together on the instant, had called out the hands, and had rushed them along to secure such openings about the deck as had not been already battened down earlier in the evening. Shouting in his fresh, stentorian voice, 'Jump, boys, and bear a hand!' he led in the work, telling himself the while that he had 'just expected this'.

But at the same time he was growing aware that this was rather more than he had expected. From the first stir of the air felt on his cheek the gale seemed to take upon itself the accumulated impetus of an avalanche. Heavy sprays enveloped the *Nan-Shan* from stem to stern, and instantly in the midst of her regular rolling she began to jerk and plunge as though she had gone mad with fright.

Jukes thought, 'This is no joke.' While he was exchanging explanatory yells with his captain, a sudden lowering of the darkness came upon the night, falling before their vision like something palpable. It was as if the masked lights of the world had been turned down. Jukes was uncritically glad to have his captain at hand. It relieved him as though that man had, by simply coming on deck, taken most of the gale's weight upon his shoulders. Such is the prestige, the privilege, and the burden of command.

Captain MacWhirr could expect no relief of that sort from anyone on earth. Such is the loneliness of command. He was trying to see, with that watchful manner of a seaman who stares into the wind's eye as if into the eye of an adversary, to penetrate the hidden intention and guess the aim and force of the thrust. The strong wind swept at him out of a vast obscurity; he felt under his feet the uneasiness of his ship, and he could not even discern the shadow of her shape. He wished it were not so; and very still he waited, feeling stricken by a blind man's helplessness.

To be silent was natural to him, dark or shine. Jukes, at his elbow, made himself heard yelling cheerily in the gusts, 'We must have got the worst of it at once, sir.' A faint burst of lightning quivered all round, as if flashed into a cavern – into a black and secret chamber of the sea, with a floor of foaming crests.

It unveiled for a sinister, fluttering moment a ragged mass of clouds hanging low, the lurch of the long outlines of the ship, the black figures of men caught on the bridge, heads forward, as if petrified in the act of butting. The darkness palpitated down upon all this, and then the real thing came at last.

It was something formidable and swift, like the sudden smashing of a vial of wrath. It seemed to explode all round the ship with an overpowering concussion and a rush of great waters, as if an immense dam had been blown up to windward. In an instant the men lost touch of each other. This is the disintegrating power of a great wind: it isolates one from one's kind. An earthquake, a landslip, an avalanche, overtake a man incidentally, as it were – without passion. A furious gale attacks him like a personal enemy, tries to grasp his limbs, fastens upon his mind, seeks to rout his very spirit out of him.

Jukes was driven away from his commander. He fancied himself whirled a great distance through the air. Everything disappeared – even, for a moment, his power of thinking; but his hand had found one of the rail-stanchions. His distress was by no means alleviated by an inclination to disbelieve the reality of this experience. Though young, he had seen some bad weather, and had never doubted his ability to imagine the worst; but this was so much beyond his powers of fancy that it appeared incompatible with the existence of any ship whatever. He would have been incredulous about himself in the same way, perhaps, had he not been so harassed by the necessity of exerting a wrestling effort against a force trying to tear him away from his hold. Moreover, the conviction of not being utterly destroyed returned to him through the sensations of being half-drowned, bestially shaken, and partly choked.

It seemed to him he remained there precariously alone with the stanchion for a long, long time. The rain poured on him, flowed, drove in sheets. He breathed in gasps; and sometimes the water he swallowed was fresh and sometimes it was salt. For the most part he kept his eyes shut tight, as if suspecting his sight might be destroyed in the immense flurry of the elements. When he ventured to blink hastily, he derived some moral support from the green gleam on the starboard light shining feebly upon the flight of rain and sprays. He was actually looking at it when its ray fell upon the uprearing sea which put it out. He saw the head of the wave topple over, adding the mite of its crash to the tremendous uproar raging around him, and almost at the same instant the stanchion was wrenched away from his embracing arms. After a crushing thump on his back he found himself suddenly afloat and borne upwards. His first irresistible notion was that the whole China Sea had climbed on the bridge. Then, more sanely, he concluded himself gone overboard. All the time he was being tossed, flung, and rolled in great volumes of water, he kept on repeating mentally, with the utmost precipitation, the words: 'My God! My God! My God! My God!'

All at once, in a revolt of misery and despair, he formed the crazy resolution to get out of that. And he began to thresh about with his arms and legs. But as soon as he commenced his wretched struggles he discovered that he had become somehow mixed up with a face, an oilskin coat, somebody's boots. He clawed ferociously, all these things in turn, lost them, found them again, lost them once more, and finally was himself caught in the firm clasp of a pair of stout arms. He returned the embrace closely round a thick solid body. He had found his captain.

They tumbled over and over, tightening their hug. Suddenly the water let them down with a brutal bang; and, stranded against the side of the wheelhouse, out of breath and bruised, they were left to stagger up in the wind and hold on where they could.

Jukes came out of it rather horrified, as though he had escaped some unparalleled outrage directed at his feelings. It weakened his faith in himself. He started shouting aimlessly to the man he could feel near him in that fiendish blackness, 'Is it you, sir? Is it you, sir?' till his temples seemed ready to burst. And he heard in answer a voice, as if crying far away, as if screaming to him fretfully from a very great distance, the one word 'Yes!' Other seas swept again over the bridge. He received them defencelessly right over his bare head, with both his hands engaged in holding.

The motion of the ship was extravagant. Her lurches had an appalling helplessness; she pitched as if taking a header into a void, and seemed to find a wall to hit every time. When she rolled she fell on her side headlong, and she would be righted back by such a demolishing blow that Jukes felt her reeling as a clubbed man reels before he collapses. The gale howled and scuffled about gigantically in the darkness, as though the entire world were one black gully. At certain moments the air streamed against the ship as if sucked through a tunnel with a concentrated solid force of impact that seemed to lift her clean out of the water and keep her up for an instant with only a quiver running through her from end to end. And then she would begin her tumbling again as if dropped back into a boiling cauldron. Jukes tried hard to compose his mind and judge things coolly.

The sea, flattened down in the heavier gusts, would uprise and overwhelm both ends of the *Nan-Shan* in snowy rushes of foam, expanding wide, beyond both rails, into the night. And on this dazzling sheet, spread under the blackness of the clouds and emitting a bluish glow, Captain MacWhirr could catch a desolate glimpse of a few tiny specks black as ebony, the tops of the hatches, the battened companions, the heads of the covered winches, the foot of a mast. This was all he could see of his ship. Her middle structure, covered by the bridge which bore him, his mate, the closed wheelhouse where a man was steering shut up with the fear of being swept overboard together with the whole thing in one great crash – her middle structure was like a half-tide rock awash upon a coast. It was like an outlying rock with the water boiling up, streaming over, pouring off, beating round – like a rock in the surf to which shipwrecked people cling before they let go – only it rose, it sank, it rolled continuously, without respite and rest, like a rock that should have miraculously struck adrift from a coast and gone wallowing upon the sea.

The *Nan-Shan* was being looted by the storm with a senseless, destructive fury: trysails torn out of the extra gaskets, double-lashed awnings blown away, bridge swept clean, weather-cloths burst, rails twisted, light-screens smashed – and two of the boats had gone already. They had gone unheard and unseen, melting, as it were, in the shock and smother of the wave. It was only later, when upon the white flash of another high sea hurling itself amidships, Jukes had a vision of two pairs of davits leaping black and empty out of the solid blackness, with one overhauled fall flying and an iron-bound block capering in the air, that he became aware of what had happened within about three yards of his back.

He poked his head forward, groping for the ear of his commander. His lips touched it – big, fleshy, very wet. He cried in an agitated tone, 'Our boats are going now, sir.'

And again he heard that voice, forced and ringing feebly, but with a penetrating effect of quietness in the enormous discord of noises, as if sent out from some remote spot of peace beyond the black wastes of the gale; again he heard a man's voice – the frail and indomitable sound that can be made to carry an infinity of thought, resolution, and purpose, that shall be pronouncing confident words on the last day, when heavens fall, and justice is done – again he heard it, and it was crying to him, as if from very, very far – 'All right.'

He thought he had not managed to make himself understood. 'Our boats – I say boats – the boats, sir! Two gone!'

The same voice, within a foot of him and yet so remote, yelled sensibly, 'Can't be helped.'

Captain MacWhirr had never turned his face, but Jukes caught some more words on the wind.

'What can – expect – when hammering through – such – Bound to leave – something behind – stands to reason.'

Watchfully Jukes listened for more. No more came. This was all Captain MacWhirr had to say; and Jukes could picture to himself rather than see the broad squat back before him. An impenetrable obscurity pressed down upon the ghostly glimmers of the sea. A dull conviction seized upon Jukes that there was nothing to be done.

If the steering-gear did not give way, if the immense volumes of water did not burst the deck in or smash one of the hatches, if the engines did not give up, if way could be kept on the ship against this terrific wind, and she did not bury herself in one of these awful seas, of whose white crests alone, topping high above her bows, he could now and then get a sickening glimpse – then there was a chance of her coming out of it. Something within him seemed to turn over, bringing uppermost the feeling that the *Nan-Shan* was lost.

'She's done for,' he said to himself, with a surprising mental agitation, as though he had discovered an unexpected meaning in this thought. One of these things was bound to happen. Nothing could be prevented now, and nothing could be remedied. The men on board did not count, and the ship could not last. This weather was too impossible.

Jukes felt an arm thrown heavily over his shoulders; and to this overture he responded with great intelligence by catching hold of his captain round the waist.

They stood clasped thus in the blind night, bracing each other against the wind, cheek to cheek and lip to ear, in the manner of two hulks lashed stem to stern together.

And Jukes heard the voice of his commander hardly any louder than before, but nearer, as though, starting to march athwart the prodigious rush of the hurricane, it had approached him, bearing that strange effect of quietness like the serene glow of a halo.

'D'ye know where the hands got to?' it asked, vigorous and evanescent at the same time, overcoming the strength of the wind, and swept away from Jukes instantly.

Jukes didn't know. They were all on the bridge when the real force of the hurricane struck the ship. He had no idea where they had crawled to. Under the circumstances they were nowhere, for all the use that could be made of them. Somehow the Captain's wish to know distressed Jukes.

'Want the hands, sir?' he cried, apprehensively.

'Ought to know,' asserted Captain MacWhirr. 'Hold hard.'

They held hard. An outburst of unchained fury, a vicious rush of the wind absolutely steadied the ship; she rocked only, quick and light like a child's cradle, for a terrific moment of suspense, while the whole atmosphere, as it seemed, streamed furiously past her, roaring away from the tenebrous earth.

It suffocated them, and with eyes shut they tightened their grasp. What from the magnitude of the shock might have been a column of water running upright in the dark, butted against the ship, broke short, and fell on her bridge, crushingly, from on high, with a dead burying weight.

A flying fragment of that collapse, a mere splash, enveloped them in one swirl from their feet over their heads, filling violently their ears, mouths, and nostrils with salt water. It knocked out their legs, wrenched in haste at their arms, seethed away swiftly under their chins; and opening their eyes, they saw the piled-up masses of foam dashing to and fro amongst what looked like the fragments of a ship. She had given way as if driven straight in. Their panting hearts yielded, too, before the tremendous blow; and all at once she sprang up again to her desperate plunging, as if trying to scramble out from under the ruins.

The seas in the dark seemed to rush from all sides to keep her back where she might perish. There was hate in the way she was handled, and a ferocity in the blows that fell. She was like a living creature thrown to the rage of a mob: hustled terribly, struck at, borne up, flung down, leaped upon. Captain MacWhirr and Jukes kept hold of each other, deafened by the noise, gagged by the wind; and the great physical tumult beating about their bodies, brought, like an unbridled display of passion, a profound trouble to their souls. One of these wild and appalling shrieks that are heard at times passing mysteriously overhead in the steady roar of a hurricane, swooped, as if borne on wings, upon the ship, and Jukes tried to outscream it.

'Will she live through this?'

The cry was wrenched out of his breast. It was as unintentional as the birth of a thought in the head, and he heard nothing of it himself. It all became extinct at once – thought, intention, effort – and of his cry the inaudible vibration added to the tempest waves of the air.

He expected nothing from it. Nothing at all. For indeed what answer could be made? But after a while he heard with amazement the frail and resisting voice in his ear, the dwarf sound, unconquered in the giant tumult.

'She may!'

It was a dull yell, more difficult to seize than a whisper. And presently the voice returned again, half submerged in the vast crashes, like a ship battling against the waves of an ocean.

'Let's hope so!' it cried – small, lonely, and unmoved, a stranger to the visions of hope or fear; and it flickered into disconnected words: 'Ship . . . This . . . Never – Anyhow . . . for the best.' Jukes gave it up.

Then, as if it had come suddenly upon the one thing fit to withstand the power of a storm, it seemed to gain force and firmness for the last broken shouts:

'Keep on hammering . . . builders . . . good men . . . And chance it . . . engines . . . Rout . . . good man.'

Captain MacWhirr removed his arm from Jukes's shoulders, and thereby ceased to exist for his mate, so dark it was; Jukes, after a tense stiffening of every muscle, would let himself go limp all over. The gnawing of profound discomfort existed side by side with an incredible disposition to somnolence, as though he had been buffeted and worried into drowsiness. The wind would get hold of his head and try to shake it off his shoulders; his clothes, full of water, were as heavy as lead, cold and dripping like an armour of melting ice: he shivered – it lasted a long time; and with his hands closed hard on his hold, he was letting himself sink slowly into the depths of bodily misery. His mind became concentrated upon himself in an aimless, idle way, and when something pushed lightly at the back of his knees he nearly, as the saying is, jumped out of his skin.

In the start forward he bumped the back of Captain MacWhirr, who didn't move; and then a hand gripped his thigh. A lull had come, a menacing lull of the wind, the holding of a stormy breath – and he felt himself pawed all over. It was the boatswain. Jukes recognized these hands, so thick and enormous that they seemed to belong to some new species of man.

The boatswain had arrived on the bridge, crawling on all fours against the wind, and had found the chief mate's legs with the top of his head. Immediately he crouched and began to explore Jukes's person upwards with prudent, apologetic touches, as became an inferior.

He was an ill-favoured, undersized, gruff sailor of fifty, coarsely hairy, short-legged, long-armed, resembling an elderly ape. His strength was immense; and in his great lumpy paws, bulging like brown boxing-gloves on the end of furry forearms, the heaviest objects were handled like playthings. Apart from the grizzled pelt on his chest, the menacing demeanour, and the hoarse voice, he had none of the classical attributes of his rating. His good nature almost amounted to imbecility: the men did what they liked with him, and he had not an ounce of initiative in his character, which was easy-going and talkative. For these reasons Jukes disliked him; but Captain MacWhirr, to Jukes's scornful disgust, seemed to regard him as a first-rate petty officer.

He pulled himself up by Jukes's coat, taking that liberty with the greatest moderation, and only so far as it was forced upon him by the hurricane.

'What is it, bos'n, what is it?' yelled Jukes, impatiently. What could that fraud of a bos'n want on the bridge? The typhoon had got on Jukes's nerves. The husky bellowings of the other, though unintelligible, seemed to suggest a state of lively satisfaction. There could be no mistake. The old fool was pleased with something.

The boatswain's other hand had found some other body, for in a changed tone he began to inquire: 'Is it you, sir? Is it you, sir?' The wind strangled his howls.

'Yes!' cried Captain MacWhirr.

IV

A LL that the boatswain, out of a superabundance of yells, could make clear to Captain MacWhirr was the bizarre intelligence that 'All them Chinamen in the fore 'tween deck have fetched away, sir.'

Jukes to leeward could hear these two shouting within six inches of his face, as you may hear on a still night half a mile away two men conversing across a field. He heard Captain MacWhirr's exasperated 'What? What?' and the strained pitch of the other's hoarseness. 'In a lump . . . seen them myself . . . Awful sight, sir . . . thought . . . tell you.'

Jukes remained indifferent, as if rendered irresponsible by the force of the hurricane, which made the very thought of action utterly vain. Besides, being very young, he had found the occupation of keeping his heart completely steeled against the worst so engrossing that he had come to feel an overpowering dislike towards any other form of activity whatever. He was not scared; he knew this because, firmly believing he would never see another sunrise, he remained calm in that belief.

These are the moments of do-nothing heroics to which even good men surrender at times. Many officers of ships can no doubt recall a case in their experience when just such a trance of confounded stoicism would come all at once over a whole ship's company. Jukes, however, had no wide experience of men or storms. He conceived himself to be calm – inexorably calm; but as a matter of fact he was daunted; not abjectly, but only so far as a decent man may, without becoming loathsome to himself.

It was rather like a forced-on numbness of spirit. The long, long stress of a gale does it; the suspense of the interminably culminating catastrophe; and there is a bodily fatigue in the mere holding on to existence within the excessive tumult; a searching and insidious fatigue that penetrates deep into a man's breast to cast down and sadden his heart, which is incorrigible, and of all the gifts of the earth – even before life itself – aspires to peace.

Jukes was benumbed much more than he supposed. He held on – very wet, very cold, stiff in every limb; and in a momentary hallucination of swift visions (it is said that a drowning man thus reviews all his life) he beheld all sorts of memories altogether unconnected with his present situation. He remembered his father, for instance: a worthy businessman, who at an unfortunate crisis in his affairs went quietly to bed and died forthwith in a state of resignation. Jukes did not recall these circumstances, of course, but remaining otherwise unconcerned he seemed to see distinctly the poor man's face; a certain game of nap played when quite a boy in Table Bay on board a ship, since lost with all hands; the thick eyebrows of his first skipper; and without any emotion, as he might years ago have walked listlessly into her room and found her sitting there with a book, he remembered his mother – dead, too, now – the resolute woman, left badly off, who had been very firm in his bringing up.

It could not have lasted more than a second, perhaps not so much. A heavy arm had fallen about his shoulders; Captain MacWhirr's voice was speaking his name into his ear.

'Jukes! Jukes!'

He detected the tone of deep concern. The wind had thrown its weight on the ship, trying to pin her down amongst the seas. They made a clean breach over her, as over a deep-swimming log; and the gathered weight of crashes menaced monstrously from afar. The break-ers flung out of the night with a ghostly light on their crests – the light of sea-foam that in a ferocious, boiling-up pale flash showed upon the slender body of the ship the toppling rush, the downfall, and the seeth-ing mad scurry of each wave. Never for a moment could she shake herself clear of the water; Jukes, rigid, perceived in her motion the ominous sign of haphazard floundering. She was no longer struggling intelligently. It was the beginning of the end; and the note of busy concern in Captain MacWhirr's voice sickened him like an exhibition of blind and pernicious folly.

The spell of the storm had fallen upon Jukes. He was penetrated by it, absorbed by it; he was rooted in it with a rigour of dumb attention. Captain MacWhirr persisted in his cries, but the wind got between them like a solid wedge. He hung round Jukes's neck as heavy as a millstone, and suddenly the sides of their heads knocked together.

'Jukes! Mr Jukes, I say!'

He had to answer that voice that would not be silenced. He answered in the customary manner: '. . . Yes, sir.'

And directly, his heart, corrupted by the storm that breeds a craving for peace, rebelled against the tyranny of training and command.

Captain MacWhirr had his mate's head fixed firm in the crook of his elbow, and pressed it to his yelling lips mysteriously. Sometimes Jukes would break in, admonishing hastily: 'Look out, sir!' or Captain MacWhirr would bawl an earnest exhortation to 'Hold hard, there!' and the whole black universe seemed to reel together with the ship. They paused. She floated yet. And Captain MacWhirr would resume his shouts. '. . . Says . . . whole lot . . . fetched away . . . Ought to see . . . what's the matter.'

Directly the full force of the hurricane had struck the ship, every part of her deck became untenable; and the sailors, dazed and dis-mayed, took shelter in the port alleyway under the bridge. It had a door aft, which they shut; it was very black, cold, and dismal. At each heavy fling of the ship they would groan all together in the dark, and tons of water could be heard scuttling about as if trying to get at them from above. The boatswain had been keeping up a gruff talk, but a more unreasonable lot of men, he said afterwards, he had never been with. They were snug enough there, out of harm's way, and not wanted to do anything, either; and yet they did nothing but grumble and com-plain peevishly like so many sick kids. Finally, one of them said that if there had been at least some light to see each other's noses by, it wouldn't be so bad. It was making him crazy, he declared, to lie there in the dark waiting for the blamed hooker to sink.

'Why don't you step outside, then, and be done with it at once?' the boatswain turned on him.

This called up a shout of execration. The boatswain found himself overwhelmed with reproaches of all sorts. They seemed to take it ill that a lamp was not instantly created for them out of nothing. They would whine after a light to get drowned by – anyhow! And though the unreason of their revilings was patent – since no one could hope to reach the lamp-room, which was forward – he became greatly distressed. He did not think it was decent of them to be nagging at him like this. He told them so, and was met by general contumely. He sought refuge, therefore, in an embittered silence. At the same time their grumbling and sighing and muttering worried him greatly, but by-and-by it occurred to him that there were six globe lamps hung in the 'tween-deck, and that there could be no harm in depriving the coolies of one of them.

The *Nan-Shan* had an athwartship coal-bunker, which, being at times used as cargo space, communicated by an iron door with the fore 'tween-deck. It was empty then, and its manhole was the foremost one in the alleyway. The boatswain could get in, therefore, without coming out on deck at all; but to his great surprise he found he could induce no one to help him in taking off the manhole cover. He groped for it all the same, but one of the crew lying in his way refused to budge.

'Why, I only want to get you that blamed light you are crying for,' he expostulated, almost pitifully.

Somebody told him to go and put his head in a bag. He regretted he could not recognize the voice, and that it was too dark to see, other-wise, as he said, he would have put a head on *that* son of a sea-cook, anyway, sink or swim. Nevertheless, he had made up his mind to show them he could get a light, if he were to die for it.

Through the violence of the ship's rolling, every movement was dangerous. To be lying down seemed labour enough. He nearly broke his neck dropping into the bunker. He fell on his back, and was sent shooting helplessly from side to side in the dangerous company of a heavy iron bar – a coal-trimmer's slice probably – left down there by somebody. This thing made him as nervous as though it had been a wild beast. He could not see it, the inside of the bunker coated with coal-dust being perfectly and impenetrably black; but he heard it sliding and clattering, and striking here and there, always in the neighbourhood of his head. It seemed to make an extraordinary noise, too – to give heavy thumps as though it had been as big as a bridge girder. This was remarkable enough for him to notice while he was flung from port to starboard and back again, and clawing desperately the smooth sides of the bunker in the endeavour to stop himself. The door into the 'tween-deck not fitting quite true, he saw a thread of dim light at the bottom.

Being a sailor, and a still active man, he did not want much of a chance to regain his feet; and as luck would have it, in scrambling up he put his hand on the iron slice, picking it up as he rose. Otherwise he would have been afraid of the thing breaking his legs, or at least knocking him down again. At first he stood still. He felt unsafe in this darkness that seemed to make the ship's motion unfamiliar, unforeseen, and difficult to counteract. He felt so much shaken for a moment that he dared not move for fear of 'taking charge again'. He had no mind to get battered to pieces in that bunker.

He had struck his head twice; he was dazed a little. He seemed to hear yet so plainly the clatter and bangs of the iron slice flying about his ears that he tightened his grip to prove to himself he had it there safely in his hand. He was vaguely amazed at the plainness with which down there he could hear the gale raging. Its howls and shrieks seemed to take on, in the emptiness of the bunker, something of the human character, of human rage and pain – being not vast but infinitely poignant. And there were, with every roll, thumps too – profound, ponderous thumps, as if a bulk object of five-ton weight or so had got play in the hold. But there was no such thing in the cargo. Something on deck? Impossible. Or alongside? Couldn't be.

He thought all this quickly, clearly, competently, like a seaman, and in the end remained puzzled. This noise, though, came deadened from outside, together with the washing and pouring of water on deck above his head. Was it the wind? Must be. It made down there a row like the shouting of a big lot of crazed men. And he discovered in himself a desire for a light, too – if only to get drowned by – and a nervous anxiety to get out of that bunker as quickly as possible.

He pulled back the bolt: the heavy iron plate turned on its hinges; and it was as though he had opened the door to the sounds of the tempest. A gust of hoarse yelling met him: the air was still; and the rushing of water overhead was covered by a tumult of strangled, throaty shrieks that produced an effect of desperate confusion. He straddled his legs the whole width of the doorway and stretched his neck. And at first he perceived only what he had come to seek: six small yellow flames swinging violently on the great body of the dusk.

It was stayed like the gallery of a mine, with a row of stanchions in the middle, and cross-beams overhead, penetrating into the gloom ahead – indefinitely. And to port there loomed, like the caving in of one of the sides, a bulky mass with a slanting outline. The whole place, with the shadows and the shapes, moved all the time. The boatswain glared: the ship lurched to starboard, and a great howl came from that mass that had the slant of fallen earth.

Pieces of wood whizzed past. Planks, he thought, inexpressibly startled, and flinging back his head. At his feet a man went sliding over, open-eyed, on his back, straining with uplifted arms for nothing: and another came bounding like a detached stone with his head between his legs and his hands clenched. His pigtail whipped in the air; he made a grab at the boatswain's legs, and from his opened hand a bright white disc rolled against the boatswain's foot. He recognized a silver dollar, and yelled at it with astonishment. With a precipitated sound of trampling and shuffling of bare feet, and with guttural cries, the mound of writhing bodies piled up to port detached itself from the ship's side and sliding, inert and struggling, shifted to starboard, with a dull, brutal thump. The cries ceased. The boatswain heard a long moan through the roar and whistling of the wind; he saw an inextricable confusion of heads and shoulders, naked soles kicking upwards, fists raised, tumbling backs, legs, pigtails, faces.

'Good Lord!' he cried, horrified, and banged-to the iron door upon this vision.

This was what he had come on the bridge to tell. He could not keep it to himself; and on board ship there is only one man to whom it is worth while to unburden yourself. On his passage back the hands in the alleyway swore at him for a fool. Why didn't he bring that lamp? What the devil did the coolies matter to anybody? And when he came out, the extremity of the ship made what went on inside of her appear of little moment.

At first he thought he had left the alleyway in the very moment of her sinking. The bridge ladders had been washed away, but an enormous sea filling the after-deck floated him up. After that he had to lie on his stomach for some time, holding to a ring-bolt, getting his breath now and then, and swallowing salt water. He struggled farther on his hands and knees, too frightened and distracted to turn back. In this way he reached the after-part of the wheelhouse. In that comparatively sheltered spot he found the second mate. The boatswain was pleasantly surprised – his impression being that everybody on deck must have been washed away a long time ago. He asked eagerly where the captain was.

The second mate was lying low, like a malignant little animal under a hedge.

'Captain? Gone overboard, after getting us into this mess.' The mate, too, for all he knew or cared. Another fool. Didn't matter. Everybody was going by-and-by.

The boatswain crawled out again into the strength of the wind; not because he much expected to find anybody, he said, but just to get away from 'that man'. He crawled out as outcasts go to face an inclement world. Hence his great joy at finding Jukes and the Captain. But what was going on in the 'tween deck was to him a minor matter by that time. Besides, it was difficult to make yourself heard. But he managed to convey the idea that the Chinamen had broken adrift together with their boxes, and that he had come up on purpose to report this. As to the hands, they were all right. Then, appeased, he subsided on the deck in a sitting posture, hugging with his arms and legs the stand of the engine-room telegraph – an iron casting as thick as a post. When that went, why, he expected he would go, too. He gave no more thought to the coolies.

Captain MacWhirr had made Jukes understand that he wanted him to go down below – to see.

'What am I to them, sir?' And the trembling of his whole wet body caused Juke's voice to sound like bleating.

'See first . . . Bos'n . . . says . . . adrift.'

'That bos'n is a confounded fool,' howled Jukes, shakily.

The absurdity of the demand made upon him revolted Jukes. He was as unwilling to go as if the moment he had left the deck the ship were sure to sink.

'I must know . . . can't leave . . .'

'They'll settle, sir.'

'Fight . . . bos'n says they fight . . . Why? Can't have . . . fighting . . . board ship . . . Much rather keep you here . . . case . . . I should . . . washed overboard myself . . . Stop it . . . some way. You see and tell me . . . through engine-room tube. Don't want you . . . come up here . . . too often. Dangerous . . . moving about . . . deck.'

Jukes, held with his head in chancery, had to listen to what seemed horrible suggestions.

'Don't want . . . you get lost . . . so long . . . ship isn't . . . Rout . . . Good man . . . Ship . . . many . . . through this . . . all right yet.'

All at once Jukes understood he would have to go.

'Do you think she may?' he screamed.

But the wind devoured the reply, out of which Jukes heard only the one word, pronounced with great energy '. . . Always . . .'

Captain MacWhirr released Jukes, and bending over the boatswain yelled, 'Get back with the mate.' Jukes only knew that the arm was gone off his shoulders. He was dismissed with his orders – to do what? He was exasperated into letting go his hold carelessly, and on the instant was blown away. It seemed to him that nothing could stop him from being blown right over the stern. He flung himself down hastily, and the boatswain, who was following, fell on him.

'Don't you get up yet, sir,' cried the boatswain. 'No hurry!'

A sea swept over. Jukes understood the boatswain to splutter that the bridge ladders were gone. 'I'll lower you down, sir, by your hands,' he screamed. He shouted also something about the smoke-stack being as likely to go overboard as not. Jukes thought it very possible, and imagined the fires out, the ship helpless . . . The boatswain by his side kept on yelling. 'What? What is it?' Jukes cried distressfully; and the other repeated, 'What would my old woman say if she saw me now?'

In the alleyway, where a lot of water had got in and splashed in the dark, the men were still as death, till Jukes stumbled against one of them and cursed him savagely for being in the way. Two or three voices then asked, eager and weak, 'Any chance for us, sir?'

'What's the matter with you fools?' he said, brutally. He felt as though he could throw himself down amongst them and never move any more. But they seemed cheered; and in the midst of obsequious warnings, 'Look out! Mind that manhole lid, sir,' they lowered him into the bunker. The boatswain tumbled down after him, and as soon as he had picked himself up he remarked, 'She would say, "Serve you right, you old fool, for going to sea." '

The boatswain had some means, and made a point of alluding to them frequently. His wife – a fat woman – and two grown-up daughters, kept a greengrocer's shop in the East End of London.

In the dark, Jukes, unsteady on his legs, listened to a faint thunderous patter. A deadened screaming went on steadily at his elbow, as it were; and from above the louder tumult of the storm descended upon these near sounds. His head swam. To him too, in that bunker, the motion of the ship seemed novel and menacing, sapping his resolution as though he had never been afloat before.

He had half a mind to scramble out again; but the remembrance of Captain MacWhirr's voice made this impossible. His orders were to go and see. What was the good of it, he wanted to know. Enraged, he told himself he would see – of course. But the boatwain, staggering clumsily, warned him to be careful how he opened that door; there was a blamed fight going on. And Jukes, as if in great bodily pain, desired irritably to know what the devil they were fighting for.

'Dollars! Dollars, sir. All their rotten chests but burst open. Blamed money skipping all over the place, and they are tumbling after it head over heels – tearing and biting like anything. A regular little hell in there.'

Jukes convulsively opened the door. The short boatswain peered under his arm.

One of the lamps had gone out, broken perhaps. Rancorous, guttural cries burst out loudly on their ears, and a strange panting sound, the working of all these straining breasts. A hard blow hit the side of the ship: water fell above with a stunning shock, and in the forefront of the gloom, where the air was reddish and thick, Jukes saw a head bang the deck violently, two thick calves waving on high, muscular arms twined round a naked body, a yellow-face, open-mouthed and with a set wild stare, look up and slide away. An empty chest clattered turning over; a man fell head first with a thump, as if lifted by a kick; and farther off, indistinct, others streamed like a mass of rolling stones down a bank, thumping the deck with their feet and flourishing their arms wildly. The hatchway ladder was loaded with coolies swarming on it like bees on a branch. They hung on steps in a crawling, stirring cluster, beating madly with their fists the underside of the battened hatch, and the headlong rush of the water above was heard in the intervals of their yelling. The ship heeled over more, and they began to drop off: first one, then two, then all the rest went away together, falling straight off with a great cry.

Jukes was confounded. The boatswain, with gruff anxiety, begged him, 'Don't you go in there, sir.'

The whole place seemed to twist upon itself, jumping incessantly the while; and when the ship rose to a sea Jukes fancied that all these men would be shot upon him in a body. He backed out, swung the door to, and with trembling hands pushed at the bolt . . .

As soon as his mate had gone Captain MacWhirr, left alone on the bridge, sidled and staggered as far as the wheelhouse. Its door being hinged forward, he had to fight the gale for admittance, and when at last he managed to enter, it was with an instantaneous clatter and a bang, as though he had been fired through the wood. He stood within, holding on to the handle.

The steering-gear leaked steam, and in the confined space the glass of the binnacle made a shiny oval of light in a thin white fog. The wind howled, hummed, whistled, with sudden booming gusts that rattled the doors and shutters in the vicious patter of sprays. Two coils of lead-line and a small canvas bag hung on a long lanyard, swung wide off, and came back clinging to the bulkheads. The gratings underfoot were nearly afloat; with every sweeping blow of a sea, water squirted violently through the cracks all round the door, and the man at the helm had flung down his cap, his coat, and stood propped against the gearcasing in a striped cotton shirt open on his breast. The little brass wheel in his hands had the appearance of a bright and fragile toy. The cords of his neck stood hard and lean, a dark patch lay in the hollow of his throat, and his face was still and sunken as in death.

Captain MacWhirr wiped his eyes. The sea that had nearly taken him overboard had, to his great annoyance, washed his sou'wester hat off his bald head. The fluffy, fair hair, soaked and darkened, resembled a mean skein of cotton threads festooned round his bare skull. His face, glistening with seawater, had been made crimson with the wind, with the sting of sprays. He looked as though he had come off sweating from before a furnace.

'You here?' he muttered heavily.

The second mate had found his way into the wheelhouse some time before. He had fixed himself in a corner with his knees up, a fist pressed against each temple; and this attitude suggested rage, sorrow, resignation, surrender, with a sort of concentrated unforgiveness. He said mournfully and defiantly, 'Well, it's my watch below now: ain't it?'

The steam gear clattered, stopped, clattered again; and the helmsman's eyeballs seemed to project out of a hungry face as if the compass card behind the binnacle glass had been meat. God knows how long he had been left there to steer, as if forgotten by all his shipmates. The bells had not been struck; there had been no reliefs; the ship's routine had gone down wind; but he was trying to keep her head north-north-east. The rudder might have been gone for all he knew, the fires out, the engines broken down, the ship ready to roll over like a corpse. He was anxious not to get muddled and lose control of her head, because the compass-card swung far both ways, wriggling on the pivot, and sometimes seemed to whirl right round. He suffered from mental stress. He was horribly afraid, also, of the wheelhouse going. Mountains of water kept on tumbling against it. When the ship took one of her desperate dives the corners of his lips twitched.

Captain MacWhirr looked up at the wheelhouse clock. Screwed to the bulk-head, it had a white face on which the black hands appeared to stand quite still. It was half past one in the morning.

'Another day,' he muttered to himself.

The second mate heard him, and lifting his head as one grieving amongst ruins, 'You won't see it break,' he exclaimed. His wrists and his knees could be seen to shake violently. 'No, by God! You won't . . .'

He took his face again between his fists.

The body of the helmsman had moved slightly, but his head didn't budge on his neck – like a stone head fixed to look one way from a column. During a roll that all but took his booted legs from under him, and in the very stagger to save himself, Captain MacWhirr said austerely, 'Don't you pay any attention to what that man says.' And then, with an indefinable change of tone, very grave, he added, 'He isn't on duty.'

The sailor said nothing.

The hurricane boomed, shaking the little place, which seemed airtight; and the light of the binnacle flickered all the time.

'You haven't been relieved,' Captain MacWhirr went on, looking down. 'I want you to stick to the helm, though, as long as you can. You've got the hang of her. Another man coming here might make a mess of it. Wouldn't do. No child's play. And the hands are probably busy with a job down below . . . Think you can?'

The steering-gear leaped into an abrupt short clatter, stopped smouldering like an ember; and the still man, with a motionless gaze, burst out, as if all the passion in him had gone into his lips: 'By Heavens, sir! I can steer for ever if nobody talks to me.'

'Oh! aye! All right . . .' The Captain lifted his eyes for the first time to the man, '. . . Hackett.'

And he seemed to dismiss this matter from his mind. He stooped to the engine-room speaking-tube, blew in, and bent his head. Mr Rout below answered, and at once Captain MacWhirr put his lips to the mouthpiece.

With the uproar of the gale around him he applied alternately to his lips and his ear, and the engineer's voice mounted to him, harsh and as if out of the heat of an engagement. One of the stokers was disabled, the others had given in, the second engineer and the donkey-man were firing-up. The third engineer was standing by the steam-valve. The engines were being tended by hand. How was it above?

'Bad enough. It mostly rests with you,' said Captain MacWhirr. Was the mate down there yet? No? Well, he would be presently. Would Mr Rout let him talk through the speaking-tube? – through the deck speaking-tube, because he – the Captain – was going out again on the bridge directly. There was some trouble amongst the Chinamen. They were fighting, it seemed. Couldn't allow fighting anyhow . . .

Mr Rout had gone away, and Captain MacWhirr could feel against his ear the pulsation of the engines, like the beat of the ship's heart. Mr Rout's voice down there shouted something distantly. The ship pitched headlong, the pulsation leaped with a hissing tumult, and stopped dead. Captain MacWhirr's face was impassive, and his eyes were fixed aimlessly on the crouching shape of the second mate. Again Mr Rout's voice cried out in the depths, and the pulsating beats recommenced, with slow strokes – growing swifter.

Mr Rout had returned to the tube. 'It don't matter much what they do,' he said, hastily; and then, with irritation, 'She takes these dives as if she never meant to come up again.'

'Awful sea,' said the Captain's voice from above.

'Don't let me drive her under,' barked Solomon Rout up the pipe.

'Dark and rain. Can't see what's coming,' uttered the voice. 'Must – keep – her – moving – enough to steer – and chance it,' it went on to state distinctly.

'I am doing as much as I dare.'

'We are – getting – smashed up – a good deal up here,' proceeded the voice mildly. 'Doing – fairly well – though. Of course, if the wheel-house should go . . .'

Mr Rout, bending an attentive ear, muttered peevishly something under his breath.

But the deliberate voice up there became animated to ask: 'Jukes turned up yet?' Then, after a short wait. 'I wish he would bear a hand. I want him to be done and come up here in case of anything. To look after the ship. I am all alone. The second mate's lost . . .'

'What?' shouted Mr Rout into the engine-room, taking his head away. Then up the tube he cried, 'Gone overboard?' and clapped his ear to.

'Lost his nerve,' the voice from above continued in a matter-of-fact tone. 'Damned awkward circumstance.'

Mr Rout, listening with bowed neck, opened his eyes wide at this. However, he heard something like the sounds of a scuffle and broken exclamations coming down to him. He strained his hearing; and all the time Beale, the third engineer, with his arms uplifted, held between the palms of his hands the rim of a little black wheel projecting at the side of a big copper pipe. He seemed to be poising it above his head, as though it were a correct attitude in some sort of game.

To steady himself, he pressed his shoulder against the white bulk-head, one knee bent, and a sweat-rag tucked in his belt hanging on his hip. His smooth cheek was begrimed and flushed, and the coal dust on his eyelids, like the black pencilling of a make-up, enhanced the liquid brilliance of the whites, giving to his youthful face something of a femin-ine, exotic, and fascinating aspect. When the ship pitched he would with hasty movements of his hands screw hard at the little wheel.

'Gone crazy,' began the Captain's voice suddenly in the tube. 'Rushed at me . . . Just now. Had to knock him down . . . This minute. You heard, Mr Rout?'

'The devil!' muttered Mr Rout. 'Look out, Beale!'

His shout rang out like the blast of a warning trumpet, between the iron walls of the engine-room. Painted white, they rose high into the dusk of the skylight, sloping like a roof; and the whole lofty space resembled the interior of a monument, divided by floors of iron grating, with lights flickering at different levels, and a mass of gloom lingering in the middle, within the columnar stir of machinery under the motionless swelling of the cylinders. A loud and wild resonance, made up of all the noises of the hurricane, dwelt in the still warmth of the air. There was in it the smell of hot metal, of oil, and a slight mist of steam. The blows of the sea seemed to traverse it in an unringing, stunning shock, from side to side.

Gleams, like pale long flames, trembled upon the polish of metal; from the flooring below the enormous crank-heads emerged in their turns with a flash of brass and steel – going over; while the connecting-rods, big-jointed, like skeleton limbs, seemed to thrust them down and pull them up again with an irresistible precision. And deep in the half-light other rods dodged deliberately to and fro, crossheads nodded, discs of metal rubbed smoothly against each other, slow and gentle, in a commingling of shadows and gleams.

Sometimes all those powerful and unerring movements would slow down simultaneously, as if they had been the functions of a living organism, stricken suddenly by the blight of languor; and Mr Rout's eyes would blaze darker in his long sallow face. He was fighting this fight in a pair of carpet slippers. A short shiny jacket barely covered his loins, and his white wrists protruded far out of the tight sleeves, as though the emergency had added to his stature, had lengthened his limbs, augmented his pallor, hollowed his eyes.

He moved, climbing high up, disappearing low down, with a restless, purposeful industry, and when he stood still, holding the guard-rail in front of the starting-gear, he would keep glancing to the right at the steam-gauge, at the water-gauge, fixed upon the white wall in the light of a swaying lamp. The mouths of two speaking-tubes gaped stupidly at his elbow, and the dial of the engine-room telegraph resembled a clock of large diameter, bearing on its face curt words instead of figures. The grouped letters stood out heavily black, around the pivot-head of the indicator, emphatically symbolic of loud exclamations: AHEAD ASTERN SLOW HALF STAND BY; and the fat black hand pointed downwards to the word FULL, which, thus singled out, captured the eye as a sharp cry secures attention.

The wood-encased bulk of the low-pressure cylinder, frowning portly from above, emitted a faint wheeze at every thrust, and except for that low hiss the engines worked their steel limbs headlong or slow with a silent, determined smoothness. And all this, the white walls, the moving steel, the floor plates under Solomon Rout's feet, the floors of iron grating above his head, the dusk and the gleams, uprose and sank continuously, with one accord, upon the harsh wash of the waves against the ship's side. The whole loftiness of the place, booming hollow to the great voice of the wind, swayed at the top like a tree, would go over bodily, as if borne down this way and that by the tremendous blasts.

'You've got to hurry up,' shouted Mr Rout, as soon as he saw Jukes appear in the stokehold doorway.

Jukes's glance was wandering and tipsy; his red face was puffy, as though he had overslept himself. He had had an arduous road, and had travelled over it with immense vivacity, the agitation of his mind corresponding to the exertions of his body. He had rushed up out of the bunker, stumbling in the dark alleyway amongst a lot of bewildered men who, trod upon, asked 'What's up, sir?' in awed mutters all round him – down the stokehold ladder, missing many iron rungs in his hurry, down into a place deep as a well, black as Tophet, tipping over back and forth like a see-saw. The water in the bilges thundered at each roll, and lumps of coal skipped to and fro, from end to end, rattling like an avalanche of pebbles on a slope of iron.

Somebody in there moaned with pain, and somebody else could be seen crouching over what seemed the prone body of a dead man; a lusty voice blasphemed; and the glow under each fire-door was like a pool of flaming blood radiating quietly in a velvety blackness.

A gust of wind struck upon the nape of Jukes's neck and next moment he felt it streaming about his wet ankles. The stokehold ventilators hummed; in front of the six fire-doors two wild figures, stripped to the waist, staggered and stooped, wrestling with two shovels.

'Hallo! Plenty of draught now,' yelled the second engineer at once, as though he had been all the time looking out for Jukes. The donkeyman, a dapper little chap with a dazzling fair skin and a tiny, gingery moustache, worked in a sort of mute transport. They were keeping a full head of steam, and a profound rumbling, as of an empty furniture van trotting over a bridge, made a sustained bass to all the other noises of the place.

'Blowing off all the time,' went on yelling the second. With a sound as of a hundred scoured saucepans, the orifice of a ventilator spat upon his shoulder a sudden gush of salt water, and he volleyed a stream of curses upon all things on earth including his own soul, ripping and raving, and all the time attending to his business. With a sharp clash of metal the ardent pale glare of the fire opened upon his bullet head, showing his spluttering lips, his insolent face, and with another clang closed like the white-hot wink of an iron eye.

'Where's the blooming ship? Can you tell me? Blast my eyes! Under water – or what? It's coming down here in tons. Are the condemned cowls gone to Hades? Hey? Don't you know anything – you jolly sailorman you . . .?'

Jukes, after a bewildered moment, had been helped by a roll to dart through; and as soon as his eyes took in the comparative vastness, peace, and brilliance of the engine-room, the ship, setting her stern heavily in the water, sent him charging head down upon Mr Rout.

The chief's arm, long like a tentacle, and straightening as if worked by a spring, went out to meet him, and deflected his rush into a spin towards the speaking-tubes. At the same time Mr Rout repeated earnestly:

'You've got to hurry up, whatever it is.'

Jukes yelled 'Are you there, sir?' and listened. Nothing. Suddenly the roar of the wind fell straight into his ear, but presently a small voice shoved aside the shouting hurricane quietly.

'You, Jukes? – Well?'

Jukes was ready to talk: it was only time that seemed to be wanting. It was easy enough to account for everything. He could perfectly imagine the coolies battened down in the reeking 'tween-deck, lying sick and scared between the rows of chests. Then one of these chests – or perhaps several at once – breaking loose in a roll, knocking out others, sides splitting, lids flying open, and all these clumsy Chinamen rising up in a body to save their property. Afterwards every fling of the ship would hurl that tramping, yelling mob here and there, from side to side, in a whirl of smashed wood, torn clothing, rolling dollars. A struggle once started, they would be unable to stop themselves. Nothing could stop them now except main force. It was a disaster. He had seen it, and that was all he could say. Some of them must be dead, he believed. The rest would go on fighting . . .

He sent up his words, tripping over each other, crowding the narrow tube. They mounted as if into a silence of an enlightened comprehension dwelling alone up there with a storm. And Jukes wanted to be dismissed from the face of that odious trouble intruding on the great need of the ship.

v

HE waited. Before his eyes the engines turned with slow labour, that in the moment of going off into a mad fling would stop dead at Mr Rout's shout, 'Look out, Beale!' They paused in an intelligent immobility, stilled in mid-stroke, a heavy crank arrested on the cant, as if conscious of danger and the passage of time. Then, with a 'Now, then!' from the chief, and the sound of a breath expelled through clenched teeth, they would accomplish the interrupted revolution and begin another.

There was the prudent sagacity of wisdom and the deliberation of enormous strength in their movements. This was their work – this patient coaxing of a distracted ship over the fury of the waves and into the very eye of the wind. At times Mr Rout's chin would sink on his breast, and he watched them with knitted eyebrows as if lost in thought.

The voice that kept the hurricane out of Jukes's ear began: 'Take the hands with you . . .' and left off unexpectedly.

'What could I do with them, sir?'

A harsh, abrupt, imperious clang exploded suddenly. The three pairs of eyes flew up to the telegraph dial to see the hand jump from FULL TO STOP as if snatched by a devil. And then these three men in the engine-room had the intimate sensation of a check upon the ship, of a strange shrinking, as if she had gathered herself for a desperate leap.

'Stop her!' bellowed Mr Rout.

Nobody – not even Captain MacWhirr, who alone on deck had caught sight of a white line of foam coming on at such a height that he couldn't believe his eyes – nobody was to know the steepness of that sea and the awful depth of the hollow the hurricane had scooped out behind the running wall of water.

It raced to meet the ship, and, with a pause, as of girding the loins, the *Nan-Shan* lifted her bows and leaped. The flames in all the lamps sank, darkening the engine-room. One went out. With a tearing crash and a swirling, raving tumult, tons of water fell upon the deck, as though the ship had darted under the foot of a cataract.

Down there they looked at each other, stunned.

'Swept from end to end, by God!' bawled Jukes.

She dipped into the hollow straight down, as if going over the edge of the world. The engine-room toppled forward menacingly, like the inside of a tower nodding in an earthquake. An awful racket, or iron things falling, came from the stokehold. She hung on this appalling slant long enough for Beale to drop on his hands and knees and begin to crawl as if he meant to fly on all fours out of the engine-room, and for Mr Rout to turn his head slowly, rigid, cavernous, with the lower jaw dropping. Jukes had shut his eyes, and his face in a moment became hopelessly blank and gentle, like the face of a blind man.

At last she rose slowly, staggering, as if she had to lift a mountain with her bows.

Mr Rout shut his mouth; Jukes blinked; and little Beale stood up hastily.

'Another one like this, and that's the last of her,' cried the chief.

He and Jukes looked at each other, and the same thought came into their heads. The Captain! Everything must have been swept away. Steering-gear-gone – ship like a log. All over directly.

'Rush!' ejaculated Mr Rout thickly, glaring with enlarged, doubtful eyes at Jukes, who answered him by an irresolute glance.

The clang of the telegraph gong soothed them instantly. The black hand dropped in a flash from STOP to FULL.

'Now then, Beale!' cried Mr Rout.

The steam hissed low. The piston-rods slid in and out. Jukes put his ear to the tube. The voice was ready for him. It said: 'Pick up all the money. Bear a hand now. I'll want you up here.' And that was all.

'Sir?' called up Jukes. There was no answer.

He staggered away like a defeated man from the field of battle. He had got, in some way or other, a cut above his left eyebrow – a cut to the bone. He was not aware of it in the least: quantities of the China Sea, large enough to break his neck for him, had gone over his head, had cleaned, washed, and salted that wound. It did not bleed, but only gaped red; and this gash over the eye, his dishevelled hair, the disorder of his clothes, gave him the aspect of a man worsted in a fight with fists.

'Got to pick up the dollars.' He appealed to Mr Rout, smiling pitifully at random.

'What's that?' asked Mr Rout, wildly. 'Pick up . . .? I don't care . . .' Then, quivering in every muscle, but with an exaggeration of paternal tone, 'Go away now, for God's sake. You deck people'll drive me silly. There's that second mate been going for the old man. Don't you know? You fellows are going wrong for want of something to do . . .'

At these words Jukes discovered in himself the beginnings of anger. Want of something to do – indeed . . . Full of hot scorn against the chief, he turned to go the way he had come. In the stokehold the plump donkeyman toiled with his shovel mutely, as if his tongue had been cut out; but the second was carrying on like a noisy, undaunted maniac, who had preserved his skill in the art of stoking under a marine boiler.

'Hallo, you wandering officer! Hey! Can't you get some of your slush-slingers to wind up a few of them ashes? I am getting choked with them there. Curse it! Hallo! Hey! Remember the articles: *Sailors and firemen to assist each other*. Hey! D'ye hear?'

Jukes was climbing out frantically, and the other, lifting up his face after him, howled, 'Can't you speak? What are you poking about here for? What's your game, anyhow?'

A frenzy possessed Jukes. By the time he was back amongst the men in the darkness of the alleyway, he felt ready to wring all their necks at the slightest sign of hanging back. The very thought of it exasperated him. *He* couldn't hang back. They shouldn't.

The impetuosity with which he came amongst them carried them along. They had already been excited and startled at all his comings and goings – by the fierceness and rapidity of his movements; and more felt than seen in his rushes, he appeared formidable – busied with matters of life and death that brooked no delay. At his first word he

heard them drop into the bunker one after another obediently, with heavy thumps.

They were not clear as to what would have to be done. 'What is it? What is it?' they were asking each other. The boatswain tried to explain; the sounds of a great scuffle surprised them: and the mighty shocks, reverberating awfully in the black bunker, kept them in mind of their danger. When the boatswain threw open the door it seemed that an eddy of the hurricane, stealing through the iron sides of the ship, had set all these bodies whirling like dust: there came to them a confused uproar, a tempestuous tumult, a fierce mutter, gusts of screams dying away, and the tramping of feet mingling with the blows of the sea.

For a moment they glared amazed, blocking the doorway. Jukes pushed through them brutally. He said nothing, and simply darted in. Another lot of coolies on the ladder, struggling suicidally to break through the battened hatch to a swamped deck, fell off as before, and he disappeared under them like a man overtaken by a landslide.

The boatswain yelled excitedly: 'Come along. Get the mate out. He'll be trampled to death. Come on.'

They charged in, stamping on breasts, on fingers, on faces, catching their feet in heaps of clothing, kicking broken wood; but before they could get hold of him Jukes emerged waist deep in a multitude of clawing hands. In the instant he had been lost to view, all the buttons of his jacket had gone, its back had got split up to the collar, his waistcoat had been torn open. The central struggling mass of Chinamen went over to the roll, dark, indistinct, helpless, with a wild gleam of many eyes in the dim light of the lamps.

'Leave me alone – damn you. I am all right,' screeched Jukes. 'Drive them forward. Watch your chance when she pitches. Forward with 'em. Drive them against the bulkhead. Jam 'em up.'

The rush of the sailors into the seething 'tween-deck was like a splash of cold water into a boiling cauldron. The commotion sank for a moment.

The bulk of Chinamen were locked in such a compact scrimmage that, linking their arms and aided by an appalling dive of the ship, the seamen sent it forward in one great shove, like a solid block. Behind their backs small clusters and loose bodies tumbled from side to side.

The boatswain performed prodigious feats of strength. With his long arms open, and each great paw clutching at a stanchion, he stopped the rush of seven entwined Chinamen rolling like a boulder. His joints cracked; he said 'Ha!' and they flew apart. But the carpenter showed the greater intelligence. Without saying a word to anybody he went back into the alleyway, to fetch several coils of cargo gear he had seen there – chain and rope. With these life-lines were rigged.

There was really no resistance. The struggle, however it began, had turned into a scramble of blind panic. If the coolies had started up after their scattered dollars they were by that time fighting only for their footing. They took each other by the throat merely to save themselves from being hurled about. Whoever got a hold anywhere would kick at the others who caught at his legs and hung on, till a roll sent them flying together across the deck.

The coming of the white devils was a terror. Had they come to kill? The individuals torn out of the ruck became very limp in the seamen's hands: some, dragged aside by the heels, were passive, like dead bodies, with open, fixed eyes. Here and there a coolie would fall on his knees as if begging for mercy; several, whom the excess of fear made unruly, were hit with hard fists between the eyes, and cowered; while those who were hurt submitted to rough handling, blinking rapidly without a plaint. Faces streamed with blood; there were raw places on the shaven heads, scratches, bruises, torn wounds, gashes. The broken porcelain out of the chests was mostly responsible for the latter. Here and there a Chinaman, wild-eyed, with his tail unplaited, nursed a bleeding sole.

They had been ranged closely, after having been shaken into submission, cuffed a little to allay excitement, addressed in gruff words of encouragement that sounded like promises of evil. They sat on the deck in ghastly, drooping rows, and at the end the carpenter, with two hands to help him, moved busily from place to place, setting taut and hitching the life-lines. The boatswain, with one leg and one arm embracing a stanchion, struggled with a lamp pressed to his breast, trying to get a light, and growling all the time like an industrious gorilla. The figures of seamen stooped repeatedly, with the movements of gleaners, and everything was being flung into the bunker: clothing, smashed wood, broken china, and the dollars, too, gathered up in men's jackets. Now and then a sailor would stagger towards the doorway with his arms full of rubbish; and dolorous, slanting eyes followed his movements.

With every roll of the ship the long rows of sitting Celestials would sway forward brokenly, and her headlong dives knocked together the line of shaven polls from end to end. When the wash of water rolling on the deck died away for a moment, it seemed to Jukes, yet quivering from his exertions, that in his mad struggle down there he had overcome the wind somehow: that a silence had fallen upon the ship, a silence in which the sea struck thunderously at her sides.

Everything had been cleared out of the 'tween-deck – all the wreckage, as the men said. They stood erect and tottering above the level of heads and drooping shoulders. Here and there a coolie sobbed for his breath. Where the high light fell, Jukes could see the salient ribs of one, the yellow, wistful face of another; bowed necks; or would meet a dull stare directed at his face. He was amazed that there had been no

4237

TYPHOON

corpses; but the lot of them seemed at their last gasp, and they appeared to him more pitiful than if they had been all dead.

Suddenly one of the coolies began to speak. The light came and went on his lean, straining face; he threw his head up like a baying hound. From the bunker came the sounds of knocking and the tinkle of some dollars rolling loose; he stretched out his arm, his mouth yawned black, and the incomprehensible guttural hooting sounds, that did not seem to belong to a human language, penetrated Jukes with a strange emotion as if a brute had tried to be eloquent.

Two more started mouthing what seemed to Jukes fierce denunciations; the others stirred with grunts and growls. Jukes ordered the hands out of the 'tween-decks hurriedly. He left last himself, backing through the door, while the grunts rose to a loud murmur and hands were extended after him as after a malefactor. The boatswain shot the bolt, and remarked uneasily, 'Seems as if the wind has dropped, sir.'

The seamen were glad to get back into the alleyway. Secretly each of them thought that at the last moment he could rush out on deck – and that was a comfort. There is something horribly repugnant in the idea of being drowned under a deck. Now they had done with the Chinamen, they again became conscious of the ship's position.

Jukes on coming out of the alleyway found himself up to the neck in the noisy water. He gained the bridge, and discovered he could detect obscure shapes as if his sight had become pre-naturally acute. He saw faint outlines. They recalled not the familiar aspect of the *Nan-Shan*, but something remembered – an old dismantled steamer he had seen years ago rotting on a mudbank. She recalled that wreck.

There was no wind, not a breath, except the faint currents created by the lurches of the ship. The smoke tossed out of the funnel was settling down upon her deck. He breathed it as he passed forward. He felt the deliberate throb of the engines, and heard small sounds that seemed to have survived the great uproar: the knocking of broken fittings, the rapid tumbling of some piece of wreckage on the bridge. He perceived dimly the squat shape of his captain holding on to a twisted bridge-rail, motionless and swaying as if rooted to the planks. The unexpected stillness of the air oppressed Jukes.

'We have done it, sir,' he gasped.

'Thought you would,' said Captain MacWhirr.

'Did you?' murmured Jukes to himself.

'Wind fell all at once,' went on the Captain.

Jukes burst out: 'If you think it was an easy job –'

But his captain, clinging to the rail, paid no attention. 'According to the books the worst is not over yet.'

'If most of them hadn't been half dead with sea-sickness and fright, not one of us would have come out of that 'tween-deck alive,' said Jukes.

'Had to do what's fair by them,' mumbled MacWhirr, stolidly. 'You don't find everything in books.'

'Why, I believe they would have risen on us if I hadn't ordered the hands out of that pretty quick,' continued Jukes with warmth.

After the whisper of their shouts, their ordinary tones, so distinct, rang out very loud to their ears in the amazing stillness of the air. It seemed to them they were talking in a dark and echoing vault.

Through a jagged aperture in the dome of clouds the light of a few stars fell upon the black sea, rising and falling confusedly. Sometimes the head of a watery cone would topple on board and mingle with the rolling flurry of foam on the swamped deck; and the *Nan-Shan* wallowed heavily at the bottom of a circular cistern of clouds. This ring of dense vapours, gyrating madly round the calm of the centre, encompassed the ship like a motionless and unbroken wall of an aspect inconceivably sinister. Within, the sea, as if agitated by an internal commotion, leaped in peaked mounds that jostled each other, slapping heavily against her sides; and a low moaning sound, the infinite plaint of the storm's fury, came from beyond the limits of the menacing calm. Captain MacWhirr remained silent, and Jukes's ready ear caught suddenly the faint, long-drawn roar of some immense wave rushing unseen under that thick blackness, which made the appalling boundary of his vision.

'Of course,' he started resentfully, 'they thought we had caught at the chance to plunder them. Of course! You said – pick up the money. Easier said than done. They couldn't tell what was in our heads. We came in, smash – right into the middle of them. Had to do it by a rush.'

'As long as it's done . . .' mumbled the Captain, without attempting to look at Jukes. 'Had to do what's fair.'

'We shall find yet there's the devil to pay when this is over,' said Jukes, feeling very sore. 'Let them only recover a bit, and you'll see. They will fly at our throats, sir. Don't forget, sir, she isn't a British ship now. These brutes know it well, too. The damned Siamese flag.'

'We are on board, all the same,' remarked Captain MacWhirr.

'The trouble's not over yet,' insisted Jukes, prophetically, reeling and catching on. 'She's a wreck,' he added, faintly.

'The trouble's not over yet,' assented Captain MacWhirr, half aloud . . . 'Look out for her a minute.'

'Are you going off the deck, sir?' asked Jukes, hurriedly, as if the storm were sure to pounce upon him as soon as he had been left alone with the ship.

He watched her, battered and solitary, labouring heavily in a wild scene of mountainous black waters lit by the gleams of distant worlds. She moved slowly, breathing into the still core of the hurricane the excess of her strength in a white cloud of steam – and the deep-toned vibration of the escape was like the defiant trumpeting of a living creature of the sea impatient for the renewal of the contest. It ceased suddenly. The still air moaned. Above Jukes's head a few stars shone into a pit of black vapours. The inky edge of the cloud-disc frowned upon the ship under the patch of glittering sky. The stars, too, seemed to look at her intently, as if for the last time, and the cluster of their splendour sat like a diadem on a lowering brow.

Captain MacWhirr had gone into the chart-room. There was no light there; but he could feel the disorder of that place where he used to live tidily. His armchair was upset. The books had tumbled out on the floor: he scrunched a piece of glass under his boot. He groped for the matches, and found a box on a shelf with a deep ledge. He struck one and, puckering the corners of his eyes, held out the little flame towards the barometer whose glittering top of glass and metals nodded at him continuously.

It stood very low – incredibly low, so low that Captain MacWhirr grunted. The match went out, and hurriedly he extracted another, with thick, stiff fingers.

Again a little flame flared up before the nodding glass and metal of the top. His eyes looked at it narrowed with attention, as if expecting an imperceptible sign. With his grave face he resembled a booted and misshapen pagan burning incense before the oracle of a Joss. There was no mistake. It was the lowest reading he had ever seen in his life.

Captain MacWhirr emitted a low whistle. He forgot himself till the flame diminished to a blue spark, burnt his fingers, and vanished. Perhaps something had gone wrong with the thing!

There was an aneroid glass screwed above the couch. He turned that way, struck another match, and discovered the white face of the other instrument looking at him from the bulkhead, meaningly, not to be gainsaid, as though the wisdom of men were made unerring by the indifference of matter. There was no room for doubt now. Captain MacWhirr pshawed at it, and threw the match down.

The worst was to come, then – and if the books were right this worst would be very bad. The experience of the last six hours had enlarged his conception of what heavy weather could be like. 'It'll be terrific,' he pronounced, mentally. He had not consciously looked at anything by the light of the matches except at the barometer; and yet somehow he had seen that his water-bottle and the two tumblers had been flung out of their stand. It seemed to give him a more intimate knowledge of the tossing the ship had gone through. 'I wouldn't have believed it,' he thought. And his table had been cleared, too; his rulers, his pencils, the inkstand – all the things that had their safe appointed places – they were gone, as if a mischievous hand had plucked them out one by one and flung them on the wet floor. The hurricane had broken in upon the orderly arrangements of his privacy. This had never happened before, and the feeling of dismay reached the very seat of his composure. And the worst was to come yet! He was glad the trouble in the 'tween-deck had been discovered in time. If the ship had to go after all, then, at least, she wouldn't be going to the bottom with a lot of people in her fighting teeth and claw. That would have been odious. And in that feeling there was a humane intention and a vague sense of the fitness of things.

These instantaneous thoughts were yet in their essence heavy and slow, partaking of the nature of the man. He extended his hand to put back the matchbox in its corner of the shelf. There were always matches there – by his order. The steward had his instructions impressed upon him long before. 'A box . . . just there, see? Not so very full . . . where I can put my hand on it, steward. Might want a light in a hurry. Can't tell on board ship *what* you might want in a hurry. Mind, now.'

And of course on his side he would be careful to put it back in its place scrupulously. He did so now, but before he removed his hand it occurred to him that perhaps he would never have occasion to use that box any more. The vividness of the thought checked him and for an infinitesimal fraction of a second his fingers closed again on the small object as though it had been the symbol of all these little habits that chain us to the weary round of life. He released it at last, and letting himself fall on the settee, listened for the first sounds of returning wind.

Not yet. He heard only the wash of water, the heavy splashes, the dull shocks of the confused seas boarding his ship from all sides. She would never have a chance to clear her decks.

But the quietude of the air was startlingly tense and unsafe, like a slender hair holding a sword suspended over his head. By this awful pause the storm penetrated the defences of the man and unsealed his lips. He spoke out in the solitude and the pitch darkness of the cabin, as if addressing another being awakened within his breast.

'I shouldn't like to lose her,' he said half aloud.

He sat unseen, apart from the sea, from his ship, isolated, as if withdrawn from the very current of his own existence, where such freaks as talking to himself surely had no place. His palms reposed on his knees, he bowed his short neck and puffed heavily, surrendering to a strange sensation of weariness he was not enlightened enough to recognize for the fatigue of mental stress.

From where he sat he could reach the door of a washstand locker. There should have been a towel there. There was. Good . . . He took it out, wiped his face, and afterwards went on rubbing his wet head. He towelled himself with energy in the dark, and then remained motionless

with the towel on his knees. A moment passed, of a stillness so profound that no one could have guessed there was a man sitting in that
cabin. Then a murmur arose.

'She may come out of it, yet.'

When Captain MacWhirr came out on deck, which he did
brusquely, as though he had suddenly become conscious of having
stayed away too long, the calm had lasted already more than fifteen
minutes – long enough to make itself intolerable even to his imagination. Jukes, motionless on the forepart of the bridge, began to speak
at once. His voice, blank and forced as though he were talking through
hard-set teeth, seemed to flow away on all sides into the darkness,
deepening again upon the sea.

'I had the wheel relieved. Hackett began to sing out that he was
done. He's lying in there alongside the steering-gear with a face like
death. At first I couldn't get anybody to crawl out and relieve the poor
devil. That bos'n's worse than no good, I always said. Thought I would
have had to go myself and haul out one of them by the neck.'

'Ah, well,' muttered the Captain. He stood watchful by Jukes's
side.

'The second mate's in there, too, holding his head. Is he hurt, sir?'

'No – crazy,' said Captain MacWhirr, curtly.

'Looks as if he had a tumble, though.'

'I had to give him a push,' explained the Captain.

Jukes gave an impatient sigh.

'It will come very sudden,' said Captain MacWhirr, 'and from over
there, I fancy. God only knows though. These books are only good to
muddle your head and make you jumpy. It will be bad, and there's an
end. If we only can steam her round in time to meet it . . .'

A minute passed. Some of the stars winked rapidly and vanished.

'You left them pretty safe?' began the Captain abruptly, as though
the silence were unbearable.

'Are you thinking of the coolies, sir? I rigged lifelines all ways across
that 'tween-deck.'

'Did you? Good idea, Mr Jukes.'

'I didn't . . . think you cared to . . . know,' said Jukes – the lurch-
ing of the ship cut his speech as though somebody had been jerking him
around while he talked – 'how I got on with . . . that infernal job. We
did it. And it may not matter in the end.'

'Had to do what's fair, for all – they are only Chinamen. Give them
the same chance with ourselves – hang it all. She isn't lost yet. Bad
enough to be shut up below in a gale –'

'That's what I thought when you gave me the job, sir,' interjected
Jukes, moodily.

'– without being battered to pieces,' pursued Captain MacWhirr with rising vehemence. 'Couldn't let that go on in my ship, if I knew she hadn't five minutes to live. Couldn't bear it, Mr Jukes.'

A hollow echoing noise, like that of a shout rolling in a rocky chasm, approached the ship and went away again. The last star, blurred, enlarged, as if returning to the fiery mist of its beginning, struggled with the colossal depth of blackness hanging over the ship – and went out.

'Now for it!' muttered Captain MacWhirr. 'Mr Jukes.'

'Here, sir.'

The two men were growing indistinct to each other.

'We must trust her to go through it and come out on the other side. That's plain and straight. There's no room for Captain Wilson's storm-strategy here.'

'No, sir.'

'She will be smothered and swept again for hours,' mumbled the Captain. 'There's not much left by this time above deck for the sea to take away – unless you or me.'

'Both, sir,' whispered Jukes, breathlessly.

'You are always meeting trouble half-way. Jukes.' Captain MacWhirr remonstrated quaintly. 'Though it's a fact that the second mate is no good. D'ye hear, Mr Jukes? You would be left alone if . . .'

Captain MacWhirr interrupted himself, and Jukes, glancing on all sides, remained silent.

'Don't you be put out by anything,' the Captain continued, mumbling rather fast. 'Keep her facing it. They may say what they like, but the heaviest seas run with the wind. Facing it – always facing it – that's the way to get through. You are a young sailor. Face it. That's enough for any man. Keep a cool head.'

'Yes, sir,' said Jukes, with a flutter of the heart.

In the next few seconds the Captain spoke to the engine-room and got an answer.

For some reason Jukes experienced an access of confidence, a sensation that came from outside like a warm breath, and made him feel equal to every demand. The distant muttering of the darkness stole into his ears. He noted it unmoved, out of that sudden belief in himself, as a man safe in a shirt of mail would watch a point.

The ship laboured without intermission amongst the black hills of water, paying with this hard tumbling the price of her life. She rumbled in her depths, shaking a white plummet of steam into the night, and Jukes's thought skimmed like a bird through the engine-room, where Mr Rout – good man – was ready. When the rumbling ceased it seemed to him that there was a pause of every sound, a dead pause in which Captain MacWhirr's voice rang out startlingly.

'What's that? A puff of wind?' – it spoke much louder than Jukes had ever heard it before – 'On the bow. That's right. She may come out of it yet.'

The mutter of the winds drew near apace. In the forefront could be distinguished a drowsy waking plaint passing on, and far off the growth of a multiple clamour, marching and expanding. There was the throb as of many drums in it, a vicious rushing note, and like the chant of a tramping multitude.

Jukes could no longer see his captain distinctly. The darkness was absolutely piling itself upon the ship. At most he made out movements, a hint of elbows spread out, of a head thrown up.

Captain MacWhirr was trying to do up the top button of his oilskin coat with unwonted haste. The hurricane, with its power to madden the seas, to sink ships, to uproot trees, to overturn strong walls and dash the very birds of the air to the ground, had found this taciturn man in its path, and, doing its utmost, had managed to wring out a few words. Before the renewed wrath of winds swooped on his ship, Captain MacWhirr was moved to declare, in a tone of vexation, as it were: 'I wouldn't like to lose her.'

He was spared that annoyance.

VI

ON a bright sunshiny day, with the breeze chasing her smoke far ahead, the *Nan-Shan* came into Fu-chau. Her arrival was at once noticed on shore, and the seamen in harbour said: 'Look! Look at that steamer. What's that? Siamese – isn't she? Just look at her!'

She seemed, indeed, to have been used as a running target for the secondary batteries of a cruiser. A hail of minor shells could not have given her upper works a more broken, torn, and devastated aspect: and she had about her the worn, weary air of ships coming from the far ends of the world – and indeed with truth, for in her short passage she had been very far; sighting, verily, even the coast of the Great Beyond, whence no ship ever returns to give up her crew to the dust of the earth. She was incrusted and grey with salt to the trucks of her masts and to the top of her funnel; as though (as some facetious seaman said) 'the crowd on board had fished her out somewhere from the bottom of the sea and brought her in here for salvage'. And further, excited by the felicity of his own wit, he offered to give five pounds for her – 'as she stands'.

Before she had been quite an hour at rest, a meagre little man, with a red-tipped nose and a face cast in an angry mould, landed from a sampan on the quay of the Foreign Concession, and incontinently turned to shake his fist at her.

A tall individual, with legs much too thin for a rotund stomach, and with watery eyes, strolled up and remarked, 'Just left her – eh? Quick work.'

He wore a soiled suit of blue flannel with a pair of dirty cricketing shoes; a dingy grey moustache drooped from his lip, and daylight could be seen in two places between the rim and the crown of his hat.

'Hallo! what are you doing here?' asked the ex second mate of the *Nan-Shan*, shaking hands hurriedly.

'Standing by for a job – chance worth taking – got a quiet hint,' explained the man with the broken hat, in jerky, apathetic wheezes.

The second shook his fist again at the *Nan-Shan*. 'There's a fellow there that ain't fit to have the command of a scow,' he declared, quivering with passion, while the other looked about listlessly.

'Is there?'

But he caught sight on the quay of a heavy seaman's chest, painted brown under a fringed sailcloth cover, and lashed with new manila line. He eyed it with awakened interest.

'I would talk and raise trouble if it wasn't for that damned Siamese flag. Nobody to go to – or I would make it hot for him. The fraud! Told his chief engineer – that's another fraud for you – I had lost my nerve. The greatest lot of ignorant fools that ever sailed the seas. No! You can't think . . .'

'Got your money all right?' inquired his seedy acquaintance suddenly.

'Yes. Paid me off on board,' raged the second mate. ' "Get your breakfast on shore," says he.'

'Mean skunk!' commented the tall man, vaguely, and passed his tongue on his lips. 'What about having a drink of some sort?'

'He struck me,' hissed the second mate.

'No! Struck! You don't say?' The man in blue began to bustle about sympathetically. 'Can't possibly talk here. I want to know all about it. Struck – eh? Let's get a fellow to carry your chest. I know a quiet place where they have some bottled beer . . .'

Mr Jukes, who had been scanning the shore through a pair of glasses, informed the chief engineer afterwards that 'our late second mate hasn't been long in finding a friend. A chap looking uncommonly like a bummer. I saw them walk away together from the quay.'

The hammering and banging of the needful repairs did not disturb Captain MacWhirr. The steward found in the letter he wrote, in a tidy chart-room, passages of such absorbing interest that twice he was nearly caught in the act. But Mrs MacWhirr, in the drawing-room of the forty-pound house, stifled a yawn – perhaps out of self-respect – for she was alone.

She reclined in a plush-bottomed and gilt hammock-chair near a tiled fireplace, with Japanese fans on the mantel and a glow of coals in the grate. Lifting her hands, she glanced wearily here and there into the many pages. It was not her fault they were so prosy, so completely uninteresting – from 'My darling wife' at the beginning, to 'Your loving husband' at the end. Slo couldn't be really expected to understand all these ship affairs. She was glad, of course, to hear from him, but she had never asked herself why, precisely.

    . . . . They are called typhoons . . . The mate did not seem to like it . . . Not in books . . . Couldn't think of letting it go on . . .

The paper rustled sharply. . . . 'A calm that lasted more than twenty minutes,' she read perfunctorily; and the next words her thoughtless eyes caught, on the top of another page, were: 'see you and the children again . . .' She had a movement of impatience. He was always thinking of coming home. He had never had such a good salary before. What was the matter now?

It did not occur to her to turn back overleaf to look. She would have found it recorded there that between 4 and 6 a.m. on 25 December Captain MacWhirr did actually think that his ship could not possibly live another hour in such a sea, and that he would never see his wife and children again. Nobody was to know this (his letters got mislaid so quickly) – nobody whatever but the steward, who had been greatly impressed by that disclosure. So much so, that he tried to give the cook some idea of the 'narrow squeak we all had' by saying solemnly, 'The old man himself had a damn poor opinion of our chance.'

'How do you know?' asked the cook contemptuously, an old soldier. 'He hasn't told you, maybe?'

'Well, he did give me a hint to that effect,' the steward brazened it out.

'Get along with you! He will be coming to tell *me* next,' jeered the old cook, over his shoulder.

Mrs MacWhirr glanced farther, on the alert.

. . . Do what's fair . . . Miserable objects . . . Only three, with a broken leg each, and one . . . Thought had better keep the matter quiet . . . hope to have done the fair thing . . .

She let fall her hands. No: there was nothing more about coming home. Must have been merely expressing a pious wish. Mrs MacWhirr's mind was set at ease, and a black marble clock, priced by the local jeweller at £3 18s. 6d., had a discreet stealthy tick.

The door flew open, and a girl in the long-legged, short-frocked period of existence, flung into the room. A lot of colourless, rather lanky hair was scattered over her shoulders. Seeing her mother, she stood still, and directed her pale prying eyes upon the letter.

'From father,' murmured Mrs MacWhirr. 'What have you done with your ribbon?'

The girl put her hands up to her head and pouted.

'He's well,' continued Mrs MacWhirr, languidly. 'At least I think so. He never says.' She had a little laugh. The girl's face expressed a wandering indifference, and Mrs MacWhirr surveyed her with fond pride.

'Go and get your hat,' she said after a while. 'I am going out to do some shopping. There is a sale at Linom's.'

'Oh, how jolly!' uttered the child, impressively, in unexpectedly grave vibrating tones, and bounded out of the room.

It was a fine afternoon, with a grey sky and dry sidewalks. Outside the draper's Mrs MacWhirr smiled upon a woman in a black mantle of generous proportions armoured in jet and crowned with flowers blooming falsely above a bilious matronly countenance. They broke into a swift little babble of greetings and exclamations both together, very hurried, as if the street were ready to yawn open and swallow all that pleasure before it could be expressed.

Behind them the high glass doors were kept on the swing. People couldn't pass, men stood aside waiting patiently, and Lydia was absorbed in poking the end of her parasol between the stone flags. Mrs MacWhirr talked rapidly.

'Thank you very much. He's not coming home yet. Of course it's very sad to have him away, but it's such a comfort to know he keeps so well.' Mrs MacWhirr drew breath. 'The climate there agrees with him,' she added, beamingly, as if poor MacWhirr had been away touring in China for the sake of his health.

Neither was the chief engineer coming home yet. Mr Rout knew too well the value of a good billet.

'Solomon says wonders will never cease,' cried Mrs Rout joyously at the old lady in her armchair by the fire. Mr Rout's mother moved slightly, her withered hands lying in black half-mittens on her lap.

The eyes of the engineer's wife fairly danced on the paper. 'That captain of the ship he is in – a rather simple man, you remember, mother? – has done something rather clever, Solomon says.'

'Yes, my dear,' said the old woman meekly, sitting with bowed silvery head, and that air of inward stillness characteristic of very old people who seem lost in watching the last flickers of life. 'I think I remember.'

Solomon Rout, Old Sol, Father Sol, the Chief, 'Rout, good man' – Mr Rout, the condescending and paternal friend of youth, had been the baby of her many children – all dead by this time. And she remembered him best as a boy of ten – long before he went away to serve his apprenticeship in some great engineering works in the North. She had seen so little of him since, she had gone through so many years, that she had now to retrace her steps very far back to recognize him plainly in the mist of time. Sometimes it seemed that her daughter-in-law was talking of some strange man.

Mrs Rout junior was disappointed. 'H'm. H'm.' She turned the page. 'How provoking! He doesn't say what it is. Says I couldn't understand how much there was in it. Fancy! What could it be so very clever? What a wretched man not to tell us!'

She read on without further remark soberly, and at last sat looking into the fire. The chief wrote just a word or two of the typhoon; but something had moved him to express an increased longing for the companionship of the jolly woman.

> If it hadn't been that mother must be looked after, I would send you your passage-money today. You could set up a small house out here. I would have a chance to see you sometimes then. We are not growing young-er . . .

'He's well, mother,' sighed Mrs Rout, rousing herself.

'He always was a strong healthy boy,' said the old woman, placidly.

But Mr Jukes's account was really animated and very full. His friend in the Western Ocean trade imparted it freely to the other officers of his liner. 'A chap I know writes to me about an extraordinary affair that happened on board his ship in that typhoon – you know – that we read of in the papers two months ago. It's the funniest thing! Just see for yourself what he says. I'll show you his letter.'

There were phrases in it calculated to give the impression of light-hearted, indomitable resolution. Jukes had written them in good faith, for he felt thus when he wrote. He described with lurid effect the scenes in the 'tween-deck.

> . . . It struck me in a flash that those confounded Chinamen couldn't tell we weren't a desperate kind of robbers. 'Tisn't good to part the Chinaman from his money if he is the stronger party. We need have been desperate indeed to go thieving in such weather, but what could these beggars know of us? So, without thinking of it twice, I got the hands away in a jiffy. Our work was done – that the old man had set his heart on. We cleared out without staying to inquire how they felt. I am convinced that if they had not been so unmercifully shaken, and afraid – each individual one of them – to stand up, we would have been torn to pieces. Oh! It was pretty complete, I can tell you; and you may run to and fro across the Pond to the end of time before you find yourself with such a job on your hands.

After this he alluded professionally to the damage done to the ship, and went on thus:

> It was when the weather quietened down that the situation became confoundedly delicate. It wasn't made any better by us having been lately

transferred to the Siamese flag; though the skipper can't see that it makes any difference – 'as long as *we* are on board' – he says. There are feelings that this man simply hasn't got – and there's an end of it. You might just as well try to make a bedpost understand. But apart from this it is an infernally lonely state for a ship to be going about the China seas with no proper consuls, not even a gunboat of her own anywhere, nor a body to go to in case of some trouble.

My notion was to keep these Johnnies under hatches for another fifteen hours or so; as we weren't much farther than that from Fu-chau. We would find there, most likely, some sort of a man-of-war, and once under her guns we were safe enough; for surely any skipper of a man-of-war – English, French, or Dutch – would see white men through as far as a row on board goes. We could get rid of them and their money afterwards by delivering them to their Mandarin or Taotai, or whatever they call these chaps in goggles you see being carried about in sedan-chairs through their stinking streets.

The old man wouldn't see it somehow. He wanted to keep the matter quiet. He got that notion into his head, and a steam windlass couldn't drag it out of him. He wanted as little fuss made as possible, for the sake of the ship's name and for the sake of the owners – 'for the sake of all concerned', says he, looking at me very hard. It made me angry hot. Of course you couldn't keep a thing like that quiet; but the chests had been secured in the usual manner and were safe enough for any earthly gale, while this had been an altogether fiendish business I couldn't give you even an idea of.

Meantime, I could hardly keep on my feet. None of us had a spell of any sort for nearly thirty hours, and there the old man sat rubbing his chin, rubbing the top of his head, and so bothered he didn't even think of pulling his long boots off.

'I hope, sir,' says I, 'you won't be letting them out on deck before we make ready for them in some shape or other.' Not, mind you, that I felt very sanguine about controlling these beggars if they meant to take charge. A trouble with a cargo of Chinamen is no child's play. I was damn tired, too. 'I wish,' said I, 'you would let us throw the whole lot of these dollars down to them and leave them to fight it out amongst themselves, while we get a rest.'

'Now you talk wild, Jukes,' says he, looking up in his slow way that makes you ache all over, somehow. 'We must plan out something that would be fair to all parties.'

I had no end of work on hand, as you may imagine, so I set the hands going, and then I thought I would turn in a bit. I hadn't been asleep in my bunk ten minutes when in rushes the steward and begins to pull at my leg.

'For God's sake, Mr Jukes, come out! Come on deck quick, sir. Oh, do come out!'

The fellow scared all the sense out of me. I didn't know what had happened: another hurricane – or what. Could hear no wind.

'The Captain's letting them out. Oh, he is letting them out! Jump on deck, sir, and save us. The chief engineer has just run below for his revolver.'

That's what I understood the fool to say. However, Father Rout swears he went in there only to get a clean pocket-handkerchief. Anyhow, I made one jump into my trousers and flew on deck aft. There was certainly a good deal of noise going on forward of the bridge. Four of the hands with the bos'n were at work abaft. I passed up to them some of the rifles all the ships on the China coast carry in the cabin, and led them on the bridge. On the way I ran against Old Sol, looking startled and sucking at an unlighted cigar.

'Come along,' I shouted to him.

We charged, the seven of us, up to the chart-room. All was over. There stood the old man with his sea-boots still drawn up to the hips and in shirt-sleeves – got warm thinking it out, I suppose. Bun-hin's dandy clerk at his elbow, a dirty as a sweep, was still green in the face. I could see directly I was in for something.

'What the devil are these monkey tricks, Mr Jukes?' asks the old man, as angry as ever he could be. I tell you frankly it made me lose my tongue. 'For God's sake, Mr Jukes,' says he, 'do take away these rifles from the men. Somebody's sure to get hurt before long if you don't. Damme, if this ship isn't worse than Bedlam! Look sharp now. I want you up here to help me and Bun-hin's Chinaman to count that money. You wouldn't mind lending a hand, too, Mr Rout, now you are here. The more of us the better.'

He had settled it all in his mind while I was having a snooze. Had we been an English ship, or only going to land our cargo of coolies in an English port, like Hong Kong, for instance, there would have been no end of inquiries and bother, claims for damages, and so on. But these Chinamen know their officials better than we do.

The hatches had been taken off already, and they were all on deck after a night and a day down below. It made you feel queer to see so many gaunt, wild faces together. The beggars stared about at the sky, at the sea, at the ship, as though they had expected the whole thing to have been blown to pieces. And no wonder! They had had a doing that would have shaken the soul out of a white man. But then they say a Chinaman has no soul. He has, though, something about him that is deuced tough. There was a fellow (amongst others of the badly hurt) who had had his eye all but knocked out. It stood out of his head the size of half a hen's egg. This would have laid out a white man on his back for a month: and yet there was that chap elbowing here and there in the crowd and talking to the others as if nothing had been the matter. They made a great hubbub amongst themselves, and whenever the old man showed his bald head on the foreside of the bridge, they would all leave off jawing and look at him from below.

It seems that after he had done his thinking he made that Bun-hin's fellow go down and explain to them the only way they could get their money back. He told me afterwards that, all the coolies having worked in the same place and for the same length of time, he reckoned he would be doing the fair thing by them as near as possible if he shared all the cash we had picked up equally among the lot. You couldn't tell one man's dollars from another's, he said, and if you asked each man how much money he brought on board he was afraid they would lie, and he would find himself a long way short. I think he was right there. As to give up the money to any Chinese official he could scare up in Fu-chau, he said he might just as well put the lot in his own pocket at once for all the good it would be to them. I suppose they thought so, too.

We finished the distribution before dark. It was rather a sight: the sea running high, the ship a wreck to look at, these Chinamen staggering up on the bridge one by one for their share, and the old man still booted, and in his shirt-sleeves, busy paying out at the chart-room door, perspiring like anything, and now and then coming down sharp on myself or Father Rout about one thing or another not quite to his mind. He took the share of those who were disabled himself to them on the No. 2 hatch. There were three dollars left over, and these went to the three most damaged coolies, one to each. We turned-to afterwards, and shovelled out on deck heaps of wet rags, all sorts of fragments of things without shape, and that you couldn't give a name to, and let them settle the ownership themselves.

This certainly is coming as near as can be to keeping the thing quiet for the benefit of all concerned. What's your opinion, you pampered mail-boat swell? The old chief says that this was plainly the only thing that could be done. The skipper remarked to me the other day, 'There are things you find nothing about in books.' I think that he got out of it very well for such a stupid man.

Joseph Conrad

The Black Mate

A GOOD many years ago there were several ships loading at the Jetty, London Dock. I am speaking here of the eighties of the last century, of the time when London had plenty of fine ships in the docks, though not so many fine buildings in its streets.

The ships at the Jetty were fine enough; they lay one behind the other; and the *Sapphire*, third from the end, was as good as the rest of them, and nothing more. Each ship at the Jetty had, of course, her chief officer on board. So had every other ship in dock.

The policeman at the gates knew them all by sight, without being able to say at once, without thinking, to what ship any particular man belonged. As a matter of fact, the mates of the ships then lying in the London Dock were like the majority of officers in the Merchant Service – a steady, hard-working, staunch, unromantic-looking set of men, belonging to various classes of society, but with the professional stamp obliterating the personal characteristics, which were not very marked, anyhow.

This last was true of them all, with the exception of the mate of the *Sapphire*. Of him the policeman could not be in doubt. This one had a presence.

He was noticeable to them in the street from a great distance; and when in the morning he strode down the Jetty to his ship, the lumpers and the dock labourers rolling the bales and trundling the cases of cargo on their hand-trucks would remark to each other:

'Here's the black mate coming along.'

That was the name they gave him, being a gross lot, who could have no appreciation of the man's dignified bearing. And to call him black was the superficial impressionism of the ignorant.

Of course, Mr Bunter, the mate of the *Sapphire*, was not black. He was no more black than you or I, and certainly as white as any chief mate of a ship in the whole of the Port of London. His complexion was of the sort that did not take the tan easily; and I happen to know that the poor fellow had had a month's illness just before he joined the *Sapphire*.

From this you will perceive that I knew Bunter. Of course I knew him. And, what's more, I knew his secret at the time, this secret which – never mind just now. Returning to Bunter's personal appearance, it was nothing but ignorant prejudice on the part of the foreman stevedore to say, as he did in my hearing: 'I bet he's a furriner of some sort.' A man may have black hair without being set down for a Dago. I have known a West-country sailor, boatswain of a fine ship, who looked more Spanish than any Spaniard afloat I've ever met. He looked like a Spaniard in a picture.

Competent authorities tell us that this earth is to be finally the inheritance of men with dark hair and brown eyes. It seems that already the great majority of mankind is dark-haired in various shades. But it is only when you meet one that you notice how rare are men with really black hair, black as ebony. Bunter's hair was absolutely black, black as a raven's wing. He wore, too, all his beard (clipped, but a good length all the same), and his eyebrows were thick and bushy. Add to this steely-blue eyes, which in a fair-haired man would have been nothing so extraordinary, but in that sombre framing made a startling contrast, and you will easily understand that Bunter was noticeable enough. If it had not been for the quietness of his movements, for the general soberness of his demeanour, one would have given him credit for a fiercely passionate nature.

Of course, he was not in his first youth; but if the expression 'in the force of his age' his any meaning, he realized it completely. He was a tall man, too, though rather spare. Seeing him from his poop indefatigably busy with his duties, Captain Ashton, of the clipper ship *Elsinore*, lying just ahead of the *Sapphire*, remarked once to a friend that 'Johns has got somebody there to hustle his ship along for him.'

Captain Johns, master of the *Sapphire*, having commanded ships for many years, was well known, without being much respected or liked. In the company of his fellows he was either neglected or chaffed. The chaffing was generally undertaken by Captain Ashton, a cynical and teasing sort of man. It was Captain Ashton who permitted himself the unpleasant joke of proclaiming once in company that 'Johns is of the opinion that every sailor above forty years of age ought to be poisoned – shipmasters in actual command excepted.'

It was in a City restaurant, where several well-known shipmasters were having lunch together. There was Captain Ashton, florid and jovial, in a large white waistcoat and with a yellow rose in his buttonhole; Captain Sellers in a sack-coat, thin and pale-faced, with his iron-grey hair tucked behind his ears, and, but for the absence of spectacles, looking like an ascetical mild man of books; Captain Bell, a bluff sea-dog with hairy fingers, in blue serge and a black felt hat pushed far back off his crimson forehead. There was also a very young shipmaster, with a little fair moustache and serious eyes, who said nothing, and only smiled faintly from time to time.

Captain Johns, very much startled, raised his perplexed and credulous glance, which, together with a low and horizontally wrinkled brow, did not make a very intellectual *ensemble*. This impression was by no means mended by the slightly pointed form of his bald head.

Everybody laughed outright, and, thus guided, Captain Johns ended by smiling rather sourly, and attempted to defend himself. It was all very well to joke, but nowadays, when ships, to pay anything at all, had to be driven hard on the passage and in harbour, the sea was no place for elderly men. Only young men and men in their prime were equal to modern conditions of push and hurry. Look at the great firms: almost every single one of them was getting rid of men showing any signs of age. He, for one, didn't want any oldsters on board his ship.

And, indeed, in this opinion Captain Johns was not singular. There was at that time a lot of seamen, with nothing against them but that they were grizzled, wearing out the soles of their last pair of boots on the pavements of the City in the heart-breaking search for a berth.

Captain Johns added with a sort of ill-humoured innocence that from holding that opinion to thinking of poisoning people was a very long step.

This seemed final, but Captain Ashton would not let go his joke.

'Oh, yes. I am sure you would. You said distinctly "of no use." What's to be done with men who are "of no use"? You are a kind-hearted fellow, Johns. I am sure that if only you thought it over carefully you would consent to have them poisoned in some painless manner.'

Captain Sellers twitched his thin, sinuous lips.

'Make ghosts of them,' he suggested pointedly.

At the mention of ghosts Captain Johns became shy, in his perplexed, sly and and unlovely manner.

Captain Ashton winked.

'Yes. And then perhaps you would get a chance to have a communication with the world of spirits. Surely the ghosts of seamen should haunt ships. Some of them would be sure to call on an old shipmate.'

Captain Sellers remarked drily:

'Don't raise his hopes like this; it's cruel. He won't see anything. You know, Johns, that nobody has ever seen a ghost.'

At this intolerable provocation Captain Johns came out of his reserve. With no perplexity whatever, but with a positive passion of credulity giving momentary lustre to his dull little eyes, he brought up a lot of authenticated instances. There were books and books full of instances. It was merest ignorance to deny supernatural apparitions. Cases were published every month in a special newspaper. Professor

Cranks saw ghosts daily. And Professor Cranks was no small potatoes either. One of the biggest scientific men living. And there was that newspaper fellow – what's his name? – who had a girl-ghost visitor. He printed in his paper things she said to him. And to say there were no ghosts after that!

'Why, they have been photographed! What more proof do you want?'

Captain Johns was indignant. Captain Bell's lips twitched, but Captain Ashton protested now.

'For goodness' sake don't keep him going with that. And by the by, Johns, who's that hairy pirate you've got for your new mate? Nobody in the Dock seems to have seen him before.'

Captain Johns, pacified by the change of subject, answered simply that Willy, the tobacconist at the corner of Fenchurch Street, had sent him along.

Willy, his shop, and the very house in Fenchurch Street, I believe, are gone now. In his time, wearing a careworn, absent-minded look on his pasty face, Willy served with tobacco many southern-going ships out of the Port of London. At certain times of the day the shop would be full of ship-masters. They sat on casks, they lounged against the counter.

Many a youngster found his first lift in life there; many a man got a sorely needed berth by simply dropping in for four pennyworth of birds'-eye at an auspicious moment. Even Willy's assistant, a red-headed, uninterested, delicate-looking young fellow, would hand you across the counter sometimes a bit of valuable intelligence with your box of cigarettes, in a whisper, lips hardly moving, thus: 'The *Bellona*, South Dock. Second officer wanted. You may be in time for it if you hurry up.'

And didn't one just fly!

'Oh, Willy sent him,' said Captain Ashton. 'He's a very striking man. If you were to put a red sash round his waist and a red handkerchief round his head, he would look exactly like one of them buccaneering chaps that made men walk the plank and carried women off into captivity. Look out, Johns, he don't cut your throat for you and run off with the *Sapphire*. What ship has he come out of last?'

Captain Johns, after looking up credulously as usual, wrinkled his brow, and said placidly that the man had seen better days. His name was Bunter.

'He's had command of a Liverpool ship, the *Samaria*, some years ago. He lost her in the Indian Ocean, and had his certificate suspended for a year. Ever since then he has not been able to get another command. He's been knocking about in the Western Ocean trade lately.'

'That accounts for him being a stranger to everybody about the Docks,' Captain Ashton concluded as they rose from table.

Captain Johns walked down to the Dock after lunch. He was short of stature and slightly bandy. His appearance did not inspire the generality of mankind with esteem; but it must have been otherwise with his employers. He had the reputation of being an uncomfortable commander, meticulous in trifles, always nursing a grievance of some sort and incessantly nagging. He was not a man to kick up a row with you and be done with it, but to say nasty things in a whining voice; a man capable of making one's life a perfect misery if he took a dislike to an officer.

That very evening I went to see Bunter on board, and sympathized with him on his prospects for the voyage. He was subdued. I suppose a man with a secret locked up in his breast loses his buoyancy. And there was another reason why I could not expect Bunter to show a great elasticity of spirits. For one thing, he had been very seedy lately, and besides – but of that later.

Captain Johns had been on board that afternoon, and had loitered and dodged about his chief mate in a manner which had annoyed Bunter exceedingly.

'What could he mean?' he asked with calm exasperation. 'One would think he suspected I had stolen something and tried to see in what pocket I had stowed it away; or that somebody told him I had a tail and he wanted to find out how I managed to conceal it. I don't like to be approached from behind several times in one afternoon in that creepy way and then to be looked up at suddenly in front from under my elbow. Is it a new sort of peep-bo game? It doesn't amuse me. I am no longer a baby.'

I assure him that if anyone were to tell Captain Johns that he – Bunter – had a tail, Johns would manage to get himself to believe the story in some mysterious manner. He would. He was suspicious and credulous to an inconceivable degree. He would believe any silly tale, suspect any man of anything, and crawl about with it and ruminate the stuff, and turn it over and over in his mind in the most miserable, inwardly whining perplexity. He would take the meanest possible view in the end, and discover the meanest possible course of action by a sort of natural genius for that sort of thing.

Bunter also told me that the mean creature had crept all over the ship on his little, bandy legs, taking him along to grumble and whine to about a lot of trifles. Crept about the decks like a wretched insect – like a cockroach, only not so lively.

Thus did the self-possessed Bunter express himself with great disgust. Then, going on with his usual stately deliberation, made sinister by the frown of his jet-black eyebrows:

'And the fellow is mad, too. He tried to be sociable for a bit, and could find nothing else but to make big eyes at me, and ask me if I believed 'in communication beyond the grave.' Communication beyond – I didn't know what he meant at first. I didn't know what to say. 'A very solemn subject, Mr Bunter,' says he. 'I've given a great deal of study to it.' "

Had Johns lived on shore he would have been the predestined prey of fraudulent mediums; or even if he had had any decent opportunities between the voyages. Luckily for him, when in England he lived somewhere far away in Leytonstone, with a maiden sister ten years older than himself, a fearsome virago twice his size, before whom he trembled. It was said she bullied him terribly in general; and in the particular instance of his spiritualistic leanings she had her own views.

These leanings were to her simply satanic. She was reported as having declared that, 'With God's help, she would prevent that fool from giving himself up to the Devils.' It was beyond doubt that Johns' secret ambition was to get into personal communication with the spirits of the dead – if only his sister would let him. But she was adamant. I was told that while in London he had to account to her for every penny of the money he took with him in the morning, and for every hour of his time. And she kept the bankbook, too.

Bunter (he had been a wild youngster, but he was well connected; had ancestors; there was a family tomb somewhere in the home counties) – Bunter was indignant, perhaps on account of his own dead. Those steely-blue eyes of his flashed with positive ferocity out of that black-bearded face. He impressed me – there was so much dark passion in his leisurely contempt.

'The cheek of the fellow! Enter into relations with . . . A mean little cad like this! It would be an impudent intrusion. He wants to enter? . . . What is it? A new sort of snobbishness, or what?'

I laughed outright at this original view of spiritism – or whatever the ghost craze is called. Even Bunter himself condescended to smile. But it was an austere, quickly vanished smile. A man in his almost, I may say, tragic position couldn't be expected – you understand. He was really worried. He was ready eventually to put up with any dirty trick in the course of the voyage. A man could not expect much consideration should he find himself at the mercy of a fellow like Johns. A misfortune is a misfortune, and there's an end of it. But to be bored by mean, low-spirited, inane ghost stories in the Johns' style, all the way out to Calcutta and back again, was an intolerable apprehension to be under. Spiritism was indeed a solemn subject to think about in that light. Dreadful, even!

Poor fellow! Little we both thought that before very long he himself . . . However, I could give him no comfort. I was rather appalled myself.

Bunter had also another annoyance that day. A confounded berthing master came on board on some pretence or other, but in reality, Bunter thought, simply impelled by an inconvenient curiosity – inconvenient to Bunter, that is. After some beating about the bush, that man suddenly said:

'I can't help thinking I've seen you before somewhere, Mr Mate. If I heard your name, perhaps –'

Bunter – that's the worst of a life with a mystery in it – was much alarmed. It was very likely that the man had seen him before – worse luck to his excellent memory. Bunter himself could not be expected to remember every casual dock-walloper he might have had to do with. Bunter brazened it out by turning upon the man, making use of that impressive, black-as-night sternness of expression his unusual hair furnished him with:

'My name's Bunter, sir. Does that enlighten your inquisitive intellect? And I don't ask what your name may be. I don't want to know. I've no use for it, sir. An individual who calmly tells me to my face that he is *not sure* if he has seen me before, either means to be impudent or is no better than a worm, sir. Yes, I said a worm – a blind worm!'

Brave Bunter. That was the line to take. He fairly drove the beggar out of the ship, as if every word had been a blow. But the pertinacity of that brass-bound Paul Pry was astonishing. He cleared out of the ship, of course, before Bunter's ire, not saying anything, and only trying to cover up his retreat by a sickly smile. But once on the Jetty he turned deliberately round, and set himself to stare in dead earnest at the ship. He remained planted there like a mooring-post, absolutely motionless, and with his stupid eyes winking no more than a pair of cabin portholes.

What could Bunter do? It was awkward for him, you know. He could not go and put his head into the bread-locker. What he did was to take up a position abaft the mizzen-rigging, and stare back as unwinking as the other. So they remained, and I don't know which of them grew giddy first; but the man on the Jetty, not having the advantage of something to hold on to, got tired the soonest, flung his arm, giving the contest up, as it were, and went away at last.

Bunter told me he was glad the *Sapphire*, 'that gem amongst ships' as he alluded to her sarcastically, was going to sea next day. He had had enough of the Dock. I understood his impatience. He had steeled himself against any possible worry the voyage might bring, though it is clear enough now that he was not prepared for the extraordinary experience that was awaiting him already, and in no other part of the world than the Indian Ocean itself: the very part of the world where the poor fellow had lost his ship and had broken his luck, as it seemed for good and all, at the same time.

As to his remorse in regard to a certain secret action of his life, well, I understand that a man of Bunter's fine character would suffer not a little. Still, between ourselves, and without the slightest wish to be cynical, it cannot be denied that with the noblest of us the fear of being found out enters for some considerable part into the composition of remorse. I didn't say this in so many words to Bunter, but as the poor fellow harped a bit on it, I told him that there were skeletons in a good many honest cupboards, and that, as to his own particular guilt, it wasn't writ large on his face for everybody to see – so he needn't worry as to that. And besides, he would be gone to sea in about twelve hours from now.

He said there was some comfort in that thought, and went off then to spend his last evening for many months with his wife. For all his wildness, Bunter had made no mistake in his marrying. He had married a lady. A perfect lady. She was a dear little woman, too. As to her pluck, I, who know what times they had to go through, I cannot admire her enough for it. Real, hard-wearing every day and day after day pluck that only a woman is capable of when she is of the right sort – the undismayed sort I would call it.

The black mate felt this parting with his wife more than any of the previous ones in all the years of bad luck. But she was of the undismayed kind, and showed less trouble in her gentle face than the black-haired, buccaneer-like, but dignified mate of the *Sapphire*. It may be that her conscience was less disturbed than her husband's. Of course, his life had no secret places for her; but a woman's conscience is somewhat more resourceful in finding good and valid excuses. It depends greatly on the person that needs them, too.

They had agreed that she should not come down to the Dock to see him off. 'I wonder you care to look at me at all,' said the sensitive man. And she did not laugh.

Bunter was very sensitive; he left her rather brusquely at the last. He got on board in good time, and produced the usual impression on the mud-pilot in the broken-down straw hat who took the *Sapphire* out of dock. The river-man was very polite to the dignified, striking-looking chief mate. 'The fine-inch manilla for the check-rope, Mr – Bunter, thank you – Mr Bunter, please.' The sea-pilot who left the 'gem of ships' heading comfortably down Channel off Dover told some of his friends that, this voyage, the *Sapphire* had for chief mate a man who seemed a jolly sight too good for old Johns. 'Bunter's his name. I wonder where he's sprung from? Never seen him before in any ship I piloted in or out all these years. He's the sort of man who don't forget.

You couldn't. A thorough good sailor, too. And won't old Johns just worry his head off! Unless the old fool should take fright at him – for he does not seem the sort of man that would let himself be put upon without letting you know what he thinks of you. And that's exactly what old Johns would be more afraid of than of anything else.'

As this is really meant to be the record of a spiritualistic experience which came, if not precisely to Captain Johns himself, at any rate to his ship, there is no use in recording the other events of the passage out. It was an ordinary passage; the crew was an ordinary crew, the weather was of the usual kind. The black mate's quiet, sedate method of going to work had given a sober tone to the life of the ship. Even in gales of wind everything went on quietly somehow.

There was only one severe blow which made things fairly lively for all hands for full four-and-twenty hours. That was off the coast of Africa, after passing the Cape of Good Hope. At the very height of it several heavy seas were shipped with no serious results, but there was a considerable smashing of breakable objects in the pantry and in the staterooms. Mr Bunter, who was so greatly respected on board, found himself treated scurvily by the Southern Ocean, which, bursting open the door of his room like a ruffianly burglar, carried off several useful things, and made all the others extremely wet.

Later, on the same day, the Southern Ocean caused the *Sapphire* to lurch over in such an unrestrained fashion that the two drawers fitted under Mr Bunter's sleeping-berth flew out altogether, spilling all their contents. They ought, of course, to have been locked, and Mr Bunter had only to thank himself for what had happened. He ought to have turned the key on each before going out on deck.

His consternation was very great. The steward, who was paddling about all the time with swabs, trying to dry out the flooded cuddy, heard him exclaim 'Hallo!' in a startled and dismayed tone. In the midst of his work the steward felt a sympathetic concern for the mate's distress.

Captain Johns was secretly glad when he heard of the damage. He was indeed afraid of his chief mate, as the sea-pilot had ventured to foretell, and afraid of him for the very reason the sea-pilot had put forward as likely.

Captain Johns, therefore, would have liked very much to hold that black mate of his at his mercy in some way or other. But the man was irreproachable, as near absolute perfection as could be. And Captain Johns was much annoyed, and at the same time congratulated himself on his chief officer's efficiency.

He made a great show of living sociably with him, on the principle that the more friendly you are with a man the more easily you may catch him tripping; and also for the reason that he wanted to have somebody who would listen to his stories of manifestations, apparitions, ghosts, and all the rest of the imbecile spook-lore. He had it all at his fingers' ends; and he spun those ghostly yarns in a persistent, colourless voice, giving them a futile turn peculiarly his own.

'I like to converse with my officers,' he used to say. 'There are masters that hardly ever open their mouths from beginning to end of a passage for fear of losing their dignity. What's that, after all – this bit of position a man holds!'

His sociability was most to be dreaded in the second dogwatch, because he was one of those men who grow lively towards the evening, and the officer on duty was unable then to find excuses for leaving the poop. Captain Johns would pop up the companion suddenly, and, sidling up in his creepy way to poor Bunter, as he walked up and down, would fire into him some spiritualistic proposition, such as:

'Spirits, male and female, show a good deal of refinement in a general way, don't they?'

To which Bunter, holding his black-whiskered head high, would mutter:

'I don't know.'

'Ah! that's because you don't want to. You are the most obstinate, prejudiced man I've ever met, Mr Bunter. I told you you may have any book out of my bookcase. You may just go into my state-room, and help yourself to any volume.'

And if Bunter protested that he was too tired in his watches below to spare any time for reading, Captain Johns would smile nastily behind his back, and remark that of course some people needed more sleep than others to keep themselves fit for their work. If Mr Bunter was afraid of not keeping properly awake when on duty at night, that was another matter.

'But I think you borrowed a novel to read from the second mate the other day – a trashy pack of lies,' Captain Johns sighed. 'I am afraid you are not a spiritually minded man, Mr Bunter. That's what's the matter.'

Sometimes he would appear on deck in the middle of the night, looking very grotesque and bandy-legged in his sleeping-suit. At that sight the persecuted Bunter would wring his hands stealthily, and break out into moisture all over his forehead. After standing sleepily by the binnacle, scratching himself in an unpleasant manner, Captain Johns was sure to start on some aspect or other of his only topic.

He would, for instance, discourse on the improvement of morality to be expected from the establishment of general and close intercourse with the spirits of the departed. The spirits, Captain Johns thought, would consent to associate familiarly with the living if it were not for the unbelief of the great mass of mankind. He himself would not care to have anything to do with a crowd that would not believe in his – Captain Johns' – existence. Then why should a spirit? This was asking too much.

He went on breathing hard by the binnacle and trying to reach round his shoulder-blades; then, with a thick, drowsy severity, declared:

'Incredulity, sir, is the evil of the age!'

It rejected the evidence of Professor Cranks and of the journalist chap. It resisted the production of photographs.

For Captain Johns believed firmly that certain spirits had been photographed. He had read something of it in the papers. And the idea of it having been done had got a tremendous hold on him, because his mind was not critical. Bunter said afterwards that nothing could be more weird than this little man, swathed in a sleeping-suit three sizes too large for him, shuffling with excitement in the moonlight near the wheel, and shaking his fist at the serene sea.

'Photographs! photographs!' he would repeat, in a voice as creaky as a rusty hinge.

The very helmsman just behind him got uneasy at that performance, not being capable of understanding exactly what the 'old man was kicking up a row with the mate about.'

Then Johns, after calming down a bit, would begin again.

'Then sensitized plate can't lie. No, sir.'

Nothing could be more funny than this ridiculous little man's conviction – his dogmatic tone. Bunter would go on swinging up and down the poop like a deliberate, dignified pendulum. He said not a word. But the poor fellow had not a trifle on his conscience, as you know; and to have imbecile ghosts rammed down his throat like this on top of his own worry nearly drove him crazy. He knew that on many occasions he was on the verge of lunacy, because he could not help indulging in half-delirious visions of Captain Johns being picked up by the scruff of the neck and dropped over the taffrail into the ship's wake – the sort of thing no sane sailorman would think of doing to a cat or any other animal, anyhow. He imagined him bobbing up – a tiny black speck left far astern on the moonlit ocean.

I don't think that even at the worst moments Bunter really desired to drown Captain Johns. I fancy that all his disordered imagination longed for was merely to stop the ghostly inanity of the skipper's talk.

But, all the same, it was a dangerous form of self-indulgence. Just picture to yourself that ship in the Indian Ocean, on a clear, tropical night, with her sails full and still, the watch on deck stowed away out of sight; and on her poop, flooded with moonlight, the stately black mate walking up and down with measured, dignified steps, preserving an awful silence and that grotesquely mean little figure in striped flannelette alternately creaking and droning of 'personal intercourse beyond the grave.'

It makes me creepy all over to think of. And sometimes, the folly of Captain Johns would appear clothed in a sort of weird utilitarianism. How useful it would be if the spirits of the departed could be induced to take a practical interest in the affairs of the living! What a help, say, to the police, for instance, in the detection of crime! The number of murders, at any rate, would be considerably reduced, he guessed, with an air of great sagacity. Then he would give way to grotesque discouragement.

Where was the use of trying to communicate with people that had no faith, and more likely than not would scorn the offered information? Spirits had their feelings. They were *all* feelings in a way. But he was surprised at the forbearance shown towards murderers by their victims. That was the sort of apparition that no guilty man would dare to poohpooh. And perhaps the undiscovered murderers – whether believing or not – were haunted. They wouldn't be likely to boast about it, would they?

'For myself,' he pursued, in a sort of vindictive, malevolent whine, 'if anybody murdered me I would not let him forget it. I would wither him up – I would terrify him to death.'

The idea of his skipper's ghost terrifying anyone was so ludicrous that the black mate, little disposed to mirth as he was, could not help giving vent to a weary laugh. And this laugh, the only acknowledgement of a long and earnest discourse, offended Captain Johns.

'What's there to laugh at in this conceited manner, Mr Bunter?' he snarled. 'Supernatural visitations have terrified better men than you. Don't you allow me enough soul to make a ghost of?'

I think it was the nasty tone that caused Bunter to stop short and turn about.

'I shouldn't wonder,' went on the angry fanatic of spiritism, 'if you weren't one of them people that take no more account of a man than if he were a beast. You would be capable, I don't doubt, to deny the possession of an immortal soul to your own father.'

And then Bunter, being bored beyond endurance, and also exasperated by the private worry, lost his self-possession.

He walked up suddenly to Captain Johns, and, stooping a little to look close into his face, said, in a low, even tone:

'You don't know what a man like me is capable of.'

Captain Johns threw his head back, but was too astonished to budge. Bunter resumed his walk; and for a long time his measured footsteps and the low wash of the water alongside were the only sounds which troubled the silence brooding over the great waters. Then Captain

Johns cleared his throat uneasily, and, after sidling away towards the companion for greater safety, plucked up enough to retreat under an act of authority:

'Raise the starboard clew of the mainsail, and lay the yards dead square, Mr Bunter. Don't you see the wind is nearly right aft?'

Bunter at once answered 'Ay, ay, sir,' though there was not the slightest necessity to touch the yards, and the wind was well out on the quarter. While he was executing the order Captain Johns hung on the companion-steps, growling to himself: 'Walk this poop like an admiral, and don't even notice when the yards want trimming!' – loud enough for the helmsman to overhear. Then he sank slowly backwards out of the man's sight; and when he reached the bottom of the stairs he stood still and thought.

'He's an awful ruffian, with all his gentlemanly airs. No more gentleman mates for me.'

Two nights afterwards he was slumbering peacefully in his berth, when a heavy thumping just above his head (a well-understood signal that he was wanted on deck) made him leap out of bed, broad awake in a moment.

'What's up?' he muttered, running out barefooted. On passing through the cabin he glanced at the clock. It was the middle watch. 'What on earth can the mate want me for?' he thought.

Bolting out of the companion, he found a clear, dewy, moonlit night and a strong, steady breeze. He looked around wildly. There was no one on the poop except the helmsman, who addressed him at once.

'It was me, sir. I let go the wheel for a second to stamp over your head. I am afraid there's something wrong with the mate.'

'Where's he got to?' asked the captain sharply.

The man, who was obviously nervous, said:

'The last I saw of him was as he fell down the port poop-ladder.'

'Fell down the poop-ladder! What did he do that for? What made him?'

'I don't know, sir. He was walking the port side. Then just as he turned towards me to come aft . . .'

'You saw him?' interrupted the captain.

'I did. I was looking at him. And I heard the crash, too – something awful. Like the mainmast going overboard. It was as if something had struck him.'

Captain Johns became very uneasy and alarmed.

'Come,' he said sharply. 'Did anybody strike him? What did you see?'

'Nothing, sir, so help me! There was nothing to see. He just gave a little sort of hallo! threw his hands before him, and over he went –

crash. I couldn't hear anything more, so I just let go the wheel for a second to call you up.'

'You're scared!' said Captain Johns.

'I am, sir, straight!'

Captain Johns stared at him. The silence of his ship driving on her way seemed to contain a danger – a mystery. He was reluctant to go and look for his mate himself, in the shadows of the main-deck, so quiet, so still.

All he did was to advance to the break of the poop, and call for the watch. As the sleepy men came trooping aft, he shouted to them fiercely.

'Look at the foot of the port poop-ladder, some of you! See the mate lying there?'

Their startled exclamations told him immediately that they did see him. Somebody even screeched out emotionally:

'He's dead!'

Mr Bunter was laid in his bunk, and when the lamp in his room was lit he looked indeed as if he were dead, but it was obvious also that he was breathing yet. The steward had been roused out, the second mate called and sent on deck to look after the ship, and for an hour or so Captain Johns devoted himself silently to the restoring of consciousness. Mr Bunter at last opened his eyes, but he could not speak. He was dazed and inert. The steward bandaged a nasty scalp-wound while Captain Johns held an additional light. They had to cut away a lot of Mr Bunter's jet-black hair to make a good dressing. This done, and after gazing for a while at their patient, the two left the cabin.

'A rum go, this, steward,' said Captain Johns in the passage.

'Yessir.'

'A sober man that's right in his head does not fall down a poop-ladder like a sack of potatoes. The ship's as steady as a church.'

'Yessir. Fit of some kind, I shouldn't wonder.'

'Well, I should. He doesn't look as if he were subject to fits and giddiness. Why, the man's in the prime of life. I wouldn't have another kind of mate – not if I knew it. You don't think he has a private store of liquor, do you, eh? He seemed to me a bit strange in his manner several times lately. Off his feed too a bit, I noticed.'

'Well, sir, if he ever had a bottle or two of grog in his cabin, that must have gone a long time ago. I saw him throw some broken glass overboard after the last gale we had; but that didn't amount to anything. Anyway, sir, you couldn't call Mr Bunter a drinking man.'

'No,' conceded the captain reflectively. And the steward, locking the pantry door, tried to escape out of the passage, thinking he could manage to snatch another hour of sleep before it was time for him to turn out for the day.

Captain Johns shook his head.

'There's some mystery there.'

'There's special Providence that he didn't crack his head like an eggshell on the quarter-deck mooring-bits, sir. The men tell me he couldn't have missed them by more than an inch.'

And the steward vanished skilfully.

Captain Johns spent the rest of the night and the whole of the ensuing day between his own room and that of the mate.

In his own room he sat with his open hands reposing on his knees, his lips pursed up, and the horizontal furrows on his forehead marked very heavily. Now and then, raising his arm by a slow, as if cautious movement, he scratched lightly the top of his bald head. In the mate's room he stood for long periods of time with his hand to his lips, gazing at the half-conscious man.

For three days Mr Bunter did not say a single word. He looked at people sensibly enough, but did not seem to be able to hear any questions put to him. They cut off some more of his hair and swathed his head in wet cloths. He took some nourishment, and was made as comfortable as possible. At dinner on the third day the second mate remarked to the captain, in connection with the affair:

'These half-round brass plates on the steps of the poop-ladders are beastly dangerous things!'

'Are they?' retorted Captain Johns sourly. 'It takes more than a brass plate to account for an able-bodied man crashing down in this fashion like a felled ox.'

The second mate was impressed by that view. There was something in that, he thought.

'And the weather fine, everything dry, and the ship going along as steady as a church!' pursued Captain Johns gruffly.

As Captain Johns continued to look extremely sour, the second mate did not open his lips any more during the dinner. Captain Johns was annoyed and hurt by an innocent remark, because the fitting of the aforesaid brass plates had been done at his suggestion only the voyage before, in order to smarten up the appearance of the poop-ladders.

On the fourth day Mr Bunter looked decidedly better; very languid yet, of course, but he heard and understood what was said to him, and even could say a few words in a feeble voice.

Captain Johns, coming in, contemplated him attentively, without much visible sympathy.

'Well, can you give us your account of this accident, Mr Bunter?'

Bunter moved slightly his bandaged head, and fixed his cold, blue stare on Captain John's face, as if taking stock and appraising the value of every feature; the perplexed forehead, the credulous eyes, the inane droop of the mouth. And he gazed so long that Captain Johns grew restive, and looked over his shoulder at the door.

'No accident,' breathed out Bunter, in a peculiar tone.

'You don't mean to say you've got the falling sickness,' said Captain Johns. 'How would you call it signing as chief mate of a clipper ship with a thing like that on you?'

Bunter answered him only by a sinister look. The skipper shuffled his feet a little.

'Well, what made you have that tumble, then?'

Bunter raised himself a little, and, looking straight into Captain Johns' eyes, said, in a very distinct whisper:

'You – were – right!'

He fell back and closed his eyes. Not a word more could Captain Johns get out of him; and, the steward coming into the cabin, the skipper withdrew.

But that very night, unobserved, Captain Johns, opening the door cautiously, entered again the mate's cabin. He could wait no longer. The suppressed eagerness, the excitement expressed in all his mean, creeping little person, did not escape the chief mate, who was lying awake, looking frightfully pulled down and perfectly impassive.

'You are coming to gloat over me, I suppose,' said Bunter, without moving and yet making a palpable hit.

'Bless my soul!' exclaimed Captain Johns with a start, and assuming a sobered demeanour. 'There's a thing to say!'

'Well, gloat then! You and your ghosts, you've managed to get over a live man.'

This was said by Bunter without stirring, in a low voice, and with not much expression.

'Do you mean to say,' inquired Captain Johns, in an awestruck whisper, 'that you had a supernatural experience that night? You saw an apparition, then, on board my ship?'

Reluctance, shame, disgust, would have been visible on poor Bunter's countenance if the great part of it had not been swathed up in cottonwool and bandages. His ebony eyebrows, more sinister than ever amongst all that lot of white linen, came together in a frown as he made a mighty effort to say:

'Yes, I have seen.'

The wretchedness in his eyes would have awakened the compassion of any other man than Captain Johns. But Captain Johns was all agog with triumphant excitement. He was just a little bit frightened too. He looked at that unbelieving scoffer laid low, and did not even dimly guess at his profound, humiliating distress. He was not generally capable of taking much part in the anguish of his fellow-creatures. This time, moreover, he was excessively anxious to know what had happened.

Fixing his credulous eyes on the bandaged head, he asked, trembling slightly:

'And did it – did it knock you down?'

'Come! am I the sort of man to be knocked down by a ghost?' protested Bunter in a little stronger tone. 'Don't you remember what you said yourself the other night? Better men than me – Ha! you'll have to look a long time before you find a better man for a mate of your ship.'

Captain Johns pointed a solemn finger at Bunter's bedplace.

'You've been terrified,' he said. 'That's what's the matter. You've been terrified. Why, even the man at the wheel was scared, though he couldn't see anything. He *felt* the supernatural. You are punished for your incredulity, Mr Bunter. You were terrified.'

'And suppose I was,' said Bunter. 'Do you know what I had seen? Can you conceive the sort of ghost that would haunt a man like me? Do you think it was a ladyish, afternoon-call, another-cup-of-tea-please apparition that visits your Professor Cranks and that journalist chap you are always talking about? No; I can't tell you what it was like. Every man has his own ghosts. You couldn't conceive . . .'

Bunter stopped, out of breath; and Captain Johns remarked, with the glow of inward satisfaction reflected in his tone:

'I've always thought you were the sort of man that was ready for anything: from pitch-and-toss to wilful murder, as the saying goes. Well, well! So you were terrified.'

'I stepped back,' said Bunter curtly. 'I don't remember anything else.'

'The man at the wheel told me you went backwards as if something had hit you.'

'It was a sort of inward blow,' explained Bunter. 'Something too deep for you, Captain Johns, to understand. Your life and mine haven't been the same. Aren't you satisfied to see me converted?'

'And you can't tell me any more?' asked Captain Johns anxiously.

'No, I can't. I wouldn't. It would be no use if I did. That sort of experience must be gone through. Say I am being punished. Well, I take my punishment, but talk of it I won't.'

'Very well,' said Captain Johns; 'you won't. But, mind, I can draw my own conclusions from that.'

'Draw what you like; but be careful what you say, sir. You don't terrify me. *You* aren't a ghost.'

'One word. Has it any connection with what you said to me on that last night, when we had a talk together on spiritualism?'

Bunter looked weary and puzzled.

'What did I say?'

'You told me that I couldn't know what a man like you was capable of.'

'Yes, yes. Enough!'

'Very good. I am fixed, then,' remarked Captain Johns. 'All I say is that I am jolly glad not to be you, though I would have given almost anything for the privilege of personal communication with the world of spirits. Yes, sir, but not in that way.'

Poor Bunter moaned pitifully.

'It has made me feel twenty years older.'

Captain Johns retired quietly. He was delighted to observe this over-bearing ruffian humbled to the dust by the moralizing agency of the spirits. The whole occurrence was a source of pride and gratification; and he began to feel a sort of regard for his chief mate. It is true that in further interviews Bunter showed himself very mild and deferential. He seemed to cling to his captain for spiritual protection. He used to send for him, and say, 'I feel so nervous,' and Captain Johns would stay patiently for hours in the hot little cabin, and feel proud of the call.

For Mr Bunter was ill, and could not leave his berth for a good many days. He became a convinced spiritualist, not enthusiastically – that could hardly have been expected from him – but in a grim, unshakable way. He could not be called exactly friendly to the disembodied inhabi-tants of our globe, as Captain Johns was. But he was now a firm, if gloomy, recruit of spiritualism.

One afternoon, as the ship was already well to the north in the Gulf of Bengal, the steward knocked at the door of the captain's cabin, and said, without opening it:

'The mate asks if you could spare him a moment, sir. He seems to be in a state in there.'

Captain Johns jumped up from the couch at once.

'Yes. Tell him I am coming.'

He thought: Could it be possible there had been another spiritual manifestation – in the daytime, too!

He revelled in the hope. It was not exactly that, however. Still, Bunter, whom he saw sitting collapsed in a chair – he had been up for several days, but not on deck as yet – poor Bunter had something startling enough to communicate. His hands covered his face. His legs were stretched straight out, dismally.

'What's the news now?' croaked Captain Johns, not unkindly, because in truth it always pleased him to see Bunter – as he expressed it – tamed.

'News!' exclaimed the crushed sceptic through his hands. 'Ay, news enough, Captain Johns. Who will be able to deny the awfulness, the genuineness? Another man would have dropped dead. You want to know what I had seen. All I can tell you is that since I've seen it my hair is turning white.'

Bunter detached his hands from his face, and they hung on each side of his chair as if dead. He looked broken in the dusky cabin.

'You don't say!' stammered out Captain Johns. 'Turned white! Hold on a bit! I'll light the lamp!'

When the lamp was lit, the startling phenomenon could be seen plainly enough. As if the dread, the horror, the anguish of the supernatural were being exhaled through the pores of his skin, a sort of silvery mist seemed to cling to the cheeks and the head of the mate. His short beard, his cropped hair, were growing not black, but grey – almost white.

When Mr Bunter, thin-faced and shaky, came on deck for duty, he was clean-shaven, and his head was white. The hands were awe-struck. 'Another man,' they whispered to each other. It was generally and mysteriously agreed that the mate had 'seen something,' with the exception of the man at the wheel at the time, who maintained that the mate was 'struck by something'.

This distinction hardly amounted to a difference. On the other hand, everybody admitted that, after he picked up his strength a bit, he seemed even smarter in his movements than before.

One day in Calcutta, Captain Johns, pointing out to a visitor his white-headed chief mate standing by the main-hatch, was heard to say oracularly:

'That man's in the prime of life.'

Of course, while Bunter was away, I called regularly on Mrs Bunter every Saturday, just to see whether she had any use for my services. It was understood I would do that. She had just his half-pay to live on – it amounted to about a pound a week. She had taken one room in a quiet little square in the East End.

And this was affluence to what I had heard that the couple were reduced to for a time after Bunter had to give up the Western Ocean trade – he used to go as mate of all sorts of hard packets after he lost his ship and his luck together – it was affluence to that time when Bunter would start at seven o'clock in the morning with but a glass of hot water and a crust of dry bread.

It won't stand thinking about, especially for those who know Mrs Bunter. I have seen something of them, too, at that time; and it just makes me shudder to remember what that born lady had to put up with. Enough!

Dear Mrs Bunter used to worry a good deal after the *Sapphire* left for Calcutta. She would say to me: 'It must be so awful for poor Winston' – Winston is Bunter's name – and I tried to comfort her the best I could. Afterwards, she got some small children to teach in a family, and was half the day with them, and the occupation was good for her.

In the very first letter she had from Calcutta, Bunter told her he had had a fall down the poop-ladder, and cut his head, but no bones broken, thank God. That was all. Of course, she had other letters from him, but that vagabond Bunter never gave me a scratch of the pen the solid eleven months. I supposed, naturally, that everything was going on all right. Who could imagine what was happening?

Then one day dear Mrs Bunter got a letter from a legal firm in the City, advising her that her uncle was dead – her old curmudgeon of an uncle – a retired stockbroker, a heartless, petrified antiquity that had lasted on and on. He was nearly ninety, I believe; and if I were to meet his venerable ghost this minute, I would try to take him by the throat and strangle him.

The old beast would never forgive his niece for marrying Bunter; and years afterwards, when people made a point of letting him know that she was in London, pretty nearly starving at forty years of age, he only said: 'Serve the little fool right!' I believe he meant her to starve. And, lo and behold, the old cannibal died intestate, with no other relatives but that very identical little fool. The Bunters were wealthy people now.

Of course, Mrs Bunter wept as if her heart would break. In any other woman it would have been mere hypocrisy. Naturally, too, she wanted to cable the news to her Winston in Calcutta, but I showed her, 'Gazette' in hand, that the ship was on the homeward-bound list for more than a week already. So we sat down to wait, and talked meantime of dear old Winston every day. There were just one hundred such days before the *Sapphire* got reported 'All well', in the chops of the Channel by an incoming mailboat.

'I am going to Dunkirk to meet him,' says she. The *Sapphire* had a cargo of jute for Dunkirk. Of course, I had to escort the dear lady in the quality of her 'ingenious friend.' She calls me 'our ingenious friend' to this day; and I've observed some people – strangers – looking hard at me, for the signs of the ingenuity, I suppose.

After settling Mrs Bunter in a good hotel in Dunkirk, I walked down to the docks – late afternoon it was – and what was my surprise to see the ship actually fast alongside. Either Johns or Bunter, or both, must have been driving her hard up Channel. Anyway, she had been in since the day before last, and her crew was already paid off. I met two of her apprenticed boys going off home on leave with their dunnage on a Frenchman's barrow, as happy as larks, and I asked them if the mate was on board.

'There he is, on the quay, looking at the moorings,' says one of the youngsters as he skipped past me.

You may imagine the shock to my feelings when I beheld his white head. I could only manage to tell him that his wife was at an hotel in town. He left me at once, to go and get his hat on board. I was mightily surprised by the smartness of his movements as he hurried up the gang-way.

Whereas the black mate struck people as deliberate, and strangely stately in his gait for a man in the prime of life, this white-headed chap seemed the most wonderfully alert of old men. I don't suppose Bunter was any quicker on his pins than before. It was the colour of the hair that made all the difference in one's judgement.

The same with his eyes. Those eyes, that looked at you so steely, so fierce, and so fascinating out of a bush of a buccaneer's black hair, now had an innocent, almost boyish expression in their good-humoured brightness under those white eyebrows.

I led him without any delay into Mrs Bunter's private sitting-room. After she had dropped a tear over the late cannibal, given a hug to her Winston, and told him that he must grow his moustache again, the dear lady tucked her feet upon the sofa, and I got out of Bunter's way.

He started at once to pace the room, waving his long arms. He worked himself into a regular frenzy, and tore Johns limb from limb many times over that evening.

'Fell down? Of course I fell down, by slipping backwards on that fool's patent brass plates. 'Pon my word, I had been walking that poop in charge of the ship, and I didn't know whether I was in the Indian Ocean or in the moon. I was crazy. My head spun round and round with sheer worry. I had made my last application of your chemist's wonderful stuff.' (This to me.) 'All the store of bottles you gave me got smashed when those drawers fell out in the last gale. I had been getting some dry things to change, when I heard the cry: "All hands on deck!" and made one jump of it, without even pushing them in pro-perly. Ass! When I came back and saw the broken glass and the mess, I felt ready to faint.

'No; look here – deception is bad; but not to be able to keep it up after one has been forced into it. You know that since I've been squeezed out of the Western Ocean packets by younger men, just on account of my grizzled muzzle – you know how much chance I had to ever get a ship. And not a soul to turn to. We have been a lonely couple, we two – she threw away everything for me – and to see her want a piece of dry bread –'

He banged with his fist fit to split the Frenchman's table in two.

'I would have turned a sanguinary pirate for her let alone cheating my way into a berth by dyeing my hair. So when you came to me with your chemist's wonderful stuff –'

He checked himself.

'By the by, that fellow's got a fortune when he likes to pick it up. It is a wonderful stuff – you tell him salt water can do nothing to it. It stays on as long as your hair will.'

'All right,' I said. 'Go on.'

Thereupon he went for Johns again with a fury that frightened his wife, and made me laugh till I cried.

'Just you try to think what it would have meant to be at the mercy of the meanest creature that ever commanded a ship! Just fancy what a life that crawling Johns would have led me! And I knew that in a week or so the white hair would begin to show. And the crew. Did you ever think of that? To be shown up as a low fraud before all hands. What a life for me till we got to Calcutta! And once there – kicked out, of course. Half-pay stopped. Annie here alone, without a penny – starving; and I on the other side of the earth, ditto. You see?

'I thought of shaving twice a day. But could I shave my head, too? No way – no way at all. Unless I dropped Johns overboard; and even then – Do you wonder now that with all these things boiling in my head I didn't know where I was putting down my foot that night? I just felt myself falling – then crash, and all dark.

'When I came to myself that bang on the head seemed to have steadied my wits somehow. I was so sick of everything that for two days I wouldn't speak to anyone. They thought it was a slight concussion of the brain. Then the idea dawned upon me as I was looking at that ghost-ridden, wretched fool: 'Ah, you love ghosts,' I thought. 'Well, you shall have something from beyond the grave.'

'I didn't even trouble to invent a story. I couldn't imagine a ghost if I wanted to. I wasn't fit to lie connectedly if I had tried. I just bulled him on to it. Do you know, he got, quite by himself, a notion that at some time or other I had done somebody to death in some way, and that –'

'Oh, the horrible man!' cried Mrs Bunter from the sofa. There was a silence.

'And didn't he bore my head off on the home passage!' began Bunter again in a weary voice. 'He loved me. He was proud of me. I was converted. I had had a manifestation. Do you know what he was after? He wanted me and him "to make a *séance*," in his own words, and to try to call up that ghost (the one that had turned my hair white – the ghost of my supposed victim), and, as he said, talk it over with him – the ghost – in a friendly way.

' "Or else, Bunter," he says, "you may get another manifestation when you least expect it, and tumble overboard perhaps, or something. You ain't really safe till we pacify the spirit-world in some way."

'Can you conceive a lunatic like that? No – say?'

I said nothing. But Mrs Bunter did, in a very decided tone.

'Winston, I don't want you to go on board that ship again any more.'

'My dear,' says he, 'I have all my things on board yet.'

'You don't want the things. Don't go near that ship at all.'

He stood still; then, dropping his eyes with a faint smile, said slowly, in a dreamy voice:

'The haunted ship.'

'And your last,' I added.

We carried him off, as he stood, by the night train. He was very quiet; but crossing the Channel, as we two had a smoke on deck, he turned to me suddenly, and, grinding his teeth, whispered:

'He'll never know how near he was being dropped overboard!'

He meant Captain Johns. I said nothing.

But Captain Johns, I understand, made a great to-do about the disappearance of his chief mate. He set the French police scouring the country for the body. In the end, I fancy he got word from his owners' office to drop all this fuss – that it was all right. I don't suppose he ever understood anything of that mysterious occurrence.

To this day he tries at times (he's retired now, and his conversation is not very coherent), he tries to tell the story of a black mate he once had, 'a murderous, gentlemanly ruffian, with raven-black hair which turned white all at once in consequence of a manifestation from beyond the grave.' An avenging apparition. What with reference to black and white hair, to poop-ladders, and to his own feelings and views, it is difficult to make head or tail of it. If his sister (she's very vigorous still) should be present she cuts all this short – peremptorily:

'Don't you mind what he says. He's got devils on the brain.'

Anatole France

The Ocean Christ

THAT year many of the fishers of Saint-Valéry had been drowned at sea. Their bodies were found on the beach cast up by the waves with the wreckage of their boats; and for nine days, up the steep road leading to the church were to be seen coffins borne by hand and followed by widows, who were weeping beneath their great black-hooded cloaks, like women in the Bible.

Thus were the skipper Jean Lenoël and his son Désiré laid in the great nave, beneath the vaulted roof from which they had once hung a ship in full rigging as an offering to Our Lady. They were righteous men and God-fearing. Monsieur Guillaume Truphème, priest of Saint-Valéry, having pronounced the Absolution, said in a tearful voice:

'Never were laid in consecrated ground, there to await the judgement of God, better men and better Christians than Jean Lenoël and his son Désiré.'

And while barques and their skippers perished near the coast, in the high seas great vessels foundered. Not a day passed that the ocean did not bring in some flotsam of wreck. Now one morning some children who were steering a boat saw a figure lying on the sea. It was a figure of Jesus Christ, life-size, carved in wood, painted in natural colouring, and looking as if it were very old. The Good Lord was floating upon the sea with arms outstretched. The children towed the figure ashore and brought it up into Saint-Valéry. The head was encircled with the crown of thorns. The feet and hands were pierced. But the nails were missing as well as the cross. The arms were still outstretched ready for sacrifice and blessing, just as he appeared to Joseph of Arimathea and the holy women when they were burying Him.

The children gave it to Monsieur le Curé Truphème, who said to them:

'This image of the Saviour is of ancient workmanship. He who made it must have died long ago. Although today in the shops of Amiens and Paris excellent statues are sold for a hundred francs and more, we must admit that the earlier sculptors were not without merit. But what delights me most is the thought that if Jesus Christ be thus come with open arms to Saint-Valéry, it is in order to bless the parish, which has been so cruelly tried, and in order to announce that He has compassion on the poor folk who go a-fishing at the risk of their lives. He is the God who walked upon the sea and blessed the nets of Cephas.'

And Monsieur le Curé Truphème, having had the Christ placed in the church on the cloth of the high altar, went off to order from the carpenter Lemerre a beautiful cross in heart of oak.

When it was made, the Saviour was nailed to it with brand new nails, and it was erected in the nave above the churchwarden's pew.

Then it was noticed that His eyes were filled with mercy and seemed to glisten with tears of heavenly pity.

One of the churchwardens, who was present at the putting up of the crucifix, fancied he saw tears streaming down the divine face. The next morning when Monsieur le Curé with a choir-boy entered the church to say his mass, he was astonished to find the cross above the churchwarden's pew empty and the Christ lying upon the altar.

As soon as he had celebrated the divine sacrifice he had the carpenter called and asked him why he had taken the Christ down from His cross. But the carpenter replied that he had not touched it. Then, after having questioned the beadle and the sidesmen, Monsieur Truphème made certain that no one had entered the church since the crucifix had been placed over the churchwarden's pew.

Thereupon he felt that these things were miraculous, and he meditated upon them discreetly. The following Sunday in his exhortation he spoke of them to his parishioners, and he called upon them to contribute by their gifts to the erection of a new cross more beautiful than the first and more worthy to bear the Redeemer of the world.

The poor fishers of Saint-Valéry gave as much money as they could and the widows brought their wedding rings. Wherefore Monsieur Truphème was able to go at once to Abbeville and to order a cross of ebony, highly polished and surmounted by a scroll with the inscription I.N.R.I. in letters of gold. Two months later it was erected the place of the former and the Christ was nailed to it between the lance and the sponge.

But Jesus left this cross as He had left the other; and as soon as night fell He went and stretched Himself upon the altar.

Monsieur le Curé, when he found Him there in the morning, fell on his knees and prayed for a long while. The fame of this miracle spread throughout the neighbourhood, and the ladies of Amiens made a collection for the Christ of Saint-Valéry. Monsieur Truphème received money and jewels from Paris, and the wife of the Minister of Marine, Madame Hyde de Neuville, sent him a heart of diamonds. Of all these treasures, in the space of two years, a goldsmith of La Rue St Sulpice, fashioned a cross of gold and precious stones which was set up with great pomp in the church of Saint-Valéry on the second Sunday after Easter in the year 18—. But He who had not refused the cross of sorrow, fled from this cross of gold and again stretched Himself upon the white linen of the altar.

For fear of offending Him, He was left there this time; and He had lain upon the altar for more than two years, when Pierre, son of Pierre Caillou, came to tell Monsieur le Curé Truphème that he had found the true cross of Our Lord on the beach.

Pierre was an innocent; and, because he had not sense enough to earn a livelihood, people gave him bread out of charity; he was liked because he never did any harm. But he wandered in his talk and no one listened to him.

Nevertheless Monsieur Truphème, who had never ceased meditating on the Ocean Christ, was struck by what the poor imbecile had just said. With the beadle and two sidesmen he went to the spot, where the child said he had seen a cross, and there he found two planks studded with nails, which had long been washed by the sea and which did indeed form a cross.

They were the remains of some old shipwreck. On one of these boards could still be read two letters painted in black, a J and an L; and there was no doubt that this was a fragment of Jean Lenoël's barque, he who with his son Désiré had been lost at sea five years before.

At the sight of this, the beadle and the sidesmen began to laugh at the innocent who had taken the broken planks of a boat for the cross of Jesus Christ. But Monsieur le Curé Truphème checked their merriment. He had meditated much and prayed long since the Ocean Christ had arrived among the fisherfolk, and the mystery of infinite charity began to dawn upon him. He knelt down upon the sand, repeated the prayer for the faithful departed, and then told the beadle and the sidesmen to carry the flotsam on their shoulders and to place it in the church. When this had been done he raised the Christ from the altar, placed it on the planks of the boat and himself nailed it to them, with the nails that the ocean had corroded.

By the priest's command, the very next day this cross took the place of the cross of gold and precious stones over the churchwarden's pew. The Ocean Christ has never left it. He has chosen to remain nailed to the planks on which men died invoking His name and that of His Mother. There, with parted lips, august and afflicted, He seems to say:

'My cross is made of all men's woes, for I am in truth the God of the poor and the heavy-laden.'

Sir Ernest Shackleton

The Voyage of the *James Caird*
From *South*

I DISCUSSED with Wild and Worsley the chances of reaching South Georgia before the winter locked the seas against us. Some effort had to be made to secure relief. Privation and exposure had left their mark on the party, and the health and mental condition of several men were causing me serious anxiety. Then the food-supply was a vital consideration. We had left ten cases of provisions in the crevice of the rocks at our first camping-place on the island. An examination of our stores showed that we had full rations for the whole party for a period of five weeks. The rations could be spread over three months on a reduced allowance and probably would be supplemented by seals and sea elephants to some extent. I did not dare to count with full confidence on supplies of meat and blubber, for the animals seemed to have deserted the beach and the winter was near. Our stocks included three seals and two and half skins (with blubber attached). We were mainly dependent on the blubber for fuel, and, after making a preliminary survey of the situation, I decided that the party must be limited to one hot meal a day.

A boat journey in search of relief was necessary and must not be delayed. That conclusion was forced upon me. The nearest port where assistance could certainly be secured was Port Stanley, in the Falkland Islands, 540 miles away, but we could scarcely hope to beat up against the prevailing north-westerly wind in a frail and weakened boat with a small sail area. South Georgia was over 800 miles away, but lay in the area of the west winds, and I could count upon finding whalers at any of the whaling-stations on the east coast. A boat party might make the voyage and be back with relief within a month, provided that the sea was clear of ice and the boat survive the great seas. It was not difficult to decide that South Georgia must be the objective, and I proceeded to plan ways and means. The hazards of a boat journey across 800 miles of stormy sub-Antarctic ocean were obvious, but I calculated that at worst the venture would add nothing to the risks of the men left on the island. There would be fewer mouths to feed during the winter and the boat would not require to take more than one month's provisions for six men, for if we did not make South Georgia in that time we were sure to go under. A consideration that had weight with me was that there was no chance at all of any search being made for us on Elephant Island.

The case required to be argued in some detail, since all hands knew that the perils of the proposed journey were extreme. The risk was justified solely by our urgent need of assistance. The ocean south of Cape Horn in the middle of May is known to be the most tempestuous stormswept area of water in the world. The weather then is unsettled, the skies are dull and overcast, and the gales are almost unceasing. We had to face these conditions in a small and weather-beaten boat, already strained by the work of the months that had passed. Worsley and Wild realized that the attempt must be made, and they both asked to be allowed to accompany me on the voyage. I told Wild at once that he would have to stay behind. I relied upon him to hold the party together while I was away, and to make the best of his way to Deception Island with the men in the spring in the event of our failure to bring help. Worsley I would take with me, for I had a very high opinion of his accuracy and quickness as a navigator, and especially in the snapping and working out of positions in difficult circumstances – an opinion that was only enhanced during the actual journey. Four other men would be required and I decided to call for volunteers, although, as a matter of fact, I pretty well knew which of the people I would select. Crean I proposed to leave on the island as a right-hand man for Wild, but he begged so hard to be allowed to come in the boat that, after consultation with Wild, I promised to take him. I called the men together, explained my plan, and asked for volunteers. Many came forward at once. Some were not fit enough for the work that would have to be done, and others would not have been much use in the boat since they were not seasoned sailors, though the experiences of recent months entitled them to some consideration as seafaring men. I finally selected McNeish, McCarthy, and Vincent in addition to Worsley and Crean. The crew seemed a strong one, and as I looked at the men I felt confidence increasing.

The decision made, I walked through the blizzard with Worsley and Wild to examine the *James Caird*. The 20-ft boat had never looked big; she appeared to have shrunk in some mysterious way when I viewed her in the light of our new undertaking. She was an ordinary ship's whaler, fairly strong, but showing signs of the strains she had endured since the crushing of the *Endurance*. Where she was holed in leaving the pack was, fortunately, about the water-line and easily patched. Standing beside her, we glanced at the fringe of the storm-swept, tumultuous sea that formed our path. Clearly, our voyage would be a big adventure. I called the carpenter and asked him if he could do anything to makę the boat more seaworthy. He first inquired if he was to go with me, and seemed quite pleased when I said 'Yes.' He was over fifty years of age, and not altogether fit, but he had a good knowledge of sailing boats and was very quick. McCarthy said that he could contrive some sort of covering for the *James Caird* if he might use the lids of the cases and the four sledge-runners that we had lashed inside the boat for use in the event of a landing on Graham Land at Wilhelmina Bay. This bay, at one time the goal of our desire, had been left behind in the course of our drift, but we had retained the runners. The carpenter proposed to complete the covering with some of our canvas, and he set about making his plans at once.

Noon had passed and the gale was more severe than ever. We could not proceed with our preparations that day. The tents were suffering in the wind and the sea was rising. The gale was stronger than ever on the following morning (April 20). No work could be done. Blizzard and snow, snow and blizzard, sudden lulls and fierce returns. During the lulls we could see on the far horizon to the north-east bergs of all shapes and sizes driving along before the gale, and the sinister appearance of the swift-moving masses made us thankful indeed that instead of battling with the storm amid the ice, we were required only to face the drift from the glaciers and the inland heights. The gusts might throw us off our feet, but at least we fell on solid ground and not on rocking floes.

There was a lull in the bad weather on April 21, and the carpenter started to collect material for the decking of the *James Caird*. He fitted the mast of the *Stancomb Wills* fore and aft inside the *James Caird* as a hog-back, and thus strengthened the keel with the object of preventing our boat 'hogging' – that is, buckling in heavy seas. He had not sufficient wood to provide a deck, but by using the sledge-runners and box-lids he made a framework extending from the forecastle aft to a well. It was a patched-up affair, but it provided a base for a canvas covering. He had a bolt of canvas frozen stiff, and this material had to be cut and then thawed out over the blubber-stove, foot by foot, in order that it might be sewn into the form of a cover. When it had been nailed and screwed into position it certainly gave an appearance of safety to the boat, though I had an uneasy feeling that it bore a strong likeness to stage scenery, which may look like a granite wall and is in fact nothing better than canvas and lath. As events proved, the covering served its purpose well. We certainly could not have lived through the voyage without it.

Another fierce gale was blowing on April 22, interfering with our preparations for the voyage. We were setting aside stores for that boat journey and choosing the essential equipment from the scanty stock at our disposal. Two ten-gallon casks had to be filled with water melted down from ice collected at the foot of the glacier. This was rather a slow business.

The weather was fine on April 23, and we hurried forward our preparations. It was on this day I decided finally that the crew for the *James Caird* should consist of Worsley, Crean, McNeish, McCarthy, Vincent, and myself. A storm came on about noon, with driving snow and heavy squalls. Occasionally the air would clear for a few minutes, and we could see a line of pack-ice, five miles out, driving across from west to east. The sight increased my anxiety to get away quickly. Winter was advancing, and soon the pack might close completely round the island and stay our departure for days, or even weeks.

Worsley, Wild, and I climbed to the summit of the seaward rocks and examined the ice from a better vantage-point than the beach offered. The belt of pack outside appeared to be sufficiently broken for our purposes, and I decided that, unless the conditions forbade it, we would make a start in the *James Caird* on the following morning. Obviously the pack might close at any time. This decision made, I spent the rest of the day looking over the boat, gear, and stores, and discussing plans with Worsley and Wild.

Our last night on the solid ground of Elephant Island was cold and uncomfortable. We turned out at dawn and had breakfast. Then we launched the *Stancomb Wills* and loaded her with stores, gear, and ballast, which would be transferred to the *James Caird* when the heavier boat had been launched. The ballast consisted of bags made from blankets and filled with sand, making a total weight of about 1000 lb. In addition we had gathered a number of round boulders and about 250 lb of ice, which would supplement our two casks of water.

The swell was slight when the *Stancomb Wills* was launched and the boat got underway without any difficulty; but half an hour later, when we were pulling down the *James Caird*, the swell increased suddenly. Apparently the movement of the ice outside had made an opening and allowed the sea to run in without being blanketed by the line of pack. The swell made things difficult. Many of us got wet to the waist while dragging the boat out – a serious matter in that climate. When the *James Caird* was afloat in the surf she nearly capsized among the rocks before we could get her clear, and Vincent and the carpenter, who were on the deck, were thrown into the water. This was really bad luck for the two men would have small chance of drying their clothes after we had got under way.

The *James Caird* was soon clear of the breakers. We used all the available ropes as a long painter to prevent her drifting away to the northeast, and then the *Stancomb Wills* came alongside, transferred her load, and went back to the shore for more.

THE VOYAGE OF THE *JAMES CAIRD*

By midday the *James Caird* was ready for the voyage. Vincent and the carpenter had secured some dry clothes by exchange with members of the shore party (I heard afterwards that it was a full fortnight before the soaked garments were finally dried), and the boat's crew was standing by waiting for the order to cast off. A moderate westerly breeze was blowing, I went ashore in the *Stancomb Wills* and had a last word with Wild, who was remaining in full command, with directions as to his course of action in the event of our failure to bring relief, but I practically left the whole situation and scope of action and decision this own judgement, secure in the knowledge that he would act wisely. I told him that I trusted the party to him, and said good-bye to the men. Then we pushed off for the last time, and within a few minutes I was aboard the *James Caird*. The crew of the *Stancomb Wills* shook hands with us as the boats bumped together and offered us the last good wishes. Then, setting our jib, we cut the painter and moved away to the north-east. The men who were staying behind made a pathetic little group on the beach, with the grim heights of the island behind them and the sea seething at their feet, but they waved to us and gave three hearty cheers. There was hope in their hearts and they trusted us to bring the help that they needed.

I had all sails set, and the *James Caird* quickly dipped the beach and its line of dark figures. The westerly wind took us rapidly to the line of pack, and as we entered it I stood up with my arm around the mast, directing the steering, so as to avoid the great lumps of ice that were flung about in the heave of the sea. The pack thickened and we were forced to turn almost due east, running before the wind towards a gap I had seen in the morning from the high ground. I could not see the gap now, but we had come out on its bearing and I was prepared to find that it had been influenced by the easterly drift. At four o'clock in the afternoon we found the channel, much narrower than it had seemed in the morning but still navigable. Dropping sail we rowed through without touching the ice anywhere, and by 5.30 pm we were clear of the pack with open water before us. We passed one more piece of ice in the darkness an hour later, but the pack lay behind, and with a fair wind swelling the sails we steered our little craft through the night, our hopes centred on our distant goal. The swell was very heavy now, and when the time came for our first evening meal we found great difficulty in keeping the Primus lamp alight and preventing the hoosh splashing out of the pot. Three men were needed to attend to the cooking, one man holding the lamp and two men guarding the aluminium cooking-pot, which had to be lifted clear of the Primus whenever the movement of the boat threatened to cause a disaster. Then the lamp had to be protected from water, for sprays were coming over the bows and our flimsy decking was by no means water-tight. All these operations were conducted in the confined space under the decking, where the man lay or knelt and adjusted themselves as best they could to the angles of our cases and ballast. It was uncomfortable, but we found consolation in the reflection that without the decking we could not have used the cooker at all.

The tale of the next sixteen days is one of supreme strife amid heaving waters. The sub-Antarctic Ocean lived up to its evil winter reputation. I decided to run north for at least two days while the wind held and so get into warmer weather before turning to the east and laying a course for South Georgia. We took two-hourly spells at the tiller. The men who were not on watch crawled into the sodden sleeping-bags and tried to forget their troubles for a period; but there was no comfort in the boat. The bags and cases seemed to be alive in the unfailing knack of presenting their most uncomfortable angles to our rest-seeking bodies. A man might imagine for a moment that he had found a position of ease, but always discovered quickly that some unyielding point was impinging on muscle or bone. The first night aboard the boat was one of acute discomfort for us all, and we were heartily glad when the dawn came and we could set about the preparation of a hot breakfast.

By running north for the first two days I hoped to get warmer weather and also to avoid lines of pack that might be extending beyond the main body. We needed all the advantage that we could obtain from the higher latitude for sailing on the great circle, but we had to be cautious regarding possible ice streams. Cramped in our narrow quarters and continually wet by the spray, we suffered severely from cold throughout the journey. We fought the seas and the winds, and at the same time had a daily struggle to keep ourselves alive. At times we were in dire peril. Generally we were upheld by the knowledge that we were making progress towards the land where we would be safe, but there were days and nights when we lay hove to, drifting across the storm-whitened seas and watching, with eyes interested rather than apprehensive, the uprearing masses of water, flung to and fro by Nature in the pride of her strength. Deep seemed the valleys when we lay between the reeling seas. High were the hills when we perched momentarily on the tops of giant combers. Nearly always there were gales. So small was our boat and so great were the seas that often our sail flapped idly in the calm between the crests of two waves. Then we would climb the next slope and catch the full fury of the gale where the wool-like whiteness of the breaking water surged around us.

The wind came up strong and worked into a gale from the north-west on the third day out. We stood away to the east. The increasing seas discovered the weakness of our decking. The continuous blows shifted the box-lids and sledge-runners so that the canvas sagged down and accumulated water. Then icy trickles, distinct from the driving sprays, poured fore and aft into the boat. The nails that the carpenter had extracted from cases at Elephant Island and used to fasten down the battens were too short to make firm the decking. We did what we could to secure it, but our means were very limited, and the water continued to enter the boat at a dozen points. Much bailing was neces- sary, and nothing that we could do prevented our gear from becoming sodden. The searching runnels from the canvas were really more unpleas- and than the sudden definite douches of the sprays. Lying under the thwarts during watches below, we tried vainly to avoid them. There were no dry places in the boat, and at last we simply covered our heads with our Burberrys and endured the all-pervading water. The bailing was work for the watch. Real rest we had none. The perpetual motion of the boat made repose impossible; we were cold, sore, and anxious. We moved on hands and knees in the semi-darkness of the day under the decking. The darkness was complete by 6 pm, and not until 7 am of the following day could we see one another under the thwarts. We had a few scraps of candle, and they were preserved carefully in order that we might have light at meal-times. There was one fairly dry spot in the boat, under the solid original decking at the bows, and we man- aged to protect some of our biscuit from the saltwater; but I do not think any of us got the taste of salt out of our mouths during the voyage.

The difficulty of movement in the boat would have had its humorous side of if had not involved us in so many aches and pains. We had to crawl under the thwarts in order to move along the boat, and our knees suffered considerably. When a watch turned out it was necessary for me to direct each men by name when and where to move, since if all hands had crawled about at the same time the result would have been dire confusion and many bruises. Then there was the trim of the boat to be considered. The order of the watch was four hours on and four hours off, three men to the watch. One man had the tiller-ropes, the second man attended to the sail, and the third bailed for all he was worth. Sometimes when the water in the boat had been reduced to reasonable proportions, our pump could be used. This pump, which Hurley had made from the Flinders bar case of our ship's standard compass, was quite effective, though its capacity was not large. The man who was attending to the sail could pump into the big outer cooker, which was lifted and emptied overboard when filled. We had a device by which the water could go direct from the pump into the sea through a hole in the gunwale, but this hole had to be blocked at an early stage of the voyage, since we found that it admitted water when the boat rolled.

While a new watch was shivering in the wind and spray, the men who had been relieved groped hurriedly among the soaked sleeping-bags and tried to steal a little of the warmth created by the last occupants; but it was not always possible for us to find even this comfort when we went off watch. The boulders that we had taken aboard for ballast had to be shifted continually in order to trim the boat and give access to the pump, which became choked with hairs from the moulting sleeping-bags and finneskoe. The four reindeer-skin sleeping-bags shed their hair freely owing to the continuous wetting, and soon became quite bald in appearance. The moving of the boulders was very weary and painful work. We came to know every one of the stones by sight and touch, and I have vivid memories of their angular peculiarities even today. They might have been of considerable interest as geological specimens to a scientific man under happier conditions. As ballast they were useful. As weights to be moved about in cramped quarters they were simply appalling. They spared no portion of our poor bodies.

Our meals were regular in spite of the gales. Breakfast, at 8 am, consisted of a pannikin of hot hoosh made fom Bovril sledging ration, two biscuits, and some lumps of sugar. Lunch came at 1 pm, and comprised Bovril sledging ration, eaten raw, and a pannikin of hot milk for each man. Tea, at 5 pm, had the same menu. Then during the night we had a hot drink, generally of milk. The meals were the bright beacons in those cold and stormy days. The glow of warmth and comfort produced by the food and drink made optimists of us all.

A severe south-westerly gale on the fourth day out forced us to heave to. I would have liked to have run before the wind, but the sea was very high and the *James Caird* was in danger of broaching to and swamping. The delay was vexatious, since up to that time we had been making sixty or seventy miles a day; good going with our limited sail area. We hove to under double-reefed mainsail and our little jigger, and waited for the gale to blow itself out. During that afternoon we saw bits of wreckage, the remains probably of some unfortunate vessel that had failed to weather the strong gales south of Cape Horn. The weather conditions did not improve, and on the fifth day out the gale was so fierce that we were compelled to take in the double-reefed mainsail and hoist our small jib instead. We put out a sea-anchor to keep the *James Caird*'s head up to the sea. This anchor consisted of a triangular canvas bag fastened to the end of the painter and allowed to stream out from the bows. The boat was high enough to catch the wind, and as she drifted to leeward the drag of the anchor kept her head to windward. Thus our boat took most of the seas more or less end on. Even then the crests of the waves often would curl right over us and we shipped a great deal of water, which necessitated unceasing bailing and pumping. Looking out abeam, we would see a hollow like a tunnel formed as the crest of a big wave toppled over on to the swelling body of water. A thousand times it appeared as though the *James Caird* must be engulfed; but the boat lived. The south-westerly gale had its birthplace above the Antarctic Continent and its freezing breath lowered the temperature far towards zero. The sprays froze upon the boat, and gave bows, sides, and decking a heavy coat of mail. This accumulation of ice reduced the buoyancy of the boat, and to that extent was an added peril but it possessed a notable advantage from one point of view. The water ceased to drop and trickle from the canvas, and the spray came in solely at the well in the after part of the boat. We could not allow the load of ice to grow beyond a certain point, and in turns we crawled about the decking forward, chipping and picking at it with the available tools.

When daylight came on the morning of the sixth day out, we saw and felt that the *James Caird* had lost her resiliency. She was not rising to the oncoming seas. The weight of the ice that had formed in her and upon her during the night was having its effect, and she was becoming more like a log than a boat. The situation called for immediate action. We first broke away the spare oars, which were encased in ice and frozen to the sides of the boat, and threw them overboard. We retained two oars for use when we got inshore. Two of the fur sleeping-bags went over the side; they were thoroughly wet, weighing probably 40 lb each, and they had frozen stiff during the night. Three men constituted the watch below, and when a man went down it was better to turn into the wet bag just vacated by another man than to thaw out a frozen bag with the heat of his unfortunate body. We now had four bags, three in use, and one for emergency use in case a member of the party should break down permanently. The reduction of weight relieved the boat to some extent, and vigorous chipping and scraping did more. We had to be very careful not to put axe or knife through the frozen canvas of the decking as we crawled over it, but gradually we got rid of a lot of ice. The *James Caird* lifted to the endless waves as though she lived again.

About 11 am the boat suddenly fell off into the trough of the sea. The painter had parted and the sea-anchor had gone. This was serious. The *James Caird* went away to leeward, and we had no chance at all of recovering the anchor and our valuable rope, which had been our only means of keeping the boat's head up to the seas without the risk of hoisting sail in a gale. Now we had to set the sail and trust to its holding. While the *James Caird* rolled heavily in the trough, we beat the frozen canvas until the bulk of the ice had cracked off it, and then hoisted it. The frozen gear worked protestingly, but after a struggle our little craft came up to the wind again, and we breathed more freely.

We held the boat up to the gale during that day, enduring as best we could discomforts that amounted to pain. The boat tossed interminably on the big waves under grey, threatening skies. Our thoughts did not embrace much more than the necessities of the hour. Every surge of the sea was an enemy to be watched and circumvented. We ate our scanty meals, treated our frost-bites, and hoped for the improved conditions that the morrow might bring. Night fell early, and in the lagging hours of darkness we were cheered by a change for the better in the weather. The wind dropped, the snow-squalls became less frequent, and the sea moderated. When the morning of the seventh day dawned, there was not much wind. We shook the reef out of the sail and laid our course once more for South Georgia. The sun came out bright and clear, and presently Worsley got a snap for longitude. We hoped that the sky would remain clear until noon, so that we could get the latitude. We had been six days out without an observation, and our dead reckoning naturally was uncertain. The boat must have presented a strange appearance that morning. All hands basked in the sun. We hung our sleeping-bags to the mast and spread our socks and other gear all over the deck. Some of the ice had melted off the *James Caird* in the early morning after the gale began to slacken, and dry patches were appearing in the decking. Porpoises came blowing round the boat, and Cape pigeons wheeled and swooped within a few feet of us. These little black-and-white birds have an air of friendliness that is not possessed by the great circling albatross. They had looked grey against the swaying sea during the storm as they darted about over our heads and uttered their plaintive cries. The albatrosses, of the black or sooty variety, had watched with hard, bright eyes, and seemed to have a quite impersonal interest in our struggle to keep afloat amid the battering seas. In addition to the Cape pigeons an occasional stormy petrel flashed overhead. Then there was a small bird, unknown to me, that appeared always to be in a fussy, bustling state, quite out of keeping with the surroundings. It irritated me. It had practically no tail, and it flitted about vaguely as though in search of the lost member. I used to find myself wishing it would find its tail and have done with the silly fluttering.

We revelled in the warmth of the sun that day. Life was not so bad, after all. We felt we were well on our way. Our gear was drying, and we could have a hot meal in comparative comfort. The swell was still heavy, but it was not breaking and the boat rode easily. At noon Worsley balanced himself on the gunwale and clung with one hand to the stay of the mainmast while he got a snap of the sun. The result was more than encouraging. We had done over 380 miles and were getting on for half-way to South Georgia. It looked as though we were going to get through.

The wind freshened to a good stiff breeze during the afternoon, and the *James Caird* made satisfactory progress. I had not realized until the sunlight came how small our boat really was. There was some influence in the light and warmth, some hint of happier days, that made us revive memories of other voyages, when we had stout decks beneath our feet, unlimited food at our command, and pleasant cabins for our ease. Now we clung to a battered little boat, 'alone, alone, all, all alone, alone on a wide, wide, sea'. So low in the water were we that each succeeding swell cut off our view of the sky-line. We were a tiny speck in the vast vista of the sea – the ocean that is open to all, and merciful to none, that threatens even when it seems to yield, and that is pitiless always to weakness. For a moment the consciousness of the forces arrayed against us would be almost overwhelming. Then hope and confidence would rise again as our boat rose to a wave and tossed aside the crest in a sparkling shower like the play of prismatic colours at the foot of a waterfall. My double-barrelled gun and some cartridges had been stowed aboard the boat as an emergency precaution against a shortage of food, but we were not disposed to destroy our little neighbours, the Cape pigeons, even for the sake of fresh meat. We might have shot an albatross, but the wandering king of the ocean aroused in us something of the feeling that inspired, too late, the Ancient Mariner. So the gun remained among the stores and sleeping-bags in the narrow quarters beneath our leaking deck, and the nomads followed us unmolested.

The eighth, ninth, and tenth days of the voyage had few features worthy of special note. The wind blew hard during those days, and the strain of navigating the boat was unceasing, but always we made some advance towards our goal. No bergs showed on our horizon, and we knew that we were clear of the ice-fields. Each day brought its little round of troubles, but also compensation in the form of food and growing hope. We felt that we were going to succeed. The odds against us had been great, but we were winning through. We still suffered severely from the cold, for, though the temperature was rising, our vitality was declining owing to shortage of food, exposure, and the necessity of maintaining our cramped positions day and night. I found that it was now absolutely necessary to prepare hot milk for all hands during the night, in order to sustain life till dawn. This meant lighting the Primus lamp in the darkness and involved an increased drain on our small store of matches. It was the rule that one match must serve when the Primus was being lit. We had no lamp for the compass, and during the early days of the voyage we would strike a match when the steersman wanted to see the course at night; but later the necessity for strict economy impressed itself upon us, and the practice of striking matches at night was stopped. We had one water-tight tin of matches. I had stowed away in a pocket, in readiness for a sunny day, a lens from one of the telescopes, but this was of no use during the voyage. The sun seldom shone upon us. The glass of the compass got broken one night, and we contrived to mend it with adhesive tape from the medicine-chest. One of the memories that comes to me from those days is of Crean singing at the tiller. He always sang while he was steering, and nobody ever discovered what the song was. It was devoid of tune and as monotonous as the chanting of a Buddhist monk at his prayers; yet somehow it was cheerful. In moments of inspiration Crean would attempt 'The Wearing of the Green'.

On the tenth night Worsley could not straighten his body after his spell at the tiller. He was thoroughly cramped, and we had to drag him beneath the decking and massage him before he could unbend himself and get into a sleeping-bag. A hard north-westerly gale came up on the eleventh day (May 5) and shifted to the south-west in the late afternoon. The sky was overcast and occasional snow squalls added to the discomfort produced by a tremendous cross-sea – the worst, I thought, that we had experienced. At midnight I was at the tiller and suddenly noticed a line of clear sky between the south and south-west. I called to the other men that the sky was clearing, and then a moment later I realized that what I had seen was not a rift in the clouds but the white crest of an enormous wave. During twenty-six years' experience of the ocean in all its moods I had not encountered a wave so gigantic. It was a mighty upheaval of the ocean, a thing apart from the big white-capped seas that had been our tireless enemies for many days. I shouted, 'For God's sake, hold on! It's got us!' Then came a moment of suspense that seemed drawn out into hours. White surged the foam of the breaking sea around us. We felt our boat lifted and flung forward like a cork in breaking surf. We were in a seething chaos of tortured water; but somehow the boat lived through it, half-full of water, sagging to the dead weight and shuddering under the blow. We bailed with the energy of men fighting for life, flinging the water over the sides with every receptacle that came to our hands, and after ten minutes of uncertainty we felt the boat renew her life beneath us. She floated again and ceased to lurch drunkenly as though dazed by the attack of the sea. Earnestly we hoped that never again would we encounter such a wave.

The conditions in the boat, uncomfortable before, had been made worse by the deluge of water. All our gear was thoroughly wet again. Our cooking-stove had been floating about in the bottom of the boat, and portions of our last hoosh seemed to have permeated everything. Not until 3 AM, when we were all chilled almost to the limit of endurance, did we manage to get the stove alight and make ourselves hot drinks. The carpenter was suffering particularly, but he showed grit and spirit. Vincent had for the past week ceased to be an active member of the crew, and I could not easily account for his collapse. Physically he was one of the strongest men in the boat. He was a young man, he had served on North Sea trawlers, and he should have been able to bear hardships better than McCarthy, who, not so strong, was always happy.

The weather was better on the following day (May 6), and we got a glimpse of the sun. Worsley's observation showed that we were not more than a hundred miles from the north-west corner of South Georgia. Two more days with a favourable wind and we would sight the promised land. I hoped that there would be no delay, for our supply of water was running very low. The hot drink at night was essential, but I decided that the daily allowance of water must be cut down to half a pint per man. The lumps of ice we had taken aboard had gone long ago. We were dependent upon the water we had brought from Elephant Island, and our thirst was increased by the fact that we were now using the brackish water in the breaker that had been slightly stove in in the surf when the boat was being loaded. Some sea-water had entered at that time.

Thirst took possession of us. I dared not permit the allowance of water to be increased since an unfavourable wind might drive us away from the island and lengthen our voyage by many days. Lack of water is always the most severe privation that men can be condemned to endure, and we found, as during our earlier boat voyage, that the salt water in our clothing and the salt spray that lashed our faces made our thirst grow quickly to a burning pain. I had to be very firm in refusing to allow anyone to anticipate the morrow's allowance, which I was sometimes begged to do. We did the necessary work dully and hoped for the land. I had altered the course to the east so as to make sure of our striking the island, which would have been impossible to regain if we had run past the northern end. The course was laid on our scrap of chart for a point some thirty miles down the coast. That day and the following day passed for us in a sort of nightmare. Our mouths were dry and our tongues were swollen. The wind was still strong and the heavy sea forced us to navigate carefully, but any thought of our peril from the waves was buried beneath the consciousness of our raging thirst. The bright moments were those when we each received our one mug of hot milk during the long, bitter watches of the night. Things were bad for us in those days, but the end was coming. The morning of May 8 broke thick and stormy, with squalls from the north-west. We searched the waters ahead for a sign of land, and though we could see nothing more than had met our eyes for many days, we were cheered by a sense that the goal was near at hand. About ten o'clock that morning we passed a little bit of kelp, a glad signal of the proximity of land. An hour later we saw two shags sitting on a big mass of kelp, and knew then that we must be within ten or fifteen miles of the shore. These birds are as sure an indication of the proximity of land as a lighthouse is, for they never venture far to sea. We gazed ahead with increasing eagerness, and at 12.30 pm, through a rift in the clouds, McCarthy caught a glimpse of the black cliffs of South Georgia, just fourteen days after our departure from Elephant Island. It was a glad moment. Thirst-ridden, chilled, and weak as we were, happiness irradiated us. The job was nearly done.

We stood in towards the shore to look for a landing-place, and presently we could see the green tussock-grass on the ledges above the surf-beaten rocks. Ahead of us and to the south, blind rollers showed the presence of uncharted reefs along the coast. Here and there the hungry rocks were close to the surface, and over them the great waves broke, swirling viciously and spouting thirty and forty feet into the air. The rocky coast appeared to descend sheer to the sea. Our need of water and rest was wellnigh desperate, but to have attempted a landing at that time would have been suicidal. Night was drawing near, and the weather indications were not favourable. There was nothing for it but to haul off till the following morning, so we stood away on the starboard tack until we had made what appeared to be a safe offing. Then we hove to in the high westerly swell. The hours passed slowly as we waited the dawn, which would herald, we fondly hoped, the last stage of our journey. Our thirst was a torment and we could scarcely touch our food; the cold seemed to strike right through our weakened bodies. At 5 am the wind shifted to the north-west and quickly increased to one of the worst hurricanes any of us had experienced. A great cross-sea was running, and the wind simply shrieked as it tore the tops off the waves and converted the whole seascape into a haze of driving spray. Down into valleys, up to tossing heights, straining until her seams opened, swung our little boat, brave still but labouring heavily. We knew that the wind and set of the sea was driving us ashore, but we could do nothing. The dawn showed us a storm-torn ocean, and the morning passed without bringing us a sight of the land; but at 1 pm, through a rift in the flying mists, we got a glimpse of the huge crags of the island and realized that our position had become desperate. We were on a dead lee shore, and we could gauge our approach to the unseen cliffs by the roar of the breakers against the sheer walls of rock. I ordered the double-reefed mainsail to be set in the hope that we might claw off, and this attempt increased the strain upon the boat. The *James Caird* was bumping heavily, and the water was pouring in everywhere. Our thirst was forgotten in the realization of our imminent danger, as we bailed unceasingly, and adjusted our weights from time to time; occasional glimpses showed that the shore was nearer. I knew that Annewkow Island lay to the south of us, but our small and badly marked chart showed uncertain reefs in the passage between the island and the mainland, and I dared not trust it, though as a last resort we could try to lie under the lee of the island. The afternoon wore away as we edged down the coast, with the thunder of the breakers in our ears. The approach of evening found us still some distance from Annewkow

Island, and, dimly in the twilight, we could see a snow-capped mountain looming above us. The chance of surviving the night, with the driving gale and the implacable sea forcing us on to the lee shore, seemed small. I think most of us had a feeling that the end was very near. Just after 6 PM, in the dark, as the boat was in the yeasty backwash from the seas flung from this iron-bound coast, then, just when things looked their worst, they changed for the best. I have marvelled often at the thin line that divides success from failure and the sudden turn that leads from apparently certain disaster to comparative safety. The wind suddenly shifted, and we were free once more to make an offing. Almost as soon as the gale eased, the pin that locked the mast to the thwart fell out. It must have been on the point of doing this throughout the hurricane, and if it had gone nothing could have saved us; the mast would have snapped like a carrot. Our backstays had carried away once before when iced up, and were not too strongly fastened now. We were thankful indeed for the mercy that had held that pin in its place throughout the hurricane.

We stood off shore again, tired almost to the point of apathy. Our water had long been finished. The last was about a pint of hairy liquid which we strained through a bit of gauze from the medicine chest. The pangs of thirst attacked us with redoubled intensity, and I felt that we must make a landing on the following day at almost any hazard. The night wore on. We were very tired. We longed for day. When at last the dawn came on the morning of May 10 there was practically no wind, but a high cross-sea was running. We made slow progress towards the shore. About 8 am the wind backed to the northwest and threatened another blow. We had sighted in the meantime a big indentation which I thought must be King Haakon Bay, and I decided that we must land there. We set the bows of the boat towards the bay and ran before the freshening gale. Soon we had angry reefs on either side. Great glaciers came down to the sea and offered no landing-place. The sea spouted on the reefs and thundered against the shore. About noon we sighted a line of jagged reef, like blackened teeth, that seemed to bar the entrance to the bay. Inside, comparatively smooth water stretched eight or nine miles to the head of the bay. A gap in the reef appeared, and we made for it. But the fates had another rebuff for us. The wind shifted and blew from the east right out of the bay. We could see the way through the reef, but we could not approach it directly. That afternoon we bore up, tacking five times in the strong wind. The last tack enabled us to get through, and at last we were in the wide mouth of the bay. Dusk was approaching. A small cove, with a boulder-strewn beach guarded by a reef, made a break in the cliffs on the south side of the bay, and we turned in that direction. I stood in the bows directing the steering as we ran through the kelp and made the passage of the reef. The entrance was so narrow that we had to take in the oars, and the swell was piling itself right over the reef into the cove; but in a minute or two we were inside, and in the gathering darkness the *James Caird* ran in on a swell and touched the beach. I sprang ashore with the short painter and held on when the boat went out with the backward surge. When the *James Caird* came in again, three of the men got ashore, and they held the painter while I climbed some rocks with another line. A slip on the wet rocks twenty feet up nearly closed my part of the story just at the moment when we were achieving safety. A jagged piece of rock held me and at the same time bruised me sorely. However, I made fast the line, and in a few minutes we were all safe on the beach with the boat floating in the surging water just off the shore. We heard a gurgling sound that was sweet music in our ears, and, peering around, found a stream of fresh water almost at our feet. A moment later we were down on our knees drinking the pure ice-cold water in long draughts that put new life into us.

Wilbur Daniel Steele

The Yellow Cat

At least once in my life I have had the good fortune to board a deserted vessel at sea. I say 'good fortune' because it has left me the memory of a singular impression. I have felt a ghost of the same thing two or three times since then, when peeping through the doorway of an abandoned house.

Now that vessel was not dead. She was a good vessel, a sound vessel, even a handsome vessel, in her blunt-bowed, coastwise way. She sailed under four lowers across as blue and glittering a sea as I have ever known, and there was not a point in her sailing that one could lay a finger upon as wrong. And yet, passing that schooner at two miles, one knew, somehow, that no hand was on her wheel. Sometimes I can imagine a vessel, stricken like that, moving over the empty spaces of the sea, carrying it off quite well were it not for that indefinable suggestion of a stagger; and I can think of all those ocean gods, in whom no landsman will ever believe, looking at one another and tapping their foreheads with just the shadow of a smile.

I wonder if they all scream – these ships that have lost their souls? Mine screamed. We heard her voice, like nothing I have ever heard before, when we rowed under her counter to read her name – the *Marionette* it was, of Halifax. I remember how it made me shiver, there in the full blaze of the sun, to hear her going on so, railing and screaming in that stark fashion. And I remember, too, how our footsteps, pattering through the vacant internals in search of that haggard utterance, made me think of the footsteps of hurrying warders roused in the night.

And we found a parrot in a cage; that was all. It wanted water. We gave it water and went away to look things over, keeping pretty close together, all of us. In the quarters the tables were set for four. Two men had begun to eat, by the evidence of the plates. Nowhere in the vessel was there any sign of disorder, except one sea-chest broken out, evidently in haste. Her papers were gone and the stern davits were empty. That is how the case stood that day, and that is how it has stood to this. I saw this same *Marionette* a week later, tied up to a Hoboken dock, where she awaited news from her owners; but even there, in the midst of all the water-front bustle, I could not get rid of the feeling that she was still very far away – in a sort of shippish other-world.

The thing happens now and then. Sometimes half a dozen years will go by without a solitary wanderer of this sort crossing the ocean paths, and then in a single season perhaps several of them will turn up: vacant waifs, impassive and mysterious – a quarter-column of tidings tucked away on the second page of the evening paper.

That is where I read the story about the *Abbie Rose*. I recollect how painfully awkward and out-of-place it looked there, cramped between ruled black edges and smelling of landsman's ink – this thing that had to do essentially with air and vast coloured spaces. I forget the exact words of the heading – something like 'Abandoned Craft Picked Up At Sea,' but I still have the clipping itself, couched in the formal patter of the marine-news writer.

> The first hint of another mystery of the sea came in today when the schooner *Abbie Rose* dropped anchor in the upper river, manned only by a crew of one. It appears that the out-bound freighter *Mercury* sighted the *Abbie Rose* off Block Island on Thursday last, acting in a suspicious manner. A boat party sent aboard found the schooner in perfect order and condition, sailing under four lower sails, the topsails being pursed up to the mastheads but now stowed. With the exception of a yellow cat the vessel was found to be utterly deserted, though her small boat still hung in the davits. No evidences of disorder were visible in any part of the craft. The dishes were washed up, the stove in the galley was still slightly warm to the touch, everything in its proper place with the exception of the vessel's papers, which were not to be found.
>
> All indications being for fair weather, Captain Rohmer of the *Mercury* detailed two of his company to bring the find back to this port, a distance of one hundred and fifteen miles. The only man available with a knowledge of the fore-and-aft rig was Stewart McCord, the second engineer. A seaman by the name of Björnsen was sent with him. McCord arrived this noon, after a very heavy voyage of five days, reporting that Björnsen had fallen overboard while shaking out the foretopsail. McCord himself showed evidences of the hardships he has passed through, being almost a nervous wreck.

Stewart McCord! Yes, Stewart McCord would have a knowledge of the fore-and-aft rig, or of almost anything else connected with the affairs of the sea. It happened that I used to know this fellow. I had even been quite chummy with him in the old days – that is, to the extent of drinking too many beers with him in certain hot-country ports. I remembered him as a stolid and deliberate sort of a person, with an amazing hodge-podge of learning, a stamp collection, and a theory about the effects of tropical sunshine on the Caucasian race, to which I have listened half of more than one night, stretched out naked on a freighter's deck. He had not impressed me as a fellow who would be bothered by his nerves.

And there was another thing about the story which struck me as rather queer. Perhaps it is a relic of my seafaring days, but I have always been a conscientious reader of the weather reports; and I could remember no weather in the past week sufficient to shake a man out of a top, especially a man by the name of Björnsen – a thorough-going seafaring name.

I was destined to hear more of this in the evening, from the ancient boatman who rowed me out on the upper river. He had been to sea in his day. He knew enough to wonder about this thing, even to indulge in a little superstitious awe about it.

'No sir-ee. Something *happened* to them four chaps. And another thing –'

I fancied I heard a sea-bird whining in the darkness overhead. A shape moved out of the gloom ahead, passed to the left, lofty and silent, and merged once more with the gloom behind – a barge at anchor, with the sea-grass clinging around her waterline.

'Funny about that other chap,' the old fellow speculated. 'Björnsen – I b'lieve he called 'im. Now that story sounds to me kind of –' He feathered his oars with a suspicious jerk and peered at me. 'This McCord a friend of yourn?' he inquired.

'In a way,' I said.

'Hm-m – well –' He turned on his thwart to squint ahead. 'There she is,' he announced, with something of relief, I thought.

It was hard at that time of night to make anything but a black blotch out of the *Abbie Rose*. Of course I could see that she was pot-bellied, like the rest of the coastwise sisterhood. And that McCord had not stowed his topsails. I could make them out, pursed at the mastheads and hanging down as far as the crosstrees, like huge over-ripe pears. Then I recollected that he had found them so – probably had not touched them since; a queer way to leave tops, it seemed to me. I could see also the glowing tip of a cigar floating restlessly along the farthest rail. I called: 'McCord! Oh, McCord!'

The spark came swimming across the deck. 'Hello! Hello, there – ah –' There was a note of querulous uneasiness there that somehow jarred with my remembrance of this man.

'Ridgeway,' I explained.

He echoed the name uncertainly, still with that suggestion of peevishness, hanging over the rail and peering down at us. 'Oh! By gracious!' he exclaimed, abruptly. 'I'm glad to see you, Ridgeway. I had a boatman coming out before this, but I guess – well, I guess he'll be along. By gracious! I'm glad –'

'I'll not keep you,' I told the gnome, putting the money in his palm

and reaching for the rail. McCord lent me a hand on my wrist. Then
when I stood squarely on the deck beside him he appeared to forget my
presence, leaned forward heavily on the rail, and squinted after my
waning boatman.

'Ahoy – boat!' he called out, sharply, shielding his lips with his
hands. His violence seemed to bring him out of the blank, for he fell
immediately to puffing strongly at his cigar and explaining in rather a
shamefaced way that he was beginning to think his own boatman had
'passed him up'.

'Come in and have a nip,' he urged with an abrupt heartiness, clapping me on the shoulder.

'So you've –'

I did not say what I had intended. I was thinking that in the old days
McCord had made rather a fetish of touching nothing stronger than beer.
Neither had he been of the shoulder-clapping sort. 'So you've got some-
thing aboard?' I shifted.

'Dead men's liquor,' he chuckled. It gave me a queer feeling in the
pit of my stomach to hear him. I began to wish I had not come, but
there was nothing for it now but to follow him into the after-house.
The cabin itself might have been nine feet square, with three bunks
occupying the port side. To the right opened the master's stateroom,
and a door in the forward bulkhead led to the galley.

I took in these features at a casual glance. Then, hardly knowing
why I did it, I began to examine them with greater care.

'Have you a match?' I asked. My voice sounded very small, as
though something unheard of had happened to all the air.

'Smoke?' he asked. 'I'll get you a cigar.'

'No.' I took the proffered match, scratched it on the side of the
galley door, and passed out. There seemed to be a thousand pans
there, throwing my match back at me from every wall of the box-like
compartment. Even McCord's eyes, in the doorway, were large and
round and shining. He probably thought me crazy. Perhaps I was, a
little. I ran the match along close to the ceiling and came upon a rusty
hook a little aport of the centre.

'There,' I said. 'Was there anything hanging from this – er – say a
parrot – or something, McCord?' The match burned my fingers and
went out.

'What do you mean?' McCord demanded from the doorway. I got
myself back into the comfortable yellow glow of the cabin before I
answered, and then it was a question.

'Do you happen to know anything about this craft's personal
history?'

'No. What are you talking about! Why?'

'Well, I do,' I offered. 'For one thing she's changed her name. And it happens this isn't the first time she's – Well, damn it all, fourteen years ago I helped pick up this whatever-she-is off the Virginia Capes – in the same sort of condition. There you are!' I was yapping like a nerve-strung puppy.

McCord leaned forward with his hands on the table, bringing his face beneath the fan of the hanging-lamp. For the first time I could mark how shockingly it had changed. It was almost colourless. The jaw had somehow lost its old-time security and the eyes seemed to be loose in their sockets. I had expected him to start at my announcement; he only blinked at the light.

'I am not surprised,' he remarked at length. 'After what I've seen and heard –' He lifted his fist and brought it down with a sudden crash on the table. 'Man – let's have a nip!'

He was off before I could say a word, fumbling out of sight in the narrow state-room. Presently he reappeared, holding a glass in either hand and a dark bottle hugged between his elbows. Putting the glasses down, he held up the bottle between his eyes and the lamp, and its shadow, falling across his face, green and luminous at the core, gave him a ghastly look – like a mutilation or an unspeakable birth-mark. He shook the bottle gently and chuckled his 'Dead men's liquor' again. Then he poured two half-glasses of the clear gin, swallowed his portion, and sat down.

'A parrot,' he mused, a little of the liquor's colour creeping into his cheeks. 'No, this time it was a cat, Ridgeway. A yellow cat. She was –'

'*Was*?' I caught him up. 'What's happened – what's become of her?'

'Vanished. Evaporated. I haven't seen her since night before last, when I caught her trying to lower the boat –'

'*Stop it!*' It was I who banged the table now, without any of the reserve of decency. 'McCord, you're drunk – *drunk*, I tell you. A *cat*! Let a *cat* throw you off your head like this! She's probably hiding out below this minute, on affairs of her own.'

'Hiding?' He regarded me for a moment with the queer superiority of the damned. 'I guess you don't realize how many times I've been over this hulk, from decks to keelson, with a mallet and a foot-rule.'

'Or fallen overboard,' I shifted, with less assurance. 'Like this fellow Björnsen. By the way, McCord –' I stopped there on account of the look in his eyes.

He reached out, poured himself a shot, swallowed it, and got up to shuffle about the confined quarters. I watched their restless circuit – my friend and his jumping shadow. He stopped and bent forward to examine a Sunday-supplement chromo tacked on the wall, and the two heads drew together, as though there were something to whisper. Of a sudden

I seemed to hear the old gnome croaking, 'Now that story sounds to me kind of –'

McCord straightened up and turned to face me.

'What do you know about Björnsen?' he demanded.

'Well – only what they had you saying in the papers,' I told him.

'Pshaw!' He snapped his fingers, tossing the affair aside. 'I found her log,' he announced in quite another voice.

'You did, eh? I judged, from what I read in the paper, that there wasn't a sign.'

'No, no; I happened on this the other night, under the mattress in there.' He jerked his head towards the state-room. 'Wait!' I heard him knocking things over in the dark and mumbling at them. After a moment he came out and threw on the table a long, cloth-covered ledger, of the common commercial sort. It lay open at about the middle, showing close script running indiscriminately across the column ruling.

'When I said "log," ' he went on, 'I guess I was going it a little strong. At least, I wouldn't want that sort of log found around *my* vessel. Let's call it a personal record. Here's his picture, somewhere –' He shook the book by its back and a common kodak blueprint fluttered to the table. It was the likeness of a solid man with a paunch, a huge square beard, small squinting eyes, and a bald head. 'What do you make of him – a writing chap?'

'From the nose down, yes,' I estimated. 'From the nose up, he will 'tend to his own business if you will 'tend to yours, strictly.'

McCord slapped his thigh. 'By gracious! that's the fellow! He hates the Chinaman. He knows as well as anything he ought not to put down in black and white how intolerably he hates the Chinaman, and yet he must sneak off to his cubby-hole and suck his pencil, and – and how is it Stevenson has it? – the "agony of composition,' you remember. Can you imagine the fellow, Ridgeway, bundling down here with the fever on him –'

'About the Chinaman,' I broke in. 'I think you said something about a Chinaman?'

'Yes. The cook, he must have been. I gather he wasn't the master's pick, by the reading-matter here. Probably clapped on to him by the owners – shifted from one of their others at the last moment; a queer trick. Listen.' He picked up the book and, running over the pages with a selective thumb, read:

'*August second*. First part, moderate southwesterly breeze –

and so forth – er – but here he comes to it:

'Anything can happen to a man at sea, even a funeral. In special to a

Chinyman, who is of no account to social welfare, being a barbarian as I look at it.

'Something of a philosopher, you see. And did you get the reserve in that "even a funeral"? An artist, I tell you. But wait; let me catch him a bit wilder. Here:

> 'It'll get that mustard-coloured – (This is back a couple of days.) Never can hear the – coming, in them carpet slippers. Turned round and found him standing right to my back this morning. Could have stuck a knife into me easy. 'Look here!' says I, and fetched him a tap on the ear that will make him walk louder next time, I warrant. He could have stuck a knife into me easy.

'A clear case of moral funk, I should say. Can you imagine the fellow, Ridgeway –'

'Yes; oh yes.' I was ready with a phrase of my own. 'A man handicapped with an imagination. You see he can't quite understand this "barbarian," who has him beaten by about thirty centuries of civilization – and his imagination has to have something to chew on, something to hit – a 'tap on the ear,' you know.'

'By gracious! that's the ticket!' McCord pounded his knee. 'And now we've got another chap going to pieces – Peters, he calls him. Refuses to eat dinner on August the third, claiming he caught the Chink making passes over the chowder-pot with his thumb. Can you believe it, Ridgeway – in this very cabin here?' Then he went on with a suggestion of haste, as though he had somehow made a slip. 'Well, at any rate, the disease seems to be catching. Next day it's Bach, the second seaman, who begins to feel the gaff. Listen:

> 'Back he comes to me tonight, complaining he's being watched. He claims the – has got the evil eye. Says he can see you through a two-inch bulkhead, and the like. The Chink's laying in his bunk, turned the other way. "Why don't you go aboard of him," says I. The Dutcher says nothing, but goes over to his own bunk and feels under the straw. When he comes back he's looking queer. "By God!" says he, "the devil has swiped my gun!" . . . Now if that's true there is going to be hell to pay in this vessel very quick. I figure I'm still master of this vessel.'

'The evil eye,' I grunted. 'Consciences gone wrong there somewhere.'

'Not altogether, Ridgeway. I can see that yellow man peeking. Now just figure yourself, say, eight thousand miles from home, out on the water alone with a crowd of heathen fanatics crazy from fright, looking around for guns and so on. Don't you believe you'd keep an eye around the corners, kind of – eh? I'll bet a hat he was taking it all in, lying there in his bunk, "turned the other way." Eh? I pity the poor cuss – Well, there's only one more entry after that. He's good and mad. Here:

'Now, by God! this is the end. My gun's gone too; right out from under lock and key, by God! I been talking with Bach this morning. Not to let on, I had him in to clean my lamp. There's more ways than one, he says, and so do I.'

McCord closed the book and dropped it on the table. 'Finis,' he said. 'The rest is blank paper.'

'Well!' I will confess I felt much better than I had for some time past. 'There's *one* "mystery of the sea" gone to pot, at any rate. And now, if you don't mind, I think I'll have another of your nips, McCord.'

He pushed my glass across the table and got up, and behind his back his shadow rose to scour the corners of the room, like an incorruptible sentinel. I forgot to take up my gin, watching him. After an uneasy minute or so he came back to the table and pressed the tip of a forefinger on the book.

'Ridgeway,' he said, 'you don't seem to understand. This particular "mystery of the sea" hasn't been scratched yet – not even *scratched*, Ridgeway.' He sat down and leaned forward, fixing me with a didactic finger. 'What happened?'

'Well, I have an idea the "barbarian" got them, when it came to the pinch.'

'And let the – remains over the side?'

'I should say.'

'And they came back and got the "barbarian" and let *him* over the side, eh? There were none left, you remember.'

'Oh, good Lord, I don't know!' I flared with a childish resentment at this catechizing of his. But his finger remained there, challenging.

'I do,' he announced. 'The Chinaman put them over the side, as we have said. And then, after that, he died – of wounds about the head.'

'So?' I had still sarcasm.

'You will remember,' he went on, 'that the skipper did not happen to mention a cat, a *yellow* cat, in his confessions.'

'McCord,' I begged him, 'please drop it. Why in thunder *should* he mention a cat?'

'True. Why *should* he mention a cat? I think one of the reasons why he should *not* mention a cat is because there did not happen to be a cat aboard at that time.'

'Oh, all right!' I reached out and pulled the bottle to my side of the table. Then I took out my watch. 'If you don't mind,' I suggested, 'I think we'd better be going ashore. I've got to get to my office rather early in the morning. What do you say?'

He said nothing for the moment, but his finger had dropped. He leaned back and stared straight into the core of the light above, his eyes squinting.

'He would have been from the south of China, probably.' He seemed to be talking to himself. 'There's a considerable sprinkling of the belief down there, I've heard. It's an uncanny business – this trans-migration of souls –'

Personally, I had had enough of it. McCord's fingers came groping across the table for the bottle. I picked it up hastily and let it go through the open companionway, where it died with a faint gurgle, out some-where on the river.

'Now,' I said to him, shaking the vagrant wrist, 'either you come ashore with me or you go in there and get under the blankets. You're drunk, McCord – *drunk*. Do you hear me?'

'Ridgeway,' he pronounced, bringing his eyes down to me and speaking very slowly. 'You're a fool, if you can't see better than that. I'm not drunk. I'm sick. I haven't slept for three nights – and now I can't. And you say – you –' He went to pieces very suddenly, jumped up, pounded the legs of his chair on the decking, and shouted at me: 'And you say that, you – you landlubber, you office coddler! You're so comfortably sure that everything in the world is cut and dried. Come back to the water again and learn how to wonder – and stop talking like a damn fool. Do know where – Is there anything in your municipal budget to tell me where Björnsen went? Listen!' He sat down, waving me to do the same, and went on with a sort of desperate repression.

'It happened on the first night after we took this hellion. I'd stood the wheel most of the afternoon – of and on, that is, because she sails herself uncommonly well. Just put her on a reach, you know, and she carries it off pretty well –'

'I know,' I nodded.

'Well, we mugged up about seven o'clock. There was a good deal of canned stuff in the galley, and Björnsen wasn't a bad hand with a kettle – a thorough-going Square-head he was – tall and lean and yellow-haired, with little fat, round cheeks and a white moustache. Not a bad chap at all. He took the wheel to stand till midnight, and I turned in, but I didn't drop off for quite a spell. I could hear his boots wandering around over my head, padding off forward, coming back again. I heard him whistling now and then – an outlandish air. Occasionally I could see the shadow of his head waving in a block of moonlight that lay on the decking right down there in front of the state-room door. It came from the companion; the cabin was dark because we were going easy on the oil. They hadn't left a great deal, for some reason or other.'

McCord leaned back and described with his finger where the illumin-ation had cut the decking.

'There! I could see it from my bunk, as I lay, you understand. I must have almost dropped off once when I heard him fiddling around out here in the cabin, and then he said something in a whisper, just to find out if I was still awake, I suppose. I asked him what the matter was. He came and poked his head in the door.

‘ "The breeze is going out," says he. "I was wondering if we couldn't get a little more sail on her." Only I can't give you his fierce Squarehead tang. "How about the tops?" he suggested.

‘I was so sleepy I didn't care, and I told him so. "All right," he says, "but I thought I might shake out one of them tops." Then I heard him blow at something outside. "Scat, you –!" Then: "This cat's going to set me crazy, Mr McCord," he says, "following me around everywhere." He gave a kick, and I saw something yellow floating across the moonlight. It never made a sound – just floated. You wouldn't have known it ever lit anywhere, just like –’

McCord stopped and drummed a few beats on the table with his fist, as though to bring himself back to the straight narrative.

‘I went to sleep,’ he began again. ‘I dreamed about a lot of things. I woke up sweating. You know how glad you are to wake up after a dream like that and find none of it is so? Well, I turned over and settled to go off again, and then I got a little more awake and thought to myself it must be pretty near time for me to go on deck. I scratched a match and looked at my watch. "That fellow must be either a good chap or asleep," I said to myself. And I rolled out quick and went abovedecks. He wasn't at the wheel. I called him: "Björnsen! Björnsen!" No answer.’

McCord was really telling a story now. He paused for a long moment, one hand shielding an ear and his eyeballs turned far up.

‘That was the first time I really went over the hulk,’ he ran on. ‘I got out a lantern and started at the forward end of the hold, and I worked aft, and there was nothing there. Not a sign, or a stain, or a scrap of clothing, or anything. You may believe that I began to feel funny inside. I went over the decks and the rails and the house itself – inch by inch. Not a trace. I went out aft again. The cat sat on the wheelbox, washing her face. I hadn't noticed the scar on her head before, running down between her ears – rather a new scar – three or four days old, I should say. It looked ghastly and blue-white in the flat moonlight. I ran over and grabbed her up to heave her over the side – you understand how upset I was. Now you know a cat will squirm around and grab something when you hold it like that, generally speaking. This one didn't. She just drooped and began to purr and looked up at me out of her moonlit eyes under that scar. I dropped her on the deck and backed off. You remember Björnsen had *kicked* her – and I didn't want anything like that happening to –’

The narrator turned upon me with a sudden heat, leaned over and shook his finger before my face.

‘There you go!’ he cried. ‘You with your stout stone buildings and your policemen and your neighbourhood church – you're so damn sure. But I'd just like to see you out there, alone, with the moon setting, and all the lights gone tall and queer, and a shipmate –' He lifted his hand overhead, the finger-tips pressed together and then suddenly separated as though he had released an impalpable something into the air.

'Go on,' I told him.

'I felt more like you do, when it got light again, and warm and sun-shiny. I said 'Bah!' to the whole business. I even fed the cat, and I slept awhile on the roof of the house – I was so sure. We lay dead most of the day, without a streak of air. But that night –! Well, that night I hadn't got over being sure yet. It takes quite a jolt, you know to shake loose several dozen generations. A fair, steady breeze had come along, the glass was high, she was staying herself like a doll, and so I figured I could get a little rest, lying below in the bunk, even if I didn't sleep.

'I tried not to sleep, in case something should come up – a squall or the like. But I think I must have dropped off once or twice. I remember I heard something fiddling around in the galley, and I hollered "Scat!" and everything was quiet again. I rolled over and lay on my left side, staring at that square of moonlight outside my door for a long time. You'll think it was a dream – what I saw there.'

'Go on,' I said.

'Call this table-top the spot of light, roughly,' he said. He placed a finger-tip at about the middle of the forward edge and drew it slowly towards the centre. 'Here, what would correspond with the upper side of the companionway, there came down very gradually the shadow of a tail. I watched it streaking out there across the deck, wiggling the slightest bit now and then. When it had come down about half-way across the light, the solid part of the animal – its shadow, you understand – began to appear, quite big and round. But how could she hang there, done up in a ball, from the hatch?'

He shifted his finger back to the edge of the table and puddled it around to signify the shadowed body.

'I fished my gun out from behind my back. You see, I was feeling funny again. Then I started to slide one foot over the edge of the bunk, always with my eyes on that shadow. Now I swear I didn't make the sound of a pin dropping, but I had no more than moved a muscle when that shadowed thing twisted itself around in a flash – and there on the floor before me was the profile of a man's head, upside down, listening – a man's head with a tail of hair.'

McCord got up hastily and stepped over in front of the state-room door, where he bent down and scratched a match.

'See,' he said, holding the tiny flame above a splintered scar on the boards. 'You wouldn't think a man would be fool enough to shoot at a shadow?'

He came back and sat down.

'It seemed to me all hell had shaken loose. You've no idea, Ridgeway, the rumpus a gun raises in a box like this. I found out afterwards the slug ricochetted into the galley, bringing down a couple of pans – and that helped. Oh yes, I got out of here quick enough. I stood there, half out of the companion, with my hands on the hatch and the gun between them, and my shadow running off across the top of the house shivering before my eyes like a dry leaf. There wasn't a whisper of sound in the world – just the pale water floating past and the sails towering up like a pair of twittering ghosts. And everything that crazy colour –

'Well, in a minute I saw it, just abreast of the mainmast, crouched down in the shadow of the weather rail, sneaking off forward very slowly. This time I took a good long sight before I let go. Did you ever happen to see black-powder smoke in the moonlight? It puffed out perfectly round, like a big pale balloon, this did, and for a second something was bounding through it – without a sound, you understand – something a shade solider than the smoke and big as a cow, it looked to me. It passed from the weather side to the lee and ducked behind the sweep of the mainsail like *that* –' McCord snapped his thumb and forefinger under the light.

'Go on,' I said. 'What did you do then?'

McCord regarded me for an instant from beneath his lids, uncertain. His fist hung above the table. 'You're –' He hesitated, his lips working vacantly. A forefinger came out of the fist and gesticulated before my face. 'If you're laughing, why, damn me, I'll –'

'Go on,' I repeated. 'What did you do then?'

'I followed the thing.' He was still watching me sullenly. 'I got up and went forward along the roof of the house, so as to have an eye on either rail. You understand, this business had to be done with. I kept straight along. Every shadow I wasn't absolutely sure of I *made* sure of – point-blank. And I rounded the thing up at the very stem – sitting on the butt of the bowsprit, Ridgeway, washing her yellow face under the moon. I didn't make any bones about it this time. I put the bad end of that gun against the scar on her head and squeezed the trigger. It snicked on an empty shell. I tell you a fact; I was almost deafened by the report that didn't come.

'She followed me aft. I couldn't get away from her. I went and sat on the wheel-box and she came and sat on the edge of the house, facing me. And there we stayed for upwards of an hour, without moving. Finally she went over and stuck her paw in the water-pan I'd set out for her; then she raised her head and looked at me and yawled. At sundown there'd been two quarts of water in that pan. You wouldn't think a cat could get away with two quarts of water in –'

He broke off again and considered me with a sort of weary defiance.

'What's the use?' He spread out his hands in a gesture of hopelessness. 'I knew you wouldn't believe it when I started. You *couldn't*. It would be a kind of blasphemy against the sacred institution of pavements. You're too damn smug, Ridgeway. I can't shake you. You haven't sat two days and two nights, keeping your eyes open by sheer teeth-gritting, until they got used to it and wouldn't shut any more. When I tell you I found that yellow thing snooping around the davits, and three bights of the boat-fall loosened out, plain on deck – you grin behind your collar. When I tell you she padded off forward and evaporated – flickered back to hell and hasn't been seen since, then – why, you explain to yourself that I'm drunk. I tell you –' He jerked his head back abruptly and turned to face the companionway, his lips still apart. He listened so for a moment, then he shook himself out of it and went on:

'I tell you, Ridgeway, I've been over this hulk with a foot-rule. There's not a cubic inch I haven't accounted for, not a plank I –'

This time he got up and moved a step toward the companion, where he stood with his head bent forward and slightly to the side. After what might have been twenty seconds of this he whispered, 'Do you hear?'

Far and far away down the reach a ferry-boat lifted its infinitesimal wail, and then the silence of the night river came down once more, profound and inscrutable. A corner of the wick above my head sputtered a little – that was all.

'Hear what?' I whispered back. He lifted a cautious finger toward the opening.

'Somebody. Listen.'

The man's faculties must have been keyed up to the pitch of his nerves, for to me the night remained as voiceless as a subterranean cavern. I became intensely irritated with him; within my mind I cried out against this infatuated pantomime of his. And then, of a sudden, there *was* a sound – the dying rumour of a ripple, somewhere in the outside darkness, as though an object had been let into the water with extreme care.

'You heard?'

I nodded. The ticking of the watch in my vest pocket came to my ears, shucking off the leisurely seconds, while McCord's finger-nails gnawed at the palms of his hands. The man was really sick. He wheeled on me and cried out, 'My God! Ridgeway – why don't we go out?'

I, for one, refused to be a fool. I passed him and climbed out of the opening; he followed far enough to lean his elbows on the hatch, his feet and legs still within the secure glow of the cabin.

'You see, there's nothing.' My wave of assurance was possibly a little over-done.

'Over there,' he muttered, jerking his head towards the shore lights. 'Something swimming.'

I moved to the corner of the house and listened.

'River thieves,' I argued. 'The place is full of –'

'*Ridgeway. Look behind you!*'

Perhaps it *is* the pavements – but no matter; I am not ordinarily a jumping sort. And yet there was something in the quality of that voice beyond my shoulder that brought the sweat stinging through the pores of my scalp even while I was in the act of turning.

A cat sat there on the hatch, expressionless and immobile in the gloom.

I did not say anything. I turned and went below. McCord was there already, standing on the farther side of the table. After a moment or so the cat followed and sat on her haunches at the foot of the ladder and stared at us without winking.

'I think she wants something to eat,' I said to McCord.

He lit a lantern and went out into the galley. Returning with a chunk of salt beef, he threw it into the farther corner. The cat went over and began to tear at it, her muscles playing with conclusive shadow-lines under the sagging yellow hide.

And now it was she who listened, to something beyond the reach of even McCord's faculties, her neck stiff and her ears flattened. I looked at McCord and found him brooding at the animal with a sort of listless malevolence. '*Quick!* She has kittens somewhere about.' I shook his elbow sharply. 'When she starts, now –'

'You don't seem to understand,' he mumbled. 'It wouldn't be any use.'

She had turned now and was making for the ladder with the soundless agility of her race. I grasped McCord's wrist and dragged him after me, the lantern banging against his knees. When we came up the cat was already amidships, a scarcely discernible shadow at the margin of our lantern's ring. She stopped and looked back at us with her luminous eyes, appeared to hesitate, uneasy at our pursuit of her, shifted here and there with quick, soft bounds, and stopped to fawn with her back arched at the foot of the mast. Then she was off with an amazing suddenness into the shadows forward.

'Lively now!' I yelled at McCord. He came pounding along behind me, still protesting that it was of no use. Abreast of the foremast I took the lantern from him to hold above my head.

'You see,' he complained, peering here and there over the illuminated deck. 'I tell you, Ridgeway, this thing –' But my eyes were in another quarter, and I slapped him on the shoulder.

'An engineer – an engineer to the core,' I cried at him. 'Look aloft, man.'

Our quarry was almost to the cross-trees, clambering up the shrouds with a smartness no sailor has ever come to, her yellow body cut by the moving shadows of the ratlines, a queer sight against the mat of the night. McCord closed his mouth and opened it again for two words: 'By gracious!' The following instant he had the lantern and was after her. I watched him go up above my head – a ponderous, swaying climber into the sky – come to the cross-trees, and squat there with his knees clamped around the mast. The clear star of the lantern shot this way and that for a moment, then it disappeared, and in its place there sprang out a bag of yellow light, like a fire-balloon at anchor in the heavens. I could see the shadow of his head and hands moving monstrously over the inner surface of the sail, and muffled exclamations without meaning came down to me. After a moment he drew out his head and called: 'All right – they're here. Heads! There below!'

I ducked at his warning, and something spanked on the planking a yard from my feet. I stepped over to the vague blur on the deck and picked up a slipper – a slipper covered with some woven straw stuff and soled with a matted felt, perhaps a half-inch thick. Another struck somewhere abaft the mast, and then McCord reappeared above and began to stagger down the shrouds. Under his left arm he hugged a curious assortment of litter, a sheaf of papers, a brace of revolvers, a grey kimono, and a soiled apron.

'Well,' he said when he had come to deck, 'I feel like a man who has gone to hell and come back again. You know I'd come to the place where I really believed that about the cat. When you think of it – By gracious! we haven't come so far from the jungle, after all.'

We went aft and below and sat down at the table as we had been. McCord broke a prolonged silence.

'I'm sort of glad he got away – poor cuss! He's probably climbing up a wharf this minute, shivering and scared to death. Over toward the gas-tanks, by the way he was swimming. By gracious! now that the world's turned over straight again, I feel I could sleep a solid week. Poor cuss! can you imagine him, Ridgeway –'

'Yes,' I broke in. 'I think I can. He must have lost his nerve when he made out your smoke and shinnied up there to stow away, taking the ship's papers with him. He would have attached some profound importance to them – remember, the "barbarian," eight thousand miles from home. Probably couldn't read a word. I suppose the cat followed him – the traditional source of food. He must have wanted water badly.'

'I should say! He wouldn't have taken the chances he did.'

'Well,' I announced, 'at any rate, I can say it now – there's another "mystery of the sea" gone to pot.'

McCord lifted his heavy lids.

'No,' he mumbled. 'The mystery is that a man who has been to sea all his life could sail around for three days with a man bundled up in his top and not know it. When I think of him peeking down at me – and playing off that damn cat – probably without realizing it – scared to death – by gracious! Ridgeway, there was a pair of funks aboard this craft, eh? Wow – yow – I could sleep –'

'I should think you could.'

McCord did not answer.

'By the way,' I speculated. 'I guess you were right about Björnsen, McCord – that is, his fooling with the foretop. He must have been caught all of a bunch, eh?'

Again McCord failed to answer. I looked up, mildly surprised, and found his head hanging back over his chair and his mouth opened wide. He was asleep.

John Masefield

A White Night

SOMETIMES when I am idle, my mind fills with a vivid memory. Some old night at sea, or in a tavern, or on the roads, or some adventure half forgotten, rises up in sharp detail, alive with meaning. The thing or image, whatever it may be, comes back to me so clearly outlined, under such strong light, that it is as though the act were playing before me on a lighted stage. Such a memory always appears to me significant like certain dreams. I find myself thinking of an old adventure, a day in a boat, a walk by still waters, the crying of curlews, or the call of wild swans, as though such memories, rather than the great events in life, were the things deeply significant. I think of a day beside a pool where the tattered reeds were shaking, and a fish leapt, making rings, as though the day were a great poem which I had written. I can think of a walk by twilight, among bracken and slowly moving deer, under a September moonrise, till I am almost startled to find myself indoors. For the most part my significant memories are of the sea. Three such memories, constantly recurring, appear to me as direct revelations of something too great for human comprehension. The deeds or events they image were little in themselves, however pleasant in the doing, and I know no reason why they should haunt me so strangely, so many years after they occurred.

One winter night, fourteen years ago, I was aboard a ship then lying at anchor in a great river. It was a fine night, full of stars, but moonless. There was no wind, but a strong tide was running, and a suck and gurgle sounded all along the ship's length, from the bows to the man-catcher. I had been dancing below-decks by lamplight with my shipmates, and had come up for a turn in the air before going to my hammock. As I walked the deck, under the rigging, with my friend, a pipe sounded from below, 'Away third cutters.' I was the stroke oar of the third cutter, and I remembered then that a man had been dining with the captain, and that he would be going ashore, and that he would need a red-baize cushion to sit upon, and a boat-rug to cover his knees. I ran below to get these things, and to haul the boat alongside from her boom. As I stepped into her with the gear, I heard the coxswain speaking to the officer of the watch. 'It's coming on very hazy, sir. Shall I take the boat's compass and the lantern?'

I noticed that it was growing very hazy. The lights of the ship were burning dim, and I could not see a long line of lights, marking a wharf, which had shone clearly but a few moments before. I put the cushion in the stern-sheets and arranged the rug for the visitor, and then stood up in my place, holding the boat to the gangway by the manrope. The coxswain came shambling down the ladder with his lantern and compass. The officer in charge of the boat came after him, with his oilskins on his arm. Then came the visitor, a tall, red-haired man, who bumped his hat off while coming through the entry-port. I could see the ship's side and the patches of yellow light at her ports, and the lieutenant standing on the gangway with his head outlined against the light.

We got out our oars and shoved off through the haze. The red-haired man took out a cigar and tried to light it, but the head of the match came off and burnt his fingers. He swore curtly. The officer laughed. 'Remember the boat's crew,' he said. In the darkness, amid the gurgle of the running water, over which the haze came stealthily, the words were like words heard in a dream. I repeated them to myself as I rowed, wondering where I had heard them before. It seemed to me that they had been said before, somewhere, very long ago, and that if I could remember where I should know more than any man knew. I tried to remember where I had heard them, for I felt that there was but a vague film between me and a great secret. I seemed to be outside a door opening into some strange world. The door, I felt, was ajar, and I could hear strange people moving just within, and I knew that a little matter, perhaps an act of will, perhaps blind chance, would fling the door wide, in blinding light, or shut it in my face. The rhythm of rowing, like all rhythm, such as dancing, or poetry, or music, had taken me beyond myself. The coxswain behind the back-board, with his head nodding down over the lantern, and the two men beneath him, seemed to have become inhuman. I myself felt more than human. I seemed to have escaped from time. We were eternal things, rowing slowly through space, upon some unfathomable errand, such as the Sphinx might send to some occult power, guarded by winged bulls, in old Chaldea.

When we ran alongside the jetty, the haze was thick behind us, like a grey blanket covering the river. I got out with the stern-fast, and held the lantern for the visitor to clamber out by. The officer ran up the jetty to a little shop at the jetty head where the ship's letters were left. The visitor thanked me for my help, and said 'Good night,' and vanished into the mist. His steps sounded on the slippery stones. They showed us that he was walking gingerly. Once he struck a ringbolt and swore. Then he passed the officer, and the two exchanged a few parting words. I thought at the time that the casual things in life were life's greatest mysteries. It seemed as though something had failed to happen; as though something – something beautiful – had been kept from the world by some blind chance or wilful fate. Who was the red-haired man, I wondered, that we, who had come from many wanderings and many sorrows, should take him to our memories for ever, for no shown cause? We should remember him for ever. He would be the august thing of that white night's rowing. We should remember him at solemn moments. Perhaps as we lay a-dying we should remember him. He had said good night to us and had passed on up the jetty, and we did not know who he was, nor what he was, and we should be gone in a few days' time, and we should never see him again. As for him, he would never think of us again. He would remember his dented hat, and his burnt finger, and perhaps, if it had been very good, his dinner.

When we shoved off again for the ship the haze was so thick that we could not see three feet in front of us. All the river was hidden in a coat of grey. The sirens of many steamers hooted mournfully as they passed up or down, unseen. We could hear the bell-signals from the hulks, half a mile away. Voices came out of the greyness, from nowhere in particular. Men hailed each other from invisible bridges. A boat passed us under oars, with her people talking. A confused noise of many screws beating irregularly, came over the muffled water. They might have been miles away – many miles or hard upon us. It is impossible to judge by sound in a haze so thick. We rowed on quietly into the unknown.

We were a long time rowing, for we did not know where we were, and the tide swept us down, and the bells and sirens puzzled us. Once we lay on our oars and rocked in a swell while some great steamer thrashed past hooting. The bells beat now near, now very far away. We were no longer human beings, but things much greater or much less. We were detached from life and time. We had become elemental, like the fog that hid us. I could have stayed in the boat there, rowing through the haze for all eternity. The grunt of the rowlocks, and the wash and drip of the oars, and the measured breath of the men behind me, keeping time to me, were a music passing harps. The strangeness and dimness of it all, and the halo round the coxswain's lantern, and the faces half seen, and the noises sounding from all sides impressed me like a revelation.

'Oars a minute,' said the coxswain. 'There's the fog-bell.'

Somewhere out of the grey haze a little silver bell was striking. It beat four strokes, and paused, and then again four strokes, and again a pause, from some place high above us. And then, quite near to us, we heard the long, shrill call of a pipe and a great stamp of feet upon hatchways.

'Good Lord! we're right on top of her,' said the officer. 'I see her boom. Ship ahoy!'

'Is that you, Carter?'

We bumped alongside, and held her there while the officer and coxswain ran up the gangway with the letters. We laid in the oars and unshipped the rudder, and a man came down the gangway for the red-baize cushion and the rug. 'Hook your boat on,' said the officer of the watch.

That is one of the memories which come back to me, when I am idle, with the reality of the deed itself. It is one of those memories which haunt me, as symbols of something unimagined, of something greater than life expressed in life. Why such a thing should haunt me I cannot tell, for the words, now they are written down, seem foolish. Within the ivory gate, and well without it, one is safe; but perhaps one must not peep through the opening when it hangs for a little while ajar.

Ralph Stock

Dead Reckoning

I HAVE killed a man because he disagreed with me.

Anything more futile it is hard to imagine in cold blood for by killing him I have proved nothing. He still holds his view. I know it because I have spoken to him *since* and he still laughs at me, though softly, compassionately, not as he laughed on that night when the absurdity happened.

Perhaps I am mad, but you shall judge. In any case, that is of no great importance, for by the time you read this, my confession – if, indeed, it is ever read – I shall have ceased to encumber the earth.

He was young and strong, and filled with that terrible self-assurance of youth that sets an older man's teeth on edge. During his short term of tuition in the schools of the South there was nothing that he had not learned to do better (in theory) than a man of fifty years' experience; and obstinate – but I must not let myself go. It is my duty to set down here precisely what happened, without prejudice, without feeling even, if that were possible. Yet as I write, my pulse quickens – I will wait a little. It is unfair to him to continue at present.

Here on this reef off the Queensland coast there are unbelievable quantities of fish. Even I have never seen so many, not of such brilliant colouring. It is possible to wade into the tepid water and catch them with the hand. I have caught hundreds today, for lack of something better to do – and set them free; for I will have no more blood on my hands, even that of a fish. Besides, what is the use? There is no drinking water here, nothing but blinding sunlight, a ridge of discoloured coral cleaving the blue mirror of the sea like a razor edge, and myself – a criminal perched upon it as upon a premature scaffold.

But I have overlooked the pickle bottle. It came to me floating, not quite empty, and corked against the flies, just as he and I had left it after the last meal. When the wreck sank, it must have risen from the fo'c'sle table and up through the hatch – it is curious that nothing else should rise – and it occurred to me that by its aid, and that of the little notebook with pencil attached which I always carry, it would be possible to set my case before the world. I must continue, or there may not be time to say all.

I am what they call an old man on Thursday Island, for none but blacks live to any age in the neighbourhood of this sun-baked tile on the roof of Australia. But I come of Old Country stock and blood will tell.

I have mixed little with others preferring the society of my only child, a daughter, to the prattlers and drinkers of a small equatorial community. Perhaps I have been too circumscribed, too isolated, from my fellow-creatures. I only know that until *he* came I was content. My small weather-board house ashore, the ketch in which I brought sandalwood from the mainland coast, were my twin worlds. In each all things were conducted according to my wishes – according, rather, to the methods I had evolved from long experience, and that their merits were borne out by results none could deny.

The house, with its small, well-tended garden, was the best on Thursday Island. My daughter, dutiful and intelligent, managed it according to my wishes, so that it ran like a well-oiled mechanism. And the ketch – that was my inviolable domain. Above and below decks, although only a twenty-ton-cargo-carrier, she would have put many a yacht to shame. There was nothing superfluous, nothing lacking. Everything aboard had its place and uses; that is how I contrived to work her single-handed for nearly ten years.

They called me a curmudgeon and a skinflint, but I could afford to smile. My cargoes were not so large as theirs, and took longer to gather, but while they were eating into their profits by paying wages and shares to lazy crews, mine came solely to myself, and never in all those years did I have a mishap. Trust an owner to look after his craft, say I, and trust none other.

Then, as I have said, *he* came. How he gained entrance I have never known, but he had a way with him, that boy, and when one evening I returned from a trip, he was sitting on the verandah with Doris. She was evidently embarrassed.

'This is Mr Thorpe, father,' she said, and went in to prepare super, which was late for the first time that I could remember.

'Indeed?' said I, and remained standing, a fact that Thorpe appeared to overlook, for he reseated himself with all the assurance in life.

'Yes,' he said in a manner that I believe is called 'breezy,' 'that is my name, Captain Brent, and I'm pleased to make your acquaintance. Have you had a good trip?'

'Passable,' said I. 'And now, if you'll excuse me, I must go in and change.'

'Oh, don't mind me,' returned Thorpe, spreading himself in the cane chair and lighting a cigarette; 'I'm quite comfortable.'

For a moment I stood speechless, then went into the house.

Doris was preparing the meal, but turned as I entered. Never before had I seen the look that I saw in her face at that moment – fear battling with resolve.

'Who is that boy?' I asked her.

'I have already told you, father,' she answered; 'he is a young man named Thorpe – Edward Thorpe.'

'Ah,' said I, momentarily at a loss, 'a young man – named Thorpe. And why does he come here?'

'To see me,' returned Doris in her quiet, even voice, but I saw that she trembled.

I took her by the arm.

'Girl,' said I, 'tell me all.'

'We love one another,' she told me, looking full into my eyes with no hint of timidity; 'we are engaged to be married.'

I could not speak. I could not even protest when, at no invitation of mine, this youth had the effrontery to come in to supper. The world – my twin worlds – rocked under my feet.

It was a terrible meal. I, speechless, at one end of the table, my daughter, pale, but courteous, at the other, and this clown sat between us, regaling us, as he no doubt thought, with anecdotes of life down South.

And this was not enough, but he must come into the kitchen afterwards and help to wash up. He said it made him feel more at home. Now, it has been my custom, ever since leaving a civilization that I abhor and finding comfort in this far corner of the earth, to help wash up when I am at home. The thing is part of the routine of life, and as such demands proper management. A nice adjustment of the water's temperature is necessary; for it too hot it may crack glass and china and ruin knife handles; and if too cold, in spite of a certain amount of soda, it fails to remove grease. Then, too, it is my invariable habit at the end to turn the wash-bowl upside down to drain, and spread the dishcloth upon it to dry. It occurs to me that these may appear small matters to some, but is not life composed of such, and do they not often turn out to be the greater? And our uninvited guest disorganized the entire routine by pathetic efforts at buffoonery such as tying one of Doris's aprons about his waist, making a napkin-ring climb his finger by a circular motion of the hand, and laughing openly at what he evidently regarded as our fads.

The spreading of the dishcloth on the wash-bowl appeared to amuse him most of all.

'I suppose you always do that,' he said.

'It is the custom in this house,' said I.

'And when you come to think of it, why not?' he reflected, with his handsome head at an angle.

'There are many things one has to come to think of before one knows anything,' said I.

And at that he laughed good-naturedly. He always laughed.

At length he went. From my easy-chair in the living-room I heard the last 'Good night' and his assured footfall on the verandah steps. Doris came straight to me. I knew she would. Perching herself on the arm of my chair, as she used to when a child, she encircled my shoulder with her arm.

'Do you hate him, father?' she asked me.

I answered her question with another.

'Do you fear me, Doris?' For the look in her face that evening had shocked me.

'I used to sometimes,' she said, 'but not now.'

'And what has worked the transformation?'

She leaned over and whispered in my ear.

I held her from me and studied her as though for the first time. She was young, beautiful, fragile, yet she was stronger than I. I am no fool. I knew that nothing I could do or say would have one particle of weight with her now. She loved, and was loved. So it is with women; and such is this miracle of a day, an hour, a fraction of time, that shatters lifelong fealty like glass.

'Then I have nothing to say,' said I.

'Nothing?' she questioned me, and again presently, 'nothing?'

And at last I heard myself muttering the absurd formula of wishes for their happiness.

It was bound to come some time. It had come, that was all, and I made the best of it. Of an evening that boy would sit with us and make suggestions for the betterment of the business – my business. He pointed out that new blood was needed – his blood. By heavens, how he talked! And there is an insidious power in words. Utter them often enough, with youthful enthusiasm behind them, and they resolve themselves into deeds.

I cannot explain even to myself how it came about, but this was the plan – to take my ketch to Sydney, where she would apparently realize an enormous sum as a converted yacht, and buy another, installing an auxiliary motor-engine with some of the profits. With an engine, and this new blood, it seemed, we were to make a fortune out of sandalwood in three years.

I wanted neither engine, new blood, nor fortune, yet in the end I gave way.

So it was that, rather late in the season, we let go moorings, he and I, and set sail for the South. For the first time in my life I had a crew. My inviolable domain was invaded. What with the thought of this, and the unworthy mission we were engaged upon, it was all I could do to look my ketch in the face. Those with the love of ships in their bones will understand.

More than once I caught Thorpe smiling at one or another of my own small inventions for the easier handling of the boat, or the saving of labour or space below; but he said nothing beyond calling them 'gadgets', a word that was new to me.

'Not a bad little packet,' he said, after the first hour of his trick at the tiller.

'I am glad to hear you say so,' said I, with an irony entirely lost on one of his calibre.

'But she ought to sail nearer the wind than his,' he added, staring up at the quivering top-sail. 'Six points won't do. Under-canvassed, that's what she is. By the way, when we get through the reef pass, what's the course?'

'Sou'-sou'-east,' said I.

'And where's your deviation card?'

'Never had to bother with one,' I told him.

He seemed thunderstruck.

'Of course, she's wooden,' he began; 'but surely -'

'The course is sou'-sou'-east,' I repeated, and went below.

From then onwards he took to reeling me off parrot-like dissertations on devioscopes, new pattern compasses, and what-not, until the sound of his voice sickened me. Amongst his other accomplishments, he had sat for a yachting master's ticket, and passed, though every one knew, it appeared, how much stiffer were the examinations nowadays than in the past, when half the men called ship's masters had no right to the title, or even knew the uses of a chronometer.

'Yet they managed to circumnavigate the globe,' I pointed out.

'By running down their latitude!' he scoffed.

'Perhaps,' said I, whereat he burst into a gale of laughter, and expressed the devout hope that I would never expect him to employ such methods.

'I expect you to do nothing but what you are told,' said I, exasperated beyond endurance. 'At the present moment you are not getting the best out of her. Give her another point, and make a note of time and distance in the scrap log hanging on yonder rail.'

'Dead reckoning,' he muttered contemptuously.

'Just that,' said I, and left him.

Why did I 'leave him'? Why did I 'go below'? At all costs I must be fair. I did both these things because I knew that he could argue me off my feet if I remained, that he knew more about deep-sea navigation than I, that I was one of those he had mentioned who are called ship's masters and have no right to the title, nor even knew the uses of a chronometer.

Such a confession is like drawing a tooth to me, but it is made. And as vindication I would point to my record - ten years, single-handed and by dead reckoning without mishap. Can an extra master show better?

As day succeeded day, the tension grew. Often I would sit on a locker gazing on my familiar and beloved surroundings and ask myself how long I could suffer them to be sneered at and despised. Trust small craft for discovering one man to another. Before three days and three nights had passed, we stood before each other, he and I, stripped to our souls. His every movement was an aggravation to me, especially when he played with the bespangled sextant and toy chronometer he had brought, and when each day, on plotting out my position on the chart according to dead reckoning, I found his, by observation, already there. I rubbed it out. I prayed that there would come such a fog as would obscure the sun and stars for ever.

And it was as though my prayer were answered, for that night we ran into a gale that necessitated heaving to. Luckily it was off the shore, and for forty-eight hours we rode it out in comparative comfort, until it died as suddenly as it had been born, and was succeeded by a driving mist that stilled the sea as though with a giant white hand.

'You see,' said Thorpe, 'dead reckoning is all right up to a point, as a check, but how do you know where you are now?'

'Can you tell me?' said I.

'Not until the mist clears,' he admitted.

'Well, then – ' said I.

He flung away from me with an impatient movement.

'These are the methods of Methuselah,' he muttered.

'Nevertheless,' I returned, the blood throbbing at my temples, 'I know our position at this moment better than any upstart yachtsman.'

He turned and looked at me strangely, then of a sudden his mouth relaxed into a smile. At that moment I could have struck him.

'There is no call for us to quarrel,' he said gently, 'but how – how can you possibly know where we have drifted to in the last forty-eight hours?'

'I have my senses,' said I, 'and to prove them we will carry on.'

'In this mist?'

'In this mist,' I thundered. 'The wind is fair, the course is now south-half-east, and you'll oblige me by taking the tiller.'

He seemed about to speak, but evidently changed his mind, and turned abruptly on his heel.

In silence we shook out the reef and got under way. In silence we remained until the end of his watch, when the mist was dispersed by a brazen sun. Thorpe at once took a sight, and again at noon, and when I had plotted our position on the chart, he was still poring over volumes of nautical tables.

Towards dusk he came to me at the tiller.

'Are you holding this course after dark?' he asked.

'That is as may be,' said I.

'Because if you are,' he went on, as though I had not spoken, 'you'll be on the Barrier Reef inside of five hours.'

'I thank you for the information,' said I, and he went below.

He knew ship's discipline; I'll say that for him. He might consider myself and my methods archaic, but he recognized my authority and carried out instructions. I am aware that up to the present my case appears a poor one, but I can convey no idea of the pitch to which I was brought by these eternal bickerings, by the innovation of another will than my own, and the constant knowledge that he was laughing at me up his sleeve.

But it was a little thing that brought matters to a climax. It is always the little things.

With a fair wind, and in these unfrequented waters, it has always been my habit to lash the tiller and eat in comfort. We were washing up after supper, or, rather, he was washing and I was drying, for the dryer puts away the utensils, and I knew better the proper place for each. At the end he tossed the dishcloth in a sodden mass upon the table and turned to go.

'The dishcloth, if you remember,' said I, 'is spread on the washbowl to dry.'

He turned and looked at me, and in his eyes I saw a sudden, unaccustomed flame leap to life.

'It'll do it good to have a change,' he said.

'I do not think so,' said I.

'Naturally,' he returned; 'but I do.'

'And who is the master of this ship?' I asked him.

'As for that, you are,' he admitted, 'but a dishcloth is another matter.' Suddenly he dropped on to a locker and laughed, though there was a nervous catch in it. 'Heavens!' he giggled, 'we're arguing over a dishcloth now!'

'And why not,' said I, 'if you don't know how to use one? Will you be so good as to put it in its proper place?'

He did not answer, but sat looking down at his naked feet.

'This is impossible,' he muttered.

'As you will,' said I.

'It can't go on; I can't stand it.'

'Do you imagine it is any pleasanter for me?' I asked him.

'And whose fault is it?'

'That is a matter of opinion,' said I; 'but in the meantime things are to be done as I wish. Kindly put the dishcloth in its proper place.'

Again he did not answer, but when he looked up it was with compressed lips.

'You are a frightful old man,' he said. Those were his words. I remember every one, and they came from him in deliberate, staccato sentences.

'You are that, though no one has dared to tell you so until this minute. You have lived in a rut of your own making so deep and so long that you don't know you're in it. That is your affair, but when you drag others in with you, it is time to speak. I rescued Doris – bless her – just in time! Why, man, can't you see? There's no light down there; you can never take a look at yourself and laugh. You have no more sense of humour than a fish. If you had, this absurd quibble could never have come to a head. We should have been sitting here laughing instead. Think of it – a dishcloth! You are my senior; I ought not to be talking like this to you, but I am; it's just been dragged out of me, and you can take it or leave it. Why not open up a bit – do something different just because it's different, admit there may be something others know that you don't, fling the dishcloth in a corner . . .'

Those were some of the things he said to me, and I stood there listening to them from a – from my future son-in-law on my own ship. It seemed incredible to me now, but I was dazed with the unexpectedness of this attack. All that remained clearly before me was the issue of the dishcloth. In the midst of his endless discourse I repeated my command, whereat he burst into another of his inane fits of laughter.

'You find it amusing,' said I in a voice I scarce recognized as my own.

'Amusing!' he chuckled. 'Think – try and think – a dishcloth!'

'And one that you will put in its proper place,' I told him.

'What makes you think that?' he said, sobering a little.

'Because I say so.'

'And if I refuse?' His face was quite grave now. He leant forward, as though interested in my reply. Somehow the sight of it – this handsome, impertinent face of his – caused a red mist to swim before my eyes.

'You will be made to,' I said.

'Ah!' was all he answered at the moment, and resumed the study of his feet. If he had remained so, all might have been well. I cannot tell. I only know that at that moment one word stood for him between life and death, and he chose to utter it.

'How?'

I tried to show him, that was all. I swear that was my sole intention. But he was obstinate, that boy. I had not thought it possible for a man to be as obstinate as he.

My weight carried him to the floor; besides, I am strong, and the accumulated fury of days and nights were behind me. He was like a doll in my hands, yet a doll that refused to squeak when pressed. There is a sail-rack in the fo'c's'le, and we were under it, my back against it, my knee at his chest; and I asked him, lying there laughing up at me, if he intended to do as I had ordered. He rolled his head in a negative. It was all he could do, and the pressure was increased. I must have asked him many times, and the answer was invariably the same. At the last something gave beneath my knee, and his jaw dropped, and no movement came from him, even from the heart.

The ripple of water past the ketch's sides brought me back to the present. I rose and stood looking down on him. As I live, it seemed that there was a smile still upon his face!

Of the rest I have no clear recollection. At one moment I was standing there trying – trying to realize what I had done; the next I was flung against the bulkhead as the ketch struck and rose – I can describe it in no other way – struck and rose. Even as I rushed on deck to be caught by a roller and hurled headlong, it seemed to me that a mocking voice called after me: 'Dead Reckoning!'

It was the Barrier Reef.

And for me it is the Barrier Reef to the end, which is not far off. When

I came to, the ketch had sunk, and I tried again to think. I have been trying ever since, and I can get no further than that I have killed him – for a dishcloth; that if by some miracle I am rescued, such is the message I shall have for Doris . . . Is it comedy or tragedy? I am not so sure now. *He* seemed to find it amusing to the very end, and he was right in some things. Perhaps he is right in this.

I never laugh? Did I not catch myself laughing aloud just now? Perhaps I am developing, somewhat late in life, to be sure, the 'sense of humour' he tells me I lack . . . I have finished. It is for you to read and judge.

The foregoing with such editing as was necessary to render it intelligible, is the message I found in a pickle bottle firmly wedged amongst the mangrove roots of a creek in the Gulf of Carpentaria. It must have been there for years.

I was duck-shooting at the time, but somehow, after happening on to this quaint document besmeared with pickle juice, my interest in the sport flagged. I wanted to know more, and there is only one way to do that on Thursday Island – ask Evans. Consequently, that evening found me, not for the first time, on his wide verandah, discussing whisky and soda, and the impossible state of the shell market.

'By the way,' I ventured presently, 'did you ever know a Captain Brent?'

'Still know him, for the matter of that,' said Evans. 'Why?'

'Then he – I mean he still lives on TI,' I stammered like a fool.

'Certainly. I used to buy his sandalwood. Buy his son-in-law's now.'

'His son-in-law's?'

Evans rolled over in his chair and grinned at me.

'What's the game?' he questioned good-naturedly. 'I never saw such a fellow.' He rolled back again. 'But, come to think of it, there might be something in him for you. The old man's ketch is the first thing I ever heard of to jump the Barrier Reef. I thought that'd make you sit up. But it's the truth. Ask Thorpe – he was aboard when she did it. He and the old man were going South for something – I forget what – and they took the Great Barrier bow on at night. It's been done before, you know, but never quite like that. Must have struck it in a narrow place or something. Anyway, Thorpe says that ketch jumped like a two-year-old, slithered through rotten coral for a bit, and plumped into deep water beyond, carried by the surf, I expect, and nothing more to show for it than a scored bilge – oh, and a couple of broken ribs – Thorpe's, not the ketch's. He was beaten up pretty considerably when we took him ashore. Is there anything else I can serve you with today, sir?'

Evans is a good fellow, but provokingly incomplete.

'Yes,' said I. 'What happened to the old man?'

'Oh, he rushed on deck at the first shock, it seems, and was promptly bowled over the side by a breaker. But there's no killing him. He just sat on the reef, thinking his ketch sunk and Thorpe dead, until someone came and took him off. Shook him up, though. He's never been quite the same since. Which is all to the good, most of us think.'

The next evening I took occasion to wander down TI's grass-grown main street, through its herds of cavorting goats, and up the galvanized hillside to where a neat little weather-board house stood well back from the road.

In the garden, enjoying the cool of the evening, were four people – a white-bearded man seated in a cane-chair, a bronzed giant, prone and smoking, on the grass, and a woman beside him, sitting as only a woman can. Curiously enough, their eyes were all turned in the same direction – to where, in short, the fourth member of the party was engaged in the solemn procession of learning to 'walk alone'. His progress towards his mother's outstretched arms was as erratic as such things usually are – a few ungainly steps, a tottering pause, and an abrupt but apparently painless collapse.

'Seven!' exclaimed the white-bearded man, with an air of personal accomplishment.

'I made it five.' grinned the giant.

'I said seven,' boomed the other, and I left them at it.

They were Captain Brent and his son-in-law, and somehow I wanted to preserve that picture of them intact.

That, too, was partly why at the summit of the hill I tore my quaint, pickle-stained document into minute fragments and scattered them to the four winds of Torres Straits.

Eden Phillpotts

The Monkey

THEY sat together forward, under scant shadows, while the *Land Crab*, a little coasting schooner, lay nearly becalmed in the Caribbean. Her sails flapped idly; hot air danced over the deck and along the bulwarks. Now and then a spar creaked lazily, or a block went 'chip, chip,' as the *Land Crab* rolled on a swell. The sun blazed over the foreyard-arm, the heat was tremendous, but Pete and Pete basked in it and loved it. Neither saw necessity for a straw of head covering; indeed Pete the greater wore no clothes at all. He sat watching Pete the less; anon he put forth a small black hand for a banana; then, with forehead puckered into a world of wrinkles and furrows, he inspected his namesake's work; and later, tired of squatting in the sun, hopped on to the bulwark and up the mizzen shrouds.

Peter the greater was a brown monkey, treasured property of the skipper; and Pete the less, now cleaning some flying-fish for the cook, was a negro boy, treasured property of nobody – a small lad, with a lean body, more of which appeared than was hidden by the rags of his shirt, and great black eyes like a dog's. He was, in fact, a very dog-like boy. When the men cursed him he cowered, and hung his head and slunk away, sometimes showing a canine tooth; when they were in merry mood he frisked and fawned and went mad with delight. But chance for joy seldom offered. He had a stern master, and an awful responsibility in the shape of Pete the greater. This active beast, under God and the skipper, was Pete's boss. The sailors said that he always touched his wool to it, and everybody knew that he talked to it for hours at a time. When the lad first came aboard, Captain Spicer put the matter in a nutshell.

'See here, nig – this monkey's your pigeon; you've just got to watch it, an' feed it, an' think of it all the time. And bear in mind as he's a darned sight more valuable than anything else aboard this ship. So keep your weather eye lifting, and remember there'll be hell round here if harm comes to Pete.'

'I's call Pete too, Cap'n sar,' the boy had answered, grinning at what had struck him as a grand joke.

'Are you? Well, you get pals with Pete number one. That's what you've got to do.'

But apes are capricious, and Pete the less found his pigeon aboard the *Land Crab* no bed of roses. For that matter the rest of the hands suffered too. Nathan Spicer was a bald-headed old man with an evil temper – one blighted by sorrow and affliction, hard to please, bad to sail with. Dick Bent, the mate, had known his captain in past years, when the sun shone on him, and he explained the position from his former knowledge.

'It's like this 'ere – Nature filled the old sweep with the milk of human kindness; then she up and sent a thunderstorm of troubles and turned it sour. I've sailed on and off with him these twenty year, and I mind when he kept his foot on his temper, an' were a very tidy member o' seafarin' society. But after his missis died and his kid died, then he – what had married old and was wrapped up in the woman – why, then he cast off all holds, and chucked religion, and wished he could see the world in hell, and done his little best to help send it there. Men gets that way when things turn contrariwise. Not but what there's good hid in him too.'

But Bent's shipmates – three mongrel negroes and two Englishmen – failed to find the buried treasure. Skipper Spicer was always the same, with painful monotony. Only the man, Duck Bent, and the monkey, Pete, could pull with him. The rest of the crew suffered variously, for the captain, though no longer young, was rough and powerful. He had outbursts of passion that presented a sorry sight for gods and men. Such paroxysms seemed likely enough to end life for him some day; and just as likely to end life for another.

The negro boy scraped out his flying-fish and cut off their tails and wings, then he peeled a pannikin of sweet potatoes and talked to his charge.

'Marse Pete,' he said gravely, 'you's a dam lucky gem'-man, sar – de mose lucky gem'man aboard de *Lan' Crab*. You frens wid cap'n a'ways. He nebber sharp wid you – nebber; but he dat sharp wid me, sar, dat I'se sore all over de backside all de time. I fink you might say word to cap'n for me. Marse Pete, for I'se mighty kind nigger to you, sar.'

The monkey was chewing another banana. It stripped off the skin with quick black fingers, filled its mouth, stuffed its cheeks;, and then munched and munched and looked at Pete. It held its head on one side as though thinking and weighing each word, and Pete felt quite convinced that it understood him. The boy himself was ten years old. He had entered the world undesired and knew little of it, save that sugar-cane was sweet in the mouth but hard to come by, honestly or otherwise. Pete the greater lived in his master's cabin, and Pete the less often heard the skipper talking to him. If the captain could exchange ideas with his monkey, surely a nigger might do so; and it comforted the boy to chatter his miseries and empty his heart to the beast. Nobody on board had time or inclination to attend to him.

'I wish you was me and me was you, sar, for I has berry bad time aboard dis boat, but you has all b'nana an' no work -an' – an' – don't be so spry, Marse Pete!' as the monkey went capering aloft. 'One day you run 'long dem spars too often and fall in de sea to Marse Shark. Den what de boss do wid me?'

It happened that Bent was lying full sprawl behind a hatchway, smoking and grinning, as he listened to these remarks. Now he lifted a funny, small head, with a red beard, and answered the question.

'Old man'd skin you, nig, and then throw you after the monkey.' he answered.

'I guess he would, sar.'

'So keep alive. Why, you might as well steal skipper's watch as let the animal there get adrift.'

The skipper came on deck and both Petes saw him at the same moment. One touched his wool and ambled forward to the galley; the other came down the ratlines head first, and leapt chattering to the captain's shoulder, a favourite perch. His master had owned the monkey five years. It belonged once to his mulattress wife; and when she was dying, she specially mentioned it and made it over to him. That and his watch were the only treasures he had in the world. With his brown wife and his home in Tobago, the man had been happy, even God-fearing, but the first baby killed its mother and, dying also, left a wrecked life behind. Nathan Spicer cared for nothing now, and consequently feared nothing. It is their interest on earth, not the stake in eternity, that makes men cowards.

II

THE *Land Crab*, delayed by light winds, was some days overdue at Trinidad, and the skipper exploded in successive volcanoes from dawn till dusk. He was always in a rage, and, as Bent observed:

'If this sight o'energy, and cussing and swearing and to helling the ship's comp'ny, was only shoved into the elements, we'd 'a' had half a gale o' wind by now. The old man'll bust 'is biler, sure as death, 'fore he's done with it.'

But the winds kept baffling, and swearing did not mend them, nor yet blows, nor yet footfall with Pete the boy. There is no reason to suppose that Skipper Spicer disliked Peter overmuch – not more than he hated any boy; but he was brutal, and needed something to kick at times. Moreover, a kick does not shown on a negro, and many imagine that it is the only way of explaining that you disagree with him.

Once the mate ventured to intercede by virtue of his long acquaintance.

'We're old pals, Cap'n,' he said, 'and meanin' no disrespect, it's like this 'ere – you're killing that little black devil. 'E's small, and you do welt that 'ard. It's cause he's a good boy I mention it. If he was a bad 'un, then I'd say, "lather on," and I'd help. But he minds his pigeon.'

'Which you'd better do likewise,' answered the skipper.

'All right, boss. Only it's generally allowed now that nigs is human, same as us, and has workin' souls also.'

'Drivel! and rot! I don't have none of that twaddle aboard this ship. I know – nobody better'n me – 'cause I was a psalm-singer myself among the best. And what's come of it? There ain't no God in these latitoods anyway, else why did he play it so dirty on me? If there's any manner of God at all, he killed my wife and my child for fun, and I don't take no stock in a God that could do that. I'll rip forrard my own way now, till he calls for my checks, which he's quite welcome to, any time – damn him. But 'tis all bunkum and mumbo-jumbo. Nobody's got a soul no more'n my monkey, so there's a end of the argument.'

'Soul or none, 'e's a deal of sense for sartin,' admitted the mate, 'a 'mazing deal of sense. An' he takes kind to t'other Pete. If 'e could talk now, I bet he'd say to give the boy a chance, off and on, to get a whole skin over his bones for a change.'

'Which if he did,' answered the other, 'I should say to him as I do to you: to mind his own blasted bus'ness.'

But the men were friends in half an hour, for a fair wind came up out of the sea at dusk, the *Land Crab* plodded along and Spicer quickly thawed.

'Darn the old tub, she makes some of them new-fangled boats look silly yet!' he said to Bent, as, a day later, they lumbered through the Dragon's Teeth to Port of Spain.

After leaving Trinidad, the little coaster proceeded to Tobago for a cargo of coconuts, and the crew viewed the circumstance with gratification, for the most heavy-witted amongst them never failed to notice how a visit to his former home softened the old man. On this occasion, as upon past trips, the palm-crowned mountains of Tobago brought a measure of peace into the skipper's heart, whilst a fair wind and a good cargo tended to improve that condition. All hands reaped benefit and to Dick Bent the captain grew more communicative than usual.

They walked the deck together one morning on the homeward passage to Barbados, and Spicer lifted a corner of the curtain hiding his past.

'Then it was good to live like, but when my missus went "west," and took the baby along with her, life changed. Now there's only two things in all creation I care a red cent about. One's a beast, t'other an old gold watch – pretty mean goods to set your heart on, but all as I've got in the whole world.'

'It's a mighty fine watch,' said Bent.

'It is, and chain too, for that matter. I was lookin' at 'em in my cabin only half an hour past.' He brightened as he thought of the trinket, and continued, 'I doubt there's many better'n me would fancy that chain across their bellies, but she – '

'Lord deliver us, look aft!' sang out the mate suddenly, interrupting and pointing to the hatch of the companion.

THE MONKEY

Spicer's monkey had just hopped up on deck, and from his black paw hung the skipper's watch and chain. Pete the greater ambled along towards the bulwark, and a sweat burst from his master's face as he called to the brute in a strange voice. But Pete was perverse. He reached the bulwark and the skipper's nerve died in him, while Bent dared not to take a step towards hastening the threatened catastrophe, or identifying himself therewith. It was a trying moment as the monkey made for his favourite perch on the mizzen rigging, and while he careered forward on all fours, the watch bumped, bumped against the ship's side. The sound brought the blood with a rush to Skipper Spicer's head. Patience was no virtue of his at the best, and he jumped forward with a curse. The man had his hand within six inches of the watch when Pete squeaked and dropped it into the sea. There was a splash, a gleam of gold, and the treasure sank, flashing and twinkling down through the blue, dwindling to a bright, submerged snake, then vanishing for ever. A great gust of passion shook the skipper and tied his tongue. He tried to swear, but could only hiss and growl like an angry beast. Then he seized the monkey by the scruff of the neck as it jumped for his shoulder, shook it and flung it overboard with a shower of oaths. A red light blinded him, he felt his temples bursting, and he reeled away below, not stopping to see a brown head rise from the foam of the splash where Pete had fallen. The monkey fought for it, as one may see a rat driven off shipboard into the deep water. Two terrified eyes gazed upwards at his home, while the *Land Crab* swept by him; his red mouth opened with a yell, and his black paws began beating the water hard as he fell astern. Presently Pete sank for the first time. Then he came up again and went on fighting.

But the skipper saw nothing. He only felt the hot blood surging through his head as he flung himself on his bunk, face downwards. For a moment he thought death had gripped him; but the threatened evil passed, and his consciousness did not depart. He guessed that he had been near apoplexy. Then thoughts came and flooded his brain with abomination of desolation. He lay with his bald head on his arms and turned his mind back into the past. He remembered so much, and every shaft of memory brought him back with a round turn to the present. There was the lemon-tree with Pete's perch on it. His wife had loved the monkey. He could see her now kissing its nose. And she had died with the gold watch ticking under her head. Her wedding ring was upon the chain of it. She had tried to put it on his little finger before she went, but it would not get over the second joint, so she had slipped it upon the watch-chain. Now God in heaven could tell what loathsome fish was nosing it under the sea. And her monkey, her last gift to him, a live meal for a shark. Now the wide world remained to him, empty – save for the thought of what he had done.

He lay heedless of time for near three hours. Then he sat up and looked round the cabin. As he did so the door opened, Bent's small head peeped in and the mate spoke:

'Fit as a fiddle, boss; only a flea or two missing.'

Then the man shut the cabin door again. But he left something behind. Pete the greater chattered and jumped to his perch in the corner, and from there on to his master's berth. He was dry, warm and much as usual apparently; and he bore no malice whatever. Spicer glared and his breath caught in his throat. Then he grabbed the brute to him till it squeaked, while Nathan snuffled horrible but grateful oaths.

There was only one soul aboard the *Land Crab* who would have gone into a shark-haunted sea to save a monkey, and he did not think twice about it. He came on deck too late to see the catastrophe, though in time to note Pete the greater in the jaws of death. Had he known how the monkey came into the Caribbean he might have doubted the propriety of attempting a rescue; but he did not know, and so he joined it, feeling they might as well die together as perish apart. The boy could swim like a duck, and as Bent lowered a boat smartly, and the sharks held off, it was not long before Pete and Pete came aboard again. But, meantime, the master in his bunk did not even know that the ship had been hove to.

They emptied the water out of Pete the monkey and dried him, and they gave Pete the negro some rum. Both were jolly in an hour; and Skipper Spicer chose to take peculiar views of the gravity of the incident. He never kicked his cabin-boy again.

James Gould Cozzens

SS *San Pedro*

Anthony supposed it was ten o'clock when the fore-and-aft bulkhead in upper hold number one stove. Two cased automobiles shifted fifteen feet to port, knocking down the wall of the port bunk-room. The wedges probably came loose when they had lain-to while wind and sea on their port quarter shook them so heavily. That helpless half-hour had been a little worse than futile, then. He went forward with Mr Eberly. The junior second officer said, 'Well, maybe the old man will feel better now. We got something wrong here all right.'

Anthony understood Mr Eberly's attitude, but he understood too Captain Clendening's earlier exasperation at their failure to find anything which would account for the list. He said nothing now, viewing the bunk-room attentively. In the working alleyway there was water over his ankles. At the half-door Mr Driscoll was still busy in a grim, conscientious silence. He had several seamen with him and they were trying to tighten the dogs with a persistence which had become, considering the simplicity of the task, merely maddening. Anthony had an impatient desire to get at that job himself and finish it up. It was too senseless. They had been working there off and on for eight hours without effecting a change. To avoid any such officiousness he turned back to Mr Eberly and said, 'We'd gone over pretty far to make them slide. This sea will have to go down before we can do much. I don't believe they'll move again.'

'Say, listen, white man,' rose a querulous voice from the fireman's forecastle beyond, 'how we sleep?'

'Pipe down!' called Anthony sharply.

'We got water, mister.'

He went up the passage. 'Oh,' he said, 'you have a port out.'

The bunk-room was running underfoot. Two electric bulbs burned, and sickly morning light came with the recurring splashes of water through the broken port. A strong smell arose; wet wool and bedding, old sweat. Wrapped in blankets, like lively mummies on shelves, forms stirred, white eyeballs rolled in the shadows. The crazy man, Quail, caught the iron bunk post above, swung himself out and down with one arm, like a chimpanzee. He landed squatly on his feet in the shallow water. 'I want to be home,' he moaned. He beat his great swinging fist on his chest; his voice rolled and boomed from the depths. 'I got those home-again blues.' His conical skull swayed from side to side. 'Home,' he chanted, 'knock on the door!'

'Lay off, nigger,' snapped Anthony. 'I'll have the carpenter in.'

'Quail, he think he swim. Long way New York, Quail.' Laughter exploded richly in the bunks.

'Quail, he feel water, he fear soap to come!'

Quail held on to the post. 'Home, just as before,' he moaned. 'Home again, to roam no more . . .'

Most of the late morning Mr MacGillivray had a crew on the ash-ejector valve. It must have worked loose during the heavy weather while they were heaved-to earlier. By noon they had it tight again, but water was pouring smoothly into the stokehole by the bunker chutes. It slopped around the dog box and washed back and forth on the plates. Perhaps a bunker-hatch cover had gone and Mr MacGillivray suggested this to the bridge. He did not know whether they had done anything about it or not but he had started a pump at half-past ten and still needed it. In fact he would have used all his pumps but he had been ordered to empty the rest of the port ballast-tanks. Meanwhile he was clearing his bilge by not more than a foot an hour and the whole place was in a mess, with pressure falling off. It was useless to tell the fire-room to shake her up. The men worked resentfully with a psychological slowness in a flooded stokehole. Mr MacGillivray wished loudly and audibly to God that they were an oil, independent of firemen with wet feet and trimmers who were constantly losing their rakes in the shallow water.

It was his only public concession to the annoyances of the situation, which were, to his mind, many. Among other things, he wouldn't get to luncheon and he had a nice crowd at his table, including two good-looking women who called him chief and knew a funny story when they heard one – well, that was the way it always worked, and probably they were seasick anyway. There would be plenty more meals when they got South and had nicer weather. At the moment it was still remarkably rough. Much rougher than there was any need for it to be, he decided, having gone above a moment for the purpose. Most of it was the half-witted way they handled the ship.

Half-past three, declared the clock on the stairs which Anthony had just passed, moving down the port alleyway of the C deck. He was going aft to find out what had been done five minutes before by a green sea taken broad on the quarter. It pooped them with a shock like a hill falling aboard. Anthony could not figure it out – how, in view of wind, weather, and the *San Pedro*'s course, it even got there. He was extraordinarily tired. In this state, the ocean became almost personified; a purposeful and malicious agent, driving its heavy assaults to the unexpected and unguarded points. At the *San Pedro*'s heavy stagger, Captain Clendening went out and looked aft? Obviously a boat had gone from the steerage super-structure, for one thing. The supports of the after-bridge were twisted. White water cascaded endlessly off the poop-deck as the fantail shook itself free. You could hear the descending crash all the way forward. He said without emphasis, 'Find out what carried away, Mr Bradell.'

Anthony went, as smartly as he could make his aching legs move. He was certain that it would prove to have been particularly, wantonly, destructive. The steerage passengers were probably in a panic. In fact, there was no reason to suppose they hadn't lost a few people overboard. Anthony reviewed these possibilities in a stupor of resentment. A figure was approaching him in the alleyway and he faltered a moment, trying to calculate by the lethargic lurch of the tilted floor whether to pass right or left.

'Hallo, Bradell,' she said. 'Such a nice day, isn't it?'

She moved a little with the shift underfoot, and managed, intentionally or not, to block the whole alleyway, so he had to halt. 'Sorry,' he said. 'I've got to get aft.'

'Listen, Bradell,' she said. 'Do something about this. Clara and tons of people are sick as dogs. And I can't even get a bath. The bath-steward says we aren't level enough. I'll be positively filthy if it keeps up many weeks.' She regarded him with clear good-humour and he saw that her eyes were blue. 'You don't look well, Bradell,' she continued critically. 'Have a sleepless night? So did I. I couldn't get my mind off you. And the food is atrocious, such of it as stays on the table. It was bad enough before.'

'Sorry,' repeated Anthony. 'Don't worry. Everything is all right.'

All the woodwork creaked and cried out with the roll. She put a hand on his arm and said, 'Good Lord, is it as bad as that?'

She seemed obscurely to cling to him, impeding his thought as well as his progress. He felt too tired to shake her off, so he said, 'No danger at all. Everything is all right.'

'Listen, Bradell,' she begged. 'Tell me how bad it is. I'll be simply furious if I find out afterwards we almost sank and I didn't even know. A girl has to have some kick out of life.'

'Everything is all right,' said Anthony, looking at her.

She frowned a little, tightening the fingers on his arm.

'I thought at first there couldn't be anything wrong,' she admitted, 'because so many of the passengers were scared. Listen, Bradell, why don't you say it's the worst storm you've seen in ninety-seven years at sea, or something?'

'No danger,' he said. 'I've got to get aft.'

'Bradell,' she pleaded. 'You don't hate me enough to go and drown all these innocent people too, do you? Besides, I told you I damn well didn't want to drown.'

'All right,' he exploded wearily. 'You won't. Don't be such a fool.'

Her face was getting whiter and whiter under the rouge. 'Listen,' she said, somewhat more huskily. 'I've got plenty of nerve, but you have to tell me one thing.' She hesitated an instant. 'Bradell, are you sure that doctor man went ashore?'

'I've got to get aft,' said Anthony, 'I can't talk to you.'

'Bradell, you weren't fooling me?'

'I can't talk to you,' said Anthony. 'Please step aside.'

'I don't know,' she said, whiter still, 'whether I'd rather have him really here, or have him not really here.' She moistened her lips.

'I've got to get aft,' said Anthony.

She moved, backing against the white-panelled wall, extending a lax arm on either side of her to grasp the hand-rail. She murmured, 'Goodbye, Bradell.'

He passed her. Although he did not look, he could feel her still there, her dark head up, leaning against the wall mutely, her blue eyes on his retreating back.

In the wireless-room Smith, the first operator, regarded Morris without favour. Morris was on duty. He had, as usual, the phones pushed off one ear. A cigarette nodded up and down as he hummed to himself. His tobacco-dyed forefinger kept the key in a vibrating, whining chatter – $QSU - QRN - QRU$ . . . The San Pedro's WPRV went on to the end. He locked his hands in back of his head and sucked at the cigarette.

'Who was that?' asked Smith, still sleepy.

'San Pablo.'

'We aren't reporting anything?'

'Having a fine time. Wish you were here. Want me to write a poem, or tell 'em the one about the stuffed monkeys?'

'It doesn't feel so good to me,' said Smith. 'Where did we get all this water?'

'Elephant charged the camera,' admitted Morris, 'but I dropped him at twenty paces. He's in the wastepaper basket.'

'Funny boy, aren't you?' marvelled Smith. 'Are we all right?'

'As advertised,' agreed Morris. 'These magnificent vessels are unsurpassed in comfort and luxury. Having been specially constructed for tropical voyaging, the ventilation of every room is perfect – just feel it,' he invited, turning up his collar. 'Running water, too,' he added, 'in every room now. Some with baths.'

'Don't, I'll die!' grunted Smith.

'Appetizing meals to delight the keen appetites aroused by the bracing sea air –' He seized a partly consumed ham sandwich from the plate beside him. 'Do take some more caviar, count,' he urged. 'It will only be thrown out.'

'Say, listen,' said Smith. 'Is that all we get to eat?'

'That? You don't even get that. That's mine. Try and find another. While you were absent they procured five tons of sea water somewhere at great expense and put them in the ranges. Didn't they consult you?'

'After the applause dies down, let's see the bridge orders.'

'Help yourself,' said Morris cordially. 'The old man keeps wanting to know where the *San Pablo* is, as if I give a damn! When I get them, he doesn't want them for anything. Their lad told me for God's sake to leave them alone. That shows how little he's been out. Nothing like a valve transmitter in unscrupulous hands, I always say. We'll bother them, if you want to know, from thirty-five to forty-five on twenty-one hundred continuous every hour for the rest of the night.'

'What's the idea?'

'Oh, just a little thing I tossed off while I was waiting. It isn't finished yet, of course, but the old man certainly liked it.'

'Listen, I'll relieve you now. Like a good sport, go down and get me a sandwich, will you?'

'Wrong,' protested Morris.

'Listen, have I got to order you?'

'No, no, don't feel that way. Accidents happen.'

'Go on, get up. You got a drag down there.'

'Say, you certainly presume on your white hairs, Lord Algy,' groaned Morris. All together now; American Marconi Company, I love you!'

The narrow promenade around the fantail had lost a long section of rail. On the port side the third-class pantry had been flushed out clean. The door was carried away; every detachable object was swept through with the rail. For the moment it would be simpler to assume that no one had been on duty there, Anthony decided. He continued around the stern. Not a square inch of glass was left in any exposed window. The stewards would have to rope off the unprotected deck, and looking for them, he put his shoulder against the starboard entry doors.

Inside, the constricted stairs came up to the third-class lounge. Furniture consisted mainly of benches fastened to the walls, but there was a big table. This had torn out the pin of the stay-chain, overturning and scattering newspapers and old magazines on the linoleum, shining with dirty water. Forty faces, black or palely negroid, lifted to Anthony. The high, miserable storm of voices quailed a moment. Then the sight of his uniform cap drove up a louder wail; partly hysterical relief at finding they were not alone in the world, partly fresh panic at the appearance of authority, in most of their minds associated with disaster and unreasonable suffering to come.

Anthony endeavoured to ignore them, but his rapid and accurate eye included them all. Some sat paralysed, bundles of their poor possessions done up in sheets resting at their feet. Others had gotten inefficiently into lifebelts. One group appeared to be praying, led by a monstrous woman with a moustache. More practical, another group had procured several bottles.

'Steward!' Anthony called.

Not understanding him, most of them joined in, too; a general lamentation. The old woman with the moustache shrieked louder. The people with bundles laid hold of them. A man with a bottle tilted it up as far as it would go.

'Pipe down!' shouted Anthony. 'Shut up! You're all right.' He realized that they did not understand him. 'No hay periculo! Basta! Basta!'

That exhausted his Spanish, but they understood at least that he was trying to talk to them. With appalling suddenness a silence fell, marred on the edges by stifled groans and sobs. They swayed visibly towards him, all eyes fastened to him, all waiting for him to perform some miracle and save them.

'No hay, periculo,' repeated Anthony. 'Esta bien.'

His broken Spanish was worse than nothing. It frightened them more. The uncertainty of his accent, the inadequacy of his words made everything he said improbable, sinister even. They were clearly cut off from the people who had them in charge, who had brought them to this extremity and alone could deliver them. The moaning swelled up again and Anthony shouted, 'Doesn't any one speak English?'

White under his black skin one man said nervelessly, 'What you like to say, senor?'

'Tell them to go back to their staterooms.'

'No, no, mister,' he wailed. 'No, no. Room full of water. People sick. People scared. No, no.'

'Tell them.'

'No, no,' he groaned. 'Ship sink. People drown. Leave those here, mister.'

'Where's the steward?'

'What you say, mister?'

'The steward!'

'No, no, mister. No, no.'

'Where is the man with the white coat?' Anthony shouted.

'Some gone. Some sick in room. Some under bed.'

'Where?' snapped Anthony. 'Show me.'

'No, no. I stay here, mister. No, no.'

Anthony did not move, but simple savagery must have shown in his face, for the man cowered away into the corner, backing against people who parted struggling to keep far from Anthony. Their shrieks swelled up again. The whole rail fabric of human relationships melted now in a mess of paralyzed muscle and brain and will. More shocking than the most murderous resistance, they became simple dead weight. They were lumps weighing some hundred and fifty pounds, too yielding to grasp, too misshapen to handle. Anthony stood dark-eyed and stiff-faced. He wanted to plant his feet in these quivering gelatinous heaps. He was shaken to the bottom – indeed there was no bottom, only the unthinkable abyss of human impotence opened under him. His brain, suspended over it, counselled him merely to kill, trample them down, destroy them, before their shocking contagion destroyed him. The blood beat up and filmed over his eyes, and he was saved by a quick, idiotic irrelevancy. He recognized that he was seeing red; that there was such a thing, no figure of speech, but a bloody mist. The childish surprise of it unsprung his nerves. He turned stiffly, grasped the rail of the stairs, and, putting one foot before another, descended. At the bottom his voice came like a croak, but he cleared it and shouted, 'Steward!'

A figure appeared uncertainly at the end of the little passage. 'Where are the others?' Anthony asked.

'In the pantry, they were,' faltered this man, glassy-eyed.

Three, maybe four, men gone, swept off and smothered somewhere in the broken wake, was a fact, literal and sharp. At once the misery of wetness and fear, the noise above, like animals crowded in a dangerous pen, became a simpler thing, pitiable. If, a moment ago, Anthony could have wished them all scoured out by the hard sea, buried away and obliterated, now he felt only their wretched humanity, their common helplessness against the inhuman ocean.

'Poor devils,' he murmured. The man's enormous eyes looked up at him. 'All right,' Anthony said. 'We can't do anything now. Buck up!'

The man opened his mouth and no sound came out, but finally he said, 'Yes, sir.'

'Unlock the passage-door there. I'll get some men down to you. Everything is all right. Go upstairs and don't let any one out. Half the rail's carried away.'

'Yes, sir.' the steward spoke more securely. He at least had the outlines of a discipline, however irregular, or casual. This framework propped him up a little, made him firm enough to grasp. Once grasped, the current of command galvanized him. His chin rose, his shaking ceased. 'Yes, sir,' he repeated quickly.

'Look alive,' said Anthony. 'We'll probably be out of this before dark.'

At nine o'clock Mr MacGillivray and his fourth engineer finished work on the extra pump. Designed for blowing ashes or supplying water to the deck fire-lines, they turned it on the stubbornly making bilge, broke the joint connection and fitted on a screen filter. That raised their available horse-power to about two hundred. As there was never anything wrong with the gear in an engine-room ruled by Mr MacGillivray, the pumps were better than seventy per cent efficient. Together they sucked up a ton of water a minute, heaved it thirty feet from the level of the fire-room plates, and dumped it over the side.

The chief viewed this arrangement, satisfied. He did not know where so much water could be coming from, but he was, he felt sure, more than a match for it. He would have his bilges dry before morning. If it came to that, he could and would pump out the whole blasted ocean. He'd have no dirty water in his department.

Presently he went above to clean up. Soaping his big hands he felt rather grumpy. As he got older he tended more and more to regard sailors, deck officers, as a not very necessary nuisance. If they ever developed a tenth of the efficiency he demanded and received from his personnel, from his main plant, from every fitting and auxiliary, there might be some sense in shipping. As it was, you took the finest turbines made by man and put them in a tin scow run by a lot of damn fools who filled it with water, ran it on its side and near shook the lagging off. He was tired now, but he certainly wasn't turning in until they got a grip on things. Though the sea was moderating, the *San Pedro* rolled heavily. The list was to twenty degrees and he didn't believe what water he had below was doing it.

Returning to his office, he put on his uniform coat and settled at the desk, his hands folded on his belly, his porcelain-blue eyes brooding. He was there when the alleyway door opened and he saw that at last the captain had come below. Mr MacGillivray got to his feet. Mr Bradell had entered with the old man. He stood at his elbow, as though he were helping him to walk, and the chief noticed that Captain Clendening moved heavily, without determination.

' 'Evening, captain,' he said shortly.

'How is it?' said Captain Clendening at last.

'We're all right,' Mr MacGillivray nodded. 'Got three pumps on. Have us dry pretty soon. Can't we do something about this list? Throws my lubrication off. Burn out a bearing somewhere, I wouldn't be surprised.' Actually he would be stunned with surprise. He had an extraordinary extra-sense for developing friction; it would be a clever bearing that burnt out in his engine-room.

'Where do you think the water's coming from, MacGillivray?' Captain Clendening asked.

Mr MacGillivray pulled his loose chin. 'It's black water,' he said. 'Must come through the coal. Don't suppose we sprung a plate?'

'I don't know,' said Captain Clendening.

Mr MacGillivray looked at him sharply. 'Aren't you trying to find out?' he asked.

'Since about four this morning,' interposed Mr Bradell, 'we haven't done anything else, chief.'

'Now, if I were you, son,' said Mr MacGillivray, 'I'd get myself in overalls and poke about the port bunkers. You can get in from the shelter-deck. Take an electric flashlight and keep it dry –'

'I'll give Bradell his orders, Mr MacGillivray,' said Captain Clendening.

'Just offering a suggestion,' said Mr MacGillivray, his mouth pouting out from the hanging folds of cheek. 'Seems to me about time something was done.'

Captain Clendening's lumpy jaw sagged down and forward. His moustache stiffened. 'By God, sir,' he roared, 'I'll have you understand, Mr MacGillivray, that I am in command of this ship. When I want your suggestions, I'll ask for them!'

'Very good,' snapped Mr MacGillivray. 'And now I'll step below, with your permission, and get on with more important matters.'

He turned his back on them. The clear snorts of his breathing sounded above the roar of the engine-room shaft for a moment. He stumped down the steel steps.

Captain Clendening swallowed audibly. 'Boy?' he said.

'Yes, sir,' said Anthony.

Captain Clendening made an uneasy gesture. 'Go down, boy,' he said. 'My apologies to Mr MacGillivray. Sort of nervous, boy. Guts are no good. Got to take care of myself. Tell him I appreciate his hard work. Tell him I rely on him absolutely and I hope he'll see fit to overlook my – my' – he faltered – 'my language, that is.'

'Yes, sir,' said Anthony. The captain's mouth worked a little and Anthony hesitated, not knowing if he were finished.

The captain's eyes came back to him, focused harder a moment. 'Mr Bradell!'

'Yes, sir.'

'Perhaps you can tell me who is in command of this vessel?'

'You are, sir,' said Anthony, dumbfounded.

'Thank you. When I give an order, I want it obeyed. What are you standing here for? Look alive, sir! I'll have no oil-tanker customs on this ship!'

IV

MIRO had gone below when Mr Bradell told him to turn in. Wind, weather; noise, no matter how relentless; discomfort very severe, he could ignore when he was ready to sleep. Now, long past midnight, he knew no such thing had disturbed him. His eyes open in the dark, he was at once alert, roused from within. Believing that an angel watched over him, he recognized instantly what had happened. This invisible being, who saw all and knew all, had bent down suddenly. Her tall shadow fell on him, her great wings fanned him.

He was not perturbed, nor was he hurried, though it could mean only that danger had become at last real and imminent. Perhaps all day danger had been mounting, like fluid in a pressure tube. Now it had crossed a mark and its crossing touched off tremendous alarms. His inquiring physical senses assured him that to every appearance nothing had changed. Slow and steady, the hammer of the engines at half-speed and time continued; the *San Pedro* rolled sluggishly; water forward bumped and crashed. A sound of movement and still calm enough voice came from the working alleyway. All the greater reason to find out, if he could, what subtler or more sinister change had caught his angel's sleepless eye, made her reach down and rouse him.

He had not taken off his boots, so he came at once to his feet. The occasional lights of the narrow wet passage, tilted badly by the list, burned dim in their heavy cups of misted glass. He proceeded to aft to the working alleyway and saw to his astonishment a dozen men from the steward's department. The half-door, he observed immediately, had carried away altogether. The carpenter was there, trying to rig a new one of boards and canvas. It was not completed and only partly in place, so when they leaned far on the list the sea came right in. One had a momentary staggering glimpse of their dull lights spilling into the void, winking on fathomless black swells almost under foot. Coming back enough to conceal this ugly phenomenon, the water already shipped surged to starboard like a miniature tidal wave. It went above the knees of the carpenter and his mate, busy with their boards.

Mr Driscoll had been absent a moment before, but Miro saw him now, buttoned up in his bridge coat, his face remarkably white in the bad light. He picked out Miro in the shadow beyond and said, 'Quartermaster?'

Miro answered, greatly relieved to find the chief officer in such alert charge.

'See if you can rout out some more men here. Get a lot of men. Any men you can.' Mr Driscoll supported himself with one hand on the clammy wall as the *San Pedro* went over and the half-door framed the black sea like a steep floor. 'Wait,' he said.

'Yes, sir.'

'Report to the bridge first. Tell the captain that the situation doesn't seem to improve. You might ask if it would be possible for him to step below here a moment. I – er –' He became conscious of the deadly silence of the men listening. 'Hurry up,' he jerked out. 'Get on with it.'

Mr Driscoll, then, was worried, too. Miro, in point of private fact, had small respect for Mr Driscoll as a seaman. He did not believe now that Mr Driscoll knew what ought to be done, nor even how to go about whatever substitute for the right thing he might have in mind. Mounting the inside stairs to the chart-room, Miro decided to report to Mr Bradell first. Mr Bradell could tell him what to do, and once sure of himself, he might discover some way to modify Mr Driscoll's designs.

He found this intention defeated, however. He appeared quietly in the door, and was dismayed to see the wheel-house almost crowded. Both Mr Eberly and Mr Sheedy were standing by. Young Mr Fenton and the third officer were close together in the corner, the fifth officer, Mr Eberly's junior, balanced himself restlessly with the roll, looking at the ceiling. Mr Bradell, his arms folded tight, the brim of his cap down over his forehead, stood beside the engine-room telegraph. The helmsman's eyes swung furtively from the binnacle to the rudder indicator and then sideways, as though appealing to Mr Bradell.

Unnoticed in the door behind, Miro considered them one after another. They were all tired, yet they were all alert, too, quiet and composed, but obviously mystified. One could deduce that they were here because they had been ordered up. They had not been told why, they had not been told what to do. No one spoke; they simply waited. It was, in its inept, mute, rather bewildered way, magnificent, and Miro appreciated this. Here was a very superior form of *tela*, a splendid, passive morale, the supreme ability to remain motionless and to appear calm; to stand endlessly ready for no one knew what.

Since Mr Bradell had the watch, it would be impossible to speak to him. Miro hesitated soundlessly, considering to whom he should speak. At this moment the port door on to the open bridge moved and Captain Clendening came in.

His face under the electric light was positively lifeless, but it had a surface shine from the spray on it. His eyes were so far swollen that they seemed to wink craftily out of slits. He stood heavy and clumsy in his wet bridge coat a moment. All glances had gone to him, but they wavered now, went away. There was a slight simultaneous movement of lips and eyes returning to careful impassivity. Mr Bradell never budged, had not looked.

Paying no attention to his waiting officers, Captain Clendening kept his face towards Miro. 'Yes?' he said.

'Chief officer reports, sir,' said Miro. 'Mr Driscoll wants to know if you can step below, sir.'

There was a general restrained stir, but no other sound.

'No,' said Captain Clendening. 'Tell him to carry on.'

The helmsman let his brown, nervous face turn. 'Helm!' said Mr Bradell. The helmsman's eyes jerked front.

In his grey-yellow face Captain Clendening's eyeballs flickered. A slight muscular contraction shook the thick cheeks. 'Turn in, Mr Eberly,' he said. 'Get some sleep. Won't want you after all.' He jerked his head towards the third and fifth officers. 'You, too,' he said. 'Turn in. Mr Sheedy, report to the chief officer.'

They all moved immediately in the grateful release of definite orders.

'Quartermaster?'

'Yes, sir.'

'Find out from the wireless-room where the *San Pablo* is.'

'Yes, sir.'

'Mr Bradell?'

'Yes, sir.'

'Can you carry on a little longer?'

'Yes, sir.'

Miro was out through the chart-room. In his ears repeated and repeated the mechanical 'Yes, sir,' 'Yes, sir.' It lost all alacrity, all smart and competent obedience. The phrase hammered and hammered. Under the senseless impact, the framework of observation – the vital initiative, the intelligence to see clearly and do quickly – cracked, crumbled to dust. Discipline, directed co-operation, ceased here to have any virtue. Habit betrayed the will and debauched the brain. Physically, the lips might stiffen with reluctance, the voice almost fail, but the mind in its extremity knew only one reply. To disaster, to stupid folly, to terrible peril which might yet be averted or resisted; to the advance of death itself, the mind acquiescent, drugged with a phrase, answered only, 'yes, sir.'

Wet wind hit Miro in the face. Beneath his feet the deck tilted away. He caught a hand-rail; he saw the dim bands of the *San Pedro*'s funnel stagger in the dark. He knew now that the *San Pedro* was certainly foundering, however slowly, and that most of those she carried might be lost.

Tuckerton, New Jersey. East Moriches, Long Island. All night rain has fallen on the Atlantic coast. Dawn is up, wet from the eastern ocean, but before six o'clock, the sullen skies were breaking. Heavy smell of wet trees, wide wet meadows, and the warm damp earth spread everywhere; through country streets, silent, but brighter; into the quiet open windows of houses still asleep. There followed presently a thin noise of bird song.

SS *SAN PEDRO*

Over the edge of the world, just about level with the drenched tree-tops, poured out the sun. Its flat, enormous shafts struck resplendent across the Eastern States. At Tuckerton, and at East Moriches, far higher than trees, slender and rigid against the fine dissolving blue, stood up the skeleton towers of the coastal wireless stations.

Under them, in the power houses, in the offices and operating rooms, some of the lights were turned off. Shifts of operators and engineers changed. The great generators, not requiring relief, spun on, subdued; but there was a sound of released voices on the beautiful air outside. An early train had tossed off New York papers, and men walking slowly home to bed lit cigarettes, looked at them, and saw there was no news worth reading.

Inside, the morning reliefs were settling down. Outside, soundless, invisible, humanly indetectable, the serene, the golden June air swelled, grew full with rising volume; the racing, screaming whine of code communication; broadcasting voices clearly relayed; early music.

At seven-fifteen, into these crowded currents which carried the immense record of the awakened world, cut faintly the *San Pedro*'s CQ – a thin plea, staccato with foreboding. From far off the Virginia Capes they were nagging at human attention; *everybody listen*. At Tuckerton, at East Moriches, the emergency operators stirred, attentive, mildly curious, as a half-hour silence settled. Just before eight o'clock came the SOS. By eight o'clock the Brooklyn Navy Yard was suspending all radio traffic. Over the whole of eastern North America the air was abruptly emptied and into this immense void the *San Pedro* called again, small and solitary; faded put; called once more, appealing this time to the Naval Compass Station at Cape May for her true bearings.

They heard it on the largest ships in the world; the white vessels of the United Fruit Co., many-decked Clyde liners, a dozen ships of the Caribbean and Southern trade, picked it up, calculating the scores of separating miles. Slow, dogged, steaming stockily, the Japanese freighter *Toledo Maru* halted a hundred miles away and came heavily about; from the North Atlantic steamship lanes a moderately fast Cunarder broke, turned south forcing her draft; a German boat, farther east, bound for New York, turned too. Just over the horizon a small sugar tramp from Cuba came abreast, passed the *San Pedro*, crawled patiently on, not being equipped with wireless.

Captain Clendening's eyeballs were finely netted with scarlet veins. There was a silver stubble of beard over his square cheeks. Beneath his short white moustache his mouth opened and shut, sucking in the cool air. He held on to the shutter of the open wheel-house window, and the cumbersome seas, whipping up the tilted well-deck forward, staggering into the port half-doors, were grey with advanced morning. The *San*

Pedro, resisting them, shook him back and forth on his feet, but he held on. He held the tighter, for he did not wish to turn around; he felt insistent, the need to look back, to survey the boat-deck again, but he put it off a moment while his head wabbled. 'Got to take care of myself,' he murmured, for he knew that he was very sick, ought to be in bed. In answer he held himself still tighter, harder, while he did turn and look back. He realized then that he could not see anything unless he went out on the open bridge end. There was, however, a quartermaster gazing at him. The man's eyes were dark, sad, deep as well. 'Order to abandon, sir?' he said softly.

Captain Clendening was stunned. He opened his mouth to roar, but his throat failed him. He could not believe that he had understood; that on his own bridge a quartermaster could be offering him a suggestion. He breathed harder, he held tighter, as though he were climbing a vertical slope. The situation was so outrageous and amazing that, still speechless, he wondered if it might not have been his imagination, for the man was saying normally, like any quartermaster, 'Chief officer reports starboard boats impractical, sir.'

He hesitated, and Captain Clendening, his mouth tight, his eyes hard ahead, continued to look at him.

'Mr Bradell asked me to say, sir, that port boats could be dropped in the lee and get off. May he reverse orders, sir?'

Captain Clendening studied him, studied his brown clear skin and melancholy liquid eyes, knew that he had noticed him often before, that this was a reliable man. 'What's your name?' he asked.

'Miro, sir,' answered the quartermaster. There was a sudden brightening of his eyes as though he were about to weep. They were all inordinately sensitive, these Southerners; particularly, intelligent ones; Captain Clendening knew. He modified his tone a little. 'Don't you know how to behave on the bridge, boy?' he said. 'Look alive and speak when you're spoken to.'

'Yes, sir,' said Miro.

'Well, what did you want?'

'About lifeboat stations, sir. Mr Bradell –'

'I gave no orders about boats,' said Captain Clendening, his voice thick in his ears. 'What are you talking about?'

The man's deep sad eyes with the far-away glint of tears stayed on him steadily. 'You will remember, sir,' he said. His voice was mild, very gentle, but distinct. 'You ordered Mr Bradell and Mr Driscoll to turn to on the boats.'

'I sent Mr Bradell forward,' said Captain Clendening. 'What's he doing with the boats?'

'Yes, sir,' assented the soft clear voice. 'That was afterwards. He has gone forward now, sir.'

'Why didn't you report at once? I'll have no tampering with –'

He found, to his amazement, that he must have been interrupted. 'I try to report, sir, for ten – twenty minutes. I have been right here, sir. I do not think that you have heard me.' The man's face was a still, tragic mask with the small deep pools of the eyes. 'Boats have broken on the side, sir. It is too –'

'Officers,' said Captain Clendening, 'will carry out their orders to the best of their ability.' He extended a hand. 'I want to go on to the bridge,' he said.

Miro came close, more like a sudden close-up in a motion-picture than ordinary movement. Miro's hard, neatly muscled shoulder steadied Captain Clendening. Very sure-footed, Miro calculated the movement of the ship, moving with it, and they were out, under the terrible white light of pale sky. Captain Clendening shook off Miro's support, holding the rail and watching the concerted movement about the lifeboats. His mouth was full of spittle, tasting brazen, or bitter, and he swallowed steadily, trying to get rid of it.

Now some one else had appeared at the wheel-house door. Captain Clendening tightened his jaw and said, 'You have your orders, Mr Fenton. Be good enough to carry them out.' The quartermaster was still gazing at him, so he added, enraged at last by the implacable sadness of the eyes, 'Get that man out of here, Mr Fenton. I'll have him in irons if he leaves his post again.'

He heard Mr Fenton's voice: '. . . get some of them away, sir?' and it occurred to him that he might not have spoken aloud in reference to the quartermaster. He saw no use in repeating it. To Mr Fenton he said automatically, 'You will await an order for general abandonment. How are the passengers?'

'Mr Eberly and Mr Sheedy are in charge, sir. Women and children mustered up. All behaving well.'

'Right,' said Captain Clendening. 'We'll have no *La Bourgogne* business here.'

Still a third man had appeared. He recognized this one as from the wireless-room. He had in his hand several papers. His voice awoke in an animated drawl. 'Yes, yes,' said Captain Clendening sharply. He did not want to listen to this, so he took the scribbled reports from the young man. 'Carry on,' he nodded, anxious to get rid of them.

In the wireless-room Smith was at the key. 'On the coil now,' he said to Morris, returning. 'When are we going to abandon?'

Morris lit a cigarette, propped himself in the tilted corner. He employed his free hand thoughtfully, scratching his red hair. 'Nobody knows,' he hummed, 'and nobody seems to care.'

'Listen,' said Smith. 'Don't wisecrack. I don't mind telling you I want to live. How's the old man?'

'He's all right,' said Morris. 'He looks pretty bad. You don't lose your ship every day, now I come to think of it, but he's playing ball.'

'What's he say?'

'Nothing,' answered Morris, 'which seems to me to be about right. They stove in another boat just now. Pretty soon we'll have to take off our shoes and stockings and wade; that is, those not otherwise engaged. I'll flip you to see who does the Casabianca stunt. We'll count Couch out, since he wouldn't be on duty anyway. Where is he, having a quiet nap?'

'Out with Mr Driscoll. He's had some experience with boats. Well–'

'If he has, he's the only one,' said Morris. 'I could tell you a good joke, only it might upset you. Let's have a half-dollar.'

'I'll stay,' said Smith. 'I'm the senior operator.'

'You're sure hell on heroism,' commented Morris, 'but I've only one cigarette left, so I might as well drown. Furthermore, what did I happen to find but a quart of Bacardi, which will take away the taste of salt water something wonderful. I'll even give you a drink if you'll lend me your boy-scout knife.'

'Now, shut up!' said Smith sharply. 'Don't get all worked up. Everything's all right. We'll float for eight hours at least and by three o'clock–'

'You must have heard Mr Eberly talking to the passengers,' admired Morris. 'That's the good joke I was going to tell you. He has them all down on the promenade-deck, and since they don't know him very well – some of them have barely met him – they think he knows what it's all about.'

'And I suppose you know a hell of a lot more?'

'I know this,' said Morris modestly. 'If we don't stop leaning over the rail, we're going to capsize. Thank God I'm not a seaman; I'd miss all the fun of expecting it.'

'You aren't so damn humorous,' said Smith.

'Get off the key,' suggested Morris, 'and let me hand these boys a few sad brave remarks.'

'Don't be an ass!' snapped Smith. 'What juice we have we'll keep. Hang on, I got the Jap boat again.'

He pencilled down letters in silence. 'You didn't bring back any new bearings, did you?' he asked Morris over his shoulder. 'They've got a ten-cent outfit with no direction finder.'

'Shoot them something snappy for a come-on,' begged Morris. 'Don't be a Western Union messenger all your life.'

'Shut up,' said Smith. His key awoke, and Morris, reading it off, translated freely. ' "Bad enough here old man position ship in hardly stay receive please hurry–'' That's right,' he applauded. 'Probably they were wondering about that last part. Probably they didn't know whether to hurry or to stop and do a little fishing.'

'For God's sake, shut up!' shouted Smith.

'Sorry,' claimed Morris. 'Didn't mean to spoil our last happy hours together. Well, before we get any more good news, I'll flip you two out of three for that space on the Memorial in Battery Park, the bottle, and all your cigarettes. Come on, boy, think of your lovin' wife.'

Smith said glumly, 'Well, at any rate I haven't got that to worry about.'

Morris's great grin of derision shone on him. 'It would be horrible,' he nodded; 'I expect you couldn't keep your mind off her if you had one. Never mind, think of your children in all parts of the world, then. What'll it be? Heads?'

Mr Eberly carried a revolver in his pocket but he found no use for it. On the appalling tilt of the promenade-deck one felt unpleasantly shut in, seeing only the pale heavens, the fast eastward drift of the melting scud to starboard; only the long jostling slide of grey water getting green to port. From above came the dull sound of boots and men working, which was comforting. So was the undisturbed solidity of the ship. Even at this awkward angle the deck underfoot was firm as rock; the steel walls, white-painted, the windows, the heavy doors, looked strong and normal enough.

Mr Eberly had all the passengers on deck now; the women and children in one compact group forward, ready for the boats which he presumed would be first down. At the after-rail, by the closed stairs, Mr Sheedy waited, holding frankly an iron stanchion. He was watching the big Negroes of the black gang, who had either come up anyway or been sent up. They gathered sullen, restless but impotent, about the hatch-covers. They hadn't yet made any real movement to approach the promenade-deck. Mr Eberly, moving with the aid of lines that he had rigged himself, passed up and down watching everybody; the groups of men smoking with affected calm; the confused herd of women where occasionally a child cried. He told them – he was careful not to do it too often – that there was absolutely no danger, and it was fine to see how they behaved; resigned, patient, doing exactly as they were asked. He had directed them to dress as warmly as possible, and he made sure that they had their ludicrous, bulky lifebelts on properly. Some of them managed to regard their appearance as amusing, and fortunately they were too ignorant to make any protest about a delay which Mr Eberly himself found inexplicable, nerve-wracking. Once he went inside with unhurried calm, waited a few minutes, and came out. 'Assistance alongside in about an hour,' he announced, with the well-sustained implication that he had been to the wireless-room.

Mr Sheedy occasionally said, addressing the invisible deck aft, 'Take your foot off the ladder, nigger, or you'll get a broken head.' Then there was a faint stir, lasting only a minute; a slight acknowledgment of this obvious hint that some other people were not quite so calm. But they all knew, they had read or been told plenty of times, that the one real danger in matters like this was simply panic. Certainly they could see no other, now that they were used to the ship's position. They believed that men who understood the situation were doing everything possible to get them off quickly and safely; they had, in fact, nothing to worry about so long as they stayed quiet and did what Mr Eberly directed them to do.

'Everything,' asserted Mr Eberly, who was still trying to explain to himself why Mr Driscoll wasted so much time on the starboard boats when it would have seemed fairly simple to Mr Eberly to let go the port ones, 'is all right.'

Driven by his consuming anxiety, he finally did find a reason. The captain must consider it wiser to try to get off as many of the starboard boats as they could first. The port ones might be handled somewhat more expeditiously if later it proved that they were pressed for time. The idea, he told himself, had much to be said for it. He was heartened, too, by the indication it gave of confidence on the bridge that they would float a long while. With the impassivity of good discipline he refrained from sending above to make inquiries which could only be useless and ridiculous. 'Try to be patient just a little longer,' he requested earnestly. 'I know this isn't very comfortable, but there's no danger. The sun,' he added with a sort of cheerfulness, 'will be out in a minute.'

From the well-deck forward Anthony could see Captain Clendening's stubborn, hatless white head against the sky. It was the one human detail in the confusion of the *San Pedro*'s superstructure. Insistently under Anthony's eyes the Negroes crouched against the cased automobiles. Their wide feet clung like stunted hands to the rivets of the deck-plates. Cords bulged out of their black necks; sweat trickled flashing under the wool on their skulls. Their enormous paws locked over levers; black hills of muscle humped across their straining shoulders; their eyes rolled white, their thick lips contracted.

Anthony looked at them through a fluctuating reddish mist. Weariness tightened his throat in rhythmic cramping retches. He would have spewed out his empty stomach if he could. Both his hands he had to keep behind him so he would not break an hysterical fist on the black stencil of an Indian's head, outstanding with the maker's name on the side of the case.

After a while he realized that men and muscle couldn't do it. They would never get that case over the side. It must be wedged. He cupped his raw hands and screamed to the bridge, 'Let me go below and make MacGillivray give me steam on the winches, sir!'

He couldn't tell whether Captain Clendening heard him, whether the old man could hear anything or understand if he did hear. The white head, stubbornly held up, wagged a little.

Anthony turned. 'Drop that. Get up number two starboard boom –' There was no one, he saw, to whom he could safely delegate authority if he wanted intelligent action, but he picked out a man finally. 'You,' he said, 'stand by to let in the valves. We'll get steam.'

At the end, the Negro called Packy released his lever. His big hands pulled it out. One moment he poised on the tilted deck, his head sunk, his black jaw swung out. Water raced up to his feet; his shoulders balanced. The steel bar drove like a battering-ram into the Indian's stencilled profile. Anthony wiped his forehead. His voice was thin as water. 'Lay off that, nigger!'

The wood had splintered at the terrible impact. Pallid sunshine from the aching white sky with the washed clouds moving fell through the broken boards, winked on nickel, on smooth cream-coloured enamel. That's an expensive car we're throwing away, thought Anthony.

He had removed his shoes to stand more securely. His feet, cold and wet in his torn socks, gave him a good grip on the slanting deck. The echo of the steel door closed behind him, and he forced himself to trot through the water in the alleyway. It caught his ankles and splashed at his knees; his unprotected heels falling hit his spine sickening jolts.

Under a raw, thin fog of vapour the engine-room depths formed an infernal swimming-pool. Like monster green hogsheads the turbine cases rose in a fantastic steel swamp. Incredible vegetation flowered; white piping; flattened-out layers of openwork footways. Stairs edged with brass rail plunged down, leading nowhere. Heavy tanks; pistons in a stiff paralysis of the final failure of almost all the auxiliary systems; transparent oil-cups with the oil at an angle in them; everything seemed to have changed places in a mechanical anarchy. Below, water moved about regularly, swaying to the sluggish roll. The engine-room shaft echoed like a sea cave. Choking with a hundred tons of brine in their throats the pumps groaned up to Anthony. Electric lights fluctuated, winked on the dirty sliding surface, steadied as the *San Pedro* came back. Anthony stumbled down the iron slant of the ladder.

There was Mr MacGillivray. He had the fire-room door tied back, and the lock-door beyond fastened, too. He braced himself between them, his eyes on the indicator dials and the bridge signal. Sometimes the water came almost to his waist. Vapour slipped out steadily above his head, licking the upper jamb. Anthony missed a step, scraped his shin open, saw the bright blood run on his foot before he landed in the water. 'Chief!'

Mr MacGillivray snatched his arm. Anthony shouted about the catch and gasp of the pumps. 'I've got to have steam.'

Mr MacGillivray's hanging cheeks were set into a cold calm. Unavoidably retreating, he had lost almost everything, but bitterly, step by step, he gave way in grim good order, contesting each point with the invading ocean. His obdurate old face was wary, undismayed. Anthony asked, 'How much steam have you got, chief?'

Mr MacGillivray's eyes came down from the dials. 'Eighty pounds!' he shouted. 'The centre boiler's just gone. Listen to it!'

Over came the *San Pedro*, heavy and deliberate, rushing water into the hot fire-box. It sounded like the crash of thin metal sheets. The outlet valves whistled harder in the darkness. Mr MacGillivray shook his finger at the fire-room. 'To their necks, some of them,' he roared. 'We can't stay much longer.'

Anthony swayed against him, looking through. A naked black back with prodigious arms bent to ease down a coal-bucket. Water swayed towards its armpits. In the upper corner a door came wide, and violent yellow light spurted in shattered columns across the liquid surface. A great shadow moved; coal crashed in, iron rang on iron, and the light went out. Up came a white back this time, another bucket.

'Electricity gone there!' roared the chief. 'Go everywhere in a minute. Tell the old man. The telephone doesn't work.'

The black figure with the dangling arms waded past. His face, his conical skull swayed into the light; he grinned; he swung his apelike arm and wagged the hand up and down. A faint boom-boom came from his chest. 'Home,' he moaned, 'knock on the door . . .'

'My God,' said Anthony, shocked, 'he's singing.'

'Sure! He's crazy!' shouted Mr MacGillivray. 'No one who wasn't crazy would be here. He's the only nigger left.'

Anthony swallowed. 'Give me pressure on a winch, chief. I got to get some cases over.'

MacGillivray stared at him, open-mouth. He laid a hand on his shoulder and shook him. 'Not do you any good. You can't use your booms in this list. Tie 'em down before you hurt some one.'

'I can try,' Anthony said, 'I got to –'

'You cannot!' bellowed MacGillivray, his amazement melted in anger. 'Hell and damnation, where are your brains, boy? You aren't at dock! Did the old man put that up to you?'

'Maybe I can work it,' protested Anthony. 'We've got to get those motors off. We –'

'Never mind them. You go up and find my fire-room crew. Tell the old man I got to have my men back.' He shook Anthony's arm with a sort of fury. 'Tell him they left. Tell him I got my engineers firing. Tell him if he wants to float to make those niggers come back here. Tell the old man we can't keep steam – tell him to come the hell down here himself!'

'He can't,' shouted Anthony. 'He's sick. He hasn't been to bed since Saturday night. What do you expect?'

'He's got no business to be sick,' yelled MacGillivray: 'Tell him I said so. Tell him we're foundering. Don't he give a damn? Don't he know we could capsize any minute? He'd lose every soul aboard. Just like that!' Mr MacGillivray's loose fingers snapped soundless in the uproar. 'Isn't he getting his passengers off?'

'We're doing everything we can,' said Anthony. 'We –'

'You are like hell!' roared MacGillivray. 'Who's in command? The old man? He's dead to the world. Had him on the phone an hour ago and he didn't know what he was talking about! Why don't Driscoll take over? Why don't you take over? Are you so damn dumb you think you're going to float for ever?'

'He's the master on this vessel,' said Anthony. 'As long as he's on the bridge giving orders, in the deck department we obey them. When we're ordered to abandon, we'll abandon. Meanwhile we keep our mouths shut.'

Mr MacGillivray stared at him. Then he spat hard into the dirty water in front of Anthony. 'Get out of here, brat! Take your play-acting upstairs! Believe me, if I was a sailor, I'd rather be drowned than have to tell people afterwards what I was doing all morning. Jesus, I hope some of you get off alive!'

Anthony turned, but Mr MacGillivray caught his shoulder suddenly. 'Listen,' he roared. 'Tell the old man! Get it into him! Ask what he's doing with four hundred human beings somebody's going to want from us afterwards. Tell him for Christ's sake use his head –'

Miro, still on the bridge, waiting for any further orders Captain Clendening might have, could not imagine what the men on the well-deck forward had in mind. He watched them release a boom from its cradle. Then they stood a moment, apparently arguing. Then with a sort of feverish violence, they scrambled above, all laid hold on the cable, and struggling hard brought the boom up, jerk by jerk. It tilted, staggered, mounted uncertain towards the perpendicular. What must surely be the idiocy of this performance did not surprise Miro so much as the energy with which they went about it. They might, of course, be contemplating something which he did not understand, but he noted that Mr Bradell was absent, and it seemed more likely that they were acting on their own initiative.

Not speaking, for he knew that the captain would not hear him, he came close and pointed insistently until Captain Clendening looked. There was a long silence, and suddenly the captain, shaking his head a little, roared out, 'On the fo'castle! Down that boom! What the devil is going on?'

Below, they wavered. Black faces turned. Out of the concealment of the deck-house under them came Mr Bradell now and he, too, turned. The boom hovered in a broken semicircle, balanced dizzily, went into a drunken side movement.

'Look alive, sir!' screamed Miro.

The boom, released, came too fast. With a blind, inert precision it swung farther left; the iron-sheathed timber struck like a well-directed club out of the anonymous skies. It knocked Mr Bradell's poised figure ten feet into the scuppers. Up to them came the final crash of the demolished tip.

Captain Clendening opened his mouth and shut it. He shook his head and said, 'Quartermaster?'

'Yes, sir,' said Miro.

'Who was that?'

'Mr Bradell, sir.'

'Bradell,' said Captain Clendening. 'Bradell.' He turned his head, continuing sharp and clearer, 'Quartermaster.'

'Yes, sir,' said Miro, whiter.

'See about him.' Captain Clendening's moustache worked stiffly. 'Don't report back here. If he's alive, get him into a boat. Don't come back here. Get him away, get him off this ship. We're foundering.'

'Yes, sir.'

Left alone, Captain Clendening was quietly aware of death like a man beside him. He thought of his lungs, bursting with sea-water, a final agony of suffocation. This his body recoiled from, his gullet tightened, bitter saliva filling his mouth. He looked about carefully, as though there might be somewhere he could go; but it was a minute, never-completed gesture, for a habit of thought, an automatic pride, interrupted him. He was exposed, on the bridge; people could see him. The slugging of his heart (too large now for his chest) he could not control, but that was hidden. He knew perfectly how he had to die, and they did, too. He wished that they might for a moment face it; he would like to know – he was distracted, not ironic – if death would still seem so proper, so necessary, to them.

There his acuter senses broke down self-defensively. An anaesthetic of poorer comprehension, a sort of mental stupor took off the momentary keen edge, veiled the face and fear of death. Deliberately, his hands heavy and inaccurate, he buttoned his bridge coat, tugged it into place. He made some motions to smooth the wrinkles from the sleeves, brushing the gold braid. After several uncertain efforts he picked up his uniform cap, and this, too, he brushed off, hitting it with his numb hand once or twice. Then he put it carefully on his head, brought the visor down, a stiff, somehow heartening, line across his vision. He stood as straight as he could, supporting himself when necessary on the rail.

From the south the sea was travelling in long swells. Miro, braced against the background of boat ten, supported Mr Bradell between his knees. He did not know what time it was; he had somehow smashed his good watch. The glass was gone and the hands snapped off; there was sea-water in it and some blood from Mr Bradell's broken head. They had more than thirty Negroes on board, and this, Miro recognized, was shameful; but he could not prevent it while he had Mr Bradell to look out for, and he told himself that if they had been the first to cut loose, he had orders to get away. Many of the other boats had been filled; one, he saw – and it frightened him more than anything else – was entirely filled with women and children. He tried to call Mr Fenton's attention to the fact that there was no one in it capable of managing it. What would they do? Mr Fenton paid no attention to him, and the men in number ten, mutinous at the delay, pushed off; with great difficulty got clear. Miro hoped that it might at least set the others an example; that they wouldn't wait any longer for an order to abandon. Otherwise, he understood, they might sink where they were, boats still attached, many people still on deck.

Mr Bradell moved between his knees and Miro was seized with distress and consternation, for it occurred to him that now Mr Bradell would realize that number ten had deliberately drawn off, leaving hundreds of people in danger of death. He said at once, 'Captain's orders to abandon, sir.'

Anthony's face had fallen apart, but it was bound up fairly well with a handkerchief and a hard web of pain. He did not realize anything; and not knowing how he got where he was, where he had been, nor for how long, Anthony made an effort to learn the time. The left arm with his wrist-watch he found to be no longer subject to his control. Pain of light on his eyes made him look up, and by the thin sun hung above him in the white sky he knew that it was close to noon. The boat, riding roughly, passed up a mound of water and let him see, amazed the *San Pedro*.

He was stupified by this sight. He had seen the *San Pedro* too often; he recognized at once that this view of her was a dream. It was impossible; it would be fatal. She could not remain like that. Here was no matter ballast-tanks could correct – her list was mortal; and at once he heard a low voice saying, '*But you do not float quite level* . . .'

He started to make a movement, to arise; and hands were instantly on him, holding him. Blood came into his mouth. A scalding void complemented his body, filling out the electric emptiness where half his face and all his shoulder should have been. Waves of heat overpowered him – so strong that with them came the imaginary smell of hot oil, the aura of the engine-room shaft. At his side, in a shabby black overcoat, he saw the horrid author of that low voice, insistent, plucking at him: 'But you do not float . . .'

This, he knew, was entirely false; he saw actually, nothing but the men forward, the gunwales, the mounting green water, literal things in a spinning blur of fever and pain – yet, in a way, Dr Percival remained; the fleshless face was steady and close, brooding on them.

Seeing thus, while not seeing, he smelt stronger than salt and blood the warmed sweetness of patchouli; he was aware of the dark, despairing blue of her eyes, the frail flippancy of her voice like a veil drawn decently over her unspeakable desire to live.

Then, violently, without escape, he knew that this was real, not a dream. The *San Pedro* was really there; the ocean was in her; the sea smothered her tremendous engines. It choked up every passage and part of her; swamped into silence the marvellous elaboration of her machines, quenched all her lights, and would in a moment drag her down like any broken metal. Water would do away quickly with everything that breathed aboard her. The boat brought him up again. Cold as he had been hot, he saw once more the *San Pedro*.

Just adequately the *San Pedro* met each swell; no wasted effort. She lay on her port side, down by the head, and took her terrible rest while the mounds of water pillowed her and washed her quietly. Like the disarray of weariness, starboard davits on the top-deck dangled out trailing ropes, suspended white boats unevenly. Expiring wisps of steam broke in curls from her flanks. She had a screw clear, pinned like a mighty metal flower on the slim cone of the starboard bracket.

There she lay in a motionless lethargy, and then without pause or warning, she went. The shooting swell rose in a hill, came quite over her bows. Her funnel inclined; water poured freely into it, into the high hoods of her ventilators. Deep in her, a hidden drum boom-boomed. Like a pool, the dark gully of her promenade-deck filled forward; steam mounted in columns through her coal-hatches. A great metallic sigh, a six-hundred-foot shudder – why hadn't her boilers blown, lifted thunderous through her exhausted sides? – she was going home, going to some deep sleep. The waters folded over her tumultuously – air, steam, the great chords booming in her hull . . .

There remained Anthony, harassed by great pain, the boat under him, Miro behind him, the black men with the oars; if there were other boats, he could not see them. Only, overhead, the vast sky, pale and white, all around the infinite empty ocean.

C. S. Forester

The Man in the Yellow Raft

In United States destroyer *Boon* the babies had grown into adolescents overnight apparently, and all the troubles associated with adolescence were making their appearance. Until now the troubles had been those of infancy, arising mostly out of simple ignorance or innocence; but after the victory that *Boon* had gained there was a very noticeable change. *Boon* had sailed from Mare Island with a ship's company of whom more than one third had been recruits, men of the best quality, all volunteers who had joined the Navy before Pearl Harbour. Boot camp had changed them very little; they had been law-abiding in intention, at least, and so interested in their new life that initiating them in their duties had been like playing nursery games with toddlers – toddlers armed with weapons their grandfathers had never dreamed of. Thanks to those weapons, they had ambushed and destroyed a Japanese cruiser, gaining a victory that had echoed round the world, and with that victory, and after three months at sea, the toddlers had grown up into teen-agers.

Now they knew everything that was worth knowing; and no one could show them anything. The attention paid to rules and conventions by their seniors was tiresome; it also marked those seniors down as conservative old men sinking into decrepitude. The community in which the recruits found themselves appeared to them to be both inelastic and old-fashioned; they were sure that from their fresh point of view they could visualize a better system. Moreover, they knew so much more about the rules and conventions now, that those among them who were merely irked in their way of life by the restrictions could think of ways of circumventing them. The infants had been pleased and proud to be playing in a group game; the teen-agers resented, consciously or unconsciously, the merging of their precious individualities into a single entity.

The consequence was – as other communities have found – the development of a wave of crime. The *Boon*, when she resumed her course and headed southwestward again across the Pacific, was engulfed in crime. The Japanese cruiser lay a thousand fathoms deep behind her,

354

THE BEST SEA STORIES

a rived wreck on the dark floor of the ocean, while the men who had
destroyed her celebrated their victory by perfectly shocking behaviour.
One heavenly still night, as the *Boon* coursed onward over the dark
swell, George Brown, the executive officer, awoke in his cabin to
hear a noise that should never be heard in a ship of war; an instantly
recognizable noise like no other. He left his bunk and went below; his
miscroscopic familiarity with every corner of the ship directed his steps
straight to the source of the noise. As he stepped across a high coaming
he heard it once more; the unmistakable sound of a pair of dice rattling
over a steel deck and bouncing back from a steel bulkhead.

'Snake eyes!' said one of the squatting group, and it was certainly
the most unlucky throw of the evening, for that was when they looked
up to find the executive officer standing over them.

'Whose money is this?' asked that officer, but no one would admit
ownership, not even when he went on: 'Nobody's? If it's unclaimed I
shall have to take charge of it for the Ship's Welfare Fund.'

They eyed him silently as he picked it up; there was a five-dollar bill,
as well as several ones and some quarters and dimes. 'Thirteen dollars
and twenty cents,' said the executive officer. 'You men can turn in
now.'

The United States Navy was not concerned with morals, viewed
simply as morals, even though there were Congressmen who wished
otherwise. The Navy was a fighting body, with victory as its aim. Victory or defeat, as well as life or death, depended on the last ounce of
effort, the highest pitch of efficiency; and the Navy had convinced itself
that craps on board could cut down the effort and reduce the efficiency
of the men. Gambling led to bitterness, to feuds; it led to a possible
relaxation of discipline between debtors and creditors, to possible
lapses from duty.

Brown looked along the line of criminals and remembered something
else. 'You, Carducci. You're due to come up to captain's mast this
morning. Aren't you?'

'Yes, sir.'

'Sleeping on watch.'

'Yes, sir.'

'This may help to explain it.'

It did nothing to explain it in the mind of Fireman 2nd Class Pietro
Carducci. His job was standing duty at the evaporator, watching the
water level, and he could see no connection between a harmless crap
game at midnight and nodding off in the four to eight. The water level
in the evaporator had remained constant, of course, and there had
been no harm done, even though he would freely admit, from his
own knowledge, that the gravest damage to the evaporator might have
ensued had the level fallen. To Fireman Carducci the linking of the two

charges was only one more example of the way in which the Navy was ready to hang a dog to which it had already given a bad name.

At captain's mast he was consoled to some extent by the misfortunes of his friend Fireman 2nd Class Clover, found guilty of a quite different crime. Clover had not turned off the tap of the shower bath, having stepped out of it to soap himself after going under to get wet. A regulation laid it down that the tap should not be left running during those thirty seconds, and Clover readily admitted that he had not observed the regulation.

'And yet you knew the order?' asked the captain. 'Wet down. Turn off. Soap down. Turn on. Rinse down. Turn off.'

'Yes, sir.'

There were several listeners who could not see any connection between fighting the Japs and the meaningless ritual the captain had just recited.

'You wasted two gallons of fresh water,' said the captain, eyeing the boy before him, whose bewilderment hid behind a sullen mask.

Two hundred men could waste four hundred gallons of fresh water a day; fifty tons in a month, and that would mean the consumption of half a ton of fuel. Captain Angell, looking over the head of the man before him, could picture in his mind's eye *Boon*, with nearly empty bunkers, crawling perforce at slowest economical speed across the Pacific, exposed at every moment to submarine attack.

He met the boy's eyes again; it was no use making a little speech along these lines. They had just sunk a Japanese cruiser with apparently the greatest of ease, and nothing at the moment could convince these lads of the importance of two gallons of fresh water.

'Five hours' extra duty,' said the captain. It was a poor way, he knew, of trying to impress the importance of water economy on Clover's mind, but it was the only way possible at present.

The captain went on to lecture Seaman 2nd Class Helder on the enormity of being late relieving watch: and the last criminal on the list was Seaman 2nd Class Kortland. The captain took special note of this man. An intelligent-looking man of sensitive expression; as a high-school graduate he was a man of some education. Of course he was a man only by courtesy of the Navy, seeing that he was still only eighteen. And his crime was something a little out of the ordinary; his battle station was in the lower handling room of the No. 1 five-inch gun, and he had apparently formed the habit of settling down there, among the live shells, for an hour or two of peace and quiet after the ship secured from morning general quarters. The captain felt a certain sympathy for him, but no one could possibly be allowed to remain unsupervised down among the ammunition, apart from all the other considerations.

'Five hours' extra duty,' said the captain.

'Mast cases dismissed,' said the executive officer.

'You know,' announced the executive officer in the wardroom later, 'the British have the right idea with their rum ration.'

'I know plenty who'd agree with you,' said Lieutenant Klein.

'What makes you say it at this moment, George?' asked the captain, taking a first sip at his coffee. 'What's the peculiar virtue of the rum ration today?'

'There's no virtue in the issue of a rum ration,' said the executive officer.

'Shame!' interjected Klein.

'But there's a lot of virtue in taking it away. What can we do to a man out here when he bucks the regulations? Extra duty? You reach a limit with that in no time – all the men have pretty well all they can do already, and you've got to be careful with their health. Restriction? They've given up hope of ever seeing port again, and restriction doesn't mean a thing. Loss of pay? Pay doesn't mean anything out here either, especially now that we've dealt with the crap games.'

'Are you telling *us*, sir?' asked Lieutenant Borglum.

'So there's no way of getting at the man who's lazy or careless, or who thinks he knows it all already. But the British can, with the rum ration. That one drink's nothing, really, to a drinking man. But leading this sort of life you come to look forward to it from day to day, just as a break in the monotony, perhaps. Take it away, and you've really done something. Next time he'll be more careful. I'm all for the rum ration, in wartime conditions anyway,' the executive officer finished.

'Maybe you have something there,' agreed Borglum.

'Maybe Josephus Daniels is turning in his grave,' said Klein. 'Are you going to bring flogging back too, sir?'

'It's just about as likely,' admitted the excutive officer.

Two days later – two days more of monotonous steaming across the featureless Pacific – Klein made a handsome admission.

'I've come round to your way of thinking, sir,' he said. 'That fellow Kortland. The man who used to hide away in the lower handling room. You know about the new offence, of course?'

'I've just published the deck court you held,' said the executive officer.

'You have? How did the captain feel about the sentence?'

'He remitted part of it. Now it stands at fifteen days' restriction.'

'Fifteen or twenty – what's the difference? It's just what you were saying. For the next fifteen days he'll watch his pals pouring ashore to enjoy themselves while he has to stay on board. Oh, yes, and he'll lose about twenty dollars in pay. A lot he cares.'

'And insubordination is a serious charge. I know he sassed the chief boatswain's mate, but what did he say?'

'I expect Trautmann had been riding him some. You know Kortland's the compartment cleaner and scullery maid for the c.p.o.'s
quarters?'

'Yes. Nice job. Doesn't stand watches.'

'He hadn't cleaned up the soap dishes in the head, and Trautmann
checked him for it.'

'Well?'

'So he flared out. He said, "I'm not a servant. I'll do it when I'm
good and ready".'

'He must be just a plain fool.'

'I'm not so sure. He lost his temper. It's not so long since he had a
mother running round after him cleaning the soap dishes.'

'Yes. But insubordination –'

There was no need to finish the sentence. With the safety of the
ship, with victory or defeat depending on instant obedience, a state of
mind must never be allowed to exist wherein it was possible to argue
back or hesitate to obey. To the two officers this was self-evident, a
part of life. It was not so evident to a recent high-school boy, however.

'Oh, well,' said the executive officer, 'tempers are short just now.
But we're making contact with the task force tomorrow. That'll be a
break in the monotony and may do everyone good. Maybe Kortland
will learn sense.'

Seaman 2nd Class Charles Kortland was not a fool, but a mixed-up
boy still, a nice-looking boy, incidentally; that fact had a bearing on the
circumstances leading up to his present state of mind. On his graduation
from high school the previous summer he had persuaded a doting
mother to allow him to anticipate the draft and enlist in the Navy. Eight
months in the service had been just enough to muddle his thinking
without making a man of him. As a handsome only child he had never
known anything except his own way; as an only child he had come to
enjoy solitude; and his doting mother had encouraged him in his belief
that there was no one in the world quite so important or quite so worthy
of every attention as Charles Kortland. And the Navy never allowed
him his own way; it offered almost no chance of enjoying solitude; and
it did not share – it laughed at – his estimate of his own importance.

His present job, as compartment cleaner to the chief petty officers'
quarters, was one many on board would have coveted; it was one of
those given in rotation, in fact, for that reason. But Kortland resented
having to clean up after other people; he had a poor opinion of chief
petty officers, which did not make it any easier, and helped to explain
the outburst which had brought him a deck court-martial. The desire
for extra sleep had not been the cause of his stolen hours in the lower
handling room; he had only wanted to get away by himself – the hardest
thing in the world in a wartime destroyer. So now he was standing

and chipping paint along with a group of other hardened criminals, completing the last hour of the sentence which had condemned him to this work before the deck court-martial. His fingers were sore by the time he was released.

'Sail ho!' yelled a lookout on the flying bridge.

'Where away?'

'Dead ahead.'

Right ahead; *Boon* had made visual contact at last with other ships of the United States Navy, after eleven days of complete solitude. The effect was felt in every part of the ship, and all to the good, as the executive officer had predicted. There were other ships to look at now, instead of an empty horizon, and disparaging comparisons to be made between them and the *Boon*. There was a tanker to refuel from, calling for considerable activity on the part of the first lieutenant and Chief Boatswain's Mate Trautmann and their party. There were new faces to be seen along the tanker's rail, and old jests to be refurbished and hurled back and forth across the foaming water that divided the two ships while the fuelling proceeded.

There was no mail – that was too much to hope for – but there was fresh bread, enough for two meals, to be hauled on board over the 'pony express'; there was ice cream, enough for a couple of dips per man, to follow. And there was a batch of new movies; from the deck of the tanker came the most stimulating comments about the new musical featuring Alice Faye, which at that moment was travelling over to *Boon* along the high line. Every eye that could be spared from duty watched the bundle with passionate anxiety until it arrived safely.

The whole world was in a turmoil, and the destiny of mankind hung in the balance. The men who lined those rails knew – if they stopped to think about it – that their lives were in imminent deadly peril, that mutilation or death might be their portion at any moment. Yet all these issues were obscured at this moment by the prospect of fresh bread, ice cream and the shadow of Miss Alice Faye upon a screen.

'Movies tonight, man!' said Seaman 2nd Class Henderson ecstatically to Seaman 2nd Class Kortland.

'Yeah,' agreed Kortland. He at least was not going to be so undignified as to display all the enthusiasm he actually felt.

An announcement over the ship's loudspeaker added to the pleasure and excitement he was concealing. 'Now hear this. Now hear this. Now that the ship has joined the task force the ship will not go to general quarters at sunset until further notice. The ship will not go to general quarters . . .'

Kortland did not bother to listen to the repetition. His quick mind was foreseeing new possibilities. The c.p.o.'s ate their dinner early. If there were no general quarters he could get through his scullery maid's duties early and could be down in the mess hall well before anyone else in the ship; he could pick himself a seat, settle himself down at leisure and view the show from a position of advantage, in comparative comfort, and without an undignified preliminary scramble.

He liked movies and tonight he would be able to enjoy them in the leisurely and privileged way that was really his due. That was how it came about that the executive officer, passing through the mess hall before the show was ready to start, grinned at the sight of the young seaman stalking down alone from the other end with an exaggerated air of owning the place, and seating himself before the centre of the screen. The exec picked him out among the crowd after the movie was over, too; the expression on his face showed how much he had enjoyed his evening.

The *Boon* was still a stepchild among destroyers; the task force to which she was attached included not one ship of her division. She was a newcomer, too, and this helped to explain why she was given the odd jobs to do, and why she was stationed on the wing of the destroyer screen that combed the sea above and below the surface, in advance of the main body, as the task force steamed steadily northward into dangerous waters. A battle had been fought in the Coral Sea; there had been losses on both sides as they groped for each other, each trying to guess at the other's objectives. The wildest stories had been told, and some of them had even proved true. While naval staffs tried to evaluate results, and while a puzzled world was coming slowly to the conclusion that the newest Japanese advance had been beaten back, this little task force was moving in to maintain an appearance of strength.

The Japanese would strike again; no one could doubt it. But the American naval staffs had already shrewdly guessed that the blow would be delivered elsewhere, against Midway, the Aleutians, against Pearl Harbor itself. There was every reason to convey the impression that the United States Navy was massing to defend New Guinea and Australia again, leaving Midway unguarded. This was the business of the little task force. Seaman 2nd Class Charles Kortland, with all his personal problems, washing dishes in the chief petty officers' pantry, was playing his part in the preliminary moves of the decisive naval battle of the war.

The sun was shining bright that morning when *Boon* secured from general quarters and Kortland came up on deck from his battle station down in the lower handling room. The sky was blue, and the sea was bluer still, with a segment of gold extending to the horizon, above which hung the golden sun; and behind, the ships stretched their long parallel wakes dazzling white against the blue. A lovely morning, and tonight he was going to see Alice Faye in the musical. He entered the chief petty officers' pantry to encounter harsh reality.

'Do you see this?' asked Chief Boatswain's Mate Trautmann. He was pointing at the garbage can, too full for the lid to close properly, and beside it the bulging paper sack that held the excess. 'I said, "Do you see this?" ' said Trautmann.

'Yes.' Kortland blurted out, for not to answer would be an additional offence.

'It's stinking already and it will have to go on stinking. Any excuse?'

Not even Kortland's quick mind could think of one in that surprised moment. He had forgotten about the garbage last night in the excitement of going to the movies. Regulations were explicit that it should only be dumped after sunset so as to leave the least traces for a scouting enemy. He had intended to return and dump the garbage after the movies and had forgotten all about it. Now it would have to stay on board all day.

'Any excuse?' repeated Trautmann.

'No.'

'You'll be at captain's mast this morning.'

And when he came up before the captain he had to stand at attention and listen to a short lecture.

'This is the third time you've been in trouble,' said the captain. 'I can't understand why an intelligent fellow like you should behave in this way. This time it will be ten hours' extra duty.'

Kortland had sense enough not to allow his feelings to appear. He could live through ten hours of paint chipping without noticing it, as long as he had the prospect of Alice Faye this evening. But before he could be dismissed the executive officer interposed.

'Excuse me, sir. Do you remember the British, sir? You –'

'Yes, I remember,' said the captain. Half an hour ago the executive officer had pointed out to him that movies meant as much to Kortland as rum to a Britisher, and had indicated a course of action. The captain went on. 'This extra duty will be served as lookout during the second dog watch for the next five days.'

There was an astonished silence at this new departure.

'Would you mind repeating that, sir?' asked the ship's yeoman, who was noting the proceedings.

The captain had no objection. He repeated what he had said, clearly and distinctly, and again there was silence.

'Mast dismissed,' said the executive officer.

Kortland was actually pale, tanned though he was, as he turned away. Some of the pallor was due to surprise and disappointment, but some of it was caused by rage. Not merely would he not get a front seat for Alice Faye but he would miss all but the end of the picture. His world fell away from him as he thought about it. When captain's mast was finished he saw the exec walking aft to inspect the after-gun mount, and he had the wild notion, momentarily, of appealing to him for his good offices in changing the order; but he knew enough about the Navy for the notion to be only momentary. And as he looked across at the exec, he had a moment of revelation. He remembered how the first night before the movies started he had met the exec's eyes before choosing his seat. That man had eyes for everything. Kortland did not understand the reference to the British which the exec had made to the captain; it might even be a code word. But that just showed he was the victim of a persecution directed with diabolical ingenuity. He felt friendless and betrayed. It was enough – nearly – to make a man weep, or to drive him to violence.

Kortland was man enough not to weep and sensible enough not to indulge in violence. Just before sunset each dog watch he climbed up to the flying bridge and took his assigned place on the starboard side to begin his dreary spell as lookout, staring out over the wide waste of blue water while the *Boon* and the rest of the task force steamed on northward, soaring slowly up the long, endless swells, and slithering down the farther slopes, the angle of meeting the swell varying irregularly with the irregular scheme of zigzagging. *Boon* was the right-hand ship of the screen, and he was the right-hand man of the ship; with misery contending with resentment in his heart he was guarding the right flank of the task force. He could hardly help but take his duties seriously, even though at the same time a dozen sonar apparatuses were probing the depths below him, and the ship's radar was scanning the horizon all round. Neither radar nor sonar could be implicitly trusted; they could not report smoke or wreckage. For that matter even after nightfall the human eye still had its uses. Even in a ship where they made silly jokes about borrowing from the British.

On the third night the sun was sinking in a clear sky over on his left hand; behind him, in fact, when he faced out to starboard and the zigzag took a westerly trend. It was dreary, monotonous work, unsuited to a thinking mind, decided Kortland as usual. A thousand hours of monotony and repetition for one hour of Alice Faye, and then to be tricked out of Alice Faye in the end. It was Alice Faye and not the Japanese who occupied his thoughts – he was like nearly every one of his shipmates in that respect.

Now the sun was hanging just above the horizon and giving perceptibly less light as it reddened. *Boon* climbed a swell, and as she hung on the summit Kortland, looking out to starboard, caught a momentary flash on the horizon. It had come and gone at once; it had been the faintest speck of light, as though a wet surface had for a second reflected the reddening sun behind him. He glued his eyes on the spot and waited. He might have been mistaken; it might have been merely a wave top. The seconds passed, lengthened into a minute. No; as the

Boon hung on the next summit there it was – a wet surface catching the light. He wondered what he should do, and it should be noted that his resentment was not in evidence as he debated with himself. He was much more preoccupied with the fear of making a fool of himself. *Boon* climbed the next swell, and there it was again, this time briefer than ever if that were possible, and redder than before. Kortland took a deep breath.

'Sail ho!' he yelled down to the bridge.

Instant tension down below; the Navy endured ten thousand hours of monotony and repetition in preparation for an hour of battle.

'Where away?' from the officer of the deck.

'Broad on the starboard beam. An – an object, sir. I saw it catch the light, sir.'

Every eye that could be spared was turned out to starboard. Only the briefest flash this time, and only Kortland, with his eyes trained in exactly the right direction, spotted it.

'There it is, sir!'

This second definite identification made up the mind of the officer of the deck.

'Captain to the bridge,' he said to the man at the voice tube.

Kortland was fully committed now. It took only a moment for the captain to reach the bridge, and a moment more for the executive officer to follow him.

'Do you think he's seeing things?' asked the captain.

'Who is it up there? Oh, it's young Kortland,' said the executive officer, and then, 'I think we can trust him.'

Half the sun was below the horizon, and darkness was increasing apace.

'Tell us what you saw again, Kortland,' hailed the captain.

'I saw something catch the light, sir. It might be wreckage.'

'Are you sure of the bearing?'

'Yes, sir.' Kortland's pointed arm indicated it with a promise of exactitude.

The sun was gone now, as the captain wrestled with his problem. As soon as it was fully night the task force was to reverse course and steam south again; it would be awkward for a detached destroyer to resume her place in the screen of darkness. But still –

The captain reached his decision. 'Keep your eye on the place, Kortland,' he said before he went to the radio telephone. 'Request permission to investigate an unidentified object to starboard, sir . . . Aye, aye, sir. Thank you.'

In the fading light *Boon* swung herself round until her jack staff was right in line with Kortland's pointed arm and then she headed forward with increased revolutions. Darker and darker it grew, and then another lookout took up the cry.

'I see it, sir! Dead ahead! A rubber life raft!' Now they could all see it.

'All engines stop.'

Boon's speed slowly diminished.

'All engines back one third.'

It was very nearly completely dark as *Boon* surged alongside; it was indeed a yellow rubber life raft whose wet side had reflected the sunset back to Kortland's eye, and lying in it was a U.S. Navy aviator; it was not until they had hoisted him on board that they could be sure he was alive. The battle of the Coral Sea had been fought ten long, long days ago. Kortland could look down upon the nearly lifeless thing swinging up on the line.

The following afternoon Kortland was mildly surprised to hear the ship's loudspeaker say his name. The call interrupted a furious train of thought; the films were to be returned tomorrow, and the whole ship's company, when consulted, had selected the Alice Faye musical as the movie to be repeated tonight. And he still had extra duty to perform, and he would miss Alice Faye for the second time.

'Seaman 2nd Class Kortland to report to the bridge immediately.'

Waiting there was the pharmacist's mate 1st class who tried to watch over the health of the entire ship's company.

'You're going to see Lieutenant Evans, the naval aviator you spotted on the rubber life raft,' said the pharmacist's mate. 'He wants to thank you. This way.'

He led the way to the captain's cabin, the one the captain never slept in at sea.

'Exec's given permission,' explained the pharmacist's mate.

The bunk there held a young man, incredibly thin, with brilliant dark eyes glittering out of a face tanned almost black, patchily, because some of that face was much whiter where ten days' beard had been shaved off.

'It was you who saved my life,' said the lieutenant. 'I want to thank you.'

'Yes, sir,' said Kortland. It was an unhelpful thing to say at this moment.

'Another night in that boat and I'd have had it,' went on the lieutenant. 'And it wasn't easy for you – they've told me about it.'

'It wasn't anything, sir,' said Kortland. He had his dignity to consider, even though the pharmacist's mate constituted the entire audience.

'We can't go on arguing about it,' said the lieutenant. 'The exec's as pleased as hell about what you did. He gave permission for me to

send for you so as to give me a chance to talk to you. I'm being transferred tomorrow. Now you tell me. What do you want? I've only got
to ask the exec and he'll give it to you. What would you like?'

Alice Faye tonight. But on the other hand there was that remark
about borrowing from the British. That rankled, although Kortland
still had no idea what it meant; yet there were other things that he
understood. He was perfectly aware, with acute telepathy, that the
exec was ready and willing to excuse him from the rest of his extra
duty. And somewhere in his subconscious there was a revolt against the
incongruity of relating the saving of a life to an exhibition of shadows
on a screen. Even though Kortland was growing up fast he was still a
mixed-up teen-ager. He opened his mouth to speak and shut it again
just in time – he had been about to say, 'To hell with the British,'
and that would have made just no sense to the lieutenant nor to the
pharmacist's mate.

'Well?' asked the lieutenant.

Kortland had to prove that the British were wrong, that the exec
was wrong, and that he himself was a man who did not care about
movies in the least.

'I don't want anything,' said Kortland. 'I don't want anything at
all.'

It was three seconds later before he remembered what else he should
have said, and he added it. 'Sir.'

Nicholas Monsarrat

The Ship that Died of Shame

THERE are a lot of things about this story that I still don't understand. I've had a good deal to do with ships – too much, maybe – and if there's one thing I know about them, it is that they are *not* alive. They are made of wood and metal, and nothing else: they don't have souls, they don't have wills of their own, they don't talk back. In fact, they're not like women at all. Writers of nautical romances may pretend – but I'd better start at the beginning.

The beginning, like almost everything in my life, goes back to the war.

My name is Bill Randall, and, if you used to read the Naval communiqués with any sort of attention during the recent contest, you might just remember it. I spent nearly all the war in Coastal Forces, which meant, for me, mucking about in motor gun-boats and having hell's own fun in the process. The Beat-up Boys, they used to call us – and the name tells you just about all you need to know. We had been hired, it seemed, for the specific purpose of nipping across to the French, Dutch, and (later) German coasts, shooting up everything in sight, and nipping back again, cheating the dawn each morning by a few short minutes.

Our targets might be anything. It depended on our own luck. Sometimes it was a coastal convoy making for the Scheldt, sometimes German E-boats, sometimes mine-layers off Calais, sometimes fishing craft, German-chaperoned, trying their luck east of the Dogger Bank. (If you even *fished* for the Germans, as far as I was concerned, you were a legitimate target.) Once it was a lighthouse, once it was a camouflaged gasometer, once (glorious moment) it was a train coming out of a tunnel north of Boulogne. We were sent over the other side to make trouble, any trouble, and we did just that, using (in Their Lordships' convenient phrase) 'the widest possible discretion' in the process.

In between times, we escorted our own East Coast convoys, and picked up clumsy RAF types who had come down into the sea, and touched off drifting mines, and acted as target-towing ships. Motor gun-boats could do anything – and that was especially true of mine, MGB 1087. Which brings us to the ship in this story.

MGB 1087 was a special honey. All gun-boats are hit-and-run weapons, of course, and mine could do both to perfection. She was a hundred feet long, with four Packard engines of 5,000 brake-horsepower, able to shove her along at nearly thirty-five knots. She was armed with a few depth-charges in case we got on the track of a submarine (we never did), six Oerlikons and eight smaller machine-guns, and two six-pounders – a gun that makes a hole approximately a foot wide in any metal, and more in a man. We had plenty of examples of both, in those wonderful years.

MGB 1087 . . . I raised that boat practically from a toy yacht, and there wasn't a better one in any flotilla operating from any base; we must have finished the war with as good a record as you could find anywhere. On the shield of the forward six-pounder – the obvious place for scoring up 'trophies' – we painted the following tally:

Mines	126
Gasometers	2
E-boats	2
Steam Locomotives	1
Aircraft	8
Trawlers	3

Those were definite kills, the fruit of hundreds of nights of watching and waiting, hundreds of hours of cutting spray and pinching cold. There seemed no harm in being proud of them.

We were also well decorated. Hoskins (my First Lieutenant – I'll tell you about him in a minute) once suggested that we enlarge the trophy list to read:

DSO	1, *and bar*
DSC	1
DSM	3

That didn't seem a very good idea, either then or now . . . But we *did* get those aircraft, and we did get those seven E-boats, and all the rest, and I suppose the medals were, in a way, the same sort of trophies. It seemed to me, though, that it needed a special kind of outlook, unusual in our job, to paint them up in black and white for all the world to see.

The ship carried a crew of twenty-two, mostly gunnery-ratings, and two officers. I was the Captain of MGB 1087; the other officer, for nearly three years, was my First Lieutenant, George Hoskins.

It's extraordinary how close you can be to a man and how many times you can owe him your life (and vice versa), and still know nothing about him. I liked Hoskins for his good qualities, exhibited on many occasions – his guts, cunning and ruthlessness, all essential 'beat-up' attributes – and I shut my mind to the rest. He ran the ship efficiently – the guns were always clean, the engines smooth as machine-oil, the ship's company well organized and well looked after. But there was always something else, something I didn't know about and didn't want to know.

Perhaps it was in his eyes. Hoskins was a small man, neat, an RNVR Lieutenant who had been some sort of salesman before the war. We were together during all those three years, and he never let me down on any of the dozens of occasions when that might have happened. He won his DSC, the one he wanted to chalk up as an advertisement on the six-pounder gun-shield; and he deserved to win it. But somehow his eyes said that the thing was *all* advertisement: that the point of the war was not really sinking E-boats and downing aircraft and killing Germans, but selling MGB 1087, and Lieutenant Commander Randall, DSO, and Lieutenant Hoskins, DSC, to the Admiralty and, through them, to the public, as the ace outfit of Coastal Forces.

In a way he had plenty of facts to support him. She *was* a wonderful ship, with a wonderful record. We *did* make the headlines, on a lot of occasions. The basic virtue of that, however, was not in the headlines, but in what we did to earn them: the actual sunk ships, the actual dead Germans, the actual few steps nearer to winning. I don't think Hoskins ever saw it like that . . .

Whenever we came back into harbour, with the dawn breaking behind us, and the ship perhaps scarred by machine-gun fire, and an entry in the deck-log such as '0125: sunk one E-boat' to tell the story of a wild, nerve-testing night, something in his eyes seemed to say: 'This ought to get us into the newspapers again. We ought to get another medal. I ought to get my half-stripe, with more money. We might even make it *two* E-boats . . .'

Hoskins had a recurrent joke (if you can call it a joke). Whenever I remarked on the way he boosted the ship's reputation, he used to answer: 'In this war, you've got to look after number one.' Number One, as you probably know, is the Navy slang for the First Lieutenant. He was the First Lieutenant.

Perhaps it wasn't a joke, after all.

My doubt of his 'genuineness' was often there, but I had only one concrete example to go on.

It was a very small matter, when you look back on it: the question as to whether or not we had shot down an aircraft, and whether we should claim it as a 'certainty'. We had been caught, one morning at first light, still on the wrong side of the Channel, and still searching for the crew of a Lancaster bomber which had come down in the sea off Dunkirk.

We never picked them up, but we were picked up ourselves – by a patrolling Ju.88 which nipped in from seawards and tried to dive-bomb us. On his way down he was squarely hit by our Oerlikons – we were *very* ready on the trigger that morning; you could see the bits flying and scattering behind him, and then he levelled off overhead, without letting his bombs go. With a thin plume of black smoke streaming out of his tail-assembly, he disappeared inshore and out of our lives.

I never thought for a moment that we could claim that Junkers as shot down, since he was still going strong, and it was obvious that he would at least reach his own coast-line. But Hoskins, writing up the deck-log as we set course for Dover, entered the incident, without batting an eyelid, as 'One enemy aircraft destroyed'.

I said: 'Oi!' and then: 'We can't put that, Number One. He was still flying for home, happy as a lark.'

Hoskins eyed me, smiling. 'A lark with a pretty sore tail . . . He'll never make it, I'm damn sure.' We both had to shout, above the sea noises and the roar of the Packards going full out. 'You saw the bits and pieces. He was on his way down.'

I shook my head. 'He was losing height very slowly. You can't call it a confirmed kill.'

'As good as.' Hoskins was still smiling, in a vaguely encouraging way, as if I only needed a bit of jollying-along to see it from his angle. 'I wouldn't give much for his chances.' But then he added: 'What's the harm, anyway?'

I stared at him – the small man, bright as a button even at five o'clock in the morning, looking up at me with those encouraging eyes. I wanted no part of any of this.

'People rely on our reports,' I said shortly. I didn't want to touch on anything more definite, like honesty or truth; though I was still keyed up after the action, and felt the thing very simply and clearly myself. 'There's a man at the Air Ministry adding these things up, and we don't want to muck up his figures.' I pointed down at the deck-log. 'Call it "damaged".'

He shrugged, looking away from me. 'We're missing a good chance.'

I didn't like that, either. 'A good chance of what?'

'I mean,' he said elaborately, 'we *did* hit it and it *was* going down, and we want to keep our *own* record straight, just as much as some chair-borne clot at the Air Ministry.'

Listening to the careful phrases, watching him, I could almost see the headlines in his eyes, the headlines he wanted so much: '*Randall and Hoskins Again: Ju.88 Destroyed in Dawn Action.*' I could almost see his private dream of the Admiral shaking hands with him, and the 'Mentioned in Despatches' citation coming by the first post in the morning . . . Without a word, I scored out his entry in the decklog, wrote in my own, and said: 'That straightens *our* record.'

Then I walked to the front of the bridge, glad as never before to feel the ship bucking under my sea-boots and the fresh air coming inboard over the dodger.

But no piece of near-crookery by Hoskins could spoil those years, nor diminish the weight of tough achievement that MGB 1087 piled up. Let me just tell you one thing we did in that ship at that time, to give you the measure of it.

It happened some months after the invasion, when our job was to look after the 'shuttle-service' of Allied shipping that went to-and-fro, to-and-fro between England and Normandy, twenty-four hours of every day of every week: keeping the men alive and the weapons served, away eastwards at the tip of the spear-head now approaching the Rhine, the place where it really mattered.

No convoys were ever so important as those cross-Channel ones – I know the Battle of the Atlantic boys will argue the toss about that, but if the flow of materials to France and Germany had ever been checked, even for half a day, we might have been driven back into the sea, and so lost the war in a prolonged and bloody stalemate. You've got to remember that there were things called V-Ones and V-Twos, robot-weapons aimed at London and tearing the heart out of it every hour on the hour, until we got a grip on the Calais coast-line . . . That invasion just had to stick.

I should explain also that it took place shortly after my wife had been killed in an air-raid, when I didn't mind what went on so long as I could hit back and draw blood. That feeling came in very useful.

We were on independent night-patrol when it happened, near the opposite coast, and drifting with our engines stopped about six miles north of Mulberry Beach. We lay a little to the side of the 'fairway' – the buoyed channel that marked the way into the landing-beaches. It was a calm night, dark, with an edge of moon still showing above the horizon.

On our hydrophones there had been, for hours on end, nothing save water noises, and the occasional boiling sound made by a near-by shoal of fish. No shipping moved within miles of us, though there was a south-bound convoy – including troopers – due to pass through our sector some time after five in the morning. Waiting and listening, for hour after hour, we did our best to believe that, in spite of the tight coastal blockade, there might still be something for us that night.

Then, a little after one o'clock, with the moon nearly down, we suddenly picked up the sound of engines coming towards us from the south – the French coast. It was a whisper at first, then a steady purring, then the loud beat that meant fast-moving diesels.

The Leading Seaman on the hydrophones pressed the earphones closer to his head for a moment, frowning. Then he said: 'Uneven beat, sir. Must be two of them. Approaching one-nine-o degrees.'

We trained our glasses and watched the bearing. One-nine-o degrees was up-moon, which gave us an initial advantage: it meant that we lay hid in an outer ring of darkness, looking towards the footlights . . . Presently something came into view – two somethings, two vague blurs in the darkness, with two slivers of light gradually widening beneath them, the creaming of their bow-waves. They were two ships, chugging towards us down the fairway as if they were driving along the Brighton Road.

They were small. They looked like us – or like E-boats.

I began to think quickly. It was far too early for our own mine-sweepers; they couldn't be other British gun-boats, because this was *our* sector; and the Yanks, however far they strayed from Omaha Beach, could hardly stray as far as this. In fact, it couldn't be *anything* belonging to our side; there was nothing due and there had been no emergency signal to alter the schedule. They *couldn't* be ours – or, if they were (for this was how I felt, after Lucille died), it was going to be just too bad for all concerned.

Hoskins, crouching by my elbow at the front of the bridge, said suddenly: 'I think they're laying mines.'

That of course was the obvious, the only answer, the sort of thing Hoskins always worked out, seconds ahead of me. I did not mind. Mine-laying E-boats in the approach channel, with a convoy on the way . . . They must have come in fast down the Dutch and French coasts, lying hid for one night on the way (though how they had got past our destroyer patrols wanted a lot of explaining), then slowed down, turned north up the marked channel, and set to work.

I called softly: 'Signalman . . .' and dictated a warning signal for the incoming convoy. They would have to send mine-sweepers on ahead, or perhaps divert it altogether. But that was someone else's worry. Ours was here, and nearly within our range.

The blurred shapes were clearer now, resolving themselves into two small ships of our own size, fifty yards apart. If they were E-boats, they would be armed like ourselves: the odds were thus two to one against us, but we had the moon and the surprise, and above all, we had M G B 1087.

I said: 'We'll go in, Number One. The starboard ship first. Then circle inshore and come back for the other one.'

Hoskins said: 'If we went between them, going very fast and firing to port and starboard at the same time, and then ducked out, they might start hammering at each other.'

That, again, was Hoskins at his best: cunning, resourceful, ready to take a chance. It *was* a chance, because if the E-boats were wide-awake, we might be caught in their cross-fire – but then again they might hold their hand for fear of hitting each other. If only we could confuse them a bit . . .

The thing suddenly clicked into place, and I said: 'As we go through, we'll drop a depth-charge between them. The spray will hang for a bit. We'll turn quickly, and fire at one of them through it. They'll both answer back – and with any luck there'll be a riot and they'll start beating each other up.'

Hoskins said: 'Genius.'

I pressed the button.

The roar with which our engines burst into life always startled me: it startled me now. 1087 jumped, then began to rip forward, the bows lifting, the spray whipping upwards and outwards. We started to weave towards the gap between the two E-boats, going our full thirty-five knots, the engines rising to a thick, solid howl as the screws took hold, and the whole ship bumping and shuddering as we drove onwards. Hoskins shouted his fire orders through the inter-com; presently I pressed the firing bell, and all our guns opened up, half on one side and half on the other as we'd arranged, the red tracer bullets fanning outwards in the darkness like the last, most decorative moment of a firework display. Other tracers – theirs – now began to come towards us, but sluggishly and wide of the mark: clearly the E-boats had been caught with their trousers way below their ankles, and we were scoring hits on both targets.

Just before we were level with them, our depth-charge went down, and then up! up! in a colossal cloud of spume and dirty water, hanging livid in the moonlight, obscuring the battlefield.

We came hard-a-port, turning behind them in a tight circle and a fifty-degree heel, and began to fire *over* one E-boat, *through* the spray cloud, *towards* the second ship. Presently the latter, confused and hurt, started to blaze away at her best friend.

We slowed and came to a stop, our guns silent. I began to laugh, standing there on the bridge watching one set of Krauts lacing into another. One could only hope that it would be a very level battle, with both sides selling their lives most dearly . . . We could see that hits were being scored by both E-boats, but the battle was *not* running level: soon the nearest E-boat, which was engaging us as well as its chum in a bemused sort of way, lost heart, and the other closed in, intent on the kill.

The kill could not be denied. There was a rumbling explosion, and the losing E-boat glowed red as though in sudden anger. Her fore-deck flickered as the flames took hold, and she began to settle in the water. The victor ceased her fire, and edged nearer, hungry for prisoners. She was probably trying to signal us all the time to get us to pick up prisoners with her.

There was something of an uproar as she found what sort of prisoners she was picking up. Shouts of wrath and pain, guttural cries of reproach, reached us across the water, sweeter than any music. While they were still sorting it all out, we started up our engines, closed in to fifty yards, and turned to starboard so that all guns were bearing. Then I pressed the firing-bell again, and we opened up with everything we had.

Two six-pounders, six 20-mm Oerlikons, eight machine-guns – it's a hell of a lot of metal in one place at one time, and it was far too much for this target. It seemed to hit that E-boat in one solid thunder-clap; there was a small pause, and then she disintegrated, with a quick, short-lived growl like an animal falling into a pit. Her main magazine bore the remnants skywards . . . There were splashes, as bits of everything fell back into the sea, and then complete silence – the silence of victory.

The score was two E-boats, two complete crews, and our only casualty a seaman who, catching his finger in the depth-charge release gear, lost a nail for King and Country.

I'd never felt so good before – or since.

Six years later I sat in the bar of the Coastal Forces Club, tankard in hand, and wondered why I was unemployable.

It was a familiar train of thought, and entirely suitable to my surroundings . . . I had always found the Coastal Forces Club depressing, not only because it was shabby and rundown, but because it was full of chaps like me – good at war, not much good at anything else, and so returning again and again, in thought and conversation, to the successful past, the only thing that was real for them.

Of course it *was* depressing, physically, with its cheap-looking bar, its indifferent servants who were always being replaced, and its members – mostly ex-RNVR types like myself – gathering there every night and getting noisy or morose over their watery beer. But though I knew all this, I never stayed away from it for more than a few days. 'Keeping up the old war-time comradeship,' we called it, slapping each other on the back and using carefully preserved slang. (The bar was the 'wardroom', the wretched rooms upstairs 'cabins', the inaccurate telephone messages 'signals'.) 'Whistling in the dark' might have been a more accurate description, for that was what we were doing: keeping close together, going through a dead ceremonial like a court in exile, because the past was our whole life, and it was now too tough outside.

But why *was* it too tough, I wondered, not for the first but for the hundredth time? What sort of men were we, that the war had been so good to us and the peace so rotten? Why was it, for example, that in 1944 I could be trusted with a ship worth ninety thousand pounds and the lives of twenty-two men, and yet, in 1950, no one would trust me with a suitcase full of samples? Why had I been able to do such skilful and accurate things six years ago, while now I could hardly put a fresh ribbon in a typewriter? Why had it all dried up so soon? Why was I, in peace-time, such a dead loss?

I was trying not to be sorry for myself, but I *was* puzzled.

I sipped my beer, not looking at the hearty types round the bar who were showing signs of wanting to sing. Life had been fine at first, when we were newly demobilized: we all had a bit of money saved up, we all had our war gratuities, we all had a future as bright as the past we had been able to conquer so royally. I 'looked around' for a bit, loafing unashamedly, and then took a job in a firm of travel agents; it was all right to begin with, except that everyone seemed to know a lot more about it than I did, and then suddenly I got sick of it, and it didn't seem worth doing any longer, and I walked out. That was the first of many such walk-outs.

I couldn't settle down anywhere. The succession of shoddy jobs multiplied, grew, faded, and disappeared behind me: I was salesman, clerk, courier, tutor, salesman, yacht-broker, club-secretary, and sales-man again. The level drifted a little lower each time: the deterior-ation, though never too marked, was always there, always progressive.

Pretty soon I stopped being choosy about jobs, and started to wheedle and to agree with everybody who might have work to offer, and to call them 'sir' again. But by then it seemed to be too late, or else I had lost the trick, or I just *looked* no good. Whatever it was, the shutters were coming down, and even the foot in the door was being squeezed out into the cold again.

Only in the Coastal Forces bar, 'keeping up the old spirit' with a lot of other dead-beats, was life anything like a living thing at all.

If Lucille had been by my side, it would all have been different; she would have taken me in hand, and organized things and seen that I climbed instead of slipped. But she wasn't by my side; she had been dead these seven years, and I *had* slipped, nearly all the way down.

Now, on this summer evening in London, I was shabby, and out of work, and broke; and I knew it all.

The man next to me, a beefy boozer who tried to sell you insurance unless you shut him up straightaway, said:

'Do you remember that show at Walcheren, when old Jack Phillips bought it?'

He droned on, while I said 'Yes' at intervals. We both knew it all by heart, and it hadn't been nearly as well-handled or as successful as we now made out. Then there was a stir at the door, and someone said: 'Of *course* I'm a member,' and a man walked in. It was George Hoskins.

We saw each other immediately. I rose, and he came across the room towards me. I said: 'Hallo, George,' and he said: 'I thought I'd find you here.'

We looked at each other. I knew well what he saw – a tall, thin man in an old grey suit, scuffed rubber-soled suède shoes, and a frayed RNVR tie. What *I* saw was very different: different from myself, and different from what the picture had been in the past.

Hoskins had blossomed. He looked enterprising, slick, confident – all the things I was not. He was well dressed, in a neat dark suit and a grey tie; he carried himself with assurance, and glanced about him with a wonderfully good-humoured air, as though to demonstrate that there was no shame in being a small man if you were a successful one also. I knew, from the past, that there must be something snide about him – that, whatever he was doing, it was not quite straightforward. But it seemed to pay all right.

I felt him taking me in, swiftly, as we faced each other in the centre of the room. His eyes, I noticed, were still encouraging, but now they were slightly ironic as well, as if we must both realize that much of the ground between us had altered. We hadn't met for five years, not since I was the Captain, and he the First Lieutenant, of MGB 1087. Things, he seemed to be saying, had moved on, hadn't they?

He looked round the bar, taking *that* all in, too. Then he said: 'Chaps still fighting the war?'

It was what I had often thought myself, but it nettled me to hear it from him. I said, shortly: 'Something like that,' and asked him what he would drink.

'A large pink gin, please.'

I ordered it, and beer for myself, rather glumly, while the other people at the bar eyed us in morose speculation. No one drank gin in the Coastal Forces Club any more. Gin was six-and-sixpence.

Hoskins faced me easily, legs crossed, one elbow on the bar – a negligent man at ease with all the world.

'Nice to see you again, Bill.' He had never called me Bill. 'What are you doing these days?'

I said: 'Nothing much.'

He nodded, as if recognizing one of his own thoughts in my answer. But he said: 'That must be nice. Wish I could afford it.'

THE SHIP THAT DIED OF SHAME

I looked at him without saying anything; the suit I was wearing, and the shoes, and the tie, had all proclaimed the answer to his remark before it was made, putting it in a special category of insult. But it might be worth sweating this sort of thing out . . . We talked idly, reminiscing in the best tradition of the Coastal Forces Club.

Presently I said: 'What are *you* doing?'

'Oh, this and that.' He waved his hand vaguely. 'You've got to scratch a living where you can, these days. It's not so easy either, with all these bloody restrictions.'

'I suppose not.' The comment meant nothing to me, but from long experience I could tell that something was coming; and I wasn't prepared to baulk him in any way, however much of a spiv he sounded.

Hoskins bent towards me. 'If you're not fixed up permanently,' he said, 'I've got an idea for a sideline that might be interesting. It needs someone like you.'

I grunted non-committally. It was nice to hear that one was needed, anywhere. I imagine that Hoskins knew that.

'It would take a boat, a first-class boat, and someone to run it. Two people, in fact – you and me.' Round us, conversation had broken out again, and his voice was now masked by others. 'A fast motor-boat, to make trips across the Channel and back.' He smiled engagingly. 'We've made enough of those in our time, God knows.'

'What sort of trips?' I asked, though I knew the answer already. 'Passengers? Freight?'

He nodded. 'You could call it that. Fast freight.'

'But what about the boat? Who'll put up the money?'

He gestured again, his eyes meeting mine with particular directness. 'I've got some friends. There are a lot of *other* people around here who don't like restrictions . . . Are you interested?'

'Yes.'

'Good show.' He smiled, as if he too knew the answers before they were given. Then he looked round the bar. 'The house should now go into secret session. Isn't there anywhere else we can talk?'

'There's a writing-room upstairs. It's usually empty.'

'O K. Let's take our glasses up.'

As I felt in my pocket to pay for the drinks, he put a pound note down on the bar and said: 'That's all right, old boy – expenses.'

On the way upstairs I said: 'I suppose you mean smuggling,' and he said: 'Yes.'

I didn't make much objection when it came down to it: I was broke, and past caring much what I did, as long as I could pay the long list of debts I owed and organize myself a bit of elbow-room. Hoskins, expanding his ideas in the down-at-heel writing-room, painted a very rosy picture of our joint future: what fun we would have, how much we could clear each trip, how enormous a demand for our services there would be, from those vague people who 'didn't care for restrictions'.

So far, life in the Welfare State had given me nothing; but all that was now to be changed. Shortages, rules, regulations, import control – these, apparently, could combine to give us a very generous living.

I thought fleetingly of England, struggling with her screwed-up economics for year after year, trying to butt her way through the post-war mess, relying on people to go fair shares and not swindle on the rations. Then I thought of myself, struggling with *my* economics; and the shabby, shoddy life which was all I had won for myself in the process.

There was no doubt which was the more compelling picture.

It would be wrong to say that I hesitated for very long; or even at all.

Sometime during the evening I said:

'I wonder if we could possibly get hold of the old ship. She'd be ideal.'

Hoskins nodded, as if once more recognizing his own thoughts. 'Funny you should say that,' he answered. 'I happen to know where she's lying. And she's for sale . . .'

It was wonderful to see MGB 1087 again; though there was no doubt that she looked like hell.

She was lying in the yacht-basin on the Lymington River in Hampshire. When Hoskins and I crossed the plank that served as a gangway and stepped aboard her, it was like stepping into the decayed past. She wore an air of old-womanish neglect: unwanted, uncared-for, unloved. The paint was blistered and flaking off, all the metalwork rusty or green verdigris; at the water-level, a filthy fringe of weed killed the clean sweep of her lines. She had nothing left to show for the proud years; if it had not been for the deep scored furrow made by a two-pounder shell in her fore-deck, I would not have recognized her, would not have claimed her as my own.

'Plenty to do,' said Hoskins, looking round him with a faint – a very faint – return of professionalism. 'But the builders swear the hull's still sound.'

'We won't need four engines,' I said. 'Too expensive to run.'

Hoskins grinned. 'And we can use the space, too.'

Down in the tiny wardroom, long closed and musty, we sat at the table where we'd both sat on hundreds of occasions in the past – sometimes safe in harbour, sometimes within gun-shot of an enemy coast – and listened to the water lapping against her bows, and planned a future for her. It wasn't going to be as worth-while as the past, but we owed it to her to make a success of it.

I worked for nearly three months down at Lymington – and that was wonderful, too. Hoskins remained in London, organizing our affairs and, I suppose, drumming up custom for the future; it was my job to dish up MGB 1087 so that she could face her curious assignment. Sometimes I caught myself thinking: all this is the First Lieutenant's job, really . . . But it was clear that the war-time roles were now reversed, and that when Hoskins had said, looking at the ship, 'There's plenty to do,' he had meant that there was plenty for *me* to do, and I'd better get on with it because that was what I was going to be paid for – by him.

It would have been irksome, a few years back, but now it was not – the intervening time had been too unsuccessful, too defeating, for me to cling even to the shreds of hierarchy. And, anyway, I soon found that I didn't really mind what label I wore, because I was working again, and close to the sea, and back home in MGB 1087.

The first things to be fixed up were the engines, which, having been grease-packed and sprayed, were still in good shape. We took two of them out; the remaining two, I calculated, would give us a speed of between twenty-five and thirty knots – enough for most emergencies. But a more important thing was to simplify the controls, since there would only be two of us aboard to work the ship. In the end we led everything up to the bridge: the steering-wheel, the engine-controls, the lighting system – they were all there under the hand of one man, leaving the other half of the crew free to sleep, or to work round the ship, or (when we came into harbour) to see to the mooring-wires or the anchor.

A general clean-up followed this reorganization: the ship was hauled out of the water, and scraped and repainted: the woodwork was sand-papered smooth, and all the metal cleaned and polished. With a spring-cleaning down below, and some extra lockers fitted in place of the two engines, that completed a refit which turned MGB 1087 from a hulk into a ship again. She wasn't a ship of war, of course: she couldn't hit her thirty-five knots, or punch holes in E-boats and aircraft, or scare the hell out of the fish with her depth-charges; but she was ship-shape once more, and clean inside and out, and workmanlike, and I knew she would not let us down.

As soon as she was ready, I telephoned Hoskins in London, and when he came down at the week-end we took her for a trial run, down-river, and out into the Solent.

It was grand to be at sea again, and we were lucky in our weather, which was clear, sunny, and calm. We crossed to the Isle of Wight, and then turned westwards down-Channel; the ship handled easily, in spite of the loss of power, and she remained as dry as a bone inside. We spent nearly the whole day at sea, alternately speeding and idling, testing her engines, her steering, her electrics, her general seaworthiness. At the end, in spite of the long lay-off, there was nowhere we could fault her.

'She's still good,' I said at last, when we had seen enough and were setting course for Lymington River once more. 'She'll take us anywhere.'

Hoskins, who had been checking the small radio we carried, joined me at the front of the bridge, where I was steering by the remote-control wheel. The spokes of this, I could not help remembering, were hollowed out – 'for small jobs', as Hoskins had put it. There were a lot of such hiding-places all over the ship covertly installed by our own carpenter ('One of the boys,' Hoskins explained): tucked inside the navigation lights, and disguised as spare petrol tanks, and hidden in a false beam down in the ward-room, and masquerading as a cold-storage space; even the pint-sized lavatory forward had a cistern that was something quite different. MGB 1087 had now become a high-class conjuring apparatus, as well as a working ship.

Hoskins looked at me and grinned suddenly. I think he had enjoyed the day, too, and our re-encounter with the past. He gestured round MGB 1087, and then at the wide horizon.

'Randall and Hoskins again, eh?' he said cheerfully.

I supposed we could call it that, in a way. In spite of the details.

From the start, Hoskins handled the business side: I was employed on a salary basis, plus a commission on 'results', which the future would determine. Hoskins did all the accounting, as well as fixing up the various jobs; and I never had any sort of complaint in that line, since, from the very beginning, we made a lot of trips, and a lot of money very fast.

'What do people need most?' Hoskins had once asked when we were working out our plans. 'That's what we want to find out – then we'll give it them.'

Put like that, our operations were practically a moral crusade, since our only aim in life was to see that people were happy. Why, we were almost on the side of the Government . . . I must say that 'what people wanted most' covered some damned queer things, particularly later on, when we started to extend a bit; but to start with, it was in a way true that we were, as smugglers, quite respectable characters.

Brandy was our principal cargo on the first few trips: that, and French wines, and nylon stockings, and tinned ham, and cigars; all the little things, you see, that make the difference between life and the 'gracious living' that one sees in the ads. I used to think what a great deal of pleasure, and how little pain, we were giving; and, at the same time, what a lot of money we were making, in this innocent fashion . . . Sometimes we made it in one quick trip – from near Dover, across the thirty-odd miles to France, and back again in one night; sometimes we took it more easily, cruising along the northern French coast, or as far south as St Malo, in the guise of English yachtsmen who could hardly bear to tear themselves away from so hospitable a playground. But as soon as we were loaded, we tore.

Hoskins had plenty of contacts in England, and plenty in France: that much I could tell, though I never asked him about the details, preferring to be just the dull sailor who ran the boat. That part did not prove difficult. We never had any trouble with MGB 1087 in those days: she handled perfectly, my coastal navigation was still adequate, and Hoskins, who could tinker effectively with most engines, kept ours running smoothly.

We had our share of excitement in other ways. Let me tell you one thing we did in that ship at that time, to give you the measure of it.

It was about four o'clock one morning, when we'd just got back from a Cherbourg trip, and were feeling our way up the Lymington River to our anchorage. There were no shore-lights, and we showed none ourselves: MGB 1087 inched her way up-stream against the gently falling tide, creeping past the stakes that marked the channel and the mud-flats that smelt richly of the sea, and the other boats at their moorings, and the beginning of the sheds and houses grouped round the anchorage. It was our own front drive, and we knew it well, even in the pitch blackness which shrouded the hour before the dawn.

It reminded me of other nights in this same ship, when we crept our way along the Dutch coast, or up the little estuaries, probing the defences, not looking for trouble, hoping for a quiet run in – and out again. Then, the enemy had been the Germans. But now . . .

We were just rounding the last bend, and shaping up for the ferryboat slipway, when a searchlight was switched on, dead ahead, and a voice shouted:

'Motor-boat ahoy! Stop your engines!'

Instinctively I swung the wheel and took the ship across to starboard: I knew we were near the right-hand riverbank, but I didn't want to risk a collision – nor another boat taking too close a look at us. But the searchlight followed our sheer to starboard; at my elbows Hoskins said softly: 'Keep her going – this looks official.' The hail was repeated, this time on a peremptory note; and knowing what was bound to happen I eased back the throttle and threw the engine out of gear.

We grounded gently on the mud, and came to rest, the stern swinging, the bows caught fast in the sucking clay.

Hoskins, not at a loss for a moment, faced the blinding searchlight, and shouted: 'You stupid clots! Where the hell do you think you're going?'

A stolid voice, unimpressed, answered: 'Take our line. We're com-ing aboard.'

There were two men, one small, one big. They brought their fast open launch alongside, and clambered aboard, with an air of compet-ence and authority which I did not relish. But we still had a part to act.

'What's this all about?' I asked peevishly, as soon as they were on deck. 'I thought we'd collide – and now we're aground.'

'You'll float off all right, at the next tide,' said the small man.

'That's not the point . . . What was the searchlight for, anyway?'

'Customs,' said the small man briefly.

Hoskins said, surprised: 'In Lymington?'

'We're not from Lymington,' said the big man. 'Let's see your log.'

A prickling silence fell, while the two of them peered at the deck-log on the chart-table. Luckily it was written up every hour – a habit from the respectable past which now paid a dividend; and there was nothing wrong with our clearance papers. But I wondered, as we waited, if Hoskins felt as tight about the throat as I did. This could be total disaster.

'Cherbourg,' said the small man presently. 'Why so late getting in?'

'We were held up,' said Hoskins. 'We could have anchored down river, but I didn't want to hang about.'

'And why no navigation lights?'

'They're fused,' answered Hoskins promptly. 'I'm sorry – I know *that* was wrong.' And then: 'Look, let's get this sorted out in comfort. Come along down to the cabin, out of the cold.'

I must say that, during the next hour, Hoskins was superb. We sat round the table, and talked and smoked; presently Hoskins produced a bottle of brandy, winking, and said: 'This hasn't paid any duty – yet,' and poured out some generous drinks. We found out where they had both been during the war, and reminisced about that, and about smuggling generally, and some of the war-time Navy scandals in connection with duty-free cigarettes . . .

The two men were suspicious – you could see that a mile off: and they were also good at their jobs and, of course, incorruptible. But to listen to Hoskins, we might have been safe in a pub ashore, with a couple of chance acquaintances who had turned out to be good company.

In spite of the ease which began to prevail, however, I found myself starting to sweat. The Customs men were certain to 'take a look round,' if only as a matter of form; and on this trip we couldn't stand even the most cursory look. Perhaps we had become careless, but this time the ship had been loaded on the supposition that we *wouldn't* run into trouble. As well as a lot of Dutch cigars and some lengths of cloth in the lockers aft, we had thirty-six dozen bottles of wine – claret and burgundy – hidden under the floor-boards, and in the fake buoyancy chambers and under the seats at the back of the bridge. We were crammed with the stuff: to all intents and purposes, MGB 1087 had red wine running out of her ears.

I began to sweat some more.

The hour passed; the convivial party must soon draw to a close. Presently, I knew, the small man would point to the brandy bottle and the cigars, and ask: 'Have you got many more of these?' and the big man would rise, and stretch, and say: 'I'll just take a look round . . .' And we would listen to him walking about, and lifting things, and then after a pause he would call out: 'Joe – just come here . . .' The party was convivial, but not convivial enough: duty lurked round the corner, and the big man and the small man were not the sort of people to forget it. No British Customs men ever were.

Hoskins said: 'Excuse me, chaps – nature calls'; and I heard him walk forward to the lavatory. There was silence round the cabin table while he was away – in spite of the brandy, my tongue was dry as bleached sand – and then he came back, and stood in the doorway, not looking at me, and said:

'It's up forward, if anyone else wants it.'

The small man nodded, and said: 'That's for me,' and disappeared. When *he* came back, the big man rose, and stretched, and said:

'I'll just take a look round before we go.'

Hoskins said: 'Sure – help yourself,' and then he suddenly looked down at this feet, and called out: 'For Heaven's sake – we're half full of water!'

It was true, like a nightmare that suddenly takes an incomprehensible turn; water was seeping across the cabin floor-boards and starting to gurgle round our feet; even as I looked, the boat gave a lurch, and more water sprayed in, in a solid cascade, from forward. MGB 1087 was awash, fore and aft.

The ensuing chaos, ably promoted by Hoskins, was our salvation.

'We must have holed ourselves when we went aground!' he shouted, and immediately, for no very clear reason, he darted up on deck, as though he could find the answer there. Then, inexplicably, all the lights went out: I could hear Hoskins blundering round above our heads, and then jumping down again, through the forward hatch. He shouted: 'It's coming in fast – you'd better get on deck!' and the Customs men, groping in the dark, stumbled up the ladder to the bridge. The ship was settling down, though it was clear that she would not settle very far: ahead of us, the moon gleamed on the uncovered part of the mud-bank that held our bows, and there could not have been more than three feet of water round our hull.

Hoskins shouted again: 'The pumps – get the pumps going!' and helped by the Customs men I started the small auxiliary pump in the after-part of the ship. There was still a lot of noise, and movement, and fluent cursing from Hoskins as he searched for the leak. Then I heard his voice once more, above the putt-putt of the motor pump, calling out: 'She doesn't seem to be holed – I wonder if it's that damned valve in the lavatory,' and then, with a loud shout like a man lighting on a burglar in the basement: 'That's it – it's been left open!'

There was another long pause, and then Hoskins joined us on deck, his sea-boots clumping like thunder. 'Just got to it in time!' he gasped, as though he had run five miles to tell us the news. And turning to the small Customs man, reproachfully: 'You have to close the inlet valve after you've used the lavatory. Otherwise it floods in – it's below the water-line.'

'Oh,' said the Customs man, crestfallen. And then: 'I'm very sorry – I didn't know.'

'I should have told you,' said Hoskins magnanimously. He looked round at the rest of us. 'There's not much harm done, anyway. She's flooded about eighteen inches all round, but I've shut the inlet valve and we can pump her out quite easily by the morning.'

'I'm very sorry,' said the Customs man again. 'I should have thought of it.'

'We'll send you a bill for a new carpet,' said Hoskins jovially. He peered down the ladder into the wardroom, where the water gently lapped and swirled. 'Looks like the party's over,' he went on. 'We'll have to doss down in the wheel-house tonight.'

'Are you sure you're OK?' asked the big Customs man, solicitously. He had not spoken for some time, and I had been afraid that he must be brooding, not without suspicion, on the turn of events; but apparently his silence was due to embarrassment only. 'We can give you a shake-down ashore, easy enough.'

'We'd better stay aboard,' said Hoskins. 'Thanks all the same, but I'd like to watch that pump. We want to get her dried out before the tide comes up again.'

We waited, in reflective silence. Perhaps it was only my conscience which made me think: they *can't* have been put off from what they were going to do – they must still want to search the ship. But it was not so. Noise, movement, crisis, and their own sense of social guilt had altered the picture altogether. When the small Customs man shifted his feet, and said: 'Well, in that case . . .' I knew that we had won the round, after all.

The two of them climbed into their launch very shortly afterwards, still apologizing, still offering hospitality, still wishing us the best of luck, and cast off. Then their boat chugged away up-river, while MGB 1087 settled comfortably on the mud, and the tide slackened, and away to the east the dawn came up to cheer us, as we stood safe on our own deck.

I ran my hand over my face – grey, bristly, at least ninety years old.

'That was a stroke of luck.'

I could just make out Hoskins, in the cold half-light, bending over the motor pump aft. He straightened up.

'You've got to keep your head, that's all.'

I was still puzzled. 'But surely that valve in the lavatory is automatic. You don't have to close it yourself.'

'It *was* automatic.' I could see him grinning as he walked towards me. 'And it is now . . . There was just a short time this evening when it kind of got stuck. Anyone who used the lavatory after me was bound to start it flooding.' And he said again, as if to a child: 'You've just got to keep your head.'

Hoskins handled the business side. Judging from the size of the cheques that went into my bank account, he was doing it very well: in one period of four months I banked nearly three thousand pounds, and the average throughout that year was over four hundred pounds a month. I could not help being aware that we were branching out, extending markedly the basis of the brandy-and-nylon run with which we had started operations. I could not help being aware, also, that we were handling some very questionable cargo in the process.

That much was obvious, simply from the look of the people who came down to see us whenever we berthed, whether it was in England or in France. Glorified barrow-boys, I would have called them, if it had not been clear that they would never do anything as straightforward as push a barrow; smart, slick young men in black overcoats and curly-brimmed hats, who manhandled their cigars and paid us out in great greasy bunches of fivers. It was not pleasant to see them aboard M G B 1087 . . . I can't claim that I gave a great deal of attention to the details of these transactions, because, basically speaking, I just didn't want to know; but I *did* know that during that time we carried, among other items, some crates labelled 'Scrap Metal' which actually held Thompson sub-machine guns: and an innocent-looking trunk crammed with faked ration-cards printed in Bordeaux; and case upon case of bottles which, though hailing from a second-rate wine merchant in Paris, yet bore the ornate practically genuine label; 'JOHN HAIGS VERY OLD SCOTCH WHISKY' . . .

When I protested, not very strongly because I was getting too deep in and too aware of that mounting bank balance, Hoskins simply said:

'We're in the cash-and-carry business – and there's plenty of both. You just leave it to me.'

I left it to him. There had been a time when I seemed to have a choice in the matter; but that time, along with a lot of other things, was vanishing.

It was during this period that I became aware of something else: that M G B 1087 was not behaving as well as she ought to.

It showed itself in little things: things that ought to have gone right and actually went wrong. Once we suffered from oiled-up plugs, which kept the engines coughing and spluttering all the way back from Calais. Once we had a steering breakdown which very nearly put us ashore between St Malo and Dinard. On another occasion we spent six precious hours of darkness, when we had hoped to clear harbour unobtrusively, trying without success to start the engines; thus losing the tide, the cover of night, and (very nearly) our clean record. Once, water in the switch-board put every moving thing out of action, and cost us five hundred pounds for an unfulfilled contract.

There was absolutely no reason why M G B 1087 should start behaving like this: she was as good as the day we bought her, both Hoskins and I lavished hours on her maintenance, and each breakdown won her a thorough overhaul. But it was certainly true that she was giving us a lot of trouble; and even when there was no ascertainable mechanical fault, she seemed to act in a curiously sluggish way, as if she were beginning to lose heart . . . I knew it was silly to endow a ship with a heart, of course. Perhaps my nerves were getting a bit out of hand, with the continual risks we were running; but that was how she seemed sometimes – human, unreliable, inexplicably disinclined to try.

One of the worst times was when the engines failed, in bad weather, when we were off the entrance to the Lymington River. Something in Hoskins's manner when we left the other side had told me that this was a special trip – which must mean either a very ticklish or a very expensive cargo; but as usual I had paid little attention to what we were carrying, and I only discovered what it was at the very end. Before I found out, we had almost run aground. M G B 1087 could not have chosen a worse moment to pack up, and if it had not been for a change of tide, which carried us away from the point again and gave us some sea-room to play with, we would have gone ashore, and probably broken up. As it was, we drifted for nearly three hours before we got going again.

As soon as we got in, Hoskins said: 'I'm taking the steering-wheel ashore for repairs. It may have to go up to London.'

I stared at him. 'The steering-wheel? There's nothing wrong with that. It's those blasted engines that keep playing us up.'

'The steering-wheel,' he repeated, with a sort of false impatience, as if he couldn't be bothered to argue.

Then I remembered the hollowed-out spokes, the hiding-place that we had never used. Light broke in.

'Why didn't you tell me?' I asked. 'What's inside?'

Hoskins said: 'Very small mink coats.'

I grinned. 'Don't be a sap. What have we brought over this time?' – Hoskins said: 'Dope.'

I thought he was still fooling. I said: 'It's you that's the dope . . .' and then the bell rang again. 'Good God! Do you mean drugs?'

Hoskins nodded. I could see that he was already gauging my mood, knowing that I was bound to kick up a fuss, not knowing how seriously I would take it. Just before I started to speak he said: 'It's *very* remunerative. I can assure you of that.'–

We did have a blazing row; but I remember it chiefly because it was the last time I objected to anything we did. I was damned angry – because I now realized without any doubt that Hoskins did not care how far he carried this game. At one point, when I said I wanted to get out there and then, he came back very toughly indeed:

'You can't get out – you're in this, boots and all, and don't you forget it!'

'But drugs,' I repeated, still appalled. 'It's so – rotten.'

He swore vividly, and then: 'Don't be so ruddy moral,' he said. 'It gets you nowhere . . . By God, I remember when I wanted to claim that Ju. 88, and you bawled me out like a blasted clergyman. I thought you'd got wise to things, these last few months.'

I said: 'Perhaps I have.'

'Well, you'd better stay that way.' He came close to me, a small man no longer unsure of himself and violently determined to keep me in his grip. 'You haven't done so badly, this last year, have you? You'd have a hard time talking yourself out of this, if it ever came to a show-down.' His eyes were holding mine with extraordinary menace. 'Don't get any funny ideas, will you? We're both in this, up to the eyebrows, and we both stay in . . . Now get that steering-wheel unshipped.'

It was, as I said, the last time I made any sort of protest.

After that, things went from bad to worse. It was as if Hoskins, given virtually a free hand, was determined to go to the very limit in order to demonstrate that he was master of a dangerous trade – and of me. I can hardly tell you the sort of jobs we did, during those horrible months.

Narcotics became nothing special in our cargo lists, and adulterated liquor a pleasing variation on an evil theme. Once there was a tough-looking woman with two terrified girls, who cried the whole way across and were taken ashore in a drugged stupor. When I asked Hoskins who they were, he said: 'Meat . . .' Once there was a coffin, a lead coffin, which we lashed to the back of the bridge – and dumped into deep water off St Catherine's Point. Once, we gave passage to some wretched stateless Jews, without papers of any sort, who went ashore at Southampton and walked straight into the arms of the police at the end of the jetty. Hoskins, when he saw this, only remarked: 'What a waste of money – their money.' I wondered if he had organized *that* as well.

Such were the outlines of this infamous period, such the sort of exploit we had worked our way up to.

Perhaps it was just a coincidence that MGB 1087 seemed to be deteriorating at the same pace during all this time; but it was certainly true that she was not the ship we had known in the old days. I found that I couldn't trust her any longer; she was like a sulky, ill-bred child whom one remembered, only a few years back, as having been a positive angel, exhibited proudly even at grown-up events . . . . Now she broke down on dozens of occasions, sometimes when it did not matter, sometimes when it mattered a great deal; she was sluggish, she wallowed heavily in any sort of a sea, she broached-to and shipped water no matter how carefully she was handled. Life aboard her had become a chancy and uncomfortable affair; and occasionally, as on one of the last trips we made in her, it was highly dangerous as well.

I remember that trip very well; except for our final one, it marked the worst thing we did in MGB 1087.

The ship had been under repair for a fortnight, down at Portsmouth, when Hoskins telephoned me from London.

'How's our little friend?' he asked, as soon as I reached the hotel call-box.

'She's OK now,' I said.

'She'd better be . . . We have a trip to make, two days from now. It's got to go like clockwork.'

'All right,' I said.

'Now, listen . . . About ten miles west of Hythe' – and he gave more particular directions – 'there's a creek running right up into the marshes. It has plenty of water at high tide. There's a side lane, off the main Folkestone road, that goes right down to the water's edge.'

I said I could find it from the chart.

'I want our friend in there, at eleven o'clock at night the day after tomorrow. Can you bring her round by yourself?'

'Yes.'

'That's fine, then.' And he repeated: 'But it's got to go like clockwork.'

'What is it this time?' I asked after a pause. I didn't really care.

'Something special.' Hoskins sounded nervous and jubilant at the same time. 'The biggest thing we've ever done.' Then I heard him laugh, unpleasantly. 'You could almost retire after this one. Does that tempt you?'

I said: 'I'll be there,' and rang off. There were no jokes between us now – and that hadn't been a joke, anyway.

Waiting with MGB 1087 among the briny, low-lying marshes, with the moon glistening on the wet fields and the seabirds crying like anguished ghosts all round me. I found myself hoping that this time something would go wrong, and that Hoskins would not show up – or that the police would do so in his place. But punctually at eleven o'clock I saw the dimmed headlights of a car turning off the main road towards me, and the purr of a heavy engine growing louder as it approached. I waited.

Presently a dark shape came into view, bumping unevenly down the rough farm lane. It was a small truck; it stopped and turned, and backed towards the ship's side, as if the whole thing had been rehearsed.

A man jumped down from the tailboard, and another – Hoskins – ran round from the driving cabin. Without a word the two of them started to unload something from the back of the truck – small oblong boxes, eight of them. Still silent, breathing deeply with the effort, they manhandled the consignment aboard, and then down into the cabin. I did my share of the work, levering the heavy shapes over the edge of the combing, and down the steep ladder.

In the faint glow from the shaded cabin-light, I saw that the boxes, wooden but securely bound with steel, were all identically marked with two intertwined letters – the Royal cypher that the Post Office used.

Not till the last one was aboard did anyone speak. Then the unidentified man said gruffly: 'Eight of them. OK?' and Hoskins answered: 'Eight. Yes.' That was all. The man walked back to the truck; the engine started; and it bumped away again towards the main road.

Hoskins, beside me on the bridge, said: 'Let's get going. I want to be in mid-Channel by daylight.'

That was a hell of a trip, the worst we had had so far. We were headed for a beach some miles to the south of Le Touquet, a safe 'outlet' which we had used many times before. We should have completed the crossing at easy speed, in time to close the French coast at dusk and keep our rendezvous at midnight. As it was, we were a full twenty-four hours late on the assignment; and only with great good luck were we able to make delivery on the other side.

I learned afterwards that the French 'contacts' were convinced we had made a break for a Spanish port, and that a reception committee had been warned to stand by at San Sebastian. Such were our friends and such our reputation. But our failure to turn up the first night was certainly none of our own choosing.

Once again, MGB 1087 just would not play. Within ten minutes of starting out, we were brought to a dead stop by weed wrapped round the screws. It took me two hours of alternate diving, hacking away for a few seconds with a knife, and then coming up for air, before I could clear it.

It had to be me that did the work, because Hoskins said he could not stay underwater at all; but perhaps it was better to have something definite to do, even something as cold, wet, and miserable as this, rather than to wait inactive for the ship to get moving again. Hoskins was in a remarkable state of nerves during all this period. We were still land-bound near the mouth of the creek, and every time a car's lights travelled along the coast road, he watched them as if they were a gun pointed at his stomach.

I wondered what on earth we could be carrying, for him to have so obvious a dose of jitters . . . But when I asked him, all he would say was: 'Don't you worry about what it is. I can tell you this, though: if we're caught with it, we'll each have about ten years to worry in – if not rather more.'

I remembered those Post Office cyphers, and the weight of the steel-bound boxes. For the first time, I really felt like a criminal on the run.

Presently we got the ship going again, and headed out into the Channel on our course for Le Touquet. Though we had lost two hours, it shouldn't have been difficult to make them up: MGB 1087 had plenty of speed in hand for an occasion like this. But now, it was clear, she had other ideas . . . Everything happened to us on that trip: an oil leak, a short circuit, dirty petrol, horrible weather, and a loose rudder-pin. The compass went completely haywire: the first shore-light we saw was Dieppe – at least seventy miles off our course. We were stopped, at one point, for nearly nine hours, while I tried to trace an electrical fault. Hoskins was seasick (that, I didn't mind). The Primus stove wouldn't work at all. The least pressure on the steering-wheel threatened to tear the rudder loose altogether.

MGB 1087, in fact, behaved all the time as though she could hardly bear to be touched.

Perhaps it sounds odd to say that I found out the reason for all this when we reached the other side. But that was how it seemed.

We made our delivery just as Hoskins must have planned, even though we were twenty-four hours late. I took MGB 1087 limping into the little bay south of Le Touquet, and ran her aground on a gently shelving beach from which we could retreat quickly if necessary. Four dark figures rose to meet us, four men who first flashed torches in our faces, as though they could hardly believe we had turned up, and then set to work unloading the boxes in total silence. When this was completed, still without a word spoken, we backed off again, and then turned quickly southwards for St Valery.

We reached harbour at first light, nearly out of fuel and dead tired. Neither of us had shut our eyes for two and a half days.

I slept late, in the little cabin under the shadow of the tall quay wall. I was roused by Hoskins clambering down the ladder, with his arms loaded. He seemed in good spirits; he carried loaves, cheese, fruit, and a copy of the *Continental Daily Mail*.

There was something in the careful way he put the paper down on the cabin table that caught my attention immediately. It was as if he were saying: 'Now you're going to find out what this is all about . . .' The paper lay between us like the dividing line of a frontier: I knew that if I picked it up and read it, I would be in Hoskin's country for ever.

'Hallo,' I said, blinking. 'What's the news?'

He grinned amiably. He said: 'You're famous. But they don't know your name yet.'

At that, I flipped the newspaper open without lifting it, and bent towards it.

There was little room for anything on the front page, save the story of the daring daylight hold-up of a Post Office van in London three days before. It made tough reading. The van had been forced into a side street by a car full of masked gunmen while on its way from the Bank of England, and the contents, a shipment of bar-gold, transferred immediately to a second waiting car. The thieves had got clean away, though not without a brief and bloody struggle. Two men had been killed, shot down in cold blood – a bank messenger, and a Post Office driver who bravely tried to tackle his assailants.

The escaping car, in an eighty-mile-an-hour chase, had knocked down a child outside Edgware Road Station; a girl of five, who was critically injured and was not expected to live. The trail had been lost somewhere in South London. It was thought that the gold might already have reached the Continent.

> The thieves, *concluded the newspaper*, have thus brought off the biggest haul of its kind for many years. Bank officials now disclose that the consignment of gold was on its way to Heathrow Airport, *en route* for America. Its value is estimated at £400,000. It was contained in eight wooden boxes, marked as usual with the Royal cypher.

We lay low for a long time after that. With the spectacular hue-and-cry which the gold robbery set in train, it was a bad moment to attract any sort of attention; and we could certainly afford to take a rest . . . We were paid, I learned from Hoskins, four thousand pounds for that trip to France – only one per cent. of the total haul, but a lot of money, anyway. With all the rest of what we had banked, it was enough for me to suggest to Hoskins, once more, that we get out and stay out.

'It can't last for ever,' I said. 'We've had hell's own luck all the time, and we've done very well out of it. I want to call it a day.'

'You can't,' he said, not for the first time. We were sitting in the Berkeley Buttery in Piccadilly, spending, elegantly, some of our winnings. 'And, anyway, what's the point? We're on to a wonderful racket. Why not make a career out of it?'

'Because we're bound to be caught in the end.'

'Why? If we do just one good job a month in future – and with the contacts I've got now, that shouldn't be hard – we can still make all the money we need. One job a month, carefully planned, isn't likely to land us in trouble.'

'They'll get wise to us in the end,' I insisted. 'In fact, I don't know why they haven't done so already. It *must* attract attention, the amount of travelling we do in the ship.'

'Don't you believe it.' Hoskins tossed back his drink and beckoned a waiter for another. 'They're not as smart as that, not by a hundred miles. As long as we keep on looking like amateur yachtsmen who can't resist the call of the sea, we're quids in.'

The call of the sea . . . The way Hoskins said it excited my special loathing. The sea did have a call for me; it had always done so; and to hear the phrase drip thus smugly from his tongue seemed to cheapen intolerably one whole side of my life.

'Well, I'm not staying in for ever,' I said shortly. 'You can do what you like. I'm getting out pretty soon.'

'That,' said Hoskins after a pause, 'would be very unwise.'

We were staring at each other across the bar table, in such naked mutual dislike that it seemed absurd that we could be committed to any joint enterprise. I found myself wondering if other criminals found that they were tied to each other in the same disgusting way . . . I knew, in the back of my mind, that what he said was true: that he held the whip-hand, and that, having made me his accomplice, he would never let me go. If I did walk out, now or at any time in the future, he would find some way of seeing that the police got on to my track. How he would do it, without involving himself at the same time, I didn't know. But I knew he *would* do it. I was in that sort of position, and he was that sort of man.

I said, feebly: 'We'll see.'

I knew then that relief must come from somewhere else: not from my own efforts, and not from Hoskins's good offices. There was no such thing as the latter. In some way, I must be rescued – by fate or by accident. Or by something.

The revolting series of crimes which came to be known as the 'Raines Murders' filled the front pages of all the English newspapers, and of many others, for several weeks. From the newspaper point of view, the story had everything: blood, sex, mystery, a quaking public, and a resounding official scandal – in that Raines had been committed to an asylum some years before, and had then been pronounced sane, and set at liberty, by a panel of Home Office doctors.

But sane or not – and it was always fun to confound the experts – the facts were that Raines had recently, within the space of ten days, criminally assaulted and then strangled four children, none of them over eight years of age, and had then disappeared completely.

He was, of course, reported from scores of places, being identified from the 'Wanted for Murder' photograph in the newspapers, which showed a pudgy, bald, egg-shaped man looking for all the world like a stage bishop. He was 'an obvious gentleman', the papers always said, with carefully manicured hands; a man, as one bereaved mother described him, who talked like kindness itself.

Kind he may have been – he was certainly free enough with bags of sweets and offers of a nice ride in his car; but 'gentleman' was a trifle off the beam. Four children was Raines's current score: four children all killed in the same unprintable way, followed by a month of nation-wide man-hunting, a torrent of clues, evidence, near-arrest, and public outcry, and then – silence.

Though it was dusk, I recognized Raines as soon as he came aboard.

Hoskins brought him down, of course, ushering him on board as if he were the rich owner's favourite son. Standing on the bridge, watching the back of Raines's head as he minced down the ladder, I found myself thinking: no, this is too much – and then I followed them below, in order to be introduced . . . I remember that handshake, across the table of the half-lit cabin, as something specially degrading; his hand – plump, smooth, slightly moist – closed round mine with an embracing warmth, as though he were sure that this small contact would make us friends. I thought of what had lain within that hand, only a few weeks before, and my throat and tongue were dry as I withdrew my own hand from his grasp. The police doctor's phrase, I remembered, had been 'manual strangulation'. Now it wasn't a phrase any more.

Raines did not speak – indeed, I never found out what sort of a voice he had. After half-rising for our greeting, he sat hunched in one corner of the wardroom, with the look of a doomed man about him – a man living in an ultimate kind of hell which, after showing him briefly the bright lights of conquest, had left him alone in a pit of fear. You're on the run, I thought, with *that* on your conscience and the police of many countries searching for you; and we are helping you because our help has been bought, and we may be the last and best friends you make on this earth.

I took one more look at the smooth bald head and the drooping, egg-shaped face below it, and then I broke for the open air.

When Hoskins joined me on the bridge:

'How could you?' I asked him, in a frenzy of disgust. 'You must be crazy!'

'It's a job.' His voice was off-hand, but I knew that he did not really feel like that about it; he realized that this was very near the last margin of evil, even for him, and the only way to endure it was to turn aside from its implications. 'He's a piece of cargo, just like anything else.'

'He's not like anything else! He's wanted for rape and murder, and he did them both – four times, with kids of seven and eight – only a few weeks back,' I swallowed. 'This is the most horrible thing we've ever done.'

'Look,' said Hoskins. He came closer to me, dropping his voice. 'We both know he hasn't a hope in hell of getting away. The police in France will pick him up, the same day as he lands. And in the meantime –' He made a curious fluttering movement of his right hand, as though he were handling bank-notes. 'In the meantime, we cash in.'

'No matter what he pays –' I began.

'Raines was a rich man,' said Hoskins, interrupting. We were both whispering now, mindful of the obscene figure sitting within a few feet of us at the bottom of the ladder. 'Look here, that man had twenty-five thousand pounds tucked away. Twenty-five thousand pounds. Now it's going to be ours – all but five thousand.'

He was watching me closely, his eyes gleaming in the darkness; probably he was trying to persuade himself as well... I knew suddenly that nothing he was saying was making any difference to me, *because it didn't have to*. I was still sick with disgust, but in the back of my mind I knew that we would make the trip as planned. It wasn't the money, it was the whole horrible machine that I was caught up in; we were in the cargo business, and Raines was cargo, and we would carry him, as we had carried liquor and drugs and dead bodies and stolen gold and illegal immigrants in the past. I knew, once more in deep disgust, that I was simply going through the motions of dissent; and that I would stay in this business, with Hoskins by my side, until the sea or the law caught us and dealt with us.

When I had said: 'This is the most horrible thing we've ever done,' I had already known that we would do it.

Something made me walk a few steps forward and peer down the ladder into the cabin again. Raines was still sitting where we had left him, his body hunched, his hands hanging slack between his thighs. He noticed my movement and his eyes rose to meet mine. There was no expression in them; I might have been exchanging glances with a slug. Yes, I am Raines, he seemed to be saying: you may not like me – nobody does – but you are taking twenty thousand pounds of my money to get me out of this. When do we start?

I drew back again and moved across to the controls. Poor old M G B 1087 . . . Just before I started the engines, I said:

'I don't think she'll stand for this.'

It began to blow as soon as we left the shelter of Lymington River; a tough, blustering south-easterly wind that was clearly going to give us a lot of trouble.

We had a long way to go – across the Solent, westward of the Isle of Wight, over to the French coast near the Cherbourg peninsula, and then south towards St Malo. That was where Raines said he wanted to be put ashore, Hoskins told me – in a country district that would give him a better chance of slipping past the police than anywhere north of Paris. So, St Malo it was to be. But before that, we had to cross about a hundred miles of the most open part of the Channel, in the teeth of a rising wind and a short, steep sea that was already seamed and flecked with white foam.

There was nowhere round the whole coast of Britain where the weather could so swiftly deteriorate.

We sailed at about ten o'clock that night, and by dawn we had crossed the Solent and were rounding the Needles, the westerly tip of the Isle of Wight. But now we started to meet the full force of the wind and the main anger of the sea. M G B 1087 began to labour, as the waves tossed her about blindly, throwing her many degrees off her course; sometimes she buried her bows deep in the trough of the sea, sometimes she rose high on the crest of a wave, and her screws, shuddering and racing wildly in the free air, shook the whole ship. Ahead of us, a lowering sky and a torn sea was now our only horizon.

We wrestled with the engines for over three hours before I began to have doubts about the outcome. Raines remained below, 'sick as a dog,' as Hoskins told me spitefully. Hoskins himself was beside me on the bridge, tending the engine-controls and occasionally taking a spell at the wheel.

We were both very tired already and drenched to the skin; though even now we had hardly left the English coast, and there were hours of this battle, and of worsening weather, ahead.

'I don't think we can do it!' I had to shout to make myself heard, bending towards Hoskins under the lee of the bridge-rail. 'We're not making more than two or three knots headway, and the sea's getting worse. If anything goes wrong with the engines, we're sunk.'

Hoskins looked round him at the flurry of foam and dark water that contained and threatened us. 'Sunk is a good word!' he shouted back, and grinned. I almost liked him at that moment. He sounded something like the old Hoskins, at his best when we were in a rough corner, with things going wrong.

But we *were* in a rough corner. M G B 1087 was now taking huge punishment with every wave, and labouring exhaustedly under it. Everything above decks ran with water, and we had shipped a lot of it below, in the cabin and the engine-space.

The wind had begun to howl at us; under the livid sky the waves seemed to race and roar against the ship, throwing themselves against her with the full shock of malice. Even if we turned round now, we would have a wild time getting back to shelter; and if we didn't turn, there would come a moment when we would bury our bows beneath tons of water for the thousandth time, and not come up again.

Tough as she was, she was not built for this sort of thing, and we knew it, and so did she.

M G B 1087 settled the question for us. Towards midday, the engines began imperceptibly to fail.

It was sea-water, I suppose; or the harm done whenever the screws raced free; or the oil-level, which was erratic; or the terrific weight of the sea surging perpetually against us. Or perhaps she was just ashamed of us all . . . Whatever it was, she started to miss successive beats, and the revolutions dropped steadily.

Hoskins and I looked at each other. In that horrible sea, the inexorable falling of the engine-speed drained the heart of its courage.

'We'll have to turn back!' I shouted. The wind was plucking the words from my mouth as I spoke them, and again I bent towards him behind the shelter of the bridge. 'Maybe she'll pick up again if she's running with the wind.'

Hoskins stared at me, his face taut. I could tell that he was starting to be afraid, as I was. We were then twenty miles south of the Needles, twenty miles from any sort of shelter; and to reach it we would have to bring M G B 1087 round, beam on to this villainous sea, with the engines failing, and then struggle for home, with all the fury of the storm on our trail. Even if she came round without mishap, we would be taking a frightful chance, running before such a gale with the cockpit being swamped by every second wave.

But the turn had to be made. If we didn't make it and make it soon, it would be too late, and we would simply keep on until we headed for the bottom.

Whether or not M G B 1087 could in the future complete the journey, she had now been beaten back in surrender, and we had to face the fact that we were in her hands.

I had a wicked time, working to bring her round; it took nearly an hour of successive attempts, with never enough power to complete the full turn. Time and again she came half-way round, until she was lying in the trough of the waves; time and again she stuck there, with the screws thrashing ineffectually, and the sea dealing her blow after blow as she lay broadside on. She would reach that certain point, with the rudder hard over and the engines feebly pulsing, but she always lacked the power to complete the half-circle and turn her stern to the wind. Time and again we would abandon the effort, and bring her bows up to the wind again, preparatory to another try, another wild stab at it.

All the while, the ship suffered fearfully: pounding, shuddering, shipping solid black cataracts of water, unloosing below decks a frightful clatter as spare gear and crockery and oil-drums broke adrift and thrashed about.

Finally she made it. There must have been a lull, or else the engines summoned a few extra revs. She did come round, after a terrible moment of indecision, and turned her back to the storming sea. Then the worst part of the voyage began.

I had a feeling that she would never live. There was something in the touch of her, in the way the wheel spun loosely in my hands, in the sound of the dying engines, that told me that M G B 1087 was not going to make harbour. Our progress grew slower and slower; far away ahead of us I could see the vague outlines of the land, but it was like a promise that would never be fulfilled – it came no nearer, grew no clearer to the eye.

More and more often the solid seas crashed down upon our stern, driving it deep under water, and then roaring along the upper deck with the sound of unloosed thunder, Hoskins and I clung helplessly to the bridge-rail; I found that my hands, clawing at the wheel, were without feeling, and my whole body cold to the bone. The engine-beat dropped further, as the whole ship was invaded and swamped. Already she seemed to have grown smaller under the triumphant attack of the sea, and shrunken in defeat.

She was lying down under it all; as if now, at last, she had had enough of us and the things we had done to her. She was not trying any more.

There was a sudden confused noise from below, above the groaning and the clatter, and the door at the head of the cabin-ladder burst open. Raines appeared. He was a fearful sight – grey-green with seasickness, glistening with terror. He had upon his face an extraordinary luminous pallor, as if he were already dead. He reminded me of the children he had killed . . . He tottered towards us, looking round about him fearfully, and gestured at the roaring sea as though he could not believe what he saw.

The engines spluttered and died.

Now we lay there helpless, taking every blow that fell, settling lower beneath the scudding spray. MGB 1087 had become a waterlogged wreck, drifting down wind uselessly as the gale screamed round her rigging and the sea slugged and slugged at her hull. Hoskins touched Raines on the shoulder, and pointed to the land, still a long way away, vaguely glimpsed through clouds of flying spray.

It was doubtful whether he meant anything special by this pointing, but Raines took it as a definite directive. He nodded, and seemed to be gathering himself together. Then, as yet another sea swept unchecked along the deck, and drenched us all, he jumped.

It was perhaps the best thing to do, though not for him. He had not the build for swimming, nor the strength, and we could only watch him drown. I had never before seen a bald head sinking lower and lower in the water, surrounded by thrashing arms. There was a moment when he seemed to be bubbling fantastically at surface-level, like a suspect, simmering egg . . . I found that I still hated him, even as he disappeared.

I hated Hoskins, too – the man who had brought us all here, who had done all this to me and to the ship. MGB 1087 was heading for the sea-bed now – full of water, all her buoyancy lost, the great weight of the keel and the engines starting to drag her down. Thus we were all dead or dying: Raines, Hoskins, the ship, and I; dying in hatred and shame and anger, amid the raging sea.

Hoskins clutched my shoulder. When I turned, his face was close to mine, and enormous – the face I had grown to loathe, constricted now with cold and fear. Honour had caught up with him – with both of us. The ship trembled under our feet, and slid lower.

Hoskins cried out: 'I can't swim.'

I wanted to laugh, but much more I wanted to save my breath. I said:

'That's all right with me,' and as the ship foundered I struck out for the shore. I never saw him again.

Well, that's the story, and probably you see what I meant when I said, at the beginning: there are things about it that I don't understand. I've got plenty of time to work it out – ten years, as Hoskins once forecast. (They traced the payment for the gold robbery to my bank account. Perhaps I was lucky – three of the principal characters were hanged.)

What made MGB 1087 lie down and die? For that was what did happen, after all – not suddenly but progressively; in spite of all the care we spent on her, she did grow less and less dependable, and in the end she just gave up, without fighting. It was as if the last trip, the worst thing we ever asked her to do, decided the matter for her.

But that's surely a fanciful idea. There was no *real* reason for her giving up, even on that final voyage; the weather was terrible, but we'd had terrible weather on lots of occasions, particularly during the war, and she had always survived it – and even seemed to thrive on it.

Of course, during the war we had to fight the weather for different reaons. There was usually a stake that the MGB 1087 could be proud of then – in fact, many such stakes, for years on end.

Perhaps it was I, and not the ship, that was at fault. Perhaps I handled her badly, or forgot things, or just lost the knack; perhaps I was ashamed of the frightful things we did, and the shame became translated into action – or lack of action.

It may have been my fault we were wrecked. I don't think so. I was always trying my very best, I'm afraid.

ACKNOWLEDGEMENTS

The Publishers wish to thank the following for permission to reprint previously published material. Every effort has been made to locate all persons having any rights in the stories appearing in this book but appropriate acknowledgement has been omitted in some cases through lack of information. Such omissions will be corrected in future printings of the book upon written notification to the Publishers.

The Hogarth Press for 'Perilous Seas' from *The Sun's Net* by George Mackay Brown.

John Farquharson Ltd for 'Bound for Rio Grande' by A.E. Dingle.

The Society of Authors as the literary representative of the Estate of W.W. Jacobs for 'The Rival Beauties' by W.W. Jacobs.

The Society of Authors as the literary representative of the Estate of John Masefield and Macmillan Publishing Company for 'A White Night' from *A Mainsail Haul* by John Masefield, © 1913 by John Masefield.

Harper & Row, Publishers, Inc., for 'The Yellow Cat' from *Land's End and Other Stories* by Wilbur Daniel Steele, © 1918 and 1946.

Harcourt Brace Jovanovich Inc. for an extract from 'S.S. *San Pedro*' by James Gould Cozzens, © 1930, 1931, 1958, 1959.

Mrs Ann Monsarrat for 'The Ship that Died of Shame' by Nicholas Monsarrat, © the Estate of Nicholas Monsarrat.